DOCTOR ZHIVAGO

Boris Leonidovich Pasternak was born in Moscow in 1890. His father was an artist and his mother was a concert pianist, and the family numbered Tolstoy, Scriabin and Rilke among their friends. He received a classical education and began to study music intensively. In 1912, he abandoned music and went to Marburg to study philosophy, but a year later he was back in Moscow having decided to give up philosophy and devote himself to poetry. He was married in 1921, and again in 1934, and lived most of his life in Moscow. In the twenties and thirties he began writing fiction, as well as attempting a more 'epic' poetry in an effort to stay in touch with the literary requirements of the new regime. At about this time, he began translating European literature into Russian. As his life became increasingly difficult this was to become his main source of income; his translations of Shakespeare and Goethe are generally regarded as masterpieces of the translator's art. With the publication of his masterpiece, *Doctor Zhivago,* in the West in 1957-8 and with his acceptance of the Nobel Prize for Literature in 1958, official pressure intensified. After an unprecedented and savage campaign of denunciation, he was forced to renounce the award. He died on 30 May 1960.

Boris Pasternak

DOCTOR ZHIVAGO

Translated from the Russian
by Max Hayward and Manya Harari

VINTAGE

Published by Vintage 2002

2 4 6 8 10 9 7 5 3 1

Copyright © Giangiacomo Feltrinelli Editore 1958
English translation copyright © Harvill 1958

First published in Great Britain by
Collins and Harvill in 1958

Vintage
Random House, 20 Vauxhall Bridge Road,
London SW1V 2SA

Random House Australia (Pty) Limited
20 Alfred Street, Milsons Point, Sydney,
New South Wales 2061, Australia

Random House New Zealand Limited
18 Poland Road, Glenfield
Auckalnd 10, New Zealand

Random House (Pty) Limited
Endulini, 5A Jubilee Road, Parktown 2193,
South Africa

The Random House Group Limited Reg. No. 954009

www.randomhouse.co.uk

A CIP catalogue record for this book
is availabl from the British Library

ISBN 0 099 44843 2

Papers used by Random House are natural, recyclable
products made from wood grown in sustainable
forests. The manufacturing processes conform to the
environmental regulations of the country of origin

Printed and bound in Great Britain by
Bookmarque Ltd, Croydon, Surrey

Translators' Note

PASTERNAK'S prose has astonishing power, subtlety and range. While always remaining simple and colloquial, it is exceptionally rich and poetic. Indeed, he makes use of sound and word association in the manner of a poet of genius. His language has a vitality which must be rare in the literature of any country and is perhaps unique in that of Russia.

Needless to say, these very qualities face the translators with difficulties which are almost insurmountable, and we have no illusions that we have done justice, even remotely, to the original.

The poems present an even greater problem than the prose. Rather than delay the publication of the book until a version has been made by an accomplished English poet who knows Russian—a work which would inevitably take a very long time —we have adopted the expedient of merely giving a literal translation of the verse without making any attempt to convey its form (other than the length of the stanzas). But clearly, in the case, for instance, of 'The Wedding Party', where the metre is that of the Russian peasant dance tune, the *chastushki*, and this conveys the mood, a literal translation has only the most limited use.

For the convenience of the reader, a cast of the principal characters is given at the beginning of the book. In addition to surnames, Russians address one another by their name and patronymic as well as by diminutives. The cast, which lists the various forms of each name, may help to prevent confusion.

A word should perhaps be added about place names. Many of those occurring in the novel have meanings which are relevant to their context. Usually such names are translated in the footnotes, but occasionally, where the style of the passage seems to require it, we have used the reverse method, putting the Russian form of the name in the footnote and its English equivalent in the text.

We trust that one day *Doctor Zhivago* will appear in Russian and fall into the hands of a translator whose talent is equal to that of its author. All that we can hope for in the meantime is that we may have given English readers some approximate idea of the merits of this great work.

Our thanks are due to Mrs. George Villiers and the Marchesa Origo for revising the English text.

Contents

CONTENTS

ZHIVAGO'S POEMS

Principal Characters in the Novel

Surname	Name and Patronymic	Diminutive	
Zhivago	Yury Andreyevich	Yura, Yurochka	
Vedenyapin	Nikolay Nikolayevich	Kolya	Uncle of Yury Zhivago
Dudorov		Nicky }	Friends of Yury Zhivago
Gordon		Misha }	
Gromeko	Alexander Alexandrovich		
Gromeko (née Krueger)	Anna Ivanovna		Wife of Alexander Gromeko
Gromeko	Antonina Alexandrovna	Tonya	Daughter of Alexander Gromeko
Guishar	Amalia Karlovna		
Guishar	Larissa Fyodorovna	Lara	Daughter of Amalia Guishar
Guishar	Rodyon Fyodorovich	Rodya	Son of Amalia Guishar
Komarovsky	Victor Ippolitovich		
Antipov	Pavel Pavlovich	Pashenka, Pasha	
Galiullin	Gimazetdin		
Galiullina	Fatima		Wife of Gimazetdin Galiullin
Galiullin	Iosif Gimazetdinovich	Yusupka	Son of Gimazetdin Galiullin
Tiverzina	Marfa Gavrilovna		
Tiverzin	Kuprian Savelyevich	Kuprik	Son of Marfa Tiverzina
Tyagunova	Pelagia	Aunt Polya	
Samdevyatov	Anfim Yefimovich		
Mikulitsin	Avercius		
Mikulitsina	Helen		Wife of Avercius Mikulitsin
Mikulitsin	Liberius Avercievich		Son of Avercius Mikulitsin
Tuntseva	Glaphira	Glasha }	Aunts of Liberius Mikulitsin
Tuntseva	Seraphima	Sima }	

PART ONE

I

The Five O'Clock Express

ON they went, singing 'Eternal Memory', and whenever they stopped, the sound of their feet, the horses and the gusts of wind seemed to carry on their singing.

Passers-by made way for the procession, counted the wreaths and crossed themselves. Some joined in out of curiosity and asked: 'Who is being buried?'—'Zhivago,' they were told.—'Oh, I see. That explains it.'—'It isn't him. It's his wife.'—'Well, it comes to the same thing. May she rest in peace. It's a fine funeral.'

The last moments flashed past, counted, irrevocable. 'The earth is the Lord's and the fullness thereof, the earth and everything that dwells therein.' The priest scattered earth in the form of a cross over the body of Marya Nikolayevna. They sang 'The souls of the just'. Then a fearful bustle began. The coffin was closed, nailed and lowered into the ground. Clods of earth drummed on the lid like rain as the grave was filled hurriedly by four spades. A mound grew up on it and a ten-year-old boy climbed on top.

Only the numb and unfeeling condition which comes to people at the end of a big funeral could account for some of the mourners' thinking that he wished to make an address over his mother's grave.

He raised his head and, from his vantage point, absently surveyed the bare autumn landscape and the domes of the monastery. His snub-nosed face was contorted. He stretched out his neck. If a wolf cub had done this it would have been obvious that it was about to howl. The boy covered his face with his hands and burst into sobs. The wind bearing down on him lashed his hands and face with cold gusts of rain. A man in black with tightly-fitting sleeves went up to the grave. This was Nikolay Nikolayevich Vedenyapin, the dead woman's brother and the uncle of the weeping boy; he was a priest who had been unfrocked at his own request.

He went up to the boy and led him out of the graveyard.

2

They spent the night at the monastery where Uncle Kolya was given a room for old times' sake. It was the eve of the Feast of the Inter-

cession of the Holy Virgin. The next day they were supposed to
travel south to a provincial town on the Volga where Uncle Kolya
worked for a publisher who produced the local progressive newspaper.
They had already bought their tickets and their things stood packed
in the cell. The plaintive hooting of engines shunting in the distance
was carried by the wind from the neighbouring railway.

It got very cold in the evening. The two windows of the cell
were at ground level and looked out on a corner of the neglected
kitchen garden, a stretch of the main road with frozen puddles on it
and the part of the churchyard where Marya Nikolayevna had been
buried earlier in the day. There was nothing in the kitchen garden
except acacia bushes round the walls and a few beds of cabbages,
wrinkled and blue with cold. With each blast of wind the leafless
acacias danced as if possessed and flattened themselves against the
path.

During the night the boy, Yura, was woken up by a knocking at
the window. The dark cell was mysteriously lit up by a flickering
whiteness. With nothing on but his shirt, he ran to the window and
pressed his face against the cold glass.

Outside there was no trace of the road, the graveyard or the
kitchen garden, nothing but the blizzard, the air smoking with snow.
It was almost as if the snowstorm had caught sight of Yura and,
conscious of its power to terrify, roared, howled and did everything
possible to attract his attention, revelling in the effect it had on him.
Turning over and over in the sky, length after length of whiteness
unwound over the earth and shrouded it. The blizzard was alone on
earth and knew no rival.

When he climbed down from the window-sill Yura's first impulse
was to dress, run outside and start doing something. He was afraid
that the cabbage patch would be buried so that no one could dig it
up, and that his mother, buried in the open field, would helplessly
sink deeper and deeper away from him into the ground.

Once more it ended in tears. His uncle woke up, spoke to him of
Christ and tried to comfort him, then yawned and stood thoughtfully
by the window. They started to dress. It was getting light.

3

While his mother was alive Yura did not know that his father had
abandoned them long ago and spent his time wenching and carousing
in Siberia and abroad, nor that he had blown the family millions to

the four winds. He was always told that his father was away on business in Petersburg or at one of the big fairs, usually at Irbit.

When his mother, who had never been strong, developed consumption, she took to going to southern France and northern Italy for treatment. Yura went with her on two of these journeys. He was often left with strangers and often passed on from one to another. He became accustomed to all these changes and against this untidy background, surrounded with continual mysteries, he was not surprised at his father's absence.

He could remember a time in his early childhood when an infinite variety of objects were still known by his surname. There were Zhivago factories, a Zhivago bank, Zhivago buildings, a Zhivago tiepin, even a cake rather like a *baba au rhum* known as a Zhivago bun, and at one time you only had to say to your sleigh driver in Moscow : 'Zhivago's !' and, rather as if you had said : 'Take me to Timbuctoo !', he carried you off in his sleigh to an enchanted kingdom at the end of the world. The park closed round you as quiet as a countryside ; crows scattered the hoar-frost as they settled on the heavy branches of the firs ; their cawing echoed like cracking wood ; pedigree dogs came running across the road out of the clearing where building was going on and where lights shone in the gathering dusk.

Suddenly it all vanished. They became poor.

4

One day in summer 1903, two years after his mother's death, Yura was driving across fields in a two-horse open carriage with his Uncle Kolya. They were on their way to see Ivan Ivanovich Voskoboynikov, a teacher and a writer of popular textbooks, who lived at Duplyanka, the estate of Kologrivov, a silk manufacturer and a great patron of the arts.

It was the Feast of the Virgin of Kazan. The harvest was in full swing but, whether because of the feast or because of the midday break, there was not a soul in sight. The half-reaped fields scorched in the sun like the half-shorn heads of convicts. Birds circled overhead. The ripe wheat stood straight up in the perfect stillness. At a distance from the road, stooks rose above the stubble, and, if you stared at them long enough, seemed to move, like land surveyors walking about on the skyline taking notes.

'Are these landlords' or peasants' fields?' Nikolay Nikolayevich asked Pavel, the publisher's odd-job man who sat sideways on the box, shoulders hunched and legs crossed to show that driving was not his regular job.

'These are the masters'.' Pavel lit his pipe, drew on it and after a long silence jabbed with the end of his whip in another direction: 'And those are ours!—Get on with you,' he shouted at the horses, whose tails and haunches he watched like an engine-driver's instrument panel. But the horses were like horses all the world over, the shaft horse pulling with the innate honesty of a simple soul while the off horse arched its neck like a swan and seemed to the uninitiated to be an inveterate idler who thought of nothing but prancing in time to the jangling of its bell [1].

Nikolay Nikolayevich had with him the proofs of Voskoboynikov's book on the land question; the publisher had asked the author to revise it in view of the increasingly strict censorship.

'People are getting pretty rough here,' he told Pavel. 'A merchant has had his throat slit and the stud farm of the *zemsky* [2] has been burned down. What do you think of it all? What are they saying in your village?'

But evidently Pavel took an even gloomier view than the censor, who wished Voskoboynikov to moderate the passionate strength of his views on the agrarian problem.

'What do you expect them to say? The peasants have got out of hand. They've been treated too well. That's no good for the likes of us. Give the peasants rope and God knows we'll all be at each other's throats in no time.—Get a move on there!'

This was Yura's second trip with his uncle to Duplyanka. He thought he knew the way and, every time that the fields ran out on either side with a thin line of forest in front and behind, he expected the road to turn right and give a fleeting view of the Kologrivov place with its ten-mile stretch of open country, the river gleaming in the distance and the railway beyond it. But each time he was mistaken. Field followed field and was in turn swallowed by forests. The succession of huge views aroused in the travellers a feeling of spaciousness and made them think and dream of the future.

The books which later made Nikolay Nikolayevich famous were still unwritten, but his ideas had already taken shape. Yet he did not know that his hour was close at hand.

Soon he was to take his place among the writers of his time—university professors and philosophers of the revolutionary movement

---

[1] The horses were harnessed as a troika less one horse. In a troika the shaft horse trots and the two off horses canter.

[2] A government official who dealt with rural matters.

—as one who, though he shared their preoccupations, had nothing in common with their way of thinking except its terminology. All of them, without exception, clung to this or that dogma, and were satisfied with words and outward appearances, but he, Father Nikolay, a priest, had been both a Tolstoyan and a revolutionary idealist and was still travelling on. He craved for an idea, inspired yet concrete, that would show a clear path and change the world for the better, an idea as unmistakable even to a child or an ignorant fool as lightning or a roll of thunder. He craved for something new.

Yura liked being with his uncle. He reminded him of his mother. Like hers, his mind moved with freedom and welcomed the unfamiliar. He had the same aristocratic sense of equality with all living things and the same gift of taking in everything at a glance and of expressing his thoughts as they first came to him and before they had lost their meaning and vitality.

Yura was glad that his uncle was taking him to Duplyanka. It was a beautiful place and this too reminded him of his mother, who had been fond of nature and had often taken him for country walks.

He also looked forward to seeing Nicky Dudorov again, though Nicky, being two years older, probably despised him. Nicky was a schoolboy who lived at the Voskoboynikovs and who, when he shook hands with Yura, jerked his arm downwards with all his might and bowed his head so low that his hair flopped over his forehead and hid half his face.

5

'The vital nerve of the problem of poverty,' Nikolay Nikolayevich read from the revised manuscript.

'"Essence" would be better, I think,' said Ivan Ivanovich, making the correction on the galleys.

They were working in the half-darkness of the covered verandah. Watering-cans and gardening tools lay about, a raincoat had been flung over the back of a broken chair and waders caked with mud, their tops dropping to the floor, stood in a corner.

'On the other hand, the statistics of births and deaths show,' dictated Nikolay Nikolayevich.

'Insert, "for the year under review",' said Ivan Ivanovich and made a note. There was a slight draught. Lumps of granite lay on the sheets as paper weights.

When they finished, Nikolay Nikolayevich wanted to leave at once.

'There's a storm coming. We must be off.'

'Nothing of the sort. I won't let you. We're going to have tea now.'

'But I must be back in town by evening.'

'It's no use arguing. I won't hear of it.'

Tea was being laid in the garden. A whiff of charcoal smoke from the samovar drifted in, smothering the smell of tobacco and heliotrope. A maid carried out a tray with clotted cream, berries and cheese cakes. It was learned that Pavel had gone off to bathe in the river and had taken the horses with him. Nikolay Nikolayevich had no choice but to submit and stay.

'Let's go down to the river while they're getting tea ready,' suggested Ivan Ivanovich.

On the strength of his friendship with Kologrivov, he had the use of two rooms in the manager's house. The lodge with its own small garden stood in a neglected corner of the park, near the old drive, now thickly overgrown with grass and no longer used except for carting rubbish to the gully which served as a refuse dump. Kologrivov, a man of advanced views and a millionaire who sympathised with the revolution, was abroad with his wife. Only his two daughters, Nadya and Lipa, with their governess and a small staff of servants were living on the estate.

A thick hedge of blackthorn separated the manager's lodge and garden from the park, with its lawns and artificial lakes, which surrounded the house. As Ivan Ivanovich and Nikolay Nikolayevich skirted the hedge, sparrows flew out of it in front of them at regular intervals in small flocks of equal size. The blackthorn swarmed with them and they filled it with an even chatter like water flowing in a pipe.

They passed the hothouses, the gardener's cottage and some stone ruins of obscure origin. They were talking about new talent in the world of letters and scholarship.

'Of course one does meet brilliant men,' said Nikolay Nikolayevich, 'but they are isolated. The fashion nowadays is all for groups and societies of every sort.—It is always a sign of mediocrity in people when they herd together, whether their group loyalty is to Solovyev or to Kant or Marx. The truth is only sought by individuals, and they break with those who do not love it enough. How many things in the world deserve our loyalty? Very few indeed. I think one should be loyal to immortality, which is another word for life, a stronger word for it. One must be true to immortality—true to Christ! But you're frowning, my poor man. As usual, you haven't understood a word.'

'Hm,' said Ivan Ivanovich. He was a thin, fair-haired man, restless as an eel and with a wicked little beard which made him look like an American of Lincoln's time; he was always bunching it up in his hand and nibbling the tip. 'I say nothing, of course. As you know, I look at these things rather differently. But while we're at it, tell me, what was it like when they unfrocked you? I bet you were scared. Didn't they anathematise you?'

'You're trying to change the subject. However, why not. . . . No, I wasn't anathematised. Cursing isn't done nowadays. There was a certain amount of unpleasantness, and there are certain consequences. For instance, I am banned from the civil service for quite a long time and I am forbidden to go to Moscow or Petersburg. But these are trifles. As I was saying, one must be true to Christ. I'll explain. What you don't understand is that it is possible to be an atheist, it is possible not to know if God exists or why He should, and yet to believe that man does not live in a state of nature but in history, and that history as we know it now began with Christ, it was founded by Him on the Gospels. Now what is history? Its beginning is that of the centuries of systematic work devoted to the solution of the enigma of death, so that death itself may eventually be overcome. This is why people write symphonies, and why they discover mathematical infinity and electromagnetic waves. Now, you can't advance in this direction without a certain upsurge of spirit. You can't make such discoveries without spiritual equipment, and for this, everything necessary has been given us in the Gospels. What is it? Firstly, the love of one's neighbour—the supreme form of living energy. Once it fills the heart of man it has to overflow and spend itself. And secondly, the two concepts which are the main part of the make-up of modern man—without them he is inconceivable—the ideas of free personality and of life regarded as sacrifice.—Mind you, all this is still quite new. There was no history in this sense in the classical world. There you had blood and beastliness and cruelty and pock-marked Caligulas untouched by the suspicion that any man who enslaves others is inevitably second-rate. There you had the boastful dead eternity of bronze monuments and marble columns. It was not until after the coming of Christ that time and man could breathe freely. It was not until after Him that men began to live in their posterity and ceased to die in ditches like dogs—instead, they died at home, in history, at the height of the work they devoted to the conquest of death, being themselves dedicated to this aim.—Ouf! I'm sweating like a pig. I might as well be talking to a blank wall.'

'That's metaphysics, my dear fellow. It's forbidden me by my doctors, my stomach won't take it.'

'Oh well, you're hopeless. Let's leave it.—Goodness, what a view, you lucky devil. Though I suppose as you live with it every day you don't see it.'

The river blazed in the sun, hurting the eyes. It shimmered, bending and unbending like sheet metal. Suddenly its surface creased. A big ferry loaded with carts, horses, and peasants and their women started for the other shore.

'Fancy, it's only just gone five,' said Ivan Ivanovich. 'There's the express from Syzran. It comes through here at five past five.'

Far out on the plain, crossing it from right to left, came a neat little yellow and blue train, made tiny by the distance. Suddenly they noticed that it stopped. White puffs of steam flurried over the engine and a moment later they heard its alarmed hooting.

'That's strange,' said Voskoboynikov. 'Something's wrong. It has no business to stop in the middle of the marsh out there. Something must have happened. Let's go and have tea.'

6

Nicky was not to be found either in the house or in the garden. Yura, left to wander aimlessly round the house while his uncle and Ivan Ivanovich worked on the verandah, guessed that he was in hiding because guests bored him and Yura was not his equal.

It was a wonderful place. Every other minute a yellow thrush made its three-note call, followed by a pause to let the whole of the clear, moist, fluting tune sink and soak into the countryside. Flower smells, caught and dazed by the stagnant air, stood in still shafts over the beds transfixed by the heat. How much it reminded him of Antibes and of Bordighera! He kept turning to right and left. Like an aural hallucination his mother's voice haunted the lawns, it was in the buzzing of the bees and the musical phrases of the birds. It made him quiver with the illusion that she was expecting him to answer, that she was calling him to her, now here, now there.

He walked towards the gully and climbed through the clean coppice overhanging its edge into the tangled alder thicket at the bottom. Down there, among the litter of fallen branches, it was dark and dank; flowers were few and the knotted stalks of mare's-tail looked like the Egyptian sceptres in his illustrated Bible.

Yura felt more and more depressed. He felt like crying. He slumped to his knees and burst into tears.

'Angel of God, my holy guardian,' Yura prayed, 'confirm me in the way of truth and tell Mama I'm all right, she's not to worry. If there is a life after death, O Lord, receive her into thy heavenly mansions where the faces of the saints and of the just shine like lamps. Mama was so good, she couldn't have been a sinner; have mercy on her, Lord, and please don't let her suffer. Mama!'—in his heart-rending anguish he called her down from heaven like a newly canonised saint and suddenly, unable to bear any more, fell down in a faint.

He was not unconscious for long. When he came to himself, he heard his uncle calling him from above. He answered and started climbing out of the gully. Suddenly he remembered that he had not prayed for his missing father, as his mother had taught him to do.

But his fainting fit had left him with such a sense of lightness and well-being that he was unwilling to risk losing it, and it occurred to him that nothing much would happen if he prayed for his father another time. 'He can wait,' he almost thought. Yura did not remember him at all.

7

In a second-class compartment of the train which had stopped in the field across the river sat Misha Gordon [1], who was travelling with his father, a lawyer from Orenburg. Misha was a boy of eleven with a thoughtful face and big dark eyes; he was in his second form at school. His father, Grigory Osipovich Gordon, was being transferred to a new post in Moscow. His mother and sisters were already there arranging the flat.

Misha and his father had been travelling for three days.

Russia with its fields, steppes, villages and towns, bleached lime-white by the sun, flew past them, wrapped in hot clouds of dust.

Lines of carts stretched along the roads; they lumbered aside at the level crossings and, from the furiously speeding train, it seemed as if the carts stood still and the horses were marking time.

At big stations the passengers jumped out and ran helter-skelter to the buffet; the sun, setting behind the station garden, lit up their feet and the wheels of the train.

All the movements in the world, taken separately, were sober and deliberate but, taken together, they were all happily drunk with the general flow of life which united and carried them. People worked and struggled, they were driven on by their individual cares and anxieties, but these springs of action would have run down and jammed the mechanism if they had not been kept in check by an over-all feeling of profound unconcern. This feeling came from the comforting

[1] In Russia Gordon often is a Jewish surname.

awareness of the interwovenness of all human lives, the sense of their flowing into one another, the happy assurance that all that happened in the world took place not only on the earth which buried the dead but also on some other level known to some as the Kingdom of God, to others as history and yet to others by some other name.

From this general rule the boy, Misha, felt himself to be a bitterly unfortunate exception. Anxiety was his mainspring and no such unconcern as the rest of the world shared, relieved and ennobled him. He knew this hereditary trait in himself and watched for it with a morbid self-consciousness. It distressed and humiliated him.

For as long as he could remember, he had never ceased to wonder how it was that a human being with arms and legs like everyone else, and with a language and way of life common to all the rest, could be so different—a being liked by so few and loved by no one. He could not understand how it was that if you were worse than other people you could not improve yourself by trying. What did it mean to be a Jew? What was the purpose of it? What was the reward or the justification of this unarmed challenge which brought nothing but grief?

When he took his problem to his father he was told that his premises were absurd, he must not argue like that, but he was offered no solution deep enough to attract him or to make him bow silently to the inevitable.

And, making an exception only for his parents, he gradually became contemptuous of all the grown-ups who had made this mess and were quite unable to clear it up. He was quite sure that when he was big he would straighten it all out.

For instance, no one could suggest that his father should not have run after that lunatic when he rushed out into the corridor, or that he should not have stopped the train when the man pushed him aside, flung open the door and threw himself, head first, out of the express like a diver leaping from a springboard into a swimming pool.

Yet now that the train had been stuck for ages, the fact that it was not just anyone but precisely Grigory Osipovich who had pulled the communication cord made it seem that the hold-up and the whole annoying business had been caused by the Gordon family.

No one knew for certain why there was such a long delay. Some said that the sudden stoppage had damaged the pneumatic brakes, others that the train had stopped on a steep gradient and the engine could not take it without getting up speed. A third view was that, as the suicide was a well-known person, his lawyer, who had been with him on the train, had insisted on officials being called from the nearest station, Kologrivovka, so that a sworn statement could be drawn up. This was why the driver's mate had climbed up the telegraph pole: the inspection trolley bringing the officials should by now be on its way.

There was a faint stench from the lavatories, not quite neutralised by eau-de-cologne, and a smell of fried chicken, a little high and wrapped in dirty, grease-stained paper. As if nothing had happened, greying Petersburg ladies with wheezy, chesty voices, who had been turned into gypsies by the combination of soot and cosmetics, powdered their faces and wiped their fingers on their handkerchiefs. When, with a coquettish wriggle of their shoulders for which the narrow passage offered an excuse, they passed the Gordons' compartment, it seemed to Misha that through their pursed lips they must be hissing: 'Gracious, what sensitive plants! They think they're a special creation! They're intellectuals! All this is too much for them!'

The body of the suicide lay on the grass by the side of the bank. Blood had streaked his forehead with a dark sign, as if crossing out his face. The dry blood did not look like his blood but like something apart from him, a piece of sticking plaster or a streak of mud or a wet birch leaf.

Knots of constantly changing onlookers and sympathisers surrounded him, while his friend and travelling companion, a thick-set, haughty lawyer, who looked like a well-bred animal in a sweaty shirt, stood over him sullenly with an expressionless face. He was dying of heat and fanning himself with his hat. In answer to all questions he shrugged his shoulders and said crossly, without even turning round: 'He was an alcoholic. What can you expect? A typical consequence of D.T.s.'

Once or twice a thin old woman in a woollen dress and lace kerchief went up to the body. She was the widow Tiverzina, two of whose sons were engine drivers and who was travelling third class on a free warrant with her two daughters-in-law. Like nuns with their mother superior, the two quiet women, their shawls pulled low over their foreheads, followed her in silence. The crowd made way for them.

Tiverzina's husband had been burned alive in a railway accident. She stood a little away from the body, where she could see it through the crowd, and sighed as if comparing the two cases: 'Each according to his fate,' she seemed to say. 'Some die by the Lord's will, but here's a fine kettle of fish, upon my soul, to die of rich living and derangement of mind!'

All the passengers came out and had a look at the corpse and only went back to their compartments for fear their belongings might get stolen.

As they jumped out on to the track and picked flowers or took a short walk to stretch their legs, they felt as if the whole place had only been brought into being by the halt and that neither the squelchy marsh nor the broad river nor the fine house and church on the steep bank opposite would have existed except for the accident.

Even the sun as it shone its evening light on the scene of the suicide, diffident like a cow from a near-by herd come to take a look at the crowd, seemed to be a stage prop, a purely local manifestation.

Misha had been deeply shaken by the event and had at first cried with shock and pity. In the course of the long journey the man who was now dead had come several times to their compartment and had talked for hours with Misha's father. He had said that he found relief in the moral decency, peace and understanding which he discovered in him and had asked him endless questions about fine points of law concerning Bills of Exchange, Deeds of Settlement, bankruptcy and fraud. 'Well I never!' he exclaimed at Gordon's answers. 'Is the law as merciful as that? My lawyer takes a much more gloomy view.'

Each time that this nervous wreck of a man calmed down, his travelling companion had come from their first-class coach to fetch him and drag him off to the restaurant car to drink champagne. This companion was the same thick-set, insolent, clean-shaven and smartly dressed lawyer who now stood over his body looking as if nothing could surprise him. It was hard to escape the feeling that his client's ceaseless agitation had somehow been to his advantage.

Misha's father had told him that the suicide had been a well-known millionaire, Zhivago, a good-natured profligate, by then half out of his mind. Unrestrained by Misha's presence, the man had talked about his late wife and his son, a boy of Misha's age, and then about his second family whom he had abandoned like the first. At this point he would remember something else, grow pale with terror and begin to mumble and lose the thread of his story.

To Misha he had shown an unaccountable affection, which probably reflected a feeling for someone else. He showered him with presents, jumping out to buy them at the big stations where the bookstalls of the first-class waiting-rooms also sold toys and local curios.

He had drunk incessantly and complained that he had not slept for three months and that as soon as he sobered up for however short a while he suffered torments unimaginable to any normal human being.

At the end, he had rushed into their compartment, seized Gordon by the hand, tried to tell him something but found he could not, and had dashed out into the corridor and thrown himself from the train.

Now Misha sat examining the small wooden box of Urals minerals which had been the last gift of the dead man. Suddenly there was a general stir. A trolley rolled up on the parallel track. A doctor, two policemen and a magistrate with a cockade in his hat jumped out. Questions were asked in cold business-like voices and notes taken. The policemen and the guards, slipping and sliding awkwardly in the sand, dragged the corpse up the embankment. A peasant woman started wailing. The passengers were asked to go back to their seats, the guard blew his whistle and the train moved on.

8

'Here's old Holy Oil,' Nicky thought savagely, looking round the room for a way of escape. The voices of the guests were outside the door and retreat was cut off. The room had two beds, his own and Voskoboynikov's. With scarcely a moment's thought he crept under the first.

He could hear them calling and looking for him outside, surprised at his absence and finally coming into the bedroom.

'Well, it can't be helped,' said Nikolay Nikolayevich. 'Run along, Yura. Perhaps your friend will turn up later and you can play with him then.' They sat talking about the student unrest in Petersburg and Moscow, keeping Nicky in his absurd and undignified confinement for close on half an hour. At last they went out on the verandah. Nicky softly opened the window, jumped out and went off into the park.

He had had no sleep the night before and was out of sorts. He was in his fourteenth year and was sick and tired of being a child. He had stayed awake all night and had gone out at dawn. The rising sun had cast the long dewy shadow of trees in loops over the parkland. The shadow was not black but dark grey like soaked felt, and it was somehow from this damp shadow on the ground, with strips of light in it like a girl's fingers, that the heady fragrance of the morning seemed to come. Suddenly a streak of quicksilver, as shiny as the dew on the grass, flowed by him a few paces away. It flowed on and on and the ground did not absorb it. Then, with an unexpectedly sharp movement, it swerved aside and hid. It was a grass snake. Nicky shivered.

He had certain oddities of character. When he was excited he talked aloud to himself, copying his mother's choice of lofty subjects and her taste for paradox.

'How wonderful to be alive,' he thought. 'But why does it always have to be so painful? God exists, of course. But if He exists, then I

25

am He.' He looked up at an aspen shaking from top to bottom, its wet leaves like bits of tinfoil. 'I'll order it to stop.' With an insane intensity of effort, he willed silently with his whole being, with every ounce of his flesh and blood : 'Be still,' and the tree at once obediently froze into immobility. Nicky laughed with joy and ran off happily to the river to bathe.

His father was the terrorist Dementiy Dudorov, condemned to death by hanging but reprieved by the Tsar and now doing forced labour. His mother was a Georgian princess of the Eristov family, a spoilt and beautiful woman, still young and always in the throes of an enthusiasm for one thing or another—risings, rebels and rebellions, extremist theories, famous actors or unhappy failures.

She adored Nicky, turned his name, Inokentiy, into a thousand impossibly tender and silly nicknames such as Inochek and Nochenka, and took him to Tiflis to show him off to her family. There, what struck him most was a straggly tree in the courtyard of their house. It was a clumsy, tropical giant, with leaves like elephant's ears which sheltered the yard from the scorching southern sky. Nicky could not get used to the idea that it was a plant and not an animal.

It was dangerous for Nicky to bear his father's terrible name. Ivan Ivanovich wished him to adopt his mother's and intended, with her consent, to petition the Tsar for permission to make the change. When Nicky was lying under the bed, indignant at all the world, he had thought also of this.—Who did Voskoboynikov think he was to meddle so outrageously with his life ? He'd teach them where they got off.

And that Nadya ! Just because she was fifteen, did that give her the right to turn up her nose and talk down to him as if he were a child ? He'd show her ! 'I hate her,' he said several times to himself. 'I'll kill her. I'll take her out in the boat and drown her.'

His mother was pretty cool too ! Of course she'd lied to him and Voskoboynikov when she went away. She hadn't gone anywhere near the Caucasus, she had simply turned round at the nearest junction and gone north to Petersburg, and was now having a lovely time with the students shooting at the police, while he was supposed to rot alive in this silly dump. But he wasn't such a fool as they thought. He'd kill Nadya, chuck school, run away to his father in Siberia and start a rebellion.

9

The pond had water-lilies growing all round the edge. The boat cut into them with a dry rustle, making a triangular rift ; the dark water showed in it like juice in a water-melon where a segment has been cut out.

Nicky and Nadya were picking the lilies. They both took hold of the same tough rubbery stem. It pulled them together, so that they knocked their heads, and the boat was dragged into shore as by a boat hook. There the stems were shorter and more tangled; the white flowers, with hearts as yellow as egg-yolk streaked with blood, dived and came up, water pouring out of them.

The children went on picking them, leaning over the side of the boat and making it tip more and more.

'I'm sick of school,' said Nicky. 'It's time I began my life—time I went out into the world and earned my living.'

'And I meant to ask you about square root equations. My algebra is so bad I was nearly kept back another term.'

Nicky decided that he was being needled. Naturally, she was putting him in his place, telling him he was a baby—talking about square root equations when he hadn't got anywhere near algebra yet.

But he did not show that he was offended and asked her with assumed indifference, realising at the same moment how silly it was:

'Who will you marry when you're grown up?'

'That's a very long way off. No one, I should think. I haven't thought about it.'

'You needn't think I'm interested.'

'Then why d'you ask?'

'You're an idiot.'

They started quarrelling. Nicky remembered his early morning misogyny and threatened to drown her if she didn't stop calling him names. 'Have a try,' said Nadya. He grabbed her across the waist. They fought, lost their balance and fell in.

They could both swim but the lilies caught at their arms and legs and they were out of their depth. Finally they felt the slime under their feet and climbed out, water streaming from their shoes and pockets. Nicky was the more exhausted of the two.

If this had happened even so recently as last spring, after the excitement they would have shouted, cursed and giggled as they sprawled side by side, wet to the skin.

But now they sat without a word, hardly breathing, overcome by the absurdity of the whole thing. Nadya seethed with silent indignation and Nicky ached all over as if his arms and legs were black and blue and he had cracked his ribs.

In the end Nadya let fall quietly, like an adult: 'You really are mad,' and Nicky said in an equally grown-up voice: 'I'm sorry.'

They walked home, leaving watery tracks like two water-carts. Their way took them up the dusty slope swarming with snakes near the place where Nicky had seen the grass snake that morning.

He remembered the excitement which had filled him in the night, and his omnipotence at dawn when he had commanded nature. What order should he give it now? he wondered. What did he want more than anything else in the world? It struck him that what he wanted most was to fall into the pond again with Nadya, and he would have given much to know if this would ever happen.

2

A Girl from a Different World

THE war with Japan was not yet finished but it was unexpectedly overshadowed by other events. Waves of revolution swept across Russia, each greater and more extraordinary than the last.

It was at this time that Amalia Karlovna Guishar, the widow of a Belgian engineer and herself a Russianised Frenchwoman, arrived in Moscow from the Urals with her two children—her son Rodyon and her daughter Larissa. She placed her son in a military academy and her daughter in a girls' high school, in the same school, as it happened, and in the same form as the one attended by Nadya Kologrivova.

Madame Guishar's husband had left her his savings, stocks which had been rising and were now beginning to fall. To stop the drain on her resources and to have something to do, she bought a small business; this was Levitskaya's dressmaking establishment near the Triumphal Arch[1]; she took it over from Levitskaya's heirs together with the firm's goodwill, its clientèle and all its seamstresses and apprentices.

This she did on the advice of Komarovsky, a lawyer who had been a friend of her husband's and was now her mainstay, a cold-blooded business man who knew the Russian business world like the back of his hand. It was with him that she had arranged her move by correspondence; he had met her and the children at the station and had driven them to the other end of Moscow, to the Montenegro Hotel in Oruzheiny Street[2] where he had booked their room; and he it was who had persuaded her to send Rodya to the military academy and Lara to the school of his choice, and who joked in an offhand way with the boy and stared at the girl so that he made her blush.

2

They stayed about a month at the Montenegro before moving into the small three-roomed flat adjoining the workshop.

[1] A poor district.   [2] Oruzheiny Street: Gun or Armoury Street.

This was the most sordid part of Moscow—slums, shady dives, the haunts of *likhachi* [1] and whole streets given up to vice.

The children were not dismayed by the dirt in the rooms, the bed bugs and the wretchedness of the furniture. Since their father's death their mother had lived in constant fear of destitution. Rodya and Lara were used to being told that they were on the verge of ruin. They realised that they were different from the children of the street, but, like children brought up in an orphanage, they had a deep-seated fear of the rich.

Their mother gave them a living example of this fear. Madame Guishar was a plump blonde of about thirty-five whose heart attacks alternated with her fits of silliness. She was a dreadful coward and was terrified of men. It was because of this that, out of sheer panic and confusion, she drifted from the embraces of one lover to those of another.

At the Montenegro the family lived in Room 23, and in Room 24 there had lived, ever since the Montenegro had been founded, the 'cellist Tishkevich, a bald, sweaty, kindly man in a wig, who joined his hands prayerfully and pressed them to his heart when he was trying to convince anyone of anything, and who played at fashionable parties and concert halls, throwing back his head and rolling his eyes in rapture. He was rarely in and spent whole days at the Bolshoi and the Conservatoire. As neighbours they helped each other out and this brought them together.

Since the presence of the children sometimes embarrassed Madame Guishar during Komarovsky's visits, Tishkevich would leave her his key so that she could use his room. Soon she took his altruism so much for granted that on several occasions she knocked on his door asking him in tears to protect her from her patron.

3

The workshop was in a single-storeyed house near the corner of Tverskaya Street, in a quarter invaded by the Brest railway with its engine depots, warehouses and lodgings for the clerks.

In one of them lived Olya Demina, a clever girl who worked at Madame Guishar's and whose uncle was a clerk at the goods-yard. She was a quick apprentice. She had been singled out by the former owner of the workshop and was now beginning to be favoured by the new one. Olya had a great liking for Lara Guishar.

[1] Fashionable cab-drivers who had an unsavoury reputation as a class because of their connection with prostitutes.

Nothing had changed since Levitskaya's day. The sewing machines whirred frantically under the tread of tired seamstresses or their hovering hands. Here and there a woman sat on a table, sewing quietly with a broad sweep of the arm as she pulled the needle and long thread. The floor was littered with scraps. You had to raise your voice to make yourself heard above the clatter of the machines and the fluted warbling of Kyril Modestovich, the canary in its cage in the window; the former owner had carried with her to the grave the secret of the bird's improbable name.

In the reception room the ladies clustered in a striking group round a table heaped with fashion journals; they stood, sat or reclined in the poses they had seen in the fashion plates, and discussed the models and the patterns. Sitting in the manager's chair at another table was Faïna Silantyevana Fetisova, a bony woman with warts in the recesses of her flabby cheeks, who was a senior cutter and Madame Guishar's assistant.

A cigarette in a bone holder clamped between her yellowed teeth, her eyes with yellow eyeballs screwed up against the yellow jet of smoke from her nose and mouth, she jotted in a notebook the measurements, orders and addresses of the clients.

Madame Guishar had no experience of running a workshop. She felt that she was not quite the boss, but the staff were honest and Fetisova reliable. All the same, these were troubled times and she was afraid to think of the future; she had moments of paralysing despair.

Komarovsky often came to see them. As he walked through the workshop on his way to their flat, startling the fashionable ladies at their fittings so that they darted behind the screens coyly parrying his jokes, the seamstresses muttered, disapproving and amused: 'Here comes his lordship,' 'Amalia's heartache,' 'old goat,' 'lady killer.'

An object of even greater hatred was his bulldog Jack; he sometimes brought it with him on a lead on which it pulled with such violent jerks that Komarovsky followed, stumbling and lurching with outstretched hands like a blind man after his guide.

One spring Jack sank his teeth in Lara's leg and tore her stocking.

'I'll do him in, the pest,' Olya whispered hoarsely into Lara's ear.

'Yes, he really is a horrid dog; but how can you do that, silly?'

'Ssh, don't shout, I'll tell you how. You know those stone Easter eggs on your Mama's chest of drawers . . .'

'Well, yes, they're made of crystal and marble.'

'That's it, that's it! Bend down and I'll whisper. You take them and dip them in lard—the filthy beast will guzzle them and choke himself, the devil. And that's that—he'll die. . . .'

Lara laughed and thought of Olya with envy. Here was a working

31

girl who lived in poverty. Such children were precocious. Yet goodness, how unspoilt and childlike she was! Jack, the eggs—where on earth did she get all her ideas? 'And why is it,' thought Lara, 'that my fate is to see everything and take it all so much to heart?'

4

'Mama is his—what's the word? . . . He's Mama's . . . They're bad words, I won't say them. Then why does he look at me like that? I'm her daughter after all.'

Lara was only a little over sixteen but her figure was completely formed. People thought she was eighteen or more. She had a clear mind and an easy nature; she was very good-looking.

She and Rodya realised that nothing in life would come to them easily. Unlike the idle and the well-to-do, they had not the leisure for premature theorising and curiosity about things which did not as yet concern them in practice. Only the superfluous is sordid. Lara was the purest being in the world.

Both of them were grateful for small mercies. They knew what everything cost and valued what they had achieved so far. People had to think well of you if you were to get on. Lara worked well at school, not because she had an abstract love of learning but because only the best pupils paid reduced fees. For similar reasons, she washed her mother's dishes and ran her errands. She moved with a silent grace, and everything about her—voice, figure, gestures, her grey eyes and her shining hair—was fitting and harmonious.

It was a Sunday in the middle of July and on holidays you could stay in bed a little longer. She lay on her back, her hands clasped behind her head.

The workshop was quiet. The window looking out on the street was open. Lara heard the rattle of a droshki in the distance turn into a smooth glide as the wheels left the cobbles for the groove of a tram track. 'I'll sleep a bit more,' she thought. The rumble of the town was like a lullaby and made her sleepy.

Lara was aware of touching the bedclothes with her left shoulder and the big toe of her right foot—these defined the space she took up in bed. Everything between her shoulder and her foot was vaguely herself—her soul or essence neatly fitting into the outline of her body and impatiently straining towards the future.

'I must go to sleep,' thought Lara, and conjured up in her imagination the sunny side of Coachmakers' Row [1] as it must be at this hour—

[1] Coachmakers' Row: Karetny Ryad.

the enormous carriages displayed on the cleanly swept floors of the coachmakers' sheds, the lanterns of cut glass, the stuffed bears, the rich life. And a little further down the street, the dragoons exercising in the yard of the Znamensky barracks—the chargers mincing in a circle, the men vaulting into the saddles and riding past, at a walk, at a trot and at a gallop—and outside, the row of children with nannies and wet-nurses gaping through the railings.

And a little further still, thought Lara, Petrovka Street. 'Good heavens, Lara, what an idea! I just wanted to show you my flat. As we're so near.'

It was the name-day of Olga, the small daughter of some friends of Komarovsky's who lived in Coachmakers' Row, and the grown-ups were having a party with dancing and champagne for the occasion. He had invited Mama, but Mama couldn't go, she wasn't feeling well. Mama had said: 'Take Lara. You're always telling me to look after Lara. Well, now you look after her.' And look after her he did— that was a joke!

It was all this waltzing that had started it. What a crazy business it was! You spun round and round, thinking of nothing. While the music played a whole eternity went by like life in a novel. But directly it stopped you had a feeling of shock, as if a bucket of cold water were splashed over you or somebody had found you undressed. Of course, one reason why you allowed anyone to be so familiar was mere showing off—to demonstrate how grown-up you were.

She could never have imagined that he danced so well. What clever hands he had, what assurance as he gripped you by the waist! But never again would she allow anyone to kiss her like that. She could never have dreamed there could be so much effrontery in any-one's lips when they were pressed for such a long time against your own.

She must stop all this nonsense. Once and for all. Stop playing at being shy, simpering and lowering her eyes—or it would end in disaster. This was where a terrible border-line lay. One step and you would be hurled into an abyss. She must stop thinking about dancing. That was the root of the evil. She must boldly refuse— pretend that she had never learned to dance or that she'd broken her leg.

5

That autumn there was unrest among the railway workers on the Moscow network. The men on the Moscow–Kazan line went on strike and those of the Moscow–Brest line were expected to join them. The decision to strike had been taken but the strike committee were still arguing about the date. Everyone on the railway knew that a strike was coming and only a pretext was needed for it to break out.

It was a cold overcast morning at the beginning of October and on that day the wages were due. For a long time nothing was heard from the accountants; then a boy came into the office with a pay sheet and a pile of labour books which had been kept back for the fines to be deducted. The cashier started handing out the pay packets. In an endless line, conductors, switchmen, joiners, drivers' mates, charwomen from the depot moved across the wasteland between the wooden buildings of the management and the station with its work-shops, warehouses, engine sheds and tracks.

The air smelt of early winter in town—of trampled maple leaves, melted snow, and warm engine soot and rye bread just out of the oven (it was baked in the basement of the station buffet). Trains came and went and were shunted, coupled and uncoupled to the waving, furling and unfurling of signal flags. The deep engine hooters roared and the horns and whistles of the guards and shunters tooted and trilled. Smoke rose in endless ladders to the sky, and hissing engines scalded the cold winter clouds with clouds of boiling steam.

Fuflygin, the Divisional Manager, and Pavel Ferapontovich Antipov, the Track Overseer of the station district, strolled up and down along the edge of the permanent way. Antipov had been pestering the repair shops about the quality of the spare parts for mending the tracks. The steel was not sufficiently tensile, the rails failed the test for strains and Antipov thought that they would crack in frosty weather. The management paid no attention to his complaints. Evidently someone was making money on the contracts.

Fuflygin wore an expensive fur-lined coat on which the piping of the railway uniform had been sewn; it was unbuttoned and showed his new civilian serge suit. He stepped cautiously along the embankment, glancing down with pleasure at the line of his lapels, the straight creases on his trousers and his well-cut shoes. What Antipov was saying came in at one ear and went out at the other. Fuflygin had his own thoughts; he kept taking out his watch and looking at it; he was in a hurry to be off.

'Quite right, quite right, my dear fellow,' he broke in impatiently, 'but that's only dangerous on the main lines or on some through-track with a lot of traffic on it. But just look at what you've got. Sidings and dead ends, nettles and dandelions. And the traffic!—at most an old shunting engine for sorting the empties. What more do you want? You must be off your head! Talk about steel! Wooden rails would do!'

Fuflygin looked at his watch, snapped the lid and gazed into the distance where a road ran towards the railway. A carriage came into sight at a bend of the road. This was Fuflygin's turn-out. His wife had come for him. The coachman drew in the horses almost at the edge of the permanent way, talking to them in a high-pitched womanish voice, like a nanny scolding fretful children: they were frightened of trains. In a corner of the carriage sat a pretty woman leaning back against the cushions with an abstracted air.

'Well, my good fellow, some other time,' said the Divisional Manager with a wave of the hand, as much as to say, 'I've got more important things than rails to think about.' The couple drove off.

6

Three or four hours later, almost at dusk, in a field some distance from the track, where no one had been visible until then, two figures rose out of the ground and, looking back over their shoulders, quickly walked away.

'Let's walk faster,' said Tiverzin. 'I'm not worried about the police getting on to us but the moment those ditherers in their hole in the ground have finished they'll come out and catch up with us. I can't bear the sight of them. What's the point of having a committee if you drag things out like this?—You play with fire and then you duck for shelter. You're a fine one yourself—siding with that lot.'

'My Darya's got typhus. I ought to be taking her to hospital. Until I've done that I can't take anything in.'

'They say the wages are being paid to-day. I'll go round to the office. If it wasn't pay-day I'd chuck the lot of you, honest to God I would, and I'd put an end to all this off my own bat, I wouldn't wait a minute.'

'And how would you do that, might I ask?'

'Nothing to it. I'd go down to the boiler room, blow the whistle, and that would be that.'

They said good-bye and went off in different directions.

Tiverzin walked along the track towards the town. He ran into people coming away from the office with their pay. There were very many of them. By the look of it, he reckoned that nearly all the station workers had been paid.

It was getting dark, the lights were on in the office. Idle workers

35

crowded in the square outside it. At the entrance to the square stood Fuflygin's carriage and in it sat Fuflygin's wife, still in the same pose as though she had not moved since morning. She was waiting for her husband, who was getting his money.

Sleet began to fall. The coachman climbed down from his box to put up the leather hood. While he tugged at the stiff struts, one leg braced against the back of the carriage, Fuflygina sat admiring the silver beads of sleet glittering in the light of the office lamps; her unblinking dreamy gaze was fixed on a point above the heads of the workers in a manner suggesting that it would, in case of need, go through them as if they were only sleet or mist.

Tiverzin caught sight of her expression and squirmed. He walked past without greeting her and decided to call for his wages later, so as not to run into her husband at the office. He crossed over to the darker side of the square, towards the workshops and the black shape of the turntable with tracks fanning out from it towards the depot.

'Tiverzin! Kuprik!' Several voices called out of the darkness. There were a lot of people outside the workshops. Inside, someone was yelling and a child was crying. 'Do go in and help that boy,' said a woman in the crowd.

As usual, the old foreman, Pyotr Khudoleyev, was walloping Yusupka [1] the apprentice.

Khudoleyev had not always been a tormentor of apprentices nor a brawling drunkard. There had been a time when, as a dashing young workman, he had attracted the admiring glances of merchants' and priests' daughters in Moscow's industrial suburbs. But Marfa, who had graduated that year from the diocesan convent school, had turned him down and had married his workmate, the engine-driver Saveliy Nikitich, Tiverzin's father.

Five years after Saveliy's fearful end (he was burnt to death in the sensational railway crash of 1883) Khudoleyev renewed his suit, but again Marfa rejected him. So Khudoleyev took to drink and rowdiness, trying to get even with a world which was to blame, so he believed, for all his misfortunes.

Yusupka was the son of Gimazetdin [2] the porter at the block of tenements where Tiverzin lived. Tiverzin had taken the boy under his wing and this made Khudoleyev dislike him even more.

'Is that the way to hold a file, you cross-eyed brat?' bellowed Khudoleyev, dragging Yusupka by the hair and pummelling the back

[1] Tartar diminutive of Joseph.
[2] A Russianised form of the Moslem name Gemal-et-Din. (Gimazetdin is a Tartar.)

of his neck. 'Is that the way to strip down a casting, you slit-eyed Tartar scamp?'

'Ow, I won't do it any more, mister, ow, I won't do it any more, ow, you're hurting me!'

'If he's been told once he's been told a thousand times; first adjust the mandrel and then screw up the chuck, but will he listen?—No, he just goes on doing it his own sweet way! Nearly broke the spindle, the bastard.'

'I didn't touch the spindle, mister, honest I didn't.'

'Why are you plaguing the boy?' asked Tiverzin, elbowing his way through the crowd.

'It's none of your business,' Khudoleyev snapped.

'I'm asking you why you plague the boy.'

'And I'm telling you to move off before there's trouble, you Socialist meddler. Killing's too good for him, the son of a bitch, he nearly broke my spindle. He should thank his lucky stars he's still alive, the slit-eyed devil—all I did was tweak his ears and pull his hair a bit.'

'So you think he should have his head torn off for this? Khudoleyev, old man, you ought to be ashamed of yourself, really, an old foreman like you! You've got grey hair but you haven't learned sense yet.'

'Move on, move on, I tell you, while you're still in one piece. I'll knock the stuffing out of you, preaching at me, you dog's arse. You were made on the sleepers, you jellyfish, under your father's very nose. I know your mother, the slut, the mangy cat, the crumpled petticoat!'

What happened next was over in a second. Both men seized the first thing that came to hand on the lathe benches, where heavy tools and lumps of iron were lying about, and would have killed each other if the crowd had not rushed in to separate them. Khudoleyev and Tiverzin stood with their heads bent down, their foreheads almost touching, pale, with bloodshot eyes. They were so angry that they could not utter a word. They were held firmly, their arms gripped from behind. Once or twice they tried to break free, twisting their bodies and dragging their workmates who were hanging on to them. Hooks and buttons went flying, their jackets and shirts slipped off, baring their shoulders. Around them was a ceaseless noisy hubbub.

'The chisel! Take the chisel away from him, he'll smash his head in. Easy now, easy now, Pyotr, old man, or we'll break your arm! What are we playing around with them for! Drag them apart and put them under lock and key and there's an end to it.'

With a superhuman effort Tiverzin suddenly shook off the men who clung to him and, breaking loose, dashed to the door. They started after him but, seeing that he had changed his mind, left him alone. He went out, slamming the door behind him, and marched off without turning round. The dark damp autumn night closed in on him. 'You try to help them and they come at you with a knife,' he muttered, striding on unconscious of his direction.

This base world of lies and fraud, in which an over-fed madam had the impertinence to stare right through a crowd of working men and where a drink-sodden victim of such ways found pleasure in taking it out of his own kind, this world was now more hateful to him than it had ever been before. He hurried on as though his pace could hasten the time when everything on earth would be as reasonable and harmonious as it was now inside his feverish head. He knew that all their strivings in the last few days, the troubles on the line, the speeches at meetings, the decision to strike—not carried out yet but at least not cancelled—were small separate stages on the great road lying ahead of them.

But at the moment he was so worked up that he wanted to run all the way without stopping to draw breath. He had not consciously worked out where he was going with his long steps, but his feet knew very well where they were taking him.

It was not until much later that Tiverzin learned of the decision, taken by the strike committee after he had left the underground shelter with Antipov, to begin the strike that very night. They had decided there and then which of them was to go where and which men would be called out.

A crowd was already moving away from the depot and the goods yard, when Tiverzin blew the hooter of the engine repair shop and its hoarse whistle burst out as though from the bottom of his heart, to drop a few seconds later to a level note. Soon this crowd was joined by the men from the boiler room, who had downed tools at Tiverzin's signal.

For many years Tiverzin thought that it was he alone who had stopped work and traffic on the line that night. Only much later, at the trial, when he was charged with complicity in the strike but not with inciting it, did he learn the truth.

People ran out asking: 'Where is everybody going? What's the hooting for?'—'You're not deaf,' came from the darkness. 'It's a fire. They're sounding the alarm. They want us to put it out.'—'Where's the fire?'—'There must be a fire or they wouldn't be sounding the alarm.'

Doors banged, more people came out. Other voices were heard.

'Fire my foot. Listen to the ignorant lout! It's a strike, that's what it is, see? Down tools, mates. Let them get some other fools to do their dirty work. Clear off home, lads.'

More and more people joined the crowd. The railway workers were on strike.

7

Tiverzin came home two days later, drawn with lack of sleep and chilled to the bone. Frost, unheard of at this time of year, had set in the night before and Tiverzin was not dressed for winter. The porter, Gimazetdin, met him at the gate.

'Thank you, Mister Tiverzin,' he babbled in broken Russian. 'You didn't let Yusupka come to harm. I will always pray for you.'

'You're crazy, Gimazetdin, who're you calling Mister? Cut it out, for goodness' sake, and say what you have to say quickly, you see how cold it is.'

'Why should you be cold? You will soon be warm, Kuprian Savelich. Me and your mother Marfa Gavrilovna brought a whole shed full of wood from the goods station yesterday—all birch—good, dry wood.'

'Thanks, Gimazetdin. If there's something else you want to tell me let's have it quickly. I'm frozen.'

'I wanted to tell you not to spend the night at home, Savelich. You must hide. The police have been here asking who comes to the house.—Nobody comes, I said, my relief comes, I said, the people from the railway but no strangers come, I said, not on your life.'

Tiverzin was unmarried and lived with his mother and his younger married brother. The tenements belonged to the neighbouring Church of the Holy Trinity. Among the tenants were some of the clergy and two *arteli* [1] of street hawkers—one of butchers, the other of green-grocers—but most of them were small clerks on the Moscow–Brest railway.

It was a stone house built round four sides of a dirty, unpaved yard. Covered wooden staircases went up the outside walls facing the yard; the dirty, slimy steps smelt of cats and sauerkraut; latrines and padlocked larders clung to the landings.

Tiverzin's brother had fought as a conscript in the war with Japan and had been wounded. Now he was convalescing at the military hospital in Krasnoyarsk and his wife and two daughters had gone

[1] Groups of workmen or small tradesmen who worked together under their own foreman and usually shared lodgings.

there to see him and to bring him home (the Tiverzins, hereditary railway workers, were natural travellers and journeyed all over Russia on free service warrants). The flat was quiet and empty except for Tiverzin and his mother.

Their flat was on the second floor. On the landing outside there was a water-butt, filled regularly by the water-carrier. Tiverzin noticed as he came up that the lid of the butt had been pushed sideways and a tin mug stood on the frozen surface of the water. 'Prov must have been round,' he grinned. 'The way that man drinks, his guts must be on fire.' Prov was Prov Afanasyevich Sokolov, the church psalmist, a relation of Tiverzin's mother.

Tiverzin jerked the mug out of the ice and pulled the handle of the door bell. A warm homely smell, steamy with cooking, billowed out to greet him.

'Hullo, Mother, you've got a good blaze going; it's nice and warm in here.'

His mother flung herself on his neck and burst into tears. He stroked her head and, after a while, gently pushed her aside.

'Nothing venture, nothing win, Mother,' he said softly. 'The line is at a standstill from Moscow to Warsaw.'

'I know, that's why I'm crying. They'll be after you, Kuprinka, you've got to get away.'

'That nice boy friend of yours, Pyotr, nearly broke my head!' He meant to make her laugh but she said earnestly: 'It's a sin to laugh at him, Kuprinka. You should be sorry for him, poor lost soul.'

'Antipov's been arrested. They came in the night, searched his flat, turned everything upside down and took him away this morning. And his Darya's in hospital with the typhus. And their kid, Pasha, who's at secondary school, is alone in the house with his deaf aunt. And they're going to be evicted. I think we should have the boy to stay with us.—What did Prov want?'

'How did you know he came?'

'I saw the water-butt was uncovered and the mug on the ice— sure to have been Prov swigging water, I said to myself.'

'How sharp you are, Kuprinka. Yes, he's been. Prov—Prov Afanasyevich. Came to borrow some logs—I gave him some. But what am I talking about, fool that I am! It went clean out of my head—the news Prov brought. Think of it, Kuprinka!—the Tsar has signed a manifesto and everything's to be turned upside down— everybody's to be treated right, the peasants are to have land and we're all going to be equal with the gentry! It's actually signed, he says, it's only got to be made public. The Synod's sent something to be put into the church service, a thanksgiving or a prayer for the Tsar, he told me what it was but I've forgotten.'

8

Pasha Antipov, whose father had been arrested as one of the organisers of the strike, came to live with the Tiverzins. He was a clean, tidy boy with regular features and red hair parted in the middle; he was always smoothing it down with a brush and straightening his tunic or the school buckle on his belt. He had a great sense of humour and an unusual gift of observation, and kept himself and everyone else in fits of laughter by his clever imitations of everything he heard and saw.

Soon after the Manifesto was published on October 17th there was a big demonstration; it started from the Tver Gate and was to march to the Kaluga Gate at the other end of Moscow. But it could be truly said of it that too many cooks spoil the broth! Several revolutionary bodies had planned it together but had quarrelled and given it up; then, on the appointed day, when they heard that people had come out all the same, they hastily sent their representatives to lead them.

In spite of Tiverzin's efforts to dissuade her, his mother joined the demonstrators, and Pasha, gay and friendly as ever, went with her.

It was a dry frosty November day with a still, leaden sky and a few snowflakes coming down one by one. They spun slowly and hesitantly before settling on the pavement like fluffy grey dust.

Down the street people came pouring in a torrent—faces, faces, faces, quilted winter coats and sheepskin hats, men and women students, old men, children, railwaymen in uniform, workers from the tramcar depot and the telephone exchange in knee boots and leather jerkins, girls and schoolboys.

For some time they sang the Marseillaise, 'Warsaw' and 'Victims they Fell'. Then a man who had been walking backwards at the head of the procession, singing and conducting with his cap which he used as a baton, turned round, put his cap on his head and listened to what the other leaders round him were saying. The singing broke off in disorder. Now you could hear the crunch of innumerable footsteps on the frozen road.

The leaders had received a message from sympathisers that Cossacks [1] were waiting to ambush the procession further down the street. The warning had been given by telephone to a chemist near by.

'What of it?' said the ringleaders. 'We must keep calm and not lose our heads, that's the main thing. We must occupy the first public building we come to, warn the people and scatter.'

An argument began about the best building to go to. Some suggested the Society of Shop Assistants, others the Technical School and still others the School of Foreign Business Correspondence.

While they were still arguing they reached the corner of a high school building, which offered shelter every bit as good as those which had been mentioned.

When they drew level with the entrance the ringleaders turned aside, climbed the steps of the semicircular porch and motioned the head of the procession to halt, but their gesture was misunderstood. The multiple doors opened and the people—coat to coat and cap to cap—moved into the entrance hall and up the stairs.

'The lecture hall, the lecture hall,' shouted a few voices in the rear, but the rest continued to press forward, scattering down corridors and straying into the schoolrooms. The leaders at last succeeded in shepherding them into the lecture hall, and tried several times to warn them of the ambush, but no one would listen. The fact of stopping and going inside a building was taken as an invitation to an impromptu meeting, which in fact began at once.

After all the walking and singing, people were glad to sit quietly for a bit and let others do their work for them, shouting themselves hoarse. The speakers, who agreed on most points, seemed all to be saying the same thing; if there were any differences between them they were overlooked in the relief of sitting down and having a rest. In the end it was the worst orator of the lot who received the most enthusiastic welcome. People made no effort to follow him and merely roared approval at every word, no one minding the interruptions and everyone agreeing out of impatience to everything he said. There were shouts of 'Shame!' and a telegram of protest was drafted; then the crowd, bored with the speaker's droning voice, stood up as one man and, forgetting all about him, poured out in a body—cap to cap and coat to coat—down the stairs and out into the street. The procession continued.

While the meeting had been taking place indoors, it had started to snow. The street was white. The snow fell thicker and thicker.

When the dragoons charged, the marchers at the rear at first knew

[1] The troops engaged in this action were dragoons, not Cossacks, but uneducated people called all mounted troops Cossacks.

nothing about it. A swelling noise rolled back to them as of great crowds shouting 'Hurrah!' and individual screams of 'Help!' and 'Murder!' were lost in the uproar. Almost at the same moment, and borne, as it were, on this wave of sound along the narrow corridor which formed as the crowd divided, there appeared the heads of riders and their horses, manes and swinging swords carried swiftly and silently above the crowd.

Half a platoon galloped through, turned, re-formed and cut into the tail of the procession. The killing began.

A few minutes later the street was practically empty. People were scattering down the side-streets. The snow was lighter. The dry evening was like a charcoal sketch. Then the sun, setting behind the houses, poked a finger round the corner and picked out everything red in the street—the red tops of the dragoons' caps, a red flag trailing on the ground and the red specks and threads of blood on the snow.

A groaning man with a split skull was crawling along the edge of the kerb. From the far end of the street to which the chase had taken them several dragoons were riding back abreast at a walk. Almost at the horses' feet Tiverzina, her shawl knocked to the back of her head, was running from side to side screaming wildly: 'Pasha! Pasha!'

Pasha had been with her all along, making her laugh by taking off the last speaker at the meeting, but had vanished suddenly in the confusion when the dragoons charged.

A blow from one of their whips had fallen on her back, and though she had hardly felt it through her thickly-wadded coat she swore and shook her fist at the retreating horsemen, indignant that they had dared to strike an old woman like herself, and in public at that.[1]

Looking anxiously from side to side she had the luck finally to spot the boy on the other side of the street. He stood in a recess between a grocer's shop and the porch of a stone house, where a group of chance passers-by had been hemmed in by a horseman who had mounted the pavement. Amused by their terror, the dragoon was giving a display of *haute-école*, backing his horse into the crowd and making it rear and paw the air slowly as in a circus turn. Suddenly he saw his comrades riding back, turned swiftly and in a couple of bounds took his place in the file.

The crowd dispersed and Pasha, who had been too frightened to utter a sound, rushed to the old woman.

Tiverzina grumbled all the way home. 'Filthy murderers! People

[1] In his autobiographical book, *Safe Conduct*, the author describes an incident in 1895 when he took part in a street demonstration and was struck by a whip.

are happy because the Tsar has given them freedom, but these damned killers can't stand it. All they want is to spoil everything, twist every word inside out.'

She was furious with the dragoons, furious with the whole world, and at the moment even with her own son. When she was in a temper it seemed to her that all the recent troubles were the fault of 'Kuprinka's bunglers and fumblers' as she called them.

'What do they want, the half-wits? They don't know themselves, just so long as they can make mischief, the vipers. Like that chatter-box.—Pasha, dear, show me again how he went on, show me, darling. —Oh! I'll burst, I'll burst. You've got him to the life.'

At home she fell to scolding her son. Was she of an age to have a curly-headed oaf on a horse beat her with a whip on her behind?

'Really, Mother, who d'you take me for? You'd think I was the Cossack captain or the head of the police.'

9

Nikolay Nikolayevich saw the fleeing demonstrators from his window. He realised who they were and looked to see if Yura were among them. But none of his friends seemed to be there, though he thought that he had caught sight of the Dudorov boy—he could not quite remember his name—that madcap who had had a bullet extracted from his shoulder not so long ago and who was evidently back again, hanging about in places where he had no business.

Nikolay Nikolayevich had recently arrived from Petersburg. He had no flat in Moscow and he did not wish to go to a hotel, so he was staying with some distant relations of his, the Sventitskys. They had given him a corner room on the mezzanine floor.

The Sventitskys were childless and the two-storeyed house which their late parents had rented from time immemorial from the Princes Dolgoruky was too big for them. It was part of the untidy cluster of buildings in various styles with three courtyards and a garden which stood on the Dolgorukys' property, a three-sided plot bounded by narrow alleys and known by the ancient name of Muchnoy Gorodok.[1]

In spite of its four windows the study was darkish. It was cluttered up with books, papers, rugs and prints. It had a balcony forming a semicircle round the corner of the house. The glass doors of the balcony were sealed for the winter.

The doors and two of the windows looked out on an alley which

Muchnoy Gorodok: Flour Town.

ran away into the distance with its sleigh tracks and crooked little houses and fences.

Purple shadows reached into the room from the garden. The trees, laden with hoar-frost, their branches like smoky streaks of candle-wax, looked in as if they wished to rest their burden on the floor of the study.

Nikolay Nikolayevich stood gazing into the distance. He thought of his last winter in Petersburg—Gapon [1], Gorky, his meeting with Witte [2], modern, fashionable writers. From that bedlam he had fled to the peace and quiet of the ancient capital to write the book he had in mind. But he was no better off.—Lectures every day—Higher Courses for Women [3], the Religious Philosophical Society, the Red Cross and the Strike Fund—not a moment in which to collect his wits. He had jumped out of the frying-pan into the fire. What he needed was to get away to Switzerland, to some remote canton, to the peace of lakes, mountains, sky and the echoing, attentive air.

Nikolay Nikolayevich turned away from the window. He felt like going out to call on someone or just to walk about the streets, but he remembered that Vyvolochnov, the Tolstoyan, was coming to see him about some business or other. He paced up and down the room, his thoughts turning to his nephew.

When Nikolay Nikolayevich had moved from his fastness on the Volga to Petersburg, he had left Yura in Moscow where he had many relations—the Vedenyapins, the Ostromyslenskys, the Selyavins, the Mikhaelises, the Sventitskys and the Gromekos. At first Yura was foisted on the slovenly old chatterbox Ostromyslensky, known among the clan as Freddy. Freddy lived in sin with his ward Motya and therefore saw himself as a disrupter of the established order and a champion of progressive thought. So little did he justify his kinsman's confidence that he even took the money given him for Yura's upkeep and spent it on himself. Yura was transferred to the professorial family of the Gromekos and was still living with them.

The atmosphere at the Gromekos' was eminently suitable, Nikolay Nikolayevich thought. Their daughter, Tonya, was Yura's age, and Misha Gordon, Yura's friend and classmate, spent most of his time with them.

'And a comical triumvirate they make,' thought Nikolay Nikolaye-

---

[1] A priest and revolutionary leader who headed the demonstration in Winter Palace Square in 1905 on what later came to be known as 'Bloody Sunday'; he was suspected of being an *agent provocateur* and killed by the revolutionaries.

[2] Prime Minister in 1905.

[3] University Courses for Women (who were not officially admitted to the universities).

vich. The three of them had soaked themselves in *The Meaning of Love* and *The Kreutzer Sonata* and had a mania for preaching chastity. It was right, of course, for adolescents to go through a frenzy of purity but they were overdoing it, they had lost all sense of proportion.

How childish and eccentric they were. Obsessed by sex, they labelled everything to do with it as 'vulgar' and used the word *ad nauseam*, blushing or growing pale as they uttered it. 'Vulgar' was applied to instinct, to pornography, to prostitution and almost to the whole physical world.

'If I had been in Moscow,' thought Nikolay Nikolayevich, 'I would not have let it go so far. Shame is necessary and within limits . . . Ah! Nil Feoktissovich, come in!' He was interrupted by the arrival of his guest.

10

A fat man came in wearing a grey Tolstoyan shirt with a broad leather belt, felt boots and trousers bagging at the knees. He looked a kindly fellow with his head in the clouds, but a pince-nez on a wide black ribbon quivered angrily on the end of his nose. He had taken off his coat in the hall but had not removed his scarf and came in with it trailing on the floor and his round felt hat still in his hand. These encumbrances prevented him from shaking hands and even from saying How-do-you-do.

'Um-m-m,' he mooed helplessly, looking round the room.

'Put them down anywhere,' said Nikolay Nikolayevich, thereby restoring Vyvolochnov's self-possession and power of speech.

Here was one of those disciples of Tolstoy in whom the teacher's restless thoughts grow shallow past redeeming and settle down to a long, unclouded rest. He had come to ask Nikolay Nikolayevich to speak at a meeting in aid of political prisoners, which was to be held at some school or other.

'I've spoken at that school already.'

'In aid of political prisoners?'

'Yes.'

'You'll have to do it again.'

Nikolay Nikolayevich jibbed a little and then gave in.

The business dealt with, Nikolay Nikolayevich did not attempt to delay his guest. He could have left at once but evidently felt that it would be unseemly and was looking for something lively and natural to say by way of parting. The conversation became strained and disagreeable.

'So you're a decadent nowadays? Going in for mysticism?'

'What do you mean?'

'It's a waste, you know. Do you remember our rural council?'

'Of course. Didn't we canvass for it together!'

'And we did some jolly good work fighting for the schools and teachers' colleges. Remember?'

'Of course. It was a splendid battle.'

'And didn't you do some work afterwards for public health?'

'For a time, yes.'

'Hm-m. — And now it's all this highbrow stuff — fauns and nenuphars and ephebes and "Let's be like the sun."[1] I can't believe it, bless me if I can—an intelligent man like you, and with your sense of humour and your knowledge of the people . . . Come, now. Or am I intruding into the holy of holies?'

'Why talk for the sake of talking? What are we arguing about? You don't know my ideas.'

'Russia needs schools and hospitals, not fauns and nenuphars.'

'No one denies it.'

'The peasants are in rags and they're starving . . .'

So the conversation jerked on. Knowing how useless it was, Nikolay Nikolayevich tried nevertheless to explain what attracted him to some of the writers of the symbolist school. Then, turning to Tolstoyan doctrines, he said:

'Up to a point I am with you, but Tolstoy says that the more a man devotes himself to beauty the further he moves away from goodness . . .'

'And you think it's the other way round—the world will be saved by beauty, is that it?—Dostoyevsky, Rozanov[2], mystery plays and what not?'

'Wait, let me tell you what I think. I think that if the beast who sleeps in man could be held down by threats—any kind of threat, whether of jail or of retribution after death—then the highest emblem of humanity would be the lion tamer in the circus with his whip, not the self-sacrificing preacher. But don't you see, this is just the point— what has for centuries raised man above the beast is not the cudgel but an inward music: the irresistible power of unarmed truth, the attraction of its example. It has always been assumed that the most important things in the Gospels are the ethical teaching and commandments. But for me the most important thing is the fact that Christ speaks in

---

[1] Title of a book of poems by K. D. Balmont.

[2] V. Rozanov, 1856–1919, whose historiosophic conceptions influenced some intellectuals in St. Petersburg and Moscow. This trend was unacceptable to Tolstoyans.

parables taken from daily life, that he explains the truth in terms of everyday reality. The idea which underlies this is that communion between mortals is immortal, and that the whole of life is symbolic because the whole of it has meaning.'

'I haven't understood a word. You should write a book about it!'

At last Vyvolochnov left. Nikolay Nikolayevich felt extremely cross. He was furious with himself for airing some of his most intimate thoughts to that blockhead upon whom they had not had the slightest effect. Then his rage, as sometimes happens, changed its target. He recalled another reason for annoyance and forgot Vyvolochnov altogether.

He did not keep a diary, but once or twice a year he would put down in a thick notebook some thought which struck him particularly. He got out the notebook now and started writing in a large, legible hand. This is what he wrote.

'Upset all day by that silly Schlesinger woman who came this morning, sat till dinner-time and for two solid hours bored me reading out that balderdash—a libretto in verse by the symbolist X to the cosmogonic symphony by the composer Y—spirits of the planets, voices of the elements, etc. etc.

'Have suddenly understood why this stuff is so deadly, so insufferable and artificial even when you come across it in *Faust*. The whole thing is an affectation, no one is genuinely interested in it. Modern man has no need of it. When he is vexed by the mysteries of the universe he turns to physics, not to Hesiod's hexameters.

'And it isn't just that the form is an anachronism, or that these spirits of earth and air only confuse what science has made clear, it's that this *genre* is wholly out of keeping with the very essence, the motivating force of present-day art.

'These cosmogonies belong to the ancient world—a world peopled so sparsely that nature was not yet overshadowed by man. Mammoths still walked the earth, dragons and dynosaurs were still fresh in people's memory. Nature hit you in the eye so plainly and grabbed you so fiercely and so tangibly by the scruff of the neck that perhaps it really was still full of gods. Those were the first pages of the chronicle of mankind, it was only just beginning.

'This ancient world ended with Rome, overpopulation put a stop to it.

'Rome was a flea market of borrowed gods and conquered peoples, a bargain basement on two tiers—earth and heaven—slaves on one, gods on the other. Dacians, Herulians, Scythians, Sarmatians, Hyperboreans. Heavy, spokeless wheels, eyes sunk in fat, bestialism, double chins, illiterate emperors, fish fed on the flesh of learned slaves. Beastliness convoluted in a triple knot like guts. There were more people in the world than there have ever been since, all crammed into the passages of the Coliseum and all wretched.

'And then, into this tasteless heap of gold and marble. He came, light-footed and clothed in light, with his marked humanity, his deliberate Galilean provincialism, and from that moment there were neither gods nor peoples, there was only man—man the carpenter, man the ploughman, man the shepherd with his flock of sheep at sunset, man whose name does not sound in the least proud [1] but who is sung in lullabies and portrayed in picture galleries the world over.'

11

The Petrovka seemed a corner of Petersburg mislaid in Moscow. The matching houses on both sides of the street, the quiet ornaments of the façades, the bookshop, the library, the cartographer, the good tobacconist, the good restaurant, its front door flanked by two round frosted gas-lamps on massive brackets, all helped to create the impression.

In winter the street glowered forbiddingly. Its inhabitants were solid, self-respecting, well-paid members of the liberal professions.

Here Victor Ippolitovich Komarovsky rented his magnificent third-floor flat reached by a wide staircase with massive oak banisters. Unseen and unheard, his housekeeper, or rather the châtelaine of his quiet fastness, Emma Ernestovna, ran it with as much efficiency as discretion, as careful to know everything as never to meddle in the details of his life, and he repaid her with the knightly delicacy to be expected of so fine a gentleman, by not receiving at home anyone— man or woman—whose presence would not have been compatible with her serene old-maidenly world. A monastic peace reigned in the flat—blinds drawn and not a speck of dust, as in an operating theatre.

On Sunday mornings Victor Ippolitovich, accompanied by his bulldog, took a leisurely walk down the Petrovka and along Kuznetsky Most, and at one of the crossroads they were joined by the actor and gambler, Constantine Illarionovich Satanidi.

They strolled on together, exchanging brief anecdotes and remarks so curt, so insignificant and so imbued with contempt for everything in the world that they could quite safely have been replaced by a growling noise, always provided that it filled the street from side to

[1] Reference to Gorky's famous saying, 'Man whose name has so proud a sound'.

side with a sound as loud as their voices, deep, shamelessly panting and as though choking with their own vibration.

12

The weather was unseasonable. Tap-tap-tap went the water drops on the metal of the drain pipes and the cornices, roof tapping messages to roof as if it were spring. It was thawing.

Lara walked all the way in a daze and only realised what had happened to her when she reached home.

Everyone was asleep. She fell back into her trance and in this abstracted state sat down at her mother's dressing table, still in her pale mauve, almost white, lace-trimmed frock and long veil borrowed for the evening from the workshop, as if it were a fancy dress. Her hands clasped upon the table, she sat facing her reflection in the looking-glass, but seeing nothing. After a while she dropped her head on her hands.

If Mama got to hear of it she would kill her. She would kill her and then she would kill herself.

How had it happened? How could it possibly have happened? It was too late now, she should have thought of it earlier.

Now she was—what was it called?—a fallen woman. She was a woman out of a French novel, though to-morrow she would go to school and sit side by side with those other girls who were like babies compared with her. O God, O God, how could it have happened?

Some day, many, many years later, when it was possible, Lara would tell Olya Demina, and Olya would hug her and burst into tears.

Outside the window the water drops lisped, the thaw muttered its spells. Down the road someone was banging on the neighbours' door. Lara sat with bowed head and quivering shoulders, weeping.

13

'That's all rubbish, Emma Ernestovna, my dear. I'm sick and tired of it.' He kept opening and shutting drawers, turning things out, throwing cuffs and collars all over the carpet and the sofa, not realising what it was he needed.

What he needed desperately was Lara and there was no possible chance of seeing her that Sunday. He paced up and down the room frantically, like a caged animal.

She had for him the unique charm of the incorporeal. Her hands astonished him like a sublime idea. Her shadow on the wall of the hotel room had seemed to him the outline of innocence. Her vest was stretched over her breast, as firmly and simply as linen on an embroidery frame.

His fingers drummed on the window pane in time to the unhurried thud of horses' hooves on the asphalted carriage-way below. 'Lara,' he whispered, shutting his eyes. He had a vision of her head resting on his arm; her eyes were closed, she was asleep, unconscious that he watched her sleeplessly for hours on end. Her dark hair was scattered and its beauty stung his eyes like smoke and ate into his heart.

His Sunday walk was not a success. He strolled a few paces with Jack, stopped, thought of Kuznetsky Most, of Satanidi's jokes, of the milling stream of his acquaintances—no, it was more than he could bear. He turned back. The dog, startled, looked up disapprovingly from ground level and waddled after him in disgust.

'What the hell can it all mean?' thought Komarovsky. 'What kind of bedevilment is it?' Could it be his conscience, or pity, or repentance? Or was he worried about her? No, he knew she was safely at home. Then why couldn't he get her out of his mind?

He walked back to his house, up the stairs and past the first landing where the heraldic ornaments at the corners of the window threw coloured patches of light at his feet; half-way up the second flight he stopped.

He must not give in to this exhausting, nagging, anxious mood. He was not a schoolboy after all. He must know what would happen if, instead of being only a toy, this girl—a mere child, the daughter of his dead friend—turned into an obsession. He must pull himself together. He must be true to himself and to his habits, otherwise everything would go up in smoke.

Komarovsky gripped the oak railing until it hurt his hand, shut his eyes a moment, then turned resolutely and went down. On the landing with its patches of coloured light the dog was waiting for him. It lifted its head like a slobbering old dwarf with hanging jowls and stared up at him adoringly.

The dog hated the girl, growled at her, bared its teeth and tore her stockings. It was as jealous of her as if it were afraid of her infecting its master with something human.

'So now you think everything is going to be just as before—Satanidi, funny stories, dirty tricks and all? All right then, take this, and this, and this.' He struck the bulldog with his stick and kicked it. Jack squealed, howled, waddled up the stairs shaking his behind and scratched at the door to complain to Emma Ernestovna.

Days and weeks went by.

14

What a bewitched circle it was! If Komarovsky's intrusion into Lara's life had only filled her with disgust she could have rebelled and broken with him. But it was not so simple.

It flattered her that a handsome man whose hair was turning grey, old enough to be her father, a man who was applauded at meetings and mentioned in the newspapers, should spend his time and money on her, take her out to concerts and theatres, tell her that she looked divine, and should generally, as they say, improve her mind.

After all she was still a schoolgirl in a brown uniform who enjoyed harmless conspiracies at school. Komarovsky's philandering in a carriage behind the coachman's back or in an opera box in full view of the audience pleased and challenged her by its mixture of secrecy and daring.

But these childishly adventurous moods were short-lived. A nagging broken-spirited horror at herself was taking root in her. Worn out by struggling with her lessons and by sleepless nights, tears and an everlasting headache, she was sleepy all day long.

15

She hated him, he was the curse of her life. Every day she went over it in her mind.

She had become his prisoner for life. How had he enslaved her? What made her submit to his wishes and satisfy his need to make her feel ashamed? What was his hold over her? His age? Or her mother's dependence on his money? Did that impress or frighten her so much? No, a thousand times no. That was all nonsense.

It was she who had a hold on him. Didn't she know how much he needed her? There was nothing to be frightened of, her conscience was clear. It was he who should be frightened and ashamed, and terrified of her giving him away. But that was just what she would never do. She lacked his treachery, his chief asset in dealing with the weak and the dependent.

This was just the difference between them. And it was this that made the whole of life so frightening. You were not blasted by thunder and lightning but by covert looks and whispered calumny. Life was all treachery and ambiguity. Any single thread was as fragile as a cobweb, but just try to pull yourself out of the net! It only held you tighter.

Even the strong are ruled by the weak and treacherous.

16

She tried sophistry. What if she were married, she asked herself, what difference would it make? But at times she was overtaken by a hopeless anguish.

How was he not ashamed to grovel at her feet and plead with her? —'We can't go on like this. Think what I have done to you! You are going to your ruin. We must tell your mother and I'll marry you.' He wept and insisted as though she were arguing and protesting. She knew that it meant nothing and hardly listened.

And he continued taking her, veiled, to dinner in the private rooms of that ghastly restaurant where the waiters and the clients undressed her with their eyes as she came in, and all she did was to ask herself: 'If he really loved me, would he so humiliate me?'

Once she had a dream. She was buried under the ground and nothing remained of her except her left side and her right foot. A tuft of grass sprouted from her left nipple and above the ground people were singing 'Black eyes and white breast' and 'Masha must not cross the river'.

17

Lara was not religious. She did not believe in ritual. But sometimes, to enable her to bear her life, she needed the accompaniment of an inward music and she could not always compose it for herself. That music was God's word of life and it was to weep over it that she went to church.

Once, at the beginning of December, when she was feeling like Katerina in *The Storm* [1], she went to pray with such a heavy heart that she felt as if at any moment the earth might open at her feet and the vaulted ceiling of the church cave in. And it would serve her right, and it would put an end to the whole thing. She was only sorry that she had taken that chatterbox Olya Demina with her.

'There's Prov Afanasyevich,' whispered Olya.

[1] A play by Ostrovsky.

'Sh-sh. Do leave me alone. What Prov Afanasyevich?'

'Prov Afanasyevich Sokolov. The one who's reading. He's our cousin twice removed.'

'Oh, the psalmist. Tiverzin's relation. Do shut up.'

They had come in at the beginning of the service. The psalm was: 'Let my soul bless the Lord and all that is within me sanctify His holy name'.

The worshippers all stood in a crowd at the altar end of the echoing, half-empty church. It was a new building. The plain glass window gave no adornment to the grey, snow-bound, busy street outside. In front of it stood the church warden paying no attention to the service and loudly reproving a deaf, half-witted beggar woman in a voice as flat and commonplace as the window and the street.

In the time it took Lara, clutching her pennies in her fist, to make her way past the worshippers without disturbing them, buy two candles for herself and Olya near the door and turn back, Prov Afanasyevich had rattled off nine of the Beatitudes at a pace suggesting that they were quite well enough known without his help.

Blessed are the poor in spirit. . . . Blessed are they that mourn. . . . Blessed are they that hunger and thirst after righteousness. . . .

Lara shivered and stood still. This was for her. He was saying: Happy are the downtrodden. They have something to say for themselves. They have everything before them. That was what He thought. That was Christ's opinion of it.

18

It was the time of the Presnya rising. The Guishars' flat was in the rebel area. A barricade was being built in Tver Street a few yards from their house. People carried buckets of water from their yard, in order to cement the stones and scrap-iron with ice.

The neighbouring yard was used by the insurgents as an assembly point, something between a Red Cross post and a soup kitchen.

Lara knew two of the boys who went to it. One was Nicky Dudorov, a friend of her school friend Nadya. He was proud, straightforward, taciturn and too much like Lara herself to interest her.

The other was Pasha Antipov who went to high school and lived with old Tiverzina, Olya Demina's grandmother. Lara could not help noticing the effect she had on the boy when she met him at the Tiverzins'. He was so childishly simple that he no more thought of hiding his joy at seeing her than if she had been some holiday landscape of birch trees, grass and clouds in which he could delight without any risk of being laughed at.

Hardly had she realised that she had an influence over him when she began unconsciously to use it, though it was not until several years later and at a much further stage in their relationship that she was to take his malleable, easy-going character seriously in hand. By then Pasha knew that he was head over ears in love with her and committed to her for life.

The two boys were playing the most terrible and adult of games, war, and in this particular war they faced not only the normal risks of battle, but the danger of exile or hanging as well. Yet the way their woollen caps were tied at the back suggested that they were children who still had, or should have, parents to look after them. It was as children that Lara thought of them. Their dangerous amusements had a bloom of innocence which they communicated to everything—to the evening, so shaggy with hoar-frost that it seemed more black than white, to the dark-blue shadows in the yard, to the house across the road where the boys were hiding and, above all, to the revolver shots which came from it. 'The boys are shooting,' thought Lara. This was how she thought not only of Nicky and Pasha but of all those who were shooting all over Moscow. 'Good, decent boys,' she thought. 'It's because they are good that they are shooting.'

19

They heard that the barricade might be shelled and that their house would be in danger. It was too late to think of going to stay with friends in some other part of Moscow, the district was surrounded; they had to find shelter in the neighbourhood. They thought of the Montenegro.

It turned out that many other people who were in the same position had also thought of it. The hotel was full up, but for old times' sake they were promised a shake-down in the linen room.

Not to attract attention by carrying suitcases, they packed the most necessary things into three bundles; then they put off moving from day to day.

Such were the patriarchal customs at the workshop that it had stayed open long after the beginning of the general strike. But one dull, cold afternoon there was a ring at the door. Someone had come to complain and to argue. The boss was asked for. Fetisova went instead to pour oil on the troubled waters. A few moments later she called the seamstresses into the hall and introduced them to the visitor. He shook hands all round, clumsily and with emotion, and went away having apparently settled something with Fetisova.

The seamstresses came back into the workroom and began tying on their shawls and pulling on their shabby winter coats.

'What has happened?' asked Madame Guishar, hurrying in.

'They're bringing us out, Madam, we're on strike.'

'But I don't see . . . What harm have I done you?' Madame Guishar burst into tears.

'Don't take on so, Amalia Karlovna. We've got nothing against you. We're very grateful to you. It's not just you and us. Everybody's doing the same, the whole world. You can't go against everybody, can you?'

They all went away, even Olya Demina and even Fetisova who whispered to Madame Guishar by way of parting that she was only staging the strike for the good of the owner and of the establishment. Madame Guishar was inconsolable.

'What black ingratitude! To think that I was so mistaken in these people! The kindness I've lavished on that brat! Well, admittedly she's only a child, she has some excuse, but that old witch!'

'They can't make an exception just for you, Mama, don't you see,' Lara tried to comfort her. 'No one bears you any malice. On the contrary. All that's being done now is done in the name of humanity, in defence of the weak, for the good of women and children. Yes, it is. Don't shake your head. You'll see, one day you and I will be better off because of it.'

But her mother could not understand. 'It's always like this,' she sobbed. 'Just when I can't think straight you come out with something that simply astounds me. People play a dirty trick on me and you say it's all for my good. No really, I must be out of my mind.'

Rodya was at school. Lara and her mother wandered about, alone in the empty house. The unlit street stared emptily into the rooms and the rooms returned its stare.

'Let's go to the hotel, Mama, before it gets dark,' Lara begged. 'Do come, Mama. Don't put it off, let's go now.'

'Filat, Filat,' they called the porter. 'Take us to the Montenegro, Filat, dear.'

'Very good, Madam.'

'Take the bundles across. And keep an eye on the house, Filat, until things sort themselves out. And please don't forget the bird seed for Kyril Modestovich, and to change his water. Here's the key. That's all, I think, and do look us up.'

'Very well, Madam.'

'Thank you, Filat. God keep you. Well, let's sit down [1] and then we must be off.'

When they came out the fresh air seemed as unfamiliar as after weeks of illness. Noises, rounded, as if polished on a lathe, rolled echoing lightly through crisp, frosty, nut-clean space. Shots and salvoes smacked, thudded and plopped, flattening the distance into a pancake.

However much Filat tried to convince them to the contrary, Lara and Amalia insisted that the shots were blanks.

'Don't be silly, Filat. Think it out for yourself. How could they be anything but blanks when you can't see anyone shooting? Who d'you think is shooting, the Holy Ghost or what? Of course they're blanks.'

At one of the crossroads they were stopped by a patrol of grinning Cossacks who searched them, insolently running their hands over them from head to foot. Their peakless caps with chin-straps were tilted jauntily over one ear; it made all of them look one-eyed.

'Wonderful,' thought Lara as she walked on. She would not see Komarovsky for as long as the district was cut off from the rest of the town. Her mother made it impossible for her to break with him. She could not say: 'Mama, please stop seeing him.' If she did that it would all come out.

And what if it did? Why should that frighten her? Oh, God! Anything, anything, if only it could end!

God! God! She would fall down in a faint with disgust. What was it she had just remembered? What was the name of that frightful picture? There was a fat Roman in it. It hung in the first of those private rooms, the one where it all began. 'The Woman or the Vase?' That was it. Of course. It was a famous picture. The fat Roman making up his mind between the woman and the vase. When she first saw it she was not yet a woman, she was not yet comparable to an expensive work of art. That came later. The table was splendidly set for a feast.

'Where do you think you are running like that? I can't keep up with you,' panted Madame Guishar. Lara walked swiftly. Some unknown power swept her on, as though she were striding on air, borne by this proud quickening force.

'How splendid,' she thought, listening to the gun shots. 'Blessed are the downtrodden. Blessed are the deceived. God speed the bullets. They and I are of one mind.'

[1] A Russian custom: before a move or a journey people sit down for a few moments for luck.

20

The brothers Gromeko had a house at the corner of Sivtsev Vrazhek [1] and another small street. Alexander Alexandrovich and Nikolay Alexandrovich Gromeko were both professors of chemistry, the one at the Petrov Academy, the other at the University. Nikolay was unmarried. Alexander had a wife Anna, *née* Krueger. Her father was an iron-master ; he owned an enormous estate in the Urals, near Yuryatin ; on it were several abandoned and unprofitable mines.

The Gromekos' house had two storeys. On the top floor were the bedrooms, the schoolroom, Alexander Alexandrovich's study and his library, Anna's sitting-room and Tonya's and Yura's rooms ; these were the living quarters. The ground floor was used for receptions. Its pistachio-coloured curtains, gleaming piano top, aquarium, olive-green upholstery and potted plants like seaweed made it look like a green, sleepily swaying sea-bed.

The Gromekos were cultivated, hospitable and great connoisseurs and lovers of music. They often held receptions and evenings of chamber music at which string quartets and piano trios were performed.

Such a musical evening was to be held in January 1906. There was to be a first performance of a violin sonata by a young composer, a pupil of Taneyev's, and a trio by Tchaikovsky.

The preparations were begun the day before. The furniture was moved round in the drawing-room. In one corner the piano tuner struck the same chord dozens of times and scattered arpeggios like handfuls of beads. In the kitchen, chickens were being plucked, vegetables cleaned and mustard mixed with olive oil for salad dressings.

Shura Schlesinger, Anna's bosom friend and confidante, had come first thing in the morning to make a nuisance of herself.

Shura was a tall thin woman with regular features and a rather masculine face which recalled the Emperor's, especially when she wore her grey astrakhan hat set at an angle ; she kept it on in the house and only slightly raised the veil pinned to it.

In times of sorrow or anxiety the two friends lightened each other's burdens. They did this by provoking one another, their conversation becoming increasingly caustic until an emotional storm burst and soon ended in tears and a reconciliation. These scenes had a tranquillising effect on both, like the application of leeches for high blood pressure.

Shura Schlesinger had been married several times but she forgot

[1] Sivtsev Vrazhek : Grey Mare's Gully.

her husbands as soon as she divorced them and took her marriages so lightly that her manner always retained the cold restlessness of a single woman.

Shura was a theosophist, but she was also an expert on the ritual of the Orthodox Church, and even when she was *toute transportée*, in a state of utter ecstasy, could not refrain from prompting the officiating clergy. 'Hear O Lord,' 'Now and ever shall be,' 'Glorious cherubim,' she muttered ceaselessly in her hoarse, staccato voice.

Shura had a knowledge of mathematics and of esoteric Indian cults, she knew the addresses of the best known teachers at the Moscow conservatoire, who was living with whom and goodness only knows what else besides. For this reason she was called in, as arbiter and organiser, on all important occasions in life.

At the appointed time the guests started to arrive. It was snowing and whenever the front door opened you could see the air rush past, as though tangled in a thousand knots by the flickering snow. The men came in out of the cold in long clumsy snow boots, and every one of them, without exception, did his best to look like a country bumpkin, but their wives, on the contrary, their faces glowing from the frost, coats unbuttoned, shawls pushed back and hair spangled with rime, impersonated hardened coquettes, sophisticated perfidy itself. 'Cui's [1] nephew,' the whisper went round as the new musician came in.

Beyond the open side doors of the ballroom the supper table gleamed, white and long as a winter road. The play of light on frosted bottles of red rowanberry vodka caught the eye. The crystal cruets on silver stands and the picturesque arrangement of game and *zakuski* [2] captured the imagination, while the very napkins, folded into stiff pyramids, and the baskets of mauve cineraria smelling of almonds seemed to whet the appetite.

Not to delay the pleasure of terrestrial food too long the company got down hastily to their spiritual repast. They sat down in rows. 'Cui's nephew,' people whispered again as the musician took his place at the piano. The concert began.

The sonata, expected to be dry, laboured and boring, fulfilled these fears and was terribly long drawn out as well.

During the interval the critic Kerimbekov and Alexander Gromeko had an argument about it, Kerimbekov running it down and Gromeko defending it, while all round them people smoked, talked and moved their chairs; till the glittering tablecloth in the next room again attracted attention and made them decide to get on with the concert.

[1] Famous Russian musician, 1835–1918.
[2] Hors-d'œuvres, including various kinds of cold meat and fish.

The pianist nodded to his partners; the violinist and Tishkevich flourished their bows and the music rose plaintively.

Yura, Tonya and Misha Gordon, who spent half his time at the Gromekos, were sitting in the third row.

'Yegorovna is making signs at you,' Yura whispered to Alexander Alexandrovich who sat immediately in front of him.

Yegorovna, the Gromekos' white-haired old servant, stood in the doorway and, by staring desperately at Yura and nodding with equal energy at Alexander Alexandrovich, tried to make Yura understand that she needed urgently to speak to the master.

Alexander Alexandrovich turned, gave her a reproachful look and shrugged his shoulders, but she stood her ground. Soon they were talking across the room by signs, like a couple of deaf-mutes. People were looking. Anna cast infuriated glances at her husband. He got up, blushing, and tiptoed round the edge of the room.

'You ought to be ashamed, Yegorovna! Really now, what's all the hurry? Well, what is it?'

Yegorovna muttered in his ear.

'What Montenegro?'

'The hotel.'

'Well, what about it?'

'They're asking for him to come back at once. There's somebody of his dying.'

'So now they're dying! I can just imagine . . . It can't be done, Yegorovna. When they've finished this piece I'll tell him. Until then I can't.'

'They've sent the waiter with a cab to fetch him. Somebody's dying, I tell you, can't you understand? It's a lady—one of the gentry.'

'And I tell you it's impossible. As if a few minutes could make all that difference.' He tiptoed back to his place with a worried frown, rubbing the bridge of his nose.

At the end of the first part, before the applause had died down, he went up to the musicians and told Tishkevich that he was needed at home, there had been some accident, they would have to stop playing. Then he turned to the audience and held up his hands for silence:

'Ladies and Gentlemen, I am afraid the trio has to be interrupted. Monsieur Tishkevich has had some bad news from home. All our sympathy is with him. He has to leave us. I wouldn't like him to go by himself at such a moment, I'll go with him in case he should need my help. Yura, my boy, go and tell Simon to bring the carriage round, he's had it ready for some time. Ladies and gentlemen, I won't say good-bye—I beg you all to stay—I won't be long.'

The boys asked to go with him for the sake of the drive through the frosty night.

21

Although the normal flow of life had been restored since December, there were still occasional shots here and there and the new fires, such as are always starting in the ordinary way, looked like the remains of the December fires burning themselves out.

The boys had never been for such a long drive before. In reality the Montenegro was a stone's throw away—only down the Smolensky Boulevard, along the Novinsky and half-way up Sadovaya Street, but the savage frost and fog had dislocated the distance and torn it apart, as if space were not the same the world over. The shaggy, ragged smoke of street fires [1], the crunch of footsteps and the whine of passing sleighs, all helped to give them the impression that they had been travelling for goodness knows how long and were on their way to some terrifyingly remote place.

Outside the hotel entrance stood a narrow, elegant-looking sleigh; the horse was covered with a cloth and had bandaged fetlocks. The driver sat hunched up in the passenger's seat trying to keep warm, his swathed head buried in his huge gloved paws.

It was warm in the hotel vestibule where the porter sat dozing behind the cloak-room counter; lulled by the hum of the ventilator, the roar of the blazing stove and the boiling samovar, he was woken up occasionally by one of his own snores.

A thickly made-up woman with a face like a dumpling stood by the mirror on the left. Her fur jacket was too light for the weather. She was waiting for someone to come down; her back to the glass, she turned her head over each shoulder to make sure that she looked all right behind.

The frozen cab-driver came in. His bulging coat made him look like a bun on a baker's sign and the clouds of steam he gave off increased the likeness. 'How much longer will you be, Mam'zel?' he asked the woman by the looking-glass. 'Why I ever get mixed up with your sort, I don't know. I don't want my horse to freeze to death.'

The hotel staff were being driven frantic; the incident in No. 23 was only one more nuisance added to their daily vexations. Every minute the bells shrilled and numbers popped up behind the long glass

---

[1] Fires are lit at crossroads in very cold weather.

panel of the box on the wall, showing which client in which room was going frantic and pestering the valet or the chamber-maid without knowing what he wanted.

At the moment the doctor was giving an emetic to that old fool Guisharova [1] and washing out her guts. Glasha, the maid, was run off her feet mopping up the floor and carrying dirty slop pails out and clean ones in. But the storm now raging in the service room had started well before this hullaballoo, before Tirashka had been sent in a cab to fetch the doctor and that wretched fiddler, before Komarovsky had arrived and so many people had cluttered up the corridor outside the door of room 23.

The trouble had started that afternoon, when someone had turned clumsily in the narrow passage leading from the pantry to the landing and had accidentally pushed the waiter Sisoy just as he was rushing out, bent double and with a fully loaded tray balanced on his right hand. The tray clattered to the floor, the soup was spilled and two soup plates and one meat plate were smashed.

Sisoy insisted that it was the washer-up who had been responsible and should pay for the damage. By now it was nearly eleven o'clock and half the staff were due to go off duty but the row was still going on.

'He's got the shakes, can't keep his hands and feet steady. All he cares about is sitting with a bottle, you'd think it was his wife, he gets pickled like a herring, and then he asks who pushed him, who spilled his soup, who smashed his crockery. Now who do you think pushed you, you devil, you Astrakhan pest, you shameless creature?'

'I have told you already, Matryona Stepanovna, to keep a civil tongue in your head.'

'And who's the one that all the fuss is about now, I ask you? You'd think it was somebody worth smashing crockery for. But it's that slut, that street-walker giving herself airs, that madam-five-bob-a-time, innocence in retirement, done so well for herself she's swigging arsenic. Of course, Madame lives at the Montenegro, wouldn't know an alley cat if she met one.'

Misha and Yura walked up and down the corridor outside Madame Guishar's room. It had all turned out quite differently from anything Alexander Alexandrovich had expected. He had imagined a clean and dignified tragedy in a musician's life. But this was the devil of a business. Sordid and scandalous, and certainly not for children.

The boys cooled their heels in the passage.

'Go in to the lady now, young gentlemen,' the valet came up to

[1] Madame Guishar's name Russianised by the hotel staff.

them and for the second time tried to persuade them in his soft un-hurried voice. 'You go in, don't worry. The lady's all right, you needn't be afraid. She's quite recovered. You can't stand here. There was an accident here this afternoon, valuable china was smashed. You can see we have to run up and down serving meals and it's a bit narrow. You go in there.'

The boys obeyed.

Inside the room, a lighted paraffin lamp which ordinarily stood on the table had been taken out of its stand and carried behind the wooden partition into the sleeping alcove. The alcove stank of bugs and had a dusty curtain to conceal it from the main room and the lobby. But the curtain had been flung aside and in the confusion no one had thought of drawing it. The lamp stood on a low stool and lit the alcove garishly from below as though by footlights.

Madame Guishar had tried to poison herself not with arsenic, as the washer-up thought, but with iodine. The room had the tart, astringent smell of green walnuts when their husks are still soft and blacken at a touch.

Behind the partition the maid was mopping up the floor, and lying on the bed was a half-naked woman; wet with tears, water and sweat, her hair stuck together, she was holding her head over a bucket and crying loudly.

The boys turned away at once, so shameful and unmannerly did they feel it was to look in her direction. But Yura had seen enough to be impressed by the fact that in certain clumsy, tense positions, in moments of strain and exertion, a woman ceases to be as she is repre-sented in sculpture and looks more like a wrestler with bulging muscles, stripped down to his shorts and ready for the match.

At last someone behind the partition had the sense to draw the curtain.

'Monsieur Tishkevich, my dear, where's your hand? Give me your hand,' the woman was saying, choking with tears and nausea. 'Oh, I have been through such horrors. I had such terrible sus-picions . . . Monsieur Tishkevich . . . I imagined . . . but happily it has all turned out to be nonsense, just my disordered imagination . . . Just think what a relief. And the upshot of it all . . . here I am . . . here I am alive . . .'

'Calm yourself, Amalia Karlovna, I beg you. . . . How awkward all this is, upon my word, how very awkward.'

'We'll be off home now,' said Alexander Alexandrovich gruffly to the children. Excruciatingly embarrassed, they stood in the door of the entrance lobby and as they did not know where to look they stared straight in front of them into the shadowy depth of the main room.

The walls were hung with photographs, there was a bookshelf filled with musical scores, a desk piled with papers and fashion journals, and, beyond the round table with a crochet cover, a girl was asleep in an armchair, one arm flung over the back and her face pressed against the cushion. She must have been dead tired to be able to sleep in spite of all the noise and excitement.

'We'll be off now,' Alexander Alexandrovich said again. There had been no sense in their coming and to stay any longer would be indecent. 'As soon as Monsieur Tishkevich comes out . . . I must say good-bye to him.'

But it was not Tishkevich who came out from behind the partition, but a thick-set, portly, self-confident man. Carrying the lamp above his head he went over to the table and replaced it on its stand. The light woke up the girl. She smiled at him, screwing up her eyes and stretching.

At sight of the stranger, Misha started and stared as if he could not take his eyes away. He pulled Yura's sleeve and tried to whisper to him, but Yura would not have it.—'You can't whisper in front of people—what will they think of you?'

Meanwhile the girl and the man were acting a dumb-scene. Not a word passed their lips, only their eyes met. But the understanding between them had a terrifying quality of black magic, as if he were the master of a puppet show and she were a puppet obedient to his every gesture.

A tired smile puckered her eyes and loosened her lips, but in answer to his amused glance she gave him a sly wink of complicity. Both of them were pleased that it had all ended so well—their secret was safe and Madame Guishar's attempted suicide had failed.

Yura devoured them with his eyes. From the half-darkness of the lobby where no one saw him he stared unblinking into the circle of lamplight. The scene between the captive girl and her master was both incommunicably mysterious and shamelessly frank. New and conflicting feelings crowded painfully in Yura's heart.

Here was the very thing which he, Tonya and Misha had endlessly discussed and had dismissed as 'vulgar', the force which so frightened and attracted them and which they controlled so easily from a safe distance by words. And now here it was, this force, in front of Yura's very eyes, concrete, real, and yet confused and veiled as in a dream, pitilessly destructive, and complaining and helpless—and where was Yura's childish philosophy now and what was he to do?

'Do you know who that man is?' said Misha when they came out into the street. Yura, busy with his thoughts, did not reply.

'He's the one who made your father drink and caused his death. The lawyer who was in the train with him—you remember, I told you.'

Yura was thinking about the girl and the future, not about his father and the past. At first he could not even understand what Misha was telling him, and anyway, it was too cold to talk.

'You must be frozen, Simon,' Alexander Alexandrovich said to the coachman. They drove home.

3

Christmas party at the Sventitskys'

ONE winter Alexander Alexandrovich gave Anna an antique
wardrobe. He had picked it up as a bargain. It was made
of ebony and so enormous that it would not go through any
door in one piece. It was brought into the house in sections; the
problem then was where to put it. It was unfitted for the reception
rooms by its function and for the bedrooms by its size. In the end, a
part of the landing was cleared for it outside the best bedroom.

Markel, the handyman, came to put it together. He brought
with him his daughter Marinka; she was six years old. Marinka
was given a piece of barley sugar. She clutched it in her sticky fingers
and stood sucking it, wheezing through her nose, and watching her
father.

At first everything went well. The cupboard grew in front of
Anna's eyes; when it was almost finished—only the top remained to
be put on—she took it into her head to help Markel. She got inside,
stood on the raised floor, slipped, and fell against one wall of the
cupboard, which was only held in place by tenons; the rope which
Markel had tied loosely round it came undone. Anna fell on her
back, together with the boards as they clattered to the ground, and
bruised herself painfully.

'Oh, madam, mistress,' Markel rushed to her. 'What made you
do that, my dear? You haven't broken any bones? Feel your bones.
It's the bones that matter, the soft part doesn't matter at all; the soft
parts mend in God's good time, and, as the saying is, they're only for
pleasure anyway.—Don't bawl, you little brute!' he rounded on the
crying Marinka. 'Wipe the snot from your nose and clear off to
your mum.—Ah, Madam, couldn't you trust me to set up that there
cupboard without you? Of course, to look at me you'd think I was
only a handyman, but to speak straight, cabinet-making is my proper
trade. I began by being a cabinet-maker. You wouldn't believe
how much furniture has passed through my hands, in a manner of
speaking—cupboards, sideboards, lacquer, walnut, mahogany. Nor
how many well-to-do young ladies have passed me by, in a manner of
speaking. Vanished from under my nose, in a manner of speaking.
And the cause of it is drink, my lady, strong spirits.'

Markel rolled up an armchair and with his help Anna sank into it, groaning and rubbing her bruises. Then he set about restoring the wardrobe. When he put the top on he said : 'Now the doors, and then it's fit for an exhibition.'

Anna did not like the wardrobe. Its shape and size reminded her of a catafalque or a royal tomb and filled her with a superstitious dread. She nicknamed it the tomb of Askold [1]; she meant the horse of Prince Oleg [2], which had caused its master's death. Owing to her unsystematic reading her association of ideas was odd.

After this accident Anna developed a pulmonary weakness.

2

Anna spent the whole of November 1911 in bed with inflammation of the lungs.

Yura, Misha Gordon and Tonya were due to graduate the following spring, Yura in medicine, Tonya in law and Misha in philosophy.

Everything in Yura's mind was mixed up together and misplaced and everything was sharply his own—his views, his habits and his inclinations. He was unusually impressionable and the freshness and novelty of his vision were remarkable.

Though he was greatly drawn to art and history, he scarcely hesitated over the choice of his career. He considered that art was no more a vocation than innate cheerfulness or melancholy were professions. He was interested in physics and natural science and believed that a man should do something useful in his practical life. He settled on medicine.

In the first year of his four-year course he had spent a term in the dissecting room ; it was deep under ground in the basement of the university. You came down the winding staircase. There was always a crowd of dishevelled students, some hard at work over their tattered textbooks surrounded by bones, or quietly dissecting, each in his corner, others fooling about, cracking jokes and chasing the rats which scurried in swarms over the stone floors. In the half-darkness of the mortuary the naked bodies of drowned women and unidentified young suicides, well preserved and untouched by decay, gleamed white as phosphorus. Injections of alum salts rejuvenated them and gave them a deceptive

---

[1] Askold was one of the founders of the Russian state; he ruled in Kiev, where he was buried.
[2] Oleg, another Prince of Kiev, was killed by a snake which came out of the skull of his favourite horse.

roundness. The corpses were cut open, dismembered and prepared, yet even in its smallest sections the human body kept its beauty, so that the wonder Yura felt in looking at the body of a girl brutally flung down upon a zinc table he also felt in gazing at her amputated arm or hand. The basement smelled of carbolic and formaldehide and was filled with the presence of mystery, the mystery of the unknown lives of these naked dead, and the mystery of life and death itself—and death was as familiar in this place as though the underground room were its home or its headquarters.

The voice of this mystery, drowning everything else, distracted Yura at his dissecting. But then a lot of things in life distracted him. He was used to it and was not put out.

Yura thought well and wrote even better. Ever since his schooldays he had dreamed of writing a book in prose, a book of impressions of life in which he would conceal, like buried sticks of dynamite, the most striking things he had so far seen and thought about. He was too young to write such a book; instead, he wrote poetry. He was like a painter who spent his life making sketches for a big picture he had in mind.

The vigour and the originality of his poems made Yura forgive himself what he regarded as the sin of their conception, for he believed that originality and vigour alone could give reality to a work of art, and that without them art was utterly useless, superfluous and a waste of time.

Yura realised how great a part his uncle had played in forming his character.

Nikolay Nikolayevich now lived in Lausanne, where several of his books had come out both in Russian and in other languages. In these books he developed his views of history as another universe—a universe built by man with the help of time and memory in answer to the challenge of death. Inspired by a new understanding of Christianity, they resulted in a new conception of art.

Misha Gordon was even more deeply affected by these ideas than Yura. It was their influence which had made him take up philosophy as his subject, and he attended lectures on theology and even played with the idea of transferring later to the theological college.

Yura advanced and developed under the influence of his uncle's theories but Misha was cramped by them. Yura allowed for the part which his racial origin played in Misha's extremist views and was too discreet to try to talk him out of his strange plans, but he sometimes wished that Misha were more empirical and closer to life.

3

One evening at the end of November Yura came home late from the university; he was tired and had eaten nothing all day. He was told that there had been a terrible scare that afternoon. Anna Ivanova had had convulsions; several doctors had seen her; at one time they had advised Alexander Alexandrovich to send for the priest but later they had changed their minds. Now she was feeling better; she was conscious and had asked for Yura to be sent to her the moment he got back. Yura went up at once.

The room showed traces of the recent commotion. A nurse was quietly arranging something on the night table. Towels and napkins, which had been used for compresses, were still lying about, damp and crumpled. The water in the slop pail was pinkish with expectorated blood, and broken ampoules and swollen tufts of cotton-wool floated on its surface.

Anna lay bathed in sweat, with parched lips. Her face had become haggard since morning.

'Can the diagnosis be wrong?' Yura wondered. 'She has all the signs of lobar pneumonia and it looks like the crisis.' After greeting her and saying the encouraging things which are always said on such occasions, he sent the nurse out of the room, took Anna's wrist to feel her pulse and reached into his coat pocket for his stethoscope. She moved her head as if to say: 'It's useless, what's the point?' He understood that it was something else she wanted. She spoke with effort.

'They said . . . last sacraments . . . Death is hanging over me . . . Any moment . . . When you go to have a tooth out you're frightened, it'll hurt, you prepare yourself . . . But this isn't a tooth . . . it's the whole of you, your whole life . . . being pulled out . . . And what does it mean? Nobody knows . . . And I am sick at heart and terrified.'

She fell silent. Tears poured down her cheeks. Yura said nothing. A moment later Anna went on.

'You're clever, talented . . . That makes you different . . . Say something to me . . . Set my mind at rest.'

'Well, what is there for me to say,' replied Yura. He fidgeted on his chair, got up, paced the room and sat down again. 'In the first place, you'll feel better to-morrow, I know the signs, I give you my word. And then death, the survival of consciousness, resurrection . . . You want to know my opinion as a scientist? Perhaps some other time?—No?—At once?—Well, as you wish. But you know, it's difficult to put into words, straight off.' And there and then he delivered a whole impromptu lecture, so that he was even astonished at himself.

'Resurrection.—In the crude form in which it is preached for the consolation of the weak, the idea doesn't appeal to me. I have always understood Christ's words about the living and the dead in a different sense. Where could you find room for all these hordes of people collected over thousands of years? The universe isn't big enough, God and good and meaning would be crowded out. They'd be crushed by all that greedy animal jostling.

'But all the time life, always one and the same, always incomprehensibly keeping its identity, fills the universe and is renewed at every moment in innumerable combinations and metamorphoses. You are anxious about whether you will rise from the dead or not, but you have risen already—you rose from the dead when you were born and you didn't notice it. Will you feel pain? Do the tissues feel their disintegration? In other words, what will happen to your consciousness? But what is consciousness? Let's see. To try consciously to go to sleep is a sure way to have insomnia, to try to be conscious of one's own digestion is a sure way to upset the stomach. Consciousness is a poison when we apply it to ourselves. Consciousness is a beam of light directed outwards, it lights up the way ahead of us so that we don't trip up. It's like the head-lamps on a railway engine—if you turned the beam inwards there would be a catastrophe.

'So what will happen to your consciousness? *Your* consciousness, yours, not anyone else's. Well, what are *you*? That's the crux of the matter. Let's try to find out. What is it about you that you have always known as yourself? What are you conscious of in yourself? Your kidneys? Your liver? Your blood vessels?—No. However far back you go in your memory, it is always in some external, active manifestation of yourself that you come across your identity—in the work of your hands, in your family, in other people. And now look. You in others are yourself, your soul. This is what you are. This is what your consciousness has breathed and lived on and enjoyed throughout your life.—Your soul, your immortality, your life in others. And what now? You have always been in others and you will remain in others. And what does it matter to you if later on it is called your memory? This will be you—the you that enters the future and becomes a part of it.

'And now one last point. There is nothing to worry about. There is no death. Death is not our department. But you mentioned talent

—that's different, that's ours, that's at our disposal. And to be gifted in the widest and highest sense is to be gifted for life.

'There will be no death, says St. John, and just look at the simplicity of his argument. There will be no death because the past is over; that's almost like saying there will be no death because death is already done with, it's old and we are tired of it. What we need is something new, and that new thing is life eternal.'

He paced up and down the room, talking. 'Go to sleep,' he said, going up to the bed and putting his hand on Anna's forehead. After a few moments she gradually went to sleep.

Yura quietly left the room and told Yegorovna to send in the nurse. 'What the devil,' he thought, 'what kind of a charlatan am I turning into now? Muttering incantations, laying on hands . . .'

Next day Anna was better.

4

Anna continued to improve. In the middle of December she tried to get up but she was still too weak. The doctors told her to stay in bed and have a really good rest.

She often sent for Yura and Tonya and would talk to them by the hour of her childhood in the Urals. She had grown up on her father's estate, Varykino, on the river Rynva. Neither Yura nor Tonya had ever been there, but, listening to her, Yura could easily imagine those twelve thousand acres of impenetrable virgin forest as black as night, and, cutting through it in sharp zigzags like knife-thrusts, the swift stream, with its rocky bed and steep cliffs on the Krueger side.

For the first time in their lives Yura and Tonya were having evening clothes made for them, Yura a dinner jacket and Tonya a light satin evening dress which only just uncovered her neck.

They were going to wear them for the first time at the traditional Christmas party at the Sventitskys' on the twenty-seventh. The suit and the dress were delivered on the same day. Yura and Tonya tried them on, were delighted, and had not yet taken them off when Anna sent Yegorovna to fetch them.

When they came in she raised herself on her elbow, looked them over and told them to turn round.

'Very nice,' she said. 'Quite lovely. I had no idea they were ready. Let me have another look, Tonya. No, it's all right, I thought the yoke puckered a bit. Do you know why I've called you?—But first I want a word with you, Yura.'

'I know, Anna Ivanovna. I know you've seen the letter, I had it sent to you myself. I know you agree with Nikolay Nikolayevich. You both think I should not have refused the legacy. But wait a moment. It's bad for you to talk. Just let me explain—though you know most of it already.

'Well, then, in the first place. It suits the lawyers that there should be a Zhivago case because there is enough money in Father's estate to cover the costs and to pay their fees. Apart from that there is in fact no legacy at all—nothing but debts and muddle—and a lot of dirty linen to be washed. If there really had been anything ⊾at could be turned into money, do you think I'd have made a present of it to the court and not used it myself? But that's just the point— the whole case is bogus. So, rather than rake up all that dirt, it was better to give up my right to a non-existent property and let it go to all that trumped-up bunch of rivals and false pretenders who were after it.

'One claimant, as you know, is a certain Madame Alice who calls herself Zhivago and lives with her children in Paris—I've known about her for a long time. But now there are various new claims—I don't know about you, but I was told of them quite recently.

'It appears that while Mother was still alive, Father became infatuated with a certain eccentric Princess Stolbunova-Enritsi. This lady has a child by him, Yevgraf, he's ten years old.

'The Princess is a recluse. She has a house just outside Omsk; she lives there and never goes out. The source of her income is un-known. I've seen a photograph of the house. It's very handsome, with five french windows and stucco medallions on the cornices. And recently I kept having the feeling that the house was staring at me nastily, out of all its five windows, right across all the thousands of miles between the Urals and Moscow, and that sooner or later it would give me the evil eye.

'So what do I want with all this—imaginary capital, false claimants, malice, envy? And lawyers?'

'All the same, you shouldn't have given it up,' said Anna. 'Do you know why I called you?' she asked again and immediately went on from where she had left off the day before. 'I've remembered his name.—You remember the forest guard I was telling you about yesterday? He was called Bacchus. Extraordinary, isn't it! A real bogey man, black as the devil, with a beard growing up to his eye-brows, and calls himself Bacchus! His face was scarred; a bear had mauled him but he had fought it off. And they're all like that out there. Such names—dissyllabic, round, sonorous! Bacchus or Lupus or Faustus. Every now and then somebody like that would be announced—perhaps Auctus—somebody with a name like a shot from your grandfather's double-barrelled gun—and we would all immediately troop downstairs from the nursery to the kitchen. And there—you can't think what it was like—you never knew who you'd find. It might be a charcoal dealer with a live bear cub, or a prospector from the far end of the estate with a specimen of the ore. And your grandfather would always give them a chit for the office. Some were given money, some buckwheat, others cartridges. The forest came right up to the windows. And the snow, the snow! Higher than the roofs!' Anna started coughing.

'That's enough, it's bad for you,' Tonya and Yura urged her.

'Nonsense, I'm perfectly all right. That reminds me. Yegorovna told me that you two are worrying about whether you should go to the party the day after to-morrow. Don't let me hear anything so silly again, you ought to be ashamed of yourselves! And you call yourself a doctor, Yura!—So that's settled, you'll go and that's that.— But to return to Bacchus. He used to be a blacksmith when he was young. He got into a fight and damaged his inside. So he made himself a set of iron guts.—Now, don't be silly, Yura. Of course I know he couldn't, you mustn't take it literally! But that's what the people said out there.'

She was interrupted by another coughing fit, a much longer one than the last. It went on and on, she could not get back her breath.

Yura and Tonya hurried across to her. They stood shoulder to shoulder by her bedside. Their hands touched. Still coughing, Anna caught their hands in hers and kept them joined a moment longer. When she was able to speak she said : 'If I die, stay together. You're meant for each other. Get married. There now, I've betrothed you,' she added and began to cry.

5

By the spring of 1906, before Lara was in the top form at school, the six months of her liaison with Komarovsky had driven her beyond the limits of her endurance. He was clever at exploiting her wretchedness and reminded her, when it suited him, of her dishonour without seeming to do so. These hints brought her to just that state of confusion to which a voluptuary needs to reduce a woman, and left her powerless to resist the nightmare of sensuality which terrified her whenever she awoke from it. The insanely contradictory world she inhabited at night was as inexplicable as black magic. Here everything was topsy-turvy and against logic; sharp pain announced itself by peals of silvery laughter, resistance and refusal meant consent, and grateful kisses covered the hand of the tormentor.

It seemed that there would be no end to it, but that spring, as she sat through a history lesson at the end of term, thinking of the holidays when even school and homework would no longer stand between her and Komarovsky, she came to a sudden decision which altered the course of her life.

It was a hot morning and a storm was brewing. Through the open classroom windows came the distant drone of the town, as monotonous as a beehive, and the shrieks of children playing in the yard. The grassy smell of earth and young leaves made your head ache like a Shrovetide surfeit of pancakes and vodka.

The lesson was about Napoleon's Egyptian campaign. When the teacher came to the battle of Fréjus, the sky blackened, cracked and was split by lightning and thunder, and clouds of dust and sand swept into the room together with the smell of rain. Two school toadies rushed out obligingly to fetch the porter to close the windows and as they opened the door the wind sent all the blotting-paper flying off the desks.

The windows were closed. The rain fell in an urban downpour, dirty with dust. Lara tore a page out of an exercise book and wrote to her neighbour, Nadya Kologrivova:

'Nadya, I want to live away from Mother. Help me to find a teaching job, as well paid as possible. You know lots of rich people.'

Nadya wrote back:

'Mother and Father are looking for a governess for Lipa. Why not come to us?—it would be wonderful. You know how fond they are of you.'

6

Lara spent three years at the Kologrivovs', as safe as in a stronghold. No one bothered her and even her mother and her brother, from whom she had become estranged, kept out of her way.

Kologrivov was a brilliant business man of a new kind. He despised and hated the decaying order with a double hatred, both as a man rich enough to outbid the treasury and as one who had risen to these fabulous heights from a humble origin. He sheltered political criminals in his house and hired lawyers to defend them; and it was said of him, as a joke, that he was so keen on subsidising the revolution

and dispossessing himself that he fomented strikes at his own factory.
Fond of shooting and a good marksman, he spent his Sundays in the
winter of 1905 in the Serebryanny woods, giving rifle training to
insurgents.

His wife, Serafima, was as remarkable a personality in her way
as he was in his. Lara was devoted to both of them and the whole
household took her to its heart.

After three years of this carefree life she received a visit from her
brother Rodya, who came to see her on business. Swaying affectedly
backwards and forwards on his long legs and, for dramatic emphasis,
talking through his nose, he told her that the cadets of his year had
collected money for a farewell gift to the head of the Academy and
entrusted it to him, asking him to choose and buy the present. This
money he had gambled away two days ago down to the last copeck.
Having told Lara, he flopped into an armchair and burst into tears.

Lara sat frozen with horror. Rodya went on through his sobs :

'Last night I went to see Victor Ippolitovich. He refused to talk
about it with me but he said, if you wished him to . . . He said that
although you no longer loved any of us, your power over him was still
so great . . . Lara, darling . . . One word from you would be
enough. . . . You realise what this means for me, what a disgrace
it is, how it affects my honour as a cadet. . . . Go to him, what does
it cost you. . . . You can't want me to make this good with my life.'

'Your life . . . Your honour as a cadet.' Indignantly, she paced
the room. 'I am not a cadet. I have no honour. You can do what
you like with me. Have you any idea what you are asking ? Do you
realise what he is making you do ? Year after year I slave away and
now you come along and sit about and don't care if everything I've
built up is scattered to the winds. To hell with you. Go ahead,
shoot yourself. What do I care ? How much do you need ?'

'Six hundred odd roubles.—Say seven hundred in round figures,'
he added after a slight hesitation.

'Rodya ! You must be mad ! Do you know what you are saying ?
You've gambled away seven hundred roubles ! Do you realise how
long it takes an ordinary person like myself to earn that much by
honest work ?'

She broke off and after a short silence said coldly, as if to a stranger :

'All right. I'll try. Come to-morrow. And bring your revolver—
the one you were going to shoot yourself with. You'll hand it over
to me. And with a good supply of bullets, remember.'

She got the money from Kologrivov.

7

Her work at the Kologrivovs' did not prevent Lara from finishing school and starting on a university course. She did well and was to graduate the following year, 1912.

In the spring of 1911 her pupil Lipa finished school. She was already engaged to a young engineer, Friesendank. He was well off and came of a good family. Her parents approved of him but were against her marrying so young. Lipa, the spoilt and wilful darling of the family, made scenes, shouted at her parents and stamped her feet.

In this wealthy household where Lara was accepted as a member of the family, no one reminded her of her debt or indeed remembered it. She would have paid it back long before if it had not been for her secret expenses.

Unknown to Pasha, she sent money to his father in Siberia, helped his querulous and ailing mother, and kept his own expenses down by paying part of his board and lodging directly to his landlady. It was she who had found him his room in a new building in Kamerger Street near the Arts Theatre.

Pasha, who was a little younger than Lara, loved her madly and obeyed hre slightest wish. After specialising in science at school he had, on her advice, studied Greek and Latin in order to take an Arts degree. It was her dream that after they had both graduated in the following year they would marry and go out as school teachers to some provincial capital in the .Urals.

In the summer of 1911 Lara went for the last time with the Kologrivovs to Duplyanka. She adored the place, she was even fonder of it than its owners. They realised this and a custom had established itself. When the hot, grimy train left them at the station, and while the luggage was being loaded on to a cart and the family took their seats in the carriage and listened to the Duplyanka coachman, in his scarlet shirt and sleeveless coat, telling them the season's local news, Lara, struck dumb by the boundless, dazed, scented silence of the country, went off to the house on foot.

The path trodden by wayfarers and pilgrims followed the railway and then turned into the fields. Here Lara stopped, closed her eyes and took a good breath of the air which carried all the smells of the huge countryside. It was dearer to her than her kin, better than a lover, wiser than a book. For a moment she rediscovered the meaning of her life. She was here on earth to make sense of its wild enchantment and to call each thing by its right name, or, if this were not within her power, then, out of love of life, to give birth to heirs who would do it in her place.

That summer she had arrived exhausted by the many duties she had undertaken. She was easily upset, irritable and ready to take offence at the slightest thing. This touchiness was quite new in her and out of keeping with her nature, which had always been singularly generous and understanding.

The Kologrivovs were as fond of her as ever and wished her to stay on with them, but now that Lipa had grown up she regarded herself as superfluous in the house. She refused her salary. They had to press it on her. At the same time, she needed the money and had no other way of getting it, since it would have been embarrassing and in practice impossible to earn it independently while living with them as their guest.

She believed her position to be unendurably false and imagined that they all found her a burden and were only putting a good face on it. She was a burden to herself and longed to run away both from herself and the Kologrivovs as fast and as far as her legs would carry her. But according to her ideas she had first to repay the money she had borrowed and at the moment she had no conceivable means of doing so. She felt that she was a hostage—all through Rodya's stupid fault—and ate her heart out in helpless exasperation.

Her nerves on edge, she suspected slights at every turn. If the Kologrivovs' friends were attentive to her, she was sure that they regarded her as a meek 'ward' and an easy prey, and if they left her alone, that meant that she did not exist for them.

Her fits of hypochondria did not prevent her from sharing eagerly in their amusements. There were immense house-parties all through the summer and she went bathing and rowing and for midnight picnics by the river, and danced and let off fireworks with the rest. She took part in amateur theatricals and, with even more zest, in shooting competitions. Short Mauser rifles were used in these contests. Her aim was good, though for target practice she preferred Rodya's light revolver. 'Pity I'm a woman,' she laughed, 'I'd have made a career as a duellist.' But the more she did to distract herself the less she knew what she wanted and the more wretched she felt.

When they came back to town after the holidays it was worse than ever, for to her other troubles were now added her tiffs with Pasha (she was careful not to quarrel with him seriously; she regarded him as her last refuge). Pasha was beginning to show a certain self-assurance. His conversation was getting a little didactic and this both amused and irritated her.

Pasha, Lipa, the Kologrivovs, the money—all her worries whirled inside her mind. She was sick and disgusted with life. It was driving her insane. She wished she could break with everything she had ever known or experienced and start on something altogether new and untried. In this mood, at Christmas in the year 1911, she arrived at a fateful decision. She would leave the Kologrivovs now, at once, and set up on her own, and she would get the money to do this from Komarovsky. It seemed to her that after all that there had been between them and the years of independence she had won for herself, he must help her chivalrously, without any demands or explanations or conditions.

With this in mind she set out for Petrovka Street on the night of the 27th. Rodya's revolver, loaded and with the safety catch off, was inside her muff. Should Komarovsky refuse or humiliate her in any way, she intended to shoot him.

She walked through the festive streets in a terrible excitement, seeing nothing, not aware of anything except the revolver shot which, already, had gone off in her heart—and in her heart it was a matter of complete indifference who the shot was aimed at. She heard it all the way to Petrovka Street, and it was aimed as much at Komarovsky as at herself, her fate and the wooden target on the oak on the Duplyanka lawn.

8

'Don't touch my muff!'

Emma Ernestovna had put out her hand to help her off with her coat; she had received her with Oh's and Ah's, telling her that Victor Ippolitovich was out but she must stay and wait for him.

'I can't. I'm in a hurry. Where is he?'

He was at a Christmas party. Clutching the scrap of paper with the address on it she ran down the familiar gloomy staircase with its stained-glass coats-of-arms and started off for the Sventitskys' house in Muchnoy Gorodok.

Only now, when she came out for the second time, did she take a look round her at the town and the winter night.

It was icy cold. The streets were covered with thick black ice, chunky like the glass bottoms of broken beer bottles. The air hurt her to breathe. It was thick with grey rime and it pricked and tickled her face like the grey frozen bristles of her fur.

Her heart thumping, she walked through the empty streets past the steaming doors of cheap eating-houses. Faces as red as sausages and horses' and dogs' heads with beards of icicles dived out of the mist. Screened with a crust of ice and snow, the windows of the houses were chalk-white, and the coloured reflections of lighted Christmas trees and the shadows of merrymakers moved across their opaque surfaces, as if a magic lantern show were being given in the street.

As she passed in front of the building where Pasha lived in Kamerger Street Lara stopped and almost broke down. 'I can't go on. I can't bear it,' she almost spoke the words aloud. 'I'll go up and tell him everything.' Pulling herself together she went in through the heavy doors of the ornate entrance.

9

Pasha, red in the face, his tongue pushing out his cheek, stood in front of the looking-glass struggling with a collar, a stud and the starched buttonhole of his shirt front. He was going to a party. So innocent was he, that Lara embarrassed him by coming in without knocking and finding him with his dressing unfinished. But he at once noticed her agitation. She could hardly keep on her feet. She advanced, pushing the hem of her skirt aside at each step as if it were water she was crossing at a ford.

He hurried towards her. 'What's the matter? What has happened?'

'Sit down beside me. Sit down, don't bother to finish dressing. I'm in a hurry, I must go in a minute. Don't touch my muff. Wait, don't look a second, turn round.'

When he obeyed she took off the jacket of her tailored suit hung it up and put the revolver in the pocket. Then she went back to the sofa.

'Now you can look. Light a candle and switch off the electricity.'

She was fond of talking in the dark by candlelight and so Pasha always kept a few spare candles. He put a new candle into the holder on the window-sill and lit it. The flame choked and spluttered, shooting off small stars, sharpened to an arrow and steadied. The room filled with soft light. On the window-pane, at the level of the flame, the ice melted leaving a black chink like a peep-hole.

'Listen, Pasha,' said Lara. 'I am in trouble, you must help me. Don't be frightened and don't question me. But don't ever think we can be like other people. You must take this seriously. I am in constant danger. If you love me, if you don't want me to be destroyed, we must not put off our marriage.'

'But that's what I've always wanted,' broke in Pasha. 'I'll marry you any day you like. But tell me plainly what is worrying you. Don't torment me with riddles.'

But Lara evaded his question and changed the subject. They talked a long time about several things which had nothing to do with her distress.

10

That winter Yura was preparing an essay on the nervous system of the eye for the University Gold Medal competition. Though he had qualified only in general medicine he had almost a specialist's knowledge of the physiology of sight. His interest in it was in keeping with other sides of his character—his creative gifts and his interest in the relation between imagery in art and the logical structure of ideas.

Just now he and Tonya were driving in a hired sleigh to the Sventitskys'.

After six years of childhood and adolescence spent in the same house they knew everything there was to know about each other and had their own ways and habits, including their way of snorting at each other's jokes and their companionable silences. Now too, they drove almost in silence, thinking their own thoughts, their lips tightly closed against the cold.

Yura was thinking about the date of his competition and that he must work harder at his essay. Then his mind, distracted by the festive, end-of-the-year bustle in the streets, jumped to other things. He had promised Gordon an article on Blok for the mimeographed student paper which he edited; young people in both capitals were mad about Blok, Yura and Gordon particularly. But not even these thoughts held his mind for long.

They drove on, their chins tucked into their collars, rubbing their frozen ears and thinking their own thoughts, but there was one thought which was in both their minds.

The scene at Anna's bedside had transformed them in each other's eyes as if they had only just been granted the gift of sight.

To Yura, his old friend Tonya, until then a part of his life which had always been taken for granted and had never needed explaining, had suddenly become the most inaccessible and complicated being he could imagine. She had become a woman. By a stretch of imagination he could picture himself as an emperor, a hero, a prophet, a conqueror, but not as a woman.

Now that Tonya had taken this supreme and most difficult task on her slender, fragile shoulders (she now seemed to him slender and fragile, though she was a perfectly healthy girl), he was filled with that ardent sympathy and shy wonder which are the beginning of passion.

The change in Tonya's attitude to Yura was equally deep.

It occurred to Yura that perhaps they should not after all have gone out. He was worried about Anna. They had been on the point of leaving when they heard that she was feeling less well; they had gone in to her, but she had ordered them off to the party as sharply as before. 'What's the weather like now?' she had asked. They had gone to the window to look out, and as they came back the net curtains had clung to Tonya's new dress, trailing after her like a wedding veil. They had all laughed, so immediately striking had been the likeness.

Yura looked round and saw what Lara had seen a little earlier. The unnaturally loud whining of the sleigh on the frozen road aroused an unnaturally long echo from the ice-bound trees of the squares and streets. The lights shining through the frosted windows turned the houses into precious caskets of smoky topaz. Inside them glowed the Christmas life of Moscow, candles burned on trees, guests milled and fooled about in fancy dress, playing hide-and-seek and hunt-the-ring.

It occurred to him that Blok was a manifestation of Christmas in the life and art of modern Russia—Christmas in the life of this northern city, Christmas underneath the starry skies of its modern streets and round the lighted trees in its twentieth-century drawing-rooms. There was no need to write an article on Blok, he thought, all you needed do was to paint a Russian version of a Dutch Adoration of the Magi with snow in it, and wolves and a dark fir forest.

As they drove through Kamerger Street Yura noticed that a candle had melted a patch in the icy crust on one of the windows. Its light seemed to fall into the street as deliberately as a glance, as if the flame were keeping a watch on the passing carriages and waiting for someone.

'A candle burned on the table, a candle burned . . .' he whispered to himself—the confused, formless beginning of a poem; he hoped that it would take shape of itself, but nothing more came to him.

11

An immemorial ritual was followed at the Sventitskys' Christmas parties. At ten o'clock, after the children had gone home, the tree was lit a second time for the young people and grown-ups and the party went on till morning. Elderly people played cards all night long in the 'Pompeiian' sitting-room, curtained off from the ballroom by heavy hangings on bronze rings. At dawn they all breakfasted together.

'Why are you so late?' asked the Sventitskys' nephew, Georges, running through the entrance hall on his way to his uncle's and aunt's rooms at the back of the flat. Yura and Tonya took off their things and looked in at the ballroom door before going to greet their hosts.

Rustling their dresses and treading on each other's toes, those who were not dancing but walking and talking moved like a black wall past the hotly breathing Christmas tree girded with tier upon tier of streaming lights.

In the centre of the room the dancers twirled and spun dizzily. They were paired off or formed into chains by a young law school student, Koka Kornakov, the son of an assistant public prosecutor, who was leading the cotillon. '*Grand rond!*' he bellowed at the top of his voice across the room, or '*Chaîne chinoise!*'—and they all followed his orders. '*Une valse, s'il vous plaît,*' he shouted to the pianist as he led his partner at the head of the first round, whirling her away and gradually slowing down in ever smaller and smaller circles, until they were hardly noticeably marking time in what was still the dying echo of a waltz; and everyone clapped, and ices and cool drinks were carried round the noisy, milling, shuffling crowd. Flushed boys and girls never stopped shouting and laughing for a moment as they gulped cold cranberry juice and lemonade, yet the moment they put down their glasses on the trays the noise was ten times louder, as if they had had a swig of something which had made them gayer still.

Without stopping in the ballroom Tonya and Yura went through to their hosts' rooms at the other end of the flat.

12

The back rooms were cluttered up with furniture which had been moved out of the ballroom and the drawing-room. Here the Sventitskys kept their Christmas workshop, their magic kitchen. There was a smell of paint and glue, and coloured wrappings and boxes of cotillon favours and spare candles were piled up on every chair.

The Sventitskys were writing names on cards for presents and for seats at the supper table, and numbers on tickets for a lottery. They were helped by Georges, but he kept losing count and getting muddled and they grumbled at him irritably. They were overjoyed at Tonya's and Yura's coming, they remembered them as children and unceremoniously set them to work.

'Felitsata Semyonovna doesn't see that this should all have been done in advance, not right in the middle of the party when the guests are there.—Look what you've done now, Georges—the empty *bon-bonnières* go on the sofa and the ones with sugared almonds on the table —you've got them the wrong way round.'

'I am so glad dear Annette is better. Pierre and I were so worried.'

'Except that she's worse, not better, darling, worse, do you understand? You always get things *devant-derrière*.'

In the end, Yura and Tonya spent half the evening with Georges and the Sventitskys behind the scenes.

13

All this time Lara was in the ballroom. She was not in evening dress and did not know anyone there, but she stayed on, either waltzing with Koka like a sleep-walker or wandering aimlessly round the room.

Once or twice she stopped and stood hesitating outside the sitting-room, hoping that Komarovsky, who sat facing the doorway, might see her. But he held his cards in front of him like a small shield in his left hand, and either really did not notice her or pretended not to. She was choking with mortification. A girl whom she did not know went in from the ballroom and Komarovsky looked at her in the way Lara remembered. The girl was flattered and flushed and smiled with pleasure. Lara crimsoned with shame and nearly screamed. 'A new victim,' she thought, seeing herself in the girl as though reflected in a looking-glass. She did not give up her plan to speak to him but decided to do it later, at a more convenient moment. Forcing herself to be calm, she went back to the ballroom.

Komarovsky was playing with three other men. The one on his left was Kornakov, the father of Koka, the elegant young man with whom Lara was again dancing: so she understood from the few words she exchanged with him. And the young man's mother was the tall dark woman in black with burning eyes and an unpleasantly snake-like neck who went backwards and forwards between the ballroom and the sitting-room, watching her son dancing and her husband playing cards. And finally Lara learned that the girl who had aroused such complicated feelings in her was the young man's sister and that her suspicions had been groundless.

She had not paid attention to Koka's surname when he had first introduced himself, but he repeated it as he swept her in the last gliding movement of the waltz to a chair before bowing himself off.

83

'Kornakov. Kornakov.' It reminded her of something. Of something unpleasant.—Yes, that was it, she had it now. Kornakov was the assistant public prosecutor at the Moscow central court who had made a fanatical speech at the trial of the group of railway men which had included Tiverzin. At Lara's wish, Kologrivov had gone to plead with him, but without success. So that was it. . . . Well, well, well. . . . How very odd. . . . Kornakov.

14

It was almost two in the morning. Yura's ears were ringing. There had been an interval with tea and *petits fours* and now the dancing had begun again. No one bothered any more to change the candles on the tree as they burned down.

Yura was standing absent-mindedly in the middle of the ballroom, watching Tonya as she danced with a stranger. She swept up to him, flounced her short satin train like a fish, and vanished.

She was very excited. During the interval, she had refused tea and had slaked her thirst with innumerable tangerines, peeling them and wiping her fingers and the corners of her mouth on a handkerchief the size of a fruit blossom. Laughing and talking incessantly, she kept taking the handkerchief out and putting it back inside her sash or her sleeve or the frilled neck of her dress.

Now, as she brushed past him, spinning with her unknown partner, she caught and pressed Yura's hand and smiled. The handkerchief she had been holding stayed in his fingers. He pressed it to his lips and closed his eyes. The handkerchief smelled equally enchantingly of tangerines and of Tonya's hand. This was something new in Yura's life, something he had never felt before, something sharp and piercing that went through his whole being from top to toe. This naïvely childish smell was like a friendly, sensible word whispered in the dark. He pressed the handkerchief to his eyes and lips, lost in its kindly smell. At that moment a shot rang out inside the house.

Everyone turned and looked at the curtain which hung between the ballroom and the sitting-room. There was a moment's silence. Then uproar broke out. Some people rushed about screaming, others ran after Koka into the sitting-room from which the sound of the shot had come, and from which still other people were emerging, weeping, arguing and all talking at once.

'What has she done, what has she done?' Komarovsky kept saying in despair.

'Borya, Borya, tell me you're alive,' Mrs. Kornakov was screaming hysterically. 'Where is Doctor Drokov? They said he's here.—Oh, but where, where is he?—How can you, how can you say it's nothing but a scratch! It proves how right I always was! He exposed those criminals! Now you see what kind of people they are. Oh, my poor darling, martyred for your convictions!—There she is, the scum, there she is; I'll scratch your eyes out, you slut, you won't get away this time!—What did you say, Monsieur Komarovsky? You? She shot at you? No, I can't bear it, this is a tragic moment, Monsieur Komarovsky, I haven't time to listen to jokes.—Koka, Koka darling! Can you believe it? She tried to kill your father. . . . Yes. . . . But Providence . . . Koka! Koka!'

The crowd rolled out of the sitting-room into the ballroom. At the head of it came Kornakov, laughingly assuring everyone that he was quite all right and dabbing with a napkin at a scratch on his left hand. They were followed by another group who seemed to be pulling Lara by the arms.

Yura was dumbfounded.—This girl again! And again in such extraordinary circumstances! And again that grey-haired man was near her. But this time Yura knew him. It was the prominent lawyer Komarovsky who had had something to do with his father's estate. There was no need to bow. They both pretended not to know each other. And the girl . . . So it was the girl who had fired the shot? At the prosecutor? Must be for political reasons. Poor thing. She was in for a bad time. How proudly beautiful she was! And those louts were pulling her along, twisting her arms as if they had caught a thief!

But at once he realised that he was mistaken. Lara was fainting, they were holding her up and almost carrying her to the nearest armchair where she finally collapsed.

Yura went up to her to help in bringing her round but then thought it would look better if he first showed some interest in the victim.

'Can I help you? I am a doctor,' he said to Kornakov. 'Show me your hand. Well, you've been lucky. It's not even worth bandaging. A drop of iodine wouldn't do any harm, though.—There's Felitsata Semionovna, she's sure to have some.'

Felitsata and Tonya were coming towards him. They looked white and shocked. They told him to leave everything and to get his coat. There had been a message from home, they were to go back at once.

Yura, imagining the worst, forgot everything else and ran for his things.

They did not find Anna alive. When they ran up the stairs to her room she had been dead for ten minutes. The cause of death had been an attack of asthma resulting from acute oedema of the lungs. This had not been diagnosed in time. The first few hours Tonya screamed and banged her head on the floor and would recognise no one. On the following day she calmed down but could only nod in answer to anything that Yura or her father said to her: the moment she opened her mouth her grief overpowered her and she began to scream again as if she were possessed.

In the intervals between the services she knelt for hours beside the dead woman, her large, fine hands clasping a corner of the coffin which stood on its dais, covered with wreaths. She noticed no one around her, but as soon as her eyes met those of her near ones she would quickly get up and hurry from the room and up the stairs, choking back her tears until she could fall on the bed and bury her stormy grief in the pillow.

What with sorrow, standing for many hours on end, lack of sleep, the deep-toned singing and the dazzling candles by night and day as well as the cold he had caught, Yura was filled with a sleepy, ecstatic, gentle befuddlement of grief and exaltation.

When his mother had died ten years earlier he had been a child. He could still remember his tears of inconsolable grief and terror. In those days his self was not important to him. He could hardly even realise that such a being as Yura existed on its own or had any value or interest. What mattered then was everything outside and around him. From every side, the external world pressed in on him, dense, undeniable, tangible as a forest, and the reason why he was so shaken by his mother's death was that, at her side, he had lost himself in the forest, and now suddenly found her gone and himself alone in it. The forest was made up of everything in the world; everything he knew was in it—clouds and shop signs and the golden tops of belfries and the bare-headed outriders who galloped before the Blessed Virgin's coach, wearing ear-flaps instead of caps out of reverence for the Holy Image [1]. Shop fronts were in it, and arcades, and the inaccessibly high starry heaven at night and the good God and the saints.

That inaccessibly lofty heaven bowed its head quite low, right down to the hem of his nurse's skirt when she was telling him about

[1] The icon of the Iverskaya Virgin was believed to be miraculous and was taken by coach to the sick and dying.

the things of God; it was close and accessible like the tops of hazel bushes in the gully when you pulled down their branches and picked the nuts. It seemed as if it dipped into the nursery wash-basin with its red and gilt flowers and, having bathed in fire and gold, transformed itself into the service at the small church in the side street where he went with his nurse. There the heavenly stars became the lights before the icons and the good God was the good Father and they all tried to fulfil their functions as best they could. But chiefly it was the real world of the grown-ups and of the town that loomed darkly like a forest all round him, and with the whole of his half-animal faith Yura believed in the God who was the keeper of that forest.

Now it was quite different. In his twelve years at school and college Yura had studied the classics and Scripture, legends and poets, history and natural science, reading all these things as if they were the chronicles of his house, his family tree. Now he was afraid of nothing, neither of life nor of death; everything in the world, each thing in it, was named in his dictionary. He felt he was on an equal footing with the universe, and the prayers for Anna now had a different sound for him from the prayers he had heard for his mother as a child. Then he had prayed in confusion, fear and pain. Now he listened to the service as if it were a personal message to him, affecting him directly. He attended to the words and expected of them a clear meaning, as of any other serious communication. And his piety had nothing in common with his feeling for the forces of the earth and sky, which he reverenced merely as his own ancestors.

16

'Holy God, Holy and Strong, Holy and Immortal, have mercy on us.' What was it? Where was he? They were taking out the coffin. He must wake up. He had fallen asleep in his clothes on the sofa at six in the morning. He was sure to have a temperature. Now they were hunting for him all over the house but no one thought of looking in the far corner of the library behind the bookshelves.

'Yura! Yura!' Markel was calling him. They were taking out the coffin. Markel would have to carry the wreaths and nowhere could he find Yura to help him, and to make things worse he had got stuck in the bedroom where the wreaths had been piled up, because the bedroom door was blocked by that of the wardrobe on the landing, which had swung open.

'Markel! Markel! Yura!' people were shouting from downstairs. Markel overcame the obstacle with one kick at the door, and ran downstairs with several wreaths.

'Holy God, Holy and Strong, Holy and Immortal,' the words drifted softly down the street and lingered; as if a feather had softly brushed the air; everything was swaying—wreaths, passers-by, plumed horses' heads, the censer swinging on its chain from the priest's hand, and the white earth under their feet.

'Yura! My God! At last.' Shura Schlesinger was shaking his shoulder. 'What's the matter with you? They're carrying out the coffin. Are you coming with us?'

'Yes, of course.'

17

The funeral service was over. The beggars, shuffling their feet in the cold, closed up in two ranks. The hearse, the gig with wreaths on it and the Kruegers' carriage stirred and swayed slightly. The cabbies drew up closer to the church. Shura Schlesinger came out, with a tear-stained face; she lifted her damp veil, and shot a searching look at the line of cabs; spotting the one in which the coffin-bearers were waiting, she summoned them with a nod and vanished with them into the church. More and more people were pouring out.

'Well, so Anna Ivanovna's passed on. She's no longer with us, gone to a better place, poor soul.'

'Yes, she's had her life, poor thing, and now she's gone to her rest.'

'Have you got a cab or are you taking the number eleven?'

'I've got pins and needles with all that standing. We'll stretch our legs a bit and then take a cab.'

'Did you see how upset Fufkov was? Looking at her, tears pouring down his face, blowing his nose, staring at her face. Standing next to her husband at that.'

'He always had his eye on her.'

So they made their way to the cemetery at the other end of town. That day the hard frost had broken. It was a still, heavy day, a day of ended frost and of departed life, a day meant for a funeral. The dirty snow looked as if it shone through crêpe and the firs behind the churchyard railings, wet and dark like tarnished silver, seemed to be the clothes of mourning.

It was in this same churchyard that Yura's mother lay buried. He had not been to her grave in recent years. He glanced in its direction and whispered, 'Mama,' almost as he might have done years before.

They walked back in solemn, picturesque groups; the meanderings of the swept paths seemed out of keeping with the sorrowful deliberation of the mourners' steps. Tonya walked on her father's arm. They were followed by the Kruegers. Tonya looked well in black.

Hoar-frost, bearded like mould, sprouted on the chains which held the crosses to the domes and on the pink walls of the monastery. Washing hung from wall to wall in the far corner of the monastery yard—shirts with heavy, sodden sleeves, sheets and peach-coloured tablecloths, wet and hanging crookedly. Yura realised that this was the part of the monastery grounds—altered in appearance by the new buildings—where the blizzard had raged that night.

Yura walked on alone, ahead of the others, stopping occasionally to let them catch up with him. In answer to the challenge of the desolation brought by death into the life of the small community whose members were slowly pacing after him, he was drawn, as irresistibly as water funnelling downwards, to dream, to think, to work out new forms, to create beauty. He realised, more vividly than ever before, that art has two constant, two unending preoccupations: it is always meditating upon death and it is always thereby creating life. He realised that this was true of all great and genuine art; it was true of that work of art which is called the Revelation of St. John, and of all those works which have been completing it throughout the ages.

With joyful anticipation, he thought of the day or two which he would set aside and spend alone, away from the university and from his home, in order to write a poem in memory of Anna. He would include in it all those random things which life would send his way—a few descriptions of Anna's best characteristics; Tonya in mourning; street incidents on the way back from the funeral; and the washing hanging in the place where he had wept as a child and the blizzard had raged.

4

The Advent of the Inevitable

LARA lay feverish and half conscious in Felitsata Semyonovna's
bed; the Sventitskys, the servants and Dr. Drokov were talking
in whispers round her.

The rest of the house was dark and empty. Only one lamp on a
bracket in the sitting-room cast its dim light up and down the long
suite of communicating rooms.

Up and down this passage Komarovsky strode with angry resolute
steps, as if he were at home and not a visitor. He would look into
the bedroom for news and tear back to the other end of the flat, past
the tree with its silver bubbles and through the dining-room, where
the table stood laden with untasted dishes and the green crystal goblets
tinkled every time a cab drove past the windows or a mouse scurried
over the table-cloth among the china.

Stormy feelings crowded in his breast. The scandal! The disgrace! He boiled with anger. His position was threatened, his
reputation was endangered by the incident. At whatever cost he
must prevent the gossip or, if the news had already spread, stop the
rumours, strangle them at birth.

Another reason for his agitation was that he had once again
experienced the irresistible attraction of this wild, desperate girl.
He had always known that she was different from everyone else.
There had always been something unique about her. But how
deeply, painfully, irreparably had he wounded her and upset her life,
and how restless and violent she was in her determination to re-shape
her destiny and start afresh!

It was clear from every point of view that he must help her—take
a room for her, perhaps—but in no circumstances must he come near
her; on the contrary, he must keep away, stand aside so as not to
overshadow her, or else with her violent nature there was no knowing
what she might do.

And what a lot of trouble still lay ahead! This wasn't the sort of
thing that did you any good. The law didn't wink at it. It was not
yet morning and hardly two hours had passed since it had all begun,
and already the police had been twice and he, Komarovsky, had had
to go to the kitchen and see the sergeant and smooth things over.

And the further it went the more complications there would be.

They would have to have proof that Lara had meant to shoot at
him and not at Kornakov. And even that wouldn't be the end of
it; she would only be cleared of one part of the charge but would
still be liable to prosecution for the rest.

Naturally he would do everything to prevent it. If the case
came into court, he would get expert evidence from a psychiatrist that
she had not been responsible for her actions at the moment when she
fired the shot and would see to it that the proceedings were dropped.

With these reflections he began to calm down. The night was
over. Streaks of light darted from room to room and dived under the
chairs and tables like thieves or bailiffs.

After a last look in the bedroom, where he was told that Lara was
no better, Komarovsky left and went to see a friend of his, Ruffina
Onissimovna Voit-Voitkovsky, a woman lawyer who was the wife of
a political *émigré*. Her eight-roomed flat was now too large for her,
she could not afford to keep it up, so she let two of the rooms. One
of them had recently become vacant and Komarovsky took it for
Lara. There she was brought a few hours later, unconscious with
brain fever.

2

Ruffina Onissimovna was a woman of advanced views, a sworn enemy
of prejudice and well disposed towards everything that she considered
'positive and vital'.

On her chest of drawers she kept a copy of the Ehrfurt programme [1] with a dedication by the author. One of the photographs on
the wall showed her husband, 'her good Voit', at a Swiss popular outing
together with Plekhanov [2], both in lustrine jackets and panama hats.

Ruffina Onissimovna took a dislike to her sick lodger at sight. She
considered Lara as an intolerable malingerer and believed her feverish
ravings to be a pretence from start to finish. She could have sworn that
Lara was impersonating some demented Gretchen in a Gothic dungeon.

She expressed her contempt for her by a breezy animation, banging doors, singing in a loud voice, tearing through her part of the
flat like a hurricane and keeping the windows open all day long.

The flat was on the top floor of a building in the Arbat [3] and
after the winter solstice its windows filled to overflowing with blue
sky as wide as a river in flood. Through half the winter the flat

[1] Programme of the German Social Democratic Party, adopted at the S.D.
congress in 1891.
[2] A leading Russian theoretician of Marxism, who lived mostly in Switzerland.
[3] A very wide street which had a market in it.

was full of the advance news of the coming spring.

A warm wind from the south blew in through the casement. Locomotives at their distant stations roared like sea-lions. Lara, lying ill in bed, filled her leisure with recollections.

Very often she remembered the evening of her arrival in Moscow from the Urals, that evening seven or eight years ago, in the days of her unforgettable childhood.

They were driving in a cab from the station, through gloomy alleys to the hotel at the other end of town. One by one the street lamps threw the humpbacked shadow of the coachman on the walls; it grew and grew till it became gigantic and stretched across the roofs; then it was cut off and it all began again from the beginning.

The eighty score bells of Moscow clanged in the darkness overhead and the trams rang their bells as they scurried through the streets, but Lara was also deafened by the lights and shop fronts, as if they too were noisy like the wheels and bells.

In their hotel room she was staggered at the sight of a water melon of incredible size. It was Komarovsky's house-warming gift and seemed to her to be a symbol of his power and wealth. When he thrust a knife into this marvel and the dark-green globe split in half, revealing its icy, sugary heart, she caught her breath in alarm, but she dared not refuse a slice; her nervousness made the fragrant pink mouthfuls stick in her throat but she forced herself to swallow them.

Just as she was intimidated by expensive food and by the night life of the capital, so she was later intimidated by Komarovsky himself —this was the real explanation of everything.

But now he had changed beyond recognition. He made no claims on her, never reminded her of the past, and never even came to see her; he kept his distance while assuring her in the most gentlemanly way of his readiness to help her.

Very different was Kologrivov's manner, when he called on her. She was delighted at his visit. Not so much because of his tall, handsome presence as the vitality and intelligence which radiated from him together with his gay, clever smile, her visitor took up half the room.

He sat down by her bedside and rubbed his hands thoughtfully. On the occasions when he was summoned to attend a ministerial meeting in Petersburg he spoke to the titled elders as if they were naughty schoolboys; but here before him lay a girl who, until recently, had been a member of his household, something like a daughter to him. As with the rest of his family, he had hardly ever exchanged with her more than a word or a glance in passing: in its very conciseness, his manner had a warmth and charm which they all recognised. He could not treat her with the same heavy indifference as an adult. Not knowing how to begin without touching on something painful, he said smilingly, as to a child: 'Well, my girl, what have you been up to? What's the idea of all this melodrama?'

He paused, examined the damp stains on the walls and ceiling and shook his head reproachfully.

'There's an international exhibition opening at Düsseldorf—painting, sculpture, flowers. I'm going. You know, it's a bit damp here. And how long do you think you're going to wander about from pillar to post without a proper place to live in? This Voit woman, between ourselves, is a pretty nasty piece of work. I know her. Why don't you move out? You've been ill in bed long enough. Time you got up. Change your room, take up something, finish your studies. There's a painter, a friend of mine, who's going to Turkestan for two years. He's got partitions up in his studio—it's more like a small flat. I think he'd hand it over furnished to somebody who'd look after it. How about my fixing it up? And there's another thing. I've been meaning to do it for a long time, it's a sacred duty . . . since Lipa . . . Here's a small sum, a bonus for her graduation. No, please. . . . No, I beg you, don't be obstinate . . . no, really you'll have to . . .'

And in spite of her protests, her tears and her struggles, he forced her before he left to accept a cheque for ten thousand roubles.

When she recovered, Lara moved to the lodgings Kologrivov had recommended, near the Smolensky Market. The flat was at the top of an elderly-looking two-storey house. There were draymen living in the other part of it and a warehouse on the ground floor. The cobbled yard was always littered with spilt oats and hay. Pigeons strutted about cooing and fluttered up noisily to the level of Lara's window; sometimes a drove of rats swarmed down the stone gutter

3

Pasha was greatly troubled about Lara. So long as she was seriously ill he was not allowed to see her, and what was he to feel? Lara had tried to kill a man who, so far as he knew, was no more than an acquaintance of hers, and this same man, the object of her attempt at murder, had afterwards shielded her from its consequences. He had warded off the punishment which hung over her. Thanks to him, she was able to continue her studies, safe and unharmed. Pasha was puzzled and tormented.

When she was better Lara sent for him and said: 'I am a bad woman. You don't know me, you have no idea what I'm like. Some day I'll tell you. I can't talk about it now; you can see for yourself, every time I try, I start crying. But you must let me be, you must forget all about me. I'm not worthy of you.'

There followed terrible scenes, each more heart-rending and unbearable than the last. All this went on while Lara was still living in Arbat Street, and Voitkovskaya, meeting Pasha in the corridor with his tear-stained face, would rush off to her room, collapse on her sofa and laugh till she had a stitch, shouting: 'Oh, I can't, I can't, it's too much! The strong silent man! The Samson!'

To deliver Pasha from this corrupting attachment, to tear out his love for her by the roots and put an end to his torment, Lara announced that she had finished with him for good, she would have nothing more to do with him because she did not love him, but in making this renunciation she sobbed so much that it was impossible to believe her.

Pasha suspected her of all the seven deadly sins, disbelieved every word she said and was ready to curse and hate her, but he loved her to distraction and was jealous of her very thoughts, and of the mug she drank from and of the pillow on which she lay. If they were not to go out of their minds, they must act quickly and firmly. They made up their minds to get married at once, without waiting for their examinations. The wedding was to be held on Low Sunday. At Lara's wish it was again put off.

They were married on Whit Monday; by then it was quite clear that they had graduated successfully. All the arrangements were made by Lyudmila Kapitonovna Chepurko, the mother of Lara's fellow-student Tusya. Lyudmila was a handsome woman with a high bosom, a fine low-pitched singing voice and a head full of innumerable superstitions, some of them picked up and others invented by herself.

The day Lara was to be 'led to the altar' (as Lyudmila purred in her gipsy voice while helping her to dress) it was terribly hot. The golden domes of churches and the freshly sanded paths in the town gardens were a screaming yellow. The birch saplings cut on Whitsun Eve hung over the church railings, dusty, their leaves rolled up into little scrolls and scorched. There was hardly a breath of air and the sunshine dazzled you and danced in bright flecks before your eyes. As if a thousand weddings were to be held that day, all the girls were in light dresses like brides and had curled their hair, and all the boys had oiled theirs and wore tight-fitting black suits in honour of the feast. Everyone was excited and everyone was hot.

As Lara stepped on the carpet leading to the altar, Lagodina, the mother of another of her friends, threw a handful of small silver coins at her feet as an omen of prosperity; and with the same intention Lyudmila had told her that when the wedding crown was held over her head, she must not make the sign of the cross with her bare fingers but cover them with the edge of her veil or a lace frill. She had also told Lara to hold her candle high in order to have authority in her house. But Lara, sacrificing her future to Pasha's, held her candle as low as she could, yet all in vain, because however low she held it, Pasha held his lower still.

Straight from the church they drove to the wedding breakfast at the studio, which had been freshly decorated by Pasha. The guests shouted: 'It's bitter!' and others responded unanimously from the end of the room: 'Make it sweet!' and the bride and bridegroom grinned shyly and kissed.[1] Lyudmila sang 'The Vineyard' in their honour, with the double refrain, 'God give you love and concord,' and a song which began 'Undo the plait, scatter the fair hair.'

When all the guests had gone and they were left alone, Pasha felt uneasy in the sudden silence. A street lamp shone from across the road and, however tightly he drew the curtains, a streak of light, as thin as a shaving, came into the room. This light gave him no rest, he felt as if they were being watched. He discovered to his horror that he was thinking more of the light than of Lara or of himself or of his love for her.

During this night, which lasted an eternity, Antipov ('Stephanie' or 'the fair maiden' as he had been called by his fellow-students) reached the heights of joy and the lowest depths of despair. His suspicions and guesses alternated with Lara's confessions. He questioned her and with each of her answers his spirit sank lower as though he were hurtling down a precipice. His wounded imagination could not keep up with her revelations.

They talked till morning. In all Pasha's life there had been no change in him so decisive and abrupt as in the course of this night. He got up a different man, almost astonished that he was still called Pasha Antipov.

4

Nine days later their friends arranged a farewell party for them, still in the same room. Both Pasha and Lara had passed their exams,

[1] A Russian custom at weddings.

both had done equally brilliantly, and both had been offered jobs in the same town in the Urals; they were setting out for it next day.

Again they drank and sang and made a noise, but this time there were only young people present.

Behind the partition which separated the living quarters from the studio there stood a big basket trunk, and another, smaller one of Lara's, a suitcase, a case of crockery and several sacks. There was a lot of luggage. Part of it was being sent next day by freight. Almost everything was packed, but there was still a little room left in the case and in the baskets. Every now and then Lara thought of something else she meant to take and put it into one of the baskets, re-arranging the top layer to make it level.

Pasha was at home and already entertaining guests by the time Lara got back from the College Registry where she had been to fetch her birth certificate and her other documents; she came up, followed by the porter with a bundle of sacking and a good stout rope for those pieces which were going by freight. She sent him away, made the round of the guests, shaking hands with some and kissing others, and went into the bedroom to change. When she came back, they clapped, sat down and the same uproar began as at the wedding breakfast a few days earlier. The more enterprising poured out vodka for their neighbours; hands and forks converged on the middle of the table where bread, hors-d'œuvres and cooked dishes were set out; speeches were made, people grunted as they drained their glasses, kept up a cross-fire of jokes and got tipsy.

'I'm dead tired,' said Lara, who sat next to her husband. 'Did you manage to get everything done?'

'Yes.'

'All the same I'm feeling wonderful. I'm so happy. Are you?'

'Of course. But that's a long story.'

As an exception Komarovsky had been allowed to join the young people's party. At the end of the evening he started to say how bereft he would feel when his two young friends left Moscow—the town would be like a desert, a Sahara; but he became so sentimental that he began to sob and had to start all over again.

He asked the Antipovs' permission to write to them and to look them up in the Urals, if he found the parting unbearable.

'That's quite unnecessary,' Lara said in a loud, absent-minded voice. 'And in general it's all quite pointless—writing, Sahara and all that. As for coming, don't think of it. With God's help you'll manage without us, we aren't such a rarity. Don't you think so, Pasha?—With luck you'll find other young friends.'

Then, suddenly forgetting what she was talking about, she got up and hurried off to the kitchen. There she took the meat mincer apart and packed the sections into the corners of the crockery case, padding them with tufts of straw. In doing this she scratched herself on the edge of the case and nearly ran a splinter into her hand.

Absorbed in what she was doing she no longer heard her guests, and she forgot all about them until they reminded her of their existence by a sudden outburst of laughter. It occurred to her that when people were drunk they always tried to impersonate people who were drunk; the more drunk they were the harder they tried and the more they over-acted.

At this moment another sound, coming from the yard, drew her to the window. She pulled the curtains and leaned out.

A hobbled horse was moving across the yard with short limping jumps. She did not know whose it was or how it had strayed into the yard. The sleeping city seemed dead. It was bathed in the grey-blue coolness of the early hours. Lara closed her eyes, carried to goodness knows what country depths and joys by the noise of the horse's hobbled steps, so unlike any other sound.

There was a ring at the door and someone got up and went to open it. Lara pricked up her ears. It was Nadya. Lara ran to meet her. Nadya had come straight from the train, so fresh, enchanting, that it seemed as if she bore with her the scent of the lilies of the valley of Duplyanka. The two friends stood speechless with emotion and could only hug each other and cry their eyes out.

Nadya had brought Lara the congratulations and good wishes of the whole family and a present from her parents. She took a jewel-case out of her travelling bag, snapped it open and held out a very beautiful necklace.

There were gasps of delight and astonishment. A guest, who had been drunk but had recovered a little, said:

'It's rose jacinths. Yes, yes, rose, believe it or not. That's what it is. It's just as valuable as diamonds.'

But Nadya said that the stones were yellow sapphires.

Lara put Nadya next to her at table and made her eat and drink. The necklace lay beside her plate and she could not stop looking at it. The stones had rolled into a hollow on the mauve cushioned lining of the case and looked now like dew and now like a cluster of small grapes.

Meanwhile those of the guests who had sobered up were again drinking to keep company with Nadya, whom they soon made tipsy.

Soon everyone in the flat was fast asleep. Most of them were going to the station with Lara and Pasha in the morning, so they stayed the night. A good many had been snoring before Nadya came, and Lara herself never knew afterwards how she came to be lying fully dressed on the sofa next to Ira Lagodina.

She was woken up in the night by voices in the yard; the owners of the horse had come to fetch it. As she opened her eyes she said to herself: 'What on earth can Pasha be doing, pottering about in the middle of the room?' But when the man she had taken for Pasha turned his head she saw an ogre's face, pock-marked and scarred from brow to chin. She realised it was a thief and tried to shout but could not utter a sound. She remembered her necklace, and, raising herself cautiously on her elbow, looked at the table where she had left it.

The necklace was still there among the breadcrumbs and empty chocolate papers; the stupid thief hadn't seen it. He was only rummaging in the suitcase she had packed so carefully and making a mess of her work; that was all she could think of at the moment, half-asleep and still tipsy as she was. Again she tried to shout and again found she couldn't. At last she dug her knee into Ira's stomach and when Ira cried out with pain she too found her voice. The thief dropped everything and ran. Some of the men jumped up and tried to chase him without quite knowing what it was all about, but by the time they got outside the door he had vanished.

The commotion woke everyone up and Lara did not allow them to go back to sleep. She made them coffee and packed them off home until it was time to go to the station.

Then she set to work, feverishly stuffing the bed linen into the baskets, strapping up the luggage and tying it with ropes, and only begging Pasha and the porter's wife not to hinder her by trying to help.

Everything got done in time. The Antipovs did not miss their train. It started smoothly, as though wafted away by the hats their friends were waving after them. When they stopped waving and bellowed something three times—probably 'Hurrah!'—the train put on speed.

5

For the third day the weather was wretched. It was the second autumn of the war. The successes of the first year had been followed by set-backs. Brussilov's Eighth Army, which had been concentrated in the Carpathians, ready to pour down the slopes into Hungary, was drawing back instead, caught by the ebb of the general retreat.

We were pulling out of Galicia, which had been occupied in the first months of the fighting.

Dr. Zhivago, until recently known as Yura but now addressed more and more often as Yury Andreyevich, stood in the corridor of the gynaecological section of the hospital, outside the door of the maternity ward to which he had just brought his wife Tonya. He had said good-bye to her and was now waiting to see the midwife and arrange a method of getting news and of being called in case of need.

He was in a hurry to be back at his own hospital. He had still to pay two sick calls on the way, and here he was, wasting precious time, staring out of the window at the slanting streaks of rain buffeted by the autumn wind like a cornfield in a storm.

It was not yet very dark. He could see the back of the hospital, the glassed-in verandahs of the private houses in the square and the branch tramline leading to one of the hospital blocks.

The rain poured with a dreary steadiness, neither hurrying nor slowing down for all the fury of the wind, which seemed enraged by the indifference of the water and shook the creeper on one of the houses as if meaning to tear it up by the roots, swinging it up into the air, and dropping it in disgust like a torn rag.

A tram with two trailers drove past the verandah to the hospital entrance. Wounded men were carried in.

The Moscow hospitals were desperately overcrowded, especially since the battle of Lutsk. The wounded were put in the passages and on landings. The general overcrowding was beginning to affect the women's wards.

Yury turned away from the window, yawning with fatigue. He had nothing to think about. Suddenly he remembered an incident at the Hospital of the Holy Cross, where he worked. A woman had died a few days earlier in the surgical ward. Yury had diagnosed echinococcus of the liver, but everyone thought him wrong. An autopsy was to be made to-day, but the interne on duty was a frightful drunkard and goodness only knew what he would make of the job.

Night fell suddenly. Nothing more was visible outside. As at the stroke of a magic wand, lights sprang up in all the windows.

The head gynaecologist came out of Tonya's ward through the narrow lobby separating it from the corridor. He was a mammoth of a gynaecologist who, whenever he was asked a question, replied by shrugging his shoulders and rolling up his eyes as much as to say that, whatever the advances of science, there were 'more things in heaven and earth, Horatio . . .'

He passed Yury with a nod and a smile, flipped his podgy hands a few times, thus conveying that there was nothing for it but patience, and went off down the corridor to have a smoke in the waiting-room.

After him came his assistant who was as talkative as the gynaecologist was taciturn.

'If I were you, I'd go home,' she told Yury. 'I'll ring you up to-morrow at the Holy Cross. It's most unlikely that anything will happen between now and then. There's every reason to expect a natural birth, there shouldn't be any need for surgical intervention. But of course the pelvis is narrow, the child's head is in the occipito-posterior position, there are no pains and the contractions are slight. All this gives grounds for anxiety. However, it's too soon to say. It all depends on how the pains develop once labour begins. Then we'll know what to expect.'

When Yury rang up the following day, the hospital porter who took the call told him to wait while he made enquiries and, after keeping him in misery for a good ten minutes, came back with the following inadequate and crudely worded information: 'They say, tell him he's brought his wife too soon, he's to take her back.'

Yury told him furiously to get someone more responsible. The nurse who finally answered said that the symptoms had been misleading, the doctor was not to worry but it might take a day or two.

On the third day he was told that labour had begun the night before, the waters had broken at dawn and there had been intense pains with short intervals since the early morning.

He rushed headlong to the hospital. As he walked down the passage to the door, which by mistake had been left half open, he heard Tonya's heart-rending screams; she screamed like the victim of an accident who was being dragged with crushed limbs from under the wheels of a train.

He was not allowed to see her. He bit his knuckle, drawing blood, and went over to the window; the same slanting rain was pouring down as yesterday and the day before.

A ward maid came out and he heard the squealing of a new-born child. 'She's safe, she's safe,' Yury muttered joyfully to himself.

'It's a son. A little boy. Congratulations on a safe delivery,' said the maid in a sing-song voice. 'You can't go in yet. When they're ready we'll show you. Then you'll have to make a big .uss of her. She's had a bad time. It being the first. There's always trouble with the first.'

'She's safe, she's safe,' Yury rejoiced, hardly taking in what the maid was telling him, or that she was including him in her congratulations as if he had played a part in what had happened.—Though what had he had to do with it in reality? Father—son; he could see nothing to be proud of in this unearned fatherhood, he could not feel anything about this gift of parenthood which had fallen on him from the sky. It was all outside his consciousness. The great thing was that Tonya, Tonya who had been in mortal danger, was now happily safe.

He had a patient living near the hospital. He went to see him and was back in half an hour. Both the doors of the lobby and of the ward were again ajar. Without knowing what he was doing, Yury darted into the lobby.

The mammoth gynaecologist in his white overall rose as though out of the ground in front of him, barring the way.

'What do you think you're doing?' he whispered breathlessly so that the patient should not hear. 'Are you out of your mind? Wounds, blood, risk of sepsis, not to speak of psychological shock! That's a nice way to behave, and you call yourself a doctor.'

'I didn't mean to. . . . Do let me have just a glance. Just from here, just through the crack.'

'Oh, well, that's different. All right, if you must. But don't let me catch you. . . . If she sees you, I'll wring your neck, there'll be murder.'

Inside the ward two women in white overalls stood with their backs to the door; they were the midwife and the nurse. Squirming on the palm of the nurse's hand lay a tender, squealing human offspring, stretching and contracting like a dark red piece of india-rubber. The midwife was putting a ligature on the navel before cutting the cord. Tonya lay on a surgical bed with a movable board in the middle of the room. The bed was rather high. Yury, exaggerating everything in his excitement, thought that she was lying, say, at the level of one of those desks at which you write standing up.

Raised higher, closer to the ceiling than is usual with ordinary mortals, Tonya lay exhausted in the cloud of her spent pain. To Yury she seemed like a barque lying at rest in the middle of a harbour after putting in and being unloaded, a barque which plied between an unknown country and the continent of life across the waters of death with a cargo of new immigrant souls. One such soul had just been landed, and the ship now lay at anchor, resting in the lightness of her empty flanks. The whole of her was resting, her strained masts and hull, and her memory washed clean of the image of the other shore, the crossing and the landing.

And as no one had explored the country whose flag she flew, no one knew the language in which to speak to her.

At Yury's hospital everyone congratulated him. He was astonished to see how fast the news had travelled.

He went into the staff room, known as the Rubbish Dump. With so little space in the overcrowded hospital, it was used as a cloakroom; people came in from outside wearing their snow-boots, they forgot their parcels and littered the floor with papers and cigarette ends.

Standing by the window, a flabby, elderly interne was holding up a jar with some opaque liquid against the light and examining it over the top of his glasses.

'Congratulations,' he said without looking round.

'Thank you. How kind of you.'

'Don't thank me. I've had nothing to do with it. Pichuzhkin did the autopsy. But everyone is most impressed—echinococcus it was. That's a real diagnostician, they're all saying. That's all everyone is talking about.'

Just then the head doctor came in, greeted them both and said: 'What the devil is happening to this place? What a filthy mess it is! By the way, Zhivago, it was echinococcus after all; just fancy, we were wrong. Congratulations. There's another thing. It's a nuisance. They've checked up on your class again. I can't stop them this time. There's a frightful shortage of medical personnel. You'll be sniffing gunpowder before long.'

6

The Antipovs had quickly settled down in Yuryatin. The Guishars were remembered with affection and this had helped Lara over the difficulties of setting up house in a new place. They had now been here four years.

Lara had her hands full and plenty to think about. She had the house to see to, as well as Katya, her daughter, who was three years old.—Marfutka, their red-haired maid, did her best but could not get all the work done.—In addition, Lara shared all Pasha's interests and taught at the girls' high school. She worked ceaselessly and was happy. This was exactly the kind of life she had dreamed of.

She liked Yuryatin. She had been born there. It stood on one of the Urals railways and on the big river Rynva, navigable except in its upper reaches.

A sign of approaching winter in Yuryatin was that people took their boats out of the river, loaded them on carts, drove them into the town and put them away in their backyards. There they lay in the open air, waiting for the spring. The sight of the boats with their light upturned bottoms in the shadows of the yards meant in Yuryatin what the migration of storks or the first snow meant in other places. Such a boat lay in the yard of the house rented by the Antipovs. Katya played in the shelter of its white hull as in a summer-house.

Lara liked Yuryatin's provincial ways, the long vowels of its northern accent and its naïvely trustful intellectuals in felt boots and grey flannel sleeveless coats. She was attracted to the soil and to simple people.

Paradoxically, it was Pasha, the son of a Moscow railway worker, who turned out to be an incorrigible metropolitan. He judged the people of Yuryatin much more harshly than Lara. He disliked them as ignorant savages; they got on his nerves.

He had an unusual gift, it now appeared, for reading quickly and remembering the information he picked up. He had read a great deal in the past, partly thanks to Lara. In the retirement of his provincial exile, he became so well read that even Lara no longer seemed to him well-informed. As for the milieu of his fellow-school-masters, he towered above them and complained that he felt stifled. Now in war time, their standard, commonplace patriotism was out of tune with his own more complicated feeling for his country.

Pasha had graduated in classics and now taught Latin and Ancient History. But from his earlier high school days he had kept a half-forgotten passion for the exact sciences, physics and mathematics, and it had now revived in him. Teaching himself at home, he had reached university standard in these subjects, and dreamed of taking his degree, transferring to some scientific branch and moving with his family to Petersburg. Studying late into the night had affected his health and given him insomnia.

His relations with his wife were good, but not sufficiently simple. Her kindness and her fussing over him oppressed him but he would not criticise her for fear that she might take some quite innocent word of his for a reproach—a hint, perhaps, that her blood was bluer than his, or that she had once belonged to someone else. He was frightened that she suspected him of having some ridiculously unfair idea about her and this prevented both of them from being natural. Each constantly tried to behave more generously than the other and this made things complicated.

To-night they were having guests—the headmistress of Lara's

school, several fellow-teachers of Pasha's, a member of an arbitration court on which Pasha too had recently served, and a few others. They were all, from Pasha's point of view, complete fools. He was amazed at Lara, who managed to be pleasant to them, and he could not believe that there was a single one of them she really liked.

After they had gone, Lara took a long time airing and tidying the rooms and washing dishes in the kitchen with Marfutka. Then she made sure that Katya was properly tucked up and Pasha asleep, quickly undressed, switched off the light and lay down next to him as simply as a child getting into bed with its mother.

But Pasha was only pretending, he was not asleep. As so often recently, he had insomnia. Knowing that he would only lie awake for hours, he got up quietly, put on his fur coat and cap over his night clothes, and went outside.

It was a clear frosty night. Thin slides of ice crackled into powder under his feet. The sky, shining with stars, threw a pale blue flicker like the flame of methylated spirit over the black earth with its clumps of frozen mud.

The Antipovs lived at the other end of town from the river harbour. The house was the last in the street and beyond it lay a field cut by a railway with a level crossing and a signal hut.

Pasha sat down on the overturned boat and looked at the stars. The thoughts to which he had become accustomed in the past few years closed in on him disturbingly. It seemed to him that sooner or later they would have to be thought out to the end and that it might as well be now.

This can't go on, he thought. He should have realised it long before they were married. Why had she allowed him as a child to take his fill of gazing at her? Even then she could make him do whatever she liked. Why hadn't he had the sense to break it off in time when she herself had insisted on it? Wasn't it clear that it was not him she loved, but only the task she had set herself and was carrying out so generously? What she loved was the image of her own heroism. But what had her mission, however meritorious or noble, to do with real family life? The worst of it was that he loved her as much as ever. She was overwhelmingly lovely. And yet—was he sure that it was love even on his side? Or was it a bewildered gratitude for her loveliness and her generosity? Who could possibly sort it all out!

So what was he to do? Set his wife and daughter free from this counterfeit life?—This was even more important than to liberate himself. Yes, but how? Divorce? Drown himself? 'What disgusting rubbish!' he rebelled indignantly. 'As if I'd ever do anything of the sort! So why rehearse this melodrama even in my mind?'

He looked up at the stars as if asking their advice. They flickered on, small or large, alone or in clusters, some blue, some rainbow-coloured. Suddenly they were blotted out and the house, the yard and Pasha sitting on his boat were thrown into relief by a harsh, darting light, as though someone were running from the field towards the gate waving a naked torch. An army train, puffing clouds of yellow, flame-shot smoke into the sky, rolled over the level crossing going westwards, as countless others had rolled by, night and day, for the past year.

Pasha smiled, got up and went to bed. He had found his answer.

7

When Lara heard of Pasha's decision she was stunned and at first would not believe her ears. 'It's madness,' she thought, 'he's raving. I won't take any notice and he'll forget it.'

But it appeared that he had been getting ready for the past fortnight. He had sent in his papers to the recruiting office, the high school had found a replacement and he had received orders to go to the military training school at Omsk.

Lara howled like a peasant woman, grabbed Pasha's hands and rolled at his feet. 'Pasha, Pasha darling,' she screamed, 'don't leave us. Don't do it, don't. It isn't too late, I'll see to everything. You haven't even had a proper medical examination, and with your heart . . . You're ashamed to change your mind? And aren't you ashamed to offer up your family to some crazy notion? You, a volunteer! All your life you've laughed at Rodya, and now you're jealous. You have to swagger about in an officer's uniform too, you have to do your own bit of sabre-rattling. Pasha, what's the matter with you? You're not yourself, I don't recognise you. What's changed you like this? Tell me honestly, for Christ's sake, without any fine phrases, is this really what Russia needs?'

Suddenly she realised that it wasn't that at all. Though she could not understand all of it, she grasped the main thing. Pasha misunderstood her attitude to him. He rebelled against the motherly feeling which all her life had been a part of her affection for him and could not see that such a love was something more, not less, than the ordinary feeling of a woman for a man.

She bit her lip and, shrinking as if she had been beaten and swallowing her tears, set about silently packing his things.

After he had left it seemed to her that the whole town was silent and even that there were fewer crows flying about in the sky. 'Madam, Madam,' Marfutka tried to call her back to herself. 'Mama, Mama,' Katya kept pulling at her sleeve.—She had had the greatest defeat of her life. Her best and brightest hopes were in ruins.

Pasha's letters from Siberia told her all about his moods. He was beginning to see things more clearly. He badly missed his wife and daughter. But within a few months he received an emergency commission as an ensign and, with equal suddenness, was sent on active service. His journey took him nowhere near Yuryatin and in Moscow he had no time to see anyone.

When he wrote from the front he sounded less depressed. He wanted to distinguish himself, so that, as a reward or as a result of some light wound, he could go home on leave and see his family. Soon he got his opportunity. Brussilov's forces had broken through and were attacking. Pasha's letters stopped coming. At first Lara was not worried. She put down his silence to the military operations, he could not write when his regiment was on the move. But in the autumn the advance slowed down, the troops were digging themselves in, yet there was still no word from him. She began to be anxious and to make enquiries, at first locally, in Yuryatin, then by post in Moscow and at his old field address. There was no reply, nobody seemed to know anything.

Together with other local ladies, Lara had been giving a hand at the military ward attached to the town hospital. Now she trained seriously and qualified as a nurse, got permission to be absent from her school for six months and, leaving the house in Marfutka's care, took Katya to Moscow. She left her with Lipa, who was living on her own, as her husband, Friesendank, was a German subject and had been interned with other enemy civilians at Ufa.

Convinced of the futility of trying to get news of Pasha in any other way, Lara had decided to go and look for him. With this in mind, she got a job as a nurse on a hospital train going to the Hungarian border and passing through the town of Liski, the last address Pasha had given her.

8

A Red Cross train, equipped through voluntary contributions collected by the Tatyana Committee of Help for the Wounded [1], arrived at

[1] A Committee presided over by the Grand Duchess Tatyana, daughter of the Tsar.

Divisional Headquarters. It was a long train mostly made up of ugly short freight trucks; in the only first-class coach came prominent people from Moscow with presents for the troops. Among them was Gordon. He knew that his childhood friend Zhivago was attached to the Divisional hospital; hearing that it was in a near-by village, he obtained the necessary permit to travel in the area just behind the lines, and got a lift in a cart going to the village.

The driver was a Byelorussian or a Lithuanian who spoke broken Russian. The current spy mania reduced his conversation to a stale official patter; discouraged by his ostentatious loyalty, Gordon travelled most of the way in silence.

At Headquarters, where they were used to moving armies and measured distances in hundred-mile stages, he had been told that the village was quite near—within fifteen miles at most; in reality, it was more like fifty.

All along the way an unfriendly grunting and grumbling came from the horizon on their left. Gordon had never been in an earthquake but he thought rightly that the sullen, scarcely distinguishable, distant sound of enemy artillery was the nearest thing to that of volcanic shocks and rumblings. Towards evening, a pink glow flared up over the skyline on that side and went on flickering until dawn.

They passed ruined villages. Some were abandoned, in others people were living in cellars deep underground. Piles of dust and rubble were aligned as once the houses had been. You could see the whole of such a burned-out settlement at a glance, like a barren waste ground. Old women scratched about in the ashes, each on the ruins of her own home, now and then digging something up and putting it away, apparently feeling as sheltered from the eyes of strangers as if their walls were still around them. They looked up at Gordon and gazed after him as he drove past, seeming to ask him how soon the world would come to its senses and peace and order be restored to their lives.

After dark the cart ran into a patrol and was ordered off the main road. The driver did not know the new cart-track. They wandered about in circles for a couple of hours without getting anywhere. At dawn they came to a village which had the name they were looking for but where no one knew anything about a hospital. It turned out that there were two villages of the same name. At last, in the morning, they found the right one. As they drove down the village street, which smelled of camomile and iodoform, Gordon decided not to stay the night but to spend the day with Zhivago and go back that evening to the railway station where he had left his other friends. But circumstances kept him here for over a week.

9

The front line had begun to move. To the south of the district where Gordon found himself, our forces had succeeded in breaking through the enemy positions. Supporting units followed, widening the gap, but they fell behind and the advanced units were cut off and captured. Among the prisoners was Lieutenant Antipov, who was obliged to give himself up when his platoon surrendered.

He was believed to have been killed by a shell and buried by the explosion. This was told on the authority of his friend, Ensign Galiullin, who had been watching through field-glasses from an observation post when Antipov led the attack.

What Galiullin had seen was the usual picture of an attacking unit. The men advanced quickly, almost at a run, across no-man's-land, an autumn field with dry broom waving in the wind and motionless spiky gorse. Their object was either to flush the Austrians out of their trenches and engage them with bayonets or to destroy them with hand grenades. To the running men the field seemed endless. The ground shifted under their feet like a bog. Their ensign was running, first in front of them, then beside them, waving his revolver above his head, his mouth split from ear to ear with hurrahs which neither he nor they could hear. At intervals they threw themselves on the ground, got up all together and ran on shouting. Each time, one or two, who had been hit, fell with the rest but in a different way, toppling like trees chopped down in a wood, and did not get up again.

'They're overshooting the target, call up the battery,' Galiullin said anxiously to the artillery officer who stood next to him.—'No, wait, it's all right.'

The attackers were on the point of engaging the enemy when the artillery barrage stopped. In the sudden silence the observers heard their own hearts beating as if they, like Antipov, had brought their men to the edge of the enemy trench and were expected within the next few minutes to perform wonders of resourcefulness and courage. At that moment they saw two German sixteen-inch shells burst in front of the attackers. Black clouds of dust and smoke hid what followed. 'Ya Allah! Finished. They're done for,' whispered Galiullin, white-lipped, believing that the ensign and his men had been killed. Another shell came down close to the observation post. Bent double, the observers hurried to a safer distance.

Galiullin had shared Antipov's dug-out. Once it was accepted that Antipov was dead, his friend was asked to take charge of his belongings and keep them for his widow, of whom there were many photographs among his things.

Galiullin, a mechanic by trade, had recently been promoted. The son of Gimazetdin, the porter at Tiverzin's block of flats, he was that very Yusupka whom, as an apprentice in the distant past, the foreman Khudoleyev had beaten up, and it was to his old tormentor that he was now indebted for his promotion.

On getting his commission, he had found himself, against his will and for no reason that he knew of, in a cushy job as garrison commander in a small town at the rear. The garrison was composed of semi-invalids whom instructors as elderly as themselves took every morning through the drill they had both forgotten. He had to supervise the drill and the changing of the guard in front of the adjutant's stores. Nothing else was expected of him. He had not a care in the world when, among the recently called-up men sent from Moscow and put under his orders, there turned up the all too familiar figure of Pyotr Khudoleyev.

'Well, well, an old friend,' Galiullin grinned sourly.

'Yes, sir,' said Khudoleyev standing to attention and saluting.

It was impossible that this should be the end of it. The very first time the lieutenant caught the private in a fault at drill he roared at him, and when it seemed to him that the man was not looking him straight in the eye but somehow sideways, he gave him a sock in the jaw and put him for two days on bread and water in the detention cell.

From now on, every move of Galiullin's smacked of revenge. But this game, in view of their respective positions and with rules enforced by the stick, was too unsporting; it was undignified. What was to be done? They could not both be in the same place. But what pretext could an officer find for transferring a private from his unit, and where, if it were not for disciplinary reasons, could he transfer him to? On the other hand, what grounds could Galiullin think of to apply for his own transfer? Justifying his request by the boredom and uselessness of garrison duty, he asked to be sent to the front. This earned him a good mark and when, in the first engagement, he showed his other qualities, it appeared that he had the makings of an excellent officer and he was quickly promoted to lieutenant.

Galiullin knew Antipov from the days of the Tiverzins, when Pasha Antipov had spent six months with them in 1905 and Yusupka had come to play with him on Sundays. There, too, he had once or twice met Lara. He had heard nothing of either of them since. When Antipov came from Yuryatin and joined the regiment, Galiullin was struck by the change in his old friend whom he had known as a shy, mischievous and girlish child and who had now turned into an arrogant and erudite hypochondriac. He was intelligent, very brave, taciturn and sarcastic. Sometimes, when Galiullin caught the melancholy expression of his eyes, he could have sworn that he saw in them, almost as though he were looking through a window, something else, perhaps an idea which possessed him, perhaps a longing for his daughter or his wife. Antipov seemed to him to be a changeling, bewitched as in a fairy tale. And now Antipov had vanished, and Galiullin was left with his papers, his photographs and the unsolved secret of his transformation on his hands.

As was bound to happen sooner or later, Lara's enquiries for her husband reached Galiullin. He meant to write to her but he was busy, he had no time to write properly and he wished to prepare her for the blow. He kept putting it off until he heard that she was herself somewhere at the front as a nurse, and by then he did not know where to address a letter to her.

10

'Will there be horses to-day?' asked Gordon every time Dr. Zhivago came home to his midday meal. They were living in a Galician peasant's cottage.

'Not a chance. Anyway, where would you go? You can't move right or left. There's a frightful muddle going on all round, nobody can make any sense of it. To the south we have outflanked the Germans in some places and broken through in others, and, I am told, several of our over-zealous units got captured. To the north, the Germans have crossed the Sventa, at a point which was supposed to be impassable; that was their cavalry, about a corps in strength. They are blowing up railways, destroying supply dumps, and my guess is that they are encircling us. That's the picture, and you talk about horses.—Come on, Karpenko,' he turned to his orderly, 'get a move on and lay the table. What are we having for dinner? Calf's foot? Splendid.'

The Medical Unit with its hospital and its dependencies was scattered all over the village, which by a miracle was still unharmed. The houses glittered with lattice windows in the western style, stretching from wall to wall, and not so much as a pane was damaged.

The end of a hot golden autumn had turned into an Indian summer. In the daytime the doctors and officers opened windows, swatted the flies crawling in black swarms along the sills and the low white ceilings, unbuttoned their tunics and overalls and, dripping with sweat, sipped scalding hot cabbage soup or tea.

At night they sat down to cards in front of the open stove, blew on the damp logs, their eyes smarting with smoke, and cursed the orderlies for not knowing how to lay a fire.

It was a still night. Gordon and Zhivago were lying on two bunks facing each other. Between them were the dinner table and the low window running the whole length of the wall. The window panes sweated; the room was hot and filled with tobacco smoke. They had opened the two end lattices to get a breath of the fresh autumn night. As usual they were talking, and as usual the skyline in the direction of the front was glowing with a pink light. The incessant chatter of gun-fire was occasionally interrupted by a deep thud which shook the ground as though a heavy steel-bound trunk were being dragged across the floor, scraping the paint. Zhivago paused for it respectfully. 'That's a Bertha, a German sixteen-inch. The shell is a little fellow that weighs sixty *puds* [1].' When they resumed their conversation he had forgotten what they had been talking about.

'What's that smell that hangs all over the village?' asked Gordon. 'I noticed it as soon as I arrived. It's a disgusting sort of sweet, cloying smell, rather like mice.'

'I know what you mean. That's hemp—they grow a lot of it here. The plant itself has that nagging, clinging, carrion smell. And then, in the battle zone, the dead often remain undiscovered in the hemp fields until they start to decay. Of course the smell of corpses is everywhere. That's only natural.—Hear that? It's the Bertha again.'

In the past few days they had talked of everything in the world. Gordon had learned his friend's ideas about the war and the spirit of the times. Zhivago had told him how hard he found it to accept the ruthless logic of mutual extermination, to get used to the sight of the wounded, particularly to the horror of certain wounds which were inflicted nowadays, and to the thought of survivors whom the technique of modern fighting had turned into lumps of mutilated flesh.

Going about with him day by day, Gordon too had seen terrible sights. He realised that it was immoral to look on idly while other people suffered with courage, to look on at their superhuman striving to overcome their fear of death and to see what they risked and paid for it. But he did not think that merely crying over them was any less immoral. He believed in behaving simply and honestly, according to the circumstances in which life placed him.

[1] One pud is 36 lb.

That it was possible to faint at the sight of wounds he knew from his own experience, when they had visited a first-aid post run by a mobile Red Cross unit just behind the front line.

They came to a clearing in a wood which had been badly damaged by artillery fire. Twisted gun carriages lay upside down in the broken and trampled undergrowth. A charger was tethered to a tree. Just inside the wood there was a house, put up by the Forestry Department; half its roof had been blown away. The forestry office was used for the first-aid post and two big grey tents had been pitched on the other side of the road which led to it.

'I shouldn't have brought you,' said Zhivago. 'The trenches are within a mile or two and our batteries are just over there, behind the wood. You can hear what's going on. So don't play the hero. I wouldn't believe you if you did. You're bound to be scared stiff, it's only natural. Any moment the position may change and they'll start shelling us.'

Tired young soldiers in enormous boots, their dusty tunics black with sweat on the chest and shoulder-blades, sprawled, some on their backs, others face down, by the side of the road. They were the survivors of a detachment which had been taken out of the front line after four days of heavy fighting and was being sent to the rear for a short rest. They lay as if they were made of stone, without energy to smile or swear, and no one turned his head when several carts came rumbling swiftly down the road. They were ammunition carts, without springs, loaded with wounded whom they jolted, cracking their bones and twisting their guts, as they jogged along at a trot to the first-aid post. There the wounded would be hastily bandaged and the most urgent cases operated on. They had been picked up in appalling numbers on the battle-field in front of the trenches half an hour ago when there was a short lull in the artillery fire. A good half of them were unconscious.

When the carts stopped in front of the office verandah, orderlies came down the steps with stretchers and unloaded them. A nurse raised the flap of one of the tents and stood looking out; she was off duty. Two men who had been arguing loudly in the wood behind the tents—their voices echoing among the tall young trees but their words indistinguishable—came out and walked along the road towards the office. One of them, an excited young lieutenant, was shouting at the other who was the Medical Officer of the mobile unit; there had been a gun emplacement in the clearing and he wanted to know where it had gone to. The doctor did not know, it was not his business; he begged him not to shout and to leave him alone—he was busy, the wounded had arrived; but the officer went on cursing the Red Cross, the gunners and the world in general. Zhivago walked up to the doctor; they greeted each other and went into the office. The lieutenant, still swearing loudly with a slight Tartar accent, untied his horse, vaulted into the saddle and galloped down the road into the wood. The nurse was still looking on.

Suddenly her expression became horrified. 'What are you doing? You're out of your minds!' she shouted at two lightly-wounded soldiers who were walking without assistance between the stretchers. She ran out towards them.

The orderlies were carrying a man who had been mutilated in a particularly monstrous way. A splinter from the shell which had mangled his face, turning his tongue and lips into a red gruel without killing him, had lodged in the bone structure of his jaw, replacing the torn-out cheek. He uttered short groans in a thin inhuman voice; no one could take these sounds for anything but an appeal to finish him off quickly, to put an end to his inconceivable torment.

The nurse got the impression that the two lightly-wounded men who were walking beside the stretcher had been so moved by his cries that they were about to pull out the iron splinter with their bare hands.

'You mustn't do that. The surgeon will do it, he has special instruments . . . if it has to be done.' (O God, O God, take him away, don't let me doubt that You exist.)

Next moment, as he was carried up the steps, the man screamed, his whole body shuddered and he died.

The man who had just died was Private Gimazetdin; the excited officer who had been shouting in the wood was his son, Lieutenant Galiullin; the nurse was Lara. Gordon and Zhivago were the witnesses. All these people were there, together, in this one place. But some of them had never known each other, while others failed to recognise each other now. And there were things about them which were never to be known for certain, while others were only to await another opportunity in order to reveal themselves.

11

In this area the villages seemed to have been miraculously preserved. They were unaccountable islands of safety in a sea of ruins. One evening at sunset Gordon and Zhivago were driving home. In one village they saw a young Cossack surrounded by a happy crowd;

the Cossack tossed a copper coin into the air and an old Jew with a grey beard and a long coat was supposed to catch it. The old man missed every time. The coin flew past his pitifully outstretched hands and fell into the mud. The old man bent down to pick it up, the Cossack slapped his bottom, the onlookers held their sides and groaned with laughter; this was the point of the entertainment. For the moment it was harmless, but no one could say for certain that it would not take a more serious turn. Every few moments the old man's wife darted out of their cottage across the road, screaming and holding out her hands, and ran back again in terror. Two small girls were watching their grandfather out of the cottage window and crying.

The driver, who thought all this extremely funny, slowed down so that the passengers could have a look. But Zhivago called the Cossack, cursed him and ordered him to stop baiting the old man.

'Yes, sir,' he said readily. 'We didn't know; we were only doing it for fun.'

Gordon and Zhivago drove on in silence until they were in sight of their own village.

'It's terrible,' said Yury. 'You can't imagine what this wretched Jewish population is going through in this war. The fighting happens to be in their Pale of Settlement [1]. And as if punitive taxation, the destruction of their property and all their other sufferings were not enough, they have to put up with pogroms, insults and the charge that they lack patriotism. And why should they be patriotic while the enemy offers them equal rights and we do nothing but persecute them? There is something paradoxical at the very root of this hatred of them. It is stimulated by the very things which should arouse sympathy—their poverty, their overcrowding, their weakness and their inability to fight back. I can't understand it. There is something fateful about it.'

Gordon did not reply.

12

And now once again they were lying on their bunks on either side of the long, low window, it was night time and they were talking.

Zhivago was telling Gordon how he had once seen the Tsar at the front.

It was Yury's first spring in the army. He was attached to a unit which held the mouth of a valley in the Carpathian Mountains,

[1] The Pale was an area in the west of Russia to which the Russian Jews, with a small number of exceptions, were confined.

blocking it to the Hungarians. The Headquarters of the unit were in the valley.

At the bottom of the valley there was a railway station. Zhivago described the look of the place, the mountains overgrown with great firs and pines, with tufts of clouds catching in their tops and sheer cliffs of grey slate and graphite showing through the forests like worn bald patches in a thick fur. It was a damp, dark April morning as grey as the slate, locked in by the mountains on all sides and therefore still and airless. Mist hung over the valley, and everything in it steamed and smoked upwards—engine smoke from the railway station and the grey mist from the fields, and the grey mountains and the dark woods and the dark clouds.

At that time the Emperor was making a tour of inspection in Galicia and it was learned suddenly that he was coming to inspect the unit of which he was the honorary Colonel. He might arrive at any moment. A guard of honour was drawn up on the station platform. After a couple of hours of suspense, two trains of the imperial suite went by quickly one after the other and soon afterwards the Tsar's train drew in.

Accompanied by the Grand Duke Nicolas, the Tsar inspected the grenadiers. Every word of his quiet greeting set off bursts and splashes of loud, echoing hurrahs, their sound spurting like water from a swinging bucket.

The Tsar, smiling and ill at ease, looked older and more tired than his image on his coins and medals. His face was listless and a little flabby. He kept glancing apologetically at the Grand Duke, not knowing what was expected of him at any given moment, and the Grand Duke, bending down respectfully, showed him the way out of his difficulty not so much by words as by moving an eyebrow or a shoulder.

Watching him on that warm grey mountain morning, Yury felt sorry for the Tsar and horrified to think that this diffident reserve and shyness were the essential attributes of the oppressor, that such weakness could kill or pardon, bind or loose.

'He should have made a speech—"I, my sword, my people,"—like Wilhelm. Something about "the people" anyway—that was essential. But, you know, he behaved in a natural, Russian way, and he was tragically above these banalities. After all, this kind of play-acting is unthinkable in Russia, isn't it—because play-acting is surely what it is? I can just accept that there were "peoples" under the Caesars—Gauls and Scythians and Illyrians and so on. But ever since, the idea has been utter fiction, a phrase for Tsars and kings and politicians to use in their speeches: "The people, my people."'

'Now the front is flooded with correspondents and journalists. They "observe", they collect gems of popular wisdom, they visit the wounded and construct new theories about the people's soul. It's a new version of Dahl [1] and just as bogus—linguistic graphomania and verbal incontinence. That's one type—and then there's the other—clipped speech, "sketches and scenes", scepticism and misanthropy. I read a piece like that the other day. I've still got it. Here it is.—"A grey day, like yesterday. Rain since morning, slush. I look out of the window and see the road. Prisoners in an endless line. Wounded. A gun is firing. It fires to-day as yesterday, to-morrow as to-day and every day and every hour." Isn't that subtle and witty! But what has he got against the gun? How odd to expect variety from a gun! Why doesn't he look at himself, shooting off the same sentences, commas, lists of facts, day in, day out, keeping up his barrage of journalistic benevolence as rapid as a squad of jumping fleas? Why can't he get it into his head that it's for him to stop repeating himself—not for the gun—that you can't make sense by dribbling nonsense out of your notebook, however long you go on, because facts don't exist until man puts into them something of his own, some measure of his own wilful, human genius—of fairy tale, of myth.'

'You couldn't be more right,' broke in Gordon. 'And now I'll tell you what I think about that incident we saw to-day.—That Cossack making a fool of the poor old patriarch—that and the thousands of other incidents like it—of course none of that is worth theorising about.—You don't have to think about it, you just have to bash in somebody's face. But the Jewish question as a whole—there, philosophy does come in. Not that I'm telling you anything new—we both got our ideas from your uncle.

'You were saying, what is a people? . . . And who does more for a people, the one who coddles them or the one who forgets all about them and simply draws them after him into universality and deathlessness by the sheer beauty of his actions?—Well, of course, there can't be any argument about that . . .

'What are all these nations we talk about anyway, now, in the Christian era? They aren't just nations—they are nations made up of individuals who have been converted, transformed.—The point about them is their transformation, not their loyalty to their ancient ways.

'Now what do the Gospels say about it?—To start with, the Gospels don't lay down the law—they aren't an assertion: "It's like

---

[1] Dahl was the compiler of a Russian dictionary which became a classic and which included a very wide list of linguistic oddities.

this and like that." The Gospels are an offer, a naïve and tentative offer: "Would you like to live in a completely new way? Would you like to enjoy spiritual beatitude?" And everybody was delighted, they all accepted, they were carried away by it for thousands of years . . .

'When the Gospels say that in the Kingdom of God there are neither Jews nor Gentiles, do they just mean that all are equal in the sight of God? I don't believe it means only that—that was known already—it was known to the Greek philosophers and the Roman moralists and the Hebrew Prophets. What the Gospels tell us is that in this new way of life and of communion, which is born of the heart and which is called the Kingdom of God, there are no nations, but only persons.

'Now you said that facts don't mean anything by themselves—not until a meaning is put into them. Well—the meaning you have to put into the facts to make them relevant to human beings is just that: it's Christianity, it's the mystery of personality . . .

'And then we were talking about the ordinary run of politicians— people who aren't interested in life as a whole, in the world as a whole, the sort of people with restricted minds who like restriction for its own sake.—They're as pleased as Punch to get everybody thinking and talking about a nicely restricted group—the more restricted the better—a people, especially if it's a small people, and best of all if it's having a bad time, so that there can be plenty of judging and weighing and settling and deciding, and getting pity to pay dividends. Well now, what more perfect example can you have of the victims of this mentality than the Jews? Their national idea has forced them, century after century, to be a people and nothing but a people—and the extraordinary thing is that they have been chained to this deadening task all through the centuries when all the rest of the world was being delivered from it by a new force which had come out of their own midst! Isn't that extraordinary? How can you account for it? Just think!—This glorious holiday from mediocrity, from the dreary, boring constriction of everyday life, was first achieved on their soil, proclaimed in their language, belonged to their race! And they actually saw and heard it and let it go! How could they do it?— How could they allow a spirit of such overwhelming power and beauty to go out of them, to leave them, so that when it was enthroned in triumph they were left behind like the empty skin it had cast aside!—In whose interests is this voluntary martyrdom? Who stands to gain by keeping it going, so that all these innocent old men and women and children, all these clever, kind, humane people should go on being mocked and beaten up throughout the centuries? And why is it that all these friends of "the people", all these writers who write on national questions, to whatever nation they belong, are always so unimaginative and so untalented? Why don't the intellectual leaders of the Jewish people ever get beyond facile *Weltschmertz* and irony? Why don't they—even if they have to burst like a boiler with the pressure of their duty—dismiss this army which is for ever fighting and being massacred nobody knows for what? Why don't they say to them: "That's enough, stop now. Don't hold on to your identity, don't all get together in a crowd. Disperse. Be with all the rest. You are the first and best Christians in the world. You are the very thing against which you have been turned by the worst and weakest among you."'

13

The following day, when Zhivago came home to dinner, he said: 'Well, you were so anxious to leave, now we're all leaving. I won't say "just your luck", because it isn't lucky that we are being hardpressed and beaten again. The way east is open, the pressure is from the west. All the medical units are under orders to get out. We'll be going to-morrow or the next day. Where to, I don't know. —And I suppose, Karpenko, Mr. Gordon's linen still hasn't been washed. It's always the same.—Karpenko will tell you he has given it to his girl to wash, but if you ask him who or where she is, he doesn't know, the idiot!'

He paid no attention to Karpenko's lying excuses nor to Gordon's apologies for borrowing his host's shirts.

'That's army life for you,' he went on. 'As soon as you get used to one place you're moved to another. I didn't like anything here when we came. It was dirty, stuffy, the stove was in the wrong place, the ceiling was too low. And now, bless me if I can remember what it was like where we came from. I feel as if I wouldn't mind spending my life in this place, staring at that corner of the stove with the sunshine on the tiles and the shadow of that tree moving across it.'

They packed without haste.

During the night they were woken up by shouts, gunfire and running footsteps. There was an angry glow over the village. Shadows flitted past the window. The landlord and his wife were getting up behind the partition. Yury sent the orderly to ask what the commotion was about.

He was told that the Germans had broken through. Yury hurried off to the hospital and found that it was true. The village was under fire. The hospital was being moved at once, without waiting for the evacuation order.

'We'll all be off before dawn,' Yury told Gordon. 'You're going in the first party, the gig is ready now, but I've told them to wait for you. Well, good luck. I'll see you off and make sure you get your seat.'

They ran down the village street, bending double and hugging the walls. Bullets whizzed past them and from the crossroads they could see shell-bursts like fiery umbrellas opening over the fields.

'What are you going to do?' asked Gordon as they ran.

'I'll follow with the second party. I have to go back and collect my things first.'

They separated at the edge of the village. The gig and several carts, which made up the convoy, moved, bumping into one another and gradually spacing out. Yury waved to his friend, who saw him for a few moments longer by the light of a burning barn.

Again keeping to the shelter of the houses, Yury hurried back. A few yards from his house he was knocked off his feet by the blast of an explosion and hit by a shell splinter. He fell in the middle of the road, bleeding and unconscious.

14

The hospital where Yury was recovering in the officers' ward had been evacuated and apparently forgotten in a small town by a railway line and close to the G.H.Q. It was a warm day at the end of February. The window near his bed was open.

The patients were killing time before dinner. They had been told that a new nurse had joined the hospital staff and would be doing her first round that day. In the bed opposite Yury's Galiullin was looking at the newspapers which had just arrived and exclaiming indignantly at the blanks left by the censorship. Yury was reading Tonya's letters which the field post had delivered in a batch. The wind rustled the letters and the papers. At the sound of a light footstep he looked up. Lara came into the ward.

Both Yury and Galiullin recognised her, though neither guessed that the other knew her and she did not recognise either of them. She said: 'How do you do? Why is the window open? Aren't you cold?' Going up to Galiullin, she asked him how he felt and took his wrist to feel his pulse, but immediately let go of it and sat down by his bed, looking at him with a puzzled expression.

'This is indeed unexpected, Larissa Fyodorovna,' he said. 'I knew your husband. We were in the same regiment. I've kept his things for you.'

'It isn't possible,' she kept saying, 'it isn't possible. You knew him! What an extraordinary coincidence. Please tell me quickly how it happened. He was killed by a shell, wasn't he, and buried by the explosion? You see I know, please don't be afraid of telling me.'

Galiullin's courage failed him. He decided to tell her a comforting lie.

'Antipov was taken prisoner. He advanced too far with his unit. They were surrounded and cut off. He was forced to give himself up.'

But she did not believe him. Shaken by the unexpectedness of the meeting and not wishing to break down in front of strangers, she hurried out into the corridor.

A few moments later she came back, outwardly collected; afraid of crying again if she spoke to Galiullin, she deliberately avoided looking at him and went over to Yury. 'How do you do. How do you feel?' she asked in an expressionless voice.

Yury had seen her agitation and her tears. He wanted to ask her why she was so upset and to tell her that he had seen her twice before in his life, once as a schoolboy and once as a student, but he was afraid of intruding on her and of her misunderstanding him. Then he suddenly remembered Christmas all those years ago, the coffin with Anna's body in it and Tonya's screams. He said instead:

'Thank you. I am a doctor. I am looking after myself. I don't need anything.'

'Why should he sound offended?' Lara wondered. She looked in surprise at the stranger with his snub nose and unremarkable face.

For several days the weather was troubled, uncertain, with a warm, talkative wind in the night, smelling of damp earth.

During these days there were strange reports from G.H.Q. and alarming rumours from the interior. Telegraphic communications with Petersburg were cut off time and again. Everywhere, at every corner, people were talking politics.

Nurse Antipova did her rounds morning and evening, exchanging a few words with each patient including Galiullin and Yury. 'What a curious creature,' she thought of Yury. 'Young and gruff. You couldn't call him handsome with his turned-up nose. But he is intelligent in the best sense of the word, alive and with an attractive mind. However, it's not my business. My business is to finish my job here as soon as possible and go back to Moscow to be near Katya, and then to apply to be released from nursing and go home to Yuryatin, back to the school. It's quite clear now what happened to poor Pasha, there isn't any hope, so the sooner I stop playing the field heroine the better. I wouldn't have landed myself here if it hadn't been to look for Pasha.'

How was Katya getting on out there, she wondered, poor orphan! and this always made her cry.

She had noticed a sharp change around her recently. Before, there had been obligations of all kinds, sacred duties—your duty to your country, to the army, to society. But now that the war was lost (and that misfortune was at the bottom of all the rest) everything seemed to have been deposed, nothing was any longer sacred.

Everything had changed suddenly—the tone, the moral climate; you didn't know what to think, who to listen to. As if all your life you had been led by the hand like a small child and suddenly you were on your own, you had to learn to walk by yourself. There was no one around, neither family nor people whose judgment you respected. At such a time you felt the need to entrust yourself to something absolute —life or truth or beauty—of being ruled by it now that man-made rules had been discarded. You needed to surrender to some such ultimate purpose more fully, more unreservedly than you had ever done in the old familiar, peaceful days, in the old life which was now abolished and gone for good.—But in her own case, Lara reminded herself, she had Katya to fulfil her need of the unconditional, her need of a purpose. Now that she no longer had Pasha, Lara would be nothing but a mother, devoting all her strength to her poor orphaned child.

Yury heard from Moscow that Gordon and Dudorov had published his book without his permission and that it was praised and regarded as showing great literary promise; and that Moscow was going through disturbed, exciting times and was on the eve of something important; there was growing discontent among the masses, grave political events were imminent.

It was late at night. Yury was terribly drowsy. He dozed intermittently and imagined that the excitement of the past days was keeping him awake. A drowsy, sleepily breathing wind yawned and stirred outside the window. The wind cried and complained: 'Tonya, Sasha, I miss you, I want to go home, I want to go back to work.' And to the muttering of the wind Yury slept and woke and slept again in a quick troubled alternation of joy and suffering, as taut and as disturbing as the changing weather, as the troubled night.

It occurred to Lara that after all the devotion Galiullin had shown to Pasha's memory, the trouble he had taken to look after his things, she had not so much as asked him who he was and where he came from. She was disgusted with herself.

To make up for her omission and not to seem ungrateful she asked him all about himself when she made her next morning round.

'Merciful goodness,' she exclaimed at what he told her. Twenty-eight Brest Street, the Tiverzins, the revolution of 1905, that winter! Yusupka? No, she couldn't remember having met him, he must forgive her. But that year, that year, and that house! Had there really, truly been such a year and such a house! How vividly it all came back to her! The gunfire and—what was it she had called it then—'Christ's opinion'! How strong, how piercingly sharp were the feelings you experienced for the first time as a child. 'Forgive me, do forgive me, Lieutenant, what did you say your name and patronymic was? Yes, yes, you did tell me once. Thank you, Osip Gimazetdinovich, I can't thank you enough for reminding me, for bringing it all back to my mind.'

All day long she went about thinking of 'that house' and almost talking to herself and exclaiming out loud.

To think of it, Brest Street, No. 28! And now they were shooting again, but how much more frightening it was now! You couldn't say: 'It's the children shooting' this time. The children had all grown up, the boys were all here, in the army, all those simple people who had lived in that house and in others like it and in villages which also were like it, they were all here. How extraordinary it was, how very extraordinary!

All the patients who were not bedridden rushed in from the other rooms, hobbling noisily on crutches or running, or walking with sticks, shouting:

'Street fighting in Petersburg! The Petersburg garrison has joined the insurgents! It's the Revolution!'

5

Farewell to the Past

THE small town to which the hospital had been evacuated was called Melyuzeyevo. It stood in the fertile, black [1] soil country. Black dust hung over it all day long like a cloud of locusts. It was raised by the troops and convoys passing through the town; they moved in both directions, some going to the front and others coming away from it, and it was impossible to tell if the war were still going on or had already ceased.

Every day Zhivago, Nurse Antipova and Galiullin found new duties growing up like mushrooms. They and a few other people from the cities, who were regarded as knowledgeable and experienced, were picked for every job that came along.

They served on the municipal council and as minor commissars in the army and the health department, and they looked upon this succession of tasks as a diversion, like an outdoor sport, or a game of blind man's buff. But more and more often they felt that it was time to stop playing and get back to their ordinary occupations and their homes.

Yury and Antipova were often brought together by their work.

2

The rain turned the black dust into coffee-coloured mud and the mud spread over the streets; most of them were unpaved.

The town was very small. At the end of almost every street you could see the bleak steppe and the dark sky, the vast countryside glowering with revolution and war.

Yury wrote to his wife:

'I've been to see some of the army units in the neighbourhood. The chaos keeps on getting worse in spite of everything they do to improve discipline and morale.

'By way of a postscript (though I might have mentioned it earlier) I must tell you that I do a lot of my work with a certain Antipova, a nurse from Moscow who was born in the Urals.

[1] Russia's richest agricultural belt is known as *chernozem* ('black soil').

'You remember the girl student who shot at the public prosecutor at that terrible party on the night of your mother's death? I think there was a trial afterwards. I remember telling you that Misha and I had once seen her, when she was still a schoolgirl, at some sordid hotel where Father took us. I can't remember why we went, only that it was a bitterly cold night. I think it was at the time of the Presnya rising.—Well, that girl was Antipova.

'I have made several attempts to go home, but it is not so simple. It is not so much the work—we could hand that over easily enough—the trouble is the actual journey. Either there are no trains at all or else they are so full that there is not a hope of getting in.

'But of course it can't go on like this indefinitely, and some of us, who have resigned or been discharged, including Antipova and Galiullin, have made up our minds that whatever happens we shall leave next week. We'll go separately, it gives us a better chance.

'So I might turn up any day out of the blue, though I'll try and send a telegram.'

Before he left, however, he received Tonya's reply. In sentences plainly broken by sobs and with tear stains and ink spots for punctuation, she begged him not to come back to Moscow but to go straight to the Urals with that wonderful nurse whose progress through life was marked by omens and events so strange that she, Tonya, with her simple ways, could not possibly compete with it.

'Don't worry about Sasha's future,' she wrote. 'You will never need to be ashamed of him. I will bring him up in those principles which as a child you saw practised in our house, this I promise you.'

Yury hastened to reply. 'You must be out of your mind, Tonya! How could you imagine such a thing? How is it that you don't know —or don't feel deeply enough—that if it were not for you, if it were not for my constant, faithful thoughts of you and of our home, I would never have survived these two terrible, devastating years of war? But words are useless. Soon we'll be together, our life will begin again, then everything will be cleared up.

'What worries me about your letter is something else. If I really gave you cause to write in such a way, my behaviour must have been ambiguous and I am at fault not only before you but before that other woman whom I have misled. I'll apologise to her as soon as she is back. She is away in the country. Local councils are being set up in the villages (apart from those at county and borough level which existed before) and she has gone to help a friend of hers who is acting as instructor in connection with these administrative changes.

'It may interest you to know that although we live in the same house I don't know to this day which is Antipova's room, I've never bothered to find out.'

3

Two main roads ran from Melyuzeyevo, one going east, the other west. One, a mud track, led through the forest to Zabushino, a small town which traded in corn and was administratively subordinate to Melyuzeyevo although it was ahead of it in many ways. The other was gravelled and went through fields, boggy in winter but dry in summer, to Biryuchi, the nearest railway junction.

In June Zabushino became an independent republic. It was set up by the local miller Blazheiko and supported by deserters from the 212th Line Regiment who had left the front at the time of the upheavals, kept their arms and come to Zabushino through Biryuchi.

The republic refused to recognise the Provisional Government and split off from the rest of Russia. Blazheiko was a sectarian who had once corresponded with Tolstoy. He called the local council an Apostolic Seat and proclaimed a new millennial kingdom where all work was to be shared and all property to be held in common.

Zabushino had always been a place of legends and exaggerations. It was mentioned in the chronicles of the Times of Troubles [1] and it stood amidst deep forests which had teemed with robbers until recent years. It was famed far and wide for the prosperity of its merchants and the fabulous richness of its soil, and from it came many of the popular beliefs, customs and oddities of speech which distinguished this whole region.

The usual wonderful tales were now being told about Blazheiko's chief assistant. He was said to have been born a deaf-mute and only to enjoy the gift of speech by a special dispensation granted him at certain times.

The republic lasted a fortnight and was overthrown before the end of June by a unit loyal to the Provisional Government. The deserters fell back on Biryuchi. Several miles of forest had once been cleared along the railway line on both sides of the junction, and there, among the old tree stumps overgrown with wild strawberries, the piles of timber depleted by pilfering and the tumble-down huts of the seasonal labourers who had cut the trees, the deserters set up their camp.

[1] Period of interregnum and civil war in the 17th century.

4

The hospital where Yury had been a patient and was now a doctor was housed in the former residence of Countess Zhabrinskaya. She had offered it to the Red Cross at the beginning of the war.

It was a two-storey house on one of the best sites of the town, at the corner of the main street and the square, known as the 'Platz', where soldiers had drilled in the old days and where meetings were held now.

Its position gave it a good view of the neighbourhood; in addition to the street and the square, it overlooked the courtyard of the house next door (owned by a poor, provincial family who lived almost like peasants), as well as the Countess's old garden at the back.

The Countess had a large estate in the district, Razdolnoye, and had only used the house for occasional business visits to the town and as a rallying point for the guests who came from near and far to stay at Razdolnoye in summer.

Now the house was a hospital, and its owner was under arrest in Petersburg, where she had lived.

Of the large staff, only two women were left: Ustinya had been the Countess's head cook and Mademoisselle Fleury had brought up her daughters, who were now married.

Grey-haired, pink-cheeked and dishevelled, Mademoiselle Fleury shuffled about in bedroom slippers and a floppy, worn-out housecoat, apparently as much at home in the hospital as she had ever been in the Zhabrinsky family. She told long stories in her broken Russian, swallowing the ends of her words, gesticulated, struck dramatic poses and burst into hoarse peals of laughter which ended in coughing fits.

She believed that she knew Nurse Antipova inside out and thought that the nurse and the doctor were bound to be attracted to each other. Steeped in the love of passionate intrigue so dear to the Latin heart, she was never so delighted as when she found them in each other's company and would shake her finger and wink slyly at them; this puzzled Lara and irritated Yury, but like all eccentrics Mademoiselle clung to her illusions and would not be parted from them at any price.

Ustinya was an even stranger character. Her clumsy pear-shaped figure gave her the look of a broody hen. Usually she weighed her words and was brisk and to the point in her speech, but her imagination was unbridled in everything to do with superstition. Born in Zabushino and said to be the daughter of the local sorcerer, she knew countless spells and would never go out without first muttering over

the stove and the keyhole to protect the house in her absence from fire
and the Evil One. Ustinya was capable of keeping quiet for years, but
once she was provoked, nothing could hold her back. Any attack on
her convictions roused her to a passionate defence of the truth.

In spite of the overthrow of the Zabushino republic the revolutionary council of Melyuzeyevo feared its anarchical influence over
the district and decided to counteract it by a campaign of enlightenment. A suitable opportunity for such activities arose in the evenings,
when peaceful and spontaneous meetings were held in the square;
they were sparsely attended by those of the citizens who had nothing
better to do and who, in the old days, had gathered for a gossip outside the fire station at the other end of the Platz. The council
encouraged them and invited local and visiting speakers to guide the
discussions. The visitors believed the tales about the talking deaf-
mute to be utterly absurd and were anxious to say so. But the small
craftsmen, the soldiers' wives and former servants in Melyuzeyevo
did not regard these stories as absurd and stood up in his defence.

Among them was Ustinya. At first shy and held back by womanly
reserve, she had gradually become bolder in refuting opinions which
Melyuzeyevo disliked and was by now an experienced public speaker
herself.

The hum of the voices in the square could be heard through the
open windows of the hospital, and on still evenings even the words
were distinguishable. If Ustinya were speaking, Mademoiselle would
rush into any room where people were sitting and implore them to
listen, taking her off without malice in her broken accent: 'Rasputi
. . . Raspu . . . Tsar . . . Zabushi . . . deaf-mu . . . traitors!
traitors!'

Mademoiselle was secretly proud of her spirited and sharp-tongued
friend; the two women were fond of each other although they never
stopped bickering.

5

Yury was making the round of the offices where he needed to get
permits and priorities for his return to Moscow and calling on his
friends and acquaintances to say good-bye.

At that time the young commissar newly appointed to the local
sector of the front was spending a few days in Meluzeyevo on his way
to the army. He was said to be a mere boy.

His appointment was connected with the renewed activity at the
front. The army was preparing to attack and everything was being

done to break the soldiers' apathy and tighten discipline. War-revolutionary tribunals had been set up and the death penalty, recently abolished, had been restored.

One of the signatures which Yury needed for his documents was that of the local town major. Usually you could not get near his office. The queue stretched half-way down the street and there was such a noise inside that no one could hear anything.

But this was not one of the reception days. The clerks sat writing silently in the peaceful office, disgruntled at the growing complication of their work, and exchanging ironic glances. Cheerful voices came from the town major's room; it sounded as if, in there, people had unbuttoned their tunics and were having refreshments.

Galiullin came out of the inner room, saw Yury and beckoned to him with exaggerated movements of his whole body, almost crouching as though for the start of a race.

Since Yury had in any case to see the town major, he went in. He found the room in a state of picturesque confusion.

The centre of the stage was held by the new commissar, the hero of the day and the sensation of the town, who, instead of being at his post, was addressing the rulers of this paper kingdom quite unconnected with staff and operational matters.

'Ah, here's another of our stars,' said the town major introducing Yury. The commissar, completely self-absorbed, did not look round, and the town major, only turning to sign the papers which Yury put in front of him and to wave him politely to a low pouffe, resumed his attitude of rapt attention.

Yury sat down. He was the only person in the room who sat like a human being. All the rest were lolling eccentrically with an air of exaggerated and assumed ease. The town major almost lay across his desk, his cheek on his fist, in a thoughtful, Byronic pose. His assistant, a massive, stout man, was perched on the arm of the sofa, his legs tucked on the seat as if he were riding side-saddle. Galiullin sat astride a chair, his arms folded on its back and his head reclining on his arms, and the commissar kept pulling himself up by his wrists on to the window-sill and jumping off and running up and down the room with small quick steps, buzzing about like a wound-up top, never still or silent for a moment. He talked continuously; the subject of the conversation was the problem of the deserters at Biryuchi.

The commissar was exactly as he had been described to Yury: thin and graceful, a boy just out of the schoolroom and burning like a candle with the flame of his ideals. He was said to come of a good family (the son of a senator, some people thought) and to have been one of the first to march his regiment to the Duma in February. He was called Gintz or Gintze—Yury had not quite caught the name— and spoke very distinctly, with a correct Petersburg accent and a slight Baltic intonation.

He wore a tight-fitting tunic. It probably embarrassed him to be so young and in order to seem older he put on a caustic expression and an artificial stoop, hunching his shoulders with their stiff epaulettes and keeping his hands deep in his pockets; this did in fact give him a stylised cavalryman's silhouette which could be drawn in two straight lines, converging downwards from the angle of his shoulders to his feet.

'There is a Cossack regiment stationed a short distance down the railway,' the town major informed him. 'It's Red, it's loyal. It will be called out, the rebels will be surrounded and that will be the end of the business. The Corps commander is anxious that they should be disarmed without delay.'

'Cossacks! Not in any circumstances,' flared up the commissar. 'This is not 1905. This is no time for historical reminiscences. Our views are diametrically opposed. Your generals are trying to be too clever.'

'Nothing has been done yet. This is only a plan, a suggestion.'

'We have an agreement with the High Command not to interfere with operational orders. I am not cancelling the order to call out the Cossacks.—Let them come.—But I'll take such steps on my side as are dictated by common sense.—I suppose they have a bivouac out there?'

'Well, yes. A camp at any rate. An armed camp.'

'Splendid. I wish to go there. You must show me this menace, this nest of robbers. They may be rebels, gentlemen, they may even be deserters, but remember, they are the people. And the people are like children, you have to know them, you have to know their psychology. To get the best out of them, you must have the right approach, you have to move them, to touch their hearts.

'I'll go and have a heart-to-heart talk with them and you'll see, they'll go back to the positions they have deserted as good as gold. You don't believe me? What will you bet on it?'

'I wonder. I hope to goodness you're right.'

'I'll say to them: "Take my own case. I am an only son, the only hope of my parents, yet I haven't spared myself. I've given up everything—name, family, position. I have done this to fight for your freedom, greater freedom than is enjoyed by any other people in the world. This I did, and so did many other young men like myself, not to speak of the old guard of our glorious forerunners, champions of the people's rights, who were sent to hard labour in Siberia or locked up in the Schlüsselburg Fortress. Did we do this for ourselves? Did we have to do it? And you, you who are no longer ordinary privates but the warriors of the first revolutionary army in the world, how have you lived up to your proud calling?—At the moment when our country is shedding her blood, when she is making a supreme effort to shake off the encircling hydra of the enemy, you have allowed yourselves to be fooled by a gang of nobodies, you have become a rabble, politically unconscious, surfeited with freedom, hooligans for whom nothing is enough. Give them an inch and they take an ell, as the saying goes, let a pig into the dining-room and it puts its trotters on the table."—Oh, I won't mince my words, I'll make them feel ashamed of themselves.'

'Oh no, that would be very risky,' the town major ventured to object, looking meaningly at his assistant.

Galiullin did his very best to dissuade the commissar from his insane idea. He knew the men of the 212th, they had been in his division at the front. But the commissar refused to listen.

Yury kept trying to get up and go. The commissar's naïveté embarrassed him, but the sly sophistication of the town major and his assistant—two shifty crooks of the worst sort—was no better. The silliness of the one was matched by the hypocrisy of the others and Yury was sickened by the torrent of their words, dull, unnecessary, such as are rejected by life itself.

How intense can be the longing to escape from the emptiness and dullness of human verbosity, to take refuge in nature, apparently so inarticulate, or in the wordlessness of long, grinding labour, of sound sleep, of true music, or of a human understanding rendered speechless by emotion!

Yury remembered his coming explanation with Nurse Antipova. It was bound to be unpleasant, but he was glad of the necessity of seeing her, even at such a price. She was unlikely to be back. But he got up as soon as he could and went out, unnoticed by the others.

6

She was back. Mademoiselle, who gave him the news, added that she was tired, she had had a quick meal and had gone up to her room saying she was not to be disturbed. 'But why not go up and knock?' Mademoiselle suggested. 'I am sure she is not asleep yet.'—

'Which is her room?'—When Mademoiselle got over her astonishment, she told him that it was at the end of the passage on the top landing, past several rooms in which the whole of the Countess's furniture was kept locked, and where Yury had never been.

It was getting dark. Outside, the houses and fences huddled closer together in the dusk. The trees advanced out of the depth of the gardens into the light of the oil-lamps shining from the windows. It was hot and sticky. The lamp-light streaming into the yard dribbled down the bark of trees like sweat.

Yury stopped at the top of the stairs. It occurred to him that even to knock on Lara's door when she was only just back and tired from her journey would be discourteous and embarrassing. Better leave the explanation for to-morrow. In the absent mood which goes with a change of mind, he walked to the other end of the passage, where a window overlooked the neighbouring yard, and leaned out.

The night was full of quiet, secret sounds. Next to him, inside the passage, a tap dripped evenly with full, slow drops. Somewhere outside the window people were whispering. Somewhere in the vegetable patch they were watering cucumber beds, clanking the chain of the well as they drew the water and poured it from pail to pail.

There was a smell of all the flowers at once, as if the earth had been unconscious all day long and were now waking.

And from the Countess's centuries-old garden, so littered with fallen branches that it was impenetrable, the dusty aromatic smell of old lime trees coming into blossom drifted in a huge wave as tall as a house.

Noises came from the street beyond the fence on the right— snatches of a song, a drunken soldier, doors banging.

An enormous crimson moon rose behind the rooks' nests in the Countess's garden. At first it was the colour of the new brick mill in Zabushino, then it turned yellow like the water-tower at Biryuchi.

And just under the window, the smell of new-mown hay, as strong as China tea, mixed with that of deadly nightshade. Down there, a cow was tethered; she had been brought from a distant village, she had walked all day, she was tired and homesick for the herd and would not yet accept food from her new mistress.

'Now, now, whoa there, I'll show you how to butt,' her mistress coaxed her in a whisper, but the cow crossly shook her head and stretched her neck mooing plaintively, and beyond the black barns of Melyuzeyevo shone the stars, and invisible threads of sympathy hung between them and the cow, as if there were cattle-sheds in other worlds where she was pitied.

Everything was fermenting, growing, rising with the yeast of life. The joy of living, like a still wind, swept in a tidal wave indiscriminately through fields and towns, through walls and fences, through wood and flesh. To escape from this overwhelming flow, Yury went out into the square to listen to the speeches.

7

By now the moon stood high. The moonlight in the square was as thick as whitewash, with broad black carpets of shadow before the pillared porches of stone buildings.

The meeting was being held across the square and Yury could have heard every word of it if he'd wished, but he was so overcome by the splendour of what he saw that he sat down on the bench outside the fire station and looked instead of listening.

Narrow dead-end streets ran off the square, as deep in mud as country lanes and lined with crooked little houses. Fences of plaited willow stuck out of the mud like the tops of lobster pots. You could see the one-eyed glint of open windows. From the small front gardens, sweaty red heads of maize with oily whiskers looked in at the windows, and single pale thin hollyhocks gazed into the distance over the fences, like women in their night-shifts whom the heat indoors had driven out for a breath of air.

The moonlit night was as astonishing as mercy or the gift of second sight. Suddenly, into this radiant, legendary stillness, there dropped the measured, choppy sound of a familiar, recently heard voice. It was a fine voice and it rang with conviction. Yury listened and recognised it at once. It was Commissar Gintz making his speech.

The municipality had evidently asked him to lend their campaign the support of his prestige and he spoke with feeling, reproving the people of Melyuzeyevo for their disorganised ways and for allowing themselves to be affected by the disintegrating influence of the bolsheviks who, he assured them, were the real instigators of the Zabushino disorders. In the same spirit as at the town major's, he reminded them of the might and ruthlessness of the enemy and of their country's hour of trial. The crowd began to heckle.

Requests not to interrupt the speaker alternated with cries of protest. The interruptions grew louder and more frequent. A man who had come with Gintz and who now assumed the role of chairman, shouted that speeches from the floor were not allowed and called the public to order. Some insisted that a citizeness who wished to speak should be allowed to do so, while others asked for silence.

A woman made her way through the crowd to the wooden crate which served as platform. She did not attempt to climb the tribune but stood beside it. The woman was known. The crowd fell silent. Its attention was caught. The woman was Ustinya.

'Now you were saying about Zabushino, Comrade Commissar,' she began, 'and about looking sharp, you told us to look sharp and not be deceived, but actually, you yourself, I heard you, all you know is how to play about with words like "bolsheviks-mensheviks", that's all you talk about, bolsheviks and mensheviks. Now all that about no more fighting and all being brothers, I call that being godly, not menshevik, and about the works and factories going to the poor, that isn't bolshevik, that's according to humanity and loving-kindness. And about that deaf-mute, we've heard quite enough about him without you. Everybody goes on and on about the deaf-mute. And what have you got against him? Just that he was dumb all that time and then he suddenly started to talk and didn't ask your permission. Well, what of it? As if it was so wonderful! Much more extraordinary things than that have been known to happen. Take the famous she-ass, for instance. "Balaam, Balaam, "she says, "listen to me, I tell you straight, don't go that way or you'll be sorry." Well, naturally, he wouldn't listen, he went on. Like you saying: "A deaf-mute." "What's the good of listening to her?" he thought. "She's only a she-ass, a dumb beast." And look how sorry he was afterwards. You all know what the end of it was.'

'What?' someone asked curiously.

'That's enough,' snapped Ustinya. 'If you ask too many questions you'll grow old before your time.'

'That's no good. You tell us,' insisted the heckler.

'All right, all right, how-and-why, you sticky burr. He was turned into a pillar of salt.'

'You've got it wrong, dearie, that was Lot. That was Lot's wife,' people shouted. Everyone laughed. The chairman called the meeting to order. Yury went to bed.

8

He saw Lara the following evening. He found her in the pantry; a pile of linen, straight out of the wringer, lay in front of her; she was ironing.

The pantry was one of the back rooms at the top, looking out over the garden. There the samovars were got ready, food was dished out and the used plates stacked in the hand-worked service-lift to be sent down to the dish washer. There, too, the lists of china, plate and glass were kept and checked, and there people spent their moments of leisure and met by appointment.

The windows were open. In the room the scent of lime blossom mixed, as in an old park, with the caraway-bitter smell of dry twigs; to it were added the charcoal fumes of the two flat-irons which Lara used alternately, putting them each in turn in the flue to keep them hot.

'Well, why didn't you knock last night? Mademoiselle told me. Though actually you were right. I couldn't have let you in, I went to bed almost at once. Well, how are you? Mind the charcoal, don't get it on your suit.'

'You look as if you've done the laundry for the whole hospital.'

'No, there's a lot of mine there. You see? You keep on teasing me about getting stuck in Melyuzeyevo. Well, this time I mean it, I'm going. I've done my washing, I'll pack my things. When I've finished I'll be off. I'll be in the Urals and you'll be in Moscow. One day somebody will ask you: "Do you happen to know a little town called Melyuzeyevo?"—"I don't seem to call it to mind."—"And who is Antipova?"—"Never heard of her."'

'That's as may be. Did you have a good journey? What was it like in the country?'

'That's a long story.—Goodness, how quickly these irons cool. Do pass me the other, do you mind? It's over there, look, just inside the flue. And could you put this one back? Thanks.—Every village is different, it depends on the villagers. In some they're industrious, they work hard, then it isn't bad. And in others I suppose all the men are drunks, and then it's desolate and terrifying.'

'What nonsense! Why should they be drunks? A lot you understand! It's just that there is no one there, all the men are in the army. What about the new councils, the revolutionary ones?'

'You're wrong about the drunkards, but we'll argue about that afterwards. The councils? There's going to be a lot of trouble with the councils. The instructions are inapplicable, there's nobody to work with. All the peasants care about at the moment is the land question. I called at Razdolnoye. What a lovely place! You should go and see it. It was burned and looted a bit last spring, the barn is burned down, the fruit trees are singed, part of the façade is damaged by smoke. Zabushino I didn't see, I didn't get there. But they all tell you the deaf-mute really exists. They tell you what he looks like, they say he's young and educated.'

'Last night Ustinya stood up for him in the Platz.'

'The moment I got back there was another lot of rubbish from Razdolnoye. If I've asked them once I've asked them twenty times to leave it alone. As if we didn't have enough of our own. And this morning the porter from the town major's office comes over with a note—they must have the silver tea-set and the crystal glasses, it's a matter of life and death, just for one night, they'll send it back. Half of it we'll never see again. It's always a loan—I know these loans. They're having a party, in honour of some visitor or something.'

'I can guess who that is. The new commissar has arrived, the one who's appointed to our sector of the front. They want to tackle the deserters, have them surrounded and disarmed. The commissar is a babe in arms. Our people want to call out the Cossacks, but he says no, he'll wring their hearts. The people, he says, are like children, and so on, he thinks it's all child's play. Galiullin tried to argue with him. He said: "Don't stir up the jungle. Leave us to deal with it in our way." But you can't do anything with a chap like that once he's got a thing into his head.—I do wish you'd listen to me. Do stop ironing a minute. We'll have some very nasty trouble here soon, it's beyond our power to prevent it. I do wish you'd leave before it happens.'

'There won't be anything, you're exaggerating. And anyway, I am leaving. But I can't just snap my fingers and say good-bye. I have to hand over properly, and the inventory must be checked. I don't want it to look as if I've stolen something and run away. And who is to take over? That's the problem. I can't tell you what I've been through with that wretched inventory, and all the thanks I get is, I'm told I've committed a fraud! I registered Zhabrinskaya's things in the name of the hospital, because that was the sense of the decree. Now they say I did it fraudulently and kept them for the owner! It's disgusting!'

'Do stop worrying about pots and rugs. To hell with them. What a thing to fuss about at a time like this. Oh, I wish I'd seen you yesterday. I was in such good form I could have explained everything in heaven and earth, I had the answer to every question. It's true, I'm not joking, I was itching to get it all off my chest. I wanted to tell you about my wife, and my son, and myself . . . Why the hell can't a grown-up man talk to a grown-up woman without being suspected of some ulterior motive! Damn all motives—ulterior or otherwise. Please go on ironing, don't pay any attention to me, I'll go on talking. I intend to talk for a long time.

'Just think what's going on nowadays! And you and I are living in these days! Do you realise what an unheard-of thing is happening? Such a thing only happens once in an eternity. Just think of it, the whole of Russia has had its roof torn off, and you and I and everyone else are out in the open! And there's nobody to spy on us.—We are free—not just free in theory, in words—it's real freedom, dropped out of the sky, freedom beyond our expectations. Freedom by accident, through a misunderstanding.

'And how huge everyone is and how disconcerted by his own size. Have you noticed? As if overwhelmed by himself, by the revelation of his greatness.

'Go on ironing, I tell you. Don't talk. You aren't bored. Let me change your iron for you.

'Last night I was watching the meeting in the square. It was an astonishing sight. Mother Russia is on the move, she can't stand still, she's restless and she can't find rest, she's talking and she can't stop. And it isn't as if only people were talking. Stars and trees meet and converse, flowers talk philosophy at night, stone houses hold meetings. It's like something out of the Gospels, don't you think? Like in the days of the apostles. Like in St. Paul—do you remember? "You will speak with tongues and prophesy. Pray for the gift of understanding."'

'I know what you mean about stars and trees holding meetings. I understand that. It's happened to me too.'

'It was partly the war, the revolution did the rest. The war made an artificial break in life—as if life could be put off for a time. What nonsense that is! The revolution broke out willy-nilly, like a breath that's been held too long. Everyone was revived, reborn, changed, transformed. You might say that everyone has been through two revolutions—his own personal revolution as well as the general one. It seems to me that socialism is the sea, and all these separate streams, these private, individual revolutions are flowing into it—the sea of life, of life in its own right. I said life, but I mean life as you see it in a work of art, transformed by genius, creatively enriched. Only now people have decided to experience it not in books and pictures but in themselves, not in theory but in practice.'

The sudden trembling of his voice revealed his rising agitation. Lara stopped ironing and gave him a grave, astonished look. It confused him and he forgot what he was saying. After a moment of embarrassed silence he rushed on, blurting out whatever came into his head.

'I have such a longing nowadays for an honest, productive life.

I so much want to be a part of all this quickening. And then, in the middle of all this general rejoicing, I come up against your puzzlingly sad, absent look, wandering in who knows what enchanted kingdom. I'd give anything for it not to be like that, for your face to tell me that you are all right, that you are pleased with life, that you don't need anything from anyone. For someone really close to you, your friend or husband (best of all if he were a soldier) to come and take me by the hand and tell me kindly to stop worrying about your fate and leave you alone. Only then, of course, I'd knock him down. . . . Sorry, I didn't mean that.'

His voice betrayed him again. He shook his head, and, with a feeling of hopeless embarrassment, got up and went to the window. Leaning on the window-sill he looked out with absent, restless, unseeing eyes into the garden veiled in darkness, and tried to collect himself.

Lara walked round her ironing-board (it was propped on the edge of the table and the other window-sill) and stopped a few paces behind him in the middle of the room. 'It's what I've always been afraid of,' she said softly, as if to herself. 'I shouldn't have . . . Don't, Yury Andreyevich, you mustn't. Oh, now just look at what you've made me do!' She ran back to the board where a scorched blouse sent up a thin stream of acrid smoke from under the iron.

'Yury Andreyevich,' she went on, thumping down the iron crossly on its stand, 'do be sensible, go off to Mademoiselle for a minute, have a drink of water and come back, my dear, and be as I've always known you till now and as I want you to be. Do you hear, Yury Andreyevich? I know you can do it. Please do it, I beg you to.'

They had no more explanations of this kind, and a week later Lara left.

9

Some time later still, Zhivago too set out for home. The night before he left there was a terrible storm. The noises of the gale and of the downpour mixed; the rain sometimes crashed straight on to the roofs and at others drove down the street with the changing wind as if lashing its way step by step.

The peals of thunder followed each other without an interval, merging into an even roar. In the blaze of lightning the street fled into the distance with bent trees fleeing in the same direction.

Mademoiselle Fleury was woken up in the night by an urgent

knocking on the front door. She sat up in alarm and listened. The knocking went on.

Could it be, she thought, that there wasn't a soul left in the hospital to get up and open the door? Did she always have to do everything, poor old woman, just because nature had made her honest and endowed her with a sense of duty?

All right, the Zhabrinskys were rich aristocrats and the house had been theirs, but what about the hospital, didn't that belong to the people, wasn't it their own? Who did they expect to look after it? Where, for instance, had the male nurses vanished to, she'd like to know. Everyone had fled—no more orderlies, no more nurses, no doctors, no one in authority. Yet there were still wounded in the house, two legless men in the surgical ward where the drawing-room used to be, and downstairs, next to the laundry, the store-room full of dysentery cases. And that devil Ustinya had gone out visiting. She must have known perfectly well that there was going to be a storm, but did that stop her? Now she had a good excuse to spend the night with strangers.

Well, thank God the knocking had stopped, they'd realised that nobody would answer, so they'd got discouraged and gone away. Why anybody should want to be out in this weather . . . Or could it be Ustinya? No, she had her key.—'Oh God, they've started again, it's too frightening.'

What pigs, all the same. Not that you could expect Zhivago to hear anything, he was off to-morrow, his thoughts were already in Moscow or on the journey. But what about Galiullin? How could he snore through all this noise? Or did he lie awake listening, counting on her to get up in the end? Counting on a weak defenceless woman to go down and open goodness only knew to whom, on this frightening night in this frightening country.

Galiullin!—she remembered suddenly. That was a good one—Galiullin! What was she thinking about, she must have been half asleep. Galiullin wasn't there, he should be a long way off by now. Hadn't she herself, with Zhivago, hidden him, and disguised him as a civilian and then told him about every road and village in the district so that he should know how to escape after that horrible lynching at Biryuchi station when they killed Commissar Gintz and chased Galiullin all the way from Biryuchi to Melyuzeyevo, shooting at him and then hunting for him all over the town?

If it hadn't been for those motor-cars, not a stone would have been left standing in Melyuzeyevo. An armoured division happened to be passing through, and it stood up for the town and got the better of those evil men.

The storm was passing over. The thunder was less continuous, more dull, more distant. The rain stopped now and then and the water could be heard still splashing softly off the leaves and down the gutters. Gleams of noiseless lightning dropped into Mademoiselle's room and lingered as if looking for something.

Suddenly the knocking at the front door, which had long since stopped, began again. Someone was in urgent need of help and was knocking repeatedly, in desperation. The wind rose again and the rain came down.

'Coming!' shouted Mademoiselle to whoever it was, and the sound of her own voice frightened her.

It had suddenly occurred to her who it might be. Sitting up and pushing her feet into slippers, she threw her dressing-gown over her shoulders and hurried to wake Zhivago; it would be less frightening to go down with him. But he too had heard the knocking and was coming down with a lighted candle. The same idea had struck both of them.

'Zhivago, Zhivago, they're knocking on the front door, I'm afraid to go down alone,' she called out in French, adding in Russian: 'You will see, it is either Lara or Lieutenant Gaiul.'

Roused by the knocking, Yury had also felt certain that it was someone he knew, either Galiullin who had been stopped in his flight and was coming back for refuge, or Nurse Antipova, prevented from continuing her journey and in consequence returning to him.

In the porch Yury gave the candle to Mademoiselle, drew the bolts and turned the key. A gust of wind burst the door open, putting out the candle and showering them with cold raindrops.

'Who is there? Who is there? Is there anybody there?' Mademoiselle and the doctor shouted in turn into the darkness, but there was no reply. Suddenly the knocking started in another place—was it at the back door or, as they now thought, at the french window into the garden?

'Seems to be the wind,' said the doctor. 'But just to make sure, perhaps you'd have a look at the back. I'll stay here in case there really is someone.'

Mademoiselle disappeared into the house, while the doctor went out and stood in the shelter of the porch. His eyes had become accustomed to the darkness and he could make out the first signs of the dawn.

Above the town, clouds raced dementedly as if pursued, so low that their tatters almost caught the tops of the trees, which bent in the same direction so that they looked like bent brooms sweeping the sky. The rain whipped the wooden wall of the house turning it from grey to black.

Mademoiselle came back. 'Well?' said Yury.

'You were right. There's no one.' She had been all round the house; a branch knocking on the pantry window had broken one of the panes and there were huge puddles on the floor, and the same thing in what used to be Lara's room—there was a sea, positively a sea, an ocean. 'And on this side, look, there's a broken shutter knocking on the casing, do you see? That's all it was.'

They talked a little and went back to their rooms, both regretting that it had been a false alarm.

They had been sure that, when they opened the door, Lara would come in, chilled through and soaked to the skin, and they would ask her dozens of questions while she took off her things, and she would go and change and come down and dry herself in front of the kitchen stove, still warm from the night before, and would tell them her adventures, pushing back her hair and laughing.

They had been so sure of it that when they locked the door the imprint of their certainty remained in the street, round the corner, like the watery wraith of this woman, or of her image which continued to haunt them.

10

It was thought that an indirect responsibility for the trouble at Biryuchi station lay with the Biryuchi telegraphist, Kolya Frolenko.

Kolya was the son of a Melyuzeyevo clockmaker and had been known in Melyuzeyevo from his earliest childhood. Mademoiselle knew him well because as a small boy he had stayed with some of the servants at Razdolnoye and had played under her supervision with her two pupils, the Countess's daughters (it was then that he learned to understand French).

Everyone was used to seeing him on his bicycle, coatless, hatless and in canvas summer shoes in any weather. Arms crossed on his chest, he free-wheeled down the road from Biryuchi, glancing up at the wires and poles to check their condition.

A few houses in Melyuzeyevo had the telephone and were connected by a branch line with the exchange at Biryuchi station. This line was controlled by Kolya from the station office. There he was up to his eyes in work, for if the station-master was away, he was in charge not only of the telephone and telegraph but also the railway signals, which were operated from the same control room.

Having to look after several mechanical instruments at once, Kolya had evolved a special style of speech, obscure, abrupt and enigmatic, which enabled him, when he chose, to avoid answering questions or getting involved in a conversation. He was said to have abused the advantage this gave him on the day of the disorders.

And it is true that, by his evasions, he had defeated all Galiullin's good intentions and, perhaps without meaning to, had given a fatal turn to the events.

Galiullin had rung up from town and asked for Commissar Gintz, who was somewhere at the station or just outside, in order to tell him that he was joining him at once, and to ask him to wait for him and do nothing until he arrived. Kolya refused to call Gintz, on the pretext that he was busy signalling to an approaching train. At the same time he used every excuse, true and untrue, to delay the train, which was bringing up the Cossacks who had been summoned to Biryuchi.

When the troops arrived all the same, he could not hide his displeasure.

The engine, crawling in under the shadow of the station, stopped immediately opposite the huge window of the control room. Kolya drew the green serge curtain with the initials of the Company woven in yellow into the border, picked up the enormous water-jug which stood on a large tray on the stone window ledge, poured some water into the plain, thick, moulded glass, drank a few mouthfuls and looked out.

The engine driver saw him from his cabin and gave him a friendly nod.

'The stinker, the louse,' Kolya thought with hatred. He put out his tongue and shook his fist. The driver not only understood him but managed to convey by a shrug of the shoulders and a nod in the direction of the train : 'What am I to do? I'd like to see what you'd have done in my place. He's the boss.'—'You're a filthy brute, all the same,' Kolya replied by gestures.

The horses were led out of the trucks, resisting and holding back. Their hooves thudded on the wooden gangway and rang out on the stone platform. They were led, rearing, across several lines.

At the end of the tracks were two rows of discarded wooden coaches. The rain had washed them clean of paint, and worms and damp had rotted them from inside, so that now they were reverting to their original kinship with the wood of the forest, which started just beyond the rolling stock, with its lichen, its birches, and the towering clouds above it.

Outside the station, the Cossacks vaulted into their saddles and galloped off to the deserters' camp in the clearing.

The rebels were soon surrounded. Although they had rifles in their huts, they were alarmed at the sight of the mounted men, who, as usual, looked taller and more imposing among the trees than they would have done in the open. The Cossacks drew their swords.

Gintz walked into the ring, leapt on to a pile of timber in the middle, and addressed the surrounded men.

He spoke of soldierly duty, of the meaning of the motherland and of many other lofty subjects. But these ideas found no sympathy among his audience. It was too large. The men had seen too much of the war, they were tired and coarsened. They had heard it all before, and months of wheedling propaganda from both Left and Right had made them cynical. Besides, they were plain folk who disliked Gintz's foreign name and Baltic accent.

Gintz felt that his speech was too long and was annoyed at himself, but he thought that he had to repeat himself in order to be clearly understood by these men, who should be grateful, and whose faces, instead, showed nothing but boredom, indifference or hostility. Gradually losing patience, he decided to speak straight from the shoulder and to bring up the threats he had so far held in reserve. Disregarding their rising murmurs, he reminded the deserters that war-revolutionary tribunals had been set up and called on them, on pain of death, to disarm and give up their leaders. If they refused, he said, they would prove that they were vile traitors, a politically unconscious swollen-headed rabble. The men had grown unused to such a tone.

Several hundred voices rose in an uproar. Some were low-pitched and almost without resentment : 'All right, all right. Pipe down. That's enough.' But there were some, raised almost to a squeal by hatred, which gained a hearing. Hysterical shouts went up :

'Listen to him laying it on, comrades ! Just like in the old days ! We haven't done with these officers' tricks yet. So we are traitors, are we ? And what about you yourself, excellency ?—Why do we bother with him ? Obviously he's a German, an infiltrator, can't you see ?—Show us your documents, blue blood.—And what are you gaping at ?' They turned to the Cossacks : 'You've come to restore order, get on with it, tie us up, make an end of us.'

But the Cossacks liked Gintz's unfortunate speech less and less. 'We're all swine to him,' they muttered. 'Fancies himself as the lord and master.' One by one they sheathed their swords. One after another they got off their horses. When most of them had dismounted, they moved in a straggly crowd towards the centre of the clearing, mixed with the men of the 212th and fraternised.

'You must get away,' the worried Cossack officer told Gintz. 'You must vanish quietly, don't let them see you go. Your car is at the level crossing, we'll send for it to meet you. Hurry.'

Gintz went, but he felt that to steal away was beneath his dignity, so he turned quite openly towards the station. He was terribly agitated, but his pride forced him to a calm, unhurried step.

He was close to the station. On the edge of the woods, within sight of the railway lines, he looked round for the first time. Soldiers with rifles had followed him. 'What do they want?' he wondered. He quickened his pace.

So did his pursuers. The distance between them remained unchanged. He saw the double wall of broken-down coaches, stepped behind them and ran. The train which had brought the Cossacks had been shunted and the lines were clear. He ran across them and leapt on to the steep platform. At the same moment the soldiers ran out from behind the derelict coaches.

Kolya and the station-master were shouting and waving to him to get into the station building, where they could save him.

But once again the sense of honour bred in him for generations, an urban sense of honour, which impelled him to self-sacrifice but was tragically irrelevant to these circumstances, barred his way to safety. His heart pounding wildly, he made a supreme effort to control his fear. He told himself: 'I must shout to them: "Come to your senses, men, you know I'm not a spy." Something human, sobering, will stop them.'

In the past few months his feeling for sincerity and heroism had unconsciously become connected with a setting of platforms and tribunes, with chairs on to which you leapt to fling your call to action, your challenge, at the serried ranks of listeners. He needed a tribune.

At the very doors of the station, under the station bell, there stood a water-butt, for use in case of fire. It was covered with a lid. Gintz jumped up on it and spoke a few heart-breakingly disconnected words to the approaching men. The insane courage of his gesture, two steps from the door where he could so easily have taken shelter, astounded them and stopped them in their tracks. They lowered their rifles.

But Gintz stepped forward to the edge of the lid, overturned it and fell in, one leg in the water, the other sticking up out of the butt.

At the sight of him sitting clumsily astride the butt, the men burst into laughter and the one in front shot Gintz in the neck. He was dead by the time the others ran up and thrust their bayonets into his body.

11

Mademoiselle rang up Kolya and told him to find Dr. Zhivago a good seat in the train to Moscow, threatening him with exposure if he did not.

Kolya was as usual conducting another conversation and, judging by the decimal fractions which embellished his speech, transmitting a message in code over a third instrument.

'Pskov, Pskov, can you hear me?—What rebels? What help? What are you talking about, Mademoiselle? Ring off, please.— Pskov, Pskov, thirty-six point naught one five.—Oh, hell, they've cut me off.—Hullo, hullo, I can't hear.—Is that you again, Mademoiselle? I've told you, I can't, speak to the station-master. All lies, fables— Thirty-six . . . Oh, hell . . . Get off the line, Mademoiselle.'

And Mademoiselle was saying:

'Don't you throw dust in my eyes, Pskov, Pskov, you liar. I can see right through you; to-morrow you'll put the doctor on the train, and I won't listen to another word from any murdering little Judases.'

12

The day Yury left it was sultry. A storm was brewing like the one that had broken two days earlier. In the station suburb, littered with the husks of sunflower seeds, the clay huts and the geese looked white and frightened under the still menace of the black sky.

The grass on the wide lawn in front of the station and stretching to both sides of it was trampled and completely hidden by a countless multitude who had been waiting weeks for trains.

Old men in coarse grey woollen coats wandered from group to group in search of news and rumours. Silent fourteen-year-olds lay on their elbows twirling peeled twigs, as if they were keeping an eye on sheep, while their small brothers and sisters scuttled about under people's feet with flying shirts and pink bottoms, and their mothers sat on the ground, their legs stretched out decorously straight in front of them, with babies packed into the tight shapeless bosoms of their brown peasant jackets.

'All scattered like sheep as soon as the shooting began,' the station-master told Yury unsympathetically as they zigzagged between the rows of bodies lying on the ground in front of the entrance and on the floors inside the station. 'In a twinkling, everybody cleared off the grass. You could see the ground again; we hadn't seen it in four months with all this gipsy camp going on; we'd forgotten what it looked like.—This is where he lay. It's a funny thing, I've seen some bad things in the war, you'd think I was used to anything. But I felt so sorry, somehow. It was the senselessness of it as much as anything. What had he done to them? But then they aren't human beings. They say he was the favourite son.—And now to the right, if you please, into my office. There isn't a chance on this train, I'm afraid, they'd squash you to death. I'm putting you on a local one. We are making it up now. But not a word about it until we start letting them in; they'd tear it apart before it was made up. You change at Sukhinichi to-night.'

13

When the secret train backed into the station from behind the railway sheds, the whole crowd poured on to the tracks. People rolled down the banks like marbles. They scrambled on to the permanent way and, pushing each other aside, jumped on to the steps and buffers or climbed in through the windows and on to the roof. The train filled up in an instant, while it was still moving, and by the time it stood by the platform, not only was it crammed but bunches of passengers hung all over it outside, from top to bottom. By a miracle, Yury managed to get on to a coupling and from there, still more unaccountably, into the corridor.

There he stayed, sitting on his luggage, all the way to Sukhinichi.

The clouds had scattered and the fields were blazing with sunshine and echoing from end to end with crickets whose chirping drowned the clatter of the wheels.

The passengers who stood by the windows kept the sun from the rest. Their long multiple shadows streaked across the floor and the seats and the partitions. As though crowded out of the compartment, they jumped out of the windows on the other side and ran and skipped along the opposite bank together with the moving shadow of the train.

All around Yury people were shouting, bawling songs, cursing and gambling. To the turmoil inside was added, whenever the train stopped, the noise of the besieging crowds outside. It rose to the pitch of a storm at sea, and, as at sea, there would be a sudden lull. In the inexplicable silence you could hear footsteps hurrying down the platform, the bustle and arguments outside the luggage van, people saying good-bye a long way off, and the quiet clucking of hens and rustling of trees in the station garden.

Then, like a message delivered on the way or like greetings from Melyuzeyevo, as though addressed personally to Yury, there drifted in the familiar aromatic smell. It came from somewhere to one side of the window and higher than the level of either garden or wild flowers, and it quietly asserted its excellence over all else. Kept from the windows by the crowd, Yury could not see the trees; but he imagined them growing somewhere very near and spreading over the carriage roofs their tranquil branches covered with dusty leaves as thick as night and sprinkled with constellations of small, glittering wax flowers.

Everywhere along the way there was the noisy crowd, and everywhere the lime trees were in blossom.

Their scent seemed to be everywhere at once and to overtake the travellers on their journey north, like a rumour flying round each siding, signal-box and half-way halt and waiting for them on arrival, established and confirmed.

14

That night at Sukhinichi, an obliging, old-style porter took Yury over the unlit tracks to the back of some unscheduled train which had just arrived, and put him in a second-class carriage.

Hardly had he unlocked it with the conductor's key and lifted Yury's luggage inside, when the conductor came and tried to throw it out, but he was mollified by Yury and disappeared.

The mysterious train was under special orders; it went fairly fast, hardly stopped at stations and had an armed guard. The carriage was almost empty.

Yury's compartment was lit by a guttering candle which stood on the small table, its flame wavering in the stream of air from the half-open window. The candle belonged to the only other passenger, a fair-haired youth who, judging by the size of his hands and feet, was very tall. His limbs were loosely jointed, as though not properly attached. He had been lying back in a corner seat by the window, but when Yury came in he sat up in a more seemly manner.

Something that looked like a floor-cloth lay under his seat. One corner of it stirred and a flop-eared setter bustled out. It inspected Yury, sniffed him over and started running up and down the compartment, throwing out its paws as loosely as its lanky master crossed his legs. Soon, at his command, it crawled back under the seat and resumed its likeness to a crumpled duster.

It was only then that Yury noticed the gun case, leather cartridge belt and bulging satchel which lay on the rack.

The young man had been out shooting.

Extremely talkative, he smiled amiably and at once engaged Yury in conversation, looking him, as he did so, literally in the mouth.

He had an unpleasant, high-pitched voice, which now and then rose to a tinny falsetto. Another oddity of his speech was that, while he was plainly Russian, he pronounced the vowel *oo* in a most outlandish manner, softening it either to the French *u* or the German *ü*. To say it at all evidently cost him considerable effort and he spoke it, straining himself to the utmost, with a slight squeal and louder than any other sound. At moments, apparently by concentrating, he managed to correct this defect, but it always came back.

'What the devil is it,' Yury wondered. 'I'm sure I've read about it, I ought to know as a doctor, but I can't think what it is. It must be some brain trouble which causes defective speech.' Whatever the cause, it struck him as so funny that he could hardly keep a straight face. 'Better go to bed,' he told himself.

He climbed up on to his top bunk. The young man offered to blow out the candle in case it should keep him awake. Yury accepted and the compartment was plunged into complete darkness.

'Shall I close the window?' Yury asked. 'You are not afraid of thieves?'

There was no reply. He repeated his question louder but there was still no answer.

He struck a match and leaned out of his bunk to see if his neighbour had gone out. That he had dropped off to sleep in so short a time seemed improbable.

He was there, however, sitting in his place and with his eyes open. He smiled at Yury's face as it hung over him.

The match went out, Yury struck another and, while it was alight, repeated his question for the third time.

'Do as you wish,' the young man replied at once. 'I've got nothing a thief would want. But perhaps leave it open. It's stuffy.'

'What an extraordinary character!' thought Yury. 'An eccentric evidently. Doesn't talk in the dark! It's most astonishing!'

15

Tired out by the events of the past week and by his early start, Yury expected to go to sleep the moment he had made himself comfortable, but he was too exhausted and stayed awake nearly till dawn.

His thoughts swarmed and whirled in the dark. They seemed to move in two main circles, two skeins which constantly tangled and untangled themselves.

In one circle were his thoughts of Tonya: their home and their former, settled life where everything, down to the smallest detail, had its poetry and its sincerity and warmth. Yury felt anxious about this life, he wanted it to be safe and whole, and after two years of separation, rushing back to it in his express train, he longed already to be there.

Here too were his loyalty to the revolution and his admiration for it, the revolution in the sense in which it was accepted by the middle classes and in which it had been understood by the students, followers of Blok, in 1905.

This familiar circle also contained the foretaste of new things. In it were those omens and promises which before the war, between 1912 and 1914, had appeared in Russian thought, art and life, in the destiny of Russia as a whole and in his own, Zhivago's.

It would be good to go back to that climate, once the war was over, to see its renewal and continuation, just as it was good to be going home.

New things were also in the other circle of his thoughts, but how different, how unlike the first! These new things were not familiar, not led up to by the old; they were unchosen, prescribed by reality and as sudden as an earthquake.

Among them was the war with its bloodshed and its horrors, its homelessness, savagery and isolation, its trials and the worldly wisdom which it taught. Here too were the lonely little towns where you were stranded by the war, and the people with whom it threw you together. Such a new thing, too, was the revolution, not the one idealised in student fashion in 1905, but this new upheaval, to-day's born of the war, bloody, pitiless, elemental, the soldiers' revolution, led by the professionals, the bolsheviks.

And among his new thoughts was Nurse Antipova, caught by the war at the back of beyond, with her completely unknown life, Antipova who never blamed anyone, yet whose very silence was almost a reproach, mysteriously reserved and so strong in her reserve. And here too was Yury's honest endeavour not to love her as whole-hearted as his striving throughout his life until now to love not only his family or his friends, but everyone else as well.

The train rushed on at full speed. The head-wind, coming through the open window, ruffled and blew dust on Yury's hair. At every station, by night as by day, the crowds stormed and the lime trees rustled.

Sometimes carts or gigs rattled up to the station out of the darkness and voices and rumbling wheels mingled with the rushing noise of trees.

At such moments Yury felt he understood what it was that made these night shadows rustle and put their heads together, and what it was that they whispered to each other, hardly turning their leaves, heavy with sleep, like faltering, lisping tongues. It was also what Yury was thinking of, turning and twisting in his bunk—news of the ever widening circles of unrest and excitement in Russia, news of the revolution, of its difficult and fateful hour and of the likelihood of its ultimate greatness.

16

Next morning Yury slept late; by the time he woke it was past eleven. 'Prince, Prince,' his neighbour was calling softly to his disgruntled dog. To Yury's astonishment they still had the compartment to themselves: no other passengers had got in.

They had left the province of Kaluga and were well into that of Moscow. The names of the stations had been familiar to Yury since his childhood.

He washed and shaved in pre-war comfort and came back to his compartment in time for breakfast, to which his strange companion had invited him. Now he had a better look at him.

What struck him most was his extreme garrulousness and that he was never still for a moment. He liked talking, and what he liked best was not communicating and exchanging ideas so much as the function of speech itself, pronouncing words and uttering sounds. As he spoke he kept jumping up as if he were on springs; he laughed deafeningly for no reason, rubbed his hands very quickly and, when all else failed to express his feelings, slapped his knees hard and rocked with laughter until he cried.

His conversation had the same peculiarities as the night before. He was curiously inconsistent, now making an unasked-for confession, now leaving the most innocent questions unanswered. He poured out incredible and disconnected facts about himself. Perhaps he lied a little; certainly he was out to impress by his extreme opinions and by denying whatever was the commonly accepted view.

It all reminded Yury of something.—This had been the radical mood of the nihilists of the last century, and a little later of some of Dostoyevsky's characters, and still more recently that of their direct descendants, the provincial intellectuals, who were often in advance of the capitals because of the earnestness which they retained and which the great cities considered old-fashioned.

The young man told him that he was the nephew of some well-known revolutionary, but that his parents were hopelessly reactionary, prehistoric, as he called them. They had a fairly large estate in a district which now adjoined the front. There the young man had grown up. His parents had been at daggers drawn with his uncle all their lives, but the uncle did not hold it against them and now used his influence to save them a good deal of unpleasantness.

His own views were like his uncle's; he was an extremist in everything, whether in life, politics or art. This too reminded Yury of Peter Verkhovensky [1]—not so much the leftism, as the corruption and the bombast. 'He'll be telling me he's a futurist next,' thought Yury; indeed the conversation did turn to futurism. 'Now it will be sport, racing horses, skating rinks or French wrestling'; in fact they spoke of shooting.

The young man had been shooting near his home. He was a crack shot, he boasted, and if it had not been for the physical defect which had kept him out of the army he would have distinguished himself by his marksmanship. Catching Yury's curious glance, he cried: 'Haven't you really noticed anything? I imagined you had guessed my trouble.'

He took two cards out of his pocket and handed them to Yury. One was his visiting card. He had a double-barrelled name, he was called Maxim Aristarkhovich Klintsov-Pogorevshikh—or plain Pogorevshikh, as he begged Yury to call him, in honour of his uncle who bore this name.

The other card was divided into squares and in each square there was a drawing of two hands variously joined and with fingers differently folded. It was an alphabet for deaf-mutes. It explained everything. Pogorevshikh was a phenomenally gifted pupil of the school of either Hartman or Ostrogradov, a deaf-mute who had reached an incredible perfection in the art of speaking not by ear but by eye, by watching the throat muscles of his teachers, and this method also enabled him to understand what other people were saying.

[1] A character in Dostoyevsky's *The Possessed*.

Putting together what he had told him about the part of the country he came from and about his shooting expedition, Yury said :

'Forgive me if this is indiscreet, you needn't tell me after all.—Have you had anything to do with setting up the Zabushino republic ?'

'But how did you guess ? . . . Did you know Blazheiko ? . . . Yes, yes ! Indeed I was connected with it !' Pogorevshikh gabbled, laughing, shaking his whole body and slapping his knees.

Pogorevshikh said that Blazheiko had been the pretext and Zabushino the chance locality for the application of his own ideas. Yury could not always follow his exposition of his philosophy ; it seemed to be partly anarchism and partly simple hunter's lies.

Imperturbable as an oracle, he prophesied disastrous upheavals which would take place in Russia in the near future. Yury privately agreed that this was not unlikely, but he was maddened by the unpleasant schoolboy arrogance of his pronouncements.

'Just a moment,' he said tentatively. 'This may all be true, what you say may happen. But it seems to me that with all that's going on—the chaos, the disintegration, the pressure from the enemy —this is not the moment to start dangerous experiments. The country has to get over one upheaval before plunging into another. There has to be something like peace and order first.'

'That's a very naïve statement,' said Pogorevshikh. 'What you call disorder is just as normal a state of things as the order you are so keen on. All this destruction—it's the right and proper preliminary stage of a wide, constructive plan. Society has not yet disintegrated sufficiently. It must fall to pieces completely, then a genuinely revolutionary government will put the pieces together on a completely new basis.'

Yury felt sick. He went out into the corridor.

The train, gathering speed, was approaching Moscow. It ran through birch-woods full of summer villas. Small roofless platforms with men and women standing on them swung sideways into the distance in a cloud of dust, turning as on a roundabout. The train hooted repeatedly and the hollow, fluty echo of the woods gurgled with its hooting.

All at once, for the first time in all these days, Yury understood quite clearly where he was, what was happening to him and what awaited him in little more than a couple of hours.

Three years of changes, moves, uncertainties, upheavals ; the war, the revolution ; scenes of destruction, scenes of death, shelling, blown-up bridges, fires, ruins—all this turned suddenly into a huge, empty, waste space. The first real event since the long interruption was this vertiginous home-coming by train, in the knowledge that his home was still safe, still existing somewhere, with every smallest stone in it dear to him. This was the point of life, this was experience, this was the quest of the adventure seekers and what artists had in mind—this coming home to your family, to yourself, this renewal of life.

The train broke out of the leafy closeness of the woods into the open. A sloping field rose from a hollow to a wide mound. It was striped horizontally with dark green potato beds; beyond them, at the top of the mound, were glass frames. Opposite the field, beyond the curving tail of the train, a dark purple cloud covered half the sky; sunbeams were breaking through it, spreading like wheel-spokes and flashing with insupportable brightness off the glass of the frames.

Suddenly, warm, heavy rain, sparkling in the sun, fell out of the cloud. It had the same hurried tempo as the speeding train knocking and thundering over the sleepers, as if it were afraid of being left behind and were trying to catch up.

Hardly had Yury noticed it when the church of Christ the Saviour [1] showed over the rim of the hill, and a moment later the domes, chimneys, roofs and houses of the city.

'Moscow,' said Yury returning to the compartment. 'It's time to get ready.'

Pogorevshikh jumped up, rummaged in his shooting bag and took out a fat duck. 'Take it,' he said, 'as a memento. I have rarely spent a day in such pleasant company.'

Zhivago's protests were unavailing. In the end he said: 'All right, I'll take it as a present from you to my wife.'

'Splendid, splendid, your wife,' Pogorevshikh kept repeating delightedly, as though he had heard the word for the first time, jerking and laughing so much that Prince jumped out and took part in the rejoicing.

The train drew into the station. The compartment became dark as if it were night. The deaf-mute held out the wild duck wrapped in a torn broadsheet.

[1] The church of St. Saviour, a Moscow landmark, built to commemorate the Napoleonic War, stood in the centre of the city. It was demolished after the revolution to make way for the Palace of Soviets, as yet not built.

6

Moscow Bivouac

SO long as he had been sitting in the train it had seemed to Yury that only the train was moving, that time stood still and it was still only midday.

But in fact it was late afternoon when his cab slowly made its way from the station through the dense crowd in Smolensky Square.

Whether it was so indeed, or Yury's memories were overlaid by the experience of other years, it seemed to him when he recalled it later that even then the crowd hung about the market only by habit, that already there was no reason for it to be there, because the stalls were covered up and not even locked and there was nothing to buy or sell in the littered square which nobody swept.

And it seemed to him that already he saw, shrinking against the walls, thin, decently dressed old men and women, who stood like a silent reproach to the passers-by, wordlessly offering what no one needed—artificial flowers, coffee percolators with glass lids and whistles, black net evening dresses and uniforms of offices that had been abolished.

Simpler people traded in more useful things : spiky crusts of stale rationed black bread, damp, dirty chunks of sugar, and ounce packets of coarse tobacco cut in half right across the label.

This unbelievable rubbish went all round the market, going up in price as it changed hands.

The cab turned into a side street. The setting sun was at their back. In front of them a dray horse clattered along, pulling an empty, bouncing cart. It raised pillars of bronze dust burning in the sunset.

At last they overtook it and went faster. Yury was struck by the quantities of old newspapers and posters, torn down from the walls and fences, littering the streets. The wind pulled them one way and hooves, wheels and feet pushed them the other.

They passed several cross-roads, and there was Yury's house at the corner of two side streets. The cab stopped.

Yury caught his breath and his heart hammered as he got out, walked up to the front door and rang the bell at the side. Nothing happened. He rang again. As there was still no reply he went on ringing at short, anxious intervals. He was still ringing when he saw that the door had been opened by Tonya and that she stood holding it wide. The unexpectedness of it so dumbfounded them both that neither of them heard the other cry out. But as the door, held wide open by Tonya, was in itself a welcome and almost an embrace, they soon recovered and rushed into each other's arms. A moment later they were both talking at once.

'First of all, is everybody well?'

'Yes, yes, don't worry. Everything is all right. I wrote you a lot of silly nonsense, forgive me. But we'll talk about that later. Why didn't you send a telegram? Markel will take your things up. I suppose you got worried when Yegorovna didn't let you in! She is in the country.'

'You're thinner. But how young you look, and so pretty! Wait a minute, I'll pay the cabby.'

'Yegorovna has gone to try and get some flour. All the other servants have been sent away. There's only one girl now, Nyusha, you don't know her, she's looking after Sasha, there's no one else. Everybody has been told you're coming, they're all longing to see you—Gordon, Dudorov, everyone.'

'How is Sasha?'

'All right, thank God. He's just woken up. If you weren't just off the train—with all this typhus about—we could have gone to him at once.'

'Is Father at home?'

'Didn't anyone write to you?—He's at the borough council from morning till night, he's the chairman. Yes, can you believe it! Have you settled with the cabby? Markel! Markel!'

They were standing in the middle of the street with Yury's basket trunk and suitcase blocking the way, and the passers-by stopped and looked them over from head to foot and stared at the cab as it pulled away from the kerb, and at the wide open front door, to see what would happen next.

But Markel, his waistcoat over his cotton shirt and his porter's cap in his hand, was already running up from the gate to welcome the young master, shouting as he ran:

'Lord almighty, if it isn't Yurochka! Well I never, so it's our darling himself! Yury Andreyevich, light of my eyes, so you haven't forgotten us, and us praying for you every day! You've honoured us, you've come home!—And what do you want?' he snapped at the onlookers. 'What's so extraordinary? Be off with you. What is there to goggle at?'

'How are you, Markel?' Yury hugged him. 'Put your cap on,

you ass. Well, what's new? How's the wife? How are the girls?'

'How should they be? They're growing, thanks be to God. As for news, you can see for yourself—while you were away doing mighty deeds, we've been busy too. Such a mess-up, such a bedlam, the devil couldn't sort it out—streets dirty, roofs leaking, bellies empty as in Lent—and all this "without annexations or contributions" [1].'

'I'll complain to Yury Andreyevich about you, Markel. He's always carrying on like this, Yurochka. I can't stand such silly talk. It's all for your benefit, he thinks you like it—he's as sharp as they make them. All right, all right, Markel, don't argue with me, I know you. You're a dark horse, Markel. It's time you learned some sense. Playing up to us as if we were shopkeepers!'

They went in. Markel carried Yury's things inside, shut the front door behind him and went on confidentially.

'Antonina Alexandrovna is vexed, you heard what she said. It's always like that. She says, you're all black inside, Markel, she says, like that stove pipe. Nowadays, she says, every little child, maybe even every pug or other lap dog knows what's what. That, of course, is true, but all the same, Yurochka, believe it or not, those who know have seen the book, the Masons' book [2], one hundred and forty years it's been lying under a stone, and now, it's my considered opinion, Yurochka, we've been sold down the river. But can I say a word? See for yourself, Antonina Alexandrovna is shaking her head at me.'

'Do you wonder? That's enough, Markel, put the things down, and that will be all. If Yury Andreyevich wants anything, he'll call you.'

2

'Thank goodness, he's gone! All right, all right, you can listen to him if you like, but I can tell you, it's all play-acting. You talk to him and you think he's the village idiot, butter wouldn't melt in his mouth, and all the time in secret he's sharpening his knife—only he hasn't quite decided yet who it's for, the poor old rascal.'

'Isn't that a bit far-fetched? I expect he's just drunk, that's all there is to it.'

'And when is he sober, I'd like to know. Anyway, I've had enough of him.—What worries me is, Sasha might go to sleep again before you've seen him. If it weren't for those typhus lice on trains . . . You haven't any lice on you?'

[1] 'Peace without annexation or contribution' was the slogan of the Socialist left.
[2] The Book of the Masons: i.e. *The Protocols of the Elders of Zion*.

'I don't think so. I travelled in luxury—positively pre-war. I'd better have a quick wash, though. I'll wash properly afterwards. Which way are you going? Don't we go through the drawing-room any more?'

'Oh, of course, you don't know. Father and I thought and thought and we decided to give up a part of the ground floor to the Agricultural Academy. It's too much to heat in winter, anyway. Even the top floor is too big. So we've offered it to them. They haven't taken it over yet, but they've moved in their library and their herbarium and their seed collections. I only hope we don't get rats with all those seeds, it's grain after all. But at the moment they're keeping the rooms spick and span. By the way, we don't say rooms any more, it's called living space nowadays. Come on, this way. Aren't you slow on the uptake! We go up the back stairs. Come along, I'll show you.'

'I'm very glad you've given up those rooms. The hospital I've been in was also in a private house. Endless suites of rooms with a little parquet flooring still left. Potted palms sticking out their paws like ghosts over the beds—some of the wounded from the battle zone used to wake up screaming—they weren't quite normal of course—shell-shocked—we had to remove the plants. What I mean is, there really was something unhealthy in the way rich people used to live. Masses of superfluous things. Too much furniture, too much room, too much refinement, too much self-expression. I'm very glad we're using fewer rooms. We should give up still more.'

'What's that parcel you've got? There's something sticking out of it, it looks like a bird's beak. It's a duck! How lovely! A wild drake! Where did you get it? I can't believe my eyes. It's worth a fortune nowadays.'

'Somebody made me a present of it on the train. I'll tell you later, it's a long story. What shall I do? Shall I leave it in the kitchen?'

'Yes, of course. I'll send Nyusha down at once to pluck and clean it. They say there will be all sorts of horrors this winter—famine, cold.'

'Yes, that's what they are saying everywhere. Just now, I was looking out of the train window—I thought, what is there in the whole world worth more than a peaceful family life and work? The rest isn't in our hands. It does look as if there is a bad time coming. Some people are trying to get out, they talk of going south, to the Caucasus, or further still. I wouldn't want to do that myself. A grown-up man is supposed to grit his teeth and share in whatever's coming to his country. But for you it's different. I wish to goodness you didn't have to go through it all. I'd like to send you away somewhere safe—to Finland perhaps.—But if we stand gossiping half an hour on every step we'll never get upstairs.'

'Wait a minute. I quite forgot to tell you. I've got a wonderful piece of news for you. Nikolay Nikolayevich is back.'

'What Nikolay Nikolayevich?'

'Uncle Kolya.'

'Tonya! It can't be! How is it possible?'

'It's true. He was in Switzerland. He came all the way round through London, via Finland.'

'Tonya! You aren't teasing me? Have you seen him? Where is he? Can't we get him now, at once?'

'Don't be so impatient. He's staying with someone in the country. He promised to be back the day after to-morrow. He's changed a lot. You'll be disappointed. He stopped in Petersburg on the way, he's gone bolshevik. Father gets quite hoarse arguing with him. We do seem to get stuck on every step. Come on. So you've also heard there's a bad time coming—what do people say?—hardships, dangers, insecurity?'

'I think so myself. Well, what of it? We'll manage, it can't be the end of everything. We'll wait and see, the same as other people.'

'They say there won't be any firewood, or water, or light. They'll abolish money. No supplies will be coming in. Now we've stopped again! Come along. Listen, they say there are wonderful iron stoves being sold in the Arbat. Small ones. You can burn a newspaper and cook a meal. I've got the address. We must buy one before they're all gone.'

'That's right. We will. Good idea. But just fancy, Uncle Kolya! I can't get over it.

'Let me tell you what I want to do. We'll set aside a corner somewhere at the top of the house, say two or three rooms, communicating ones, and we'll keep those for ourselves and Father and Sasha and Nyusha, and we'll give up all the rest of the house. We'll put up a partition and have our own door, like in a flat. We'll put one of those metal stoves in the middle room, with a pipe through the window, and we'll do all our laundry, and our cooking, and our entertaining, all in this one room. Like that we'll make the most of the fuel, and who knows, with God's help, we'll get through the winter.'

'Of course we'll get through it. There's no question. That's a splendid idea.—And you know what? We'll have a house-warming.

We'll cook the duck and we'll invite Uncle Kolya.'

'Lovely. And I'll ask Gordon to bring some alcohol. He can get it from some laboratory or other. Now look, this is the room I was thinking of. All right? Put your suitcase down and go down and get your basket. We could ask Dudorov and Shura Schlesinger to the house-warming as well. You don't mind? You haven't forgotten where the lavatory is? Go and put a little disinfectant on. While you do that I'll go in to Sasha and send Nyusha down, and when we're ready I'll call you.'

3

The most important novelty for him in Moscow was his little boy. Yury had been called up almost as soon as the child was born, so that he hardly knew him.

One day, while Tonya was still in hospital, Yury came to see her; he was already in uniform and was shortly leaving Moscow. He arrived at the babies' feeding time and was not allowed in.

He sat down in the waiting-room. From the nursery, at the end of the passage beyond the maternity ward, came the squealing chorus of ten or twelve babies' voices. Several nurses came down the corridor, hurrying so that the new-born babies should not catch cold, taking them bundled up like parcels, one under each arm, to their mothers.

'Wa, wa,' yelled the babies all on one note, almost impassively, without feeling, as if it were all in the day's work. Only one voice stood out from the others. It was also yelling 'wa, wa', and it did not express any more suffering than the rest, but it was deeper and seemed to shout less out of duty than with a deliberate, cold hostility.

Yury had already decided that his child was to be called Alexander —Sasha for short—in honour of his father-in-law. For some reason he imagined that the voice he had singled out was that of his son; perhaps it was because this particular cry had its own character and seemed already to contain the future personality and destiny of a particular human being; it had its own sound-colouring which included the child's name, Alexander, so Yury fancied.

He was not mistaken. It turned out later that this had in fact been Sasha's voice. It was the first thing he knew about his son.

The next thing was the photograph Tonya sent him to the front, of a fat, jolly-looking child with its mouth in a cupid's bow, standing on a blanket, bandy-legged and with its fists up as if it were doing a peasant dance. Sasha was a year old at the time and just beginning to walk; now he was two and was learning to talk.

Yury picked up his suitcase, put it on the card-table by the window and began to unpack. What had the room been used for in the past, he wondered. He could not recognise it. Tonya must have changed the furniture or the wallpaper or redecorated it in some way.

He took out his shaving kit. A bright full moon stood between the pillars of the church belfry exactly opposite the window. When it lit up the top layer of clothes and books inside the suitcase, the light in the room changed and he realised where he was.

It had been the lumber room in the old days. Broken chairs and tables had been stowed away in it, and here Anna had kept her family archives and the trunks where winter clothes were stored in summer. In her lifetime the corners were piled up to the ceiling with junk and the children were not allowed in. Only at Christmas or Easter— when huge crowds of children came to parties and the whole of the top floor was thrown open to them—was it unlocked and they played robbers in it, hiding under the tables, dressing up and blackening their faces with cork.

Yury stood thinking of all this, then he went down the back stairs to get his basket trunk from the hall.

In the kitchen Nyusha squatted on her haunches in front of the stove, plucking the duck on a piece of newspaper. When Yury came in carrying his trunk, she jumped up with a shy graceful movement, blushing crimson, shook the feathers from her apron, greeted him, and offered to help him. He thanked her, saying he could manage, and went up. His wife called him from a couple of rooms further on : 'You can come in now, Yura.'

He went in to see Sasha.

The nursery was Tonya's old schoolroom. The boy in the cot was not nearly so handsome as in his photograph, but he was the living image of Yury's mother, the late Marya Nikolayevna Zhivago, a more striking likeness than any of the portraits Yury had kept.

'Here's Daddy, here's your Daddy, wave your hand like a good boy,' Tonya was saying. She lowered the side of the cot to make it easier for Yury to kiss the child and pick it up.

Little Sasha let the bristly stranger, who perhaps frightened and repelled him, get quite close and bend over him, then he jerked himself upright, clutching the front of his mother's dress with one hand and angrily swung the other and slapped him in the face. Terrified by his own daring, he then threw himself into Tonya's arms and burst into bitter tears.

'Naughty, naughty,' Tonya scolded him. 'You mustn't be like that, Sashenka. What will Daddy think ? He'll think Sasha is a bad boy. Now, show how you can kiss, kiss Daddy. Don't cry, silly, it's all right.'

'Let him be, Tonya,' Yury begged her. 'Don't bother him and don't upset yourself. I know the kind of nonsense you are thinking—that it's not for nothing, it's a bad sign—but that's all rubbish. It's so natural. The boy has never seen me. To-morrow he'll have a good look at me and we'll make friends and you'll see, we'll get on splendidly.'

Yet he went out of the room depressed and with a feeling of ill-omen.

4

During the next few days he realised how isolated he was. It was no one's fault, he thought. He had simply got what he had asked for.

His friends had become strangely dim and colourless. Not one of them had kept his own outlook, his own world. They had been much more vivid in his memory. He must have over-estimated them in the past.

It had been easy enough to do so, as long as the order of things had been such that people with means could indulge their follies and eccentricities at the expense of the poor. The fooling, the right to idleness enjoyed by the few while the majority suffered, could itself create an illusion of genuine character and originality.

But how quickly, once the lower classes had risen and the rich had lost their privileges, had these people faded! How effortlessly, how happily, had they given up the habit of independent thought—which at this rate could never in fact have been genuinely theirs!

The only people with whom Yury now felt at home were Tonya, her father and two or three of his colleagues, people in plain, ordinary jobs who got on with them decently and modestly without fuss or rhetoric.

The party with duck and vodka was given as planned, a few days after his return. By then he had seen most of those who came to it, so that the dinner was not in fact the occasion of their reunion.

The large duck was an unheard-of luxury in those hungry days, but there was no bread to go with it, and because of this its splendour was somehow pointless—it was even a little disagreeable.

The spirits (a favourite black market currency) had been brought by Gordon in a medicine bottle with a glass stopper. Tonya hugged it to herself and diluted the alcohol in small portions with more or less water according to her fancy. The mixture, always too weak or too strong, seemed for some reason to be more intoxicating than if it had been consistently stronger, and this also was annoying.

But the saddest thing of all was that their party was out of keeping with the conditions of the times. You could not imagine anyone in the houses across the street eating or drinking in the same way at the same time. Out there, beyond the windows, lay dumb, dark, hungry Moscow; its shops were empty, and, as for game and vodka, people had forgotten even to think about such things.

And so it seemed that the only real way of living was to live like everyone else, to be lost in other people's lives without leaving a trace, and that an unshared happiness was not happiness, so that duck and vodka when they seemed to be the only duck and vodka in town were not even duck and vodka.

Neither did they get much comfort from their guests. Gordon had been all right in the days when he had thought his heavy thoughts and expressed them in his gloomy, hesitating words. He was Yury's best friend and he had been popular at school.

But now he had taken a dislike to his mental image of himself and was trying, most unsuccessfully, to improve on it. He made a point of being jolly, told one supposedly funny story after another and kept saying 'What fun !' and 'How amusing !', words which did not belong to his vocabulary because Gordon had never looked upon life as an entertainment.

While they were waiting for Dudorov he told the current gossip about Dudorov's marriage. Yury had not yet heard it.

It seemed that Dudorov had been married for about a year and had then separated from his wife. The far-fetched humour of the story lay in that it had all started with Dudorov being called up by mistake. While he was serving and his case was being investigated, he had go into endless trouble through being absent-minded and forgetting to salute officers.

For months after his release he kept seeing epaulettes everywhere and jerking up his arm ; he was more distracted than ever and almost in a state of nervous collapse. Just at that time, so the story went, he had met two girls, two sisters, at a river station on the Volga—they were waiting for the same steamer as he was—and in a fit of absent-mindedness brought on by the sight of the many uniforms milling around them, and by the hangover from his army days, he had fallen in love with the younger of the two and hastily proposed to her. 'Isn't it fun !' said Gordon, but he had to cut short the end of his story as the voice of its hero was heard outside the door. Dudorov came in.

He had changed the opposite way. He had been unstable and erratic as a weathercock; now he had become an earnest scholar.

When, as a boy, he had been expelled from school for complicity in the escape of a political prisoner, he had wandered about from art school to art school but had in the end landed at the classical faculty. Later than his friends, he had taken his degree during the war, and had been kept on as a lecturer in Russian and world history. He was now writing a book on the land policy of Ivan the Terrible and another on Saint-Just.

He discoursed amiably on every subject, his voice never rising or falling from its quiet, rather nasal pitch and his eyes dreamily fixed on one point as if he were lecturing.

Towards the end of the evening, when the party was going full swing with everyone shouting and arguing, Shura Schlesinger burst in and teased them all as usual, adding to the general noise and excitement. Dudorov, who had been Yury's childhood friend but had never said 'thou' to him, asked him several times, still addressing him as 'you', whether he had read Mayakovsky's poems, 'War and Peace' and 'My Spine is a Flute'.

Missing Yury's reply in all the noise, he asked him again a little later: 'Have you read "My Spine is a Flute" and "Man"?'

'I told you once, you don't listen. I've always liked Mayakovsky. He is a sort of continuation of Dostoyevsky. Or rather, he's a Dostoyevsky character writing lyrics—one of his young rebels, the "Raw Youth" or Hippolyte or Raskolnikov. What an all-devouring poetic energy! And his way of saying a thing once and for all, implacably, straight from the shoulder! And above all, the way he takes a good bold swing and chucks it all at the face of society and a bit further somewhere, into outer space!'

But the great attraction of the evening was, of course, Uncle Kolya. Tonya had been mistaken in thinking that he was out of town, he had come back the day of his nephew's return. They had met a couple of times already and had got over their initial Oh's and Ah's and had talked and laughed together to their hearts' content.

The first time had been on a dull, grey night with a drizzle as fine as watery dust. Yury went to see him at his hotel. The hotels were already refusing to take people in except at the insistence of the town authorities, but Nikolay Nikolayevich was well known and had kept some of his old connections.

The hotel looked like a lunatic asylum left in the charge of the patients—empty, chaotic and abandoned to chance.

Through the large window of the unswept room the huge square looked in, deserted and terrifying, more like a square in a dream at night than the one plainly to be seen in front of the hotel.

For Yury the encounter was a tremendous, unforgettable event. He was seeing the idol of his childhood, the teacher who had dominated his mind as a boy.

His grey hair suited Uncle Kolya, and his loose foreign suit fitted him well; he was very young and handsome for his years.

Admittedly, he was overshadowed by the grandeur of the events; seen beside them he lost in stature. But it never occurred to Yury to measure him by this yardstick.

He was surprised at Uncle Kolya's calm, at his light and detached tone when speaking of politics. He was more self-possessed than most Russians could be at that time. It marked him as a new arrival and it seemed old-fashioned and a little embarrassing.

But a lot they cared about such things in those intoxicating first few hours of their reunion! It was something very different from politics which made them laugh and cry and throw their arms round each other's necks and talk breathlessly and choke with excitement.

What brought them together was the fact that they both had the temperament of creative artists, and although they were also kinsmen, and the past arose and lived again between them, and memories surged up, and they spoke of the new events and circumstances in each other's lives, the moment it came to the most important, to what is known only to those who have an aptitude for creative work, all differences and all other ties between them vanished—they were neither uncle and nephew nor an older and a younger man—there remained only the kinship of energy to energy, of first principle to first principle.

Not for ten years had Nikolay Nikolayevich talked of the problems of writing and the meaning of a writer's task so relevantly or with any-one whose ideas corresponded so closely to his own. Nor had Yury met with so much understanding, stimulation or encouragement.

So they shouted, rushed up and down the room and clutched their heads, or stood in deep silence by the window, drumming on the glass, shaken and exalted by the rightness of each other's intuition and the depth of the mutual understanding which it proved.

That was how their first meeting went; but since then they had seen each other in company, and among other people Uncle Kolya was unrecognisable.

He was conscious of being a guest in Moscow, and he liked the feeling, though whether it was Petersburg he regarded as his home, or some other place, remained uncertain. He enjoyed being lionised as a drawing-room politician, and possibly he imagined that political salons in the style of Madame Roland's in Paris on the eve of the Convention should now exist in Moscow.

Calling on his women friends at their hospitable flats in quiet Moscow back streets, he teased them and their husbands in the kindest way on their limited, local and retarded outlook. He was as proud of his familiarity with the newspapers as once of his apocryphal and Orphic learning.

It was said that he had left an inconclusive love affair, much unfinished business and an unfinished book in Switzerland and had only come for a dip into the whirlpool, meaning, if he came out safe and sound, to make a bee-line again for his beloved Alps.

He was pro-bolshevik and often mentioned two left-wing Social Revolutionaries who shared his views, journalists who wrote under the pseudonyms Miroshka Pomor and Sylvia Coterie.

'It's frightful, what you've come down to, Nikolay Nikolayevich,' Yury's father-in-law growled at him, 'with all your Miroshkas; it's a proper cesspool. And then that Lydia Pokori.'

'Coterie,' corrected Nikolay Nikolayevich, 'and Sylvia.'

'Pokori or Potpourri, it's all the same thing. What's in a name.'

'All the same, it happens to be Coterie,' Nikolay Nikolayevich insisted patiently. They had dialogues of this sort :

'What are we arguing about ? It's so obvious that it makes you blush to have to prove it. It's the A.B.C. of everything.—For centuries the mass of the people have lived impossible lives. Take any history book. Whatever it was called, feudalism and serfdom or capitalism and industry, it was a state of things which was unnatural and unjust. This has been known for a long time and the world has been preparing for an upheaval which would bring light to the people and put everything in its proper place.

'You know perfectly well that it's quite useless tinkering with the old structure, you have to dig right down to the foundations.—I don't say the whole building won't collapse as a result.—What of it ? The fact that it's frightening won't prevent its happening. It's a question of time. How can you dispute it ?'

'That's not the point, that's not what I was talking about.' Alexander Alexandrovich lost his temper and the argument flared up.

'Your Potpourris and Miroshkas are people without a conscience. They say one thing and do another. Anyway, where's your logic ? It's a complete non-sequitur. No, wait a minute, I'll show you something,' and he would start hunting for some newspaper with an article in it which contradicted itself, banging the drawers of the writing table and using all this noisy fuss to work up his eloquence.

Alexander Alexandrovich liked something to get in his way when he was talking, the distraction made an excuse for his mumbling and his hums and haws. His fits of talkativeness came on him when he was looking for something he had lost—say hunting for his second snow boot in the dimly lighted cloakroom—or as he stood at the bathroom door with a towel over his arm, or at table, as he was passing a heavy serving dish or pouring wine into the glasses of his friends.

Yury loved listening to him. He adored the familiar, old-Moscow sing-song and the soft, purring Gromeko *r*'s.

Alexander Alexandrovich's upper lip with its little cropped moustache protruded above his lower lip in just the same way as his butterfly tie stuck out from his neck; there was something in common between the two and it somehow gave him a touching, childishly confiding look.

On the night of the party Shura Schlesinger arrived very late; she had come straight from a meeting and was wearing a suit and a man's cap. She came striding into the room and burst into complaints and accusations as she shook hands.

'How are you, Tonya? How are you, Alexander? You must admit it's disgusting. The whole of Moscow knows he's back, everyone is talking about it and you are the last to tell me. Well, I suppose I'm not good enough. Where is he anyway, our Yura? Let me get at him.—Well, how are you? I've read it, it's wonderful, I didn't understand a word but it's full of talent, you can tell at once.—How are you, Nikolay Nikolayevich?—I'll see you in a moment, Yura dear, I've got to talk to you.—Hullo, children. You're here too, Gogochka, Goosey-Goosey-Gander' (this to a distant relation of the Gromekos, a fervent admirer of every rising star, who was known as Goosey because of his idiot laugh and as the Tapeworm on account of his height and thinness). 'Eating and drinking, are you? I'll soon catch you up. Well, my dears, you've simply no idea what you're missing. You don't know anything, you haven't seen a thing. If you only knew what's happening, what's being done in the world! You go and have a look at a real mass meeting, with real workers, real soldiers, not out of books. Just try and say a word to them about fighting the war to a victorious end! They'll give you a victorious end! I've just been listening to a sailor—Yura darling, you'd simply have gone crazy! The passion! The single-mindedness!'

Shura kept being interrupted. Everyone was shouting. She moved over to Yury, clasped his hand and, with her face close to his, shouted like a megaphone above the din:

'Let me take you along, Yura darling, let me show you real people. You must, you simply must get the feel of the soil, like Antheus. Why are you staring at me like that? I'm an old war horse, didn't you know? An old Bestuzhev student.[1] I've seen the inside of a prison, I've fought on the barricades.—Well, of course, what did you think?—But honestly, we don't know the people at all. I've just come from there, I was right in the thick of it. I'm fixing up a library for them.'

She had had a drink and was obviously getting tipsy. But Yury's head was also going round. He never noticed how it happened that Shura was now at one end of the room and he at the other; he was standing at the head of the table and apparently, quite unexpectedly to himself, making a speech. It took him some time to get silence.

'Ladies and gentlemen . . . I should like . . . Misha! Gogochka! Tonya, what am I to do, they won't listen! Ladies and gentlemen, let me say a word or two. We are about to see something unheard-of, unbelievable. Before it overtakes us, here is what I wish you. When it happens, may God grant us not to lose each other and not to lose our souls. Gogochka, you can cheer afterwards, I haven't finished. Come away from there, come and listen carefully.

'In this third year of the war the conviction has formed among the people that the difference between those in the front line and those at the rear must sooner or later be abolished. The sea of blood will rise until it reaches every one of us and submerges all who stayed out of the war. The revolution is this flood.

'When this happens it will seem to you, as it seemed to us in the army, that life has stopped, that there is nothing personal left, that there is nothing going on in the world except killing and dying. If we survive into the days when chronicles and memoirs of this time are being written, we shall see from reading those recollections that, in these five or ten years, we have experienced more than other people do in a century. I don't know if the people will rise of themselves and advance spontaneously like a tide, or if everything will only be done in their name. Such a huge event cannot be asked for its credentials, it has no need to give dramatic proof of its existence, we'll take it on trust. It would be mean and petty to try to dig for the causes of Titanic happenings. Indeed they haven't any. It's only in a family quarrel that there is a beginning—and after people have pulled each other's hair and smashed the crockery they try to think who it was that started it. What is truly great is without beginning,

[1] A student following the Bestuzhev University Courses for women. Many of the students were left-wing.

like the universe. It confronts us suddenly as if it had always been there or as if it had dropped out of the sky.

'I also think that Russia is destined to become the first socialist country since the beginning of the world. When this happens it will stun us for a long time, and when we come to ourselves we shall still be only half-conscious and with half our memory gone. We'll have forgotten what came first and what followed and we won't look for the causes of the inexplicable. The new order of things will be all round us and as familiar to us as the woods on the skyline or the clouds over our heads. There will be nothing else left.'

He said a few more things, and by then he had sobered up completely, yet when he sat down he could still not hear exactly what was being said to him and replied at random. He knew that they were all showing him their affection but he felt a crushing weight of distress. He said:

'Thank you, thank you. I appreciate your feelings. I don't deserve them. Don't be so quick with your love. It's as though you were laying in stores of affection in case you have to love even more in the future.'

They all laughed and clapped, taking it for a deliberate witticism, while he had no idea what he was saying, so great was his foreboding of misfortune and his feeling of powerlessness over the future, however great his thirst for goodness and his capacity for happiness.

The guests were leaving. They had long, tired faces. Their yawns, clenching and unclenching their jaws, made them look like horses.

As they said good-bye they drew the curtains and pushed the windows open. There was a yellowish dawn in the wet sky filled with soiled, earthy-pea-green clouds. 'Looks as if there's been a storm while we were chattering,' said someone.—'I was caught in the rain on my way, I only just got here,' Shura confirmed.

In the deserted side street it was still dark and the dripping of the water from the trees alternated with the insistent chirruping of drenched sparrows.

It thundered once as if a plough had been dragged right across the sky. Then silence. Then four loud, delayed thuds, like overgrown potatoes being flung out of the soft, newly dug beds in autumn.

The thunder cleared a space in the dusty, smoke-filled room. All at once, like electrical currents, the component elements of life became perceptible: air and water, need for joy, earth, sky.

The side street filled with the voices of the departing guests. They had started an argument of some sort in the house and were still arguing in exactly same way in the street. Gradually the voices became softer in the distance and at last faded away.

'How late it is,' said Yury. 'Let's go to bed. The only people I love in the world are you and Father.'

5

August had gone by and now September was nearly over. Winter was at hand and in the world of men the air was heavy with something as inexorable as the coming death of nature. It was on everybody's lips.

Food and logs had to be got in. But in those days of the triumph of materialism, matter had become an abstract notion, and food and firewood were replaced by the problems of alimentation and fuel supply.

The people in the towns were as helpless as children in the face of the unknown—of that unknown which swept every known usage aside and left nothing but desolation in its wake—although it was the offspring and creation of the towns.

People were still talking and deceiving themselves as their daily life struggled on, limping and shuffling to its unknown destination. But Yury saw it as it was, he could see that it was doomed, and that he and such as he were sentenced to destruction. Ordeals were ahead, perhaps death. Their days were counted, and these days were running out before his eyes.

What saved his reason were the everyday details of his life, his work, his worries. His wife, his child, the need to earn, the humble daily ritual of his practice, these were his salvation.

He understood that he was a pygmy before the monstrous machine of the future. He both feared and loved that future and was secretly proud of it, and, as though for the last time, as if saying good-bye, was avidly aware of the trees and clouds and of the people walking in the streets, of the great Russian city struggling through misfortune —and he was ready to sacrifice himself to make things better but was powerless to do anything.

The sky and the people usually struck him just as he was crossing the Arbat at the corner of Old Coachyard Street, near the pharmacy of the Russian Medical Society.

He was back in his job at the hospital. It was still called the Hospital of the Holy Cross although the community of that name had been dissolved—no one had so far thought of a more suitable name.

The staff had already divided up into camps. There were the moderates, whose obtuseness annoyed him and who thought him dangerous, and the people who had gone further in their politics and who considered him not Red enough, so that he didn't please anyone.

In addition to his normal duties, the Director had put him in charge of statistics. Endless questionnaires went through his hands, endless forms had to be filled in. Death rate, sickness rate, the earnings of the staff, the level of their political consciousness and their part in the elections, the perpetual shortage of fuel, food, medicines, everything had to be checked and reported.

Yury worked at his old table by the staff-room window; it was stacked with charts and forms of every size and shape. He had pushed them to one side; occasionally he took a few moments off, not only for his medical notes, but for his 'Manikins and Men', a gloomy diary of those days consisting of prose, verse and what-have-you, coloured by his feeling that half the world had ceased to be itself and was playing goodness only knew what part.

The light room with its white painted walls was full of the creamy sunshine of those golden autumn days which follow the Assumption, when the first frosts strike at dawn and winter-tits and magpies dart into the bright-leaved thinning woods. On such days the sky rises to its topmost height and an icy, dark-blue radiance from the north steals into the transparent air between sky and earth. Everything in the world becomes more visible and more audible. Every sound is carried, iced and ringing, into immense distance. The country opens out as if to show the whole of life for years ahead. This clarity would be insupportable if it were not so short-lived, coming at the end of the brief autumn day just before the early dusk.

Such was now the light in the staff-room, the light of an early autumn sunset, as juicy, glassy, watery as a ripe Granny Smith.

Yury sat at his desk writing, pausing to think and dip his pen in the ink, while silent birds flew past the tall staff-room window, throwing shadows on his hand as it moved over the page and on the table with its forms and on the staff-room walls, and silently vanishing.

The chemistry demonstrator came in; he was a stout man who had dropped so much weight that his skin hung on him in folds. 'The maple leaves are nearly all gone,' he said. 'When you think how they stood up to all the rain and wind, and now a single morning frost has done all that!'

Yury looked up. The mysterious birds darting past the window had been maple leaves all the time. They soared away from the trees, keeping their height, then, turning into curved orange stars, fell at a distance on the lawn.

'Have the windows been fixed with putty?'

'Not yet.' Yury went on writing.

'Isn't it time they were?'

Yury was absorbed in his work and did not answer.

'Pity Tarasyuk's gone,' went on the chemist. 'He was worth his weight in gold, Tarasyuk was. Patch your boots or mend your watch —he'd do anything. And he could get you anything in the world. Now we'll have to do the windows ourselves.'

'There's no putty.'

'You can make some. I'll give you the recipe.' He explained how you made putty with linseed oil and chalk. 'Well, I'll leave you now. I suppose you want to get on with your work.'

He went off to the other window and bent over his bottles and specimens. 'You'll spoil your eyes,' he said a moment later. 'It's getting dark. And they won't give you any light. Let's go home.'

'I'll work another twenty minutes or so.'

'His wife is a ward-maid here.'

'Whose wife?'

'Tarasyuk's.'

'I know.'

'Nobody knows where he is himself. He prowls about all over the country. Last summer he came twice to see his wife, now he's away again. He's building the new way of life. He's one of those soldier-bolsheviks, you see them everywhere, walking about in the streets, travelling in trains. And shall I tell you something about them?— Take Tarasyuk. He can turn his hand to anything. Anything he does, he has to do it well. That's what happened to him in the army—he learned to fight, just as he'd learn any other trade. He became a first-class shot. He has excellent reflexes, good co-ordination between eyes and hands. He was decorated—not for courage or brains but for always hitting the mark. Well, anything he takes up, it becomes a passion with him, so he took to fighting in a big way. He could see what a rifle does for a man—it gives him power, it brings him distinction. He wanted to be a power in himself. A man with a rifle isn't just a man like any other. In the old days such men turned into bandits. You just try and take Tarasyuk's rifle away from him now! Well, then there came the slogan, "Turn your bayonets against your masters", so Tarasyuk turned. That's the whole story. There's Marxism for you.'

'That's the most genuine kind—straight from life. Didn't you know?'

The chemist went back to his test-tubes.

'How did you get on with the stove specialist?' he asked.

'I'm most grateful to you for sending him. A most interesting man. We spent hours talking Hegel and Croce.'

'Naturally! Took his doctorate in philosophy at Heidelberg. What about the stove?'

'That's not so good.'

'Still smoking?'

'Never stops.'

'He can't have fixed the chimney right. The pipe ought to go out through a flue. Did he let it out through the window?'

'No, through the flue. But it still smokes.'

'Then he can't have found the right air vent. If only we had Tarasyuk! But you'll get it right in the end. Moscow wasn't built in a day. Getting a stove to work isn't like playing the piano, it takes skill. Have you got your logs in?'

'Where am I to get them from?'

'I'll send you the church porter. He's a fuel thief. Takes fences to pieces and turns them into firewood. But you'll have to bargain with him.—No, better the rat catcher.'

They went down to the cloakroom, put their coats on and went out.

'Why the rat catcher? We haven't any rats.'

'That's got nothing to do with it. I'm talking about logs. The rat catcher is an old woman who is doing a big trade in logs. She's got it all set up on a proper business footing—buys up whole houses for fuel. Goodness, it's dark, mind your step. In the old days I could have taken you blindfold anywhere in this district, I knew every stone, I was born near here. But since they've started knocking down the fences I can hardly find my way about even by day. It's like being in a strange town. On the other hand, some extraordinary places have come to light. Have you noticed? Little Empire houses you never knew were there, with a round green table and garden chairs still rotting away on the lawn. The other day I passed a place like that, a sort of little wilderness at a crossing of three streets, and there was an old lady poking about with a stick—she must have been about a hundred. "Hullo, Granny," I said, "are you looking for worms to go fishing?" I was joking, of course, but she took it quite seriously. "No, not worms," she said, "mushrooms." And it's true, you know, the town is getting to be like a forest. There's a smell of rotten leaves and mushrooms.'

'I think I know where you mean—between Silver Street[1] and Silent Street[2], isn't it? The strangest things are always happening to

<hr>

[1] Silver Street: Serebryannaya.   [2] Silent Street: Molchannaya.

me there—either I meet someone I haven't seen in twenty years, or I find something. They say it's dangerous, and no wonder; there's a proper rabbit warren at the back, a whole network of alleys leading to the old thieves' dens near Smolensky. Before you know where you are, they've stripped you to the skin and vanished.'

'And look at those street lamps—they give hardly any light at all. No wonder they call them bruisers. Mind you don't bump yourself.'

6

All sorts of incidents did indeed happen to Yury at the crossroads near Silver Street. One cold dark night, shortly before the October battles, he came across a man lying unconscious on the pavement. He lay right across the kerb, with his arms and legs flung out and his head against a lamp-post. When Yury tried to rouse him he groaned and mumbled a few words, something about a pocket-book. He had been attacked and robbed. His head was knocked about, but Yury found that no bones were broken.

He went to the chemist's shop in the Arbat, rang up for the cab which the hospital used in emergencies and took the patient to the casualty ward.

The wounded man turned out to be a prominent political leader. Yury saw him through his illness and for years afterwards this man acted as his protector, getting him out of several misunderstandings in those days which were so heavy with suspicion.

7

Tonya's plan had been adopted and the family had settled for the winter in three rooms on the top floor.

Sunday was a cold, windy day, dark with heavy snow clouds. Yury was off duty.

The fire was lit in the morning and the stove began to smoke. Nyusha struggled with the damp logs. Tonya, who knew nothing about stoves, kept giving her contradictory advice. Yury, who did know, tried to interfere but his wife took him by the shoulders and gently pushed him out: 'Don't you meddle in this. You'll only pour oil on the flames.'

'Oil would be all right. The trouble is, there is neither oil nor fire.'

'And don't make jokes. This isn't the right time.'

The trouble with the stove upset everyone's plans. They had all hoped to get their chores done before dark and have a free afternoon, but now dinner would be late, Tonya could not wash her hair and various other schemes had to be abandoned.

The fire smoked more and more. As the wind rose, the smoke blew down the chimney and hung about the room in a sooty cloud like a black monster in a magic wood.

Finally Yury drove everyone out into the two other rooms, opened the window, took out half the logs and spaced out the rest, putting chips and birchwood shavings between them.

The air burst in, the curtain swayed and flew up, the papers blew off the desk, a door banged down the passage and the wind started a cat-and-mouse game with what was left of the smoke.

The logs blazed and crackled. The stove gurgled with the flames and came out in spots of red-hot metal like a consumptive flush. The air cleared.

The room grew lighter. The windows steamed over. Yury had fixed them with putty made according to the chemist's recipe and they gave off a warm, greasy smell. An acrid smell of scorching fir bark and the fresh, toilet-water scent of aspen came from the logs drying by the stove.

Nikolay Nikolayevich burst into the room as impetuously as the wind.

'They're fighting in the street. The Cadets are fighting for the Provisional Government against the garrison soldiers who are backing the bolsheviks. They're skirmishing all over the place, you can't count the focal points of the insurrection. I got into trouble coming here—once at the corner of Big Dmitrovka and once at the Nikitsky Gate. Now you can't get through at all, you have to go round. Come on, Yura, put your coat on and come out. You've got to see it. This is history. This happens once in a lifetime.'

But he stayed talking for a couple of hours. Then they had dinner, and by the time he was ready to go home and was dragging Yury out, Gordon burst in, in exactly the same way and with much the same news.

Things had moved on, however. Gordon spoke of increasing rifle fire and of passers-by killed by stray bullets. According to him, all the traffic had stopped. He had got into the side street by a miracle, but the way had closed behind him.

Nikolay Nikolayevich refused to believe him and dashed out, but was back in a minute. He said bullets were whistling down the street, knocking chips of brick and plaster off the corners. There was not a soul outside. All traffic had stopped.

That week, little Sasha caught a cold.

'If I've said it once, I've said it a hundred times, he's not to play near the stove,' Yury scolded. 'It's much worse to let him get too hot than too cold.'

Sasha had a sore throat and a temperature. He had a special, overwhelming terror of being sick, and when Yury tried to examine his throat he pushed away his hand, clenching his teeth, yelling and choking. Neither threats nor arguments had the slightest effect on him. At one moment, however, he gave a large incautious yawn and Yury took advantage of his carelessness to dart in with a teaspoon and hold down his tongue for long enough to get a look at his purple larynx and swollen tonsils covered with white spots. The spots worried him.

He managed, by means of a similar manœuvre, to get a specimen and, as he had a microscope at home, was able to examine it. Luckily it was not diphtheria.

But on the third night Sasha had an attack of nervous croup. His temperature shot up and he could not breathe. Yury was helpless to relieve his suffering and could not bear to watch it. Tonya thought the child was dying. They carried him about the room in turn and this seemed to make him better.

They needed milk and soda water for him. But the street fighting was at its height. Gun and rifle fire never ceased for a moment. Even if Yury had crossed the battle zone at the risk of his life, he would not have found anyone about in the streets beyond it. The city had stopped living till the position was decided.

Yet the outcome was already clear. Rumours came from all sides that the workers were getting the upper hand. Groups of Cadets were fighting on but they were cut off from each other and from their command.

The Sivtsev district was held by soldiers' units who were pressing on towards the centre. Soldiers from the German front and young working boys sat in a trench they had dug down the side street; they were already getting to know the people who lived in the street and joked with those who came and stood outside their gates. There was beginning to be a little movement in this part of the town.

Gordon and Nikolay Nikolayevich, who had got stuck at the Zhivagos', were released from their three days' captivity. Yury had been glad of their presence during Sasha's illness and Tonya forgave them for adding to the general disorder. But they had felt obliged to repay the kindness of their hosts by entertaining them with ceaseless chatter; Yury felt exhausted by it and was glad to see them go.

8

They received a message that their guests had got home safely but that it was too early to speak of the town being at peace. Fighting was still going on in places and several districts were still closed. Yury could not go to the hospital. He missed his work and the research notes and the manuscript which he had left in the drawer of the staff-room desk.

Only within their own small neighbourhood did people come out in the morning and walk a short distance to buy bread or to stand in a crowd round some lucky stranger with a bottle of milk, asking him where he had got it.

Now and then the firing started up again all over the town. It was believed that the two sides were negotiating and that the gun fire died down or increased according to whether the negotiations looked like succeeding or failing.

One evening in late October (according to the old calendar) Yury went, without any particular necessity, to call on one of his colleagues. The street was almost empty; he met hardly anyone on his way. He walked quickly. The first thin powdery snow was coming down, scattered by a rising wind.

He had turned down so many side streets that he had almost lost count of them when the snow thickened and the wind turned into a blizzard, the kind of blizzard that whistles in a field, blanketing it with snow, but which, in town, buffets about at its wits' end as if it had lost its way.

There was something in common between events in the moral and the physical world, between disturbances near and far, on earth and in the sky. Here and there came volleys from islands of half-broken resistance. Bubbles of dying fires rose and broke on the skyline. And the snow too bubbled and funnelled in the wind and smoked on the wet stones under Yury's feet.

A newsboy running with a thick batch of freshly printed papers under his arm and shouting 'All the latest!' overtook him at one of the crossroads.

'Keep the change,' said Yury. The boy peeled a damp sheet off the batch, thrust it into his hand and vanished in the snowstorm.

Yury stopped under a street light to read the headlines. The paper was a late extra, printed on one side only; it gave the official announcement from Petersburg that a Soviet of People's Commissars had been formed and that Soviet power and the Dictatorship of the Proletariat were established in Russia. There followed the first decrees of the new government and various brief news items received by telegraph and telephone.

The blizzard slashed at Yury's eyes and covered the printed page with a grey, rustling, snowy gruel, but it was not the snowstorm that prevented Yury from reading. He was shaken and overwhelmed by the greatness of the moment and the thought of its significance for centuries to come.

Since he had to go on reading all the same, he looked round for a better lit and more sheltered spot. He found that he was standing once again at the bewitched crossroads of Silver and Silent Streets, in front of a tall, five-storey building with a glass-fronted door and a spacious, well-lit hall.

He went in and stood under the ceiling light, reading the news.

Footsteps sounded above him. Someone came slowly half-way down the stairs, stopped as if hesitating, then turned and ran up again to the first-floor landing. A door opened somewhere and two voices welled out, so distorted by echoes that it was impossible to tell if men or women were speaking. Then the door banged and the same steps ran down, this time resolutely.

Yury was absorbed in his paper and had not meant to look up, but the stranger stopped so suddenly at the foot of the stairs that he raised his head.

Before him stood a boy of about eighteen, in a reindeer cap and a stiff reindeer coat worn as in Siberia, fur-side out. He was dark and had narrow Kirghiz eyes. His face had something aristocratic about it, the fugitive spark and reticent delicacy which give an impression of remoteness and are sometimes found in people of a complex, mixed parentage.

The boy seemed to mistake Yury for someone else. He looked at him, puzzled and shy, as if he knew him but could not make up his mind to speak. To put an end to the misunderstanding Yury measured him with a cold, discouraging glance.

The boy turned away, confused, and went to the entrance. There he stopped and looked back once again before going out and banging the heavy glass door shut behind him.

Yury left a few minutes after him. His mind was full of the news; he forgot not only the boy but the colleague he had meant to visit and turned straight for home. But he was distracted on the way by another incident; it was one of those details of everyday life which assumed an inordinate importance in those days.

Not far from his house he stumbled in the dark over a pile of timber. There was a state institution of some sort in the street, and the timber, which looked like a dismantled wooden house from the outskirts of the town, must have been supplied to it for fuel. Not all of it would go into the yard and the rest had been left on the kerb. A sentry with a rifle was on duty by this mountain of logs; he paced up and down the yard and occasionally looked outside the gate.

Without thinking twice, Yury took advantage of a moment when the watchman's back was turned and the wind had raised a cloud of snow into the air to creep up on the dark side, avoiding the lamplight, carefully loosen a beam from the very bottom and pull it out; he loaded it with difficulty on his back and, immediately ceasing to feel its weight (your own load is not a burden), crept off, hugging the shadow of the walls, and brought the wood safely home.

Its arrival was timely; they had run out of firewood. The beam was chopped up, the logs were stacked, Yury lit the stove and squatted in front of it in silence, while Alexander Alexandrovich moved up his armchair and sat warming himself.

Yury took the broadsheet out of the side pocket of his coat and held it out to him:

'Seen this? It's quite something. Have a look.'

Still squatting on his heels and poking the logs, he talked to himself.

'What splendid surgery! You take a knife and you cut out all the old stinking sores. Quite simply, without any nonsense, you take the old monster of injustice which has been accustomed for centuries to being bowed and scraped and curtseyed to, and you sentence it to death.

'This fearlessness, this way of seeing the thing through to the end, has a familiar national look about it. It has something of Pushkin's blazing directness and of Tolstoy's bold attachment to the facts.'

'Pushkin you said? Wait a second. Let me finish. I can't read and listen at the same time,' broke in Alexander Alexandrovich under the mistaken impression that Yury was addressing him.

'And the real stroke of genius is this.—Suppose you told someone to go and create a new world, to start a new era—they would ask you first to clear a space. They would wait for the old centuries to finish before they started to build the new one, they'd want to see a balance sheet, a round figure, a clean page.

'But here, they don't bother with anything like that—"Here it is. Take it or leave it." This new thing, this marvel of history, this revelation is exploded right into the very thick of daily life without the slightest consideration for its course. It doesn't start at the beginning, it starts in the middle, without any specified delays, simply on the first week-day that comes along, right in the middle of the rush hour. That's real genius. Only real greatness can be so misplaced and so untimely.'

9

Winter came, just the kind of winter that had been foretold. It was not as terrifying as the two winters that followed it but it was already of the same sort, dark, hungry and cold, spent in watching the destruction of all that was familiar and the changing of all the foundations of life, and in inhuman efforts to keep hold of life as it slipped out of your grasp.

There were three of them, one after the other, three such terrible winters; and not all that now seems to have happened in the winter of 1917 to 1918 really happened then—some of it may have been later. These three winters which followed one another have now merged into one and it is difficult to tell them apart.

The old life and the new ways did not yet interlock. They were not as yet at daggers drawn, as when the civil war broke out a year later, but neither did they have enough connection with each other. They were like two parts of a puzzle put down side by side and which could not be made to fit.

Everywhere there were new elections: for the running of housing, trade, industry and municipal services. Commissars were being appointed to each, men in black leather jerkins, with unlimited powers and an iron will, armed with means of intimidation and revolvers, who shaved little and slept less.

They knew the slinking bourgeois breed, the average holders of cheap government stocks, and they spoke to them without the slightest pity and with Mephistophelean smiles, as to petty thieves caught in the act.

These were the people who reorganised everything in accordance with the plan, and company after company, enterprise after enterprise became bolshevised.

The Hospital of the Holy Cross was now known as the Second Reformed. Many things had changed in it. Part of the staff had been dismissed and others had resigned because they did not find the work sufficiently rewarding. These were doctors with a fashionable practice and high fees, great talkers and darlings of society, who left out of self-interest but claimed that they had made a civic gesture of protest and looked down on those who had stayed on. Zhivago had stayed.

In the evenings he and Tonya had conversations of this sort:

'Don't forget Wednesday, at the Doctors' Union, they'll have two sacks of frozen potatoes for us in the basement. I'll let you know what time I can get away. We'll have to go together and take the sledge.'

'All right, darling, there's plenty of time. Why don't you go to bed now? It's so late. I wish you'd rest, you can't do everything.'

'There's an epidemic on. Exhaustion lowers resistance to disease. You and Father look terrible. We must do something. If only I knew what. We don't take enough care of ourselves. Listen, Tonya. You aren't asleep?'

'No.'

'I'm not worried about myself, I've got nine lives, but if by any chance I should get ill, you will be sensible, won't you, you mustn't keep me at home. Get me into the hospital at once.'

'Don't talk like that, darling. Pray God you'll keep well. Anyway, we'll cross our bridges when we come to them.'

'Remember, there aren't any honest people left, or any friends. Still less any people who know their business. If anything should happen, don't trust anyone except Pichuzhkin. That's if he's still there, of course. You aren't asleep?'

'No.'

'The pay wasn't good enough, so off they went, now it turns out they had principles and civic sentiments. You meet them in the street, they hardly shake hands, just raise an eyebrow: "So you're working for *them*?"—"I am," I said, "and may it not displease you, I am proud of our privations and I respect those who honour us by imposing them on us."'

10

Most people's meals consisted of boiled millet and fish soup made of herring heads, followed by the rest of the herring as a second course; there was also gruel made by boiling wheat or rye. This was to be the staple food of the majority for a long time to come.

A woman professor, who was a friend of Tonya's, taught her to bake bread in their Dutch stove. The idea was to sell some of the bread and so cover the cost of heating the big stove as in the old days, instead of using the metal cooker which continued to smoke and gave hardly any heat.

Tonya's bread was good but nothing came of her commercial plans. They had to go back to the wretched cooker. They were in a very bad way indeed.

One morning, after Yury had gone to work, Tonya put on her shabby winter coat—she was so run down that she shivered in it even in warm weather—and went out 'hunting'. There were only two logs left.

She wandered about the alleys in the neighbourhood where you could sometimes catch a peasant from one of the villages outside Moscow selling vegetables and potatoes. In the main streets, peasants with loads were liable to be arrested.

Soon she found what she was looking for. An enormous young man in a peasant's coat walked back with her, pulling a sledge which looked as light as a toy, and followed her cautiously into the yard.

Covered up by sacking inside the sledge was a load of birch logs no thicker than the balusters of an old-fashioned country house in a 19th-century photograph. Tonya knew their worth: birch only in name, the wood was of the poorest sort and too freshly cut to be suitable for burning. But as there was no choice, it was pointless to argue.

The young man carried five or six armloads up to the living-room and took in exchange Tonya's small cupboard with looking-glass doors. He carried it down and packed it in his sledge to take away as a present for his wife. Hinting at a future deal in potatoes, he asked the price of the piano.

When Yury came home he said nothing about Tonya's purchase. It would have been more sensible to chop up the cupboard, but they could never have brought themselves to do it.

'There's a note for you on the table, did you see it?' asked Tonya.

'The one sent on from the hospital? Yes, I've had the message already. It's a sick call. I'll certainly go. I'll just have a rest and go. But it's pretty far. It's somewhere near the Triumphal Arch. I've got the address.'

'Have you seen the fee they are offering you? You'd better read it. A bottle of German cognac or a pair of stockings! What sort of people are they, do you imagine? They don't seem to have any idea of how we live nowadays. *Nouveaux riches*, I suppose.'

'Yes, that's certainly from a supplier.'

Suppliers, or concessionnaires or agents, were the names given to small private entrepreneurs who got government contracts for supplying various goods. The state had abolished private trade but it gave them certain facilities at moments of economic crisis.

They were not former men of substance or dismissed heads of old firms—such people did not recover from the blow they had received. They were a new category of business men, people without roots who had been dredged up from the bottom by the war and the revolution.

Yury had a drink of hot water and saccharine whitened with milk and went off to see his patient.

Deep snow covered the street from wall to wall, in places up to the level of the ground-floor windows. Silent half-dead shadows moved all over this expanse, carrying a little food or pulling it along on sledges. There was almost no other traffic.

Old shop signs still hung here and there. They were unconnected with the small co-operatives below them. These shops were all empty and locked, their windows barred or boarded up.

The reason they were locked and empty was not only that there were no goods but that the reorganisation of all sides of life, including trade, had so far remained largely on paper and had not yet affected such trifling details as these boarded-up shops.

11

Yury found the house at the end of Brest Street, near the Tver Gate.

It was an old brick barrack of a house built round a courtyard and with covered wooden stairs running up the courtyard walls.

That day the tenants were at their general meeting, which had been fixed well in advance and was attended by a woman delegate from the Borough Soviet, when a military commission turned up to check arms licences and to search for unlicensed weapons. The lodgers had to go back to their flats and await their turn, but the head of the commission asked the delegate of the Borough Soviet not to go away, as the search would not take long and the meeting could be resumed afterwards.

When Yury arrived, the commission had indeed almost finished, but the flat to which he was going had not yet been searched. Yury was stopped on the landing by a soldier with a rifle, but the head of the commission heard them arguing and ordered the search to be put off until after the doctor had examined his patient.

The door was opened by the master of the house, a polite young man with a pale olive complexion and dark melancholy eyes. He was agitated by a number of things—his wife's illness, the impending search, and his profound reverence for medical science and its representatives.

To save the doctor time and trouble he wished to give him a

brief summary of the case, but his very haste made his speech long and disconnected.

What the doctor saw was a mixture of luxury flat and bargain basement; most of the furniture had been bought in a hurry as an investment against rapid inflation, and consisted of broken-up suites and unrelated single objects originally intended for pairs.

The young man thought his wife's illness had been caused by nervous shock. He explained with many digressions that they had recently bought an antique chiming clock. Its mechanism was past repair and they had bought it for a song merely as a remarkable example of the clock-maker's art (he took the doctor into the next room to see it). And all at once the clock, which had not been wound for years, started of itself, played its complicated minuet of chimes and stopped. His wife was terrified, the young man said, she was convinced that her last hour had struck, and now there she was, delirious; she did not recognise him and she neither ate nor drank.

'So you think it's nervous shock,' Yury said doubtfully. 'Could I see her?'

They went into another room which had a porcelain ceiling lamp, a wide double bed and two mahogany bedside tables. A small woman with big black eyes lay on the edge of the bed, the eiderdown pulled up over her chin. When she saw them, she freed one arm from under the bedclothes and waved them back, the loose sleeve of her dressing-gown falling back to her armpit. Then, as if she were alone in the room, she began to sing something sad in a low voice, which upset her so much that she cried, whimpering like a child and begging to 'go home'. When Yury came up to the bed she turned her back on him and refused to let him touch her.

'I ought to examine her,' said Yury, 'but it doesn't really matter. It's quite clear that she's got typhus—rather badly at that, poor thing; she must be feeling pretty wretched. My advice to you is, put her in a hospital. I know you'd see to it that she had everything she needed at home, but it's most important that she should have constant medical supervision in the first few weeks. Could you get hold of any sort of transport—a cab or even a cart? Of course she'll have to be well wrapped up. I'll give you an admission order.'

'I'll try, but wait a moment. Can it really be that? What a dreadful thing!'

'I'm afraid so.'

'Look, I know I'll lose her if I let her go—couldn't you possibly look after her here? Come as often as you possibly can—I'd be only too happy to pay you anything you like.'

'I am sorry, I've told you: what she needs is constant supervision. Do as I say. I really am advising you for her good.—Now, do your damnedest to get hold of a cab and I'll write out the order. I'd better do it in your house-committee room. The order has to have the house stamp on it, and there are a few other formalities.'

12

One by one, the tenants, muffled up in shawls and fur coats, had returned to the unheated basement which had once been a warehouse for eggs and was now used by the house committee as its board room.

An office desk and several chairs stood at one end of it. As there were not enough chairs, old empty wooden egg crates, turned upside-down, had been placed in a row to form a bench. A pile of them as high as the ceiling towered at the far end of the room. In a corner there was a heap of shavings stuck into lumps with frozen yolk which had dripped from broken eggs. Rats bustled noisily inside the heap, making an occasional sortie into the middle of the stone floor and darting back.

Each time this happened a fat woman tenant climbed, squealing, on to a crate; daintily holding up her skirt and drumming with the heels of her fashionable boots, she shouted in a deliberately hoarse tipsy voice:

'Olya, Olya, you've got rats all over the place. Get away, you filthy brutes. Ai-ai-ai! look at them, they understand, the horrors, look at how they snap their wicked teeth. Ai-ai-ai! it's trying to climb up, it'll get under my skirt, I'm so frightened! Look the other way, gentlemen. Sorry, I forgot, you're comrade citizens nowadays, not gentlemen.'

Her astrakhan cape hung open over the three quaking layers of her double chin and rich, silk-swathed bosom and stomach. She had once been the belle of her circle of small tradesmen and shop clerks, but now her small pig eyes were hardly more than slits between her swollen eyelids. A rival had once tried to splash her with vitriol but had missed, and only a drop or two had ploughed traces, so slight as to be almost becoming, on her cheek and at one corner of her mouth.

'Stop yelling, Khrapugina. How can we get on with our work?' said the woman delegate of the Borough Council, who had been elected chairman and was sitting behind the desk.

The delegate had known the house and many of the lodgers all her life. Before the meeting she had had an unofficial talk with Aunt

Fatima, the caretaker, who had once lived with her husband and children in a corner of the filthy basement, but who now had only her daughter with her and had been moved into two light rooms on the first floor.

'Well, Fatima, how are things going?' the delegate had asked.

Fatima complained that she could not cope with such a big house and so many lodgers all by herself, and that she got no help because, although each family was supposed to take it in turn to clean the stairs and the door steps, not one of them did it.

'Don't worry, Fatima, we'll show them. What kind of a house committee is this anyway? They're hopeless. Criminal elements are given shelter, people of doubtful morals stay on unregistered. We'll get rid of them and elect another. I'll make you house-manageress, only don't make a fuss.'

Aunt Fatima begged to be let off, but the delegate refused to listen.

Looking round the room and deciding that enough people were present, she called for silence and opened the meeting with a short introductory speech. She condemned the slackness of the house committee, proposed that candidates should be put up for the election of a new one and went on to other business.

In conclusion she said casually:

'So that's how it is, comrades. Frankly speaking, this is a big house, it's suitable for a hostel. Look at all the delegates who come to town to attend conferences, and we don't know where to put them. It's been decided to take over the building for a Borough Council hostel for visitors from the country and to call it the Tiverzin Hostel, in honour of Comrade Tiverzin who lived here before he was deported, as everyone knows. No objections? Now as to dates. There's no hurry, you've got a whole year. Working people will be rehoused, others must find accommodation for themselves and are given a year's notice.'

'We're all working people! Every one of us! We're all workers,' people shouted from every side, and one voice sobbed out: 'It's Great-Russian chauvinism! All the nations are equal now! I know what you're hinting at.'

'Not all at once, please. Who am I to answer first? What have nations got to do with it, Citizen Valdyrkin? Look at Khrapugina, you can't think there's a question of nationality involved in her case, and we are certainly evicting her.'

'You are, are you! Just you try and evict me, we'll see about that! You crushed sofa! You crumpled bedsheet!' Khrapugina screamed, calling the delegate by every idiotic name she could think of in the heat of the quarrel.

'What a she-devil!' Aunt Fatima was indignant. 'Haven't you any shame?'

'Don't you meddle, Fatima, I can look after myself,' said the delegate. 'Stop it, Khrapugina, I know all about you. Shut up, I tell you, or I'll hand you over to the authorities at once, before they catch you making vodka and keeping a thieves' den.'

The uproar was at its height when Yury came into the room. He asked the first person he could get to listen if he could see a member of the house committee; the other held up his hands like a trumpet in front of his mouth and shouted above the noise:

'Ga-li-ull-li-na! You're wanted.'

Yury could not believe his ears. A thin elderly woman with a slight stoop—Aunt Fatima—came up to him; her face would have been enough to tell him that she was Galiullin's mother. He did not, however, identify himself at once, but said:

'One of your lodgers has got typhus' (he told her the name). 'There are various precautions that have to be taken to prevent it spreading. And another thing, the patient has to be taken to the hospital. I'll make out an admission order; the house committee has to stamp it. How and where can we do that?'

She thought he meant, 'How is the patient to get to the hospital?' and replied: 'There's a cab coming from the Borough Council for Comrade Demina, that's the delegate. She's very kind, Comrade Demina, I'll tell her, she's sure to let your patient have the cab. Don't worry, Comrade Doctor, we'll get her there all right.'

'That's wonderful. Actually I only meant where could I write out the order. But if there's a cab as well . . . May I ask you, are you the mother of Lieutenant Galiullin? We were in the same unit at the front.'

Galiullina started violently and grew pale. She caught hold of Yury's hand: 'Come outside. We'll talk in the yard.'

As soon as they were outside the door she said quickly: 'Talk softly, for God's sake. Don't ruin me. Yusupka's taken the wrong road. Judge for yourself—what is he? He was an apprentice, a worker. He ought to understand—simple people are much better off now, a blind man can see that, nobody can deny it. I don't know what you feel yourself, maybe it would be all right for you, but it's a sin for Yusupka, God forgive him. Yusupka's father was a private, he was killed; they say his face was shot off, and his arms and legs.'

Her voice shook; she waited till she was more calm, then she went on:

'Come. I'll get you the cab. I know who you are. He was

here for a couple of days. He told me. He said you knew Lara Guishar. She was a good girl, I remember her, she used to come and see us. What she's like now, I don't know—who can tell with you people? It's natural for gentry to stick together. But for Yusupka it's a sin. Come, let's ask for the cab. I'm sure Comrade Demina will let you have it. You know who Comrade Demina is? She's Olya Demina, a seamstress she was, worked for Lara's Mama, that's who she is, and she's from here too. From this very house. Come along.'

13

It was quite dark. The darkness was all round them. Only the small round patch of light from Demina's pocket torch jumped from snow-drift to snow-drift four or five paces ahead, confusing them rather than lighting their way. The darkness was all around them, and they had left behind them the house where so many people had known Lara, where she had often come as a girl and where, they said, Antipov, her husband, had grown up.

'Will you really find your way without a torch, Comrade Doctor?' Demina was playfully patronising. 'If not, I'll lend you mine. It's a fact, you know, I had a real crush on her when we were little girls. They had a dressmaking establishment. I was an apprentice in the workshop. I've seen her this year. She stopped on her way through Moscow. I said: "Where are you off to, silly? Stay here. Come and live with us. We'll find you a job." But it wasn't any good, she wouldn't. Well, it's her business. She married Pasha with her head, not with her heart; she's been daft ever since. Off she went.'

'What do you think of her?'

'Mind—it's slippery. I don't know how many times I've told them not to throw the slops out of the door—might as well talk to a wall.—What do I think of her? How do you mean, think? What should I think? I haven't any time to think.—Here's where I live.—One thing I didn't tell her—her brother, who was in the army, I think they've shot him. As for her mother, my mistress she used to be—I'll see that she's all right. Well, I've got to go in—good-bye.'

So they parted. The light of Demina's little torch shot into the narrow stone entrance and ran on, lighting up the stained walls and the dirty stairs while Yury was left surrounded by the darkness. On his right lay Garden Triumph Street[1], on his left Garden Coach Street[2].

---

[1] Garden Triumph Street: Sadovaya Triumfalnaya.
[2] Garden Coach Street: Sadovaya Karetnaya.

Running into the black snowy distance, they were no longer streets but cuttings in the jungle of stone buildings, like cuttings through the dense forests of Siberia or the Urals.

At home it was light and warm.

'Why are you so late?' asked Tonya. 'An extraordinary thing happened while you were out,' she went on before he could reply. 'Really quite unaccountable.—Yesterday Father broke the alarm clock—I forgot to tell you—he was terribly upset, it was the only clock in the house that worked. He tried to mend it, he tinkered and tinkered with it, but it was no good. The clock-maker round the corner wanted a ridiculous price—three pounds of bread. I didn't know what to do and Father was completely in the dumps. Well, about an hour ago—can you believe it?—there was a sudden ringing—such a piercing, deafening noise, we were all frightened out of our wits! It was the alarm clock! Can you imagine such a thing! It had started up again, all by itself.'

'My typhus hour has struck,' laughed Yury. He told her about his typhus patient and the chiming clock.

14

But Yury did not get typhus until much later. In the meantime the Zhivagos were tried to the limits of endurance. They had nothing and they were starving. Yury went to see the party member he had once saved, the one who had been the victim of a robbery. This man helped him so far as he could, but the civil war was beginning and he was hardly ever in Moscow; besides, he regarded the privations people were suffering in those days as only natural, and himself went hungry, though he concealed it.

Yury tried the couple in the house in Brest Street—his former typhus patient and her husband, the 'supplier'—but in the intervening months the young man had disappeared and nothing was known about his wife either. Galiullina was out when Yury called, most of the lodgers were new, and Demina was at the front.

One day he received an allocation of logs at the official price. He had to fetch them from the Vindava Station. Walking home along the endless stretches of Meshchanskaya Street [1]—keeping an eye on the driver of the cart loaded with his unexpected treasure—he noticed that the street looked quite different; he found that he was swaying from side to side, his legs were refusing to carry him. 'This is it,' he thought,

[1] Meshchanskaya: Bourgeois Street.

'I'm done for, it's typhus.' The driver picked him up when he fell down and slung him on top of the logs. Yury never knew how he got home.

15

He was delirious at intervals for almost a fortnight. He dreamed that Tonya had put two streets on his writing-table, Garden Coach Street on his left and Garden Triumph Street on his right, and had lit the table lamp; its warm orange glow lit up the streets and now he could write. So he was writing.

He was writing what he should have written long ago and had always wished to write, but never could. Now it came to him quite easily, he wrote eagerly and said exactly what he wanted to say. Only now and then a boy got in his way, a boy with narrow Kirghiz eyes, in an unbuttoned reindeer coat worn fur-side out, as in the Urals or Siberia.

He knew for certain that this boy was the spirit of his death or, to put it quite plainly, that he was his death. Yet how could he be his death if he was helping him to write a poem? How could death be useful, how was it possible for death to be a help?

The subject of his poem was neither the entombment nor the resurrection but the days between; the title was 'Turmoil'.

He had always wanted to describe how for three days the black, raging, worm-filled earth had assailed the deathless incarnation of love, storming it with rocks and rubble—as waves fly and leap at a sea coast, cover and submerge it—how for three days the black hurricane of earth raged, advancing and retreating.

Two lines kept coming into his head:

'We are glad to be near you.'
and
'Time to wake up.'

Near him, touching him, were hell, corruption, dissolution, death; yet equally near him were the spring and Mary Magdalene and life.— And it was time to awake. Time to awake and to get up. Time to arise, time for the resurrection.

16

He began to get better. At first he took everything for granted like a half-wit. He remembered nothing, he could see no connection between one thing and another and was not surprised at anything. His wife fed him on white bread and butter and sugared tea; she gave him coffee. He had forgotten that such things did not exist and he enjoyed their taste like poetry or like fairy tales, as something right and proper for a convalescent. Soon, however, he began to think and wonder.

'How did you get all this?' he asked Tonya.

'Your Granya got it for us.'

'What Granya?'

'Granya Zhivago.'

'Granya Zhivago?'

'Well yes, your brother Yevgraf, from Tomsk. Your half-brother. He came every day while you were ill.'

'Does he wear a reindeer coat?'

'That's right. So you did see him. You were unconscious nearly all the time. He said he had run into you on the stairs in some house or other. He knew you—he meant to speak to you, but apparently you frightened him to death! He worships you, he reads every word you write. The things he got for us! Rice, currants, sugar! He's gone back now. He wants us to go there too. He's a strange boy, he's a bit enigmatic. I think he must have some sort of connection with the government. He says we ought to go away for a year or two, get away from the big towns, "go back to the land" for a time, he says. I thought of the Krueger place. I asked him what he thought, and he said it was a very good idea. We could grow vegetables and there's the forest all round. There isn't any point in dying without a struggle, like sheep.'

In April that year Zhivago set out with his whole family for the former Varykino estate, near the town of Yuryatin, far away in the Urals.

7
The Journey

IT was the end of March. As usual the last few days of this month were the first warm days of the year, a false spring to be followed by a much colder spell.

The Zhivagos were getting ready to leave. To disguise the reason for the bustle, they told the tenants who now swarmed like sparrows in the house that the flat was being spring-cleaned for Easter.

Yury was against the journey. He had so far thought that it would come to nothing and had therefore made only tentative objections, but the time had evidently come for him to say what he really thought.

He did this at a family council made up of himself, Tonya and her father. 'Do you think I'm wrong?' he asked them at the end. 'Do you still insist on going?'

'You say that we must manage as best we can for the next couple of years,' said Tonya, 'until the new system of land tenure is established and we can get a plot to grow vegetables outside Moscow. But how are we to last out until then? That's the really interesting point and you haven't told us.'

'It's sheer madness,' her father backed her up.

'All right,' Yury gave in. 'What bothers me is the complete uncertainty. We are going blindfold, into the blue, to a place we know nothing about. Of the three people who lived in Varykino, Mother and Grandmother are dead and Grandfather is being held as a hostage, that is if he is still alive.

'You know he made some sort of a deal in the last year of the war, sold the forests and the factories or else put the title-deeds in the name of someone else, a bank or a private person, I don't know. In fact we don't know anything. Who does the estate belong to now? I don't mean whose property is it, I don't care a damn, but who is responsible for it? Who runs it? Is the timber being cut? Are the factories working? And, above all, who is in power in that part of the country, or rather, who will be by the time we get there?

'You are relying on Mikulitsin, the old manager, to see us through, but who is to tell us if he is still there? Or even if he is still alive?

Anyway, what do you know about him except his name—and that we only remember because Grandfather had such difficulty in pronouncing it.

'However, I don't want to go on raising difficulties. You have made up your minds and I've agreed. There is no point in putting it off. We must just find out exactly what one does about travelling nowadays.'

2

Yury went to the Yaroslavsky Station to find out.

Endless queues of passengers moved across the halls along gangways between wooden handrails. Below them, lying on the stone floors, were people in grey army coats, who coughed, spat, rolled over and spoke in unexpectedly loud voices, miscalculating the amplifying echo of the vaults.

They were mostly typhus patients whom the overcrowded hospitals often discharged the day after the crisis. Yury, as a doctor, had often had to do this himself, but he had no idea that there could be so many of these unfortunates or that they were forced to seek refuge in railway stations.

'You must get a priority,' a porter in a white apron told him. 'Then you must come every day to ask if there is a train. Trains are as rare as gold nowadays, it's a question of luck. And, of course' (he rubbed his two fingers with his thumb) 'a little flour or something . . . Wheels don't run without oil, you know, and what's more' (he tapped his Adam's apple) 'you won't get far without a little vodka.'

3

About that time Alexander Alexandrovich was called in several times to act as consultant to the Higher Economic Council, and Yury to treat a member of the government who was dangerously ill. They were both paid in what was then the highest currency, chits on the first of the newly introduced closed-consumer shops.

The shop was an old army warehouse next to the Monastery of St. Simon. The doctor and the professor went through the monastery and the barrack-yard and straight through a low stone door into a vaulted cellar. It sloped down and widened at its further end, where a counter ran across from wall to wall; behind it stood an attendant, weighing, measuring and handing out goods with calm unhurried movements, crossing off the items on his list with broad pencil strokes, and occasionally replenishing his stock from the back of the store.

There were not many customers and it soon came to their turn. 'Containers,' said the storekeeper, glancing at the chits. The professor and the doctor held out several pillow-cases, both large and small, and, with bulging eyes, watched them being filled with flour, cereals, macaroni, sugar, fats, soap, matches and paper packets which were found later to contain Caucasian cheese.

Overwhelmed by the storekeeper's generosity and anxious not to waste his time, they hurriedly stuffed their bundles into big sacks and slung them over their shoulders.

They came out of the vault intoxicated, not by the mere thought of food, but by the consciousness that they too were of use in the world and did not live in vain, and had deserved the praise and thanks which Tonya would shower on them at home.

4

While the men disappeared for whole days into government offices, chasing travel documents or registering the flat, so that they should be able to come back to it on their return to Moscow, Tonya sorted the family belongings.

Walking up and down the three rooms now officially assigned to the Zhivagos, she weighed even the smallest article twenty times in her hand with a preoccupied air before deciding whether to put it into the pile of things they were taking with them. Only a small part of their luggage was intended for their personal use, the rest would serve as currency on the way and in the first weeks after their arrival.

The spring breeze came in through the open window, tasting faintly of newly cut white bread. Cocks were crowing and children playing and shouting in the yard. The more the room was aired, the more noticeable became the smell of mothballs from the open trunks in which their winter clothes had been packed.

The choice of things to be taken or left behind was dictated by an elaborate theory, based on the observations of those who had left earlier and communicated by them to their friends at home. Reduced to a few simple, all-important rules, it guided Tonya's actions, almost as if a secret voice coming from outside the window with the squeals of children and the chirruping of sparrows, were whispering instructions to her.

'Lengths for dresses,' said the voice, 'but luggage is checked on the way, so this is dangerous, unless they are tacked up to look like clothes. Materials of all kinds, clothes, preferably coats if not too worn. No trunks or baskets (there won't be any porters); be sure to take nothing useless and tie up everything in bundles small enough for a woman or a child to carry. Salt and tobacco have been found very useful, but risky. Money in kerenkas [1]. Documents are the hardest thing to carry safely.' And so on and so on.

5

On the day before they left there was a snowstorm. Grey clouds of spinning snow flew up into the sky, came back to earth as a white whirlwind and blew away into the dark distance of the street, shrouding it in white.

All the luggage was packed. The flat, with such things as remained in it, was being left in the care of an elderly couple; they were a former shop assistant and his wife, relations of Yegorovna's who lived in Moscow and who, last winter, had helped Tonya to trade clothes and furniture for potatoes and logs.

(Markel could not be trusted. At the militia post which he had selected as his political club he did not actually say that his former masters sucked his blood, but he accused them, instead, of having kept him in ignorance all these years and deliberately concealed from him that the world is derived from the apes.)

Tonya took the couple on a final survey of the house, fitting keys to locks, opening and shutting drawers and cupboards and thinking of last-minute instructions.

The chairs and tables had been pushed against the walls, the curtains taken down, and there was a pile of bundles in the corner. The rooms, bare, stripped of their winter comfort and watched through the bare windows by the storm, reminded each of them of past sorrows. Yury thought of his mother's death, and Tonya and Alexander Alexandrovich of the death and funeral of Anna. They felt unreasonably as if it were their last night in the house and they were never to see it again, and although, to avoid distressing one another, they did not speak of their foreboding, it saddened them and they struggled with tears as they looked back over their life under this roof.

In spite of all this, Tonya did her best to keep up appearances by

[1] Paper money introduced by the Kerensky Government.

carrying on an endless conversation with the caretaker's wife. She exaggerated in her mind the favour which the couple were doing her and, anxious not to seem ungrateful, kept apologising, going next door and coming back with presents for the woman—blouses and lengths of cotton and silk prints. The materials were all dark with light check or polka-dot patterns, and the street, as it looked in through the bare windows on this farewell evening, was also dark with its checkerwork of bricks and polka dots of snow.

6

They left the house at dawn. The other tenants should have been asleep but one of them, Zevorotina, was incurably fond of organising social events and woke them all up shouting: 'Attention! Attention! Comrades! Hurry up! Come and say good-bye to the former[1] Gromekos!'

They all poured out on to the back porch (the front door was kept boarded up nowadays) and stood in a semicircle, as though for a photograph.

They yawned and shivered and tugged at the shabby coats they had thrown over their shoulders, and stamped about in the huge felt boots they had hastily pulled on over their bare feet.

Markel had already managed to get drunk on some suicidal brew he had succeeded in obtaining even in those 'dry' days, and hung like a corpse over the worn railings of the porch, which threatened to collapse under him. He insisted on carrying the luggage to the station and was very much offended when his offer was refused; at last they got rid of him and came out into the side street.

It was still dark. The wind had fallen and the snow fell thicker than the night before. Large, woolly snowflakes drifted down lazily and hung above the ground, hesitating to settle.

In the Arbat it was lighter. Here the snow came down like a white stage curtain as wide as the street, slowly descending and swinging its fringe round the legs of the passers-by, so that they quite lost the sense of moving forward and felt they were marking time.

There was not a soul about except the travellers, but soon they were overtaken by a cab with a snow-white nag and a driver who looked as if he had been rolled in dough; for a fabulous sum (worth less than a copeck in those days) he took them to the station with their luggage. Only Yury, at his own request, was allowed to walk.

[1] Russian equivalent of *ci-devant*.

7

He found Tonya and her father already standing in one of the endless queues. Nyusha and Sasha were walking about outside and occasionally looked in to see if it were time to join the grown-ups; they gave off a strong smell of paraffin, which had been thickly smeared on their necks, wrists and ankles as a protection against lice.

The queues went up to the gates of the platforms, but in fact the passengers had to board the train a good half mile further down the line. There were not enough cleaners and the station was filthy, and the tracks in front of the platforms were unusable because of dirt and ice. The trains stopped further out.

Tonya waved to Yury and, when he was close enough, shouted instructions as to where he was to get their travel warrants stamped.

'Show me what they've put,' she asked him when he came back. He held out a wadge of papers across the hand-rail.

'That's for the special coach,' said the man behind her in the queue, reading over her shoulder.

The man in front of her was more explicit. He was one of those sticklers for form who in every possible circumstance know the appropriate regulation, and are able to discuss it impersonally and accept it without question.

'This stamp,' he explained, 'gives you the right to claim seats in a coach with classes, that is to say a passenger coach, if there is a passenger coach on the train.'

The whole queue joined in at once.

'Passenger coach indeed! If you can get a seat on the buffers you must be thankful nowadays!'

'Don't listen to them,' said the formalist. 'I'll explain, it's quite simple. As all special trains have been abolished there is only one type of train, the same for all—army, convicts, cattle, people—it's all one and the same train. Why mislead the man?' he turned to the crowd. 'Words don't cost anything, you can say what you like, but you should say it clearly, so that he can understand.'

'A lot you've explained!' he was shouted down. 'A lot you've said when you've told him he's got stamps for the special coach! You should look at a man first, before you start explaining. How can anyone with such a face go in the special coach? The special coach is full of sailors. A sailor has a trained eye and a gun. He takes a look at him and what does he see?—A member of the propertied classes! Worse than that—a doctor, former gentry. He pulls out his gun—and good-bye.'

There is no knowing to what lengths the sympathy aroused by the doctor's case would have gone if the crowd had not turned its attention to something else.

For some time people had been looking curiously through the enormous plate-glass windows at the tracks, which were roofed in for several hundred yards. The falling snow could be seen only beyond the far end of the roofs; seen so far away, it looked almost still, sinking to the ground as slowly as bread-crumbs, thrown to fishes, sink through water.

During the past half-hour unidentified figures had been strolling into the distance along the tracks, singly or in groups. At first they were taken for railwaymen attending to their duties, but now a whole mob rushed out, and from the direction in which they were running there appeared a small cloud of smoke.

'Open up the doors, you crooks!' yelled voices in the queue. The crowd stirred and swung against the doors, those at the back pushing those in front.

'Look what's going on! Here they've locked us in, and yet out there, some bastards have found a way round and jumped the queue. Open up, you devils, or we'll bust the gates! Come on, mates, let's push!'

'They needn't envy that lot, the fools,' said the omniscient legalist. 'Those men are conscripts, called up for forced labour from Petrograd. They were going to be sent to Vologda from the Northern Station, but they've been diverted to the eastern front. They're not travelling of their own free will. They're under escort. They'll be digging trenches.'

8

They had been three days on the way but had not moved far from Moscow. The cold weather went on. Outside the window, tracks, fields, woods and village roofs, all were deep in snow.

The Zhivagos had been lucky enough to get a corner to themselves on the top tier of bunks, right up against the long bleary window underneath the ceiling, and here they had settled down in a family group.

Tonya had never travelled in a freight truck before. It stood high above the ground and had heavy sliding doors. The first time they got in Yury lifted the women in his arms, but later they learned to climb in and out by themselves.

The coach looked to Tonya no better than a stable on wheels and she had expected it to fall apart at the first jolt. But for three days they had been jolted back and forth and from side to side as the train had changed speed or direction, for three days the wheels had rattled quickly underneath them like the sticks on a mechanical toy drum, and they were still safe. Her apprehensions had been groundless.

The train had twenty-three coaches (the Zhivagos were in coach fourteen). When it stopped at country stations, only the front or middle or tail stood beside the short platform.

Sailors were in front, free passengers in the middle, and the labour conscripts in eight coaches at the back. There were about five hundred of them, people of all ages, conditions and professions.

They were a remarkable sight—rich, smart lawyers and stockbrokers from Petersburg side by side with cabbies, floor polishers, bath attendants, Tartar rag-and-bone merchants, escaped lunatics, shopkeepers, and monks, all lumped together with the exploiting classes.

The lawyers and stockbrokers sat in their shirt-sleeves round the red-hot iron stoves, telling each other endless stories, joking and laughing. They were people with connections. They felt no anxiety; they had influential relations pulling strings for them at home, and if it came to the worst, they could buy themselves off later on.

The others, in boots and kaftans, or barefoot and in long shirts worn outside their trousers, with or without beards, stood at the half-open doors of the airless truck, holding on to the sides or to the boards nailed across the opening, and gazed sullenly at the peasants and the villages by the wayside, speaking to no one. They had no influential friends. They had nothing to hope for.

There were too many conscripts for the trucks allotted to them and the overflow had been put among the free passengers, including those of coach fourteen.

9

Whenever the train stopped, Tonya sat up cautiously so as not to knock her head on the ceiling, and looked down through the crack of the door to see if it were worth while to go out. This depended on the size of the station, the probable length of the halt and the consequent likelihood of profitable barter.

So it was on this occasion. The train had awoken her from a doze by slowing down. The number of points and switches over which it bumped and rattled suggested that the station was fairly large.

She rubbed her eyes, tidied her hair and, after rummaging at the bottom of a bundle, pulled out a towel embroidered with cockerels, horse collars and wheels.

Yury, who had also woken up, helped her down from the bunk. Signal huts and lamp-posts drifted past the door, followed by trees holding out napkins of snow hospitably towards the train [1]. Long before it had stopped, sailors jumped off into the untrodden snow and raced round the corner of the station building to where peasant women were usually to be found trading illegally in food.

The sailors' black uniforms with bell-bottom trousers and ribbons fluttering from their peakless caps gave an air of reckless speed to their advance and made other people give way as before the onrush of racing skiers or skaters.

Round the corner, girls and women from villages near-by, hiding behind each other and as excited as if they were at the fortune-teller's, stood in single file in the shelter of the station wall, selling cucumbers, cottage cheese, platterfuls of boiled beef and rye pancakes kept hot and savoury in quilted napkins. Muffled up in shawls tucked inside their sheepskins, the women blushed a fiery red at the sailors' jokes, but they were terrified of them, for it was generally sailors who formed the units organised to fight against speculation and the forbidden 'free market'.

They were soon, however, rescued from their embarrassment as the train stopped and civilian passengers joined the crowd. Trade became brisk.

Tonya walked down the file, inspecting the wares, her towel flung over her shoulder, as if she were only going to the back of the station to wash in the snow. Several women had called out: 'Hey, what do you want for your napkin?' but she continued on her way, escorted by her husband.

At the end of the row there was a woman in a black shawl with a crimson pattern. She saw the embroidered towel and her bold eyes lit up. Glancing round cautiously, she sidled up to Tonya and, un-covering her wares, whispered eagerly: 'Look at this. I bet you haven't seen that in a long while. Like it? Don't think about it too long or it will be gone. Like to give me your napkin for a half-one?'

Tonya missed the last word.

'What do you mean, my dear?'

The woman meant half a hare, roasted whole from head to tail and chopped in two. She held it up. 'I'm telling you, I'll give you

[1] Traditionally, bread and salt were offered on a napkin as a sign of welcome to guests.

a half-one for your napkin. What are you staring at? It isn't dog's meat. My husband is a hunter. It's hare all right.'

They exchanged their goods. Each believed that she had had the best of the bargain. Tonya felt as ashamed as if she had swindled the peasant woman, while she, delighted with her deal, called a friend, who had also sold out her wares, and made off with her, home to their village while the going was good, striding down the snowy path into the distance.

At this moment there was an uproar in the crowd. An old woman was screaming: 'Hey you! Where are you off to? Where's my money? When did you pay me, you shameless thief? Look at him, greedy pig, you call him and he doesn't even bother to turn round. Stop! Stop, I tell you, Mister Comrade! I've been robbed! Stop, thief! There he goes, that's him, catch him!'

'Which one?'

'That one, the one who's clean-shaven and grinning.'

'Is that the one with the hole in his sleeve?'

'Yes, yes, catch him, the Saracen!'

'The one with the patched elbow?'

'Yes, yes. O, dear Lord, I've been robbed.'

'What's going on here?'

'Fellow over there bought some milk and pies, filled his belly and went off without paying, so the old woman is crying.'

'That shouldn't be allowed. Why don't they go after him?'

'Go after him! He's got straps and cartridge belts all over him. He'll go after you.'

10

There were several conscripts in coach fourteen. With them was their guard, Voronyuk. Three of the men stood out from the rest. They were Prokhor Pritulyev who had been a cashier in a government wine-shop in Petersburg, the 'casher' as he was called; Vassya Brykin, a sixteen-year-old boy apprenticed to an ironmonger; and Kostoyed-Amursky, a grey-haired revolutionary belonging to the labour-co-operative party, who had been in all the penal settlements of the old régime and was now discovering those of the new.

The conscripts who had all been strangers when they were picked up were gradually getting to know each other. It turned out that the 'casher' and Vassya, the apprentice, came from the same part of the country—the Vyatka province—and also that the train would be going through their district.

Pritulyev came from Malmysh. His hair was close-cropped and he was pock-marked, squat and hideous. His grey tunic, black with sweat under the arms, fitted him snugly like a fleshy woman's bodice. He would sit for hours as silent as a graven image, thoughtfully scratching the warts on his hands until they bled and suppurated.

One afternoon, a few months earlier, he had been walking down the Nevsky when he became involved in a militia round-up at the corner of Liteyny Street. He had to show his papers and was found to hold a fourth-class ration-book, the kind issued to non-workers on which nothing could ever be bought. He was consequently detained, with many others who were arrested for the same reason, and taken under escort to barracks. His party was to be sent, like the one preceding it, to dig trenches on the Archangel front, but was diverted on its way and sent East through Moscow.

Pritulyev had a wife in Luga, where he had worked before the war. She heard of his misfortune at second hand and, imagining him to be on his way north, rushed off to Vologda (the junction for Archangel) to look for him and try to obtain his release. But the unit had not gone there and she might just as well have stayed at home. You didn't know where you were any more these days.

In Petersburg, where he had been transferred at the beginning of the war, Pritulyev had lived with a certain Pelagia Tyagunova. At the time he was arrested they had been for a walk and had just said good-bye, she to go home and he to keep an appointment somewhere else; looking down Liteyny Street he could still see her back disappearing among the crowd.

She was a plump middle-class woman with a stately carriage, beautiful hands and thick hair which she wore in a plait and occasionally tossed, sighing, over her shoulder. This Pelagia was now in the coach, for she had chosen of her own free will to accompany him on his journey.

It was difficult to know what it was that attracted women to such a dull and ugly man but certainly they clung to him. In a coach further forward there was another woman friend of his, Ogryskova, a bony girl with white eyelashes who had somehow wangled her way on to the train and whom Tyagunova called 'the squirt', 'the snout' and many other unpleasant names.

The two rivals were at daggers drawn and avoided one another carefully. Ogryskova never appeared in coach fourteen and it was indeed a puzzle to know how she ever managed to meet the object of her passion; but perhaps she was content merely to gaze on him from afar on the occasions when all the passengers got out to help refuel the engine.

Vassya's story was quite different. His father had been killed in the war and his mother had sent him to Petersburg to be apprenticed to his uncle.

The uncle kept a private shop in Apraksin Market. One day last winter he had been summoned by the local Soviet to answer a few questions. He mistook the door and walked into the office of the Labour Corps selection board. The room was full of conscripts; after a while soldiers came in, surrounded the men and took them to the Semyonovsky barracks for the night and to the station in the morning.

The news of so many arrests spread and the prisoners' families came to say good-bye to them. Among them were Vassya and his aunt. His uncle begged the guard (the Voronyuk who was now in coach fourteen) to let him out to take leave of his wife. The guard refused unless he could provide a hostage. The uncle and aunt offered up Vassya. Vassya was put inside and his uncle was let out. This was the last he ever saw of his aunt or uncle.

When the trick was discovered, Vassya, who had suspected nothing, burst into tears, grovelled at Voronyuk's feet, kissed his hands and begged him to let him go, but it was no good. It was not that Voronyuk was a harsh man by nature, but discipline was very strict in these troubled times; he answered for the number of his charges with his life and the numbers were checked by roll-call. That was how Vassya came to be in the labour corps.

The co-operativist, Kostoyed, who had always enjoyed the respect of his jailers and succeeded in being on good terms with them whatever the government, had more than once called the attention of the head of the convoy to Vassya's intolerable situation. The head of the convoy admitted that it was a terrible misunderstanding but said there were formal difficulties in the way of his doing anything until they arrived; he promised to do his best afterwards.

Vassya was an attractive boy with regular features, who looked like a royal page or an angel in a picture. He was unusually innocent and unspoilt. His favourite occupation was to sit on the floor at the feet of his elders, looking up at them, his hands clasped round his knees, and listen to their talk or to the tales of their adventures. By watching the muscles of his face, as he only just restrained himself from tears or choked with laughter, you could almost follow the conversation.

12

The Zhivagos had invited the co-operativist Kostoyed to dinner. He sat in their corner, sucking a leg of hare with a loud wheezing noise. He was very much afraid of draughts and changed his position several times until he at last found one that suited him. 'That's better,' he said. He finished his drumstick, sucked his fingers clean, wiped them on his handkerchief, thanked his hosts and said : 'Your window doesn't fit properly, it ought to be sealed up with putty.—But to go back to our discussion, of course roast hare is an excellent thing, but to conclude from this that the peasants are flourishing is rash, to say the least, if you'll forgive my saying so.'

'O come,' said Yury. 'Look at all these stations we stop at. The trees and the fences are still standing, they haven't been chopped down for firewood. And the markets! And the women! Think how wonderful!—At least somewhere life is still going on and people are pleased with it. Not everyone is wretched. Isn't that a justification of everything?'

'It would be if it were so, but it simply isn't. How can you think it is? You should just look at what is going on in the interior, anywhere fifty or a hundred miles from the railway. The peasants are in revolt, there are ceaseless risings. You'll say that they are fighting the Reds or Whites indiscriminately, whoever may be in power, that they are simply against any established authority because they don't know what they want. Allow me to differ. The peasant knows very well what he wants, better than you or I do, but he wants something quite different.

'When the revolution came and woke him up, he decided that this was the fulfilment of his dream, his ancient dream of living anarchically on his own land by the work of his hands, in complete independence and without owing anything to anyone. Instead of that, he found he had only exchanged the old oppression of the tsarist state for the new, much harsher yoke of the revolutionary super-state. Can you wonder that the villages are restless and can't settle down! And you say they are happy! No, there are a lot of things you don't know, my dear fellow, and I am afraid it looks as if you didn't want to know them.'

'O all right, I dare say I don't.—Why, for goodness' sake, do I have to know everything and worry myself sick over every blessed thing? History hasn't consulted me, I have to put up with whatever happens, so why shouldn't I ignore the facts? You tell me it's unrealistic. But where is reality in Russia to-day? My belief is that it's been frightened out of existence. It's true that I want to believe that the peasants are better off and the villages are prosperous.—If I can't believe that, then what am I to do? Who am I to believe, what am I to live by? I've got to go on living, I've got a family.'

He made a despairing gesture and, leaving the argument to his father-in-law, moved away and hung his head over the edge of the bunk to look at what was going on below.

The 'casher' Pritulyev and his friend Pelagia were deep in conversation with Vassya and Voronyuk the guard. Very soon the train would be approaching Vassya's and Pritulyev's country, and Pritulyev was remembering the way to his village, the station and the road you took according to whether you were going on by horse or on foot, and at the sound of all the magical, familiar village names, Vassya repeated them with shining eyes as if they were a spell.

'You get off at Dry Ford?' he choked with excitement. 'And then you go on to Buysky?'

'That's right, you take the Buysky road.'

'That's what I say—Buysky—Buysky village. Of course I know it, that's our turning, you turn right and right again. That's to get to us, to Veretenniki. And your way must be left, away from the river, isn't it? You know the river Pelga? Well, of course! That's our river. You keep following the river, on and on, and away up on the cliff on the right, overhanging that same river Pelga, there's our village, Veretenniki! It's right up on the edge and it's ste-e-e-ep! It makes you giddy, honest to God it does. There's a quarry down below, for mill stones. That's where my mother lives, in Veretenniki, and my two sisters. Sister Alya. And Sister Arya. . . . Mother is a bit like you, Aunt Polya, she's young and fair. Uncle Voronyuk! Please, Uncle Voronyuk, for Christ's sake, please, I beg you, for God's sake . . . Uncle Voronyuk!'

'Well, what? Uncle, uncle, I know I'm not your aunt. What do you expect me to do? Am I mad? If I let you go, that would be the end of me, Amen. They'd put me up against a wall.'

Pelagia Tyagunova sat looking thoughtfully out of the window, stroking Vassya's reddish hair. Now and then she bent down to him and smiled as if she were telling him: 'Don't be silly. This isn't something to talk to Voronyuk about in front of everyone. Don't worry, have patience, it will be all right.'

13

Curious incidents began to happen when they left Central Russia behind on their way east. They were going through disturbed country, through districts where armed bands were in control and past villages where risings had recently been put down.

The train would halt in the middle of nowhere and a security patrol would inspect the passengers' papers and luggage.

Once they stopped at night but no one came in and no one was wakened.

Yury wondered if there had been an accident and went out to see.

It was dark. For no reason, it seemed, the train had stopped in the middle of an ordinary stretch with firs on either side of the track. Other passengers, who had come out and were stamping their feet in the snow, told Yury that there was nothing wrong but that the driver refused to go on, saying that this stretch was dangerous and should first be inspected by trolley; spokesmen for the passengers had gone to reason with him and if necessary to grease his palm, and sailors were also taking a hand in it and would undoubtedly get their way.

The snow round the head of the train was lit up at intervals, as by a bonfire, by fiery flashes from the engine or the glowing coals in the tender. By this light several dark figures were now seen to be running to the front of the engine.

The first of them, presumably the driver, reached the far end of the running board, leapt over the buffers and vanished as if the earth had swallowed him. The sailors who were chasing him did exactly the same thing: they too leapt and vanished.

All this aroused the curiosity of several passengers, including Yury, and they went to see.

Beyond the buffers, where the track opened out before them, they were met by an astonishing sight. By the side of the permanent way, the top half of the driver's body stuck out of the deep snow into which he had fallen. His pursuers stood in a semicircle round him, like hunters round their quarry; like him, they were buried in snow up to their waists.

'Thank you, comrades, fine stormy petrels [1] you are,' the driver was shouting. 'A fine sight, sailors chasing a fellow worker with guns! All because I said the train must stop.—You be my witnesses, comrade passengers, you can see what kind of a place this is. Any-

---

[1] Stormy petrels: the revolution began with a rising among the sailors of the Baltic Fleet. The reference is to this incident and also to Gorky's story of that name.

body might be roaming round unscrewing the bolts.—To hell with you, you bloody bastards, and your mothers and your grandmothers, for all I care! It's for you I was doing it, so that nothing should happen to you, and that's all the thanks I get for my trouble! Go on, go on, shoot me down! Here I am—you be my witnesses, comrade passengers, I'm not running away.'

Bewildered voices rose from the group. 'Pipe down, old man. . . . They don't mean it. . . . Nobody would let them. . . . They're only doing it to frighten you. . . .' Others urged him on: 'That's right, Gavrilka, stand up for yourself! Let them have it!'

The first sailor to scramble out of the snow was a red-haired giant with a head so huge that it made his face look flat. He turned to the passengers and spoke in a deep, quiet, unhurried voice with a Ukrainian accent, his composure oddly out of keeping with the scene.

'Beg pardon, what's all this thermidor [1] about? Mind you don't catch a chill in this cold, citizens. It's windy. Why not go back to your seats and keep warm?'

The crowd gradually dispersed. The giant went up to the driver who was still agitated and said:

'We've had enough of your hysteria, comrade driver. Get out of the snow. Full steam ahead and look sharp.'

14

Next day the train, creeping at a snail's pace for fear of running off the tracks, which the wind had powdered with snow and which no one had cleared, pulled up beside a lifeless, burned-out ruin. This was all that was left of the station, Lower Kelmes, its name still faintly legible on its blackened front.

Beyond it lay a deserted village blanketed in snow. This too was damaged by fire. The end house was charred, the one next to it sagged where its corner timbers had fallen in; broken sledges, fences, rusty pieces of metal and smashed furniture were scattered all over the street; the snow was dirty with soot and black patches of earth showed through icy puddles bristling with half-burnt logs, where efforts had been made to pour water on the flames or to beat them out.

The place was not in fact as dead as it looked; there were a few people still about. The station-master rose out of the ruins and the

---

[1] The reference is to the French Revolution; the word, in its Russianised form, is used by the 'politically conscious' sailor to mean 'commotion'.

guard jumped down from the train and commiserated with him. 'I suppose the village caught fire and the station burned with it?'

'Good day to you and welcome. Yes, we certainly had a fire, but that wasn't the worst of it.'

'I don't follow.'

'Better not try.'

'You don't mean Strelnikov!'

'I do.'

'Why? What had you done?'

'We didn't do anything, it was our neighbours, but we got punished for good measure. You see that village over there—that's Lower Kelmes in the Ust-Nemdinsk district—it was all because of them.'

'And what crime had they committed?'

'Pretty well all the seven deadly sins. Dissolved their Poor Peasants' Committee, that's one, refused to supply horses to the Red Army, that's two (and they're all Tartars, mind you, horsemen), resisted the mobilisation decree—that makes three at any rate.'

'Yes, I see. I quite see. So they were shelled?'

'Naturally.'

'From the armoured train?'

'Of course.'

'Very sad. Still, it's none of our business.'

'In any case, it's all over. But the news I have for you isn't very good either—I'm afraid you'll have to stay here for a couple of days.'

'You're joking. I'm taking troops to the front.'

'I'm not joking at all. We've had a blizzard for a solid week— snowdrifts all along the line and no one to clear it. Half the village has run away. I'll put the rest of them on the job, but it won't be enough.'

'Curse and damnation! What the hell am I going to do now?'

'We'll get it cleared in time.'

'How deep is the snow?'

'Not too bad. It varies. The worst patch is in the middle. There's a cutting about two miles long, there we'll certainly have trouble. Further on, the forest has kept the worst of the snow off the line. And on this side it's open country, so the wind has blown some of it away.'

'Hell, what a mess. I'll get the passengers on to it.'

'That's what I was thinking!'

'We mustn't touch the sailors. But there's a whole corps of labour conscripts as well as the free passengers, about seven hundred in all.'

'That's more than enough. We'll start the moment we get the shovels. We are a bit short of them, so we've sent to the near-by villages for more. They'll be here in no time.'

'God, what a misfortune! Do you think we'll manage?'

'Of course we will. They say cities are captured by weight of numbers and this is only a railway after all. Don't worry.'

15

The work of clearing the line took three days and all the Zhivagos, even Nyusha, took part in it. These were the best three days of the journey.

The country had a closed, secretive look. There was something about it that reminded one of the rising of Pugachev as seen by Pushkin and of the savage Asia of Aksakov's sketches. The ruins added to the air of mystery; so did the suspicious wariness of the remaining villagers who were frightened of informers and avoided the passengers; they were silent even among themselves.

The workers were divided into gangs, the labour conscripts kept apart from the civilians. The whole site was surrounded by security troops.

This stretch of railway was divided into sections, each gang was allocated to a section and all were sent to their places and began to work at the same time. Hills of snow between the sections hid the gangs from one another and were left untouched until the end.

The workers spent all day in the open, going back only to sleep. It was fine and frosty and the shifts were short, as there were not enough shovels. It was sheer pleasure.

Yury's section of the track had a fine view. The country to the east dipped down into a valley and rose in waves as far as the horizon.

On the top of a hill there was a house exposed to all the winds; its trees must have shaded it in summer, but they could not give it any shelter now with their frosty lacework.

The snow smoothed and rounded all contours. It could not quite conceal the winding bed of a stream which in spring would rush down to the viaduct below the railway bank, but which at present was tucked up in the snow, like a child in its cot with its head under the eiderdown.

Was there anyone living in the house on the hill, Yury wondered, or was it standing empty and falling into ruins, allocated to some land committee? What had happened to the people who had once lived there? Had they fled abroad? Or perished at the hands of the peasants? Or had they been popular and thus been allowed to stay in the district as technical specialists? And if they had stayed, had Strelnikov spared them, or had they shared the fate of the kulaks?

The house teased his curiosity but kept its sorrowful silence. Questions were not in order in these days and no one ever answered them.

But the sun sparkled on the blinding whiteness and Yury cut clean slices out of the snow, starting landfalls of dry diamond fires. It reminded him of his childhood. He saw himself in their yard at home, dressed in a braided hood and black sheepskin fastened with hooks and eyes sewn into the curly fleece, cutting the same dazzling snow into cubes and pyramids and cream buns and fortresses and cave cities. Life had had a splendid taste in those far-off days, everything had been a feast for the eyes and for the stomach!

But at this time, too, during their three days of work in the open air, the workers had a feeling of pleasantly full stomachs. And no wonder. At night they were issued with great chunks of hot fresh bread (no one knew where it came from or by whose orders); it had a tasty crisp crust, shiny on top, cracked at the side and with bits of charcoal baked into it underneath.

16

They became almost fond of the ruined station, as of a mountain shelter on a climbing holiday. Its shape, its site, the details of its damage remained in Yury's memory.

Every evening they returned to it when the sun—out of loyalty to old habits—set, just as it had always done, behind the birch outside the telegraphist's window.

A part of the outside wall had fallen in and cluttered up the room, but the window was still there and the corner opposite remained untouched, with its coffee-coloured wallpaper, the tiled stove with a round vent and a copper lid, and the inventory of the office furniture in a black frame. Exactly as before the disaster, the setting sun crept over the tiles and lit a warm brown glow on the paper and hung the shadow of the birch on a hook like a woman's scarf.

At the back of the building the waiting-room had been destroyed, but its locked door still had a notice on it, pinned up in the first days of the February Revolution or not long before; it said:

'Passengers in need of medicines and bandages are requested temporarily not to worry. For obvious reasons, am sealing door, of which am giving notice hereby.
Signed: Medical Attendant,
Ust-Namdinsk District, So-and-so.'

When finally the snow mounds between the sections of the track were cleared, the line could be seen flying into the distance as straight and level as an arrow. Hills of cleared snow gleamed on both sides of the track, white against the black walls of the forest.

Groups of men with shovels were standing at intervals all along the way. Seeing each other for the first time, they were astonished to see how many they were.

17

Although it was late and would soon be dark, the train was expected to leave within a few hours. Yury and Tonya went out for the pleasure of seeing the cleared line once again. But there was no one on it any more. They looked into the distance, exchanged a few words and turned back.

On the way to their coach they heard the voices of two women who were quarrelling violently, and recognised them as those of Ogryskova and Tyagunova; they were moving in the same direction as themselves but on the other side of the train, hidden by the endless line of coaches. The women seemed hardly ever to be level with Yury and Tonya, but always to outstrip them a little or to fall behind.

They were evidently so excited that their strength failed them, and, judging from the way their voices rose to a shriek and died down to a whisper, either their legs refused to carry them, or else they kept stumbling and falling into snowdrifts. Tyagunova seemed to be chasing Ogryskova and hitting her with her fists whenever she caught up with her. She called her every name she could think of, and her genteel, melodious voice made her insults sound infinitely more shameless and coarse than would have been the swearing of a man.

'You slut, you drag-tailed whore,' she screamed. 'I can't move an inch without seeing you flouncing up and down. Isn't my old fool enough for you, without you having to make eyes at a babe-in-arms?'

'So Vassya is your legal wedded husband too, is he? That's a good one!'

'I'll give you legal husband, you filthy plague! One more word from your dirty gob and I'll murder you.'

'Now, now, keep your fists to yourself. What on earth do you want?'

'I want to see you dead, you *nid-d'amour*, you cat on heat, you shameless bitch!'

'That's what I am, is it? Well, naturally, I'm nothing but a cat, a bitch, compared with such a grand lady as you! Born in the gutter, married in a ditch, laid by a rat and a hedgehog for a brat! . . . Help! Help! Murder! She'll murder me! Help a poor orphan, help a poor defenceless girl!'

'Come along,' Tonya hurried on. 'I can't bear to listen to it, it's too disgusting. They'll end up by doing something really awful.'

18

All at once the weather and the scenery changed. The plains ended and the track wound up hills and terraces through mountain country. The incessant north wind dropped and a warm breath came from the south as from an oven.

Here the woods grew on escarpments projecting from the mountain slopes, and when the railway crossed them, the train had to climb sharply uphill until it reached the middle of the wood and then steeply down. The train creaked and puffed on its way into the wood, hardly able to drag itself along, as if it were a very old forest guard walking in front and leading the passengers, who turned their heads from side to side and observed whatever was to be seen.

But as yet there was nothing to see. The woods were still deep in their winter sleep and peace. Only here and there a branch would rustle and shake itself free of the burden of the settling snow as though it were ridding itself of a collar.

Yury was overcome with drowsiness. All these days he lay in his bunk and slept and woke and thought and listened. But there was nothing yet to hear.

19

While Yury slept his fill, the spring was heating and melting the whole of that enormous quantity of snow which had fallen all over Russia: all that snow which had fallen in Moscow on the day they left, and had continued to fall all along the way since then; all that snow which they had spent three days clearing off the line; all that thick, deep layer of snow which had settled as far as the eye could see over the immense distances of hills and plains.

At first the snow melted quietly and secretly from inside. But by the time half the gigantic work of melting it was done, it could not be hidden any longer and the miracle became visible. Waters came rushing out from below, singing loudly. The forest stirred in its impenetrable depth, and everything in it awoke.

There was plenty of room for the water to play. It flung itself down the rocks, filled every pool to overflowing and spread. It roared and smoked and steamed in the forest. It streaked through the woods, sinking into the snow which hindered its movement; hissing on level ground or hurtling down and scattering into dusty spray. The earth was saturated. Ancient pine-trees, perched on dizzy heights, drank moisture almost from the clouds and it foamed and dried a rusty white at their roots like beer-foam on a moustache.

The sky, drunk with spring and giddy with its fumes, thickened with clouds. Low clouds, drooping at the edges like felt, sailed over the woods, and rain leapt from them, warm, smelling of soil and sweat, and washing the last of the black armour-plating of ice from the earth.

Yury woke up, stretched, raised himself on one elbow and looked and listened.

20

As they approached the mining region, there were more and more settlements, the runs were shorter, the halts more frequent. More people got on and off at the small stations. Instead of settling down and going to sleep, those who had only a short way to go found seats anywhere, near the door or in the middle of the coach, and sat up arguing in low voices about local matters intelligible only to themselves.

From the hints dropped by such local people in the past three days, Yury gathered that here the Whites were getting the best of the fighting and had seized or were about to seize Yuryatin, and also that, unless he had misheard the name, or his old friend had a namesake, the White forces were led by Galiullin whom he had last seen in Melyuzeyevo.

Not wishing to alarm his family by these unconfirmed rumours he said nothing to them for the time being.

Yury woke up in the early hours of the night, filled with an obscure happiness so strong that it had aroused him. The train was standing still. The station was bathed in the glassy dusk of a white night. Something subtle and powerful in this luminous darkness suggested a vast and open landscape, as though the station were high up on a mountain range.

People walked along the platform past the carriage speaking softly and treading as silently as shadows. Yury was moved by this evidence of a pre-war consideration for the sleeping passengers.

In reality he was mistaken. There was the same din of shouting voices and stamping boots on this platform as on any other. But there was a waterfall near by. Its freshness and freedom widened the expanse of the night and it was this that had filled Yury with happiness in his sleep. The incessant noise of the falling water dominated every other sound and created the illusion of quietness.

Knowing nothing of its existence but soothed and braced by it, Yury fell fast asleep.

Two men were talking underneath his bunk.

'Well, have they had their tails twisted yet? Are they keeping quiet now?'

'The shopkeepers, you mean?'

'Yes, the corn-dealers.'

'Feed out of your hand! As soon as a few were bumped off by way of example, all the others became as good as gold. A fine has been imposed on the district.'

'How much?'

'Forty thousand puds.'

'That's a likely tale!'

'What should I tell you a lie for?'

'Forty thousand rotten pumpkins!'

'Forty thousand puds of corn.'

'That was smart!'

'Forty thousand of the finest ground corn.'

'Well, so what? It's rich soil. Right in the thick of the corn trade. From here on, along the Rynva till you get to Yuryatin, it's village after village, wharf after wharf, one wholesaler after another.'

'Don't shout. You'll wake people up.'

'All right.' He yawned.

'How about going to sleep? Looks as if we're moving.'

The train, however, stayed where it was. But the rumble of another train approached swiftly from behind, bursting into a deafening roar and obliterating the sound of the waterfall as it drew level, and an old-fashioned express thundered past along the parallel track; it hooted, winked its tail light and vanished in the distance ahead.

'That's bad. Goodness knows when we'll be off now.'

'Yes. It won't be soon.'

'It's a special armoured train. Must be Strelnikov.'

'Must be him.'

'He's a wild beast when it comes to counter-revolutionaries.'

'He's after Galeyev.'

'Who's that?'

'Hetman Galeyev. They say he's outside Yuryatin with a Czech covering force. He's seized the harbours, the rotten turnip, and he's hanging on. Hetman Galeyev.'

'Never heard of him!'

'Or it may be Prince Galileyev. I can't quite remember the name.'

'There aren't any such princes. Must be Ali Kurban. You've mixed them up.'

'May be Kurban.'

'That's more like it.'

22

Towards morning Yury woke up again. He had again dreamed of something pleasant and a feeling of joy and liberation remained with him.

Again the train was at a standstill; perhaps it was the same station as before, but it might not have been. Once more there was the sound of a waterfall, possibly a different waterfall but more probably the same one.

He went back to sleep almost at once and as he was dozing off he dimly heard the sound of running feet and of some commotion. Kostoyed was quarrelling with the commander of the convoy and they were shouting at each other. The air was even more pleasant than before. It had a breath of something new in it, something that had not been there earlier, something fabulous, connected with the spring, white, blackish, insubstantial, scattered, like a snow flurry in May when the wet melting flakes, falling on the earth, turn it black rather than white.—'Transparent, blackish-white, sweet-smelling.—Bird-cherry,' Yury guessed in his sleep.

23

Next morning Tonya said :

'Really, Yura, you're extraordinary, you're a mass of contradictions. Sometimes a fly will wake you up and you can't get back to sleep till morning, and here you slept through all this row and I simply couldn't get you to wake up. Pritulyev and Vassya have escaped, just think of it ! And so have Tyagunova and Ogryskova ! Can you imagine such a thing ! Wait, that isn't all. Voronyuk as well. It's true, I tell you, he's run away. Now listen.—How they managed it, together or separately, and in what order—it's all a complete mystery. Voronyuk, of course, I understand—once he found the others had gone, he would have to try to save his skin. But what about the rest ? Did they really all vanish of their own free will, or was somebody done away with ? For instance, if the women are to be suspected, did Tyagunova kill Ogryskova or was it the other way round ? Nobody knows. The commander of the labour unit has been running up and down the train like a lunatic. "You're not to start the train. I order you in the name of the law not to move till I've caught my prisoners." And the train commandant shouted back : "I'm taking troops up to the front, I'm not waiting for your lousy crew. I wouldn't dream of it." So then they both went for Kostoyed. "You, a syndicalist, an educated man, how could you sit by and let a plain soldier, an ignorant child of nature, act in such a reckless manner ! And you a populist ¹ !" And Kostoyed gave them as good as he got. "That's interesting," he says. "The prisoner has to look after his guard, does he ? Well, really, the day that happens the hens will start to crow." I was shaking you as hard as I could : "Yura ! Wake up ! There's been an escape !" But it was not the slightest good. If a gun had gone off in your ear you wouldn't have heard it. . . . But I'll tell you more later. . . . Oh, do look ! Father, Yura, look how lovely !'

Through the opening in the window, where a pane had been taken out, they could see the country covered with spring floods from end to end. Somewhere a river had burst its banks and the water had come right up to the railway. It looked as if the train were actually gliding upon it.

Here and there the surface of the water had turned to a metallic blue ; over all the rest of it the hot morning sun was chasing smooth, glassy patches of light, as smooth and oily as melted butter which

¹ Populists : Left-wing idealists who devoted themselves to 'work among the people'.

a cook brushes with a feather on a pie crust.

In this shoreless flood were sunk the pillars of the white clouds, their pediments submerged together with the fields, the hollows and the bushes.

And somewhere in the middle of the flood there was a narrow strip of land with a row of trees doubled by their reflection in the water and suspended between earth and sky.

'Look, a family of ducks,' said Alexander Alexandrovich.

'Where?'

'Near the island. More to the right. Damn, they've flown. We've frightened them.'

'Yes, I see them now,' said Yury. 'I must have a talk with you some time, Alexander Alexandrovich. Some other time. . . . All the same, I'm very glad our conscripts and the women made up their minds. And I'm sure there wasn't any murder. They just ran— like the water.'

24

The white northern night was ending. Everything was clearly visible, the mountain, the thicket and the ravine, but as if they did not quite believe in themselves and existed only in a fairy tale.

The wood, which had several blossoming bird-cherries in it, was only just coming into leaf. It grew under an overhanging cliff, on a narrow ledge which itself ended in a precipice.

The waterfall, though not far away, could be seen only from the edge of the ravine beyond the thicket. Vassya Brykin, the escaped conscript, had tired himself out with joy and terror looking at it.

There was nothing comparable to the waterfall anywhere in the neighbourhood. It was unique and this made it terrible, transformed it into a being endowed with life and consciousness, perhaps that of the dragon or winged serpent of these parts, who levied tribute and preyed upon the countryside.

Half-way down, it broke on a sharp rock and divided in two. The upper part was almost motionless, but the two lower columns swayed slightly from side to side, as if the waterfall were continually slipping and righting itself, shaken but always recovering its balance.

Vassya had spread his sheepskin on the ground and was lying at the edge of the thicket. When the light became more definite, a large bird with heavy wings flew down from the mountain, soared in a smooth circle round the wood and settled on a pine close to where he lay. He looked up, enchanted, at its dark blue throat and grey-blue breast and whispered its Urals name, *ronzha*. Then he got up, picked up his sheepskin, flung it over his shoulders and crossed the clearing to speak to his companion.

'Come on, Auntie Polya. Goodness, how cold you are! I can hear your teeth chattering. Well, what are you staring at, why are you so frightened? We've got to go, I'm telling you, we must get to a village. Work it out for yourself. They'll hide us in a village, they won't harm their own kind. We've had nothing to eat for two days, we'll die out here. Uncle Voronyuk must have raised a frightful hullabaloo, they must all be out looking for us. We have to go, Auntie; to put it plainly, we've got to run. I just don't know what to do with you, Auntie—not a word out of you for two whole days. You worry too much, honest to God you do. What are you so unhappy about? It isn't as if you'd meant to push Auntie Katie off the train; you didn't push Katie Ogryskova, you just caught her sideways, by accident—I saw you. She picked herself up off the grass—I saw her with my own eyes—and she got up and ran away. She and Uncle Pritulyev are sure to catch us up. We'll all be together again. The great thing is to stop worrying, then you'll find your tongue again.'

Tyagunova got up, took Vassya's hand and said softly: 'Come along, my dear.'

25

Their timbers creaking, the coaches climbed up the steep hill. Below the embankment there was a thicket, its tops not quite reaching the level of the track. Lower still were fields. The floods had only just withdrawn, leaving sand and pieces of timber scattered about untidily. The logs must have been washed down from somewhere higher up the hill where they had been stacked.

The young coppice below the embankment was still almost as bare as in winter. Only in the buds, which spattered it all over like candle grease, was there something not in accord with the rest, something superfluous and untidy; perhaps dirt or an inflammation causing them to swell; and this untidiness, superfluity and dirt were the signs of life which had already set the most forward of the trees on fire with its green leafy flame.

Here and there an upright birch stood martyred, pierced by the teeth and arrows of its twin unfolding leaves, and you knew its smell by just looking at it: it smelled of its shiny resin which is used for making lacquer.

Soon the train drew level with the place where the logs washed down by the flood might have been stacked. A cutting through the wood came into sight at a bend of the track; it was heaped with chips and shavings and had a pile of large timber in the middle. The engine braked and the train shuddered and stopped at the point it had reached on the curve of the hill, bending slightly outwards from a wide arc.

A few short barking hoots and shouts came from the engine, but the passengers did not need these signals to know that the train had stopped in order to take in fuel.

The doors rolled open and a crowd the size of the population of a small town poured out; only the sailors stayed in their coaches for they were excused all fatigues.

There was not enough small firewood in the clearing to fill the tender and some of the large timber had to be cut down to the right size. The engine crew had saws as part of their equipment and these were issued to volunteers, one to each pair, Yury and his father-in-law among them.

Grinning sailors stuck their heads out of their carriage doors. The recruits were a curious mixture of middle-aged working men, straight from their emergency training, and boys just out of naval college, who looked as if they had got in by mistake among the staid fathers of families and who joked and played the fool with the older sailors to keep themselves from thinking. All of them knew that their hour of trial was at hand.

Jokes and guffaws followed the work parties.

'Hey, Grandfather! I'm not shirking, I'm too young to work, my nanny won't let me.' 'Hey, Martha, don't saw off your skirt, you'll catch cold!' 'Hey, young one, don't go to the wood, come and be my wife instead!'

26

There were several trestles in the clearing; Yury and Alexander Alexandrovich went up to one of them and began to saw.

This was the moment of spring when the earth comes out of the snow looking much as when the snow had trapped it six months earlier. The wood smelled of damp and was heaped with last year's leaves like an unswept room where people have been tearing up letters, bills and receipts accumulated for years.

'Don't go so fast, you'll tire yourself,' said Yury, giving a slower and more even movement to the saw. 'And what about having a rest?'

The wood echoed to the hoarse ringing of other saws; somewhere, very far away, a nightingale was trying out its voice; at longer intervals a thrush whistled as if blowing dust out of a flute, and even the engine steam rose into the sky warbling like milk boiling up on a nursery spirit stove.

'What did you want to speak to me about?' asked Alexander Alexandrovich. 'Do you remember? We were going past the island, the ducks flew away and you said you wanted to speak to me some other time.'

'Oh yes. . . . Well, I don't quite know how to put it shortly. I was thinking that we are going in deeper and deeper. The whole of this region is in turmoil. We don't know what we'll find when we get there. Perhaps we ought to talk things over just in case. . . . I don't mean about our convictions—you can't say much about them in five minutes in a spring wood. Besides we know each other too well. You and I and Tonya and many others like us, we make up our own world these days, the only difference between us is in the degree of our awareness of it. What I mean is that perhaps we ought to agree in advance on how to behave, so that we need never blush for each other or make each other feel ashamed.'

'I know what you mean. I like the way you put it. I'll tell you. Do you remember that night, in winter, in the middle of a snow-storm, when you brought me the paper with the first government decrees? You remember how unbelievably direct and uncompromising they were? It was that single-mindedness that appealed to us. But such things keep their original purity only in the minds of those who have conceived them, and then only on the day they are first published. By the day after, the casuistry of politics has turned them inside out. What can I say to you? The régime is hostile to us, its philosophy is alien to me, I have not been asked if I consent to all these changes. But I have been trusted, and my own actions, even if they were not freely chosen, put me under a certain obligation.

'Tonya keeps asking if we'll arrive in time to plant our vegetables. I don't know. I don't know the soil or the climate in the Urals; the summer is so short I can't think how anything ever ripens in time.

'But after all, it is not for the sake of market gardening that we are going all this enormous distance. No, we had better face things honestly, our object is quite different. We are going to try to subsist in the modern fashion, taking our share in the squandering of old Kreuger's properties, his factories and machines. We are not going to rebuild his fortune, but, like everyone else and in the same incredibly chaotic way, we'll fritter it away and lend a hand in the collective squandering of thousands for the sake of earning a copeck's worth of living. Not that I would take back the estate on the old terms as a gift, not if you gave me my weight in gold. That would be as foolish as to start running about naked or trying to forget the alphabet. No, the age of property in Russia is over, and anyway, we Gromekos lost our acquisitive passion a generation ago.'

27

It was too hot and stuffy in the carriage to sleep. Yury's pillow was soaked in sweat. Carefully, not to wake the others, he got down from his bunk and rolled back the carriage doors.

Sticky damp heat struck him in the face as if he had walked into a cobweb in a cellar. 'Mist,' he guessed. 'To-morrow will be scorching hot. That's why it is so airless, and so heavy and oppressive now.'

It was a big station, possibly a junction. Besides the mist and the stillness, there was a feeling of emptiness, of neglect, as if the train had been lost and forgotten. It must be standing right at the back of the marshalling yard, so far back that if, at the other end of the maze of tracks, the earth were to open and swallow up the station building, no one in the train would be any the wiser.

Two sounds could be heard faintly in the distance.

At the back, where they had come from, there was a rhythmic splashing, as if clothes were being rinsed or the wind flapped a heavy damp flag agains: a pole.

From ahead there came an even rumbling which made Yury, with his experience of the war, prick up his ears. 'Artillery,' he decided after listening to the calmly echoing, low, sustained note.

'That's it, we're right at the front,' he nodded to himself as he jumped down from the carriage. He walked a few steps forward. Two carriages further up the train broke off; the rest of the coaches had been uncoupled and had gone away together with the engine.

'So that was why they were so keyed up yesterday. They had a feeling they would be thrown straight in as soon as we arrived.'

He walked round the front carriage meaning to cross the rails and look for the main part of the station, but a sentry with a rifle rose in his path.

'Where are you going? Got a pass?' he said softly.

'What is this station?'

'That's as may be. Who are you?'

'I am a doctor from Moscow. My family and I are passengers on this train. Here are my papers.'

'You can stuff them up your ——. I'm not such a fool as to try to read in the dark. There's a mist—can't you see? And I don't need any papers to know what kind of a doctor you are. There are more of your doctors shooting twelve-inch guns at us. Bash your brains out, I would, but it's too soon for that. Get back now, while you're still in one piece.'

'He's taking me for someone else,' thought Yury. Clearly, it was no use arguing, better follow his advice before it was too late. He turned and walked back.

The gunfire had died away behind him. There, behind him, was the east. There the sun had risen in a drift of mist and was peering dully through floating shadows, like a naked man through clouds of steam at the baths.

Yury walked down the length of the train and passed the end coach. His feet sank deeper and deeper into soft sand.

The even sound of splashing came nearer. The ground sloped steeply down. He stopped, trying to make out the indistinct shapes in front of him; the mist made them unnaturally large. One more step and the hulls of beached boats came up out of the dark. Before him was a wide river, its lazy ripples splashing slowly, wearily against the sides of fishing smacks and the planks of landing stages down the shore.

A figure rose from the beach.

'Who gave you permission to prowl around?' asked another sentry with a rifle.

'What is this river?' shot out Yury, though he had firmly determined not to ask any more questions.

By way of answer the sentry put his whistle to his mouth, but he was saved the trouble of using it by the first sentry, whom it was meant to summon but who had evidently been following Yury without a sound and now joined his mate. They stood talking.

'There's no doubt about it. You can tell this kind of a bird at a glance. "What's this station?" "What's this river?" There's dust in your eyes! What do you say? Shall we take him straight to the jetty or to the train first?'

'I say to the train. See what the boss says.—Your documents,' he barked at Yury. Grabbing the bunch of papers in his fist and calling back to someone, 'Keep an eye on him,' he strode away with the first sentry towards the station.

The third figure, whom Yury had not so far made out, was evidently a fisherman. He had been lying on the beach but he now grunted, stirred and set about enlightening Yury on his position.

'It's lucky for you they're taking you to the boss. It may be your salvation. But you mustn't blame them. They're only doing their duty. The people are on top nowadays. Perhaps it's even for the best in the long run, though there isn't much to be said for it now. They've made a mistake, you see. They've been hunting, hunting all the time for a certain man. So they thought it was you. That's him, they thought, that's the enemy of the Workers' State, we've got him. A mistake, that's all it is. What you must do if anything happens is to insist on seeing the boss. Don't you let these two get away with anything. They're politically conscious; it's a misfortune, Lord help us. They'd think nothing of doing away with you. So, if they say "Come along," mind you don't go. Say you want to see the boss.'

From the fisherman Yury learned that the river was the famous waterway the Rynva, and that the station by the river served Razvilye, an industrial suburb of the town of Yuryatin. He also learned that Yuryatin, which lay a couple of miles upstream, seemed now to have been recaptured from the Whites. And that there had been trouble in Razvilye, and that this seemed also to have been put down, the reason for the great stillness all around being that the station area had been cleared of civilians and strictly cordoned off. He learned finally that the coaches of some of the trains at the station were used as army headquarters and that among them was the special train of Army Commissar Strelnikov, to whom the two sentries had gone to report.

A third sentry now came from the direction in which the two others had gone; he was distinguished from them chiefly by the fact that he pulled his rifle after him, the butt trailing on the ground, or propped it up in front of him like a tipsy friend who needed his support. This guard now took Yury to the commissar.

28

Sounds of laughter and movement came from one of the two coupled coaches to which the guard, after giving the password to the sentry, took Yury, but they ceased the moment the two men came in.

The guard led Yury down a narrow passage to a wide central compartment. It was a clean, comfortable room where tidy, well-dressed people worked in complete silence. Yury had had a very different idea of the background of Strelnikov, the famous non-party military expert who was the pride and terror of the region.

But no doubt, the real centre of his activities lay elsewhere, closer to the staff H.Q. and to the field of military operations. This could only be his personal suite, his private office and sleeping quarters.

Hence the stillness, rather like the quiet of a hydro with cork floors and attendants in soft slippers.

The office was the old dining-car, carpeted and with several desks in it.

'One moment,' said a young officer whose desk was by the door. He nodded absent-mindedly, dismissing the guard, who left, rattling his rifle butt on the metal strips nailed across the floor of the passage. After this, everyone felt free to forget Yury's existence and paid him no further attention.

From where he stood at the entrance Yury could see his papers lying on a desk at the far end of the room. The desk was occupied by a man who was older than the rest and who looked like an old-style colonel. He was an army statistician of some sort. Mumbling to himself, he consulted reference books, studied field maps, checked, compared, cut out and pasted things in. After looking round at every window in the room he announced: 'It's going to be hot,' as though forced to this conclusion only by the examination of all of them.

An army electrician was crawling about on the floor mending a broken connection. When he reached the desk by the door the young officer got up to make room for him. At the next table a typist in an army leather jerkin was struggling with her typewriter; its carriage had slipped sideways and got stuck. The young officer stood over her and examined the cause of the mishap from above, while the electrician crawled in under her desk and examined it from below. The old-style colonel got up and joined them and all four busied themselves with the typewriter.

This made Yury feel better. These people must know his fate better than he did; it was hardly likely that they would be so unconcerned and so busy with trifles in the presence of a man whom they considered doomed.

'And yet who knows?' he reflected. 'Why are they so unconcerned? Guns are going off and people are dying and they calmly forecast the temperature—not the heat of the battle but of the weather. Perhaps after all they have seen so much that they have no sensibility left.'

For something to look at, he stared across the room through the window opposite.

He could see the edge of the tracks and higher up the hill the station and the suburb of Razvilye.

Three flights of unpainted wooden steps led from the platform to the station building.

At the end of the tracks there was a graveyard for old engines. Locomotives without tenders, with smoke stacks shaped like the tops of knee-boots or like drinking-cups, stood stack to stack amid piles of scrap.

The engine graveyard below and the human graveyard above, the crumpled iron of the tracks and the rusty iron of the roofs and shop signs of the suburb made up a single picture of neglect and age under the white sky scalded by the early morning heat.

Living in Moscow, Yury had forgotten how many shop signs there still were in other towns and how much of the façades they covered. Some of those he was seeing now were so large that he could read them easily from where he stood, and they came down so low over the slanting windows of the sagging, one-storeyed buildings that the crooked little houses were almost hidden by them, like the faces of village children in their fathers' peaked caps.

The mist had gone from the west and now what remained of it in the east stirred, swayed and parted like the curtain of a stage.

And there, on a hill above Razvilye and a mile or two beyond it, stood a large town, the size of a provincial capital. The sun gilded its colours and the distance simplified its lines. It clung to the summit of the hill in tiers, house by house and street by street, with a big church in the middle on the top, as in a cheap colour print of a desert monastery or of Mount Athos.

'Yuryatin,' thought Yury excitedly. 'The town I used to hear about so often from Anna and from Nurse Antipova. How strange that I should see it in these circumstances!'

At that moment the attention of the military was diverted from the typewriter to something they could see through one of the other windows and Yury looked round.

A group of prisoners was being taken under guard up the station steps. Among them was a boy in a school uniform who was wounded in the head. He had received first-aid but a trickle of blood seeped through the bandage, and he kept smudging it with his hand over his dark, sweaty face. Walking between two Red Army men at the tail of the procession, he attracted notice not only by his resolute air, his good looks and the pathos of so young a rebel's plight, but by the utter absurdity of his own and his two companions' gestures. They were doing exactly the opposite of what they should have done.

He was still wearing his school cap. It slithered continually from his bandaged head and, instead of taking it off and carrying it in his hand, he rammed it back each time, disturbing the bandage and the wound, and in this his two guards assisted him with readiness.

There was something symbolical in this absurd action, so contrary to common sense, and, impressed by its significance, Yury longed to rush out and address the boy in the words which were boiling up inside him. He longed to shout to him and to the people in the railway coach that salvation lay not in loyalty to forms and uniforms, but in throwing them away.

He turned away; Strelnikov came in with long, vigorous strides and stood in the middle of the room.

How was it possible that he, a doctor, with his thousands of acquaintances, had never until this day come across a personality so well defined as this man? How was it that they had never been thrown together, that their paths had never crossed?

For some unknown reason, it was clear at once that this man was a finished product of the will. So completely was he himself, the self he chose to be, that everything about him struck one immediately as a model of its kind—his well-proportioned, handsomely set head, his eager step, his long legs, his knee-boots, which may well have been muddy but which looked clean, and his grey serge tunic which may have been creased but looked as if it were made of the best linen and had just been pressed.

Such was the irresistible effect of his brilliance, his unaffected ease and his sense of being at home in any conceivable situation on earth.

He must certainly, Yury thought, be possessed of a remarkable gift, but it was not necessarily the gift of originality. His talent, which showed itself in his every movement, might equally be one of imitation.

In those days everyone modelled himself on someone else—imitating the heroes of history or those who had caught men's imagination by winning fame at the front or in the street fighting, or those who had great prestige with the people, or this or that comrade who had achieved distinction, or simply each other.

Strelnikov politely concealed any surprise or annoyance he might have felt at Yury's presence. He addressed his staff, treating him as one of themselves.

He said: 'Congratulations. We have driven them back. It all

seems more like playing at war than like serious business, because they are as Russian as we are, only stuffed with nonsense—they won't give it up, so we have to beat it out of them. Their commander was my friend. His origin is even more proletarian than mine. We grew up in the same house. He has done a great deal for me in my life and I am deeply indebted to him. And here am I rejoicing that we have thrown them back beyond the river and perhaps even further.—Hurry up with that connection, Guryan, we need the telephone, we can't possibly manage only with messengers and the telegraph.—Isn't it getting hot! I managed to get in an hour's sleep all the same. Oh yes! . . .' He turned to Yury, remembering that he had been woken up to deal with some nonsense in connection with this man.

'This man?' Strelnikov thought, looking him over sharply. 'Nonsense! He's nothing like him. Fools!' He laughed and said to Yury: 'My apologies, Comrade. They mistook you for someone else. My guards made a mistake. You are free to go.—Where is the comrade's labour book?—Ah, here are your papers. May I just have a glance . . . Zhivago . . . Zhivago . . . Doctor Zhivago . . . Moscow. . . . All the same, shall we go to my room for a moment? This is the secretariat; I'm in the next coach. This way, I won't keep you long.'

30

Who, in reality, was Strelnikov?

That he should have reached and held his position was remarkable, for he was a non-party man and, though born in Moscow, had been totally unknown: he had gone straight from the university to a school-teaching job in the provinces, and in the war he had been captured and reported missing, believed killed. He had only recently come back from prison in Germany. He was put forward and vouched for by Tiverzin, a railway worker of advanced political views, in whose family he had lived as a child. Those who controlled appointments were impressed by him: in those days of inordinate rhetoric and political extremism his unbridled revolutionary fervour fitted the spirit of the times and stood out by its sincerity and its fanaticism, neither borrowed nor accidental, but his own, deliberately fostered by him and developed by the circumstances of his life.

He justified the confidence of the authorities.

His fighting record over the past few months included the burning of Lower Kelmes (where Yury's train had been stopped by the snow), the suppression of the Gubassovo peasants who had put up armed resistance to food levies, and of the men of the 14th line regiment, who had plundered a food convoy. He had also dealt with the 'Razin'[1] soldiers who had started a rebellion in the town of Turkatuy and gone over to the Whites, and with the rebellion at Chirkin Us, where a loyal commander had been killed.

In each case he had achieved complete surprise and had investigated, tried, sentenced and enforced his sentences with speed, harshness and resolution.

He had brought the local epidemic of desertions under control and reorganised the recruiting bodies. As a result, conscription went ahead and the Red Army reception centres were feverishly busy.

Finally, when the White pressure from the north increased and the position became admittedly grave, Strelnikov was entrusted with new responsibilities, military, strategic and operational. His activities produced immediate results.

Strelnikov ('the Shooter') knew that rumour had nicknamed him Razstrelnikov, 'the Executioner'. He took it calmly, he was disturbed by nothing.

His father was a worker who had been sent to prison for taking part in the revolution of 1905. He did not himself participate in the revolutionary movement in those years, at first because he was too young, and later, at the university, because young men who come from a poor background value higher education more and work harder than the children of the rich. The ferment among other students left him unmoved. He accumulated an immense amount of information and, after taking his degree in arts, educated himself later in science and mathematics.

Exempted from the army, he enlisted as a volunteer, was commissioned, sent to the front, captured and, on hearing of the revolution in Russia, escaped in 1917 and came home. He had an unusual power of clear and logical reasoning, and he was endowed with great moral purity and sense of justice; he was ardent and honourable.

But to the task of a scientist breaking new ground, his mind would have failed to bring an intuition for the incalculable: the capacity for those unexpected discoveries which shatter the barren harmony of empty foresight.

And in order to do good to others he would have needed, besides the principles which filled his mind, an unprincipled heart,—the kind of heart that knows of no general cases, but only of particular ones, and has the greatness of small actions.

Filled with the loftiest aspirations from his childhood, he had

[1] Stenka Razin was the leader of a popular uprising in the 17th century.

looked upon the world as a vast arena where everyone competed for perfection, keeping scrupulously to the rules. When he found that this was not a true picture, it did not occur to him that his conception of the world order might be over-simplified. He nursed his grievances and with them the ambition to judge between life and the dark forces which distort it, and to be life's champion and avenger.

Embittered by his disappointment, he was armed by the revolution.

31

'Zhivago,' repeated Strelnikov when they were settled in his room. 'Zhivago. . . . Trade, I think. Or gentry. . . . Well, of course, a Moscow doctor. . . . Going to Varykino.—That's strange, why should you leave Moscow for such an out-of-the-way lair?'

'That's just the idea. In search of quiet, retirement and obscurity.'

'Dear me, how romantic! Varykino? I know most of the places here. That used to be Krueger's estate. You aren't related to him by any chance? You don't happen to be his heir?'

'Why the irony? Being his "heir" has nothing to do with it. Though it is true that my wife . . .'

'Ah, so you see! But if you're feeling nostalgic for the Whites I'm going to disappoint you. We've cleared the district.'

'Are you still making fun of me?'

'And then, a doctor. An army medical officer. And we're at war. That really is my business. You're a deserter. The greens [1] are also seeking refuge in the woods.—Your reasons?'

'I have been twice wounded and invalided out.'

'Next you'll be handing me a reference from the People's Commissariat of Education or Health to prove that you are a Soviet citizen or a "sympathiser" or "entirely loyal". These are apocalyptic times, my dear sir, this is the Last Judgment. This is a time for angels with flaming swords and winged beasts from the abyss, not for sympathisers and loyal doctors. However, I told you you were free, and I won't take back my word, but remember, it's for this once. I have a feeling that we'll meet again, and that then our conversation will be quite different. Take care.'

Yury was not put out either by the challenge or the threat. He said:

'I know what you think of me. From your point of view you are

[1] A term used to denote anarchistic people, chiefly peasants, who fought both the Reds and the Whites.

right. But the point you wish me to discuss with you is one I have been arguing with an imaginary accuser all my life, and it would be odd if I had not by now reached some conclusion. Only I could not put it into a couple of words. So if I am really free, permit me to leave, without having it out with you. If I am not, then you must decide what to do with me. I have no excuses to make to you.'

They were interrupted by the telephone. The line had been repaired. Strelnikov picked up the receiver.

'Thanks, Guryan. Now be a good fellow and send somebody along to see Comrade Zhivago to his train. I don't want any more accidents. And give me the Razvilye Cheka Transport Department.'

When Zhivago had gone, Strelnikov telephoned the railway station.

'There's a schoolboy they've brought in, keeps pulling his cap over his ears and he's got a bandaged head, it's disgraceful.—That's right.—He's to have medical aid if he needs it.—Certainly.—Yes, like the apple of your eye, you'll be responsible to me personally.— Rations, too, if necessary. That's right. Now, let's get down to business. . . . I'm still talking, don't cut me off. Damn, there's somebody else on the line. Guryan! Guryan! They've cut me off.'

He gave up trying to finish his conversation for the time being. 'It might be one of my prep school boys,' he thought. 'Fighting us, now he's big.' He counted up the years since he had stopped teaching, to see if the boy could indeed have been his pupil. Then he looked out of the window towards the skyline and searched for the part of Yuryatin where he and his wife had lived. Suppose his wife and daughter were still there! Couldn't he go to them? Why not now, this very minute? Yes, but how could he? They belonged to another life. First he must see this one through, this new life, then he could go back to the one that had been interrupted. Some day he would do just that. Some day. But when, when?

PART TWO

8

Arrival

THE train which had brought the Zhivagos was still standing in the station siding, screened by other trains, but that morning, for the first time, they felt that their connection with Moscow had snapped and was ended.

From now on they were in a different territory, in a new and different provincial world which had a centre of gravity of its own.

It was clear at once that here people lived closer together than they did in Moscow or Petersburg. Although the station area was cordoned off and officially closed to civilians, passengers for the local trains had managed, in some unaccountable way, to 'filter through' (as we would say now). They had already crammed the coaches and they crowded in the doorways or strolled or stood about in front of them.

All of them, without exception, were acquainted; they waved and called out as soon as they caught sight of each other and they exchanged greetings as they passed. Their speech and dress, their food and manners, were all a little different from those of people in the capitals.

How did they earn their living? Yury wondered. What were their interests and their material resources, how did they cope with the difficulties of the times and how evade the laws?

It was not long before he learned the answer.

2

Escorted by the sentry who dragged his rifle after him or used it as a walking stick, Yury went back to his carriage.

It was a steaming hot day. The rails and the carriage roofs looked as if they were melting. The earth, black with oil, had a yellow shimmer like gilt.

The sentry's rifle ploughed a furrow in the dust and occasionally clinked against the sleepers.

'The weather has settled down,' he was saying, 'time to sow the spring corn—oats, millet—it's a golden time for the crops. It's too early for the buckwheat, though. Where I come from we sow the buckwheat on the feast of Akulina. I'm not from these parts, I come from Morzhansk, near Tambov. Eh, Comrade Doctor, if it wasn't for this civil war and this plague of a counter-revolution, do you think I'd be wasting my time in strange parts at this season? The class war has run between us like a black cat [1] and just look at what it does to us.'

3

Hands were stretched out of the carriage to help him up.

'Thanks, I can manage.'

Yury climbed in and hugged his wife.

'At last! Well, thank God, thank God, it's all ended like this,' she kept saying over and over again. 'Actually, we knew you were all right.'

'What do you mean, you knew I was all right?'

'The sentries came and told us what was going on. How otherwise do you think we could have borne the suspense? As it is, Father and I nearly went out of our minds. There he is, he's fast asleep, you can't wake him. He fell asleep like a log after all the excitement. There are several new passengers. I'll introduce you in a moment. But listen first to what everybody's talking about—they are all congratulating you on your lucky escape.—Here he is,' she suddenly turned and introduced her husband over her shoulder to one of the new passengers who was hemmed in by the crowd at the back of the carriage.

'Samdevyatov,' the stranger introduced himself, raising his soft hat over other people's heads and pushing his way forward through the press of bodies.

'Samdevyatov,' thought Yury. 'With a name like that he ought to have come straight out of an old Russian ballad, complete with a bushy beard, a smock and a studded belt. But this is the local Arts Club. Greying curls, moustache, goatee . . .'

'Well, did Strelnikov give you a fright?' said Samdevyatov. 'Be honest.'

'No, why? We had an interesting talk. Certainly he has a powerful personality.'

---

[1] According to the Russian superstition, a black cat running between two people means that they will quarrel.

'I should think so. I've got some idea of what he's like. He's not from our parts. He's one of you Moscow people. Like most of our innovations. They're all imported from the capital. We wouldn't have thought of them ourselves.'

'Yury, darling, Anfim Yefimovich knows everyone,' Tonya said. 'He's heard about you and about your father and he knew my grandfather—he knows everyone!—I suppose you must have met the schoolteacher, Antipova?' she slipped in casually, and Samdevyatov replied with as little expression: 'What about Antipova?' Yury heard, but did not take it up, and Tonya went on: 'Anfim Yefimovich is a bolshevik, so take care, darling, you'll have to be on your best behaviour.'

'Really?' said Yury. 'I'd never have thought it. I'd have taken you for an artist of some sort.'

'My father kept a coaching inn. He had seven troikas on the road. But I went to the university, and it's true that I'm a Marxist.'

'Listen to what Anfim Yefimovich told me, Yura, and by the way, if you don't mind my saying so, Anfim Yefimovich, your name and patronymic is a real tongue-twister!—Listen, darling, to what he told me—we've been tremendously lucky.—Yuryatin Central can't take the train—part of the town is on fire and the bridge has been blown up, you can't get through. So our train is going to be switched to another line, and that line happens to be just the one we want, it's the one for our station, for Torfyanaya. Isn't it wonderful!—We don't have to change and lug all our stuff from one station to another, we'll just stay in the train. On the other hand, Anfim Yefimovich says we'll be shunted backwards and forwards for hours before we really start off.'

4

Tonya was right. Coaches were coupled and uncoupled and the train was shifted endlessly from one congested line to another where other trains blocked its way into the open country.

The town lay in the distance, partly hidden by folds of land. Only now and then did its roofs, the chimneys of its factories and the crosses on its belfries show on the skyline. One of its suburbs was on fire. The smoke drifted across the sky, looking like a horse's mane blowing in the wind.

Yury and Samdevyatov sat on the floor of the carriage, their legs dangling over the side. Samdevyatov kept pointing into the distance and explaining what they saw to Yury. Every now and then the train would put on speed and drown his voice and he would lean across, bringing his mouth close to Yury's ear, and repeat what he had said, shouting himself hoarse.

'That's the "Giant" Cinema they've set on fire. The cadets were holding it, though they'd surrendered earlier on. In general, the fighting isn't over yet, by any means. You see those black dots on the belfry? Those are our people, sniping at the Czechs [1].'

'I can't see a thing. How can you see them at such a distance?'

'That's the artisans' quarter, Khokhriki, burning over there. Kholodeyevo, the part where the shops are, is further on. I'm interested because our inn is there. Luckily the fire is only on the outskirts and it doesn't look like spreading to the centre.'

'What did you say?'

'I said the centre is untouched so far, the centre of the town—the cathedral, the library. . . . Our name, Samdevyatov, is a Russian form of San Donato. We're supposed to be descended from the Demidovs [2].'

'I still can't hear.'

'I said Samdevyatov is a form of San Donato. They say we are a branch of the Demidov family, the Princes Demidov San Donato. But it may be just a family legend. This place here is called Spirka's Dell. It's full of villas and places to which people come on a spree. Funny name, isn't it?'

In front of them lay a valley criss-crossed by branch tracks. Telegraph poles strode away to the horizon, like giants in seven-league boots, and the broad winding ribbon of a highway competed in beauty with the railway. It vanished over the skyline, reappeared in a broad arc at a turning and again vanished.

'That's our famous highway. It runs right across Siberia. The convicts used to sing songs about it. Now it's the operational base of the partisans. . . . You'll like it here, you know, it's not at all bad. You'll get so used to it, you'll miss it when you go away. . . . The town has various odd features. Our water pumps, for instance. The women queue up for water at the crossroads, it's their open-air club all through the winter.'

'We are not going to live in town. We're going to Varykino.'

[1] The Czechoslovak Legion took part in the events in Eastern Russia and Siberia in 1918–1920.
[2] A Demidov opened the first mines in the Urals under a concession from Peter the Great. His descendant in the 19th century received the title of Prince San Donato from the Vatican.

'I know. Your wife told me. All the same you'll be coming into town on business. I guessed who your wife was the moment I saw her. She's the living image of old Krueger—eyes, nose, forehead—just like her grandfather. Everyone here remembers him.'

There were round red oil tanks on the skyline, and large advertisements on wooden hoardings. One of them caught Yury's eye; it was repeated twice and read: *Moreau & Vetchinkin. Seed drills. Threshing machines.*

'That was a good firm. Their agricultural machinery was first-rate.'

'I can't hear. What did you say?'

'A good firm, I said. Can you hear?—a good firm. They made agricultural machinery. It was a limited liability company. My father was a shareholder.'

'I thought you said he kept an inn.'

'So he did. That didn't prevent him from having shares. Very shrewd investments he made, too. He had money in the "Giant" Cinema.'

'You sound as if you were proud of it?'

'Of my father being shrewd? Of course I am.'

'But what about your Marxism?'

'Good Lord, what has that got to do with it? Why on earth should a man, because he is a Marxist, be a drooling booby? Marxism is a positive science. It's a doctrine of reality, a philosophy of history.'

'Marxism a science? Well, it's taking a risk, to say the least, to argue about that with a man one hardly knows, but all the same . . . Marxism is not sufficiently master of itself to be a science. Science is more balanced. You talk about Marxism and objectivity. I don't know of any teaching more self-centred and further from the facts than Marxism. Ordinarily, people are anxious to test their theories in practice, to learn from experience, but those who wield power are so anxious to establish the myth of their own infallibility that they turn their back on truth as squarely as they can. Politics mean nothing to me. I don't like people who are indifferent to the truth.'

Samdevyatov took Yury's words for the bravado of a witty eccentric and listened with a smile.

The train was still shunting. Every time it reached the 'go' signal, a woman with a milk-can tied to her belt, who was on duty at the points, put away her knitting, bent down, switched the signal lever and sent the train back to town in reverse. As it slowly rolled away she sat up and shook her fist at it.

Samdevyatov took this personally. 'Why does she do that?' he wondered. 'Her face is familiar. Can it be Glasha Tuntseva? No, I don't think it can be Glasha. She looks too old. Anyway, what has she got against me? I suppose, what with Mother Russia in the throes of her upheavals and the railways in a muddle, the poor old thing is having a thin time, so she thinks I'm to blame and shakes her fist at me. Oh well, to hell with it!—As though I didn't have other things to think about.'

At long last the woman waved her flag, shouted something to the engine driver and let the train past the signals, out into the open country, but as the fourteenth coach sped by she stuck her tongue out at the two windbags sitting on the floor; she was sick of the sight of them. Again Samdevyatov looked thoughtful.

5

When the suburbs of the burning town, with its round oil tanks, telegraph poles and hoardings, had vanished in the distance giving way to a landscape of woods and low hills, with occasional glimpses of the highway, Samdevyatov said:

'Let's go back to our seats. I have to get off soon and your station is the next but one. Mind you don't miss it.'

'I suppose you know all this neighbourhood very well?'

'Like my own backyard. Up to a hundred-mile radius. I'm a solicitor, you know. Twenty years of practice. I'm always travelling about on business.'

'Even now?'

'Certainly.'

'But what kind of business can there be in these days?'

'Anything you please. Old unfinished deals, commercial operations, breaches of contract. Any amount of work, I'm up to the eyes in it, it's enough to make your hair stand on end.'

'But haven't all such things been annulled?'

'Of course they have, nominally. But in practice there are all sorts of incompatible demands. On the one hand nationalisation, and on the other, fuel for the Town Soviet and haulage for the Provincial Economic Council. And everyone wants to live. These are the peculiarities of the transitional period, when there is still a gap between theory and practice. It's at a time like this that you need shrewd, resourceful people like myself. Blessed is the man who doesn't see too much. Also, an occasional clout on the snout doesn't come amiss, as my father used to say. Half the province depends on me for its livelihood. I'll be dropping in at Varykino about timber one of these days. Not just yet though. You can't get there except by horse, and my horse is lame. Otherwise you wouldn't catch me jolting along on this pile of scrap. Look at the way it crawls, the brute. Calls itself a train! I might be useful to you in Varykino. I know those Mikulitsins of yours inside out.'

'You know why we are going there, what our plan is?'

'More or less. I can imagine.—Back to the land, the eternal call of Mother Nature. The dream of living by the sweat of your brow.'

'What's wrong with it? You sound disapproving.'

'It's naïve and idyllic, but why not?—Good luck to you. Only I don't believe in it. It's Utopia. Arts and crafts.'

'How do you think Mikulitsin will receive us?'

'He won't let you over the threshold, he'll drive you out with a broomstick, and he'll be quite right! He's in a fine pickle as it is. Idle factories, runaway workers, no means of livelihood, no food, and then you turn up! If he murders you, I shan't blame him!'

'There you are. You are a bolshevik, and yet even you admit that what's going on isn't life—it's lunacy, it's an absurd nightmare.'

'Of course I do. But don't you see that it's a matter of historical inevitability? It has to be gone through.'

'Where is the inevitability?'

'Are you a child, or are you just pretending? Have you dropped from the moon? Gluttons and parasites sat on the backs of the starving workers and drove them to death, and you imagine things could stay like that? And what about all the other forms of outrage and tyranny? Don't you understand the rightness of the people's anger, of their desire to live in justice, of their search for truth? Or do you think a radical change was possible through the Duma, by parliamentary measures, and that we can do without a dictatorship?'

'We are talking at cross purposes and even if we argued for a hundred years we'd never see eye to eye. I used to be very revolutionary-minded, but now I think that nothing can be gained by violence. People must be drawn to good by goodness. But let's drop the subject. About the Mikulitsins—if we are to expect what you suggest, then why are we going? We should turn back.'

'Nonsense! To begin with, they are not the only people in the world. And secondly, Mikulitsin is criminally kind, kind to excess. He'll make a fuss and refuse and resist, and then he'll melt. He'll give

you the shirt off his back and share his last crust of bread with you.
I know him like the back of my hand.' And Samdevyatov told Yury
Mikulitsin's story.

6

'Mikulitsin arrived here twenty-five years ago from Petersburg. He
had been a student at the Technological Institute. He had got into
trouble and was deported and sent here under police supervision.
He got a job as manager at Krueger's works and married. There were
four sisters here in those days—one more than in Chekhov's play—
the Tuntsevas; Agrippina, Avdotya, Glaphira (Glasha) and Seraphima
(Sima). All the young men were after them. Mikulitsin married the
eldest.

'Before long they had a son. From love of liberty his fool of a
father christened him Liberius. Liberius, Libby for short, grew up a
bit wild but he had all sorts of unusual gifts. When the war came he
was fifteen. He faked the date on his birth certificate and made off
to the front as a volunteer. His mother, who was anyway delicate,
couldn't stand the shock. She took to her bed and didn't get up
again. She died the year before last, just before the revolution.

'At the end of the war Liberius came back as a hero with three
medals and, of course, he was a fully bolshevised delegate from the
front.—Have you heard about the " Forest Brotherhood " ? '

'No, I'm afraid not.'

'In that case there's no sense in telling you the story, half the
point is lost. And there isn't any point in your staring out of
the window at the highway either. What's so remarkable about the
highways nowadays?—The partisans. And what are the partisans?—
They are the backbone of the revolutionary army in the civil war,
a force which arose out of the conjunction of two factors: on the
one hand, the political organisation which assumed the leadership of
the revolution, and on the other, the rank and file of the army who
refused to obey the old authorities once the war was lost. Out of
these two things the partisan army came into being. Most of them
are middle peasants[1], but you find all sorts of people—poor peasants,
unfrocked monks, sons of kulaks up in arms against their fathers.
There are anarchist idealists, people on the run without passports,
and boys expelled from school for having had affairs with women.

[1] According to the Leninist theory the peasants were divided into three categories
—rich peasants classified as kulaks, those of average means known as 'middle peasants'
and poor or landless peasants.

And German and Austrian prisoners of war tempted by the promise of freedom and repatriation.—Well, one of the units of this great people's army is called the Forest Brotherhood, and the Forest Brotherhood is commanded by Comrade Forester, and Comrade Forester is Libby, Liberius Avercievich, the son of Avercius Mikulitsin.'

'You don't really mean it?'

'Yes! I do indeed.—But to go on about Avercius. After his wife's death he married again. His second wife, Helen, is an *ingénue*, both by nature and intention. She went straight from school to the altar and is still quite young, but she already pretends to be younger still—prattles, twitters, butter wouldn't melt in her mouth. The moment she sees you, she puts you through an exam: "When was Suvorov born? When are the two sides of a triangle equal to the third?" And if she can trip you up, she's overjoyed. But you'll see for yourself in a few hours.

'The old man has his own peculiarities. He was going to be a sailor. He studied marine engineering. He's clean-shaven, never takes his pipe out of his mouth, talks through his teeth in a slow, friendly voice, has the pipe-smoker's jutting lower jaw and cold grey eyes.—Oh, and a detail I almost forgot—he's a Social Revolutionary and was elected regional delegate to the Constituent Assembly [1].'

'That is surely very important! So father and son are at daggers drawn? Political opponents?'

'In theory, of course they are. But in practice there is no quarrel between the Forest and Varykino. However, to go on with the story. The three remaining Tuntsev sisters—Mikulitsin's sisters-in-law by his first marriage—live in Yuryatin to this day, all confirmed spinsters; but times have changed and so have the girls.

'The eldest, Avdotya, is an assistant at the Public Library.—Dark, pretty, desperately shy, blushes scarlet at the slightest thing. She has a terrible time at the library.—It's dead silent, and the poor girl has chronic hay fever—gets sneezing fits and looks as if she'd like to drop through the floor.—All nerves.

'The next one, Glasha, is the family's blessing. Terrific drive, a wonderful worker, doesn't mind what she does. Libby, Comrade Forester, is supposed to take after his aunt Glasha. One day she's a seamstress or she's working in a stocking factory, then before you know where you are she's turned herself into a hairdresser. You saw the woman at the points, who shook her fist at us?—Bless me, I

---

[1] The Constituent Assembly was formed after the February Revolution under the Provisional Government and was overthrown by the bolsheviks when they failed to obtain a majority in it.

thought, if it isn't Glasha gone to work on the railways!—But I don't think, after all, it was her, she looked too old.

'And then there's the youngest, Sima. She's their cross. She gives them no end of trouble. She's an educated girl, well read, used to go in for poetry and philosophy. But since the revolution—what with all the general uplift, speeches, demonstrations—she's become a bit touched in the head, she's got religious mania. The sisters lock her up when they go to work but she jumps out of the window and off she goes down the street, collecting crowds, preaching the Second Coming and the end of the world.—Well, it's time I stopped talking, we're nearly there. This is my station. Yours is next. You'd better get ready.'

After he had gone Tonya said to Yury: 'I don't know about you, but I feel he's been sent to us by fate. I think he'll play some helpful part in our lives.'

'I hope so, darling. But it worries me that everybody recognises you as Krueger's granddaughter and that Krueger is so well known. Even Strelnikov, the moment I said "Varykino", asked me in his disagreeable way if we were Krueger's heirs.

'It looks to me as if after leaving Moscow to escape notice, we are going to be even more conspicuous here. Not that there is anything to be done about it and there certainly isn't any sense in crying over spilt milk. But we'd better lie low and behave very unassumingly. Altogether I have an unpleasant foreboding . . . But we must be nearly there. Let's wake up your father and get ready.'

7

Tonya stood on the platform at Torfyanaya station counting her family and her luggage over and over to make sure that nothing had been left on the train. The well-trodden sand of the platform was firm under her feet but the anxiety not to miss the station remained with her, and the clatter of the wheels was still in her ears although the train was standing motionless before her eyes. This prevented her from seeing, hearing or taking in anything properly.

Passengers who were continuing their journey were calling out good-bye and waving to her from the coach, but she never noticed them. Nor did she notice that the train was leaving, and only realised that it had gone when she found herself looking at the green fields and the blue sky across the empty track.

The station was built of stone and had benches on either side of the entrance. The Zhivagos were the only travellers who had got out at Torfyanaya. They put their luggage down and sat on one of the benches.

They were struck by the silence, emptiness and tidiness of the station. It seemed strange not to be surrounded by a milling, cursing mob. History had not caught up with this remote provincial life which had yet to become as savage as in the capitals.

The station lay hidden in a birch wood. (When the train drew in it had grown as dark inside the carriage as if it were evening.) Now the shadows of the scarcely stirring trees moved lightly over their hands and faces, over the ground and the station walls and roofs, and over the platform with its clean, damp yellow sand. It was cool in the thicket and the singing of the birds in it had an equally cool sound. Candid and bare as innocence, it pierced and carried through the wood from end to end. The thicket was crossed in two directions by the railway and a country road, and both were overshadowed by the loose, long sleeves of its drooping and swaying branches.

All at once Tonya saw and heard; everything reached her consciousness at the same time—the ringing bird calls, the pure woodland solitude and the flowing, unruffled stillness. She had prepared a speech in her mind: 'I couldn't believe that we would really get here safely, darling. Your Strelnikov, you know, could quite easily have played the gentleman to your face and then sent a telegram to have us all arrested as soon as we got out of the train. I don't believe in their noble sentiments, my dear, it's all a sham.' But quite different words broke from her at the sight of the enchanting scene before her. 'How lovely!' she cried out. She could not say any more. She broke into tears.

At the sound of her crying a little old man in a station-master's uniform came out and shuffled across to them. Touching the peak of his red-topped cap, he asked politely:

'Would the young lady like something from the station medicine chest for her nerves?'

'It's nothing. Thank you. She'll be all right in a moment,' said Alexander Alexandrovich.

'It's the anxiety and the worry of the journey that does it—it's well known. And then this African heat which is so rare in our latitude. And then on top of everything else the happenings in Yuryatin.'

'We saw the fire from the train as we went by.'

'You're from Russia ¹, if I'm not mistaken?'

¹ European Russia, as distinct from Siberia.

'From the very heart of it.'

'From Moscow! Little wonder then that the lady's nerves are upset. They say there isn't a stone left standing.'

'Not quite as bad as that. People exaggerate. But we've certainly had a difficult time. This is my daughter, and that's her husband, and that's their little boy. And this is his nanny, Nyusha.'

'How do you do. How do you do. Delighted. I was rather expecting you. Anfim Yefimovich Samdevyatov telephoned from Sakma. Dr. Zhivago is coming with his family from Moscow, he said, and would I please give them every possible assistance. So that's who you are, I expect?'

'No, Dr. Zhivago is my son-in-law, there he is. I'm not a doctor. I'm a professor of agronomy and my name is Gromeko.'

'Pardon me. My mistake. I am very glad to make your acquaintance.'

'So you know Samdevyatov?'

'Who doesn't know Anfim Yefimovich, the wonder worker! He's our only hope—our one prop. If it weren't for him we'd have all been dead long ago. Give them every possible assistance, he said. Very good, I said. I promised I would. So if you need a horse or anything? Where are you bound for?'

'We want to get to Varykino. Is it far from here?'

'Varykino! That's why I keep wondering who your daughter reminds me of! So it's Varykino you want! That explains everything! Ivan Ernestovich Krueger and I built this road together. I'll see to the horse right away. I'll call one of the men and we'll see about a cart.—Donát! Donát! Take these things into the waiting-room for the time being. And how about a horse? Run over to the tea-room and see what can be done. Bacchus was hanging round here this morning. See if he's still there. Tell them, four passengers for Varykino. They're new arrivals. They've got hardly any luggage, tell them. And look sharp about it. . . . And now, lady, may I give you a piece of fatherly advice? I purposely didn't ask you how closely you were related to Ivan Ernestovich Krueger. Be very careful what you say about it. You can't be hail-fellow-well-met with everyone in times like these.'

At the mention of Bacchus the travellers looked at each other in amazement. They remembered Anna's tales about the fabulous blacksmith who had made himself an indestructible set of steel bowels and the many other local legends she had told them.

8

The horse was a white mare which had recently foaled and the driver, a lop-eared old man with floppy hair, as white as a white owl. For some reason everything about him was white: his new birch-bark shoes had not yet grown dark and his linen shirt and trousers had faded with age.

The foal, curly-haired and black as night, like a painted toy, ran after its mother, kicking out its soft-boned legs.

The travellers clung to the sides of the cart as it jolted over the ruts. Their hearts were at peace. Their dream was coming true, they were almost at the end of their journey. The last hours of the still, clear day lingered generously with a lavish splendour.

Their way led sometimes through woods and sometimes across open fields. Driving through the forest, they were thrown into a heap every time the cart-wheel hit a root, and they sat hunching their shoulders, frowning and clinging together. But in the open fields where space itself seemed to salute them out of the fullness of its heart, they sat up, relaxed and held up their heads.

It was hilly country. The hills, as always, had their own expression. They rose huge and dark in the distance, like proud shadows, keeping a silent watch on the travellers. But a comfortingly rosy light followed them across the fields, soothing them and giving them hope.

Everything pleased and astonished them, above all the unceasing chatter of their cranky old driver, in whose speech archaic idioms, traces of Tartar influence and local oddities of language mixed with those of his own invention.

Whenever the foal lagged behind, the mare stopped and waited for it; soon it caught up with her in graceful, wave-like bounds; then, walking up to the cart clumsily on its long legs set too close together, stretched its long neck and pushed its tiny head under the shaft to suck at the mare's teats.

'But I don't understand,' Tonya shouted to Yury; she shouted slowly for fear that her teeth, which chattered with the shaking of the cart, should bite off the tip of her tongue at some sudden jolt. 'Can this be the same Bacchus Mother used to tell us about? You remember all that stuff about the blacksmith who had had his guts crushed in a fight and made himself a set of new ones?—Bacchus Iron-Belly. Of course I know it's only a tale, but can it have been told about this actual man?'

'No, of course not. To begin with, as you say, it's only a tale, a legend, and then Mother told us that even the legend was over a hundred years old when she was young. But don't talk so loud. You don't want to hurt the old man's feelings.'

'He won't hear anything, he's deaf. And if he did, he wouldn't understand—he's not quite right in the head.'

'Hey, Fyodor Nefyodich!' the old man shouted to his horse, addressing it for some reason by a male name and patronymic, although he knew quite as well as did his passengers that it was a mare. 'Curse this heat! Like unto the children of Abraham in the Persian furnace! Gee-up, you underfed devil! It's you I'm talking to, Mazepa[1].'

Sometimes, without warning, he would burst into snatches of old jingles which must have been made up at the Krueger factories in the old days.

> 'Good-bye, factory yard and gate,
> Good-bye, ore and iron plate,
> The master's bread is stale to me
> And I am sick of drinking water.
> A swan is swimming past the shores,
> He uses feet instead of ores.
> It isn't wine that makes me sway,
> It is that Vanya's gone away
> To be a soldier.
> Don't grieve, Masha, I'm no fool,
> I'm no fool, I'm no clown,
> I'm off to town
> To work for Sentetyurikha.'

'Eh, you God-forsaken beast. Look at that carrion. I give her the whip and she gives me the lip! Eh, Fedya Nefedya, are you making up your mind to go?—That forest, it's called the *tayga*[2], there's no end to it. And there's no end of peasant folk inside it, the Forest Brotherhood is there.—Eh, Fedya Nefedya, have you stopped again, you devil!'

All at once he turned and looked Tonya straight in the eye.

'Where are your brains, young woman? Did you think I didn't know who you were? You're simple-minded, dearie, that I can see. Strike me dead if I didn't recognise you! Certainly I recognised you! Couldn't believe my eyes—you're the living image of Grigov' (this

---

[1] Hetman of Ukrainian Cossacks in the time of Peter the Great.
[2] Siberian virgin forest.

was his version of Krueger's name). 'You wouldn't be his grand-daughter, would you? Who could tell a Grigov if not me! I've spent my life working for him, I know all about him. I did every kind of job for him—worked in the mines as a woodman, and at the winch above ground, and in the stables.—Gee-up, get a move on! Stopped again, like she had no legs! Angels in China! Can't you hear I'm talking to you?

'Well now, you were asking if I'm that same blacksmith Bacchus. You're simple, my dear, such big eyes and no brain! Your Bacchus—he was called Postanogov, Postanogov Iron-Belly—he went to his grave more than two score years ago. But my name is Mekhonóshin. Our Christian names are the same but our surnames are different.'

Little by little the old man told them what they had already heard from Samdevyatov about the Mikulitsins. He spoke of Mikulitsin's second wife as 'his second' and of the first as 'an angel', 'a white cherub'. When he came to the partisan leader, Liberius, and learned that his fame had not yet reached Moscow and that the Forest Brotherhood was unknown there, he could hardly believe it:

'They've not heard? They haven't heard of Comrade Forester? Angels in China, then what has Moscow got ears for?'

Evening was coming, and their shadows, growing longer and longer, ran ahead of them. They were driving through flat, treeless country. Here and there, in lonely bunches, stood tall stringy stalks of goose-foot, willow herb and thistle tipped with flowering tufts. Lit from ground-level by the setting sun, they rose to a ghostly height, looking like mounted sentinels, widely spaced out and keeping motionless watch in the plain.

The valley stretched far into the distance; there it ended in a tall range of hills. A stream or a gully could be imagined at the foot of the mountains; they stood across the travellers' path like a wall, as if the sky over there were enclosed by ramparts and the road were leading to a gate.

At the top of the ridge stood a long, low white house.

'See that look-out up on the hill?' said Bacchus. 'That's where your Mikulitsins live. And down below there's a gully, Shutma it's called.'

Two rifle shots rang out from the hills, followed by a rolling, drumming echo.

'What's that? It wouldn't be the partisans, would it, Grandpa, shooting at us?'

'Bless you, no! Partisans! That's Mikulitsin scaring the wolves away in the Shutma.'

9

Their first meeting with the Mikulitsins took place in the yard of the manager's house. It was a painful scene which began in silence and ended in noisy confusion and absurdity.

Helen, Mikulitsin's wife, was coming home across the yard from her evening walk in the woods. The rays of the setting sun, as golden as her golden hair, trailed behind her through the wood from tree to tree. She had on a light summer dress. She was flushed from her walk and was wiping her face with her handkerchief. Her straw hat hung at the back of her neck from an elastic stretched across her bare throat.

Her husband was coming to meet her from the side of the ravine; he had just climbed up from it with his gun, which he meant to clean, as he had noticed that there was something wrong with it.

Suddenly, into the midst of this peaceful setting Bacchus rolled up smartly with a loud clatter of cart wheels over the cobbles, bringing his surprise.

The passengers got out and Alexander Alexandrovich, humming and hawing and taking off and putting on his hat, began to explain.

Their hosts were struck dumb with amazement. Their genuine speechlessness lasted for several minutes; so did the sincere and appalled confusion of their wretched guests, who were dying of shame. The position could not have been made clearer, whatever had been said, not only to those directly involved but to Sasha, Nyusha and Bacchus; their painful embarrassment communicated itself even to the mare, the foal, the golden rays of the setting sun and the gnats buzzing and swarming round Helen's face and neck.

The silence was finally broken by Mikulitsin. 'I don't understand. I don't understand a thing and I'll never understand. What do you think this is?—The south, where the Whites are, and there is plenty of bread? Why did your choice fall on us? What on earth has brought you here—here of all places?'

'Has it occurred to you, I wonder, what a responsibility this is going to be for Avercius Stepanovich?'

'Don't interrupt, Helen. She's quite right. Did you stop to think what a burden you would be imposing on us?'

'But Heavens above! You misunderstand us. What are we talking about? There is no question of intruding on you, of upsetting your peace of mind. What we need is a very small thing.

All we're thinking of is a corner in any old empty, tumbledown hut and a strip of land that happens to be going to waste because nobody wants it, so that we can grow our food. And a cartload of firewood from the forest when there's no one to see us take it. Is this really asking so much, is it such an imposition?'

'No, but the world is a big place. What has this to do with us? Why should we be chosen for this honour, rather than anyone else?'

'Because we've heard of you and we hoped that you'd have heard of us, so that we would not be coming to complete strangers.'

'Ah! So it's because of Krueger! Because you are related to him! How can you even bring yourselves to admit such a thing at a time like this?'

Mikulitsin had regular features. He tossed his hair back and took great strides, planting his feet squarely on the ground; in summer he wore a Russian shirt tied with a silk, tasselled cord. He was the kind of man who, in the old days, might have become a pirate on the Volga. In more recent times such people have created the type of the eternal student, the dreamer turned schoolmaster.

Mikulitsin had devoted his youth to the liberation movement, to working for the revolution, and his only fear had been that he would not live to see it or that, when it came, it would be too moderate, not bloody enough for his radical dream. Now it had come, it had exceeded his boldest expectations, but he, the born and faithful champion of the proletariat, who had been among the first to set up a Works Committee and to hand over the control of the factory to the men, had been left high and dry; so far from being at the centre of affairs, here he was, in a remote village from which the workers, some of whom were mensheviks, had fled! And now what was this ridiculous nonsense on top of everything? These uninvited survivors of Krueger's family seemed to him Fate's crowning joke, a deliberate trick. It filled his cup to overflowing.

'This is beyond all reason. It's inconceivable! Do you realise the danger you will put me in? I suppose I must be mad. I don't understand. I don't understand a thing and I never shall.'

'I wonder if you realise what a volcano we are already sitting on?'

'Just a moment, Helen. My wife is quite right. Things are bad enough without you. It's a dog's life, a bedlam. I am caught between two fires—between those who make my life a misery because my son is a Red, a bolshevik, a people's darling, and those who want to know why I was elected to the Constituent Assembly. Nobody is pleased, I have no one to turn to. And now you! A nice thought, to have to face a firing squad on your account!'

'Oh, come! Really! Be sensible, for goodness' sake!'

A little later he relented and said:

'Well, there isn't any point in squabbling in the yard. We can go inside. Not, of course, that I can see any good coming of it, but we see as in a glass darkly. Anyhow, we aren't janissaries, we aren't heathens, we won't drive you out into the forest to be eaten by bears. I think, Helen darling, we'd better put them in the palm room for the moment, next to the study. We'll see later where they can settle down; we might find them a cottage in the park. Do come inside.—Bring their things in, Bacchus, give the guests a hand.'

Bacchus did as he was told, muttering:

'Mother of God! They've got no more stuff than pilgrims! Nothing but little bundles, not a single trunk.'

10

In the evening it turned cold. They washed and the women got the room ready for the night. Sasha, who unconsciously expected to hear his childish utterances greeted with raptures and therefore prattled obligingly, was upset because for once he had no success, no one took any notice of him. He was disappointed that the black foal had not been brought into the house, and when his mother snapped at him and told him to be quiet, he burst into sobs, afraid that he might be sent back to the baby shop where, he believed, his parents had bought him. His fear was genuine and he wanted to share it with everyone round him, but it was taken for nonsense and on this occasion failed to charm. Ill at ease in a strange house, the grown-ups seemed to him to be in more than their usual hurry; they went about silently absorbed in their tasks. Sasha was offended and had a fit of what nannies call tantrums. He was made to eat and put to bed with difficulty. When at last he was asleep, Ustinya, the Mikulitsins' maid, took Nyusha to her room to have supper and to be initiated into the secrets of the household. Tonya and the men were invited to evening tea with the Mikulitsins.

Yury and his father-in-law first went out on the verandah for a breath of air.

'What a lot of stars!' said Alexander Alexandrovich.

It was very dark. Standing only a couple of yards apart, the two men could not see each other. Lamp light streamed from a window behind them into the ravine; in its shaft shrubs, trees and other vague shapes rose cloudily in the cold, damp air. But Yury and Alexander were outside this light and it only thickened the darkness round them.

'First thing to-morrow, Yura, we must have a look at the hut he's got in mind for us, and if it's any good, we must start repairing it at once. Then, by the time we've got it fitted up, the ground will have thawed out and we can start digging the beds without losing any time. Did I hear him say he'd let us have some seed potatoes?'

'He certainly did. He promised us other seed as well. I heard him say so with my own ears. As for the hut, we saw it as we were crossing the park. You know where it is? It's that wooden building at the back, you can hardly see it for nettles. I pointed it out to you, do you remember? I thought it would be a good place for the seed-beds. It looked to me as if there might have been a flower garden there once, at least it seemed like that from a distance; of course I may have been mistaken. The soil in the old flower-beds must have been well manured; I imagine it might still be pretty good.'

'I don't know, we'll have a look to-morrow. I should think it's rank with weeds and hard as stone by now. There must have been a kitchen garden somewhere, belonging to the house. It may not be in use now. We'll find out to-morrow. Probably there's still ground frost in the mornings. There's sure to be a frost to-night. Anyway, what bliss to be here at last—that's something to be thankful for. It's a good place. I like it.'

'They are nice people. He especially. She's a bit affected. There is something in herself she doesn't like. That's why she talks such a lot and why she makes herself out even sillier than she is. It's as if she were in a hurry to distract your attention from her looks before you've had time to get a bad impression. And her forgetting to take off her hat and wearing it round her neck isn't absent-mindedness either—it really becomes her.'

'Well, we'd better go back or they'll think us rude.'

On their way to the dining-room where their hosts and Tonya were having tea at the round table under the hanging lamp, they crossed Mikulitsin's dark study.

It had an enormous window, as wide as the wall, overlooking the ravine. Earlier on, while it was still light, Yury had noticed the view from it over the gully and the plain beyond, which they had crossed with Bacchus. In front of the window stood a draughtsman's table which also took up the width of the wall. A gun, lying lengthways on it and yet leaving plenty of room at either end, drew attention to its size.

Now, as they went through, Yury once more thought with envy of the window, the size and position of the table and the spaciousness of the well-furnished room; and it was the first thing he spoke of to his hosts as he entered the dining-room:

'What a wonderful place you have! What a splendid study, it must be a perfect place to work in, a real inspiration!'

'A glass or a cup? And do you like it strong or weak?'

'Yura, do look at this. It's a stereoscope. Avercius Stepanovich's son made it when he was a child.'

'He still hasn't grown up and settled down, even though he has captured district after district for the Soviets from Komuch.'

'What's Komuch?'

'It's the army of the Siberian Government, it's fighting to restore the power of the Constituent Assembly.'

'We've been hearing praise of your son all day long. You must be very proud of him.'

'Those stereoscopic photographs of the Urals—they are his work too, and he took them with a home-made camera.'

'Wonderful biscuits! Are they made with saccharine?'

'Good gracious no! Where would we get saccharine in our wilderness? It's honest-to-God sugar. Didn't you see me putting sugar in your tea?'

'Of course! I was looking at the photographs and I didn't see you. And I do believe it's real tea!'

'Certainly! It's jasmine tea.'

'How on earth do you get it?'

'We have a sort of flying carpet. A friend of ours. He's a public figure of the new type. Very left-wing. He's the official representative of the Provincial Economic Council. He takes our timber to town and gets us flour and butter through his friends. Pass me the sugar, Civvy' (this was her pet name for Avercius). 'And now, I wonder, can you tell me the year of Griboyedov's death?'

'He was born in 1795, I think. But just when he was killed I don't remember.'

'More tea?'

'No, thank you.'

'Now here's something for you. Tell me the date of the Treaty of Nymwegen and which countries signed it?'

'Don't badger them, darling. They've hardly recovered from their journey.'

'And now this is what I'd like to know. How many kinds of lenses are there, and when are the images real, reversed, natural or inverted?'

'How do you come to know so much about physics?'

'We had an excellent science master in Yuryatin; he taught

both in the boys' school and in ours. I can't tell you how good he was. Simply wonderful. It was all so clear when he explained it. Antipov his name was. He was married to a teacher too. All the girls were mad about him, they all fell in love with him. He went off to the war as a volunteer and was killed. Some people say this scourge of ours, Commissar Strelnikov, is Antipov risen from the dead. But it's only a silly rumour, of course. It's most improbable. Though, who can tell, anything is possible. A little more tea?'

9

Varykino

IN winter, when Yury had more time, he began to keep a diary. He started with a quotation from Tyutchev:

> 'What a summer, what a summer!
> This is magic indeed.
> And how, I ask you, did it come to us
> Unsought and undeserved?'

'Very often, last summer, I felt just like that. What happiness it is to work from dawn to dusk for your family and yourself, to build a roof over their heads, to till the soil to feed them, to create your own world, like Robinson Crusoe, in imitation of the Creator of the universe, and to bring forth your life, as if you were your own mother, again and again.

'So many new thoughts come into your head when your hands are busy with hard physical work, when your mind has set you a task which can be achieved by physical effort and which brings its reward in joy and success, when for six hours on end you dig or hammer, scorched by the life-giving breath of the sky. And it isn't a loss but a gain that these transient thoughts, intuitions, analogies, are not put down on paper but forgotten. The town hermit, whipping up his nerves and his imagination with strong black coffee and tobacco, doesn't know the strongest drug of all—good health and real need.

'I am not going further than this. I am not preaching a Tolstoyan doctrine of simplicity and "back to the land"; I am not trying to think out my own solution to the agrarian problem or to correct the socialist view of it. All I am doing is establishing a fact; I am not building a system on our own case. It is too fortuitous and our economy is too mixed; we are not in fact self-supporting; what we produce ourselves—potatoes and vegetables—is only a small part of what we need; the rest we get elsewhere.

'Our use of the land is illegal. We have taken the law into our own hands and we conceal what we are doing from the State. The wood we cut is stolen, and it is no excuse that we steal from the State or that the property belonged to Krueger. We are saved by Mikulitsin who covers up for us (he lives in much the same way as we do) and by being far from the town where, thank goodness, they don't know, so far, what we are up to.

'I keep quiet about being a doctor, because I don't want to restrict my freedom. But there is always some good soul somewhere who gets to know that there is a doctor in Varykino. So they trudge twenty miles to look for me, and bring a hen or a few eggs or a little butter by way of a fee, and in the end I can't refuse to accept it, because people don't believe that medicine is effective unless they pay for it. So my practice brings in a little. But our chief mainstay, Mikulitsin's and mine, is Samdevyatov.

'He is a fantastically complicated character. I can't make him out. He is a genuine supporter of the revolution and he fully deserves the confidence of the Yuryatin Soviet. With all the powers they have given him he could requisition the Varykino timber without so much as telling Mikulitsin or myself, and he knows that we couldn't do a thing. On the other hand, if he felt like robbing the State, he could fill his pocket and again there wouldn't be a murmur from anyone. There is no one he would need to bribe or share with, so what is it that makes him take such care of us—the Mikulitsins and the station-master and ourselves and almost everyone in the district? There isn't a moment when he isn't rushing off somewhere and getting hold of something to bring us. He is just as much at home with Dostoyevsky's *Possessed* as with the *Communist Manifesto*, and he talks about them equally well. I suppose if he didn't complicate his life on this generous and reckless scale he would be bored to death.'

2

A little later Yury wrote:

'We are living in two rooms in a wooden annexe at the back of the old house. In Anna Ivanovna's childhood Krueger used it for special members of the household staff—the dressmaker, the housekeeper and the retired nanny.

'It was pretty dilapidated when we came but we repaired it fairly quickly. With the help of those who know about such things we rebuilt the stove, which serves both rooms. We have rearranged the flues and it gives more heat.

'In this part of the grounds the old garden has vanished, obliterated by new growth. But now that the winter has killed everything and the living no longer conceals the dead, the past can be seen more clearly in snowy outline.

'We have been lucky. The autumn was dry and warm. It gave us time to dig up the potatoes before the rains and the cold weather. Not counting those we gave back to Mikulitsin, we had twenty sacks. We put them in the biggest bin in the cellar and covered them with old blankets and hay. We also put down two barrels of salted cucumbers and two of sauerkraut prepared by Tonya. Fresh cabbages hang in pairs from the timbers. There are carrots buried in dry sand, and radishes and beet and turnips, and peas and beans are stored in the loft. There is enough firewood in the outhouse to last us till the spring.

'I love the warm, dry winter breath of the cellar, the smell of earth, roots and snow that hits you the moment you raise the trap, as you go down in the early hours before the winter dawn, a weak, flickering light in your hand.

'You come out; it is still dark. The door creaks, or perhaps you sneeze, or the snow crunches under your foot, and hares start up from the far cabbage patch and leap away, leaving the snow criss-crossed with tracks. In the distance dogs begin to howl and it takes a long time before they quieten down. The cocks have finished their crowing and have nothing left to say. Then dawn breaks.

'As well as hares, the unending snowy plain is also patterned by the tracks of lynxes; they stretch across it neatly, like strings of beads. The lynx walks like a cat, putting one paw down in front of the other, and they say it travels many miles in a night.

'Traps are set for them, but instead of the lynxes, the wretched hares get caught and half-buried in the snow, and are taken out frozen stiff.

'At the beginning, during the spring and summer, we had a very hard time. It was all we could do to struggle along. But now we can relax in the winter evenings. Thanks to Samdevyatov who gets us paraffin, we sit round a lamp. The women sew or knit, Alexander Alexandrovich or I read aloud. The stove is hot and I, as the appointed stoker, watch for the right moment to close the damper so as not to waste any heat. If a charred log prevents the fire from drawing properly, I run out with it smoking in my hand and fling it as far as possible into the snow. It flies through the air like a torch, throwing off sparks and lighting up the white square lawns of the sleeping park, and then buries itself, hissing, in a snowdrift.

'We read and re-read *War and Peace*, *Eugene Onegin* and Pushkin's other poems, and Russian translations of Stendhal's *Rouge et Noir*, Dickens's *Tale of Two Cities* and Kleist's short stories.'

3

As spring approached Yury wrote:

'I believe Tonya is pregnant. I told her; she doesn't believe me but I feel sure of it. The early symptoms are unmistakable, I don't have to wait for the later, more certain, signs to know.

'A woman's face changes at such a time. It isn't that she becomes plain but her looks are not quite under her control. She is already at the disposal of the future which she carries within her, she is no longer only herself. Her loss of control over her appearance makes her seem physically bewildered; her face dims, her skin coarsens, her eyes shine in a different way, not as she wants them to; it is as if she couldn't quite cope with all these things and has neglected them.

'Tonya and I have never drifted apart and this year of work has brought us even closer together. I have noticed how quick, strong and tireless she is, how cleverly she plans her work so as to waste as little time as possible between one job and another.

'It has always seemed to me that every conception is immaculate and that this dogma, concerning the Mother of God, expresses the idea of all motherhood.

'At the moment of child-birth, every woman has the same aura of isolation, as though she were abandoned, alone. At this vital moment the man's part is as irrelevant as if he had never had anything to do with it, as though the whole thing were gratuitous.

'It is the woman, by herself, who brings forth her progeny, and carries it off upstairs, to some top storey of life, a quiet, safe place for a cradle. Alone, in silence and humility, she feeds and rears the child.

'The Mother of God is asked to "pray zealously to her Son and her God", and the words of the psalm are put into her mouth: "My soul doth magnify the Lord and my spirit hath rejoiced in God my Saviour. For he hath regarded the low estate of his handmaiden: for, behold, from henceforth all generations shall call me blessed." It is because of her child that she says this, He will magnify her ("for He that is mighty hath done to me great things"); He is her glory. Any woman could say it. For every one of them, God is in her child. Mothers of great men must have this feeling particularly, but then, at the beginning, all women are mothers of great men—it isn't their fault if life disappoints them later.'

4

'We go on endlessly re-reading *Eugene Onegin* and the poems. Samdevyatov came yesterday and brought a lot of presents—nice things to eat and oil for the lamps. We have endless discussions about art.

'I have always thought that art is not a category, not a realm in which there are innumerable concepts and varied phenomena, but that, on the contrary, it is something concentrated, strictly limited. It is a principle which comes into every work of art, a force applied to it and a truth worked out in it. And I have never seen it as form but rather as a hidden, secret part of content. All this is as clear to me as daylight. I feel it in every bone of my body, but it's terribly difficult to express or to define it.

'A work of art can appeal to us in all sorts of ways—by its theme, subject, situations, characters. But above all it appeals to us by the presence in it of art. One is much more shaken by the presence of art in *Crime and Punishment* than by Raskolnikov's crime.

'There is no plurality in art. Primitive art, the art of Egypt, Greece, our own—it is all, I think, one and the same art throughout, an art which remains itself through thousands of years. You can call it an idea, a statement about life, so all-embracing that it can't be split up into separate words ; and if there is so much as a particle of it in any work which includes other things as well, it outweighs all the other ingredients in significance and turns out to be the essence, the heart and soul of the work.'

5

'A slight chill, a cough, probably a temperature. Short of breath all day, constriction of the larynx, a lump in my throat. It's a bad business. It must be my heart. First warnings of heredity on my mother's side—she had a bad heart all her life. Can it really be that ? So soon ? If it is, I can't count on a long life.

'A slight smell of burning in the room. A smell of ironing. Tonya is ironing ; every now and then she gets a coal out of the stove and puts it in the iron and the lid of the iron snaps over it like a set of teeth. It reminds me of something, but I can't think what. Bad health makes me forgetful.

'To celebrate Samdevyatov's gift of soap we have had two washing days, and Sasha has been running wild. As I write he sits astride the cross-bar under the table and, imitating Samdevyatov, who takes him out in his sleigh whenever he comes, pretends that he is giving me a ride.

'As soon as I feel better I must go to the town library and read up the ethnography of the region. They say the library has had several important donations and is exceptionally good. I feel like writing. But I'll have to hurry. It will be spring before we know where we are—and then there'll be no time for reading or writing.

'Headache gets worse and worse. I slept badly. Had a muddled dream of the kind you forget as soon as you wake up. All that remained in my memory was the part that woke me up. It was a woman's voice, I heard it in my sleep, so clearly that it echoed all round me. I remembered it and kept hearing it in my mind and going through the list of our women friends—I tried to think of someone who spoke in that deep, moist, heavy, soft voice. It didn't belong to any of them. I thought it might be Tonya's, and that I had become so used to her that I no longer heard the tone of her voice. I tried to forget that she was my wife and to become sufficiently detached to find out. But it wasn't her voice either. It remains a mystery.

'About dreams. It is usually taken for granted that you dream of something which has made a particularly strong impression on you during the day, but it seems to me it's just the contrary.

'Often it's something you paid no attention to at the time—a vague thought that you didn't bother to think out to the end, words spoken without feeling and which passed unnoticed—these are the things which return at night, clothed in flesh and blood as characters in dreams, as if to force you to make up for having neglected them in your waking hours.'

6

'A clear frosty night. Unusual brilliance and coherence of everything. Earth, sky, moon and stars, all seem riveted together by the frost. Shadows of trees lie across the paths, so clear-cut that they seem carved in relief. You keep thinking you see dark figures endlessly crossing the paths, now here, now there. Big stars hang on the branches like blue lanterns. Small ones are all over the sky like daisies in a summer field.

'We go on discussing Pushkin. The other night we talked about the poems he wrote at school. What a lot depends on the choice of meter!

'So long as he was writing long lines, impressing the town of Arzamas was the limit of his ambition. Mythology, bombast, worldly wisdom, epicureanism, sophistication—all put on—all that was to keep up with the grown-ups and throw dust in his uncle's eyes.

'But as soon as he stopped imitating Ossian and Parny and changed from "Recollections of Tsarskoye Selo" to "A Small Town" or "Letter to my Sister", or "To my Inkwell" (written later in Kishinev), or "To Yudin", the whole of Pushkin was already there.

'It's as if the air, the light, the noise of life, of real substantial things burst into his poetry from the street as through an open window. Concrete things—things in the outside world, things in current use, names of things, common nouns—burst in and take possession of his verse, driving out the vaguer parts of speech. Things and more things, lined up in rhymed columns on the page.

'As if these tetrameters, which later became so famous, were units on a yardstick used to measure Russia's life, as if he took the measure of the whole of her existence, as you draw the outline of a foot or give the size of a hand to make sure that the glove or the shoe will fit.

'Later, in much the same way, the rhythm of spoken Russian, the intonations of ordinary speech were echoed in the trimeters and dactyls of Nekrassov.'

7

'I should like to be of use as a doctor or a farmer, and at the same time to be at work on something lasting, something fundamental; I should so very much like to be writing a work of art or science.

'Every man is born a Faust with a longing to embrace and experience and express everything in the world. Faust became a scientist thanks to the mistakes of his predecessors and contemporaries. Progress in science follows the laws of repulsion—every step forward is made by reaction against the delusions and false theories prevailing at the time. That Faust was an artist he owed to the example of his masters. Forward steps in art are made by attraction, through the artist's admiration and desire to follow the example of the predecessors he admires most.

'What is it that prevents me from being useful as a doctor or a writer? I think it is not so much our privations or our wanderings or our constantly changing and unsettled lives, as the power in our day of rhetoric, of the cliché—all this "dawn of the future", "building a new world", "torch-bearers of mankind". The first time you hear it you think: "What wealth of imagination!" But in fact the reason it is so pompous is that there is no imagination at the back of it, because the thought is second-rate.

'The fabulous is never anything but the commonplace touched by the hand of genius. The best object lesson in this is Pushkin. What an ode to honest work, duty and the common round! The words "bourgeois" [1] and "middle class" [1] have become terms of abuse nowadays, but Pushkin forestalled the criticism in his "Family Tree": "A bourgeois, a bourgeois [2] is what I am," and again in "Onegin's Journey":

> "Now my ideal is the housewife
> My greatest wish, a quiet life,
> A fat tureen of cabbage soup."

'What I have come to like best in the whole of Russian literature is the childlike Russian quality of Pushkin and Chekhov, their shy unconcern with such high-sounding matters as the ultimate purpose of mankind or their own salvation. It isn't that they didn't think about these things, and to good effect, but they always felt that such important matters were not for them. While Gogol, Tolstoy and Dostoyevsky worried and looked for the meaning of life and prepared for death and drew up balance-sheets, these two were distracted, right up to the end of their lives, by the current, individual tasks imposed on them by their vocation as writers, and in the course of fulfilling these tasks they lived their lives, quietly, treating both their lives and their work as private, individual matters, of no concern to anyone else. And these individual things have since become of concern to all, their work has ripened of itself, like apples picked green from the trees, and has increasingly matured in sense and sweetness.'

8

'First signs of spring. Thaw. The sleepy air smells of buttered pancakes and vodka as at Shrovetide. A sleepy, oily sun blinking in the forest, sleepy pines blinking their needles like eyelashes, oily puddles shining at noon. The countryside yawns, stretches, turns over and goes back to sleep.

'Chapter 7 of *Eugene Onegin* describes the spring, Onegin's house deserted in his absence, Lensky's grave by the stream at the foot of the hill.

[1] *Obyvatel; Meshchanin*: neither word has its exact equivalent in English. *Obyvatel* means literally a man who lives in a place with the implication that he takes no responsible part in its affairs (whatever class he belongs to). *Meshchanin* is closer to 'petit bourgeois'.   [2] *Meshchanin*.

"The nightingale, spring's lover,
Sings all night. The wild rose blooms."

Why "lover"? Well, it's a natural thing to say, it's fitting. "Lover"
is right. And then, he needed it for the rhyme.—Or was he really
thinking of Nightingale the Robber, the one in the ballad? "Robber
Nightingale, the son of Odimantiy".

"At his nightingale whistle,
At his wild forest call,
The grass is all a-tremble,
The flowers shed their petals,
The dark forest bows down to the ground
And all good people fall down dead."

'We came to Varykino in early spring. Soon the trees grew green
—alder and hazel and wild cherry—especially in the Shutma, the
hollow below Mikulitsin's house. And soon after that the nightingales
began to sing.

'Once again I wondered at the difference between their song and
that of all other birds, at the wide gulf left unbridged by nature
between the others and the wealth and singularity of theirs. Such
variety and power and resonance! Turgenev talks about it somewhere—that whistling, as if the demon of the woods were playing his
flute. There were two phrases that stood out particularly. One was a
luxurious, greedily repetitive "tiokh-tiokh-tiokh". At the sound of it,
the thicket, all covered with dew, shivered as though with pleasure.
The other was grave, imploring, an appeal or a warning: "Wake up!
Wake up!¹"

9

'Spring. Nearly time for the spring sowing. No time to write, not
even to keep a diary. It was good while it lasted. I'll put it aside
until next winter.

'The other day—and then it really was Shrovetide—right in the
middle of the spring floods, a sick peasant drove his sledge into the
yard through the mud and slush. I told him I had stopped practising,
I had none of the proper medicines or instruments. But it was no
good, he went on and on.—"Help me. My skin is bad. Have pity
on my sick body."—What could I do? A heart is not a stone. I
told him to take his clothes off. He had lupus. As I was examining
him I glanced at the bottle of carbolic on the window ledge (don't

¹ *Ochnees! Ochnees!*

ask me where it comes from—that or the few other things I couldn't do without—everything comes from Samdevyatov). Then I saw there was another sledge in the yard. I thought at first it was another patient. But it was my brother, Yevgraf, who had dropped in on us out of the blue. The family took charge of him—Tonya, Sasha, Alexander Alexandrovich. Later I came out and joined them. We showered him with questions. Where had he come from? How had he come? As usual, he was evasive, he smiled, shrugged, spoke in riddles.

'He stayed a fortnight, went often to Yuryatin and then vanished as if the earth had swallowed him. I realised while he was staying with us that he had even more influence than Samdevyatov and that his work and his connections were even more mysterious. What is he? What does he do? Why is he so powerful? He promised to make things easier for us so that Tonya should have more time for Sasha and I for practising medicine and for writing. We asked him how he proposed to do this.—He smiled. But he has been as good as his word. There are signs of change in our conditions.

'It really is extraordinary. He is my half-brother. We bear the same name. And yet I know virtually nothing about him.

'For the second time he has burst into my life as my good genius, my rescuer, resolving all my difficulties. Perhaps in every life there has to be, besides the other characters involved in it, a secret, unknown force, a figure who is almost symbolical and who comes unsummoned to the rescue, and perhaps in mine Yevgraf, my brother, plays the part of this hidden spring of life.'

At this point Yury's diary breaks off: he never took it up again.

10

Yury looked through the books he had taken out at the reading-room of the Yuryatin public library. The reading-room had many windows and could seat about a hundred people. Long tables stood in rows which ended by the windows. The library closed at dusk; in the spring the town had no lighting. But Yury was not affected by this, since, in any case, he never stayed in town later than the dinner hour. He would leave the horse which Mikulitsin had lent him at Samdevyatov's inn, read all morning and then ride back to Varykino in the afternoon.

Before he began visiting the library Yury had hardly ever been to Yuryatin; he had nothing in particular to do there, and he hardly knew it. Now, as the reading-room gradually filled with local inhabitants, some of whom sat down next to him and others further away, he felt as if he were getting to know the town by standing at one of its crossroads, and as if not only the people were coming into the room, but the houses and the streets in which they lived were also meeting there.

The actual Yuryatin, real and not imagined, could be seen out of the windows. In front of the largest, the one in the middle of the row, there stood a tank of boiled water. When the readers felt like having a rest, they went out on the landing to smoke or they gathered round the tank, drank the water, emptied the cup into the basin and crowded by the window, admiring the view over the town.

The readers were of two kinds. The majority belonged to the local intelligentsia, the rest were of more humble origin.

The intellectuals, mostly women, were poorly dressed and had a neglected, hang-dog look and long, sickly faces which for one reason or another—whether through hunger, jaundice or dropsy—were puffy. They had always been used to reading, they knew the attendants personally and felt at home in the library.

The common people looked well and handsome, and were neatly dressed in their best clothes; they came in shyly and diffidently as though they were entering a church; they made more noise than the others, not because they did not know the rules but because in their anxiety not to make a sound they could not control their lively feet and voices.

The librarian and his two assistants sat on a daïs in a recess in the wall opposite the windows, separated from the rest of the room by a counter. One of the assistants was a cross-looking woman who wore a woollen shawl and who kept putting on her pince-nez and taking it off, apparently in accordance with mood rather than need. The other, in a black silk blouse, seemed to have a weak chest, for she breathed and spoke through her handkerchief and never took it away from her nose and mouth.

The staff had the same long, puffy, flabby faces as the intellectuals, and the same loose skin, earthy and greenish like salted cucumbers or grey mould. They took it in turn to explain the rules in whispers to new readers, sorted the order slips, fetched the books and took them back, and in the intervals worked on some report or other.

Through an unaccountable association of ideas started by the sight of the real town outside the window and the imaginary one inside the room, as well as by the swollen faces round him, which made it seem as though everyone had goitre, and somehow reminded him of the face of the surly woman in charge of the Yuryatin station signals on the morning of his arrival, Yury remembered the distant panorama of the town and Samdevyatov beside him on the carriage floor and

Samdevyatov's comments and explanations. He tried to connect these explanations, given him so far outside the town, with his immediate surroundings, now that he was at the centre of the picture, but he could not remember enough of what Samdevyatov had told him.

11

Yury was sitting at the end of the room furthest from the door. In front of him were several reports on local zemstvo statistics and some reference books on the ethnography of the region. He had tried also to get two books on the history of the Pugachev rebellion but the librarian in the silk blouse had whispered that no one reader could take out so many volumes at the same time and that he would have to give back some of the journals and reference books before taking out the other works which interested him.

So he applied himself to his unsorted pile of books with more haste and industry than before, in order to set aside those which he really needed and exchange the rest for the historical books he wished to read. He was leafing through the manuals and going over the chapter headings, wholly concentrated on his work and not looking about him. The crowd of readers did not distract him. He had had a good look at his neighbours; those on his left and right were fixed in his mind, he knew they were there without raising his eyes, and he no more expected them to leave the reading-room before him than he expected the houses and churches outside the window to move from their accustomed places.

The sun, however, did change its place. It had moved all round the room from the east corner and was now shining through the windows in the south wall straight into the eyes of the nearest readers.

The librarian with the chronic cold came down from her daïs and went over to the windows. They had goffered white blinds which softened the light pleasantly. She pulled them all down except one. The last window was still in the shade. Coming to it, she pulled the cord to open the sash but was overcome with a fit of sneezing.

After she had sneezed ten or twelve times Yury guessed that she was Mikulitsin's sister-in-law, one of the Tuntsev girls of whom Samdevyatov had spoken. He raised his head and looked in her direction, as most of the readers had already done.

Now he noticed a change in the room. At its further end there was a new reader. Yury immediately recognised Antipova. She was sitting with her back to him, speaking in a low voice to the librarian with a cold, who stood leaning over her and whispering back. The conversation seemed to have a good effect on the librarian. It indeed appeared to cure her instantly, and not only her cold but also her strained and nervous expression vanished. With a warm, grateful glance at Lara she took the handkerchief she had been ceaselessly pressing to her mouth away from her face, put it in her pocket and went back to her seat behind the partition, happy, self-confident and smiling.

The incident marked by this touching detail was noticed by several people in different parts of the room; they too smiled, looking at Lara with approval. From these trivial signs Yury gathered how well Antipova was known and liked in the town.

12

Yury's first impulse was to go across and speak to her. But a shyness and lack of simplicity, entirely alien to his nature, had, in the past, crept into his relationship with her and now held him back. He decided not to disturb her, and not to interrupt his work. To avoid the temptation of looking at her, he turned his chair sideways, so that its back was almost against his table; he tried to concentrate on his books, holding one in his hand and another on his knees.

But his thoughts were worlds away from the subject he was reading. Suddenly he realised that the voice he had once heard in a dream on a winter night in Varykino had been Lara's. The discovery took him so much by surprise that he jerked his chair back, making a noise which startled his neighbours, and stared at her.

He saw her side-face, almost from the back. She wore a light check blouse with a belt and she sat, lost in her book, utterly absorbed in it, like a child, her head bent slightly over her right shoulder. Occasionally she stopped to think, looked up at the ceiling or straight in front of her, then again propped her cheek on her hand and wrote in her notebook with a swift, sweeping movement of her pencil.

Yury noticed again what he had observed long ago in Melyuzeyevo. 'She has no coquetry,' he thought. 'She does not wish to please or to look beautiful. She despises all that side of a woman's life, it's as though she were punishing herself for being lovely. But this proud hostility to herself makes her more attractive than ever.

'How well she does everything! She reads not as if reading were the highest human activity, but as if it were the simplest possible thing, a thing which even animals could do. As if she were carrying water from a well or peeling potatoes.'

These reflections calmed him. In fact he had rarely known such peace. His mind stopped darting from subject to subject. He could not help smiling; Lara's presence affected him in the same way as it had affected the nervous librarian.

No longer worried about the angle of his chair nor afraid of distractions, he worked for an hour or so with even greater concentration than before her arrival. He went through the whole pile of books in front of him, setting aside those he needed most, and e. n had time to read a relevant article he found in one of them. Then, deciding that he had done enough for the day, he gathered up all his books and took them back to the desk. With an easy conscience and without any ulterior motive he reflected that, after his hard morning's work, he deserved to take time off to see an old friend and that he could legitimately allow himself the pleasure of meeting her. But when he stood up and looked round the room, Lara was no longer there.

The books she had just returned were still lying on the counter where he had put his own. They were textbooks on Marxism. She must be re-educating herself politically before going back to her teaching job.

On her order slips which stuck out between the pages of the books was written her address. Yury took it down, surprised by its oddity: 'Merchant Street[1], opposite the House of Caryatids.' He asked another reader what this meant and was told that the habit of describing a house by its relation to the 'House of Caryatids' was as current in Yuryatin as the habit in Moscow of calling a district by the name of its parish church.

The 'House of Caryatids' was a dark, steel-grey building with statues of the Muses holding cymbals, lyres and masks decorating its façade. A merchant had built it in the last century as his private theatre. The merchant's heirs had sold it to the Merchants' Guild, which gave its name to the street, and the whole district was known by the name of the house. It was now used by the Party's Town Committee and the lower part of its façade, where posters and programmes had hung in the old days, now displayed government proclamations and decrees.

13

It was a cold windy afternoon at the beginning of May. Yury had been to the library, finished what he had to do in town and was going home, when he suddenly changed his plans and went to look for Lara.

The wind often held him up, raising clouds of dust and sand in front of him. He turned aside, bowing his head and screwing up his eyes,

[1] Merchant Street: Kupecheskaya.

waited for the dust to stop blowing and continued on his way.

Lara lived at the corner of Merchant Street opposite the dark, blue-grey House of Caryatids which he now saw for the first time. It did indeed live up to its name and made a strange, disturbing impression on him.

Mythological female figures, half as big again as human beings, stood in a row all round it at the level of the top floor. Between two gusts of dusty wind it seemed to him as if all the women in the house had come out on the balcony and were looking down at him over the balustrade.

There were two entrances to Lara's house, one door in Merchant Street, the other round the corner in the alley. Not knowing that there was a front entrance, he went in from the side street.

As he turned in at the gate the wind whirled dust and rubbish into the sky, hiding the way into the yard. Through this black curtain several hens, chased by a cock, fled clucking from under Yury's feet.

When the dust settled he saw Lara by the well. She had filled two buckets and hung them on a yoke across her left shoulder. Her hair was carelessly tied in a kerchief knotted in front to keep the dust off, and she was holding her billowing skirt down between her knees. She started for the house, but was stopped by another gust which tore the kerchief from her head and carried it off to the far end of the fence, where the hens were still cackling.

Yury ran after it, picked it up and brought it back to her. She looked amazed but remained natural as always in her manner and made no dramatic gesture of surprise. All she said was: 'Zhivago!'

'Larissa Fyodorovna!'

'What on earth are you doing here?'

'Put your buckets down. I'll carry them for you.'

'I never stop half-way, I never leave what I do unfinished. If it's me you've come to see, come along.'

'Who else should I come to see?'

'How should I know?'

'All the same, let me take those buckets. I can't be idle while you do the work.'

'You call that work? Leave them alone. You'll only splash the stairs. Better tell me what brought you here. You've been more than a year in the district and you never found a moment to come till now.'

'How do you know?'

'The world is full of rumours. Besides, I saw you in the reading-room.'

'Why didn't you speak to me?'

'Don't tell me you didn't see me.'

Swaying a little under the weight of the lightly swinging buckets, she walked in front of him through the low vaulted entrance. Here she bent down, put the pails down on the earth floor, took the yoke off her shoulder, straightened up and dried her hands with a small handkerchief.

'Come, I'll take you through the inside passage to the front hall. It's lighter. You'll have to wait a moment. I'll take the buckets up the back stairs and tidy up a bit. I won't be long. Look at our smart stairs—cast-iron steps with an open-work pattern. It's an old house. The shelling has shaken it a bit: you can see where the masonry has come loose. See this crack in the brickwork?—That's where Katya and I leave the key of the flat when we go out. Keep it in mind. You might come one day when I'm out—you can open the door and make yourself at home till I come back. You see, there it is, but I don't need to use it now. I'll go in the back way and open the door from inside. Our only trouble is rats. There are swarms and swarms of them, and you can't get rid of them. It's these old walls. Cracks and crevices all over the place. I stop up all the rat holes I can see but it doesn't do much good. Perhaps you'd come one day and help me? The cracks between the skirting and the floor-boards need stopping up. How about it? Well, you stay on the landing and think about something. I shan't be long, I'll call you in a minute.'

Waiting for her to call him, he looked round at the peeling walls and the cast-iron steps. He told himself: 'In the reading-room I thought she was absorbed in her reading with the ardour she would give to a real, hard physical task. Now I see that the reverse is also true: she carries water from the well as lightly and effortlessly as if she were reading. There is the same ease and harmony in everything she does, as if, way back in her childhood, she had taken a flying start in life and everything had followed of itself, as naturally as a result flows from a cause. All this is in the line of her back when she bends down and in her smile as it parts her lips and rounds her chin, and in her words and in her thoughts.'

'Zhivago!' Lara called down from the top landing. He went up.

14

'Give me your hand and do as I tell you. We have to go through two dark rooms piled with furniture—you'll bump into something and hurt yourself.'

'It is a maze. I'd never have found my way. Why is it like this? Is the flat being redecorated?'

'Oh no, nothing like that. That's not the reason. The flat belongs to someone else, I don't even know who it is. I had my own flat in the school building. When the school was taken over by the Town Housing Department Katya and I were given part of this one. The old tenants had gone away, leaving all their furniture. There was an awful lot of it. I don't want other people's things, so I put it all into these two rooms and whitewashed the windows to keep out the sun.— Don't let go of my hand or you'll get lost. Here we are, we turn right. Now we're out of the maze—here's my door. It will be lighter in a second. Mind the step.'

As he followed her into the room he was struck by the view from the window facing the door. It looked out on the yard and over the low roofs of the houses beyond it, to the common by the river; the common belonged to the municipality. Goats and sheep grazed on it, their wool sweeping the ground like coat-tails. There too was the familiar hoarding: *Moreau & Vetchinkin. Seed drills. Threshing machines*.

Reminded of the day of his arrival from Moscow, he began at once describing it to Lara and, forgetting that Strelnikov was said to be her husband, told her, unthinkingly, of his meeting with him. This part of his story made a deep impression on her.

'You saw him! How extraordinary! I won't tell you now, but really it is extraordinary. It's as if you were predestined to meet. I'll tell you all about it some time, you'll be amazed. He seems to have made a good rather than a bad impression on you?'

'Yes, on the whole. He ought to have repelled me. We had actually passed through the country where he had brought death and destruction. I expected to see a bashi-bazook or a revolutionary Jack the Ripper, but he was neither. It's a good thing when a man is different from your image of him. It shows he isn't a type. If he were, it would be the end of him as a man. But if you can't place him in a category, it means that at least a part of him is what a human being ought to be. He has a grain of immortality.'

'They say he is not a party member.'

'Yes, I think that's true. I have often wondered since what it is that makes him attractive. I think it is because he is a doomed man. He'll come to a bad end and he will atone for the evil he has done. Revolutionaries who take the law into their own hands are horrifying, not as criminals, but as machines that have got out of control, like a run-away train. Strelnikov is as mad as the rest, but he has been driven mad by life and suffering, not by books. I don't know his secret, but I feel sure he has one. His alliance with the bolsheviks is accidental. They put up with him so long as he happens to be going their way and they can use him. The moment they don't need him they'll throw him out and trample on him quite mercilessly, as they have done with other military experts.'

'You think so?'

'I feel sure of it.'

'But is there no escape for him? Couldn't he run away?'

'Where could he run to, Larissa Fyodorovna? You could do that in the old days, under the tsars. But just you try nowadays!'

'You've made me feel sorry for him. You've changed, you know. You used to speak more calmly about the revolution, you were less harsh about it.'

'The point is, Larissa Fyodorovna, that there are limits to everything. In all this time something definite should have been achieved. But it turns out that those who inspired the revolution aren't at home in anything except change and turmoil: that's their native element; they aren't happy with anything that's less than on a world scale. For them, transitional periods, worlds in the making, are an end in themselves. They aren't trained for anything else, they don't know about anything except that. And do you know why there is this incessant whirl of never-ending preparations? It's because they haven't any real capacities, they are ungifted. Man is born to live, not to prepare for life. Life itself—the gift of life—is such a breathtakingly serious thing!—Why substitute this childish harlequinade of adolescent fantasies, these schoolboy escapades? But enough of this. It's my turn to ask questions. We arrived on the morning of the local upheaval. Were you in it?'

'I should think I was! There were fires all round us, it's a wonder the house didn't burn down. It was pretty badly shaken, as I told you. To this day there's an unexploded shell in the yard. It's just inside the gate. Looting, shelling, all kinds of horrors—as at every change of government. But by then we were used to it, it wasn't the first time. And I can't tell you what went on under the Whites! Murders, vengeance, extortions, blackmail—a real orgy! But I haven't told you the most extraordinary thing.—Our Galiullin! He turned up with the Czechs as a sort of Governor-General.'

'I know. I heard about it. Did you see him?'

'Very often. You can't think how many people I managed to save thanks to him, how many I hid. To give him his due he behaved perfectly, like a gentleman, not like all those small fry—little upstart Cossack captains, police sergeants and what not. Unfortunately it was the small fry who set the tone, not the decent people. Galiullin helped me a lot, bless him. We are old friends, you know. When I was a little girl he lived in a block of tenements next door to us and I was always in and out. Most of the tenants were railway workers. I saw a lot of poverty as a child. That's why my attitude to the revolution is different from yours. It's closer to me. There's a lot of it I understand from the inside. But to think that Galiullin, that the son of a door-keeper should become a White colonel!—or it may have been a general.—There aren't any soldiers in my family, I don't know much about army ranks. And by profession, as you know, I am a history teacher. . . . Anyway, that's how it was. We managed to help quite a lot of people between us. I used to go and see him. We talked about you. I've always had friends and connections in every government—and also sorrows and disappointment from all of them. It's only in bad novels that people are divided into two camps and have nothing to do with each other. In real life everything gets mixed up! Don't you think you'd have to be a hopeless nonentity to play only one role all your life, to have only one place in society, always to stand for the same thing?—Ah, there you are!'

A little girl of about eight came in, her hair done up in finely braided plaits. Her narrow eyes had a sly, mischievous look and went up at the corners when she laughed. She knew her mother had a visitor, she had heard his voice outside the door, but she thought it necessary to put on an air of surprise. She curtsied and looked at Yury with the fearless, unblinking stare of a lonely child who had started to think early in life.

'My daughter, Katya. I hope you'll be friends!'

'You showed me her photograph in Melyuzeyevo. How she's grown and changed since then!'

'I thought you were out. I didn't hear you come in.'

'I took the key out of the crack and there was an enormous rat in it—as big as this! You should have seen me jump! I nearly died of fright.'

She made a comical face, opening her eyes wide and rounding her mouth like a fish out of water.

'Off you go now. I'll get Uncle Yury to stay to dinner and take the kasha [1] out of the oven. I'll call you when it's ready.'

'Thank you, I wish I could stay. But we have dinner at six since I've started coming to town and I try not to be late. It takes me over

[1] Gruel made of buckwheat.

three hours to get home—nearly four. That is why I came so early. I'm afraid I'll have to go soon.'

'You can stay another half-hour.'

'I'd love to.'

15

'And now, as you have been so frank with me, I'll be frank with you. The Strelnikov you met is my husband, Pasha Antipov—Pasha whom I went to look for at the front and in whose death I so rightly refused to believe.'

'I am not surprised you think so. I heard something of the sort myself, but I didn't believe it for a moment. That is why it went clean out of my mind when I was talking to you and I spoke so freely. It's sheer nonsense. I've seen this man. How could anyone connect him with you? What have you in common with him?'

'All the same, it's true. Strelnikov is my husband, Antipov. Most people think so and I agree with them. Katya knows it and is proud of her father. Strelnikov is his pseudonym—he has to live under an assumed name, like all active revolutionaries. For some reason he may not live or work under his own name.

'And it was he who took Yuryatin and shelled us. He knew we were here, but for fear of giving himself away, he never once tried to find out if we were alive. Of course it was his duty. If he had asked me I would have told him to do just that. All the same . . . You might say that my being safe and the Town Council giving me a reasonable place to live in shows that he is secretly looking after us. But that he should actually have been here and resisted the temptation to come and see us—it's inconceivable! It isn't human, it's some kind of Roman civic virtue, one of those things they've thought up nowadays. But I mustn't let myself be influenced by your way of looking at things. You and I don't really think alike. There is something intangible, marginal, we both understand and feel in the same way. But on the wide issues, in our philosophy of life, it's better for us to stay on different sides. But to go back to Strelnikov.

'Now he's in Siberia, and you are right—I have heard him accused of things that make my blood run cold. He is in Siberia, in command of one of our most advanced positions and he is fighting and beating poor old Galiullin, his childhood friend and his comrade in arms in the German war. Galiullin knows who he is and he knows that I am his wife but he has had the tact—I can't value it too highly—

never to make me feel it, though goodness knows he goes mad with rage at the sound of Strelnikov's name.

'That's where he is now, in Siberia. But he was here for a long time, living in that railway carriage where you saw him. I kept hoping I'd run into him by accident. Sometimes he went to the staff headquarters; they were in the building where Komuch—the Constituent Assembly army—used to have its headquarters. And it was an odd trick of fate—the entrance was through the wing where Galiullin used to see me. I was always going there to ask him to help somebody or to stop some horrible business or other. For instance, there was that affair at the Military Academy; it caused a great stir at the time.—If an instructor was unpopular the cadets ambushed him and shot him, saying he was a bolshevik sympathiser. And then there was the time when they started beating up the Jews. Incidentally—it always strikes me—if you are an intellectual of any kind and live in town, as we do, half your friends are bound to be Jews. Yet in times when there are pogroms, when all these terrible, despicable things are done, we don't only feel sorry and indignant and ashamed, we feel wretchedly divided, as if our sympathy came more from the head than from the heart and had an after-taste of insincerity.

'It's so strange that these people who once brought about the liberation of mankind from the yoke of idolatry, and so many of whom now devote themselves to its liberation from injustice, should be powerless to achieve their own liberation from themselves, from the yoke of their loyalty to an obsolete, antediluvian designation which has lost all meaning—that they should not rise above themselves and dissolve among all the rest, whose religion they have founded and with whom they would have so much in common if they knew them better.

'Of course it's true that persecution forces them into this futile and disastrous pose, this shamefaced, self-denying isolation, which brings them nothing but misfortune. But I think some of it also comes from a kind of inward senility, the fatigue of centuries. I don't like their ironical whistling in the dark, the workaday poverty of their outlook, their timid imaginations. It's as irritating as old men talking of old age or sick people about sickness. Don't you agree?'

'I haven't thought about it much. I have a friend, Misha Gordon, who thinks like you.'

'Well, I used to go along to this place hoping to catch Pasha on his way in or out. In tsarist times the Governor-General used to have his office in that part of the building. Now there is a notice on the door: "Complaints." You may have seen it? It's the prettiest place in the town. The square in front of it is paved with wooden blocks and across the square there is the town garden, full of maples, hawthorn, honeysuckle. There was always a queue in the street outside the door; I used to stand there and wait. Of course I didn't try to jump the queue, I didn't say I was his wife. After all, our names are different. And you don't suppose an appeal to sentiment would move them! Their ways are quite different. Do you know that his own father, Pavel Ferapontovich Antipov, a former political convict, an old worker, is quite near here, in a settlement along the highway, where he lived in exile. And his friend Tiverzin is there too. They are both members of the local revolutionary committee. Well, can you believe it, Pasha hasn't been to see his father and he hasn't told him who he is. And his father takes it for granted, he isn't a bit hurt. If his son is kept "under cover" then that's as it should be, he can't see him and that's all there is to it. They are made of stone, these people, they aren't human, with all their rules and principles.

'Even if I had managed to prove that I was his wife, it wouldn't have done me any good! What do wives matter to them at a time like this? The workers of the world, the remaking of the universe, that's something! But what's a wife? Just an individual biped, of no more importance than a flea or a louse!

'His A.D.C. used to come out and ask people what they wanted to see him for and let some of them in. But I never told him my name and when he asked me what my business was I always said it was personal. Of course, I knew I was wasting my time. The A.D.C. would shrug his shoulders and give me a suspicious look. I never once saw him.

'I suppose you think he can't be bothered with us, he doesn't love us, he's forgotten us? Well, you are wrong. I know him too well. I know just what he wants, and it's just because he loves us. He can't bear to come back to us empty-handed. He wants to come back as a conqueror, full of honour and glory, and lay his laurels at our feet. Just like a child!'

Katya came in again. Lara snatched her up and much to her astonishment started swinging her round, tickling and hugging her.

16

Yury was riding home from Yuryatin. He had made this journey countless times. He was so used to the road, that he was no longer aware of it, he hardly saw it.

Soon he would come to the crossroads in the forest where the way

straight on led to Varykino and a path turned off to a fishing village on
the river Sakma; here stood yet another hoarding advertising agricultural machinery; as usual, he would reach the crossroads at dusk.

It was now more than two months since that day when he went to
town as usual but, instead of returning home the same afternoon, spent
the night at Lara's and later told his family that he had been kept on
business and had stayed at Samdevyatov's inn. He had long been calling Lara by her Christian name and saying 'thou' to her, though she
still called him Zhivago. Yury was deceiving Tonya and what he
concealed from her was becoming increasingly grave and illicit. This
was something unheard-of between them.

He worshipped Tonya. Her peace of mind meant more to him
than anything in the world. He was ready to defend her honour and
was more sensitive to anything touching it than her father or herself. In
defence of her pride he would have torn anyone apart with his own
hands. And yet now he was offending against it himself.

At home he felt like a criminal. His family's ignorance of the
truth, their unchanged affection, were a mortal torment to him. In
the middle of a conversation he would suddenly be numbed by the
recollection of his guilt and cease hearing a word of what was being said.

If this happened during a meal, his food stuck in his throat and he
put down his spoon and pushed away his plate. 'What is wrong
with you?' Tonya would ask, puzzled. 'You must have had some
bad news when you were in town. Has anyone been arrested? Or
shot? Tell me. Don't be frightened of upsetting me. You'll feel
better when you've told me.'

Had he been unfaithful to her because he preferred another
woman? No, he had made no comparison, no choice. He did not
believe in 'free love' or in the 'right' to be carried away by his senses.
To think or speak in such terms seemed to him degrading. He had
never 'sown wild oats', nor did he regard himself as a superman with
special rights and privileges. Now he was crushed by the weight of
his guilty conscience.

'What next?' he sometimes asked himself, and hoped wretchedly for
some impossible, unexpected circumstance to solve his problem for him.

But at this moment things had changed. He had decided to cut
the knot and he was going home with a solution. He would confess
everything to Tonya, beg her to forgive him and never see Lara again.

Not that everything was quite as it should be. He felt now that he
had not made it clear enough to Lara that he was breaking with her
for good, for ever. He had announced to her that morning that he
intended to confess everything and that they must stop seeing one

another; but now he had the feeling that he had softened it all down and not made it sufficiently definite.

Lara had realised how unhappy he felt and had no wish to upset him further by a painful scene. She tried to listen to him as calmly as she could. They were talking in one of the empty front rooms. Tears were running down her cheeks, but she was no more conscious of them than the stone statues on the house across the road felt the rain running down their faces. She kept saying softly: 'Do as you think best, don't worry about me. I'll get over it.' She was saying it sincerely, without any false generosity, and as she did not know that she was crying, she did not wipe away her tears.

At the thought that Lara might have misunderstood him, and that he had left her with a wrong impression and false hopes, he nearly turned and galloped straight back, to say what he had left unsaid and, above all, to take leave of her much more warmly, more tenderly, in a manner more suitable to a last farewell. Controlling himself with difficulty, he continued on his way.

As the sun went down, the forest was filled with cold and darkness. It smelled of damp leaves. Swarms of gnats hung in the air as still as floats, humming sadly on a constant, high-pitched note. They settled on his face and neck and he kept swatting them, his noisy slaps keeping time with the sounds of riding—the creaking of the saddle, the heavy thud of hooves on the squelching mud and the dry salvoes bursting from the horse's guts. In the distance, where the sun was refusing to go down, a nightingale began to sing.

'Wake up! Wake up!' it called entreatingly; it sounded almost like the summons on the eve of Easter Sunday: 'Awake, O my soul, why dost thou slumber.'

Suddenly Yury was struck by a very simple thought. What was the hurry? He would not go back on the promise he had given himself, the confession would be made, but who said that it must be made that day? He had not said anything to Tonya yet, it was not too late to put it off till after he had been to town once again. He would finish his conversation with Lara, with such warmth and depth of feeling that it would make up for all their suffering. How splendid, how wonderful! How strange that this had not occurred to him before!

At the thought of seeing Lara once more his heart leapt for joy. In anticipation he lived through his meeting with her.

The wooden huts and pavements on the outskirts of the town . . . He was on his way to her. In a moment he would leave the wooden lanes and waste plots for the stone and stucco streets. The small suburban houses flashed by like the pages of a book, not when you turn them over one by one with your forefinger, but when you hold your thumb on the edge of the book and let them all swish past at once. The speed was breath-taking. And over there was her house, at the far end of the street, under the white gap in the rain clouds where the sky was clearing towards the evening. He so much loved the little houses in the streets which led to her that he could have picked them off the ground and kissed them! Those crooked one-eyed attics slammed on to the roofs! And the lamps and icon-lights reflected in the puddles and shining like berries! And her house under the white rift of the sky. There he would again receive the white, God-made gift of beauty from the hands of its creator. A dark muffled figure would open the door, and the promise of her nearness, unowned by anyone in the world, and guarded and cold as a white northern night, would reach him like the first wave of the sea as you run down over the sandy beach in the dark.

Yury dropped his reins, leaned forward in his saddle, flung his arms round the horse's neck and buried his face in its mane. Taking this display of affection for an appeal to its strength, the horse broke into a gallop.

As it bounded, its light hooves only now and then touching the ground, it seemed to Yury that, besides the joyful thudding of his own heart, he heard shouts, but he thought he was imagining it.

A shot fired at close range deafened him. He sat up, snatched at the reins and pulled. Checked in full flight, the horse side-stepped, backed and went down on its haunches ready to rear.

In front of him were the crossroads. The sign, *Moreau & Vetchinkin. Seed Drills. Threshing Machines*, was lit by the rays of the setting sun. Three horsemen blocked his way—a boy in a school cap and a tunic with two cartridge belts, a cavalryman in an officer's greatcoat and fur cap, and a fat man oddly clothed, as for a fancy-dress ball, in quilted trousers and a wide-brimmed clerical hat pulled low over his forehead.

'Don't move, Comrade Doctor,' said the cavalryman, who was the eldest of the three. 'If you obey orders, you will be perfectly safe. If you don't—no offence meant—we'll shoot you. The surgeon attached to our unit has been killed and we are conscripting you as a medical worker. Get down and hand the reins over to this young man. And let me remind you: if you try to escape we shan't stand on ceremony.'

'Are you Comrade Forester, Mikulitsin's son Liberius?'

'No, I am his chief liaison officer, Kammenodvorsky.'

10

The Highway

THERE were towns, villages and Cossack settlements along the
highway. It was the ancient mail road, the oldest highway
in Siberia. It cut through the towns like a knife, slicing them
in half like a loaf of bread along the line of their main streets. As
for the villages, it swept through them without a backward glance,
scattering them right and left, leaving the huts drawn up in a straight
row or bent into an arc or buckled by a sudden turn.

In the distant past, before the railway came to Khodatskoye, the
mail was rushed along the highway by troikas. Caravans of tea,
bread and pig-iron travelled one way and convicts under guard, on
foot, were driven the other. They walked in step, jangling their
fetters—lost, desperate souls as terrible as heavenly lightning—and
around them rustled the dark, impenetrable forest.

Those who lived along the highway were like one family. Friendship and marriage linked village to village and town to town. Khodatskoye stood at a crossing of the road and the railway; it had engine
repair shops and other workshops connected with the upkeep of the
line, and there, crowded into barracks, the poorest of the poor lived
and sickened and died. Political prisoners, who had technical quali-
fications and had served their term of hard labour, were allowed to
settle in Khodatskoye as 'free' exiles and to work as skilled mechanics.

The Soviets which had been set up all along the line in the first
days of the revolution had long since been overthrown. For some
time the Siberian Provisional Government had maintained itself in
power, but now its rule had been replaced throughout the region by
that of Admiral Kolchak, Supreme Commander of the Whites.

2

At one stage of the journey the road kept climbing uphill, giving an
ever wider view over the country. It seemed as if there would be no
end to the slow ascent or to the widening of the horizon, but when
tired horses and passengers stopped for a rest they found that they
had reached the summit of the hill. The road went on over a bridge
and the river Kezhma swirled beneath it.

277

Beyond the bridge, on an even steeper rise, they could see the brick walls of the Monastery of the Exaltation of the Cross. The road wandered round the lands of the monastery and zigzagged uphill, through the outskirts of the town of Holycross [1].

When it reached the centre of the town it skirted the monastery grounds once again, for the green-painted iron door of the monastery gave on to the main square. The icon over the arched gate was framed by the legend in gold letters: 'Rejoice, O, life-giving Cross, O unconquerable victory of piety.'

It was Holy Week, the end of Lent; winter was almost over. As a first sign of the thaw the roads were turning black, but the roofs were still wearing their tall, white, overhanging snow bonnets.

To the small boys who had climbed up to the belfry to watch the bell-ringers, the houses down below looked like small white boxes jumbled close together. Little black people, hardly bigger than dots, walked among the houses and stopped in front of them. They stopped to read the decree calling up three more age groups; its text had been posted up on the walls by order of Admiral Kolchak.

3

Many unexpected things had happened in the night. It had turned unusually warm for the time of year, and a drizzle was coming down, so fine and airy that it seemed to drift away in mist before it reached the earth. But this was an illusion. In reality there was enough rain-water to stream, warm and swift, along the ground—which had turned black all over and glistened as if it sweated—and to wash it clean of the remaining snow.

Stunted apple-trees, covered with buds, reached miraculously across the garden fences. Drops of water dripped from them, and the drumming of the water on the wooden pavements could be heard right across the town.

Tomik, the puppy, chained up for the night in the photographer's yard, squealed and yelped, and the crow in the Galuzins' garden, perhaps irritated by the noise, cawed loud enough to keep the whole town awake.

In the lower part of Holycross, three cart-loads of goods had been brought to the merchant, Lyubeznov, who refused to accept delivery, saying it was a mistake, he had never ordered the stuff. The dray-

[1] Holycross: Krestovozdvizhensk (literally, town of the Exaltation of the Cross).

men, as it was so late, were begging him to put them up for the night, but he cursed and sent them to the devil and refused to open the gate. This row could also be heard from one end of the town to the other.

At the seventh hour by the Church's reckoning and at one in the morning by the clock, a dark low sweet humming drifted from the deepest of the monastery bells, which hardly stirred. It mixed with the dark drizzle in the air. It drifted from the bell, sinking and dissolving in the air, as a clump of earth, torn from the river bank, sinks and dissolves in the water of the spring floods.

It was the night of Maundy Thursday. Almost indistinguishable in the distance, behind the network of rain, candles, lighting a face here, a forehead or a nose there, stirred and moved across the monastery yard. The fasting congregation was going to Matins.

A quarter of an hour later, steps sounded on the wooden pavement coming from the church. This was Galuzina, the grocer's wife, going home, although the service had only just begun. She walked at an uneven pace, now running, now slowing down and stopping, her shawl over her head and her fur coat unbuttoned. She had felt faint in the stuffy church and had come out into the fresh air, but now she was ashamed and sorry that she had not stayed to the end, and because, for the second year running, she was not fasting in Lent. But this was not the chief cause of her worry. The mobilisation order posted up that day affected her poor, silly boy, Teryoshka. She tried to drive the thought of it from her head, but the white patches in the darkness were there to remind her at every turn.

Her house was only just round the corner, but she felt better out of doors and was not in a hurry to go back into the airless rooms.

The stormy sadness of her thoughts oppressed her. Had she tried to think them all out aloud, one by one, she would not have had sufficient words or time enough till dawn. But out here, in the street, these comfortless reflections flew at her in clusters, and she could deal with all of them together, in the short while it took her to walk a few times from the monastery gate to the corner of the square and back.

It was almost Eastertide and there was not a soul in the house; they had all gone away, leaving her alone. Well, wasn't she alone? Of course she was. Her ward Ksyusha didn't count. Who was she anyway? 'Another's soul is a dark pool,' as the saying goes. Perhaps she was a friend, or perhaps she was an enemy or a secret rival. She was supposed to be the daughter of her husband's first wife by another marriage. Her husband, Vlas, said that he had adopted her. But suppose she was his natural daughter? Or suppose she wasn't his daughter at all but something else? Could you ever see into a man's heart? Though, to give Ksyusha her due, there was nothing wrong with her. She had brains, looks, manners—much more brains than either poor stupid Teryoshka or his father!

So here she was, abandoned, deserted in Holy Week. They had all scattered, everyone had gone his way.

Vlas was gallivanting up and down the highway, making speeches to the new recruits, exhorting them to mighty feats of arms. Instead of looking after his own son, the fool, and saving him from his mortal peril!

And Teryoshka too had dashed away from home on the eve of the great feast. He had gone to their relations in Kuteiny village to amuse himself and forget his troubles. The poor lad had been expelled from school. They had kept him back an extra year in almost every other form, and now that he was in the eighth they had to kick him out!

Oh, how depressing it all was! Oh Lord! Why had everything gone so wrong? It was so disheartening, she felt like giving up, she had no wish to live. What had caused all this misery? Was it the revolution? No, oh no! It was the war. The war had killed off the flower of Russia's manhood, and now there was nothing but rotten, good-for-nothing rubbish left.

How different it had been in her father's time! Her father had been a contractor. Sober, literate. They had lived off the fat of the land. She and her two sisters, Polya and Olya, as fine a pair of girls as you could hope to meet and as well matched as their names. And master carpenters had called on their father, every one a fine, upstanding figure of a man. At one time, she and her sisters—the things they would think of!—had got it into their heads to knit scarves in six colours of wool. And, believe it or not, such good knitters they were that their scarves had become famous all over the province! And everything in those days had been fine and rich and seemly—church services and dances and people and manners—everything had rejoiced her heart, for all that her own family were simple people who came of peasant and worker stock. And Russia too had been a marriageable girl in those days, courted by real men, men who would stand up for her, not to be compared with this rabble nowadays. Now everything had lost its gloss, nothing but civilians left, lawyers and Yids clacking their tongues day and night. Poor old Vlas and his friends thought they could bring back those golden days by toasts and speeches and good wishes! But was this the way to win back a lost love? For that you had to move mountains!

4

By now she had crossed the square and walked as far as the market-place more than once. From there her house was half-way down the street on the left, but every time she came to it, she changed her mind about going in and turned back into the maze of alleys adjoining the monastery.

The market-place was the size of a large field. In times gone by, it had been crowded on market days with peasants' carts. At one end of it was St. Helen Street [1]: the other, curving in a crescent, was lined with small buildings, one or two storeys high, used for warehouses, offices and shops.

There, she remembered, in more peaceful times, Brukhyanov, a cross old bear in spectacles and a long frock coat, who dealt in leather, oats and hay, cartwheels and harness, would read the penny paper as he sat importantly on a chair outside his great, fourfold iron doorway.

And there, in a small dim window, a few pairs of beribboned wedding candles and posies in cardboard boxes gathered dust for years, while in the small room at the back, empty of either furniture or goods except for a pile of large round cakes of wax, thousand rouble deals were made by the unknown agents of a millionaire candle manufacturer who lived nobody knew where.

There, in the middle of the row of shops, was the Galuzins' large grocery store with its three windows. Its bare, splintery floor was swept morning, noon and night with used tea leaves; Galuzin and his assistants drank tea all day long. And here Galuzina, as a young married woman, had often and willingly sat behind the cash desk. Her favourite colour was a violet-mauve, the colour of church vestments on certain solemn days, the colour of lilac in bud, the colour of her best velvet dress and of her set of crystal goblets. It was the colour of happiness and of her memories, and Russia, too, in her virginity before the revolution, seemed to her to have been the colour of lilac. She had enjoyed sitting behind the cash desk because the violet dusk in the shop, fragrant with starch, sugar and purple blackcurrant sweets in glass jars, had matched her favourite colour.

Here at the corner, beside the timber yard, stood an old, grey, weather-board house which had settled on all four sides like a dilapidated coach. It had two storeys and two front doors, one at either end. Each floor was divided in two; downstairs were Zalkind's chemist's shop on the right and a notary's office on the left. Above the chemist lived the old ladies' tailor, Schmulevich, with his big

[1] St. Helen's Street: Yeleninskaya.

family. The flat across the landing from Schmulevich and above the notary was crammed with lodgers whose trades and professions were stated on cards and signs covering the whole of the front door. Here watches were mended and shoes cobbled; here Kaminsky, the engraver, had his workroom and two photographers, Zhuk and Strodakh, worked in partnership.

As the first floor premises were overcrowded, the photographers' young assistants, Blazhein, a student, and Magidson, who retouched the photographs, had fixed up a dark room at one end of the large woodshed in the yard. To judge by the angry red eye of the lamp winking blearily in the dark room window, they were working there now. It was underneath this window that the puppy, Tomik, sat on his chain and yelped, so that you could hear him right across the square in St. Helen Street.

'There they all are in a pack, the whole Sanhedrin,' thought Galuzina as she passed the grey house. 'It's a den of filth and beggary.' And yet, she reflected at once, her husband was wrong to hate the Jews so much. It was not as if these people were the lords of the land, they were not important enough to affect Russia's destinies. Though it was true that if you asked old Schmulevich why he thought the country was in such turmoil and disorder, he wriggled, twisted his ugly face into a grin and said: 'That's Leibochka [1] up to his tricks.'

Oh, but what nonsense was she wasting her time thinking about! Did they matter? Were they Russia's misfortune? The towns were the trouble. Not that the country stood or fell by the towns, but the towns were educated, and the country people had had their heads turned; they envied the education of the towns and tried to copy their ways and could not catch up with them, so now they were neither one thing nor the other.

Or perhaps it was the other way round, perhaps ignorance was the trouble?—An educated man can see through walls, he can guess everything that happens in advance, while the rest of us are like people in a dark wood. We only miss our hats when our heads have been chopped off.—Not that the educated people were having an easy time nowadays. Look at the way the famine was driving them out of the towns! Try to sort it all out! Even the devil couldn't make head or tail of it!

All the same, it was the country people who knew how to live. Look at her relations, the Selitvins, Shelaburins, Pamphil Palykh, the brothers Modykh. They relied on their own hands and their own heads, they were their own masters. The new farmsteads along the

---

[1] Yiddish diminutive for Leo, *i.e.* Leo Trotsky.

highway were a lovely sight. Fifteen dessyatins [1] of arable, sheep, horses, pigs, cows, and enough corn in the barns for three years ahead! And their farming machines!—They even had harvesters! Kolchak was buttering them up, trying to get them on his side, and so were the commissars, to get them into the forest army. They had come back from the war with George Crosses [2] and everyone was after them, wanting to employ them as instructors. Commissioned or not, if you knew your job you were always in demand. You could always find your feet.

But it was time she went home. It simply wasn't decent for a woman to be wandering about the streets so late. It wouldn't have mattered so much if she had been in her own garden. But it was so muddy, it was like a bog. Anyway, she thought, she felt a little better now.

Utterly confused by her reflections and having quite lost the thread of them, Galuzina went home. But before she went inside, she stood for a while in the porch, going over a few more things in her mind.

She thought of the people who were lording it in Khodatskoye nowadays; she knew more or less what they were like, they were former political exiles from the capitals, men like Tiverzin, Antipov, the anarchist 'Black Banner' Vdovichenko, the local locksmith 'Mad Dog' Gorsheny. They were cunning and they knew their own minds, they had stirred up plenty of trouble in their day, they were sure to be plotting something again now. They couldn't live unless they were up to something. They had spent their lives dealing with machines and they were cold and merciless as machines themselves. They went about in sweaters and jerkins, they smoked through bone cigarette-holders and they drank boiled water for fear of catching something. Poor Vlas was wasting his time; these men would turn everything upside-down, they would always get their way.

Then she thought about herself. She knew she was a simple woman but with a mind of her own, intelligent and young for her age; taken all round she was not a bad person. But none of her qualities cut any ice in this God-forsaken hole—nor anywhere else for that matter. The indecent song about the silly old woman Sentetyurikha came into her mind; it was well known throughout the Urals, but only the first two lines could be quoted:

> 'Sentetyurikha, she sold her cart
> And bought a balalaika . . .'

---

[1] One *dessyatina*: 2·7 acres.
[2] The St. George Cross was the highest military decoration in Tsarist Russia.

After this came nothing but obscenities. They sang it in Holycross, aiming it, she suspected, at herself.

She sighed bitterly and went into the house.

5

She went straight to her bedroom, without stopping in the hall to take off her coat. The room looked out on the garden. Now, at night, the shadowy forms inside the room and in the garden outside the window were almost alike, as if they repeated each other. The limp drooping shapes of the curtains were like the limp, drooping shapes of the dark, leafless trees with their blurred outlines. In the garden where the winter was almost over, the dark purple glow of the coming spring, bursting out of the ground, warmed the taffeta darkness of the night. And by a similar interaction of two elements, the airless darkness inside the room with its dusty curtains was coloured and softened by the dark violet glow of the coming Feast.

The Virgin in the icon, freeing her dark slim hands from the silver mount, held them up, seeming to hold in each the first and last letters of her Greek name, Μήτηρ θεοῦ [1]. The garnet-coloured icon lamp, dark as an inkwell in its gold bracket, scattered its star-shaped light, splintered by the cut glass, on the bedroom carpet.

Taking off her coat and shawl, Galuzina made an awkward movement and felt her old pain, a stitch in her side under her shoulder blade. She gave a frightened cry and began to mutter: 'Mighty protectress of the sorrowful, chaste Mother of God, help of the afflicted, shelter of the universe . . .' Half-way through the prayer she burst into tears.

When the pain died down she began to undo her dress but the hooks at the back slipped through her fingers and got lost in the soft crinkled stuff. She had difficulty in finding them.

Her ward Ksyusha woke up and came into the room.

'Why are you in the dark, Mother? Shall I bring a lamp?'

'No, don't. There's enough light.'

'Let me undo your dress. Don't tire yourself.'

'My fingers are all thumbs, I could cry. And that tailor didn't have the sense to sew the hooks on so that you can get at them. Blind as a bat he is! I've half a mind to rip them all off and throw them in his ugly face.'

[1] Mother of God.

'How well they sang at the monastery! It's so still, you could hear it from the house.'

'The singing was all right, but I'm not feeling so well, my girl. I've got that stitch again—here and here. Everywhere . . . It's such a nuisance, I don't know what to do.'

'The homoeopath, Stydobsky, helped you last time.'

'He's always telling you to do something impossible. He's a quack, your homoeopath, he's no good. That's one thing. And the other thing is that he's gone away. He's gone, I tell you, he's left the town. And he isn't the only one, they've all rushed off just before the holiday—as if they expected an earthquake or something.'

'Well then, what about that Hungarian doctor, the one who is a prisoner of war—his treatment did you good.'

'That's no use either. I tell you, there isn't a soul left. Kerenyi Lajos is with the other Hungarians on the other side of the demarcation line [1]. They've conscripted him for the Red Army.'

'But you know, Mother, you're imagining a lot of it. Your heart is in a nervous condition. In a case like yours suggestion can do wonders; it's what the peasants do, after all. Do you remember that soldier's wife who whispered away your pain? What was her name?'

'Well, really! You must take me for an utter, ignorant fool! It wouldn't surprise me if you sang "Sentetyurikha" behind my back.'

'Mother! How can you say such a thing! It's a sin. You ought to be ashamed of yourself. You'd much better help me to remember that woman's name. It's on the tip of my tongue. I shan't have any peace till it comes back to me.'

'She has more names than petticoats. I don't know which is the one you're thinking of. They call her Kubarikha and Medvedikha and Zlydarikha and I don't know how many other names besides. She isn't around here any more either. She's gone. She's vanished.— They locked her up in the Kezhma jail for practising abortion and making pills and powders of some sort, but, as you can imagine, she was bored, so she hopped it, broke out of prison and got away somewhere to the East. I tell you—everyone has run away—Vlas and Teryoshka and your Aunt Polya—Pelagia of the loving heart. Apart from the two of us, fools that we are, there isn't an honest woman left in town. I'm not joking. And no medical help of any sort or kind left to us. If anything happened, you couldn't get a doctor for love or money anywhere. They say there's one in Yuryatin, some famous professor from Moscow, the son of a Siberian merchant who committed suicide. But just when I was thinking of sending

[1] Outside the territory held by the Whites.

for him, the Reds cut the road in twelve places . . . Now, off to bed with you, and I'll try and get some sleep too. By the way, that student of yours, Blazhein, he's turned your head.—What's the good of saying no?—you're blushing like a beetroot.—He'll be sweating all night long over some photographs I gave him to develop, poor boy. They don't sleep in that house and they keep everyone else awake as well. Their Tomik is barking, you can hear him all over the town, and our wretched crow is cawing its head off up in the apple tree. Looks as if I'll have another sleepless night . . . Now what are you so cross about? Don't be so touchy. What are students for if not for girls to fall in love with!'

6

'What's that dog howling for? Go and see what's the matter with it. It can't be making all that noise for nothing. Wait a minute, Lidochka, quiet, blast you! I've got to find out what is going on or we'll have the police on us before we know where we are. Stay here, Ustin, and you, Sivobluy. We can manage without you.'

Lidochka, the representative of the Central Committee, did not hear the partisan leader asking him to stop and continued his weary patter:

'By its policy of looting, requisitioning, violence, shooting and torture the bourgeois militarist régime in Siberia is bound to open the eyes of those who still deceive themselves. It is not only hostile to the working class but, in fact, to the whole of the toiling peasantry. The toiling peasantry of Siberia and the Urals must understand that only in alliance with the proletariat of the towns and with the soldiers, only in alliance with the Kirghiz and Buryat poor peasants . . .'

At last Lidochka became aware of the interruptions, stopped, wiped his sweaty face with his handkerchief and closed his tired puffy eyes.

'Have a rest. Have a drink of water,' whispered those who were standing closest to him.

The worried partisan leader was being reassured:

'What's all the fuss about? Everything is in order. The signal lamp is in the window and the look-out, if I may use a picturesque expression, has his eyes glued to space. I don't see why we shouldn't go on with the discussion. Go on, Comrade Lidochka.'

The logs kept in the large shed in the photographers' yard had been moved aside and the illegal meeting was being held in the cleared space in the middle of the shed, screened from the dark room at the entrance by a wall of logs as high as the ceiling. In case of emergency, there was a way of escape through a trap-door to an underground passage which came out in a lonely alley at the back of the monastery.

The speaker had a dull olive complexion, and a beard from ear to ear; he wore a black calico cap on his bald head. He suffered from nervous perspiration and constantly poured with sweat. His cigarette kept going out and he re-lit it greedily in the stream of hot air over the paraffin lamp. Bending low over his scattered papers, he looked them over nervously with his short-sighted eyes, as if he were sniffing at them, then he continued in his flat, tired voice:

'Only through the Soviets can this alliance between the poor in the towns and the poor in the country be achieved. Whether he wishes it or not, the Siberian peasant will now pursue the end for which the workers of Siberia began to fight long ago. Their common goal is the overthrow of the hateful autocracy of admirals and hetmans, and the establishment, by means of an armed rising, of the power of the peasants' and soldiers' Soviets. And in fighting the officer and Cossack hirelings of the bourgeoisie, who are armed to the teeth, the insurgents will have to wage conventional front-line warfare. The struggle will be long and stubborn.'

Once again he stopped, wiped his face and closed his eyes. In defiance of the rules someone in the audience got up, raised his hand and asked permission to make a comment.

The partisan leader or, to be more exact, the commander of the Kezhma group of the trans-Uralian partisan units, sat in a provocatively free-and-easy attitude under the speaker's very nose; he kept interrupting him in the rudest manner and showed him no respect whatever. It was hard to believe that so young a soldier—he was little more than a boy—could be in charge of whole armies and that his men obeyed him and looked up to him with veneration. He sat with his hands and feet wrapped in the skirts of his cavalry greatcoat; its top, thrown back over his chair, showed his ensign's tunic with dark patches on the shoulders where the epaulettes had been removed.

On either side of him stood a silent bodyguard of his own age in white sheepskin coats grown a little grey, with curly lamb's-wool edging. Their fine, stony faces revealed nothing except blind loyalty to their chief and readiness to serve him at whatever cost. Taking no part in the discussion and unmoved by any of the issues raised in it, they neither spoke nor smiled.

There were a dozen to fifteen other people in the room. Some were standing, others sitting on the floor; they leaned against the walls of caulked logs, their legs stretched out in front of them or their knees drawn up under their chins.

Three or four were guests of honour and sat on chairs. They were old workers, veterans of the revolution of 1905. Among them were Tiverzin, morose and greatly changed since his Moscow days, and his friend, old Antipov, who always agreed with every word he said. Numbered among the gods at whose feet the revolution had laid its gifts and its burnt offerings, they sat silent and grim as idols; they were men in whom everything alive and human had been driven out by political conceit.

There were other figures too in the room who deserved attention, such as that pillar of Russian anarchism, 'Black Banner' Vdovichenko. Never resting for a moment, he kept sitting down on the floor and getting up again or pacing backwards and forwards and stopping in the middle of the shed; a fat giant of a man, with a big head, a big mouth and a lion's mane of hair, who had been an officer in the war with Japan if not in the earlier one with Turkey, he was a dreamer eternally absorbed in his fantasies.

Because of his limitless good nature and colossal size which kept him from noticing anything smaller than himself, he failed to give sufficient attention to what was going on, misunderstood all that was said and, mistaking the views of his opponents for his own, agreed with everything.

Next to him on the floor sat his friend Svirid, a trapper. Although he was not a tiller of the soil, Svirid's peasant earthiness showed through the opening of his dark cloth shirt which he bunched in his hand together with the cross he wore round his neck, pulling it about and scratching his chest with it. He was half-Buryat [1], warm-hearted and illiterate; he had thin, plaited hair, a sparse moustache and a still sparser beard. His face was always creased in a smile, and his Mongol features made him look older than his years.

The speaker, who was touring Siberia on a military mission from the Central Committee, mentally surveyed the vast territory he had still to cover. He was uninterested in most of the men he was addressing. But as an old revolutionary and, from his childhood, a champion of the people, he gazed almost with adoration at the young commander who sat facing him. Not only did he forgive him his lack of manners, which he regarded as the expression of a genuinely revolutionary temperament, but he delighted in his insolence, rather as an infatuated woman might be pleased by the brazen coarseness of a masterful lover.

The partisan leader was Mikulitsin's son, Liberius. The speaker was a former member of the co-operative labour party, Kostoyed

[1] One of the Turkic tribes in Siberia.

Amursky, who had once been a social revolutionary. He had revised his views, admitted his past errors, recanted them in several detailed statements, and had not only been received into the Communist Party but had, soon afterwards, been entrusted with his present responsible task.

He was chosen for it—though he was anything but a soldier—partly as a tribute to his long years of revolutionary service and his ordeals in tsarist prisons, and partly on the assumption that, as a former member of the co-operative party, he knew the mood of the peasant masses in the insurgent regions of Siberia. For the purpose of his mission this presumed knowledge was regarded as more important than military experience.

His change of political convictions had altered his looks and manners beyond recognition. No one could remember him as either bald or bearded in the old days.—But then, perhaps it was all only a disguise! He was under strict orders from the party to remain under cover. His underground names were Berendey or Comrade Lidochka.

There was a brief commotion raised by Vdovichenko's premature statement that he agreed with the Central Committee's instructions which had just been read. When it had died down, Kostoyed went on :

'In order to embrace the growing movement of the peasant masses as widely as possible, it is essential to establish contact at once with all the partisan units operating on the territory of the Party Provincial Committee.'

He then spoke of arrangements for secret meeting places, passwords, codes and means of communication, and went over the whole ground in detail.

'The units must be informed of the location of stores of arms, food and equipment belonging to the Whites and of centres where they keep large sums of money, as well as of the precautions taken to ensure their safety.

'It is essential to work out to the last detail all questions concerning the organisation of partisan detachments, their commanders, war-comradely discipline, conspiratorial work, contact with the outside world, behaviour towards the local population, war-revolutionary field tribunals, and the tactics of sabotage on enemy territory, such as, for example, the destruction of bridges, railway lines, steamships, barges, stations, workshops with all their technical equipment, telegraph offices, mines and food supplies.'

Liberius could bear it no longer. All that had been said seemed to him to be the ravings of an amateur and to be devoid of any relevance to his work.

'A very fine lecture,' he said. 'I shall take it to heart. I suppose we must accept all this without a word of protest, unless we wish to lose the support of the Red Army?'

'Of course you must.'

'And what am I to do with your schoolboy's crib, my dear Lidochka, when my forces, blast your eyes—three regiments including artillery and cavalry—have been campaigning for months and routing the enemy?'

'How wonderful! What strength!' thought Kostoyed.

The argument was interrupted by Tiverzin who disliked Liberius's impertinent tone.

'Pardon me, Comrade Speaker, there is something which is unclear to me. I may have put down one of the points in the instructions incorrectly. May I read it out—I should like to be sure. "It is most desirable that war veterans who were at the front and belonged to soldiers' organisations at the time of the revolution should be drawn into the committee. It is desirable that the membership of the committee should include one or two N.C.O.'s and one military technician." Have I put it down correctly, Comrade Speaker?'

'Perfectly. Word for word.'

'Then allow me to say this. I find the point concerning military specialists disquieting. We workers who took part in the revolution of 1905 are not used to trusting army people. There are always counter-revolutionary elements among them.'

There were cries of 'That's enough! The resolution! Let's have a resolution! It's time to go home, it's late.'

'I am in agreement with the majority,' said Vdovichenko in a deep, rumbling voice. 'Putting it poetically, civic institutions should be founded on democracy, they should grow up from below, like seedlings which are planted and take root in the soil. You can't hammer them in from above like stakes for a fence. This was precisely the mistake of the Jacobin dictatorship and the reason why the Convention was crushed by the Thermidorians.'

'It's as clear as daylight,' Svirid, his friend and fellow-wanderer, backed him up. 'Any little child can see it. We should have thought of it earlier, now it's too late. Now our business is just to fight and to push on for all we're worth. How can we turn back, now we've started? We've made our bed and we must lie on it.'

'The resolution! The resolution!' people were repeating on all sides. They talked on a little longer, but what they said made less and less sense, and finally at dawn the meeting broke up. They went home one by one, taking the usual precautions.

There was a picturesque place along the highway, where the swift little river Pazhinka divided the two villages of Kuteiny Posad and Maly Yermolay, the one running down a steep hill and the other scattered in the valley below it. In Kuteiny a farewell party was being given for the new recruits conscripted by Kolchak, and in Yermolay the medical board under Colonel Strese had, after the Easter break, resumed its examination of those in the area liable to conscription. Mounted militia and Cossacks were stationed in the village for the occasion.

It was the third day of an unusually late Easter week and an unusually early spring, warm and without a breath of wind. Tables spread with food and drink for the recruits stood under the open sky in Kuteiny, a little off the highway so as not to block the traffic. Placed end to end but not quite in a straight line and covered with white cloths hanging to the ground, they meandered down the street like a long white sausage.

The villagers had pooled their resources to provide the entertainment. The main dishes were the remnants of the Easter food, two smoked hams and several *kulich* and *paskhas* [1]. At intervals all along the tables there were bowls of pickled mushrooms, cucumbers and sauerkraut, plates of home-baked bread cut into thick chunks and dishes piled with Easter eggs. Most of the eggs were coloured pink or light blue.

Broken eggshells, pink and light blue with a white lining, littered the new grass round the tables. Pink and light blue were the shirts of the young men and the dresses of the girls. And pink clouds sailed in the blue sky, slowly and gracefully, as though the sky were moving with them.

Wearing a pink shirt with a silk sash, and pointing his toes right and left, Vlas Galuzin clattered down the steps of Pafnutkin's house on the slope above the highway, ran down to the tables and began his speech:

'For want of champagne, I drink to you, my lads, in our own home-made vodka. A long life and happy years to you, young men who are setting forth to-day. I should like to give you many other toasts. Gentlemen recruits! May I have your attention! The

---

[1] *Kulich* is a cake shaped like a large bun; *paskha* is a sweet consisting chiefly of cottage cheese, sugar and currants, made in the shape of a pyramid and decorated with icing. They are served for breakfast on Easter Sunday to mark the end of the Lenten fast.

way of the cross which stretches out before you is the defence of our motherland against the ravishers who flood her fields with fratricidal blood. The people cherished the hope of peacefully debating the conquests of the revolution, but the party of the bolsheviks, being the slaves of foreign capital, dispersed the Constituent Assembly, which was the people's highest hope, by brute force of bayonets; and now the blood of the defenceless flows like a river. Young men who are setting forth to-day, to you is entrusted the outraged honour of our arms! We have covered ourselves in shame and we are in debt to our gallant Allies. For not only the Reds, but also Germany and Austria, are raising their brazen heads once again. God is with us, lads. . . .' He was still speaking when his voice was drowned by acclamations. He raised the glass of raw vodka to his lips and sipped. It gave him no pleasure. He preferred wine and was used to finer flavours. But the consciousness that he was making a sacrifice to the public good filled him with satisfaction.

'He's a great one for speeches, your old man! Milyukov can't be compared to him. Honest to God!' said Goshka Ryabikh in a tipsy voice amidst the drunken babble at the table to his friend Teryoshka—Terenty Galuzin—who sat next to him. 'He certainly is a fine fellow! But I suppose it's not for nothing he's working so hard. I expect he'll get you off conscription as a reward.'

'Shame on you, Goshka! How can you think such a thing! Get me off conscription, indeed! I'd like to see him try! I'll get my papers the same day as you do, and that'll be that. We'll serve in the same unit . . . They've kicked me out of school, the bastards. Mother's eating her heart out. I suppose I won't get a commission now . . . Father certainly does know how to make a speech. He hits it off every time. And the extraordinary thing is, it's a completely natural gift of his. He's had no education.'

'Have you heard about Sanka Pafnutkin?'

'Yes. Is it really such a terrible infection?'

'Incurable. He's got it till it finishes him off. It's his own fault. We warned him not to go. You have to be very careful who you get mixed up with.'

'What will happen to him now, Goshka?'

'It's an awful business. He wanted to shoot himself. He's been called up, he's having his medical now in Yermolay. I suppose they'll take him. Before that, he said he'd go off and join the partisans—"to avenge the ills of society".'

'You know, Goshka, you talk about an infectious disease, but if you don't go to them, you might get another disease.'

'I know what you mean. You've got it yourself by the looks of it. But that isn't a disease, it's a secret vice.'

'I'll punch your nose for saying things like that, Goshka. That's a nice way to talk to a friend, you rotten liar!'

'Calm down, it was only a joke. What I wanted to tell you was this—I went to Pazhinsk for Easter, and there was a visiting lecturer there, an anarchist, very interesting he was. He talked about the Liberation of the Personality. I liked that, it was good stuff. I'll join the anarchists, I'll —— your mother if I don't. There's an inner force in us, he said. It has to wake up. Sex, he said, and character, he said, those are the manifestations of animal electricity. How do you like that? A genius, he was. . . . But I'm pretty well pissed. People bawling their heads off all round, it's enough to deafen a man. I can't stick it any longer, so shut up, Terenty; dry up, I tell you.'

'All right, but just tell me one thing, Goshka. I still don't know all those words about socialism. What's the expression *sabotazhnik*[1], for instance? What does it mean?'

'I'm an expert on all those words, but I tell you, Terenty, I'm drunk, leave me alone. A *sabotazhnik* is someone who belongs to the same gang. A *vataga* is a gang, isn't it? Well, if you say savatzhnik, it means you belong to the same vataga. Do you understand, you mug?'

'That's what I thought it was—a swear word . . . But you were talking about that electric force. I've heard about it. I was thinking of ordering an electric truss from Petersburg—cash on delivery—I saw it in an advertisement. "To increase your vigour", it said. But then there was another revolution, so there were other things to think about . . .'

Terenty did not finish his sentence. The roar of drunken voices around the table was drowned by a loud, echoing explosion not far away and was for a moment cut short. Then it broke out much louder and more confused than before. Some people jumped up from their seats and those who were least unsteady remained on their feet. Others tried to stagger away but slumped down under the table and began to snore. Women wailed. There was general pandemonium.

Vlas stood looking round for the culprit. It seemed to him in the first moments that the bang had come from somewhere in the village, perhaps even from somewhere quite close to the tables. The veins in his neck stood out, his face went purple, and he bawled: 'Who is the Judas in our ranks? Who has committed this outrage? Who's

[1] Saboteur.

been chucking hand-grenades about? I'll throttle him with my own hands, the reptile, even if it's my own son. Citizens, we will not allow anyone to play such jokes on us. We must cordon off the village. We'll find the villain, we won't let him get away.'

At first they listened to him, then their attention was distracted by a pillar of black smoke slowly rising into the sky from the Rural District hall in Maly Yermolay, and they all rushed to the edge of the ravine to look across the river at what was happening in the valley.

The hall was on fire. Several recruits—one of them barefoot and naked except for his trousers—ran out of the building with Colonel Strese and the other officers of the selection board. Mounted Cossacks and militiamen, leaning low out of their saddles and swinging their whips, their horses writhing under them like snakes, galloped backwards and forwards through the village, hunting for someone. Many people were running up the road to Kuteiny, pursued by the urgent flurry of the church bells ringing the alarm.

The situation developed with terrifying speed. At dusk Colonel Strese, apparently convinced that his quarry had left Yermolay, rode up with his Cossacks to Kuteiny, surrounded the village with patrols and began to search every cottage and every house.

Half the recruits were by now dead to the world. They had stayed on at the party and were snoring, slumped on the ground, or with their heads on the tables. By the time it became known that the militia were in the village it was already dark.

Several young men, including Terenty and Goshka, took to their heels, made their way through backyards to the nearest barn, and, kicking and jostling each other, crawled underneath the floor through a narrow gap at the bottom of the wall. In the dark and the commotion they had not been able to make out whose barn it was, but now, judging by the smell of fish and paraffin, it seemed to be the one used as a warehouse by the village shop.

The young men had nothing on their conscience and it was foolish of them to hide; most of them had merely run away on the spur of the moment, because they were drunk and had lost their heads. A few, however, had kept company which now seemed to them compromising and might, they were afraid, lead to their undoing if it were known. It was true that their friends were nothing worse than hooligans, but you never knew: anything might have a political angle nowadays. Hooliganism was considered a sign of black reaction in the Soviet zone, while in the White zone it was regarded as bolshevism.

They found that they were not alone in the barn, others had got in before them; the space between the ground and the floor was

crammed with people from both villages. Those from Kuteiny were
dead drunk. Some were snoring and grinding their teeth and moaning in their sleep, others were being sick. It was pitch dark and
airless and the stench was terrible. To conceal their hide-out, those
who had come last had blocked the gap in the wall. After a time the
snores and grunts ceased, the drunks settled down to sleep quietly
and there was complete silence except for an urgent, persistent whispering in one corner, where Terenty and Goshka huddled in panic
with Koska, a quarrelsome, truculent boy from Yermolay.

'Not so loud,' Koska was saying. 'You'll give us all away, you
snotty devil. Can't you hear?—Strese's crowd are prowling up and
down. They've been to the end of the street, now they're coming
back. There they are. Don't breathe or I'll strangle you . . . Lucky
for you they've gone by . . . What the devil did you have to come
here for? What did you have to hide for, blockhead? Who on earth
would have laid a finger on you?'

'I heard Goshka yelling "Hide", so I crawled in here.'

'Goshka's got good reason to hide. His whole family is in trouble,
they're all under suspicion. They've got relations working at the
railway yards in Khodatskoye, that's why . . . Don't fidget, keep
still, you fool. People have been throwing up and shitting all over
the place—if you move you'll get the mess all over us. Can't you
smell the stink? Do you know why Strese is racing round the village?
He's looking for people from outside, from Pazhinsk, that's what
he's doing.'

'How did all this happen, Koska? How did it all start?'

'Sanka started it—Sanka Pafnutkin. We were all at the recruiting
office, lined up naked, waiting for the doctor. When it came to
Sanka's turn he wouldn't undress. He was a bit drunk when he
came into the office. The clerk told him politely to take his clothes
off, even saying "you" to him. Sanka snapped his head off. "I
won't undress," he says, "I won't show my private parts to everybody." As if he were ashamed. And then he sidles up to the clerk
and hits him in the jaw. And then, believe it or not, before you
could so much as blink, Sanka bends down, grabs the office table by
the leg and turns it over. Bang it goes on the floor with everything
that was on it, inkstand and army lists and all! Then Strese comes
in shouting: "I am not going to put up with any hooligans. I'm
not having any bloodless revolution here. I'll teach you to be dis-
respectful to the law in an official place. Who's the ringleader?"

'Sanka yells: "Grab your things, Comrades. It's all up with us,"
and he goes to the window and puts his fist through it. I pick up my

things and run after him, putting them on as I run. Out he rushes into the street and goes like the wind; I went after him and so did one or two others. We all ran as fast as our legs would carry us, and they came after us, yelling and shouting. But if you ask me what it's all about—nobody can make head or tail of it.'

'But what about the bomb?'

'What about it?'

'Well, who threw it?—the bomb or the grenade or whatever it was.'

'Good Lord! You don't think we did?'

'Who did, then?'

'How should I know? It must have been someone else. Somebody saw all this hullaballoo going on and said to himself: "Why shouldn't I blow the place up on the sly, while that racket is going on?—they'll suspect the others." It must have been someone "political", one of those "politicals" from Pazhinsk, the place is full of them . . . Quiet! Shut up! Can't you hear—Strese's men are coming back. That'll be the end of us. Keep quiet, I tell you.'

Voices could be heard approaching down the street; boots creaked, spurs clanked.

'Don't argue. You can't fool me,' came the crisp, commanding voice of the colonel speaking with Petersburg precision. 'I am certain that there was somebody talking over there.'

The mayor of the village of Yermolay, an old fisherman, Otvyazhistin, went on arguing:

'You must have been hearing things, Your Excellency. And why shouldn't people be talking in a village? It isn't a churchyard. Maybe they were talking. The houses are full of people. People aren't dumb animals. Or perhaps the devil was shaking someone in his sleep.'

'Now then! Stop playing the village idiot! The devil indeed! You've all been getting too big for your boots here. You'll be getting so clever you'll talk yourselves into bolshevism next.'

'Merciful goodness, how can you say that, Your Excellency, Mister Colonel! Our village oafs are so ignorant, they can't read the prayer book! What would they want with bolshevism!'

'That's how you all talk, until you're caught. Have the shop searched from top to bottom. Turn everything inside out, and mind you look under the counters.'

'Yes, Your Excellency.'

'I want Pafnutkin, Ryabikh and Nekhvalenikh, dead or alive. I don't care if you have to fetch them up from the bottom of the sea.

And that Galuzin puppy as well. I don't care how many patriotic speeches his Papa makes. He can talk the hind leg off a donkey, but he won't catch us napping. There's bound to be something fishy when a shopkeeper goes round making speeches. It's suspicious. It's unnatural. We have information that the Galuzins hide political criminals and hold illegal meetings in their house in Holycross. Get me that brat. I haven't yet decided what to do with him, but if there's anything against him I won't think twice about stringing him up as a lesson to the others.'

The searchers moved away. When they were quite far away, Koska whispered to Terenty who was nearly dead with fright:

'Hear that?'

'Yes,' he whispered in a changed voice.

'Well, there's only one place for me and you and Sanka and Goshka now, and that's the forest. I don't mean we'll have to stay there for good—just until they calm down. Then we'll see, we may be able to come back.'

II

Forest Brotherhood

IT was almost two years since Yury had been taken prisoner by the
partisans. The limits of his freedom were very ill defined. The
place of his captivity was not surrounded by walls; no guard was
kept over him and no one watched his movements. The partisan force
was constantly on the move; it did not keep itself apart from the local
populations through whose lands and settlements it passed; it mixed
and indeed dissolved in them.

It looked as if Yury's captivity, his dependence, were an illusion,
as though he were free, and merely failed to take advantage of his
freedom. His captivity, his dependence, were not in fact different from
other forms of compulsion in life, which are often equally invisible and
intangible, and which also seem to be non-existent and to be merely
a figment of the imagination, a chimera. But although he was not
fettered, chained or watched, Yury had to submit to his unfreedom,
imaginary though it appeared.

Each of his three attempts at escaping from the partisans had ended
in capture. He did not suffer any penalties, but he was playing with
fire, and he did not try again.

He was favoured by the partisan chief, Liberius Mikulitsin, who liked
his company and made him sleep in his tent. Yury found this enforced
companionship irksome.

2

During this period, the partisans were constantly moving to the East.
At times this movement represented an advance and was part of the
general campaign to drive Kolchak from Western Siberia; at other
moments, when the Whites struck from the rear and threatened to
encircle the Reds, the same eastward marches turned into flight. For
a long time Yury could not make any sense of it.

Their course lay parallel to the highway and occasionally they
followed it. The villages and small towns along the way were Red or
White according to the fortunes of war. It was difficult to tell by
looking at them in whose power they lay at any particular moment.

While the peasant army was passing through a settlement, everything else in it sank into insignificance. The houses on both sides of the road seemed to shrink into the ground and the riders, horses, guns and big, jostling men, splashing through the mud, looked taller than the houses.

One day, when they were in a small town called Pazhinsk, Yury went to the chemist to take charge of a stock of British medical supplies, which had been abandoned by a White officers' unit under General Kappel and had now been seized as booty by the partisans.

It was a bleak, rainy afternoon with only two colours to it—wherever the light fell it was white, everywhere else it was black; and Yury's mood was of the same bleak simplification unsoftened by half-tones.

The road, completely destroyed by the passage of armies, was nothing but a river of black mud. It could only be forded in a few places, which could be reached by hugging the houses for hundreds of yards. It was in these circumstances that Yury met Pelagia Tyagunova, who had been his travelling companion in the train from Moscow three years earlier.

She recognised him first. It took him some moments to remember the woman who kept looking at him from across the street, as from the opposite bank of a canal, with an expression suggesting a readiness to greet him if he knew her or to remain anonymous if he did not.

Finally he did remember her, and, together with the picture of the overcrowded freight-truck, the labour conscripts and their guards and the woman with a plait over her shoulder, there flashed into his mind an image of his family. Sharp details of the journey crowded in on him and the faces of his dear ones, whom he desperately missed, rose vividly in his memory.

He nodded to Pelagia to go further up the street, where there were stepping-stones, and, walking in the same direction, crossed the road and greeted her.

She told him many things about the past two years. Reminding him of Vassya, the boy with the handsome, unspoilt face, who had been unjustly conscripted and who had shared their carriage, she described her stay with his mother in their village, Veretenniki. She had been very happy among them, but the village treated her as an outsider. Then she had been falsely accused of having a love affair with Vassya and had in the end to leave if she were not to be pecked to death. She had settled with her married sister, Olga Galuzina, in the town of Holycross. Rumours that Pritulyev had been seen in the neighbourhood had brought her to Pazhinsk. The rumour had proved false and she had found herself stranded in the little town where she had later got work.

In the meanwhile, misfortune had overtaken her friends. Vere-tenniki had been raided in reprisal for withholding food supplies. It was said that Vassya's house had been burned down and that a member of his family had perished. And in Holycross, Pelagia's brother-in-law, Vlas Galuzin, had either been put in jail or shot, no one knew for certain, and her nephew had vanished. Her sister had starved for some time but was now working for her keep as a servant in a family of peasants who were their relations.

It so happened that Pelagia had a job as dish-washer at the very chemist's whose stock Yury was about to requisition. All the chemist's dependants, including herself, were faced with ruin by this measure, but Yury was powerless to prevent it. Pelagia was present at the taking over of the stock.

Yury's cart pulled up at the back of the shop. Sacks, cases and bottles, packed in plaited osier, were carried out.

As well as the people, the chemist's thin, mangy horse watched the removal sadly from its stable. The rainy day was drawing to its close. The sky cleared a little. Hemmed in by the clouds, the setting sun peered out and splashed the yard with dark bronze rays, ominously gilding the puddles of liquid dung. The wind could not stir them, the liquid manure was too heavy to move. But the rain-water on the road rippled and shone vermilion.

The troops moved on along the street, walking or riding round the deeper pools. The requisitioned supplies were found to contain a whole jar of cocaine, to which the partisan chief had recently become addicted.

3

What with typhus in winter and dysentery in summer, as well as an increase in the number of wounded now that the fighting was renewed, Yury was up to his eyes in work.

In spite of setbacks and frequent retreats, the ranks of the partisans were continually swollen by new insurgents from the settlements through which the peasant army passed, and by deserters from the enemy. In the eighteen months Yury had spent with his unit, it had grown to ten times its original size and had now actually reached the strength of which Liberius had boasted at the meeting in Holycross.

Yury had several newly appointed but experienced orderlies and two chief assistants, both former prisoners of war—Kerenyi Lajos, a Hungarian communist, who had been a medical officer in the Austrian army, and a Croat, Angelar, who was partly trained as a doctor. Yury spoke German with Kerenyi Lajos; Angelar understood a little Russian.

4

According to the Red Cross International Convention, army medical personnel must not take part in the military operations of the belligerents. But on one occasion Yury was forced to break this rule. He was in the field when an engagement started and had to share the fate of the combatants.

The front line, where he was caught by enemy fire, was on the edge of a forest. He threw himself down on the ground next to the unit's telephonist. The forest was at their back, in front of them was a field, and across this open, undefended space the Whites were attacking.

The Whites were now close enough for Yury to see their faces. They were boys, recent volunteers from the civilian population of the capitals, and older men mobilised from the reserve. The tone was set by the youngsters, first-year students from the universities and topform schoolboys.

None of them was known to Yury, yet many of them looked familiar. Some reminded him of his school friends and he wondered if they were their younger brothers; others he felt he had noticed in a theatre crowd or in the street in years gone by. Their expressive faces attracted him—they seemed to be his own people, his own kind.

Their response to duty, as they understood it, filled them with an ecstatic bravery, unnecessary and provocative. Advancing in widely scattered formation and excelling the parade ground smartness of the Guards, they walked defiantly upright, neither running nor throwing themselves on the ground, although the terrain was irregular enough to give them cover. The bullets of the partisans mowed them down.

In the middle of the wide, bare field there was a dead tree, blasted by lightning, charred by fire, or scorched and splintered in the course of some earlier battles. Each of the advancing volunteers glanced at it, fighting the temptation to stop behind it for shelter and a surer aim, then, casting the thought aside, walked on.

The partisans had a limited supply of cartridges and were under orders, confirmed by a regional agreement, not to engage superior forces and to fire only at short range.

Yury had no rifle; he lay on the grass watching the course of the engagement. All his sympathies were on the side of these heroic children who were meeting death. With all his heart he wished them success. They belonged to families who were probably akin to him in spirit, in education, moral discipline and values.

It occurred to him to run out into the field and give himself up, and so get his release. But it was too dangerous.

While he was running with his arms raised above his head he could be shot down from both sides, struck in the breast and in the back, by the partisans in punishment for his treason and by the Whites through a misunderstanding of his motives. He knew this kind of situation, he had been in it before, he had considered all the possibilities of such escape plans and had discarded them as futile. So, resigning himself to his divided feelings, he lay on his belly on the grass, his face towards the clearing, and watched, unarmed, the fortunes of the battle.

But to look on inactively while this mortal struggle raged all round was impossible, it was beyond human endurance. It was not a question of loyalty to the side which held him captive or of defending his own life, but of submitting to the order of events, to the laws governing what was happening before his eyes. To remain outside it was against the rules. You had to do what everyone was doing. A battle was going on. He and his comrades were being shot at. He had to shoot back.

So, when the telephonist at his side jerked convulsively and then lay still, he crawled over to him, took his cartridge belt and rifle and, going back to his place, emptied the gun, shot after shot.

But as pity prevented him from aiming at the young men whom he admired and with whom he sympathised, and simply to shoot into the air would be too silly, he fired at the blasted tree, choosing those moments when there was no one between his sights and his target. He followed his old technique.

Setting the sights and gradually improving his aim as he pressed the trigger slowly and not all the way down, as if not in fact intending to release the bullet, so that in the end the shot went off of itself and as it were unexpectedly, he fired with the precision of old habit at the dead wood of the lower branches, lopping them off and scattering them round the tree.

But alas! however carefully he tried to avoid hitting anyone, every now and then some young man would move into his firing-line at the crucial moment. Two of them he wounded and one who fell near the tree seemed to have lost his life.

At last the White command, convinced of the uselessness of the attack, ordered a retreat.

The partisans were few. Part of their main force was on a march and others had engaged a larger enemy detachment some way off.

Not to show their weakness, they refrained from pursuing the retreating Whites.

Yury's assistant, Angelar, joined him in the clearing with two orderlies carrying stretchers. Telling him to attend to the wounded, Yury bent over the telephonist in the vague hope that he might still be breathing and could be revived. But when he undid his shirt and felt his heart, he found that it had stopped.

An amulet hung by a silk cord from the dead man's neck. Yury took it off. It contained a sheet of paper, worn and rotted at the folds, sewn into a piece of cloth.

Written on the paper, which almost fell apart in Yury's fingers when he unfolded it, were excerpts from the ninetieth Psalm [1] with such changes in the wording as often creep into popular prayers through much repetition, making them deviate increasingly from the original text. The Church Slavonic was transcribed in Russian letters.

The words of the psalm, 'to live in the help of the Most High', had become the title, 'Live Help'. The verse 'Nothing shalt thou have to fear from the arrow that flies by daylight' was changed into the encouragement: 'Fear not the arrow of flying fight.' Where the psalm says, 'He acknowledges my name,' the paper said, 'Late my name,' and 'In affliction I am at his side, to bring him . . .' had turned into 'Soon into the night with him.'

The text was believed to be miraculous and a protection against bullets. It was worn as a talisman by soldiers in the last imperialist war. Decades later prisoners were to sew it into their clothes and mutter its words in jail when they were summoned at night for interrogation.

Leaving the telephonist, Yury went out into the field to the young White Guardsman whom he had killed. The boy's handsome face bore the marks of innocence and all-forgiving suffering. 'Why did I kill him?' thought Yury.

He undid the boy's coat and opened it. Some careful hand—probably his mother's—had embroidered his name and surname, Seryozha Rantsevich, in cursive letters on the lining. From the opening of Seryozha's shirt there slipped out and hung on a chain a cross, a locket and some other small flat gold case, rather like a snuff-box, dented as if a nail had been driven into it. A paper fell out. Yury unfolded it and could not believe his eyes. It was the same ninetieth Psalm but this time printed in its full and genuine Slavonic text.

At this moment Seryozha stirred and groaned. He was alive.

---

[1] The 91st in the Authorised Version of the Bible. The above quotations have been taken from the Douai Version, as they are nearer to the Russian.

It turned out afterwards that he had only fainted as the result of a slight internal injury. The bullet had been stopped by his mother's amulet and this had saved him.—But what was to be done with this unconscious man now?

It was a time when savagery was at its height. Prisoners did not reach headquarters alive and enemy wounded were knifed in the field.

Given the fluid state of the partisan force, with its high turnover of deserters to and from the enemy, it was possible, if the strictest secrecy were kept, to pass Rantsevich off as a recently enlisted ally.

Yury took off the clothes of the dead telephonist and, with the help of Angelar, in whom he confided, exchanged them for those of the boy.

He and Angelar nursed Seryozha back to health. When he was quite well they released him, although he did not conceal from them that he meant to go back to Kolchak's army and continue fighting the Reds.

5

In the autumn, the partisans took up quarters in Fox's Thicket, a steep wooded hill with a swift stream foaming round three sides of it and biting into the shores.

The Whites had wintered in it the year before and had dug themselves in with the help of the neighbouring villagers, but they had left in the spring without destroying their fortifications. Now their dugouts and communication trenches were used by the partisans.

Yury shared a dugout with Liberius Mikulitsin, who had kept him awake by chattering for two nights running.

'I wonder what my esteemed parent, my respected Papa, is doing at this moment.'

'God, how I hate this buffoonery,' Yury sighed to himself. 'And he's the living image of his father.'

'Judging from our previous talks, you got to know him quite well. You seem to have formed a not unfavourable opinion of him. What have you to say on the subject, my dear sir?'

'Liberius Avercievich, to-morrow we have the pre-election meeting. And there is the trial coming up of the orderlies who have been distilling vodka—Lajos and I have still to go through the evidence. And I haven't slept for two nights. Can't we put this conversation off? I'm dead tired.'

'All the same, just tell me what you think of my aged parent.'

'To begin with, your father is quite young. I don't know why you talk about him like that. Well, all right, I'll tell you. As I've often said to you, I don't know much about the various shades of socialist opinion and I can't see much difference between bolsheviks and other socialists. Your father is one of those to whom Russia owes her recent disorders and disturbances. He is a revolutionary type, a revolutionary character. Like yourself, he represents the principle of ferment in Russian life.'

'Is that meant as praise or blame?'

'Once again, I beg you to put off this discussion to a more convenient time. And I must really draw your attention to your excessive consumption of cocaine. You have been wilfully depleting the stock of which I am in charge. You know perfectly well that it is needed for other purposes, not to mention the fact that it is a poison and I am responsible for your health.'

'You cut the study circle again last night. You have an atrophied social sense, just like an illiterate peasant woman or an inveterate bourgeois. And yet you are a doctor, you are well read, I believe you even write. How do you explain it?'

'I don't. I expect I am too stupid; it can't be helped. You should be sorry for me.'

'Why the false modesty? If instead of using that ironic tone you took the trouble to find out what we do in our classes, you wouldn't be so supercilious.'

'Heavens, Liberius Avercievich, I'm not being supercilious. I have the utmost respect for your educational work. I've read the discussion notes you circulate. I know your ideas on the moral improvement of the soldier—they're excellent. All you say about what the soldier's attitude should be towards his comrades, to the weak, the helpless, to women, and about honour and chastity—it's almost the teaching of the Dukhobors [1]. All that kind of Tolstoyism I know by heart. My own adolescence was full of these aspirations towards a better life. How could I laugh at such things?

'But, firstly, the idea of social betterment as it is understood since the October Revolution doesn't fill me with enthusiasm. Secondly, it is so far from being put into practice, and the mere talk about it has cost such a sea of blood, that I am not at all sure if the end justifies the means. And lastly, and above all, when I hear people speak of reshaping life it makes me lose my self-control and I fall into despair.

'Reshaping life! People who can say that have never understood a thing about life—they have never felt its breath, its heart—however much they have seen or done. They look on it as a lump of raw material which needs to be processed by them, to be ennobled by their

[1] Communities which practised principles similar to those of Tolstoy.

touch. But life is never a material, a substance to be moulded. If you want to know, life is the principle of self-renewal, it is constantly renewing and remaking and changing and transfiguring itself, it is infinitely beyond your or my theories about it.'

'And yet, you know, if you came to our meetings, if you kept in touch with our splendid, our magnificent people, you wouldn't feel half so low. You wouldn't suffer from this melancholia. I know what it comes from. You see us being beaten and you can't see a ray of hope ahead. But one should never panic, my dear chap. I could tell you much worse things—to do with me personally, not to be made public for the moment—and yet I don't lose my head. Our set-backs are purely temporary, Kolchak is bound to lose in the end. You mark my words. You'll see. We'll win in the long run. So cheer up!'

'It's unspeakable,' thought Yury. 'How can anyone be so dense, so childish! I spend my time dinning into him that our ideas are diametrically opposed; he has captured me by force, he is keeping me against my will, and yet he imagines that his set-backs fill me with dismay and that his hopes can cheer me up! How can anyone be as blind as this? For him, the fate of the universe hangs on the victory of the October Revolution!'

Yury said nothing, merely shrugging his shoulders; this, however, made it plain that Liberius's naïveté had exasperated him so much that he could hardly control himself. Nor did this escape Liberius's notice.

'"You are angry, Jupiter, that means you must be wrong,"' he said.

'Do, for God's sake, understand once and for all that none of this means anything to me.—"Jupiter" and 'Never panic" and "Anyone who says A must say B" and "The Moor has done his work, the Moor can go"—none of these clichés, these vulgar commonplaces, appeal to me. I'll say A but I won't say B—whatever you do. I'll admit that you are Russia's liberators, her shining lights, that without you she would be lost, sunk in misery and ignorance, but I still don't give a damn for any of you, I don't like you and you can all go to the devil.

'Those who do your thinking for you go in for proverbs, but they've forgotten one proverb—"You can take a horse to the water but you can't make it drink," and they've got into the habit of liberating and showering benefits on just those people who haven't asked for it. I suppose you think I can't imagine anything in the world more pleasant than your camp and your company. I suppose I have to bless you for keeping me a prisoner and thank you for liberating me from my wife, my son, my home, my work, from everything I hold dear and that makes life worth living for me!

'There is a rumour going round that some unknown force—not a

Russian force—has raided and sacked Varykino. Kamennodvorsky doesn't deny it. They say your people and mine managed to escape. Apparently some sort of mythical slit-eyed warriors in wadded coats and fur hats crossed the Rynva in a terrible frost, and calmly shot every living soul in the place and vanished as mysteriously as they had come. Do you know anything about it? Is it true?'

'Nonsense. All lies. False rumours.'

'If you are as kind and generous as you claim to be when you lecture on the moral improvement of the soldiers, then let me go.— I'll go and look for my family—I don't know where they are, I don't even know if they are alive or dead. And if you won't do that, then shut up for goodness' sake and leave me alone, because I am not interested in anything else and I won't answer for myself if you go on. Anyway, what the hell, haven't I the right to go to sleep?'

Yury lay down flat on his bunk, his face in his pillow, doing his utmost not to listen to Liberius justifying himself and comforting him once more with the prospect of a final victory over the Whites before the spring. The civil war would be over, there would be peace, liberty and prosperity, and no one would dare to detain Yury a moment longer. But until then he must be patient. After all, they had made all the sacrifices and done all the waiting, it wasn't much to have to wait a few months longer, and anyhow, where could he go at present? For his own good he must be prevented from going anywhere alone.

'Just like a gramophone record, blast him!' Yury raged in silent indignation. 'He can't stop. Why isn't he ashamed of chewing the same cud all these years? How can he go on listening to the sound of his own voice, the wretched dope-fiend? Day and night he goes on. God, how I hate him! As God is my witness, I'll murder him some day.

'Tonya, my darling, my poor child! Where are you? Are you alive? Dear Lord, she was to have her baby quite soon. How did she get through the confinement? Have we got a son or a daughter? My dear ones, what is happening to you all? Tonya, you are my everlasting reproach. Lara, I daren't speak your name for fear of gasping out my life. O God! O God!—And that loathsome, unfeeling brute is still talking! One day he'll go too far and I'll kill him, I'll kill him.'

6

The Indian summer was over. It was a clear, golden, autumn day. At the western end of Fox's Thicket the wooden turret of a blockhouse built by the Whites still rose above the ground. Here Yury had arranged to meet his Hungarian assistant Lajos to discuss various service matters. He arrived on time and, waiting for his friend, strolled along the edge of the crumbling earthworks, climbed into the watch-tower and looked out of the slits in front of the now empty machine-gun nests at the wooded distance beyond the river.

The autumn clearly marked the frontier between the firs and pines and the deciduous trees. Between the gloomy, bristling walls of near-black pines the leafy thickets shone, flame and wine-coloured, like small mediaeval towns with painted and gold-roofed palaces built of the timber cut down in the thickness of the forest.

The earth at Yury's feet, inside the trench and in the ruts of the forest road, was hard with ground frost and heaped with the small, tight scrolls of dry willow leaves, rolled up like shavings. The autumn smelled of these brown bitter leaves and of many other gingery spices. Greedily he breathed in the mixed peppery smell of chilled apples, bitter dry twigs, sweetish damp earth and that of the blue September mist which smoked like the fumes of a recently extinguished fire.

He did not hear Lajos come up behind him.

'How are you, colleague?' he said in German. They talked about their business.

'There are three points. First, the court-martial of the orderlies who have been distilling vodka; secondly, the reorganisation of the field ambulance and the medical stores; and thirdly, my proposal for the field treatment of mental illnesses. I don't know if you agree with me, my dear Lajos, but, from what I observe, we are going mad and our modern forms of insanity are infectious.'

'It's a very interesting question. I'll come to it in a moment. But first I'd like to mention something else. There is unrest in the camp. There is sympathy with the vodka distillers. Besides, the men are worried about their families who are fleeing from the Whites. As you know, there's a convoy coming, with wives, children and old people, and some of the partisans have refused to leave the camp until it comes.'

'I know. We'll have to wait for them.'

'And all this on the eve of the election of a joint command for our unit and several others so far independent of us. I think that the only possible candidate is Comrade Liberius. But some of the young people are putting Vdovichenko forward. He is supported by a group, alien to us in spirit, which belongs to the circle of the vodka distillers—sons of shopkeepers and kulaks, deserters from Kolchak. They are the ones who are making the most noise.'

'What do you think will happen at the trial?'

'I think they will be condemned to death, but the sentence will be suspended.'

'Well, let's get down to business. First, the field ambulance.'

'All right. But I must tell you that I am not surprised at your suggestion for preventive psychiatry. I believe in it myself. We are faced with the rise and spread of a form of psychic illness which is typical of our time and is directly caused by the historical circumstances. We have a case of it in the camp—Pamphil Palykh, a former private in the tsarist army, a man with a high revolutionary consciousness and an innate class sense. The cause of his trouble is his anxiety for his family in the event of his being killed and their falling into the hands of the Whites and being made to answer for him. It's a very complex mentality. I believe his family is one of those who are coming in the convoy. I don't know enough Russian to question him properly. You could find out from Angelar or Kamennodvorsky. He ought to be examined.'

'I know Palykh very well. At one time we often came across each other at army council meetings. Dark and cruel, with a low forehead.—I can't think what good you see in him. He was always for extreme measures, shooting and punishing. I've always found him repulsive. Still, I'll take it up.'

7

It was a clear and sunny day, the weather had been still and dry for a whole week.

The usual rumble of noise hung over the large camp, rather like the distant roar of the sea. There were footsteps, voices, axes chopping wood, the ringing of an anvil, the barking of dogs, the neighing of horses and the crowing of cocks. Crowds of sunburnt, white-toothed, smiling men moved about the forest. Those who knew the doctor nodded to him, others passed him by without a greeting.

The men had refused to strike camp until their families, who were fleeing from their homes, had caught up with them, but now the fugitives were expected shortly and preparations for the move were being made. Things were being cleaned and mended, crates nailed down and carts counted and checked over.

There was a large clearing in the middle of the wood where meetings were often held; it was a sort of mound or barrow on which the grass had been trodden down. A general meeting had been called that day for some important announcement.

Many of the trees in the forest had not yet turned yellow. In its depths they were still fresh and green. The afternoon sun, sinking behind the forest, pierced it with its rays, and the leaves, transparent as glass, shone with a green flame.

On an open space outside his tent Kamennodvorsky, the chief liaison officer, was burning papers, discarded rubbish from General Kappel's records which had fallen into his hands, as well as his own partisan files. The fire, with the setting sun behind it, was as transparent as the leaves; the flames were invisible and only the waves of shimmering heat showed that something was burning.

Here and there the woods were brilliant with ripe berries—bright tassels of lady's-smock, brick-red alderberries and clusters of viburnum which changed from white to purple. Tinkling their glassy wings, dragon-flies, as transparent as the flames and the leaves, sailed slowly through the air.

Ever since his childhood Yury had been fond of woods seen at evening against the setting sun. At such moments he felt as if he too were being pierced by blades of light. As if the gift of the living spirit were streaming into his breast, piercing his being and coming out by his shoulders like a pair of wings. The archetype, which is formed in every child for life and seems for ever after to be the inward image of his personality, arose in him in its full primordial strength and compelled nature, the forest, the afterglow and everything else visible to be transfigured into a similarly primordial and all-embracing likeness of a girl. 'Lara.' Closing his eyes, he whispered and thought, addressing the whole of life, all God's earth, all the sunlit space spread out before him.

But the everyday, current reality was still there: Russia was going through the October Revolution and Yury was a prisoner of the partisans. Absent-mindedly he went up to Kamennodvorsky's fire.

'Burning your records? Not finished yet?'

'There's enough of this stuff to burn for days.'

Yury stirred a heap of papers with his boot. It was the White Staff Headquarters' correspondence. It occurred to him that he might come across some mention of Rantsevich. But all he saw were boring, out-of-date communiqués in code. He kicked another heap. It proved to be an equally dull collection of minutes of partisan meetings.

Kamennodvorsky took a paper from his pocket and handed it to Yury:

'Here are your marching orders for the medical unit. The convoy with the partisans' families is quite near and our dissensions inside the camp will be settled by this evening, so we can expect to move any day now.'

Yury glanced at the order and groaned :

'But you're giving me less transport than last time and there are all those extra wounded. Those who can will have to walk, but there are few of them and what am I to do with the stretcher cases ? And the stores and the bedding and the equipment ?'

'You'll have to manage somehow—have to cut your coat according to your cloth. Now another thing. It's a request from all of us. Will you have a look at a comrade of ours ?—tried, tested, devoted to the cause and a splendid soldier. There's something wrong with him.'

'Palykh ? Lajos told me.'

'Yes. Go and see him. Examine him.'

'He's a mental case ?'

'I suppose so. He says he has "the creeps".—Hallucinations evidently. Insomnia. Headaches.'

'All right, I might as well go and see him now, since I'm free at the moment. When does the meeting start ?'

'I think they're coming now. But why bother ? As you see, I'm not going either. They'll manage without us.'

'Then I'll go and see Pamphil. Though I can hardly keep my eyes open, I'm so sleepy. Liberius Avercievich likes to philosophise at night ; he has worn me out with his talk. Where do I find Pamphil ?'

'You know the birch copse beyond the rubbish pit ?'

'Yes, I think I know it.'

'You'll find some commanders' tents in a clearing. We've put one of them at Pamphil's disposal. He's got his family coming ; they're in the convoy. That's where you'll find him—in one of the tents—he's got battalion commander status—as a reward for revolutionary merit.'

8

On his way to see Pamphil, Yury was overcome with fatigue. It was the cumulative effect of several sleepless nights. He could go back to his dugout and lie down but he was afraid of staying there, for at any moment Liberius might come in and disturb him. He stopped in a glade strewn with leaves from the surrounding woods. They lay in a checker-board pattern and so did the low rays of the sun falling on their golden carpet. This double, criss-cross brightness made your head spin and sent you to sleep like small print or a monotonous mutter.

Yury lay down on the silkily rustling leaves, his head on his arm and his arm on a pillow of moss at the foot of a tree, and dozed off at once. The dazzle of light and shadow which had put him to sleep now covered him with its patchwork so that his body, stretched on the ground, was indistinguishable from the sunlight and the leaves, invisible as if he had put on a magic cap.

But very soon the very force of his desire and need for sleep aroused him. Direct causes are effective only within the limits which are valid for them; beyond these they produce the opposite effect. His wakeful consciousness, not finding any rest, worked feverishly in a vacuum. Thoughts whirled and wheeled inside his head, his mind was knocking like a faulty engine. This inner confusion worried and exasperated him. 'That swine Liberius,' he thought indignantly. 'As if there weren't enough things in the world to drive people mad; he has to take a sane man and deliberately turn him into a neurotic by keeping him a prisoner and boring him with his friendship and his chatter. I'll kill him one of these days.'

Folding and unfolding like a scrap of coloured stuff, a brown speckled butterfly flew across the sunny side of the clearing. Yury watched it sleepily. Choosing a background colour nearest to its own, it settled on the brown speckled bark of a pine tree and disappeared into it, vanishing as completely as Yury, hidden by the play of light and shadow, had vanished.

His mind turned to its accustomed round of thoughts—he had mentioned them indirectly in many of his medical works—they concerned will and purpose as superior forms of adaptation; mimicry and protective colouring; the survival of the fittest and whether natural selection is indeed the way to the development and birth of consciousness. And what was subject? What was object? How was their identity to be defined? His reflections led him from Darwin to Schelling, from the butterfly to modern painting and impressionist art. He thought of creation, creatures, creativeness, craft and cunning.

Once again he fell asleep, but woke up a moment later. A soft, muffled conversation had disturbed him. The few words he overheard were enough to tell him that it concerned some secret and illicit plan. He had not been seen, the conspirators had no suspicion of his presence. The slightest movement might cost him his life. Yury shammed dead and listened.

Some of the voices he recognised. They were those of the scum of the partisans, hangers-on such as Goshka, Sanka, Koska and their usual follower Terenty Galuzin, young good-for-nothings who were at the bottom of every kind of outrage and disorder. Zakhar was also there, an even more sinister personality, who was mixed up in the vodka affair, but was not being prosecuted for the time being because he had denounced the chief offenders. What surprised Yury was the presence of Sivobluy, a partisan of the crack 'silver unit' who was one of the Commander's bodyguards. In keeping with a tradition going back to Stenka Razin and Pugachev, this favourite, known to be in the confidence of the chief, was nicknamed 'the hetman's ear' [1]. Evidently he too was in the conspiracy.

The plotters were negotiating with envoys from the advanced positions of the enemy. The delegates were inaudible, so softly did they speak to the traitors, and Yury could only guess that they were speaking when an occasional silence seemed to interrupt the whispering.

Zakhar, the drunkard, was doing most of the talking, cursing foully at every other moment in his hoarse, wheezing voice. He seemed to be the ringleader.

'Now, you others, listen. The chief thing is, we've got to keep it quiet. If anybody talks—you see this knife?—I'll slit his guts. Is that clear? You know as well as I do, we're stuck. There's no way out for us. We've got to earn our pardon. We've got to work such a trick as nobody's seen before.—They want him taken alive. Now they say their boss Gulevoy is coming.' (They corrected him —'Galiullin'—but he did not catch the name and said 'General Galeyev'.) 'That's our chance. There won't be another like it. Here's their delegates. They'll tell you all about it. They say we've got to take him alive. Now you tell them, you others.'

Now the envoys were speaking. Yury could not catch a word, but from the length of the pause he judged that they explained the proposal in detail. Zakhar spoke again.

'Hear that, mates? You see what a nice fellow he is. Why should we take the rap for him? He isn't even a man—he's a half-wit, a monk or a hermit. You stop grinning, Terenty. I'll give you something to grin about, you sod. I wasn't talking about you. I'm telling you—he's a hermit, that's what he is. Let him have his way and he'll turn you all into monks—he'll have you gelded. What does he tell you?—No cursing, no getting drunk, all this stuff about women. How can you live like that? To-night we'll get him down to the ford. I'll see that he comes. Then we'll all fall on him together. It won't be hard.—There's nothing to it. What's difficult is that they want him alive. Tie him up, they say. Well, I'll see; if it doesn't work out that way I'll deal with him myself, I'll finish him off with my own hands. They'll send their people along to help.'

[1] 'Hetman's ear'—the captain's spy.

He went on explaining the plan but gradually they moved away and Yury ceased to hear them.

'That's Liberius they're plotting to hand over to the Whites or kill, the swine,' he thought with horror and indignation, quite forgetting how often he had himself wished his tormentor dead. How was it to be prevented? He decided to go back to Kamennodvorsky and tell him of the plot without mentioning any names, and also to warn Liberius.

But when he got back, Kamennodvorsky was no longer burning papers, only his assistant was keeping an eye on the smouldering fire to prevent it spreading.

The crime did not take place. It was forestalled. The conspiracy, as it turned out, was known. That day it was uncovered and the plotters were seized. Sivobluy had played the role of *agent provocateur*. Yury felt even more disgusted.

9

It became known that the partisans' families were now within a day's journey of the camp. The partisans were getting ready to welcome them and soon afterwards to move on. Yury went to see Pamphil Palykh.

He found him at the entrance to his tent, an axe in his hand. In front of him was a tall heap of birch saplings; he had cut them down but had not yet stripped them. Some had fallen where they stood and, toppling with their whole weight, had dug their sharp splintered wood deep into the damp ground. Others he had dragged from a short distance and piled on top of the rest. Shuddering and swaying on their springy branches, the saplings lay neither on the ground nor close together. It seemed as though, with outstretched arms, they were fending off Pamphil, who had cut them down, and blocking his way into his tent with a tangled thicket of branches and green leaves.

'It's for my dear guests,' explained Pamphil. 'My wife and my children. The tent is too low. And the rain comes through. I've cut these down for joists to make a roof.'

'I shouldn't count on their allowing you to have them in your tent, Pamphil. Who has ever heard of civilians, women and children, being allowed to live inside a camp? They'll stay with the wagons somewhere just outside; you'll be able to see them as much as you like in your spare time, but I shouldn't think they'll be allowed to live in your tent.—But that isn't what I've come about. They tell me you're getting thin, you can't eat or sleep, is that true? I must say you look all right. Though you could do with a hair-cut.'

Pamphil was a huge man with black tousled hair and beard and a bumpy forehead in two tiers; a thickening of his frontal bone, like a ring or a steel band pressed over his temples, gave him a beetling, glowering look.

When, at the beginning of the revolution, it had been feared that, as in 1905, the upheaval would be an abortive event affecting only the educated few and leaving the deeper layers of society untouched, everything possible had been done to spread revolutionary propaganda among the people to disturb them, stir them up and lash them into fury.

In those early days, men like Pamphil, who needed no encouragement to hate intellectuals, officers and gentry with a savage hatred, were regarded by enthusiastic left-wing intellectuals as a rare find and were greatly valued. Their inhumanity seemed a marvel of class consciousness, their barbarism a model of proletarian firmness and revolutionary instinct. By such qualities Pamphil had established his fame and he was held in great esteem by partisan chiefs and party leaders.

To Yury this gloomy and unsociable giant, with his poor and narrow interests and his soullessness, seemed a degenerate, a man who was not quite sane.

'Come into the tent,' said Pamphil.

'No—why? It's pleasanter out in the open. Anyway I couldn't get in.'

'All right. Have it your own way. We can sit on the timber.'

They sat down on the springy saplings and Pamphil told Yury the story of his life. 'They say a tale is soon told. But my story is a long one. I couldn't tell it all in three years. I don't know where to begin.

'Well, I'll try. My wife and I. We were young. She looked after the house. I worked in the fields. It wasn't a bad life. We had children. They took me for the army. They sent me to the war. Well, the war. What should I tell you about the war? You've seen it, Comrade Doctor.—Then the revolution came. I saw the light. The soldiers' eyes were opened. We heard that it wasn't only the foreigners who were enemies. We had enemies at home too. "Soldiers of the world revolution, down your rifles, go home, turn against the bourgeois!" And so on. You know it all yourself, Comrade Army Doctor. Well, to go on. Then came the civil war. I joined the partisans. Now I'll have to leave out a lot or I'll never end. After all that, what do I see now, at the present moment? That bastard, he's brought up the two Stavropolsk regiments from the Western front, and the first Orenburg Cossack as well. I'm not a child, am I? Don't I understand? Haven't I served in the army? It's a bad business, doctor, it's all up with us. What he wants to do, the swine, is to fall on us with all that scum. He wants to surround us.

'But I've got a wife and children. If he comes out on top, how are they going to get away from him? They're innocent, of course, they're right outside it all, but he won't bother his head about that. He'll get hold of my wife and he'll tie her up and he'll start tormenting her on my account; he'll torture my wife and children; he'll break every bone in their bodies; he'll tear them apart. And you ask, why don't I sleep. A man could be made of steel, but it's enough to drive you off your head.'

'What an odd fellow you are, Pamphil. I can't make you out. For years you've been away from them, you didn't even know where they were and you didn't worry. Now you're going to see them, and instead of being happy, you're getting ready to sing at their funeral.'

'That was before, now it's different. He's beating us, the White bastard. Anyway, it isn't me we're talking about. I'm done for. I'll soon be dead. But I can't take my little ones with me into the next world, can I? They'll stay and they'll fall into his heathen hands. He'll squeeze the blood out of them drop by drop.'

'Is that why you've got "the creeps"? I was told you keep seeing things.'

'Well, doctor. I haven't told you everything. I've kept back the most important thing. Now, I'll tell you the whole truth if you want it, I'll say it to your face but you mustn't hold it against me.

'I've done away with a lot of your kind, there's a lot of officers' blood on my hands. Officers, gentry. And it's never worried me. Spilt like water. Names and numbers all gone out of my head. But there's one little fellow I can't get out of my mind; I killed that brat and I can't forget it. Why did I have to kill him? He made me laugh, and I killed him for a joke, for nothing, like a fool.

'In the February revolution that was, in Kerensky's time. We were having a mutiny. We were near a railway station. We'd left the front. They sent a young fellow, an agitator, to talk us into going back. So we should fight on to victory. Well that little cadet came to talk us into being good. Just like a chicken he was. "Fight on to victory"—that was his slogan. He got up on a water-butt shouting that slogan; the water-butt was on the railway platform. He got up there, you see, so as to make his call to battle come from higher up, and suddenly the lid turned upside down under him and he fell right in. Right into the water. You can't think how funny he looked. Made me split my sides laughing! I was holding a rifle. And I was laughing my head off. Couldn't stop. It was just as if he was tickling me. And then, I raised my rifle and took aim and shot him down, bang. I can't think how it happened. Just as though somebody had pushed me.

'Well, that's the reason I've got the creeps. I dream about that station at night. At the time it was funny. Now I'm sorry.'

'Was that at Biryuchi station near the town of Melyuzeyevo?'

'Can't remember.'

'Were you in the Zibushino rising?'

'Can't remember.'

'Which front were you on? Was it the western front? Were you in the West?'

'Somewhere like that. It could have been in the West. I can't remember.'

Iced Rowanberries

THE convoy with the partisans' families, complete with children and belongings, had long been following the main partisan force. After it, behind the wagons, came vast herds of cattle, mainly cows—several thousand of them.

With the arrival of the women-folk a new figure appeared in the camp. This was Kubarikha, a soldier's wife who was a cattle healer—and also, secretly, a witch. She went about in a little pancake hat cocked sideways on her head and a pea-green Royal Scots Fusiliers greatcoat, which formed part of the British equipment supplied to Admiral Kolchak, and she assured everyone that she had made them over from a prisoner's cap and overalls and that the Reds had liberated her from Kezhma jail where, for some unknown reason, Admiral Kolchak had kept her.

The partisans had moved from Fox's Thicket to a new camping ground. They were only supposed to stay there until the neighbourhood had been reconnoitred and suitable quarters found for the winter. But changed circumstances forced them to spend the winter there.

This new camp was quite unlike the old one. The forest round it was dense and in places impenetrable *tayga*. On one side, beyond the camp and the highway, there was no end to it. In the early days after the move, while the tents were being pitched and Yury had more leisure, he had explored it in several directions and had convinced himself that one could easily get lost in it. Two places had struck him in the course of these excursions and remained in his memory.

One was on the edge of the *tayga*, just outside the camp. The forest was autumn bare, so that you could see right into it as through an open gate. Here a splendid, solitary, rusty rowan had alone kept its leaves. Growing on a mound which rose above the low, sucking, hummocky marsh, it reached into the sky, holding up the flat round shields of its hard crimson berries against the leaden menace of winter. Small winter birds with feathers as bright as frosty dawns—bullfinches and tom-tits—settled on it and picked the largest berries, stretching out their necks and throwing back their heads to swallow them.

There seemed to be a close living connection between the birds and the tree, as if the rowan had watched them for a long time, refusing to do anything, but had in the end had pity on them: as though, like a foster mother, she had unbuttoned herself and offered them her breast, smiling as much as to say: 'Well, all right, all right, eat me, have your fill.'

The other place was even stranger. This was on a height which broke away steeply to one side. Looking down into the ravine you felt that at the bottom there should be something different from what there was on top—a stream or a hollow or a wild field overgrown with seedy, uncut grass. But in fact it was a repetition of the same thing, only at a giddy depth, as if the forest had simply taken its tree-tops down into the ground at your feet, sinking to a different level. There had probably been a landslide there at some time.

It was as if the grim, giant forest, marching at cloud level, had stumbled, lost its footing and hurtled down, all in one piece; and it might have dropped right through the earth, if it had not, by a miracle, saved itself at the last moment—so there it was now, safe and sound, rustling below.

But what made the top of the ravine remarkable was not only this. All along its edge it was locked in by granite boulders standing on end, looking like the flat stones of a dolmen. As soon as Yury came across this stony platform he felt convinced that it was not of natural origin but bore the mark of human hands. It might well have been an ancient temple where prayers and sacrifices had once been offered by unknown worshippers to pagan gods.

It was here that the death sentence against eleven ringleaders of the conspiracy and two orderlies, condemned for distilling vodka, was carried out, one cold, sullen morning.

A guard of twenty of the most loyal partisans, stiffened by members of Liberius's bodyguard, brought the condemned men to this spot. Then they closed around them in a semicircle, rifle in hand, and, advancing at a quick, jostling pace, drove them to the edge of the arena, where there was no way out, except over the precipice.

Questioning, long detention and the degradations they had suffered had removed all human likeness from the faces of the prisoners. Black, bristling and haggard, they were as terrible as ghosts.

They had been disarmed when they were first arrested, and it had not even occurred to anyone to search them again before the execution. Such a search would have seemed both superfluous and vile, a gratuitous mockery of men so close to death.

But now, suddenly, Rzhanitsky, a friend of Vdovichenko, who walked beside him and who, like him, was an old anarchist, fired three shots at the guards, aiming at Sivobluy. He was an excellent marksman but his hand shook in his excitement and he missed. The same discretion and pity for their former comrades which had prevented the search now kept the guards from falling on him or shooting him down at once for his attempt. Rzhanitsky had three unspent bullets left in his revolver but, maddened by his failure and perhaps, in his agitation, forgetting that they were there, he flung his Browning against the rocks. It went off a fourth time, wounding one of the condemned men, the orderly Pachkolya, in the foot.

Pachkolya cried out, clutched his foot and fell down, screaming with pain. The two men nearest him, Sanka Pafnutkin and Koska Gorazdykh, raised him and, seizing him by the arms, dragged him on, so that he should not be trampled by his comrades, who no longer knew what they were doing. Unable to put down his wounded foot, Pachkolya hopped and limped towards the rocky ledge where the doomed men were being driven, and screamed incessantly. His inhuman shrieks infected the others with his panic and broke down their self-control. What followed was unimaginable. There arose a storm of abuse, of lamentation, prayers and curses.

Terenty Galuzin, who still wore his yellow-braided school cap, removed it, fell on his knees and, still kneeling, edged backward, following the rest of the men towards the terrible stones. Bowing repeatedly to the ground before the guards and sobbing his heart out, he pleaded with them in a half-conscious, sing-song voice:

'Forgive me, comrades, I'm sorry, I won't do it again, please let me off, don't kill me. I haven't lived yet. I want to live a little longer, I want to see my mother just once more. Please let me off, mates, please forgive me. I'll do anything for you. I'll kiss the ground under your feet. Oh, help, help, Mother, I'm done for!'

Someone else, hidden in the crowd, chanted:

'Good comrades, kind comrades! How is this possible? In two wars we fought together! We stood up and fought for the same things! Let us off, mates. We'll repay your kindness, we'll be grateful to you all our lives, we will prove it to you by our deeds.—Are you deaf or what? Why don't you answer? Christ is not in you!'

Others screamed at Sivobluy:

'Judas! Christ-killer! If we are traitors, you are a traitor three times over, you dog, may you choke. You killed your lawful tsar to whom you took your oath, you swore loyalty to us and you betrayed us. Mind you kiss your devil, your Forester, before you betray him! You'll betray him all right!'

On the verge of the grave, Vdovichenko remained true to himself as he had been throughout his life. His head high, his grey hair streaming in the wind, he addressed Rzhanitsky as one *communard* to another, in a voice loud enough to be heard by all :

'Don't humble yourself! Your protest will not reach them. These new oprichniki[1], these master craftsmen of the new torture chambers will never understand you! But don't lose heart. History will tell the truth. Posterity will nail the Bourbons of the commissarocracy to a pillar of shame, it will pillory their dark deeds. We die as martyrs at the dawn of the world revolution. Hail, revolution of the spirit! Hail, universal anarchy!'

A volley of twenty shots, discharged at some command caught only by the riflemen, mowed down half the condemned, killing most of them outright. The rest were shot down by another salvo. The boy, Terenty Galuzin, twitched longest, but finally he too lay still.

2

The idea of moving further east for the winter was not given up easily. Patrols were sent out to survey the country beyond the highway, along the Vytsk-Kezhma watershed. Liberius was often absent, leaving Yury to himself.

But in fact it was too late for the partisans to move anywhere and they had nowhere to go to. This was the time of their worst set-backs. The Whites, resolving, on the eve of their own destruction, to deal a crushing blow at the irregular forest units and have done with them once and for all, had encircled them and were pressing them from every side. The position would have been catastrophic for the Reds had the radius of the encirclement been smaller. They were protected by its size, for the approaching winter made the *tayga* impenetrable and prevented the enemy from bringing in his flank units to besiege the peasant army more closely.

To move, however, had become impossible. They could, indeed, have broken through to new positions had any plan existed which offered specific military advantages. But no such definite plan had been worked out. People were getting to the end of their tether. Junior commanders lost heart and with it their influence over their subordinates. Senior commanders met nightly in council and put

[1] The 'security troops' of Ivan the Terrible.

forward conflicting solutions. The idea of shifting camp had finally to be abandoned in favour of fortifying the present positions in the heart of the *tayga*. Their advantage was that the deep snow made them inaccessible in winter, particularly as the Whites were ill supplied with skis. The immediate task was to dig in and lay in large stores.

The camp quartermaster reported a severe shortage of flour and potatoes. Cattle, however, were plentiful and he foresaw that the staple food in winter would be milk and meat.

There was a shortage of winter clothing; some of the partisans went about half dressed. It was decided to kill off all the camp dogs and people with experience as furriers were set to making dog-skin jackets, to be worn with the fur side out.

Yury was denied the use of transport for bringing in the wounded. The carts were kept for more important needs. The last time the partisans had moved camp the wounded were carried thirty miles by stretcher.

The only medicines he still had were quinine, Glauber salts and iodine. The iodine, however, was in the form of crystals and had to be dissolved in alcohol before it could be used for dressings or operations. The destruction of the vodka still was now regretted and those of the distillers who had been acquitted at the trial as less guilty than the rest were asked to mend it or construct a new one. The manufacture of alcohol was now started again, officially, for medical purposes. The news was greeted with nods and winks. Drunkenness broke out again and contributed to the general demoralisation.

The alcohol produced was almost 100 per cent pure. At this strength it was suitable for dissolving crystals and also for preparing tincture of quinine; this was used in the treatment of typhus when it again became endemic at the onset of the cold weather.

3

Yury went to see Pamphil and his family. His wife and three children (two girls and a boy) had spent the whole of the past summer in flight on dusty roads under the open sky. They were terrified by their experiences and they lived in expectation of new terrors. All four had light hair, faded to flax colour by the sun, and grave eyebrows, white against their tanned and weathered faces. But while the children were too young to show the marks of their tribulations, the mother's face had become lifeless. Strain and fear had narrowed her lips to a thread and set her dry, regular features in an immobility of suffering and defensiveness.

Pamphil was devoted to all of them and loved his children to distraction. He surprised Yury by his skill in carving toy rabbits, cocks and bears for them, using a corner of his finely sharpened axe blade.

With the arrival of his family he had cheered up and begun to recover. But now the news had got about that the presence of the families was considered bad for discipline, and they were going to be sent, under proper escort, to winter quarters at some distance from the camp, which would thus be relieved of its useless burden of civilians. There was more talk about this plan than actual preparation for carrying it out, and Yury doubted if it would ever be put through, but Pamphil's spirits fell and his 'creeps' came back.

4

Before winter finally set in, the camp went through a period of disturbances—anxieties and uncertainties, confused, threatening situations and absurd, illogical events.

The Whites had completed the encirclement according to plan. They were headed by Generals Vitsyn, Quadri and Bassalygo, who were known far and wide for their harshness and unyielding resolution, and whose names alone terrified the refugees inside the camp as well as the peaceful population still remaining in its native villages at the rear of the encircling troops.

The enemy had no means of tightening his grip. The partisans had no reason to worry on this count, but it was impossible for them to remain inactive. Their acceptance of the situation was bound to strengthen the enemy's morale. However safe they were inside their trap, they had to make a sortie, if only as a military demonstration.

A strong force was set aside for this purpose and concentrated against the western arc of the circle. As a result of several days' hard fighting, it inflicted a defeat on the Whites and broke through to their rear.

This breach opened a way to the camp in the *tayga*, and through it poured a stream of new refugees; these were not related to the partisans. Terrified by the punitive measures of the Whites, the whole peasantry of the surrounding countryside had fled from their homes and now sought to join the peasant army, whom they regarded as their natural protectors.

But the camp was anxious to get rid of its own dependants and unwilling to assume the burden of newcomers and strangers. Envoys were sent to meet the fugitives and to divert them to a village on the river Chilimka. The village was called Dvory [1] because of the farmsteads which had grown up round its mill. There it was proposed to settle the refugees for the winter and to send the supplies which were being set aside for them.

While these steps were being taken, however, events followed their own course and the camp command could not keep up with them.

The enemy had closed the breach in his positions, and the unit which had broken through was now unable to get back into the *tayga*.

To add to the worries of the partisans, the women refugees were behaving in a very strange manner. The dense forest made it difficult to find them, and while envoys were trying to head them off, the women invaded the forest, chopping down trees, building roads and bridges and achieving prodigies of resourcefulness on their way.

None of this was in accordance with the ideas of the partisan command and Liberius found his plans turned upside down.

5

It was this that put him in such a temper as he stood talking to the trapper, Svirid, near the highway which crossed the edge of the *tayga* at this point. Several members of his staff stood on the highway, arguing about whether to cut the telegraph line which ran beside the road. The right to make the final decision belonged to Liberius but, for the moment, he was deep in conversation with Svirid and kept signing to the others to wait for him.

Svirid had been deeply shocked by the shooting of Vdovichenko, whose only crime had been that his influence rivalled that of Liberius and brought dissension into the camp. Svirid wished he could leave the partisans and go back to his old, private, independent life. But this was out of the question. He had made his choice, and were he to leave his Forest Brothers now he would share Vdovichenko's fate.

The weather was horrible. A sharp, scudding wind swept torn clouds, as black as flying soot, low over the earth. Snow fell from them in insane white flurries, instantly shrouding the distance and sheeting the earth in white; but the next minute, the white sheet was consumed, melted to cinders, and the earth came up as black as coal under the black sky splashed with slanting streaks of distant

[1] Dvory: Homesteads (Dvor: literally 'yard', by extension 'homestead').

showers. The earth could not absorb any more water, and when at times the clouds parted like windows opening with a cold, glassy sheen to air the sky, the unabsorbed water on the ground answered and the open windows of its pools and puddles shone with the same glitter.

The rain skimmed and smoked over the pinewoods; their resinous needles were as waterproof as oilcloth. The telegraph wires were threaded with raindrops which hung close together like beads and seemed never to fall down.

Svirid was one of those who had been sent to meet the fleeing women. He wished to tell his chief something of what he had seen: the confusion resulting from orders all equally inapplicable to the circumstances and conflicting with each other; the terrible deeds committed by the weakest of the women, who despaired and lost all faith. Trudging on foot, loaded with sacks, bundles and babies, exhausted young mothers who had lost their milk, driven out of their minds by the horrors of the journey, abandoned their children, shook the corn out of their sacks on to the ground and turned back. Better, they said, to fall into the clutches of the enemy than be torn to pieces by the forest beasts.

The stronger women, on the contrary, showed courage and self-control in a measure unknown to men.

Svirid had many other things to tell his chief. He wished to warn him of the threat of a rising, more dangerous than the one that had been put down, which hung over the camp, but he was slow at the best, and Liberius, by hurrying him, quite deprived him of the power of speech. The cause of Liberius's impatience was not only that his friends were calling and waving to him from the highway, but that during the past fortnight he had been given similar warnings again and again, and by now he knew them by heart.

'Give me time, Comrade Chief. I am no good at finding words. They stick in my teeth, they choke me. What I say is, go to the women's camp and order them to stop their nonsense. Otherwise, I ask you, what is this going to be—"All against Kolchak!" or a civil war among the women?'

'Get on with it, Svirid. You see I'm wanted. Don't spin it out.'

'And now there's that she-devil, Kubarikha, Satan only knows what she is. She says: "Put me down as a woman ventilator to look after the cattle . . ."'

'Veterinary, you mean.'

'That's what I say—a woman ventilator to cure cattle of wind. But she's not looking after cattle now, the heretic, the devil's reverend mother! She says masses for the cows and turns young refugee wives from their duty. "You've only yourselves to blame for your miseries," she says to them. "That's what comes of hitching up your skirts and running after the Red Flag. Don't do it again."'

'What refugees are you talking about—ours, from the camp, or some other kind?'

'Others, of course. The new ones, the strangers.'

'But they had orders to go to Dvory. How have they got here?'

'Dvory! That's a good one. Dvory's burned out, mill and all, nothing left of it but cinders. That's what they saw when they got there—not a living thing, nothing but ashes and ruins. Half of them went off their heads, they yelled and howled and turned straight back to the Whites, and the other half turned this way.'

'But how do they get through the *tayga*, through the swamps?'

'What are saws and axes for? Some of our chaps, who were sent to guard them, helped them a bit. Twenty miles of road they've cut, so they say. Bridges and all, the pests! Talk about women! They've done things that would take us a month of Sundays!'

'That's a fine thing, twenty miles of road! And what are you looking so pleased about, you jackass? That's just what the Whites want, a highway into the *tayga*! Now all they have to do is to roll in their artillery!'

'A diversionary force—send a diversionary force, that'll do the trick.'

'I can do my own thinking, thank you.'

6

The days were getting shorter, it was dark by five. Towards dusk Yury crossed the highway where Liberius had stood talking to Svirid a few days earlier. He was on his way back to the camp. Near the clearing where the mound and the rowan tree marked the camp boundary he heard the bold, challenging voice of Kubarikha, his 'rival', as he jokingly called the cattle healer. She was singing a rollickingly gay jingle and her voice had a raucous, boisterous screech in it. Judging by the peals of approving laughter which kept interrupting her, there was a crowd of men and women listening. Then came silence. The people must have dispersed.

Thinking herself alone, Kubarikha sang a different song, softly, as if to herself. Yury, who was cautiously making his way in the dusk along the footpath which skirted the swamp in front of the rowan, stopped in his tracks. It sounded like an old folk-song but he did not know it; perhaps Kubarikha was improvising.

An old Russian folk-song is like water in a weir. It looks as if it were still and were no longer flowing but in its depths it is ceaselessly rushing through the sluice-gates and its stillness is an illusion.

By every possible means—by repetitions and similes—it attempts to stop or to slow down the gradual unfolding of its theme, until it reaches some mysterious point, then it suddenly reveals itself. In this insane attempt to stop the flow of time, a sorrowful, self-restraining spirit finds its expression.

Kubarikha was half singing, half speaking:

> 'As a hare was running about the wide world,
> About the wide world, over the white snow,
> He ran, the lop-eared hare, past a rowan tree,
> Past a rowan tree and complained to her:
> Have I not, I—lop-eared hare, a timorous heart,
> Frightened of the wild beast's tracks,
> The wild beast's tracks, the wild wolf's hungry belly.
> Pity me, O rowan bush! O fair rowan tree!
> Do not give thy beauty to the wicked enemy,
> The wicked enemy, the wicked raven.
> Scatter thy red berries to the wind,
> Scatter them in handfuls to the wind, and let it carry them
> Over the wide world, over the white snow.
> Fling them, roll them to my native town,
> To the far end of the street, the last house,
> The last house in the street, the last window, the room
> Where she hides in hermit solitude,
> My dear, my longed for love.
> Whisper to my grieving love, my bride,
> A warm, an ardent word.
> I, a soldier, languish in captivity,
> Homesick, I—poor soldier, kept in foreign parts.
> I'll escape out of my bitter durance,
> I will go to my red berry, my fair love.'

7

Agatha, Pamphil's wife, had brought her sick cow to Kubarikha. The cow had been separated from the herd and tethered to a tree by a rope tied to her horns. Her mistress sat on a tree stump by her fore-legs and Kubarikha, on a milking-stool, by her hind legs.

The rest of the countless herd was crammed into a glade, hemmed in all round by the dark forest of triangular firs, as tall as hills and rising from their spreading lower branches as if they squatted on fat bottoms on the ground.

The cows were almost all black and white and belonged to some Swiss breed popular in Siberia. They were exhausted—no less exhausted than their owners—by their privations, their endless journeys and the intolerable overcrowding. Rubbing flank to flank and maddened by the lack of space, they forgot their sex and reared and climbed on top of one another, pulling up their heavy udders with an effort and roaring like bulls. The heifers who were covered by them broke away from underneath and rushed off into the forest, tails in the air and trampling shrubs and branches. Their herdsmen—old men and children—ran shrieking after them.

And as if they too were hemmed in by the tight circle of tree-tops in the winter sky above the glade, the black and white clouds reared and piled and toppled as chaotically as the cows.

The knot of curious onlookers who stood at a distance annoyed the witch and she measured them from top to toe with an evil look. But it was beneath her dignity as an artist to admit that they disturbed her, so she decided not to notice them. Yury watched her from the back of the crowd; she did not see him.

This was the first time he was able to take a good look at her. She wore her usual forage-cap and pea-green British Army greatcoat with its crumpled collar. But the haughty and passionate expression, which gave a youthful fire and darkness to this ageing woman's eyes, plainly spoke of her complete indifference to what she happened to wear or be without.

What astonished Yury was the change in Pamphil's wife. Her eyes were almost starting out of their sockets and her neck was as long and thin as a cart-shaft. She had aged so much in the past few days that Yury hardly recognised her, such was the effect upon her of her secret terrors.

'She doesn't give any milk, dearie,' she was saying. 'I thought she might be in calf, but then she would have had milk by now and she still hasn't any.'

'Why should she be in calf? You can see the scab of anthrax on her udder. I'll give you some herbal oil to rub it with. And of course I'll whisper to her.'

'My other trouble is my husband.'

'I'll charm him back, so he won't stray. That's easy. He'll stick to you, so you won't be able to get rid of him. What's your third trouble?'

'It isn't that he strays. That would be nothing. The misfortune is that he clings to me and the children with all his might, and that breaks his heart. I know what he thinks. He thinks they'll divide the camp. They will send us one way and him another. And we'll fall into the hands of Bassalygo's men and he won't be there and we won't have anyone to stand up for us. And they'll torture us, they'll rejoice at our torments. I know his thoughts. I'm afraid he'll do away with himself.'

'I'll think about it. I will find a way to end your grief. What's your third trouble?'

'I haven't a third one. That's all there is—my cow and my husband.'

'Well, you are poor in sorrows, dearie. See how merciful God has been to you! Such as you are hard to find, like a needle in a haystack. Only two sorrows in your poor heart, and one of them a fond husband! Well, let's begin. What will you give me for the cow?'

'What will you take?'

'I'll have a loaf of bread and your husband.'

The onlookers burst out laughing.

'Are you joking?'

'Too much, is it? All right, I'll do without the loaf. We'll settle for your husband.'

The laughter grew louder.

'What's the name? Not your husband's, your cow's.'

'Beauty.'

'Half the herd is called that. All right. We'll start with God's blessing.'

She recited the spell for the cow. At first she was indeed concerned with the cow, but after a while she got carried away and gave Agatha a whole set of instructions on witchcraft. Yury listened spellbound, just as, when he first arrived in Siberia from European Russia, he had listened to the flowery chatter of the driver Bacchus.

The woman was saying:

'Auntie Margesta, come and be our guest. Come on Wednesday, take away the pest, take away the spell, take away the scab. Ringworm, leave the heifer's udder. Stand still, Beauty, do your duty, don't upset the pail. Stand as still as a hill, let milk run and rill. Terror, terror, show your mettle, take the scurvy, take the scab, throw them in the nettles. Strong as a lord is the sorcerer's word.

'You see, Agatha, my dear, you have to know everything—bidding and forbidding, the word for escaping and the word for safe-keeping. You have to know what everything is. Now you, for example, you look over there and you say to yourself: "There's a forest." But what there is over there is the forces of evil fighting the angelic hosts—they're at war like your men with Bassalygo's.

'Or take another example, look over there where I'm pointing. You're looking the wrong way, dearie, use your eyes, not the back of your head, look where my finger is pointing. That's right! Now, what do you think that is? You think it's two twigs that the wind has tangled together? Or a bird building its nest? Well, it isn't either. That there thing is a proper devil's toy, a garland the water spirit started weaving for her daughter. She heard people coming along, and that frightened her, so she left it half done, but she'll finish it one of these nights, you'll see.

'Or again, take your red banner. You think it's a flag, isn't that what you think? Well, it isn't a flag. It's the purple kerchief of the death woman—she uses it for enticing. And why for enticing? She waves it and she nods and winks and entices young men to come and be killed to death, then she sends famine and plague. That's what it is. And you believed her. You thought it was a flag. You thought it was saying: "Come to me, all ye poor and protarians of the world."

'You have to know everything nowadays, Agatha, my girl, every single thing. What every bird is and every stone and every herb. That bird, for example, that's a starling. And that beast is a badger.

'Now, another thing, suppose you take a fancy to someone, you just tell me. I'll make him pine for you, whoever he is—your Forester, that rules over you, if you like, or Kolchak or Prince Ivan [1]—anyone. You think I'm boasting? Indeed I am not. Now look, I'll tell you. When the winter comes with blizzards and whirlwind and snowspouts chasing each other in the fields, I will stick a knife into such a pillar of snow, right up to the hilt, and when I take it out of the snow, it will be red with blood. Have you ever heard of such a thing? Well, there you are! And you thought I was boasting. Now, how can it be, you tell me, that blood should come out of a snowspout that is made of nothing but wind and snow? That's just it, dearie, that whirlwind isn't just wind and snow, it's a werewolf, a changeling that's lost its little warlock child and is looking for it—it goes about the fields crying and looking for it. That is what I struck with my knife, that is why there is blood on it. Now, with that knife I can cut away the

[1] A traditional Russian fairy-tale prince.

footprint of any man, and I can sew it, with a silk thread, on to your skirt, and that man—whoever he be, Kolchak, or Strelnikov, or any new tsar they set up—will follow you step by step wherever you go. And you thought I was telling lies! You thought it was: "Come to me, all ye poor protarians of the world."

'And many other things there are, such as stones raining from heaven, so that a man may go forth out of his house and the stones rain upon him. Or, as some have seen, horsemen riding through the sky, the horses' hooves hitting the tops of the houses. Or as sorcerers prophesied of old, saying: "In this woman there is corn, in that one honey, in a third marten fur." And the knight opened the shoulder of the woman, as if it were a casket, and with his sword he took out of her shoulder-blade a measure of corn or a squirrel or a honeycomb.'

No deep and strong feeling, such as we may come across here and there in the world, is unmixed with compassion. The more we love, the more the object of our love seems to us to be a victim. Occasionally, a man's compassion for a woman exceeds all measure, and his imagination removes her from the realm of possible happenings and places her in situations which are never encountered in life. He sees her at the mercy of the surrounding air, of the laws of nature and of the centuries which preceded her.

Yury was sufficiently well read to realise that Kubarikha's last words had been the opening passage of an ancient chronicle, either of Novgorod or Ipatyevo, but so distorted by the errors of copyists and the repetitions of sorcerers and bards that its original meaning had been lost. Why then should the nonsensical images thus handed down have gripped and moved him with the force of real events?

. . . Lara's left shoulder was half open. Like a key turning in the lock of a secret safe, the sword unlocked her shoulder-blade and, opening the cavity of her soul, revealed the secrets she kept in it. Memories of strange towns, streets, rooms, countrysides, unrolled like a film, like a skein, a bundle of skeins of ribbons tumbling out.

How well he loved her, and how lovable she was, in exactly the way he had always thought and dreamed and needed. Yet what was it that made her so lovely? Was it something that could be named and singled out in a list of qualities? A thousand times no! She was lovely by virtue of the matchlessly simple and swift line which the Creator at a single stroke had drawn round her, and in this divine outline she had been handed over, like a child tightly wound up in a sheet after its bath, into the keeping of his soul.

And what had happened to him now, where was he? In a Siberian forest, with the partisans who were encircled and whose fate he was to share. What an unbelievable, absurd predicament. There was a mist in Yury's head and before his eyes. Everything misted over. At that moment, instead of the expected snow there came a drizzle. Like a huge banner stretching from one side of a city street to the other, there hung before him in the air, from one side of the forest glade to the other, the greatly magnified image of a single, astonishing, deified head. It wept, and the rain kissed and watered it.

'Go along now,' said the witch to Agatha. 'I have charmed your cow, she will get well. Pray to the Mother of God who is the abode of light and the book of the living word.'

8

There was fighting on the western edges of the *tayga*. But the *tayga* was so immense that the battles were like border warfare on the edges of its kingdom, and the camp, hidden in its heart, so full of people that however many went away to fight, there seemed always to be more left.

The noise of the distant battles hardly ever reached the camp. Then, suddenly, several shots rang out in the forest and turned at once into a quick, ragged fusillade. People started up and ran quickly to their tents or wagons and a general commotion began, with everyone hurrying to get his equipment.

It proved to be a false alarm. But then a growing crowd of partisans streamed towards the place where the shots had been heard.

They stood round a bleeding stump of a man who was lying on the ground. His right arm and left leg had been chopped off. It was inconceivable how, with his remaining arm and leg, he had crawled into the camp. The chopped-off arm and leg were tied in terrible bleeding chunks on to his back, together with a small wooden board; on it, a long inscription stated, with many words of abuse, that the atrocity was in reprisal for similar atrocities committed by such and such a Red unit—a unit which had no connection with the Forest Brotherhood. It was added that the same treatment would be meted out to all the partisans unless, by a given date, they submitted and gave up their arms to the representatives of General Vitsyn's army corps.

Though fainting from loss of blood, the dying man told them in a faltering voice of the tortures and executions perpetrated by Vitsyn's investigating and punitive squads. His own sentence of death had been allegedly remitted; instead of hanging him, they had cut off his arm and leg in order to send him into the camp and strike terror among the partisans. They had carried him as far as the outposts of the camp; there they had put him down and ordered him to crawl, urging him on by shooting into the air.

He could hardly move his lips. The men around him bent down low to make out his words. He was saying:

'Look out, comrades. He has broken through.'

'Patrols have gone out in strength. There's a big engagement going on. We'll hold him.'

'There's a gap. He wants to surprise you. I know . . . I can't go on, mates. I'm nearly finished.'

'Rest a bit. Keep quiet.—Can't you see it's bad for him, you butchers!'

The man started again:

'He went to work on me, the devil. He said: "You will wash in your blood until you tell me who you are." And how was I to tell him that a deserter is just what I am? I was running from him to you.'

'You keep saying—he. Who was it that got to work on you?'

'Let me just get my breath . . . I'll tell you. The Hetman is Bekeshin. The Colonel, Strese. Vitsyn's men. You don't know out here what it's like. The whole town is groaning. They boil people alive. They cut strips out of them. They take you by the scruff of the neck and push you inside, you don't know where you are, it's pitch black. You grope about—you are in a cage, inside a railway coach. There are more than forty people in the cage, all in their underclothes. From time to time they open the door and grab whoever comes first—out he goes. They grab you like one grabs a chicken to cut its throat. I swear to God. Some they hang, some they beat with iron rods, some they question. They beat you to shreds, they put salt on the wounds, they pour boiling water on you. When you vomit or shit, they force you to eat it. As for children, and women, O God!'

The wretched man was at his last gasp. He cried out and died without finishing his tale. They all knew it at once and took off their caps and crossed themselves.

That evening, the news of a still more terrible incident flew round the camp.

Pamphil had been one of the crowd surrounding the dying man. He had seen him, heard his words and read the menacing inscription on the board.

His constant fear for his family in the event of his own death rose to a new climax. In his imagination he already saw them handed over to slow torture, watched their faces distorted by pain and heard their groans and cries for help. In his desperate anguish—to prevent their future sufferings and to end his own—he killed them himself, felling his wife and his three children with that same, razor-sharp axe which he had used to carve toys for the two little girls and the boy who had been his favourite.

The astonishing thing was that he did not kill himself immediately afterwards. Yury wondered what alternative he could be thinking of. What could he look forward to? What intentions could he have, what plans? Clearly, his life was ended. It was also clear that he was insane.

While Liberius, Yury and the members of the army council sat on his case, discussing what was to be done with him, he roamed freely about the camp, his head hung low over his chest, his dirty-yellow eyes glowering unseeingly. A dull, vague smile of inhuman, unconquerable suffering never left his face.

No one was sorry for him. Everyone avoided him. Some people said he should be lynched but they got no support.

There was nothing in the world left for him to do. At dawn he vanished from the camp, fleeing from himself like a dog with rabies.

9

High winter came with its grinding frosts. Torn, seemingly disconnected sounds and shapes rose out of the icy mist, stood still, moved and vanished. The sun was not the sun to which the earth was used, it was a changeling. Its crimson ball hung in the forest and from it, stiffly and slowly as in a dream or in a fairy tale, amber-yellow rays of light as thick as honey spread and, catching in the trees, froze to them in mid-air.

Invisible feet in felt boots, touching the ground softly with padded soles, yet making the snow screech angrily at every step, moved in all directions, while the hooded and fur-jacketed torsos belonging to them sailed separately through the upper air like heavenly bodies.

Friends stopped and spoke, their faces close together, flushed as at the baths, with beards bristling like iced loofahs. Clouds of dense, clammy steam puffed out of their mouths, too large for the clipped, frost-bitten words they accompanied.

Walking along the footpath Yury met Liberius, who stopped him.

'Hullo, stranger! Come to my dugout this evening. Stay the night. We'll have a good talk. There's some news.'

'Is the courier back? Any news from Varykino?'

'Not a word about your people or mine. This, however, leads me to the comforting conclusion that they must have got away in time, otherwise we would be sure to have heard something. We'll talk about it to-night. I'll be expecting you.'

Coming into the dugout that evening, Yury repeated his question :

'What have you heard about our families? Only tell me that.'

'You never want to see further than your nose. So far as I know, they are safe and sound. But the point is that the news is first rate. Have some cold veal.'

'No thanks. Come on now, don't change the subject.'

'Are you sure you won't? Well, I'll have a bite. Though bread and vegetables are what we really need. There's a lot of scurvy about. We should have got in more nuts and berries last autumn when the women were there to pick them. Well, as I was saying, our affairs are in excellent shape. What I've always prophesied is coming true. The worst is over. Kolchak's forces are retreating all along the line. They are breaking up. Now do you see? What did I always tell you? Do you remember how you used to moan?'

'When did I moan?'

'All the time. Especially when we were being pressed by Vitsyn.'

Yury recalled the autumn, the shooting of the rebels, Pamphil's killing of his wife and children, the whole senseless murderous mess to which there seemed to be no end. White and Red atrocities rivalled each other in savagery, outrage breeding outrage. The smell of blood was in Yury's nose and throat, it choked him, it nauseated him, it made his head go round and his eyes swim. That wasn't moaning, it was something quite different, but how could he explain it to Liberius?

The dugout was lit by torches made of sticks stuck into a metal holder. They gave off an aromatic smell of charcoal. As a stick burned down, the cinder dropped into a bowl of water standing underneath, and Liberius lit a fresh one.

'See what I have to burn? There's no more oil. And the wood is too dry, it burns too quickly. Sure you won't have some veal? About the scurvy. What are you waiting for, to call a staff meeting and give us a lecture on scurvy and the means of dealing with it?'

'Stop tormenting me, for God's sake. What exactly do you know about our families?'

'I've told you. There is nothing certain in the report. But I didn't finish telling you what I've learned from the latest communiqués. The civil war is over. Kolchak's forces are smashed. The main part of the Red Army is in pursuit, it is driving him eastwards, along the railway, into the sea. Another part of it is hurrying over this way and we are joining forces to mop up the scattered remnants of the Whites in the rear. The whole of southern Russia is clear of the enemy. Well, why aren't you glad? Isn't that enough for you?'

'I am glad. But where are our families?'

'Not in Varykino, and that's a very lucky thing. Not that there is any confirmation of that crazy business Kamennodvorsky told you about—you remember that rumour last summer about mysterious strangers raiding Varykino?—I always thought it was nonsense. All the same the village is deserted. So it looks as if something did happen after all, and it's a very good thing they got out in time, as they evidently did. That's what the few remaining inhabitants think, according to my source.'

'And Yuryatin? What happened there? Who is holding it?'

'That's another cock-and-bull story. It can't possibly be true.'

'What's that?'

'They say the Whites are still there, but that's a sheer impossibility. I'll show you, you'll see for yourself.'

He put another stick in the holder and, getting out a tattered map and folding it so that the district he was talking about was on top, explained the position, pencil in hand.

'Look. All these are sectors where the Whites have been thrown back—here, and here, and here, all over this region. Do you follow?'

'Yes.'

'So they can't possibly be anywhere near Yuryatin, because if they were, with their communications cut, they couldn't possibly avoid being captured. Even their commanders couldn't be as stupid as that —any child can see it. Why are you putting on your coat? Where are you going?'

'I'll be back in a moment. There's a lot of smoke here and I've got a headache. I'll just go out for a breath of air.'

When he was outside, Yury swept the snow off the wooden block which served as a seat at the entrance to the dugout and sat down, his elbows on his knees and his head propped on his fists.

The *tayga*, the camp, his eighteen months among the partisans, went clean out of his head. He forgot all about them. Memories of his dear ones filled his mind and crowded out all else. He tried to guess their fate; images rose before him, each more frightening than the last.

Here was Tonya walking through a field in a blizzard with Sasha in her arms. She kept wrapping him up in a blanket, her feet sinking in the deep snow. She dragged herself out, using all her strength, but the blizzard knocked her down; she stumbled and fell and got up, too weak to stand on her feet, the wind buffeting her and the snow covering her up. Oh, but he was forgetting. She had two children with her, Sasha and the baby. Both her hands were busy, like those of the fugitives at Chilimka who broke down and went mad with grief and strain.

She had both her hands full and there was no one near to help her. Sasha's father had vanished, no one knew where he was. He was away, he had always been away, all his life he had stood aside from them. What kind of a father was he? Was it possible for a real father always to be away? And what about her own father? Where was Alexander Alexandrovich? And Nyusha? And the others? Better not ask, better not think about it.

Yury got up and turned to go back into the dugout. Suddenly his thoughts took a different direction and he changed his mind about returning to Liberius.

Long ago he had put away a pair of skis, a bag of biscuits and some other things he would need if a chance should ever come of making his escape. He had buried them in the snow just outside the camp at the foot of a tall pine. To make doubly sure of finding it he had marked the tree with a notch. Now he turned and walked along the footpath trodden between the snowdrifts in the direction of his buried treasure.

It was a clear night with a full moon. He knew where the sentries were posted and at first avoided them successfully. But when he came to the clearing with the mound and the rowan tree, a patrolman hailed him from a distance, took a run on his skis and, standing straight up on them, glided swiftly towards him.

'Halt or I shoot! Who are you? Password.'

'What's come over you, man? Don't you know me? I'm the camp doctor, Zhivago.'

'Sorry, Comrade Zhelvak. I didn't recognise you, no offence meant. All the same, Zhelvak or not, I'm not letting you go any further. Orders are orders.'

'As you wish. The password is "Red Siberia" and the reply, "Down with the Interventionists".'

'That's better. Go ahead. What are you chasing after at this time of night? Anyone sick?'

'I was thirsty and I couldn't sleep. I thought I'd go out for a breath of air and eat some snow. Then I saw the rowan with iced berries on it. I want to go and pick a few.'

'Isn't that just like a gentleman's folly! Who's ever heard of picking berries in winter! Three years we've been beating the nonsense out of the gentry but they're still the same. All right, go and pick your berries, you lunatic. What do I care?'

And as swiftly as he had come, the sentry took a run, stood straight up on his long skis and whistled over the untrodden snow into the distance beyond the bare winter shrubs as thin as thinning hair.

The footpath brought Yury to the foot of the rowan whose name he had just invoked.

It was covered half in snow, half in frozen leaves and berries and it held out two white branches welcomingly. He remembered Lara's strong white arms and seized the branches and pulled them to him. As if in answer, the tree shook snow all over him. He muttered senselessly:

'I'll find you, my beauty, my love, my rowan tree, my own flesh and blood.'

It was a clear night with a full moon. He made his way further into the *tayga*, to the marked tree, dug his things out and left the camp.

Opposite the House of Caryatids

MERCHANT Street rambled crookedly downhill, overlooked
by the houses and churches of the upper part of Yuryatin.
At one corner there was a dark grey building with caryatids. The huge square stones of the lower part of its façade were
black with freshly posted sheets of government newspapers and
proclamations. Small groups of people stood in front of it, reading in
silence.

There had been a thaw but now it was dry and frosty. Now it was
light at a time of day when recently it had been dark. The winter
had gone; its place had been taken by the light which lingered on
into the evenings. The light was exhilarating, disturbing and alarming.

The Whites had gone, surrendering the town to the Reds. The
terrors of the war, shelling and bloodshed, had ceased. This too was
disturbing, like the going of the winter and the lengthening of the
spring days.

One of the proclamations pasted on the wall and still readable by
the light of the longer day announced that:

'Labour books are obtainable by those qualified at the cost of 50
roubles each, at the Food Office, Yuryatin Soviet, No. 5 October Street
(formerly Governor-General Street), Room 137.

'Anyone without a labour book, or filling in his or her labour book
incorrectly, or (still worse) making false statements, will be prosecuted
with the utmost rigour under the wartime regulations. Detailed
instructions for the correct use of labour books are printed in I.N.I.K.[1]
No. 86 (1013) for the current year and are posted up at the Yuryatin
Food Office, Room 137.'

Another proclamation stated that the town had ample food supplies. These, it alleged, were merely being hoarded by the bourgeoisie
with the object of disorganising distribution and creating chaos. It
ended with the words:

'Anyone found hoarding food will be shot on sight.'

A third announcement read:

'Those who do not belong to the exploiting class are admitted to

[1] Gazette of the Yuryatin Executive Committee.

membership of Consumer Communes. Details are obtainable at the Food Office, Yuryatin Soviet, No. 5 October Street (formerly Governor-General Street), Room 137.'

Members of the forces were warned :

'Anyone who fails to surrender his arms or who continues carrying them without having the appropriate new permit will be prosecuted with the utmost severity of the law. New permits are obtainable at the Office of the Yuryatin Revolutionary-Military Committee, No. 6 October Street, Room 63.'

2

The group in front of the building was joined by an emaciated, wild-looking man, black with dirt, with a birch-bark satchel on a stick over his shoulder. There was not yet any white in his long, shaggy hair but his bristly, reddish beard was greying. This was Doctor Yury Zhivago. His fur coat must have been taken from him on the road, or perhaps he had bartered it for food. His thin, tattered, short-sleeved jacket was certainly the result of an exchange.

All he had left in his satchel was the remnant of a crust of bread which someone had given him out of charity in a village near the town and a piece of pork fat. He had reached Yuryatin earlier, but it had taken him an hour to trudge from the outskirts to this corner of Merchant Street, so great was his weakness and so much had the last few days of the journey exhausted him. He had often stopped, and he had had to force himself not to fall on his knees and kiss the stones of this town which he had despaired of ever seeing again ; the sight of it filled him with happiness like the sight of a friend.

For almost half his journey on foot across Siberia he had followed the railway track, all of it out of action, neglected and covered with snow. Train after train, abandoned by the Whites, stood idle, stopped by the defeat of Kolchak, by running out of fuel and by snowdrifts. Immobilised for good and buried in the snow they stretched almost uninterruptedly for miles on end. Some of them served as fortresses for armed bands of robbers or as hide-outs for escaping criminals or political fugitives—the involuntary vagrants of those days—but most of them were communal mortuaries, mass graves of the victims of the cold and of the typhus raging all along the railway line and mowing down whole villages in its neighbourhood.

In those days it was true, if ever, that 'man is a wolf to man'. Traveller turned off the road at the sight of traveller, stranger meeting stranger killed for fear of being killed. There were isolated cases of cannibalism. The laws of human civilisation were suspended. The laws which men obeyed were jungle laws; the dreams they dreamed were the prehistoric dreams of cave-dwellers.

Every now and then Yury would see lonely shadows stealing along the ditch or scurrying across the road ahead of him. He avoided them carefully whenever he could, but many of them seemed familiar. He felt as if he had seen them all at the partisan camp. On one occasion this was true. The boy, who darted out of a snowdrift which concealed an International Sleeping Coach, relieved himself and darted back, was indeed a member of the Forest Brotherhood. It was Terenty Galuzin who was believed to have been shot dead. In reality he had only been wounded and had lost consciousness. When he had come to himself he had crawled away from the place of execution, hidden in the forest until he recovered from his wounds and was now making his way home to Holycross under an assumed name, hiding in the buried carriages and fleeing at the sight of human beings.

The incidents of Yury's journey had the strangeness of the transcendental, as if they were snatches torn from lives on other planets which had somehow drifted to the earth. Only nature had remained true to human history and had kept the aspect which contemporary artists had portrayed.

Now and then there was a quiet, pale-grey, dark-rose evening, with birches, black and fine as script against the afterglow, and black streams, faintly clouded over with grey ice, flowing between steep white banks of snow blackened at the edges, where the running water had corroded them. Such, in an hour or two, would be the evening in Yuryatin, frosty, grey, transparent and as gentle as pussy-willows.

Yury meant to read the notices posted up on the House of Caryatids, but his eyes kept wandering to the third-floor windows of the house across the street. These were the windows of the rooms in which the furniture left by the old tenants had been stored. They had once been white-washed; now, although the frost had filmed them at the edges, Yury could see that the glass was transparent; the chalk had evidently been washed off. What did this mean? Had the old tenants returned? Or had Lara moved, and did the flat have new tenants, and was everything completely changed?

The uncertainty was unbearable. Yury crossed the road, went in and climbed the staircase which he knew so well. How often at the camp had he not remembered every turn of it and every scroll of the open-work pattern of the cast-iron steps! In one place you could look through it down into the lumber room in the basement, where old chairs and broken pails and tin tubs had been stacked. When he came to it and found that everything was unchanged, Yury felt like thanking the staircase for its loyalty to the past.

There had been a door bell once, but it had broken and stopped ringing before Yury had left. He was just about to knock, when he noticed that there was now a padlock on the door, hanging from two rings; they had been roughly screwed into the old oak panels with their fine carving which in places had come away. Such vandalism would not have been countenanced in the old days. There would have been a fitted lock and it would have worked, or a locksmith would have come and mended it. This trivial sign spoke of the general deterioration of things which had gone a great deal further in his absence.

Yury felt certain that neither Lara nor Katya would be there, even if they were still alive, and even if they still lived in Yuryatin. He was prepared for the most bitter disappointments, and it was only to relieve his conscience that he decided to look for the key in the hollow between the bricks, where a rat had so much frightened Katya. He kicked at the wall to make sure of not putting his hand on one now. He had not the slightest hope of finding anything. The hollow was closed by a brick. He removed it and felt inside. Miraculously it had a key and a note in it. The note was written on a fairly big sheet of paper. Yury took it to the window on the landing. Still more miraculously, more unbelievably, the note was addressed to him! He read it quickly:

'Lord, what happiness! They say you are alive and have come back. Someone saw you near the town and rushed over to tell me. I take it you'll go straight to Varykino, so I'm going there myself with Katya. But just in case, I'm leaving the key in the usual place. Wait for me, don't go. You'll see I am using the front rooms now. The flat is rather empty, I've had to sell some of the furniture. I've left a little food, boiled potatoes mostly. Put the lid back on the saucepan with a weight on it, to keep the rats out. I'm mad with joy.'

He read to the bottom of the page, and did not notice that the letter continued on the back. He pressed it to his lips, folded it and put it into his pocket with the key. Mixed with his immense joy, he felt a sharp, stabbing pain. Since Lara was going to Varykino, and not even bothering to explain, it must be that his family were not there. He felt not only anxious because of this, but unbearably wounded and sad on their behalf. Why hadn't she said a single word of how and where they were?—just as if they didn't exist at all!

But it was getting darker, and he had still many things to do while it was light. The most urgent was to read the texts of the decrees posted on the wall of the House of Caryatids. It was no joke in those days to be ignorant of the regulations, it might cost you your life. Without going into the flat or taking off his satchel, he went down, crossed the road and looked over the large space covered with various announcements.

3

There were newspaper articles, reports of speeches at meetings and decrees. Yury glanced at the headings. 'Requisitioning, assessment and taxation of members of the propertied classes.' 'Establishment of workers' control.' 'Establishment of factory and works committees.' These were the regulations which the new authorities had issued on entering the town, in place of those which they had found in force. No doubt they were intended as a reminder of the uncompromising nature of the régime, in case it should have been forgotten under the Whites. But their unending monotony, their endless repetitions, made Yury's head go round. What period did they belong to? That of the first upheaval? or that of some re-establishment of the régime after a White rebellion? Had they been written last year? Or the year before? Only once in his life had this uncompromising language and single-mindedness filled him with enthusiasm. Was it possible that he must pay for that one moment of rash enthusiasm all his life by never hearing, year after year, anything but these unchanging, shrill, crazy exclamations and demands, ever more lifeless, meaningless and unfulfillable as time went by? Was it possible that in one short moment of over-sensitive generosity he had allowed himself to be enslaved for ever?

His eyes lit on a fragment of one report:

'The news of the famine shows up the unbelievable inactivity of the local organisations. There are glaring abuses, there is speculation on a gigantic scale.—And what are our factory and works committees doing? Only mass searches in the commercial districts of Yuryatin and Razvilye, only terror applied in all its harshness, down to the shooting of speculators on the spot, can deliver us from famine.'

'How lucky to be so blind!' thought Yury. 'To be able to talk of bread when it has long since vanished from the earth! Of propertied classes and speculators when they have long since been abolished by decree! Of peasants and villages when there aren't any peasants or villages in existence! Have they no memory? Don't they remember their own plans and measures? Have they forgotten that by these measures they have left no stone standing upon stone? What kind of people must they be to go on raving with this never-cooling, feverish ardour, year in, year out, of things which are non-existent, of themes which have long vanished, and to know nothing, to see nothing, of the reality which surrounds them?'

Yury's head was spinning. He fainted and fell down unconscious in the street. When he came to himself and people helped him to get up and offered to take him where he wished to go, he thanked them and refused, saying he had only to cross the road, he lived opposite.

4

He went up again and this time he unlocked the door of Lara's flat. It was still light on the landing, hardly darker than before he had gone out. He was glad that the sun was giving him time.

The click of the key in the lock started pandemonium inside. The uninhabited flat greeted him with the clang and rattle of falling tin pans. Rats, scuttling off the shelves, flopped on the floor and scattered. They must have bred here in their thousands. Yury felt sick and helpless to deal with this abomination and decided to barricade himself for the night in one room with a closely fitting door, where he could stop the rat holes with broken glass.

He turned left to the part of the flat which he did not know, crossed a dark passage and came into what was evidently Lara's own room, a light room with two windows facing the street. Directly opposite the window was the grey building with the caryatids; groups of people stood with their backs to him, reading the announcements.

The light in the room was of the same quality as outside, it was the same new, fresh evening light of early spring. This seemed to make the room a part of the street: the only difference was that inside it was a little colder.

His sudden weakness earlier that afternoon as he approached the town and walked through it an hour or two before, had made Yury think that he was ill. Now, the sameness of the light in the house and in the street exhilarated him with equal suddenness. Bathed in the same chilled air as the passers-by, he felt a kinship with them, an identity with the mood of the town, with life in the world. This dispelled his fears. He no longer expected to be ill. The transparency of the spring evening, the all-penetrating light, were a good augury, a promise of generous fulfilment of distant and far-reaching hopes. All would be well, he would achieve all he wanted in life, he would find and reunite and reconcile them all, he would think everything out and find all the right words. He waited for the joy of seeing Lara as an immediate proof that all the rest would follow.

A wild excitement and uncontrollable restlessness took the place of his earlier fatigue. In reality this animation was an even more convincing symptom of approaching illness than his recent weakness.

He wanted, before he settled down, to have a haircut and shave off his beard. He had looked for a barber earlier, on his way through town. But some of the barber's shops he had known before stood empty, others had changed hands and were used for other business and the rest were closed. He had no razor of his own. Scissors would have done the job, but though he turned everything upside-down on Lara's dressing-table, in his haste he could not find any.

Now it occurred to him that there had once been a tailor's workshop in Spassky Street : if it still existed and he got to it before closing time, he might borrow a pair of scissors.

5

His memory had not failed him. The workshop was still there, with its entrance on the street and a window running the whole length of the frontage. The seamstresses worked in full view of the passers-by. You could see right in to the back of the room.

It was packed with sewing women. In addition to the regular workers there were probably ageing local ladies who knew how to sew and had obtained jobs in order to become entitled to the labour books mentioned in the proclamation on the wall of the grey building.

It was easy to tell them from the professionals. The workshop made nothing but army clothes : padded trousers and jackets, and parti-coloured fur coats made of the skins of dogs of different breeds such as Yury had seen on the partisans. This work, more fitted to furriers, was particularly hard on the amateurs, whose fingers looked all thumbs as they pushed the stiffly folded hems through the sewing-machines.

Yury knocked on the window and made signs that he wished to be let in. The women replied by signs that no private orders were accepted. Yury persisted. The women motioned him to go away and leave them alone, they had urgent work to do. One of them made a puzzled face, held up her hand, palm up, like a little boat, in a gesture of annoyance, and asked with her eyebrows what on earth he wanted. He snipped two fingers like scissor blades. This was not understood. They decided it was some impertinence, that he was mimicking them and making fun of them. Standing out there, torn and tattered and behaving so oddly, he looked like a madman. The girls giggled and waved him on. At last he thought of going round the house, through the yard and knocking on the back door.

6

It was opened by a dark, elderly, severe woman in a dark dress who might have been the head seamstress.

'What a pest you are! Can't you leave us alone? Well, come on, what is it you want?'

'I want scissors. Don't be so surprised. I'd like to borrow a pair of scissors to cut my hair and my beard. I could do it here and give them back to you at once; it wouldn't take a minute. I'd be terribly grateful.'

The woman looked astonished and mistrustful. She clearly doubted his sanity.

'I've just arrived from a long journey. I wanted to get a haircut but there isn't a single barber's shop open. So I thought I'd do it myself, but I haven't any scissors. Could you lend me some?'

'All right. I'll give you a haircut. But I warn you. If you've got something else in mind—any tricks such as changing your appearance to disguise yourself for political reasons—don't blame us if we report you. We're not risking our lives for you.'

'For heaven's sake! What an idea!'

She let him in and took him into a side room no bigger than a cupboard; next moment he was in a chair, a sheet swathed round him and tucked under his chin, just like at the barber's. The seamstress went out of the room and came back with a pair of scissors, a comb, clippers, a strop and a razor.

'I've done every kind of job in my life,' she explained, noticing her client's astonishment. 'At one time I was a hairdresser. I learned haircutting and shaving when I was a nurse in the other war. Now we'll snip off that beard and then we'll have a shave.'

'Could you cut my hair very short, please.'

'I'll do my best. Why are you pretending to be so ignorant, an educated man like you? As if you didn't know that we have a ten-day week now, and to-day is the seventeenth of the month and the barbers have their day off on every date with a seven in it!'

'Honestly I didn't know. I've told you, I've just come from a long way off. Why should I be pretending?'

'Don't fidget or you'll get cut. So you've just arrived? How did you come?'

'On my two feet.'

'Along the highway?'

'Partly, and partly along the railway track. I don't know how many trains I've seen, all buried in the snow. Luxury trains, special trains, every kind of train you can think of.'

'There, just this little bit to snip off and it's finished. Family business?'

'Heavens, no! I worked for the former union of credit co-operatives as their travelling inspector. They sent me on an inspection tour to Eastern Siberia and there I got stuck. No chance of a train, as you know. There was nothing for it but to walk. Six weeks it took me. I can't begin to tell you all I've seen on the way.'

'If I were you, I wouldn't begin. I see I'll have to teach you a thing or two. Have a look at yourself first. Here's a mirror. Take your hand from under the sheet and hold it. All right?'

'I don't think it's quite short enough. Couldn't you take off a bit more?'

'It won't stay tidy if it's any shorter. As I was saying, don't start telling anything at all. It's much better to keep your mouth shut. Credit co-operatives, luxury trains, inspection tours—forget all about such things. It isn't the moment for them. You could get into no end of trouble. Better pretend you are a doctor or a school teacher. There now—that settles your beard. Now we'll give you a close shave. Just a spot of lather and you'll be ten years younger. I'll go and boil the kettle.'

'Whoever can she be?' Yura wondered. He had a feeling he had some connection with her—something he had seen or heard, someone she reminded him of—but he could not think who it was.

She came back with the hot water.

'Now we'll have a shave. As I was telling you, it's much better not to say a word. Speech is of silver, silence is gold. That has always been true. And your special trains and credit co-operatives—better think of something else, say you are a doctor or a teacher. As for the sights you've seen, keep that to yourself. Who are you going to impress nowadays? Am I hurting you?'

'A little.'

'It scrapes a bit, I know—it can't be helped. Just a little bit of patience, my dear. Your skin isn't used to the razor and your beard is very tough. I won't be a minute. Yes. There's nothing people haven't seen. They've been through everything. We've had our

347

troubles, too. The things that went on under the Whites! Murder, rape, abduction, man-hunts. There was one little lordling who took a dislike to an ensign. He sent soldiers to ambush him in a wood outside the town, near the Krapulskys' place. They got him and disarmed him and took him under guard to Razvilye. In those days Razvilye was the same as the regional Cheka is nowadays—a place of execution.—Why are you jerking your head like that? It scrapes, does it? I know, my dear, I know. It can't be helped. Your hair is just like bristles. There's just this one bad place. Well, the ensign's wife was in hysterics. Kolya! Kolya! What will become of my Kolya! Off she went, straight to the top, to General Galiullin. That's in a manner of speaking, of course. She couldn't get direct to him. You had to pull strings. There was somebody in the next street over there who knew how to reach him, an exceptionally kind woman, very sensitive, not like anyone else, always stood up for people. You can't think what went on all over the place, lynchings, atrocities, dramas, crimes of passion. Just like a Spanish novel.'

'That's Lara she's talking about,' thought Yury. But he kept prudently silent and did not ask for details. Her absurd remark about the Spanish novel again oddly reminded him of something—precisely by its absurdity, its irrelevance—but he still couldn't think what it was.

'Now, of course, it's all quite different. Admittedly there's any amount of investigations, informing, shooting and so on. But the idea is quite different. To begin with, it's a new government, it's only just come into power, it hasn't got into its stride yet. And then, whatever you say, they are on the side of the common people, that's their strength. In our family we are four sisters, counting myself, all working women. It's natural that we should have a leaning towards the bolsheviks. One sister died. Her husband was a political exile, worked as manager at one of the local factories. Their son—my nephew that is—he's at the head of the peasant forces—he's quite a celebrity.'

'So that's who she is,' Yury realised. 'Liberius's aunt, Mikulitsin's sister-in-law, the one who is a local legend, barber—seamstress—signal woman—Jack of all trades!' But he decided to say nothing so as not to give himself away.

'My nephew was always drawn to the people, ever since his childhood. He grew up among the workers at the factory. Perhaps you've heard of the Varykino factories?—Now look at what I've done, fool that I am. Half your chin is smooth and the other half is bristly. That's what comes of talking. Why didn't you stop me? Now the lather's dry and the water is cold. I'll go and warm it up.'

When she came back, Yury asked:

'Varykino, that's somewhere miles out in the country, isn't it? That should have been safe enough in all these upheavals.'

'Well, it wasn't exactly safe. They had it worse than we did in some ways. They had some sort of armed bands out there, nobody quite knows what they were. They didn't speak our language. They went through the place, house by house, shot everyone they found and went off again, without so much as a by-your-leave. The corpses just lay there in the snow. That was in the winter, of course. Do stop jerking your head, I nearly cut you.'

'You were saying your brother-in-law lived in Varykino. Was he there when all this happened?'

'No, God is merciful. He and his wife got out in time—that's his second wife. Where they are, nobody knows, but it's certain that they escaped. There were some new people there as well, strangers from Moscow. They left even earlier. The younger of the two men, a doctor, the head of the family, he's missing. That's in a manner of speaking, of course, it was called "missing" to spare their feelings. Actually he must be dead—sure to have been killed. They kept looking and looking for him, but he never turned up. In the meantime, the other one, the older of the two, he was called back home. A professor he was, an agronomist. The government called him back, I was told. They all stopped in Yuryatin on their way to Moscow, just before the Whites came back. Now you're at it again, twisting and jerking. You really will make me cut your throat. You certainly get your money's worth out of your barber, my dear man.'

So they were in Moscow!

7

'In Moscow! In Moscow!' The words echoed in his heart at every step of the cast-iron stairs as he climbed them for the third time. The empty flat again met him with the hellish din of scampering, flopping, racing rats. It was clear to Yury that, however tired he was, he would never go to sleep unless he could keep this foulness away from him. The first thing before settling down for the night was to stop the rat holes. Fortunately there were fewer of them in the bedroom than in the rest of the flat where the floor boards and skirtings were in a worse state. But he had to hurry. It was growing dark. It was true that a lamp stood on the kitchen table—perhaps in expectation of his coming it had been taken down from its bracket and half filled with paraffin, and a match box with a few matches had been left near it. But it was better to save both the matches and the paraffin. In the bedroom he found a small oil lamp; the rats had been at the oil but a little was left.

In some places the skirting had come away from the floor. It took him a little over an hour to fill the cracks with broken glass. The door fitted well and once it was closed the bedroom should be rat proof.

There was a Dutch stove in a corner of the room, with a tiled cornice not quite reaching the ceiling. In the kitchen there was a stack of logs. Yury decided to rob Lara of a couple of armfuls and, getting down on one knee, he gathered them up and balanced them on his left arm. Carrying them into the bedroom, he stacked them near the stove and had a look inside to see how it worked and in what condition it was. He had meant to lock the door, but the latch was broken; he wedged it firmly with paper; then he laid the fire at his leisure and lit it.

As he put in more logs he noticed that the cross-section of one of them was marked with the initials 'K. D.'. He recognised them with surprise. In the old Krueger days when timber rejected by the factories was sold for fuel, the boles were stamped before they were cut up into sections, to show where they came from. 'K. D.' stood for Kulabish Dale in Varykino.

The discovery upset him. These logs in Lara's house must mean that she was in touch with Samdevyatov and that he supplied her, as he had once supplied Yury and his household with all their needs. He had always found it irksome to accept his help. Now his embarrassment at being in his debt was complicated by other feelings.

It was hardly likely that Samdevyatov helped Lara out of sheer goodness of heart. He thought of Samdevyatov's free-and-easy ways and of Lara's feminine impulsiveness. There must surely be something between them.

The dry Kulabish logs crackled merrily and stormed into a blaze and, as they caught, Yury's blind jealousy turned from the merest suppositions into certainty.

But so tormented was he on every side that one anxiety drove out another. He had no need to banish his suspicions; his mind leapt from subject to subject, and the thought of his family, flooding it again, submerged his jealous fantasies.

'So you are in Moscow, my dear ones?' It seemed to him now that the seamstress had given him an assurance of their safe arrival. 'So you made all that long journey once again, and this time without me. How did you manage on the way? Why was Alexander Alexandrovich called back? Was it to return to his chair at the

Academy? How did you find the house? How silly of me! I don't even know if the house still stands. Lord, how hard and painful it all is! If only I could stop thinking. I can't think straight. What's the matter with me, Tonya? I think I'm ill. What will become of us? What will become of you, Tonya, Tonya, darling Tonya? And Sasha? And Alexander Alexandrovich? And myself? Why hast Thou cast me off, O Light everlasting! Why are we always separated, my dear ones? Why are you always being swept away from me? But we'll be together again, we'll be reunited, won't we, darling? I'll find you, even if I have to walk all the way to you. We'll see each other, we'll be together, we'll be all right again, won't we?

'Why doesn't the earth swallow me up, why am I such a monster that I keep forgetting that Tonya was to have another child and that she has surely had it! This isn't the first time I've forgotten it. How did she get through her confinement? To think that they all stopped in Yuryatin on their way to Moscow! It's true that Lara didn't know them, but here is a complete stranger, a seamstress, a hairdresser who has heard all about them, and Lara says nothing about them in her note. How could she be so careless, so indifferent? It's as strange as her saying nothing about knowing Samdevyatov.'

Yury now looked round the room with a new discernment. All its furnishings belonged to the unknown tenants who had long been absent and in hiding. There was nothing among them of Lara's and they could tell him nothing of her tastes. The photographs on the walls were of strangers. All the same, he suddenly felt uncomfortable under the eyes of all these men and women. The clumsy furniture breathed hostility. He felt alien and unwanted in this bedroom.

What a fool he had been to keep remembering this house and missing it, what a fool to have come into this room, not as into an ordinary room but as if into the heart of his longing for Lara! How silly this way of feeling would seem to anyone outside! How different was the way strong, handsome, practical, efficient men, such as Samdevyatov, lived and spoke and acted! And why should Lara be expected to prefer his weakness and the dark, obscure, unrealistic language of his love? Did she need his turmoil? Did she herself wish to *be* that which she *meant* to him?

And what did she mean to him? Oh, that was easy! He knew that perfectly well.

A spring evening . . . the air is punctuated with scattered sounds. The voices of children playing in the streets come from varying distances as if to show that the whole expanse is alive. The expanse is Russia, his incomparable mother; famed far and wide, martyred, stubborn, extravagant, crazy, irresponsible, adored, Russia with her eternally splendid, disastrous and unpredictable gestures. Oh, how sweet it was to be alive! How good to be alive and to love life! And how he longed to thank life, thank existence itself, directly, face to face, to thank life in person.

This was exactly what Lara was. You could not communicate with life, but she was its representative, its expression, the gift of speech and hearing granted to inarticulate being.

And all that he had just reproached her with in the moment of his confusion was a thousand times untrue. She was perfect and irreproachable.

Tears of admiration and repentance filled his eyss. Opening the oven door, he poked the fire; he pushed those of the logs which were ablaze and had turned into pure heat to the back and brought forward into the draught those that were less well alight. Leaving the door open, he sat before the open flames, delighting in the play of light and the warmth on his face and hands. The warmth and light brought him completely to his senses. He missed Lara unbearably and he longed for something which could bring him into touch with her at that very moment.

He drew her crumpled letter from his pocket. It was folded so that the back of the page he had read earlier was outside, and now he saw that there was something written on it. Smoothing it out, he read it by the dancing firelight:

'You know that your people are in Moscow. Tonya has had a little girl.' After that several lines were crossed out, then: 'I've crossed it out because it's silly to write about it. We'll talk to our heart's content when we meet. I'm rushing out, I must get hold of a horse. I don't know what I'll do if I can't. It's so difficult with Katya . . .' The rest of the sentence was smudged and illegible.

'She got the horse from Samdevyatov,' Yury reflected calmly. 'If she had anything to conceal, she wouldn't have mentioned it.'

8

When the fire had burned down Yura closed the flue and had something to eat. After that he felt so sleepy that he lay down on the sofa without undressing and at once fell fast asleep. The loud, insolent noise of the rats behind the walls and the door did not reach him. He had two bad dreams, one after the other.

He was in Moscow in a room with a glass door. The door was locked. For greater safety he was keeping hold of it by the handle and pulling it to himself. From the other side, his little boy, Sasha, dressed in a sailor suit and cap, was beating on it, crying his heart out and begging to be let in. Behind the child, splashing him and misting the door with its spray, there was a waterfall. It was making a tremendous noise. Either the water was pouring from a burst pipe (a usual occurrence in those days) or else the door was a barrier against some wild countryside, a mountain gorge filled with the sound of a raging torrent and the millennial cold and darkness of its caves.

The noise of the tumbling water terrified the boy. It drowned his cries but Yury could see him trying, over and over again, to shout the word 'Daddy!'

Yury's heart was breaking. With all his being he longed to pick the child up, to hide him in his arms and run away with him as fast as his feet would carry him.

Yet, with tears pouring down his face, he kept hold of the handle of the door and pulled it to himself, shutting out the child, denying him, and this out of a false sense of honour, a false sense of duty to another woman, who was not the child's mother, and who might at any moment come into the room through another door.

He woke up sweating and in tears. 'I've got a temperature, I'm ill,' he thought. 'This isn't typhus. This is some sort of exhaustion which is taking the form of a dangerous illness, an illness with a crisis ; it will be like any serious, infectious disease, and it only remains to be seen which is going to win, life or death. But I'm too sleepy to think.' He dropped off to sleep again.

Now he dreamed of a dark winter morning ; the lamps were lit and he was in some crowded Moscow street. Judging by the early morning traffic, the trams ringing their bells and the yellow pools of lamplight on the grey snow of the dawn-lit street, it was before the revolution. He dreamed of a big flat with many windows, all on the same side of the house, probably no higher than the third storey, with drawn curtains reaching to the floor.

Inside, people were lying about asleep in their clothes as in a railway carriage, and the rooms were untidy like a railway carriage, with half-eaten legs and wings of roast chicken and other remnants of picnic foods scattered about on greasy bits of newspaper. The shoes which the many friends, relations, callers and homeless people, all sheltering in the flat, had taken off for the night were standing in pairs on the floor. The hostess, Lara, in a dressing-gown tied hastily round her waist, moved swiftly and silently from room to room, hurrying about her duties, and Yury was following her, step by step, muttering dreary, irrelevant explanations and generally making a nuisance of himself. But she no longer had a moment to give him and took no notice of his mutterings except that she turned to him now and then with a tranquil, puzzled look or burst into her inimitable, candid, silvery laughter.—This was the only form of communication that remained between them. But how distant, cold and compellingly attractive was this woman to whom he had sacrificed all he had, whom he had preferred to everything, and in comparison with whom nothing had any value!

9

Something other than himself wept and complained in him and shone with gentle words in his darkness. His soul sorrowed for him and he too grieved for himself.

'I am ill,' he recollected in moments between sleep, delirium and unconsciousness. 'I must be having typhus after all. It must be some special form of typhus which isn't described in the textbooks. I ought to get myself something to eat or I'll die of starvation.'

But as soon as he so much as raised himself on his elbow he realised that he was incapable of moving, and fainted or fell asleep.

'How long have I been lying here?' he asked himself once. 'When I first went to sleep on the sofa it was early spring, but now the windows are so thick with hoar-frost that the room is quite dark.'

Rats were making a din in the kitchen, rattling the plates, scurrying up the walls and flopping down and squealing in their disgusting, pitiful contralto voices.

When he woke up again the snowy windows had filled with the light of dawn or sunset, glowing like red wine through a crystal glass.

Once he thought he heard voices near him and was terrified, imagining that he was going mad. Crying with self-pity, he complained that Heaven had abandoned him. 'Why hast Thou cast me off, O Light everlasting, and cast me down into the darkness of hell?'

Suddenly he realised that he was neither dreaming nor delirious but that, in sober truth, he was lying, washed and in a clean shirt, not on the sofa but in a freshly made bed, and that the person who was crying with him, sitting beside him, leaning over him, her hair mingling with his and her tears falling with his own, was Lara; he fainted with joy.

10

He had complained that Heaven had cast him off, but now the whole breadth of heaven leaned low over his bed holding out two strong, white, woman's arms to him. His head swimming with joy, he drifted into happiness, as though losing his senses.

All his life he had been active, doing things about the house, looking after patients, thinking, studying, writing. How good it was to stop doing, struggling, thinking !—to leave it all for a time to nature, to become her thing, her concern, the work of her merciful, wonderful, beauty-lavishing hands.

He soon recovered. Lara fed him, nursed him, built him up by her care, her snow-white loveliness, the warm, living breath of her whispered conversation.

Their low-voiced talk, however unimportant, was as full of meaning as the Dialogues of Plato.

Even more than by what they had in common, they were united by what separated them from the rest of the world. They were both equally repelled by what was tragically typical of modern man, his shrill textbook admirations, his forced enthusiasm, and the deadly dullness conscientiously preached and practised by countless workers in the field of art and science in order that genius should remain extremely rare.

They loved each other greatly. Most people experience love, without noticing that there is anything remarkable about it.

To them—and this made them unusual—the moments when passion visited their doomed human existence like a breath of time-lessness were moments of revelation, of ever greater understanding of life and of themselves.

11

'Of course you must go back to your family. I don't want to keep you a day more than is necessary. But just look at what is going on. You don't know how much things have changed while you were ill. As soon as we became part of Soviet Russia we were swallowed up in her disintegration. Our supplies are sent to Moscow—for them it's a drop in the ocean, all these truck-loads simply vanish down a bottomless pit—and in the meantime nothing is left for us. There are no mails, there is no passenger service, all the trains are used for grain. There's a lot of grumbling going on in town, like there was before the Gayda rising, and once again, as a reply to the open dis-content, the Cheka is running amok.

'How could you travel, weak as you are? You're nothing but skin and bone! Do you really imagine you could go on foot? You would never get there. When you are stronger, it will be quite different.

'If you take my advice, you'll get a job for the time being. Work at your own profession—they'd like that. You might get something in the regional health service.

'You'll have to do something. As it is, it doesn't look too good.—Your father was a Siberian millionaire who committed suicide, your wife is the daughter of a local landowner, and you are a fugitive from the partisans. You can't get round it—you left the ranks of the revolutionary army—it amounts to desertion. It would be dangerous for you to be unemployed. I am not in a much better position myself. I'll have to do something too. I'm living on a volcano as it is.'

'How do you mean? What about Strelnikov?'

'It's just because of him. I told you before what a lot of enemies he has. Now that the Red Army is victorious those non-party soldiers who got too near the top and knew too much are done for.—Lucky if they're only thrown out and not wiped out. Pasha is particularly vulnerable, he is in very great danger. You know he was out in the East. I've heard that he's run away and is hiding. They're hunting for him. But don't let's talk about it. I hate crying, and if I say another word I know I'll howl.'

'You were very much in love with him? You still are?'

'Well, darling, I married him, he's my husband. He has a wonderful, upright, shining personality. I am very much at fault that our marriage went wrong. It isn't that I ever did him any harm, it wouldn't be true to say that. But he is so outstanding, so big, he has such immense integrity—and I'm no good at all, I'm nothing in comparison with him. That's where my fault lies. But please don't let's talk about it now. I'll tell you more some other time, I promise you I will.

'How lovely your Tonya is. Just like a Botticelli. I was there when she had her baby. We got on splendidly. But please let's not talk about that either just at the moment!

'As I was saying, let's both get jobs. We'll go out to work every morning, and at the end of the month we'll collect our salaries in billions of roubles. You know, until quite recently the old Siberian bank-notes were still valid. Then they were abolished and for a long time, all the time you were ill, we had no currency at all! Honestly we hadn't! Just imagine it! We managed somehow, and now they say a whole train-load of new bank-notes has arrived, at least forty truckfuls! They are printed on big sheets in two colours, red and blue, and divided into little squares. The blue squares are worth five million roubles each and the red ones ten. They are badly printed, they fade and the colours are smudged.'

'Yes, I've seen that kind of money. It was put into circulation in Moscow just before we left.'

12

'Why were you so long in Varykino? Is there anybody there? I thought there wasn't a soul, that it was quite empty. What kept you so long?'

'Katya and I were cleaning your house. I thought you'd go there the moment you got back and I didn't want you to see it in the state it was in.'

'Why, what sort of state is it in? Is it so bad?'

'It was untidy, dirty, we put it straight.'

'How curt and evasive! I feel there's something you are not telling me. But just as you like, I won't try to get it out of you. Tell me about Tonya. What did they call the little girl?'

'Masha, in memory of your mother.'

'Tell me all about them.'

'Please, not now. I've told you, I still can't talk about it without crying.'

'That Samdevyatov who lent you the horse, he's an interesting character, don't you think so?'

'Very.'

'I know him quite well, you know. He was in and out of the house when we lived there. It was all new to us and he helped us to settle in.'

'I know, he told me.'

'He must be useful to you too? You see a lot of him?'

'He positively showers me with kindness! I don't know what I should do without him.'

'I can imagine it! And I suppose you two are good friends and he drops in when he likes!'

'All the time! Naturally!'

'And you like him? Sorry. I shouldn't have asked you that. I've got no business to question you. That was going too far! I apologise.'

'Oh, that's all right! I suppose what you really mean is, what kind of terms are we on? Is there anything more between us than friendship? Of course there isn't! He has done a tremendous amount for me, I am enormously in his debt, but if he gave me my weight in gold, if he gave his life for me, it wouldn't bring me a step nearer to him. I have always disliked that kind of man, I have nothing whatever in common with them. These resourceful, self-confident, masterful characters—in practical things they are invaluable, but in matters of feeling I can think of nothing more horrible than all their impertinent, male complacency! It certainly isn't my idea of life and love! Actually, as a person Anfim reminds me of someone else, someone infinitely more repulsive. It's his fault that I've become what I am.'

'I don't understand. What do you think you are? What have you got in mind? Explain to me. You are the best person in the world.'

'How can you, Yura darling! I am talking seriously and you pay me compliments, as though we were in a drawing-room. What am I like? There's something broken in me, there's something broken in my whole life. I discovered life much too early, I was made to discover it, and I was made to see it from the very worst side—a cheap, distorted version of it—through the eyes of an elderly roué. One of those useless, self-satisfied egoists of the old days who took advantage of everything and allowed themselves whatever they fancied.'

'I think I understand. I thought there was something. But wait a moment. I can imagine your suffering as a child, a suffering much beyond your years, the shock to your inexperience; a very young girl's sense of outrage. But all that is in the past. What I mean is that it isn't for you to make yourself unhappy about it now, it's for people who love you, people like myself. It's I who should be tearing my hair because I wasn't with you to prevent it, if it really makes you unhappy. It's a curious thing. I think I can only be really jealous —deadly, passionately jealous—of someone I despise and have nothing in common with. A rival whom I look up to makes me feel something different. I think if a man whom I understood and liked were in love with the same woman as myself I wouldn't feel a grievance or want to quarrel with him, I would feel a sort of tragic brotherhood with him. Naturally, I wouldn't dream of sharing the woman I loved. But I would give her up and my suffering would be something different from jealousy—less raw and angry. It would be the same if I came across an artist who was doing the same sort of thing as I do and doing it better. I would probably give up my own efforts,

I wouldn't want to duplicate his and there would be no point in going on if his were better.

'But that wasn't what we were talking about. I don't think I could love you so much if you had nothing to complain of and nothing to regret. I don't like people who have never fallen or stumbled. Their virtue is lifeless and it isn't of much value. Life hasn't revealed its beauty to them.'

'It's this beauty I'm thinking of. I think that to see it your imagination has to be intact, your vision has to be childlike. That's what I was deprived of. I might have had my own vision of life if I hadn't, right from the beginning, seen it stamped with someone else's cheap view of it. And that isn't all. It's because of the intrusion into my life, right at the start, of this immoral, selfish nonentity, that when later on I married a man who was really big and remarkable and who loved me and whom I loved, my marriage was destroyed.'

'Wait a moment before you tell me about your husband. I am not jealous of him. I told you I can only be jealous of my inferiors. Tell me first about this other man.'

'Which man?'

'This monster. The one who spoiled your life. Who was he?'

'A fairly well-known Moscow lawyer. A friend of my father's. When Father died and we were very badly off he supported my mother. He was unmarried, rich. I've probably made him sound a lot more interesting than he is by painting him so black. He couldn't be more ordinary. I'll tell you his name if you like.'

'You needn't. I know it. I saw him once.'

'Really?'

'One evening at your hotel, the night your mother took poison. It was late at night. You and I were both still at school.'

'Oh, I remember. You came with someone else. You stood in the shadow, in the entrance lobby. I don't know if I would have remembered on my own, but I think you reminded me of it once, it must have been in Melyuzeyevo.'

'Komarovsky was there.'

'Was he? Quite possible. You were quite likely to find me with him. We were often together.'

'Why are you blushing?'

'At the sound of Komarovsky's name coming from you. I've got unused to hearing it, I was taken by surprise.'

'There was a school friend of mine who came with me that night and this is what he told me. He recognised Komarovsky as a man he had seen once before in the most unusual circumstances. It

happened that as a child, during a journey, this boy, Misha Gordon,
witnessed the suicide of my father—the millionaire industrialist. They
were in the same train. Father threw himself out of the moving train
meaning to end his life and was killed. Father was accompanied on this
journey by Komarovsky, who was his lawyer. He made Father drink,
he got his business into a muddle, he brought him to the point of
bankruptcy and drove him to suicide. It was his fault that my father
killed himself and that I was left an orphan.'

'It isn't possible! How extraordinary! Can it really be true?
So he was a tragic influence in your life too! It brings us even closer,
doesn't it! It's as if it were all predestined!'

'He is the man of whom I shall always be incurably, insanely
jealous.'

'How can you say such a thing? Don't you see, it isn't just that
I don't love him, I despise him.'

'Can you know yourself as well as that? Human nature is so
mysterious and so full of contradictions. Perhaps there is something
in your very loathing of him that keeps you bound to him more surely
than to any man whom you love of your own free will, without
compulsion.'

'What a terrible thing to say! And as usual, the way you put it
makes me feel that this thing, monstrous and unnatural as it is, is
perhaps true. But how dreadful if it is!'

'Don't be frightened. Don't listen to me. I only meant that I
am jealous of what is dark, unconscious, the thing you can't communicate with, that you can't guess about. I am jealous of your
hairbrush, of the drops of sweat on your skin, of the germs in the air
you breathe which could get into your blood and poison you. And
in exactly the same way as though he were an infectious illness, I am
jealous of Komarovsky who will take you away from me some day,
just as certainly as death will some day separate us. I know this
sounds like a lot of confused nonsense, but I can't say it more clearly.
I love you beyond mind or memory or measure.'

13

'Tell me more about your husband. He is "One writ with me in
sour misfortune's book." That's Shakespeare.'

'Where did he say that?'

'In *Romeo and Juliet*.'

'I told you a lot in Melyuzeyevo when I was looking for him, and then here, when I heard how his men arrested you and took you to his train. I may have told you—or perhaps I only thought I did —how I once saw him from a distance when he was getting into his car. But you can imagine how many guards there were round him! I found him almost unchanged. The same handsome, honest, resolute face, the most honest face I've ever seen in my life. The same manly, straightforward character, not a shadow of affectation or play-acting. And yet I did notice a difference, and it worried me.

'It was as if there was something abstract in his expression—it made him colourless. As if a living human face had become an embodiment of a principle, the image of an idea. It upset me dreadfully when I noticed it. I realised that this had happened to him because he had handed himself over to something lofty but deadening and pitiless, which wouldn't spare him in the end. It seemed to me that he was marked with a sign and that here was the sign.—But perhaps I'm muddled. Perhaps I'm influenced by what you said when you described your meeting with him. After all, quite apart from what we feel for each other, I am influenced by you in so many ways!'

'Tell me about your life with him before the revolution.'

'Very early, when I was still a child, I was greatly moved by purity, it had a great attraction for me. Pasha was the fulfilment of this longing. You know we grew up almost in the same house.— Pasha and Galiullin and I. When Pasha was a little boy, he was infatuated with me. He used to blush or turn pale whenever he saw me. I probably shouldn't be talking like this, but it would be worse to pretend I didn't know. It was the kind of all-absorbing childish passion that a child conceals because his pride won't let him show it, but one look at his face is enough to tell you all about it. We saw a lot of each other. He and I were as different as you and I are alike. I chose him there and then in my heart. I decided that as soon as we were old enough I would marry this enchanting boy and in my mind I became engaged to him.

'You know, it's extraordinary how gifted he is! His father was an ordinary signalman, or a railway guard, I don't know which, and by sheer brains and hard work Pasha reached, I was going to say the level, but it's more like the summit, of present-day academic learning in two subjects—classics and mathematics! After all, that's something, you know!'

'But then what went wrong with your married life, if you were so fond of each other?'

'That's a terribly difficult thing to answer. I'll try and tell you. But you know it's absurd for me to explain to you who are so wise what is happening to human life in general, and to life in Russia, and why families get broken up, including yours and mine. Goodness, it isn't as if it were a question of individuals, of being alike or different in character, of loving or not loving! Everything established, settled, everything to do with home and order and the common round, has crumbled into dust and been swept away in the general upheaval and reorganisation of the whole of society. The whole human way of life has been destroyed and ruined. All that's left is the bare, shivering human soul, stripped to the last shred, the naked force of the human psyche for which nothing has changed because it was always cold and shivering and reaching out to its nearest neighbour, as cold and lonely as itself. You and I are like the first two people on earth who at the beginning of the world had nothing to cover themselves with—at the end of it, you and I are just as stripped and homeless. And you and I are the last remembrance of all that immeasurable greatness which has been created in the world in all the thousands of years between their time and ours, and it is in memory of all that vanished splendour that we live and love and weep and cling to one another.'

14

She was silent for a while, then she went on more calmly:

'I'll tell you. If Strelnikov became Pasha Antipov again, if he stopped raging and rebelling; if time turned back; if by some miracle, somewhere, I could see the window of our house shining, the lamplight on Pasha's table and his books, even if it were at the end of the earth—on my knees I would crawl to it. Everything in me would respond. I could never hold out against the call of the past, of loyalty. There is nothing I wouldn't sacrifice, however precious. Even you. Even our love, so happy, so natural, so much a part of me. Oh, forgive me! I don't mean that. It isn't true!'

She threw herself into his arms, weeping. But very soon she controlled herself and, wiping away her tears, she said:

'Isn't it the same call of duty that drives you back to Tonya? O God, how poor we are! What will become of us? What are we to do?'

When she had recovered she went on:

'But I haven't answered your question about what it was that broke up our happiness. I came to understand it very clearly afterwards. I'll tell you. It isn't only our story. It has become the fate of so many others.'

'Tell me, my love, you who are so wise.'

'We were married two years before the war. We were only just beginning to make a life for ourselves, we had just set up our home when the war broke out. I believe now that the war is to blame for everything, for all the misfortunes that followed and that dog our generation to this day. I remember quite well how it was in my childhood. I can still remember a time when we all accepted the peaceful outlook of the last century. It was taken for granted that you listened to reason, that it was right and natural to do what your conscience told you. For a man to die by the hand of another was a rare, an exceptional event, something quite out of the ordinary run. Murders happened in plays, newspapers and detective stories, not in everyday life.

'And then there was the jump from this calm, innocent, measured way of living to blood and tears, to mass insanity and to the savagery of daily, hourly, legalised, rewarded slaughter.

'I don't suppose this ever goes unpunished. You must remember better than I do the beginning of disintegration, how everything began to break down all at once—trains and food supplies in towns, and the foundations of home life and conscious moral standards.'

'Go on. I know what you'll say next. What good sense you make of it all! It's a joy to listen to you.'

'It was then that falsehood came into our Russian land. The great misfortune, the root of all the evil to come, was the loss of faith in the value of personal opinions. People imagined that it was out of date to follow their own moral sense, that they must all sing the same tune in chorus, and live by other people's notions, the notions which were being crammed down everybody's throat. And there arose the power of the glittering phrase, first tsarist, then revolutionary.

'This social evil became an epidemic. It was catching. And it affected everything, nothing was left untouched by it. Nor did we escape its influence in our home. Something went wrong in it. Instead of being natural and spontaneous as we had always been, we began to be idiotically pompous with each other. Something showy, artificial, forced, crept into our conversation—you felt you had to be clever in a certain way about certain world-important themes. How could Pasha, who was so discriminating, so exacting with himself, who distinguished so unerringly between reality and appearance, how could he fail to notice the falsehood which had crept into our lives?

'But this is where he made his fatal, terrible mistake. He mistook the spirit of the times, the social, universal evil, for a private and domestic one. He listened to our clichés, to our unnatural official tone, and he thought it was because he was second-rate, he was a nonentity, that we talked like this. I suppose you find it incredible that such absurd, trivial things could matter so much in our married life.—You can't imagine how important they were, what foolish things this childish nonsense made him do.

'Nobody asked him to go to the war, he went because he imagined himself to be a burden to us, so that we should be free of him. That was the beginning of all his madness. Out of a sort of misdirected, adolescent vanity, he took offence at things at which one doesn't take offence. He sulked at the course of events. He quarrelled with history. To this day he is trying to get even with it. That's what makes him so insanely provocative. It's this stupid ambition that drives him to his death. God, if I could only save him!'

'How pure and strong is your love for him! Go on, go on loving him. I'm not jealous of him. I won't stand in your way.'

15

Summer came and went, almost unnoticed. Yury recovered and, while planning to go to Moscow, took up not one, but three temporary jobs. The rapid fall in the value of money made it difficult to make ends meet.

Every morning he got up at cock-crow, left the house and walked down Merchant Street, past the 'Giant' Cinema as far as the former printing press of the Urals Cossack Army, now renamed the Red Compositor. At the corner of Gorodskaya Street the door of the town hall bore the notice, 'Complaints'. He crossed the square, turned into Buyanovka Street and, coming to the hospital, went in through the back door to the out-patients' department of the Army Section where he worked. This was his main job.

Most of his way from Lara's to the hospital lay in the shadow of overhanging trees, past curious little timber houses with steep roofs, decorated doors and carved and painted patterns round the windows. The house next to the hospital, standing in its own garden, was the hereditary domain of the widow of the merchant Goreglyadov. Its walls were covered with glazed, diamond-cut tiles, like the ancient boyar houses in Moscow.

Three or four times during his ten-day week Yury attended the board meetings of the Yuryatin Health Service in Myassky Street.

At the other end of town stood the former Institute of Gynaecology, founded by Samdevyatov's father in memory of his wife who had died in childbirth, now renamed the Rosa Luxemburg Institute; there Yury lectured on general pathology and one or two optional subjects, as part of the new, shortened course of medicine and surgery.

Coming home at night, hungry and tired, he found Lara in the thick of her domestic jobs, cooking or washing. In this prosaic, worka-day aspect of her being, dishevelled, with her sleeves rolled and her skirts tucked up, she almost frightened him by her regal beauty and dignity, more breath-taking than if he had found her on the point of going to a ball, taller, as if grown in height, in high-heeled shoes and in a long, low-cut gown with a sweeping, rustling skirt.

She cooked or washed and used the soapy water to scrub the floors, or, more quietly, less flushed, mended and pressed linen for the three of them. Or when the cooking, washing and cleaning had all been got out of the way, she gave lessons to Katya. Or with her nose in her textbook worked at her own political re-education, in order to qualify for her old teaching job at the new, reorganised school.

The nearer he was drawn to Lara and her daughter, the less he ventured to take domesticity for granted and the stricter was the control imposed on his thoughts by his duty to his family and the pain of his broken faith. There was nothing offensive to Lara or Katya in this limitation. On the contrary, this attitude on his part con-tained a world of deference which precluded vulgar familiarity.

But the division in him was a sorrow and a torment and he became accustomed to it only as one gets used to an unhealed and frequently reopened wound.

16

After two or three months of living like this, one day in October Yury said to Lara:

'You know it looks as if I'll be forced to resign from my jobs. It's always the same thing—it happens again and again. At first everything is splendid.—"Come along. We welcome good, honest work, we welcome ideas, especially new ideas. What could please us better? Do your work, your research, struggle, carry on."

'Then you find in practice that what they mean by ideas is nothing but words—claptrap in praise of the revolution and the régime. I'm sick and tired of it. And it's not the kind of thing I'm good at.

'I suppose they are right from their point of view. Of course, I'm not on their side. Only I find it hard to accept the view that they are radiant heroes and I myself am a mean little fellow who sides with tyranny and obscurantism. Have you ever heard of Nikolay Vedenyapin?'

'Well, of course! Both before you came and from what you told me yourself. Sima Tuntseva often speaks of him, she's a great admirer of his. To my shame, I haven't read any of his books. I'm not fond of philosophical essays. I think a little philosophy should be added to life and art by way of spice, but to make it one's speciality seems to me as strange as feeding on nothing but pickles. But I'm sorry, I've distracted you with my nonsense.'

'No, actually it's very much what I think myself. Well, about my uncle, I'm supposed to have been corrupted by his influence. One of my sins is a belief in intuition. And see how ridiculous—they all shout that I'm a marvellous diagnostician—and as a matter of fact it's true that I don't often make mistakes in diagnosing a disease— well, what is this immediate grasp of a situation as a whole supposed to be if not the intuition they find so detestable?

'Another thing is that I am obsessed by the problem of mimicry, of mimesis—the outward adaptation of an organism to the colour of its environment. I think it throws an astonishing light on the relationship between the inward and the outward world.

'Well, I dared to mention this in my lectures. Immediately there was a chorus: "Idealism, mysticism, Goethe's nature philosophy, neo-Schellingism."

'It's time I got out. I'll stay on at the hospital until they throw me out, but I'll resign from the Institute and the Health Department. I don't want to worry you, but from time to time I have the feeling that they might come and arrest me any day.'

'God forbid. It hasn't come to that yet, fortunately. But you are right. It would do no harm to be more careful. As I've noticed it, whenever this régime comes to power it goes through certain regular stages. In the first stage it's the triumph of reason, of the spirit of criticism, the fight against prejudice and so on.

'Then comes the second stage. The accent is all on the dark forces, the false sympathisers, the hangers-on. There is more and more suspicion—informers, intrigues, hatreds. You are perfectly right that we are entering on the second stage.

'I'll give you an example. The local revolutionary tribunal has had two new members transferred to it from Khodatskoye—two old political convicts from among the workers, Tiverzin and Antipov.

'They both know me perfectly well, in fact one of them is quite simply my father-in-law. And yet it's only since their arrival, quite recently, that I've really begun to tremble for Katya's and my life.

Antipov doesn't like me, and I believe them both to be capable of anything. It would be quite like them to destroy me and even Pasha one of these days in the name of higher revolutionary justice.'

The sequel to this conversation took place very soon. A search was carried out by night at the home of the widow Goreglyadova, at 48 Buyanovka Street, next door to the hospital. A cache of arms was found and an anti-revolutionary plot uncovered. Many people were arrested and the wave of searches and arrests continued. It was whispered that some of the suspects had escaped across the river. 'Though what good will it do them?' people said. 'There are rivers and rivers. Now the Amur, for instance, at Blagoveshchensk—you jump in and swim across and you are in China!—that really is a river. That's quite a different matter.'

'The air is getting thick,' said Lara. 'Our time of safety is over. They are sure to arrest us, you and me. And then what will become of Katya? I am a mother, I can't let this misfortune happen, I must think of something. I must have a plan. It's driving me out of my mind.'

'Let's try and think. Though what is there we can do in a case like this? Isn't it beyond our power to avert this blow? Isn't it a question of fate?'

'We certainly can't escape: there's nowhere to go. But we could get out of the limelight. We might go to Varykino, for instance. I keep thinking of the house there. It's very lonely and neglected, but we would be less in the way than here, we wouldn't attract so much attention. Winter is coming on. I wouldn't at all mind spending it there. By the time they got round to us we'd have gained a year of life: that's always something. Samdevyatov would keep us in touch with the town. Perhaps he'd even help us to go into hiding. What do you think? It's true, there isn't a soul there, it's empty and desolate, at least it was when I was there in March. And they say there are wolves. It's rather frightening. But then people, anyway people like Tiverzin and Antipov, are more frightening than wolves these days.'

'I don't know what to say. Haven't you been urging me all this time to go to Moscow, telling me not to put it off? That's easier now. I asked at the station. Apparently they've stopped worrying about black marketeers. Not everyone whose papers aren't in order is taken off the train. They shoot less, they've got tired.

'It worries me that I've had no reply to my letters to Moscow. I ought to go there and see what's happening to them—you keep telling me yourself. But then how am I to take what you say about

Varykino? You surely wouldn't go to such an out-of-the-way place by yourself?'

'No, of course. Without you it would be impossible.'

'And yet you tell me to go to Moscow?'

'Yes, you must go.'

'Listen. I've got a wonderful plan!—Let's go to Moscow, all three of us.'

'To Moscow? You're mad! What should I do in Moscow? No, I have to stay, I must be near here. It's here that Pasha's fate is going to be decided. I must wait for him and be within reach if he needs me.'

'Well, then, let's think about Katya.'

'We were talking about her with Sima—Sima Tuntseva, she comes to see me sometimes.'

'Yes, I know, I've often seen her.'

'In your place I'd have fallen in love with her at once. I don't know where you men keep your eyes! She's such a dear!—Pretty, graceful, clever, educated, kind, sensible.'

'Her sister gave me a haircut the day I arrived—Glaphira, the seamstress.'

'I know. They both live with their eldest sister, Avdotya, the one who's a librarian. They are a good, honest working family. I thought of asking them—if it comes to the worst, if you and I are arrested—if they wouldn't have Katya and look after her.'

'Only if there really isn't any other way out. Pray God it won't come to that.'

'They say Sima is a bit odd—not quite right in the head. It's true she doesn't seem quite normal, but that's only because she's so deep and original. You and she are extraordinarily alike in your views. I think I should be quite happy about Katya if Sima brought her up.'

17

Once again Yury had been to the station and had again come back empty-handed. Everything was still undecided. He and Lara were faced with the unknown. The weather was cold and dark as before the first snow. The sky, where you could see more of it at the cross-roads, had a wintry look.

Lara had a visitor, Sima. They were talking but their conversation was more like a lecture delivered by Sima to her hostess. Yury did not want to be in their way. He also wanted to be alone a little. He lay down on the sofa in the next room. The door between the two rooms was open; there was a curtain over it from lintel to floor but he could hear what they were saying.

'I'll go on with my sewing but don't take any notice, Sima dear. I'm listening, I am all ears. I read history and philosophy in my time at college. I like your way of looking at things very much. Besides, it comforts me to listen to you. We haven't slept much the last few nights, worrying about Katya. I know it's my duty as her mother to see to it that she's safe if anything happens to us. I ought to think it out calmly and sensibly but I'm not very good at that. It makes me sad to realise it. I'm sad because I'm tired and haven't slept enough. It steadies me to listen to you. Besides, it's going to snow any minute. I like to listen to a long, wise discourse when it's snowing. Have you noticed that, if you glance at the window when it's snowing, you always feel as if someone were coming across the garden to the house? Go on, Sima dear. I'm listening.'

'Where did we leave off last time?'

Yury did not catch Lara's reply. Now Sima was speaking:

'I don't like such words as "culture" and "epoch". They are confusing. I prefer to put it another way. As I see it, man is made up of two parts, of God and work. Each succeeding stage in the development of the human spirit is marked by the achievement over many generations of an enormously slow and lengthy work. Such a work was Egypt. Greece was another. The theology of the Old Testament prophets was a third. The last in time, not so far replaced by anything else and still being achieved by all that is inspired in our time, is Christianity.

'To show you the completely new thing which it brought into the world in all its freshness—not as you know it and are used to it but more simply, immediately, unexpectedly—I should like to go over a few extracts from the liturgy—only very few and shortened at that.

'A lot of liturgical texts bring together the concepts of the Old and the New Testaments and put them side by side. For instance, the burning bush, the exodus from Egypt, the children in the fiery furnace, Jonah and the whale, are compared to the virgin birth and the resurrection of Christ.

'These comparisons bring out, very strikingly, I think, the way in which the Old Testament is old and the New is new. Quite a lot of texts compare the virgin birth to the crossing of the Red Sea by the Jews. For instance, one verse begins: "The likeness of the virgin bride was once drawn in the Red Sea," and goes on to say that "as the sea was impassable after its crossing by the Israelites, the

Immaculate was incorrupt after the birth of the Emmanuel." That is to say, the sea became again impossible to cross by land after the passage of the Jews, and the virginity of Mary remained intact after the birth of Our Lord. A parallel is drawn between the two events.— What kind of events are they? Both are supernatural, both are equally recognised as miracles. But there is a difference between the two miracles—a difference in the kind of thing people thought of as miraculous in these two different periods, the one ancient and primitive, the other new, post-Roman, more advanced.

'In one case you have a national leader, the patriarch Moses, ordering the sea to withdraw, and at the stroke of his magic staff it parts and allows a whole nation—countless numbers, hundreds of thousands of people—to go through, and when the last man is across, it closes up again and submerges and drowns the pursuing Egyptians. The whole picture is in the ancient style—the elements obeying the magician, great jostling multitudes like Roman armies on the march, a people and a leader. Everything is visible, audible, deafening, tremendous.

'In the other case you have a girl—a very commonplace figure who would have gone unnoticed in the ancient world—quietly, secretly, bringing forth a child, bringing forth life, bringing forth the miracle of life, the "life of all" as he was afterwards called. The birth of her child is not only illegitimate from the standpoint of the scribes, it is also against the laws of nature. She gives birth not of necessity but by a miracle, by an inspiration. And from now on, the basis of life is no longer to be compulsion, it is to be that very same inspiration—this is what the New Testament offers—the unusual instead of the commonplace, the festive instead of the workaday, inspiration instead of compulsion.

'You can see what an enormously significant change it is. Why should a private human event, completely unimportant if judged by ancient values, be compared to the migration of a whole people? Why should it have this value in the eyes of heaven?—For it is through the eyes of heaven that it must be judged, it is before the face of heaven and in the sacred light of its own uniqueness that it all takes place.

'Something in the world had been changed. Rome was at an end. The reign of numbers was at an end. The duty, imposed by armed force, to live unanimously as a people, as a whole nation, was abolished. Leaders and nations belonged to the past.

'They were replaced by the doctrine of personality and freedom. The story of a human life became the life story of God and filled the universe. As it says in the liturgy for the Feast of the Annunciation,

Adam tried to be a god and failed, but now God was made man so that Adam should be made God.

'I'll come back to this in a minute,' said Sima. 'I'd like to digress a little.—In everything to do with the care of the workers, the protection of the mother, the struggle against the power of money, our revolutionary era is a wonderful era of new, lasting, permanent achievements. But as to its interpretation of life and the philosophy of happiness which it preaches—it's simply impossible to believe that it is meant to be taken seriously, it's such a comical remnant of the past. If all this rhetoric about leaders and peoples had the power to reverse history, it would set us back thousands of years to the Biblical times of shepherd tribes and patriarchs. But fortunately it cannot do this.

'Now a few words about Christ and Mary Magdalene—this isn't from the Gospels but from the prayers on one of the days in Holy Week, I think it's Tuesday or Wednesday. You know it all, Larissa Fyodorovna, I only want to remind you of something.

'As you know, the word passion in Church Slavonic means, in the first place, suffering, the passion of Christ—"Christ taking up his passion". The liturgy also uses it in its later Russian meaning of lusts and vices.—"My soul is enslaved by passions, I have become like the beasts of the field," "Being cast out of paradise, let us become worthy to be readmitted to it by refraining from our passions," and so on. It may be wrong of me, but I don't like the Lenten texts on the curbing of the senses and the mortification of the flesh. They are curiously flat and clumsy and without the poetry of other spiritual writings. I always think they were composed by fat monks who didn't keep their Rule! Not that I care if they broke it and deceived other people or if they lived according to their conscience—it's not the monks I'm concerned with, but the actual content of these passages.— All this remorse gives too much importance to various infirmities of the flesh and to whether it is fat or famished—it's disgusting. It seems to me to raise something impure, unimportant and second-rate to a dignity which does not belong to it.—Forgive me for all these digressions.

'It has always interested me that Mary Magdalene is mentioned on the very eve of Easter, on the threshold of the death and resurrection of Christ. I don't know the reason for it, but this reminder seems to me so timely at the moment of his taking leave of life and before he takes it up again. Now look at the way the reminder is made—what genuine passion there is in it and what a ruthless directness.

'There is some doubt as to whether this does refer to the

Magdalene or to one of the other Marys, but anyway, she begs Our Lord:

'"Unbind my debt, as I unbind my hair."—It means: "As I loosen my hair, do Thou release me from my guilt." Could any expression of repentance, of the thirst to be forgiven, be more concrete, more tangible?

'And later on in the liturgy of the same day there is another, more detailed passage, and this time it almost certainly refers to Mary Magdalene.

'Again she grieves in a terribly tangible way over her past and over the corruption which it rooted in her, so that every night it comes to life in her once more. "The flaring up of lust is to me like night, the dark, moonless zeal of sin." She begs Christ to accept her tears of repentance and be moved by the sincerity of her sighs, so that she may dry His most pure feet with her hair—reminding Him that in the rushing waves of her hair Eve took refuge when she was overcome with fear and shame in paradise. "Let me kiss Thy most pure feet and water them with my tears and dry them with the hair of my head, which covered Eve and sheltered her when, her ears filled with sound, she was afraid in the cool of the day in paradise." And immediately after all this about her hair, she exclaims: "Who can fathom the multitude of my sins and the depth of Thy judgment?" What familiarity, what equal terms between God and life, God and the individual, God and a woman!'

18

Yury had come home tired from the station. It was his day off and usually he slept enough that day to last him the nine others of the ten-day week. He lay back on the sofa and from time to time stretched himself out on it. But although he listened to Sima through a haze of oncoming drowsiness, her reflections delighted him. 'Of course, she's taken it all from Uncle Kolya's books,' he thought. 'But all the same how intelligent she is and how gifted.'

He got up and went to the window. It looked out on the yard, like the window of the room next door where Lara and Sima were now muttering inaudibly.

It was getting dark and it looked like snowing. Two magpies flew in from the street and fluttered round looking for a place to settle, their feathers ruffled by the wind. They perched on the lid of the rubbish bin, flew up on the fence, flew down on the ground and hopped about the yard.

'Magpies for snow,' thought Yury. At the same moment Sima said aloud in the other room:

'Magpies for news. You'll have guests, or else a letter.'

A little later someone pulled the handle of the door bell which Yury had mended. Lara came out from behind the curtain and walked swiftly through to the hall to open the door. Yury heard her talking to Sima's sister, Glaphira.

'You've come for your sister? Yes, she's here.'

'No, I didn't come for her, though we might as well go home together if Sima is ready. I've brought a letter for your friend. It's lucky for him that I once had a job at the post office. I don't know how many hands it's been through, it's from Moscow and it's been five months on the way. They couldn't find the addressee. At last they thought of asking me and I knew, of course—he once came to me for a haircut.'

The long letter, written on many sheets of paper, creased and soiled in the tattered envelope which had been opened at the post office, was from Tonya. Yury found it in his hands without knowing how it had got there; he had not seen Lara holding it out to him. When he began reading it he was still conscious of being in Yuryatin, in Lara's house, but gradually, as he read on, he lost all awareness of it. Sima came out, greeted him and said good-bye; he said the right things automatically but paid no attention to her, and never noticed when she left the house. After a while, he completely forgot his surroundings.

'Yura,' Tonya wrote, 'do you know that we have a daughter? We have christened her Masha in memory of your mother.

'Now about something else.—Several prominent people, professors who belonged to the Cadet party and right-wing socialists, Milyukov, Kizewetter, Kuskova and several others, including your Uncle Kolya, my father and the rest of us, are being deported from Russia.

'This is a misfortune, especially in your absence, but we must accept it and thank God that our exile takes so mild a form at this terrible time when things could have been so much worse for us. If you were here, you would come with us. But where are you? I am sending this letter to Antipova's address; she'll give it to you if she finds you. I am tortured by not knowing if the exit permit we are getting as a family will be extended to you later on, when, if God is willing, you are found. I have not given up believing that you are alive and that you will be found. My heart tells me that this is so, and I trust it. Perhaps by then, by the time you reappear, conditions in Russia will be milder, and you will manage to get a separate visa for yourself, and we shall all be once more together in the same place. But as I write this, I don't myself believe in the possibility of so much happiness.

'The whole trouble is that I love you and that you don't love me. I keep trying to discover the meaning of this judgment on me, to understand it, to see the reason for it. I look into myself, I go over our whole life together and everything I know about myself, and I can't find the beginning, and I can't remember what it is I did and how I brought this misfortune on myself. You have a false, unkindly view of me, you see me in a distorting mirror.

'As for me, I love you. If only you knew how much I love you. I love all that is unusual in you, the inconvenient as well as the convenient, and all the ordinary things which, in you, are made precious to me by being combined in an extraordinary way; your face which is made beautiful by your expression, though perhaps it would be plain without it, your intelligence and your talent which replace your will—for you have no will. All of it is dear to me and I know of no one better than you in the world.

'But listen, this is what I want to say to you. Even if you had been less dear to me, even if I had liked and admired you less, I would still have thought that I loved you, the dreadful fact that I was indifferent would have been hidden from me. Out of sheer terror of inflicting on you such a humiliating, such an annihilating punishment, I would have unconsciously taken care not to realise that I didn't love you. Neither you nor I would ever have known it. My own heart would have hidden it from me, because not to love is almost like murder and I could never have had the strength to deal such a blow to anyone.

'Nothing is definitely settled yet, but we are probably going to Paris. I'll be in those distant lands where you were taken as a child and where Father and my uncle were brought up. Father sends you his greetings. Sasha has grown a lot; he is not particularly good-looking but he is a big, strong boy; and whenever we speak of you he cries bitterly and won't be comforted. I can't go on. I can't stop crying. Well, good-bye. Let me make the sign of the cross over you and bless you for all the years ahead, for the endless parting, the trials, the uncertainties, for all your long, long and dark way. I am not blaming you for anything, I am not reproaching you, make your life as you wish, only so that you are all right.

'Before we left the Urals—what a terrible and fateful place it turned out to be for us—I got to know Larissa Fyodorovna fairly well. I am thankful to her for being constantly at my side when I was having a difficult time and for helping me through my confinement.

I must honestly admit that she is a good person, but I don't want to be a hypocrite—she is exactly the opposite of myself. I was born to make life simple and to look for sensible solutions, she—to complicate it and confuse the way.

'God keep you, I must stop. They have come for the letter, and it's time I packed. O Yura, Yura, my dear, my darling, my husband, my children's father, what is happening to us? Do you realise that we'll never, never see each other again? Now I've written it down, do you realise what it means? Do you understand, do you understand? They are hurrying me and it's as if they had come to take me to my death. Yura! Yura!'

Yury finished reading and raised his eyes. They were absent, tearless, dry with grief, emptied by suffering. He neither saw nor was aware of anything round him.

Outside it was snowing. The snow, swept by the wind, fell thicker and thicker, and faster and faster, as if it were trying to catch up with something, and Yury stared out at it, not as if he were looking at the snow, but as if he were still reading Tonya's letter; and as if the whiteness flickering past him were not the small dry snow stars but the blanks between the small black letters, white and endless.

Involuntarily he cried out and clutched his breast. He felt that he was fainting, hobbled the few steps to the sofa and fell down on it unconscious.

14

Again Varykino

WINTER had settled in. It was snowing hard as Yury walked back from the hospital. Lara met him in the hall.

'Komarovsky is here,' she said in a lost, shocked voice. She stood looking bewildered as if she had been struck.

'Where? Here in the flat?'

'No, of course not. He came this morning and he said he would come back to-night. He'll be here soon. He wants to have a word with you.'

'Why has he come?'

'I didn't understand all he said. He said he was going to the Far East and that he had come out of his way to see us. Particularly to see you and Pasha. He said we were in great danger, all three of us, you and Pasha and I. And that he alone could save us, if we followed his advice.'

'I am going out. I don't want to see him.'

Lara burst into tears and tried to throw herself at his feet and hug his knees, but he forced her to get up.

'Please do stay in, for my sake,' she implored him. 'It isn't that I'm frightened of being alone with him, but I do so hate it. Do save me from having to see him by myself. Besides, he is so practical and experienced—he might really have some advice to give us. I realise how he must disgust you, but do please put your feelings aside and stay.'

'What is the matter with you, darling? Don't be so upset. What are you trying to do? Don't keep falling on your knees. Get up now, and cheer up. You really must get rid of this bogey—he's frightened you to death. You know I'm with you. Of course I'll stay. I'll cheerfully kill him for you if you tell me to.'

Night came on in about half an hour. It was completely dark. It was now six months since all the rat holes had been stopped up and Yury kept watching out for new ones and blocking them in time. They also kept a big, fluffy tom-cat who spent his time in contemplation, looking enigmatic. The rats were still in the house but they were now more cautious.

Waiting for Komarovsky, Lara cut some slices of black rationed bread and put a plate with a few boiled potatoes on the table. They had decided to receive him in the old dining-room which they still used for their meals. The large, heavy, dark oak table and sideboard were part of its original furniture. Standing on the table was a bottle of castor oil with a wick in it, which they used as a portable lamp.

Komarovsky came in out of the dark December night, covered with snow. Slices of it fell from his hat, coat and boots and melted into puddles on the floor. His moustache and beard, plastered with it, made him look like a clown (he had been clean-shaven in the old days). He wore an old but good-looking suit with well-creased pin-striped trousers. Before saying how-do-you-do he spent a long time combing his wet hair with a pocket comb and drying his moustache and eyebrows with a handkerchief. Then, silently and with a portentous expression, he stretched out both his hands—the left one to Lara and the right one to Yury.

'Let us assume we are old acquaintances,' he turned to Yury. 'I was a great friend of your father's, as you probably know. He died in my arms. I keep looking at you to see if there is any likeness. But I don't think you take after him. He was an expansive man, spontaneous and impulsive. You must be more like your mother. She was a gentle dreamer.'

'Larissa Fyodorovna asked me to see you. She said you had some business with me. I agreed, but our meeting is not of my choice and I don't consider that we are acquainted. So shall we get on with it? What is it you want?'

'I am so happy to see you both, my dears. I understand everything, absolutely everything. If I may say so, you are wonderfully suited to each other. A perfect match.'

'Please stop. I'll thank you to mind your own business. We haven't asked for your sympathy. You forget yourself.'

'Don't flare up so fast, young man. Perhaps after all you do take after your father. He used to lose his temper just like that. Well, my children, I offer you my best wishes. Unfortunately, however, you really are children—not just in a manner of speaking, but completely ignorant and thoughtless children. In two days here I've learned more about you than you know or suspect about yourselves. Without knowing it, you are walking on the edge of a precipice. Unless you do something about it, the days of your freedom and perhaps even of your lives are numbered.

'There exists a certain communist style, Yury Andreyevich. Few people measure up to it. But no one flouts that way of life and thought as openly as you do. Why you have to flirt with danger, I can't imagine. You are a mockery of that whole world, an insult to it. If at least your past were your own secret—but there are people from Moscow who know you inside out. Neither of you is at all to the liking of the local priests of Themis. Comrades Antipov and Tiverzin are busy sharpening their claws.

'However, you are a man, Yury Andreyevich, you are your own master and you have a perfect right to play the fool and risk your life if you feel like it. But Larissa Fyodorovna is not a free agent. She is a mother, she has a child's life in her hands, and she can't go about with her head in the clouds.

'I wasted all my morning trying to get her to take the situation seriously. She wouldn't listen to me. Will you use your influence? She has no right to play with her daughter's safety. She must not disregard my arguments.'

'I've never in my life forced my views on anyone. Certainly not on those who are close to me. Larissa Fyodorovna has every right to listen to you or not as she thinks fit. It's a matter for her alone. Apart from that, I have no idea what you are talking about. I haven't heard what you call your arguments.'

'You remind me more and more of your father—just as stubborn. Well, I'll tell you. But it's a fairly complicated business, so you'll have to be patient with me and not interrupt.

'Big changes are being planned at the top.—Yes, really, I have it from a most reliable source and you can take it that it's true. What they have in mind is a switch-over to a more democratic course, a concession to legality, and this will come about quite soon.

'But just because of it, the members of punitive agencies, whose jobs are due to be abolished, are in a great hurry to square their local accounts, so before the end there will be a period of greater savagery than we have yet seen. You are marked down for destruction, Yury Andreyevich. Your name is on the list—I am telling you this in all seriousness, I've seen it myself. You must think of saving yourself before it is too late.

'But all this is by way of introduction. I am coming to the point.

'Those political forces which are still faithful to the Provisional Government and the disbanded Constituent Assembly are concentrating in the Maritime Province on the Pacific Coast. Various prominent people are getting together—members of the Duma, the more prominent members of the old zemstvos and other public figures, business men and industrialists, as well as the remnants of the volunteer armies.

'They intend to form a Far Eastern republic, and the Soviet Government winks at it, because at the moment it would suit it to have a buffer between Red Siberia and the outside world. The republic is to have a coalition government. More than half the seats, at the insistence of Moscow, will go to Communists. When it suits them, they will stage a *coup d'état* and bring the republic to heel. The plan is quite transparent but it gives us a certain breathing-space—we must make the best of it.

'At one time before the revolution, I used to look after the affairs of the Merkulovs, the Arkharov Brothers and several other banks and trading firms in Vladivostok. They know me there, and an envoy came to see me on behalf of the shadow cabinet to offer me the post of Minister of Justice in the future government. This was done secretly but with unofficial Soviet approval. I accepted and I am on my way there now. All I've just told you is happening with the tacit consent of the Soviet Government, but not so openly that it would be wise to talk about it much.

'I can take you and Larissa Fyodorovna with me. From there, you can easily get a boat and join your family overseas. You know, of course, that they have been expelled from the country. It caused a great stir; the whole of Moscow is still talking about it.

'I have promised Larissa Fyodorovna to save Strelnikov. As a member of an independent government recognised by Moscow, I can look for him in Eastern Siberia and help him to cross over into our autonomous region. If he does not succeed in escaping, I'll suggest that he should be exchanged for someone who is in Allied custody and is of interest to the Moscow Government.'

Lara had followed Komarovsky's explanation with difficulty, but when he came to the arrangements for the safety of Yury and of Strelnikov, she pricked up her ears. Blushing a little, she said to Yury:

'You see, darling, how important all this is for you and for Pasha.'

'You are too trusting, my dear. You can't take a half-formed plan for an accomplished fact. I don't say Victor Ippolitovich is deliberately misleading us, but so far he has only told us about castles in the air. For my part,' he turned to Komarovsky, 'thank you for the interest you take in my affairs, but you surely don't imagine that I am going to let you run them? As for Strelnikov, Lara will have to think it over.'

'All it comes down to,' said Lara, 'is whether we go with him or not. You know perfectly well I wouldn't go without you.'

Komarovsky sipped the diluted alcohol which Yury had brought from the hospital, chewed boiled potatoes and became more and more tipsy.

2

It was getting late. Every time the wick was trimmed it spluttered and burned brightly, lighting up the room, then the flame died down and the shadows returned. Yury and Lara were sleepy, they wanted to talk things over by themselves and go to bed, but Komarovsky stayed on. They were irked by his presence as they were irked by the sight of the heavy oak sideboard and by the December darkness outside the windows.

He was looking not at them but over their heads, his glazed eyes riveted on some distant point and his drowsy, slurred voice grinding on and on, tedious and interminable. His latest hobby-horse was the Far East. He was explaining the political importance of Mongolia. Yury and Lara, who were not interested in the subject, had missed the point at which he had got on to it and this made his explanations even more boring. He was saying:

'Siberia—truly a New America as it is often called—has immense possibilities. It is the cradle of Russia's future greatness, the gauge of our progress towards democracy and political and economic health. Still more pregnant with future possibilities is our great Far Eastern neighbour, Outer Mongolia. What do you know about it? You yawn and blink shamelessly, and yet Mongolia has nearly a million square miles and untold mineral wealth; it is a virgin land, which tempts the greed of China, and Japan and the United States. They are all ready to snatch at it to the detriment of our Russian interests —interests which have been recognised by all our rivals, whenever there has been a division of that remote quarter of the globe into spheres of influence.

'China exploits the feudal-theocratic backwardness of Mongolia through her influence over the llamas and *khutukhts*. Japan backs the local princes, the *hoshuns*. Red Russia has found an ally in the *hamjils*—the Revolutionary Association of Insurgent Mongolian Shepherds. I myself would like to see a really prosperous Mongolia governed by a freely elected *hurultaï*. What should interest you personally is that once you are across the Mongolian border, the world is at your feet—you are as free as air.'

His wordy harangues got on Lara's nerves. Finally, bored to tears and tired out, she held out her hand to him and said abruptly, with undisguised hostility:

'It's late and it's time for you to go. I am sleepy.'

'Oh come, you aren't going to be so inhospitable as to throw me out at this hour of the night! I don't believe I can find my way—I don't know the town and it's pitch dark.'

'You should have thought of that earlier instead of sitting on and on. No one asked you to stay so late.'

'Why are you so sharp with me? You haven't even asked me if I have anywhere to stay.'

'It doesn't interest me in the slightest. You are perfectly well able to look after yourself. If you are angling for an invitation to stay the night—I'll certainly not put you in the room where we and Katya sleep, and the other rooms are full of rats.'

'I don't mind them.'

'Well, it's your look-out.'

3

'What is wrong, darling? You don't sleep for nights on end, you don't touch your food, you go about all day looking like a ghost. What are you thinking about all the time? You mustn't let your worries get so much on top of you.'

'Izot, the watchman from the hospital, has been round again—he goes to see the washer-woman downstairs; they are having a love affair. So he dropped in on the way to give me a cheerful piece of news! "It's jug for your bloke," he says. "Any day now."—"How do you know?" I asked him.—"Oh it's quite certain, I heard it at the Pelican." The Pelican is the Ispolkom[1], as you probably guess.' They both laughed.

'He's quite right,' said Yury. 'It might happen any day and it's time we vanished. The problem is where to go. We must slip away quietly, so there is no question of going to Moscow—we couldn't make the arrangements for the journey without attracting attention. Listen, my darling. Why don't we, after all, do what you suggested in the first place? We'll go to Varykino and lie low—at any rate for a week or two or a month.'

'Thank you, thank you, my dear. Oh, how glad I am! I understand how much you dislike the idea. But we wouldn't live in your house. You couldn't possibly face that—the sight of the empty rooms, the regrets, the comparisons with the past. Don't I know what it means to build one's happiness on the sufferings of others, to trample on what

---

[1] *Ispol*nitelny *Komitet* : Executive Committee of the Town Council.

is dear to one, and holy. I'd never accept such a sacrifice from you. But anyhow, there is no question of that. Your house is in such a bad state that it would be difficult in any case to make the rooms fit to live in. I was thinking of the house where the Mikulitsins lived.'

'All that is true enough and I am grateful to you for being so considerate and sensitive. But wait a minute. I keep meaning to ask you and forgetting. What has happened to Komarovsky? Is he still here or is he gone? Since that time I quarrelled with him and threw him out I've heard nothing more of him.'

'I don't know anything either. But who cares! What do you want with him?'

'I am beginning to think more and more that we should not, both of us, have taken the same attitude to his idea. We are not in the same position. You have your daughter to think of. Even if you wanted to share my danger, you have no right to do it.

'But about Varykino. Of course, to go to that wilderness in winter, without food, without strength or hope—it's utter madness. But why not, my love! Let's be mad, if there is nothing except madness left to us. We'll eat humble pie once again. We'll ask Samdevyatov to lend us a horse. And we'll ask him, or not even him but the black marketeers who work under his orders, to let us have flour and potatoes on credit, for what our credit is still worth. And we'll persuade him not to take advantage of the favour he's doing us by coming to see us at once but to wait until later: not to come until he needs his horse. Let's be alone for a little while. Let's go, my heart. And we'll cut and use more logs in a week than a careful housewife would use in a year in peaceful times.

'Forgive me for not being able to speak calmly. I so much wish I didn't get pompous with you! But after all it's true, isn't it, that we haven't any choice. Put it how you like, but death is really knocking at our door. Our days are really numbered. So at least let us take advantage of them in our own way. Let us use them up saying good-bye to life, let us be alone together for the last time before we are parted. We'll say good-bye to everything we held dear, to the way we looked at things, to the way we dreamed of living and to what our conscience taught us, and to our hopes and to each other. We'll speak to one another once again the secret words we speak at night, great and peaceful like the name of the eastern ocean. It's not for nothing that you stand at the end of my life, my secret, forbidden angel, under the skies of wars and turmoil, you who arose at its beginning under the peaceful skies of childhood.

'That night, as a schoolgirl in your coffee-coloured uniform, in the shadow of your room at the hotel, you were already as you are now, you were just as overwhelmingly lovely.

'Later, I have often tried to name and to define the enchantment of which you sowed the seeds in me—that gradually fading light and dying sound which have spread throughout the whole of my being and have become to me the means of understanding everything else in the world through you.

'When you—a shadow in a schoolgirl's dress—arose out of the shadows of that room, I—a boy, ignorant of you—with all the torment of the strength of my response, at once understood: this scraggy little girl was charged, as with electrical waves, with all the femininity in the world. Had I touched you at that moment with so much as the tip of my finger, a spark would have lit up the room and either killed me on the spot or filled me for the rest of my life with a magnetic flow of plaintive longing and sorrow. I was full to the brim with tears, I wept and blazed inwardly. I was mortally sorry for myself, a boy, and still more sorry for you, a girl. The whole of my astonished self asked: if such is the torment of being charged with the energy of love, what must be the torment of being a woman, of being this energy, of being its source?

'There. At last I've told you. It's enough to drive one mad. And the whole of me is in this.'

Lara lay dressed on the edge of her bed. She was feeling ill, she had curled up and covered herself with a shawl. Yury sat on a chair beside her, speaking slowly, with long pauses. Sometimes she raised herself on her elbow, propped her chin on her hand and gazed at him open-mouthed. At other times she buried her head in his shoulder and cried silently with joy, without noticing her tears. At last she leaned out of bed, put her arms round him and whispered happily:

'Yury, my darling, how clever you are, how you know everything, how you guess everything. Yury, darling, you are my strength and my refuge, God forgive me the blasphemy. Oh, I am so happy. Let's go, my darling, let's go. Out there I'll tell you something I have on my mind.'

He thought that she imagined herself to be pregnant and that she was probably wrong. He said:

'I know.'

4

They left town on the morning of a grey, winter day. It was a week-day and people in the streets were going about their business. They saw many people they knew. On the hilly crossroads, women who had no wells in their yards were queueing up for water at the old water pumps, their yokes and buckets on the ground beside them. Yury drove round them carefully, checking Samdevyatov's spirited, smoky-yellow mare. The sleigh kept gliding off the cambered road on to the pavements, icy with splashed water, and hitting the lamp-posts.

Galloping at full tilt, they caught up with Samdevyatov who was walking down the street, and passed him without looking back to see if he had recognised them or his mare or whether he had anything to say to them. A little further on they passed Komarovsky and again swept by without a greeting.

Glasha Tunsteva shouted to them right across the street:

'What lies people tell! They said you had left yesterday. Going for potatoes?' and, signalling that she could not hear what they replied, waved them good-bye.

They slowed down only for Sima, and this was on an awkward slope where it was difficult to stop; the horse kept pulling at the reins. Sima, muffled up from head to foot in several shawls and looking as stiff as a log, hobbled out into the middle of the road to say good-bye and wish them a good journey.

'When you come back we must have a talk,' she said to Yury.

At last they left the outskirts of the town. Although Yury had been on this road in winter he mostly remembered it as it was in summer and he hardly recognised it now.

They had pushed their sacks of food and other bundles deep into the hay in the front of the sleigh and had tied them down with rope. Yury drove either kneeling upright on the floor of the sleigh like the local peasants, or sitting with his legs, warm in Samdevyatov's felt boots, hanging over the side.

In the afternoon when, as usual in winter, the day seemed on the point of ending long before sunset, Yury mercilessly whipped up the horse and it shot forward like an arrow. The sleigh pitched and tossed on the uneven road, like a ship in a storm. Lara and Katya were bundled up in their fur coats so that they could hardly move. Swinging round corners and bumping over ruts, they rolled from side to side and down into the hay like sacks, shrieking with laughter. Sometimes Yury drove the sleigh into the snowy banks on purpose, for a joke, and tipped them all out harmlessly into the snow. After being dragged for a few yards by the reins he stopped the horse, righted the sleigh and was rapped over the knuckles by Lara and Katya who climbed back, laughing and scolding.

'I'll show you the place where I was stopped by the partisans,'

Yury told them when they had left the town far behind, but he was unable to keep his promise, because the wintry bareness of the woods, the dead quiet and the emptiness all round had changed the country beyond recognition. 'Here it is,' he soon shouted, mistaking the first of the Moreau and Vetchinkin signs, which stood in a field, for the one in the forest where he had been captured. When they galloped past the second, still in its old place in the thicket at the crossroads by the turning to the Sakma, it was indistinguishable from the dazzling lacework of hoar frost which made the forest look like black and silver filigree, so they missed the signpost.

They swept into Varykino at dusk and, as the Zhivagos' house came first, they stopped in front of it. They burst in like robbers, hurrying because soon it would be dark. But inside it was dark already, so that Yury never saw half the destruction; half the abomination. Part of the furniture he remembered was still there; Varykino was empty and there was no one to complete the damage. He could see no personal belongings; but as he had not been there when his family had left, he could not tell how much they had taken with them. In the meantime Lara was saying:

'We must hurry up. It will be dark in a moment. We have no time to stand about thinking. If we are to stay here, the horse must go into the barn, the food into the porch and I'll fix this room up for ourselves. But I'm against it. We talked it all out before. It will be painful for you and therefore also for me. What was this room, your bedroom? No, the nursery. There's your son's cot. It would be too small for Katya. On the other hand, the windows are whole, there are no cracks in the walls or ceiling, and the stove is marvellous. I admired it last time I came. So if you insist on our staying here—though I am against it—I'll take off my coat and set to work at once. The first thing is to get the stove going, and to stoke and stoke and stoke; we'll need to keep it in day and night for at least three days. But what is it, my darling? You don't say a word.'

'In a moment. I'm all right. I'm sorry . . . No, really, you know, perhaps we'd better have a look at the Mikulitsins' house.'

They drove on.

5

The Mikulitsins' door was padlocked. Yury wrenched off the lock together with its screws and splinters of wood. Here again they rushed in hurriedly, going straight into the inner rooms without undressing, still in their coats, hats and felt boots.

They were immediately struck by the tidiness of certain parts of the house, particularly of Mikulitsin's study. Someone must have been living here until recently, but who? The Mikulitsins? But in that case, where had they gone to, and why had they put a padlock on the door instead of using their keys? Besides, if the Mikulitsins had been living in the house for long periods, wouldn't the whole of it have been tidy and not only some of the rooms? Everything spoke of an intruder, but who could it have been?—Neither Yury nor Lara was worried about the mystery or racked their brains to solve it. There were plenty of half-looted houses nowadays, and plenty of fugitives. 'Some White officer on the run,' they told each other. 'If he comes back we'll come to some arrangement. There's plenty of room for all of us.'

And once again, as so long before, Yury stood spellbound in the door of the study, so spacious and so austerely comfortable with its large, convenient table by the window, so conducive to patient, fruitful work.

Among the outhouses in the yard were the stables built on to the barn, but they were locked and Yury did not bother to break in, since, in any case, they might not be fit to use. The mare could spend the night in the barn, which opened easily. He unharnessed the horse, left it to cool down and brought it water from the well. The hay from the sledge which he had meant to give it had rubbed to dust under their feet. Luckily there was a little left in the loft over the barn.

They lay down without undressing, using their fur coats for blankets, and fell into a deep, sound, enjoyable sleep, like children who had been running and playing all day in the open air.

6

From the moment they got up, Yury kept glancing at the table which stood so temptingly by the window. His fingers itched for paper and pen. But he put off writing until the evening; he would wait until Lara and Katya had gone to bed. Until then he would have his hands full, even if no more than two of the rooms were to be made habitable.

In looking forward to the evening he had no important work in mind. It was merely that the passion to write possessed him.

He had to scribble something. For a beginning, he would put down old unwritten thoughts, just to get into trim. Later, he hoped, if he and Lara managed to stay on, there would be time for something new and more worth while.

'Are you busy? What are you doing?'

'Stoking and stoking. What is it?'

'I want a tub to wash the linen in.'

'We'll run out of logs if we go on heating at this rate. I must have a look in our old woodshed, there might be some left—who knows. If there is, I'll bring it over. I'll do that to-morrow.—A tub, you said. I'm sure I've seen one somewhere, I can't think where.'

'So have I, and I can't think where, either. It must have been somewhere it had no business to be, that's what makes one forget. Well, never mind. I'm heating up a pot of water for scrubbing the floors. What's left I'll use for my washing and Katya's. You might as well give me yours too. We'll have baths in the evening, when we've settled in, before we go to bed.'

'Thank you. I'll get my things now. I've moved all the heavy furniture away from the walls, as you wanted.'

'Good. I'll rinse the clothes in the washing-up basin as we can't find the tub. But it's greasy, I'll have to scrub it.'

'As soon as the stove is properly stoked up, I'll go through the rest of the cupboards. I keep finding more things in the desk and the chest of drawers—soap, matches, paper, pencils, pens, ink. And the lamp on the table is half-full of paraffin. I am sure the Mikulitsins didn't have any, it must come from somewhere else.'

'What luck! It's our mysterious lodger. Just like something out of Jules Verne. But here we are gossiping again, and my copper's boiling.'

They bustled and dashed about from room to room, their hands never still or empty for a moment, running into one another and stumbling over Katya, who was always under their feet. She mooned about, getting in the way of their work and sulking when they scolded her. She shivered and complained of the cold.

'These poor modern children,' thought Yury, 'victims of our gipsy life, wretched little fellow-vagabonds.' Aloud he said:

'Cheer up, my dear. You can't be cold—that's rubbish; the stove is red hot.'

'The stove may be feeling warm but I'm cold.'

'Well then, you'll have to be patient till this evening. I'll get a huge blaze going and you heard Mama say she'll give you a hot bath. And now you play with these, catch.' He took all Liberius's old toys out of the chilly lumber room and dumped them on the floor, some whole, some broken, bricks and cubes, trains and engines, boards with squares and pictures or numbers on them for games with dice and counters.

'What can you be thinking of, Yury Andreyevich!' Katya protested like a grown-up. 'They aren't mine. And they are for a baby. I'm too big.'

But the next moment she had made herself comfortable in the middle of the rug and all the toys had turned into bricks for a house for Nina, the doll she had brought with her from town It was a much more sensible and settled home than any of the temporary lodgings in other people's houses in which she had spent most of her life.

Lara watched her from the kitchen. 'Look at that instinct for domesticity. It just shows, nothing can destroy the longing for home and for order. Children are more honest, they aren't frightened of the truth, but we are so afraid of seeming to be behind the times that we are ready to betray what is most dear to us, and praise what repels us, and say yes to what we don't understand.'

'Here's the tub,' said Yury, coming in out of the dark porch. 'It certainly wasn't in its place. It was standing under the leak in the ceiling. I suppose it's been there since last autumn.'

7

For dinner, Lara, who had started on the provisions they had brought and had cooked enough for three days, served an unheard-of feast of potato soup and roast mutton and potatoes. Katya ate till she could eat no more, giggling and getting more and more naughty, and afterwards, warm and with her tummy full, she curled up in her mother's shawl on the sofa and went to sleep.

Lara, hot and tired from the oven, and almost as sleepy as her daughter, was pleased with the success of her cooking. She was in no hurry to clear up and sat down to have a rest. When she was sure that Katya was asleep she sprawled over the table with her head on her fist and said:

'I'd slave and be happy if only I knew it was getting us somewhere, if it wasn't all for nothing. You'll have to keep reminding me that we came here to be together. Because, strictly speaking, if you look at it honestly, what are we doing, what is all this? We've raided someone else's house, we've broken in and made ourselves at home, and now we bustle round like mad so as not to see that this isn't life, but a stage set—it isn't real, it's all "pretend", as children say, a child's game, enough to make a cat laugh.'

'But, darling, isn't it you who insisted on our coming? Don't you remember how long I held out against it?'

'Certainly I did. I don't deny it. So now I'm at fault! It's all right for you to think twice and hesitate, but I have to be logical and consistent all the time. You come in, you see your child's cot and you nearly faint. That's your right, but I'm not allowed to be worried, to be afraid for Katya, to think about the future, everything has to give way before my love for you.'

'Lara, my darling! Pull yourself together. Think. It's not too late to go back on your decision. I was the first to tell you to take Komarovsky's plan more seriously. We have a horse. If you like, we'll go straight back to Yuryatin tomorrow. Komarovsky is still there, we saw him—and incidentally I don't think he saw us. I'm sure we'll still find him.'

'I've hardly said a word and you're annoyed. But tell me, am I so wrong? We might just as well have stayed in Yuryatin if we weren't going to hide better than this. If we really meant to save ourselves we should have had a sensible plan, properly thought out, and that after all is what Komarovsky offered us. Disgusting as he is, he isn't a fool, he's well informed and practical. We are in greater danger here than anywhere else. Just think!—alone on a boundless, wind-swept plain! If we were snowed under in the night we couldn't dig ourselves out in the morning! Or suppose our fairy godmother, our mysterious visitor, turns out to be a bandit and comes to slit our throats! Have you a gun at least? I thought not! You see? What terrifies me is your thoughtlessness, and you've infected me with it as well. I simply can't think straight.'

'But what do you want? What do you want me to do now?'

'I don't know myself what to say. You must always keep me under your thumb. You must keep reminding me that I'm your loving slave and that it's not my business to think or argue. I'll tell you how I see it. Your Tonya and my Pasha are a thousand times better than we are, but that isn't the point. The point is that the gift of love is like any other gift. However great it is it needs a blessing to express itself. You and I, it's as though we had been taught to love in heaven and sent down to earth together to see if we had learned what we were taught. What we have together is a supreme harmony—no limits, no degrees, everything is of equal value, everything gives joy, everything has become spirit. But in this wild tenderness which lies in wait for us at every moment there is something childishly untamed, forbidden. It's a destructive wilfulness hostile to domestic peace. It's my duty to be afraid of it and to distrust it.'

She threw her arms round his neck, struggling with her tears.

'Don't you see, we are not in the same position? You were given wings to fly above the clouds, but I'm a woman, mine are given me to stay close to the ground and to shelter my young.'

What she said pleased him immensely but he did not show it for fear of appearing sentimental.

'It's quite true that there is something false and strained about this camp life we lead. You are perfectly right. But it isn't we who invented it. This frantic dashing about from pillar to post is what is happening to everyone, it's in the spirit of the times.

'I've been thinking about it myself all day. I should like to do everything possible to stay here for some time. I can't tell you how I'm longing to get back to work. I don't mean farming. That's what we were doing here before; we took it on as a family and we succeeded. But I wouldn't have the strength to do it again. I have something else in mind.

'Things are gradually settling down. Perhaps one day they'll start publishing books again.

'This is what I was thinking. Couldn't we come to an arrangement with Samdevyatov—we'd have to give him profitable terms, of course —so that he should keep us here for six months at his expense on condition that I spend this time writing a book, say a textbook on medicine, or something literary, perhaps a collection of poems? Or I might translate some famous classical book from a foreign language. I'm good at languages. I saw an advertisement the other day; there's a publisher in Petersburg who is doing nothing but translations. I'm pretty sure this sort of work will have a money value. I'd be very happy doing something of that kind.'

'I am glad you reminded me. I was also thinking of something like that to-day. But I have no faith in our future here. On the contrary, I have a presentiment that we'll soon be swept away, somewhere further still. But so long as we have this breathing space, I want to ask you a favour. Will you give up a few hours in the next few evenings, and put down all the poems you have recited to me at different times? Half of them you've lost and the rest you've never written down and I am afraid you'll forget them and they'll be lost too, as you say has often happened to you before.'

8

At the end of the day they had a good wash in plenty of hot water and Lara bathed Katya. Feeling blissfully clean Yury sat down at the table before the window, his back to the room where Lara, wrapped in her bath towel and smelling of soap, her hair twisted up into a turban with another Turkish towel, was putting Katya to bed and tucking her up. Enjoying the foretaste of concentrated work, he took in all that was going on around him with a happy, relaxed attentiveness.

It was one in the morning when Lara, who had been pretending, finally went to sleep. Her nightdress and Katya's, like the freshly washed and ironed linen on the beds, shone with lace and cleanliness. Even in those days Lara managed somehow to get starch.

The stillness which surrounded Yury breathed with happiness and life. The lamplight fell softly yellow on the white sheets of paper and gilded the surface of the ink in the inkwell. Outside, the frosty winter night was pale blue. To see it better, Yury stepped into the cold dark room next door and looked out of the window. The light of the full moon bound the snowy plain like white of egg or stiffened whitewash. The splendour of the frosty night was inexpressible. Yury's heart was at peace. He came back into the warm, well-lit room and began to write.

Careful to convey the living movement of his hand in his flowing writing, so that even outwardly it should not lose expression and grow numb and soulless, he set down, gradually improving them and moving further and further away from the original as he made copy after copy, the poems which he remembered best and which had taken the most definite shape in his mind, 'Christmas Star', 'Winter Night' and a number of others close to them in *genre* which later were to be forgotten, lost and never found by anyone.

From these old, completed poems he went on to others which he had begun and left unfinished, getting into their tone of voice and sketching the sequels, though without the slightest hope of finishing them now. Finally he got into his stride and, carried away, he started on a new poem.

After two or three stanzas and several images by which he was himself astonished, his work took possession of him and he experienced the approach of what is called inspiration. At such moments the correlation of the forces controlling the artist is, as it were, stood on its head. The ascendancy is no longer with the artist or the state of mind which he is trying to express, but with language, his instrument of expression. Language, the home and dwelling of beauty and meaning, itself begins to think and speak for man and turns wholly into music, not in the sense of outward, audible sounds but by virtue of the power and momentum of its inward flow. Then, like the current of a mighty river polishing stones and turning wheels by its very movement, the flow of speech creates in passing, by the force of its own laws, rhyme and rhythm and countless other forms and formations, still more important and until now undiscovered, unconsidered and unnamed.

At such moments Yury felt that the main part of his work was not being done by him but by something which was above him and controlling him: the thought and poetry of the world as it was at that moment and as it would be in the future. He was controlled by the next step it was to take in the order of its historical development; and he felt himself to be only the pretext and the pivot setting it in motion.

This feeling relieved him for a time of self-reproach, of dissatisfaction with himself, of the sense of his own nothingness. He looked up, he looked around him.

He saw the two sleeping heads on their snow-white pillows. The purity of their features, and of the clean linen and the clean rooms, and of the night, the snow, the stars, the moon, surged through his heart in a single wave of meaning, and roused in him a joyful sense of the triumphant purity of being.

'Lord! Lord!' he whispered, 'and all this is for me? Why hast Thou given me so much? Why hast Thou admitted me to Thy presence, why allowed me to stray into Thy world, among Thy treasures, under Thy stars and to the feet of my luckless, reckless, uncomplaining love?'

At three in the morning Yury looked up from his papers. He came back from his remote, selfless concentration, home to reality and to himself, happy, strong, peaceful. All at once the stillness of the open country stretching into the distance outside the window was broken by a mournful, dismal sound.

He went into the unlit room next door, but while he had been working the window had frosted over. He dragged away the roll of carpet which had been pushed against the front door to stop the draught, threw his coat over his shoulders and went out.

He was dazzled by the white flame playing on the shadowless, moonlit snow and could at first see nothing. Then the long, whimpering, deep-bellied baying sounded again, muffled by the distance, and he noticed four long shadows, no thicker than pencil strokes, on the edge of the snow-field just beyond the gully.

The wolves stood in a row, their heads raised and their muzzles pointing towards the house, baying at the moon or at its silver reflection on the windows. But scarcely had Yury realised that they were wolves when they turned and trotted off like dogs, almost as if they could read his thoughts. He lost sight of them before he noticed the direction in which they had vanished.

'That's the last straw!' he thought. 'Is their lair quite close? Perhaps in the gully. And Samdevyatov's horse is in the barn! They must have scented it.'

He decided not to upset Lara for the time being by telling her. Going back, he shut all the doors between the cold rooms and the heated part of the house, pushed rugs and clothes against the cracks to keep out the draughts, and went back to his desk. The lamplight was bright and welcoming as before. But he was no longer in the mood to write. He couldn't settle down. He could think of nothing but wolves and of looming dangers and complications of every kind. Besides, he was tired.

Lara woke up. 'Still at work, my love?' she whispered in a voice heavy with sleep. 'Burning and shining like a candle in the night. Come and sit beside me for a moment. I'll tell you my dream.'

He put out the light.

9

Another day of quiet madness went by. They had found a toboggan in the house and Katya, bundled up in her coat, glided, shrieking with laughter, down the unswept paths from the snow-chute Yury had made for her by packing the snow tight with his spade and pouring water to cover it with ice. Endlessly, she climbed back to the top of the mound, pulling the toboggan by a string, her smile never leaving her face.

It was freezing; the frost was hardening, but it was sunny. The snow was yellow at noon, with orange seeping like an aftertaste into its honey-colour at sunset.

All the washing and bathing which Lara had done the day before had made the house damp. The steam had darkened the windows with crumbly rime and had streaked the wallpaper. The rooms were dark and uncosy. Yury carried logs and water and went on with his inspection of the house, making more and more discoveries, as well as helping Lara with her endless housework.

In the rush of some task or other their hands would meet and join and then they set down whatever they were carrying, weak and giddy, all thoughts driven from their heads. And the moments went by until it was late and, horrified, they both remembered that Katya had been left on her own much too long or that the horse was unwatered and unfed, and rushed off, conscience-stricken, to make up for lost time and make good what they had left undone.

Yury had not slept enough; there was a pleasant haze in his head, like tipsiness, and he ached all over with a gentle weakness. He waited impatiently for the evening, to go back to his interrupted writing.

Half the groundwork was being done for him by the drowsiness which filled him and veiled his surroundings and his thoughts. The vagueness in which everything was bathed was a stage on the way to the precision of the final form. Like the confusion of a first rough draft, the dragging emptiness of the day was a necessary preparation for the night.

His weary idleness left nothing untouched or untransformed. Everything underwent a change and assumed a different aspect.

Yury felt that his dream of remaining in Varykino would not come true, that the hour of his parting with Lara was at hand; he would inevitably lose her and with her the will to live and perhaps life itself. He was sick at heart, yet his greatest torment was his impatience for the night, his longing so to express his anguish that others should weep.

The wolves he had been remembering all day long were no longer wolves on the snowy plain under the moon: they had become a theme, they represented the hostile force which intended his and Lara's destruction and was resolved to drive them from Varykino.

The thought of this hostility developed in him, so that by the evening it loomed like a prehistoric beast or dragon whose tracks had been discovered in the Shutma and who thirsted for Yury's blood and lusted after Lara.

The evening came on and Yury lit the lamp on the table. Lara and Katya went to bed early.

What he had written the night before fell into two parts. Clean copies—improved versions of earlier poems—were set out in his best copperplate hand. New work was written in an illegible scrawl full of gaps and abbreviations.

In deciphering these scribbles he went through the usual disappointments. Last night these rough passages had astonished him and moved him to tears by certain unexpectedly successful lines. Now, on re-reading these very lines, he was saddened to find that they were strained and glaringly far-fetched.

It had been the dream of his life to write with an originality so covert, so discreet, as to be outwardly unrecognisable in its disguise of current, customary forms of speech. All his life he had struggled after a language so reserved, so unpretentious as to enable the reader or the hearer to master the content without noticing the means by which it reached him. All his life he had striven to achieve an unnoticeable style, and had been appalled to find how far he still remained from his ideal.

Last night he had tried to convey, by means so simple as to be almost faltering and bordering on the intimacy of a lullaby, his feeling of mingled love and anguish, fear and courage, in such a way that it should speak for itself, almost independently of the words.

Looking over these rough sketches now, he found that they needed a connecting theme to give unity to the lines, which were incoherent for lack of it. He crossed out what he had written and began to write down the legend of St. George and the Dragon in the same lyrical form. He started with a broad, spacious pentameter, but its harmony, derived from the metre itself and independent of the sense, annoyed him by its slick, humdrum sing-song. He gave up the pompous rhythm and the caesura and cut down the lines to four beats, as you cut out useless words in prose. The task was now more difficult but more attractive. The writing was livelier but still too verbose. He forced himself to still shorter lines. Now the words were crammed in their tetrameters and Yury felt wide awake, roused, excited; the right words to fill the short lines came, prompted by the measure. Things hardly named assumed form by suggestion. He heard the horse's hooves ringing on the surface of the poem as you hear the trotting of a horse in one of Chopin's Ballades. St. George was galloping over the boundless spaces of the steppe. He could watch him growing smaller in the distance. He wrote in a feverish hurry, scarcely able to keep up with the words as they poured out, always to the point and of themselves tumbling into place.

He had not noticed that Lara had got out of bed and come across to the table. She seemed very thin in her long nightdress and taller than she really was. He started with surprise when she stood beside him, pale, frightened, stretching out her hand and whispering:

'Do you hear? A dog howling. Even two of them, I think. Oh, how terrible! It's a very bad omen. We'll bear it somehow till the morning and then we'll go, we'll go! I won't stay here a moment longer.'

An hour later, after much persuasion, she quietened down and fell asleep. Yury went outside. The wolves were nearer than the night before. They vanished even more swiftly and again before he could make out in which direction they had made off. They had stood in a huddle and he had not had time to count them, but it seemed to him that there were more of them.

10

It was the thirteenth day of their stay at Varykino. There was nothing new or different about it. The wolves had again howled in the night

—they had vanished in the middle of the week, but had come back. Lara, still mistaking them for dogs, again determined to leave, afraid of the omen. A hard-working woman unused to pouring out her feelings all day long or to the luxury of extravagant tenderness, her calm, balanced moods alternated with anxious fits of restlessness.

They had gone over the same scene again and again, so that when that morning, in the second week of their stay, Lara had begun to pack for the return journey, it seemed as if the week and a half since their arrival had never been.

It was again damp and dark in the rooms, this time because the weather was overcast. The frost was less keen and, judging from the look of the dark, low clouds, it would snow at any moment. Yury was exhausted by the physical and mental strain of too many sleepless nights. His legs were weak and his thoughts were in a muddle; shivering with cold and rubbing his hands, he walked about from room to room, waiting to see what Lara would decide and what he would have to do in consequence.

She did not know herself. Just then she would have given anything to exchange their chaotic freedom for a daily round, however strenuous but laid down once and for all, for work and obligations, so that they could live a decent, honest, sensible life.

She began her day as usual by doing the beds, sweeping, dusting and making breakfast. Then she started to pack and asked Yury to harness the horse; she had firmly resolved to go.

Yury did not argue. It was madness to return to town, where the wave of arrests must have reached its peak, but it was equally madness to remain, alone and unarmed, in this winter desert with its own hazards.

Besides, there was hardly an armful of hay left in the barn or the sheds. Of course, had it been possible to settle down for a long stay, Yury would have travelled round the district looking for new ways of getting food and fodder, but it wasn't worth it for a few uncertain days. He gave up the thought and went to harness the horse.

He wasn't good at it—Samdevyatov had taught him how to do it but he kept forgetting—still, he managed it, though clumsily. He strapped the yoke to the shafts, wound the slack and knotted the end of the metal-studded strap round one of them, then, one leg braced against the horse's flank, pulled the two ends of the stiff collar tight and fastened them. At last he led the horse to the porch, tethered it and went inside to call Lara.

She and Katya had their coats on and everything was packed, but Lara was in great distress. Wringing her hands and on the verge of tears, she begged him to sit down a moment and, throwing herself into a chair and getting up again, spoke incoherently in a high-pitched plaintive sing-song, stumbling over her words and interrupting herself repeatedly to ask him if he didn't agree with her:

'I can't help it, I don't know how it's happened, but you can see for yourself, we can't possibly go now, so late, it will be dark soon, we'll be caught in the darkness in your terrible wood. Don't you think so? I'll do whatever you tell me to, but I simply can't make up my mind to go—something tells me not to, but do whatever you think best. Why don't you say something? We've wasted half the day, goodness knows how. To-morrow we'll be more sensible. How would it be if we stayed one more night? And to-morrow we'll get up early and start at first light, at six or seven. What do you think? You'll light the stove and write one more evening and we'll have one more night here—wouldn't that be lovely, wouldn't that be wonderful? O God, have I done something wrong again?'

'You're exaggerating. Dusk is a long way off, it's quite early. But have it your way. We'll stay. Only calm yourself, don't be so upset. Come now, let's take off our coats and unpack. And Katya says she's hungry, we'll have something to eat. You are quite right, there would have been no point in going so suddenly, with so little preparation. But don't be so upset and don't cry. I'll light the stove in a moment. But before I do that I might as well take the sleigh, as it's at the door, and fetch what's left of the logs in our old woodshed, we've run out. Don't cry now. I'll be back soon.'

11

Several sets of sleigh tracks led up to the woodshed of the Zhivagos' house; Yury had made them on his earlier journeys and the snow over the threshold was trampled and littered from his last visit two days before.

The sky, which had been cloudy since the morning, had cleared. It was colder again. The old park, stretching into the distance, surrounded the house and the yard, and the grounds came right up to the barn as if to have a look at Yury and remind him of something. The snow was deep that winter. It came up over the threshold so that the lintel seemed lower and the shed hunchbacked. Snow overhung the roof almost touching Yury's head, like the brim of a gigantic mushroom hat. Just above it, as if spiked into the snow, stood the new moon, shining with a grey blaze down the cutting edge of its crescent.

So dark and sad was it in Yury's heart that, although it was early in the afternoon and full daylight, he felt as if he were standing late at night in some dark forest of his life, and the new moon, shining almost at eye level, was an omen of separation and an image of solitude.

He was so tired that he could hardly stand. He threw the logs out of the doorway on to the sledge in smaller armfuls than usual; the touch of the icy wood sticky with snow hurt him through his gloves. The work did not make him feel any warmer. Something within him had broken and come to a standstill. He cursed his luckless fate and prayed for Lara, that God might spare the life of the lovely, sad, humble and simple-hearted woman he loved. And the new moon stood over the barn blazing without warmth and shining without giving light.

The mare turned its head in the direction of the Mikulitsins' house and whinnied, at first softly, timidly, then louder, with assurance.

'What's that for?' Yury wondered. 'Is she pleased or frightened? Not frightened, horses don't neigh out of fear, and she wouldn't be such a fool as to signal to the wolves if she had scented them. She must be looking forward to going home.—Hold on a moment, we'll soon be off.'

He added chips for kindling to the logs, and strips of bark curled like boot leather, covered the load with sacking, lashed it to the sleigh with a rope and turned back, walking at the horse's head.

The mare neighed again, this time in answer to another horse neighing in the distance. 'What can that be? Is it possible that Varykino is not as deserted as we thought?' It never occurred to him that they had guests or that the neighing came from in front of Mikulitsin's house. He was taking the sleigh round the back of the farm buildings and the house was hidden from him by snowy folds of land.

Taking his time—why should he hurry?—he stacked the wood and, unhitching the mare, left the sleigh in the barn. Then he took the mare to the stables, put her in the far stall where there was less draught and stuffed the few remaining handfuls of hay into the rack of the manger.

He felt uneasy as he walked home. In front of the porch stood a roomy peasant sleigh with a sleek black foal harnessed to it, and walking up and down beside it was an equally sleek, plump stranger who gave the horse an occasional slap and had a look at its fetlocks.

There were voices coming from the house. Neither wishing to eavesdrop nor being close enough to hear more than an occasional word, Yury, nevertheless, involuntarily stopped dead and listened. He recognised the voice of Komarovsky talking to Lara and Katya. They were apparently in the first room near the door. They were arguing, and, judging from the sound of her voice, Lara was upset and crying, now violently contradicting and now agreeing with him.

Something made Yury feel that just then Komarovsky was speaking about him, saying something to the effect that he should not be trusted ('serving two masters' Yury thought he heard), that it was impossible to tell if he were more attached to Lara or his family, that Lara must not rely on him because if she did she would be 'running with the hare and hunting with the hounds' and would 'fall between two stools'. Yury went in.

As he had thought, they were in the first room on the right, Komarovsky in a fur coat down to his ankles, Lara holding Katya by her coat collar, trying to fasten it but not finding the hooks and shouting at her not to wriggle, and Katya protesting: 'Gently, Mama, you'll choke me.' They were all three standing in their outdoor clothes, ready to leave. When Yury came in, Lara and Komarovsky rushed to meet him, speaking together:

'Where have you been all this time? We need you so badly!'

'How are you, Yury Andreyevich? As you see, in spite of the rude things we said to each other last time, I'm with you once again, though you didn't invite me.'

Yury said how-do-you-do.

'Where on earth have you been?' Lara asked again. 'Now listen to what he says and decide quickly for both of us. There's no time to waste. We must be quick.'

'But why are we all standing? Sit down, Victor Ippolitovich. How do you mean, darling, where have I been? You know I went to fetch the wood, and afterwards I saw to the horse. Victor Ippolitovich, do sit down, please.'

'Well, aren't you amazed to see him? How is it you don't look surprised? There we were, regretting that he had gone away and that we hadn't jumped at his offer, and now here he is, right under your very eyes, and you don't even look surprised! But what is even more astonishing is what he has to tell us now.—Tell him, Victor Ippolitovich.'

'I don't know what Larissa Fyodorovna has in mind. One thing I must explain is this: I deliberately spread the rumour that I had left, but I stayed on to give you and Larissa Fyodorovna more time to think over what we had discussed, and perhaps come to a less rash decision.'

'But we can't put it off any longer,' broke in Lara. 'Now is the perfect time to leave. And to-morrow morning . . . But let Victor Ippolitovich tell you himself.'

'One moment, Lara dear. Why should we all stand about in our coats? Let's take them off and sit down. After all, these are serious things we have to talk about, we can't settle them in a minute. I am afraid, Victor Ippolitovich, our discussion has touched on something personal; it would be ludicrous and embarrassing to go into it. But the fact is that while I have never considered going with you, Lara's case is different. On the rare occasions when our anxieties were not the same and we remembered that we were not one person but two, I have always told her that she ought to give your suggestion more thought. And in fact, she has never stopped thinking about it; she has come back to it again and again.'

'But only on condition that you come with us,' Lara intervened.

'It is as difficult for you as it is for me to think of our being separated, but perhaps we ought to put our feelings aside and make this sacrifice. Because there's no question of my going.'

'But you haven't heard anything yet, you don't know . . . Listen to what Victor Ippolitovich says . . . To-morrow morning—Victor Ippolitovich.'

'Larissa Fyodorovna is evidently thinking of the news which I have already told her. In the sidings at Yuryatin, an official train of the Far Eastern Government is standing under steam. It arrived yesterday from Moscow and is leaving to-morrow for the East. It belongs to our Ministry of Communications. Half the carriages are Wagons-Lits.

'I have to go by this train. Several seats have been put at my disposal for my assistants. We could travel in great comfort. There won't ever be another chance like this again. I realise that you are not in the habit of speaking lightly, you are not the man to go back on your decisions and you have made up your mind not to go with us. But, all the same, shouldn't you reconsider it for Larissa Fyodorovna's sake? You heard her say that she won't go without you. Come with us, if not to Vladisvostok, then at least as far as Yuryatin —and there we shall see.—Only we must really hurry up—there is not a moment to lose. I have a coachman with me—I don't drive myself—and there isn't room for five of us in my sleigh. But I understand you have Samdevyatov's horse—didn't you say you had gone with it to fetch the logs? Is it still harnessed?'

'No, I've unharnessed it.'

'Well, then, harness it again as quickly as you possibly can. My coachman will help you . . . Though, come to think of it, why trouble—let's forget about your sleigh, we'll manage with mine, we'll squeeze in somehow. Only let's hurry, for heaven's sake. You only need to pack the most essential things for the journey—whatever comes to hand first. There's no time to fuss with packing when it's a question of a child's life.'

'I don't understand you, Victor Ippolitovich. You talk as if I had agreed to come. Go and good luck to you, and let Lara go with you if she wishes. You needn't worry about the house. I'll clean it up and lock it after you've gone.'

'What are you talking about, Yura? What's all this nonsense? You don't even believe it yourself. "If Lara wishes" indeed! As if you didn't know perfectly well that I shan't go without you and I shan't make any decision on my own. So what's all this pompous stuff about your locking up the house?'

'So you are quite adamant?' said Komarovsky. 'In that case, with Larissa Fyodorovna's permission, I should like to have a couple of words with you, if possible alone.'

'Certainly. If it's so important, we can go into the kitchen. You don't mind, darling?'

12

'Strelnikov has been captured, condemned to death and shot.'

'How ghastly! Are you really sure?'

'It's what I've been told, and I am convinced it's true.'

'Don't tell Lara. She'll go out of her mind.'

'Of course I won't. That's why I asked to speak to you alone. Now that this has happened, she and Katya are in imminent danger. You must help me to save them. Are you quite sure you won't go with us?'

'Quite sure. I've told you already.'

'But she won't go without you. I simply don't know what to do. You'll have to help me in a different way. You'll have to pretend, let her think that you might be willing to change your mind, look as if you might allow yourself to be persuaded. I can't see her saying good-bye and leaving you, either here, or at the station at Yuryatin. We'll have to make her think that you are coming after all, if not now, then later, when I've arranged another opportunity for you to travel. You'll have to pretend that you'll be willing to take it. You'll have to convince her of this even if you have to perjure yourself.— Though this is no empty offer on my part—I swear to you on my

401

honour that at the first sign you give me I'll get you out to the East, and I'll arrange for you to go on from there anywhere you like.— But Larissa Fyodorovna must believe that you are at least coming to see us off. You'll simply have to make her believe that. For instance, you might pretend that you are going to get your sleigh ready and urge us to start at once, without waiting for you, not to waste any time—you'll say you'll catch us up as soon as you are ready.'

'I am so appalled by the news about Strelnikov that I haven't really taken in all you have said. But you are right. According to our present-day logic, once they have settled accounts with Strelnikov, Lara's and Katya's lives are also threatened. One or other of us is certain to be arrested, so we'll be parted anyway. At that rate it might indeed be best that you should separate us, and take them away, as far away as possible. I am saying this but it doesn't make much difference, things are already happening your way. Probably in the end I'll break down and crawl to you and beg you for Lara, and life, and safety, and a sea passage to my family and be happy to receive it all at your hands. But give me time to sort it out. I am completely overwhelmed by what you've told me. I am crushed and dazed and I can't think or reason properly. It may be that by giving in to you I am making a disastrous, irreparable mistake which will horrify me all my life. But all I can do now is to agree blindly and obey you as if I had no will of my own . . . Very well, then, for her sake I'll go out now and tell her that I'll get the sleigh ready and catch up with you, but in fact I shall stay behind . . . There's one thing, though.—How can you go now, when it will soon be dark? The road runs through woods, and there are wolves, take care . . .'

'I know. Don't worry. I've got a gun and a revolver. I've brought a drop of spirits too, by the way, to keep the cold out. Would you like some?—I've got plenty.'

13

'What have I done? What have I done? I've given her up, re-nounced her, given her away. I must run after them. Lara! Lara!

'They can't hear. The wind is against me and they are probably talking at the tops of their voices. She has every reason to feel happy, reassured. She has no idea of the trick I've played on her.

'She is thinking, it's wonderful that things have gone so well, they couldn't be better. Her absurd, obstinate Yura has relented at last, thank heavens; we are going to a nice, safe place, where people are more sensible than we are, where you can be sure of law and order. Suppose even, just to be awkward, he doesn't come on to-morrow's train, Komarovsky will send another to fetch him, and he'll join us in no time at all. And at the moment, of course, he's in the stables, hurrying, excited, fumbling with the harness, and he'll rush after us full tilt and catch up with us before we get into the forest.

'That's what she must be thinking. And we didn't even say good-bye properly, I just waved to her and turned back, trying to swallow my pain as if it were a piece of apple stuck in my throat, choking me.'

He stood in the porch, his coat over one shoulder. With his free hand he was clutching the neck of the slender wooden pillar just under the roof as if he meant to strangle it. His whole attention was concentrated on a point in the distance. There a short stretch of the road could be seen climbing uphill, bordered by a few sparse birches. The low rays of the setting sun fell on this open space, and there the sleigh, now hidden in a shallow dip, would become visible at any moment.

'Good-bye, good-bye,' Yury said over and over again mindlessly, as he waited for it, driving the silent words out of his breast into the frosty evening air. 'Good-bye, my only love, my love for ever lost.'

'They're coming, they're coming,' he whispered through dry, blenched lips, as the sleigh shot like an arrow out of the dip, swept past the birches one after another, gradually slowing down, and—O joy!—stopped at the last tree.

His heart thumped with such a wild excitement that his legs were giving way and he felt weak and faint, his whole body soft as cloth like the coat slipping from his shoulder. 'O God, is it Thy will to give her back to me? What can have happened? What is going on out there near the sunset? What can be the meaning of it? Why are they standing still? No. It's finished. They've moved. They're off. She must have stopped for a last look at the house. Or perhaps to make sure that I had left? That I was chasing after them? They've gone.'

With luck, if the sun didn't go down first (he wouldn't see them in the dark), they would flash past once again, for the last time, on the other side of the ravine, across the field where the wolves had howled two nights before.

And now this moment also had come and gone. The dark-red

sun still hung, round as a ball, above the blue snowdrifts on the skyline, and the snowy plain greedily sucked in its juicy pineapple light,
when the sleigh swept into sight and vanished. 'Good-bye, Lara, until
we meet in the next world, good-bye, my love, my inexhaustible, everlasting joy. I'll never see you again, I'll never, never see you again.'

It was getting dark. Swiftly the bronze-red patches of sunset on
the snow faded and went out. The soft, ashy distance filled with lilac
dusk turning to deep mauve, and its smoky haze smudged the fine
tracery of the roadside birches lightly hand-drawn on the pink sky,
pale as though it had suddenly grown shallow.

Grief had sharpened Yury's vision and quickened his perception
a hundredfold. The very air surrounding him seemed unique. The
evening breathed compassion like a friendly witness of all that had
befallen him. As if there had never been such a dusk before and
evening were falling now for the first time in order to console him
in his loneliness and bereavement. As if the valley were not always
girded by woods growing on the surrounding hills and facing away
from the horizon, but the trees had only taken up their places now,
rising out of the ground on purpose to offer their condolences.

He almost waved away the tangible beauty of the hour like a
crowd of persistent friends, almost said to the lingering afterglow:
'Thank you, thank you, I'll be all right.'

Still standing on the verandah, he turned his face to the closed
door, his back to the world. 'My bright sun has set': something was
repeating this inside him, as if to learn it by heart. He had not the
strength to say these words out loud.

He went into the house. A double monologue was going on in
his mind, two different kinds of monologue, the one dry and business-
like, the other, addressed to Lara, like a river in flood.

'Now I'll go to Moscow,' ran his thoughts. 'The first job is to
survive. Not let insomnia get the better of me. Not go to bed at
all. Work all through the night till I drop. Yes, and another thing,
light the stove in the bedroom at once, not to freeze to-night.'

But there was also another inward conversation. 'I'll stay with
you a little, my unforgettable delight, for as long as my arms and my
hands and my lips remember you. I'll weep for you so that my
lament will be lasting and worthy of you. I'll write your memory
into an image of infinite pain and grief. I'll stay here till this is done,
then I too will go. This is how I'll trace your image. I'll trace it
on paper as the sea, after a fearful storm has churned it up to its
foundations, leaves the traces of the strongest, furthest-reaching wave
on the shore. Seaweed, shells, pumice, all the lightest debris, all

those things of least weight which it could lift from its bed, are cast up in a broken line on the sand. This line endlessly stretching into the distance is the tide's high-water mark. This is how you were cast up in my life, my love, my pride, this is how I'll write of you.'

He came in, locked the door behind him and took off his coat. When he came into the bedroom which Lara had tidied up so well and so carefully that morning, and which her hurried packing had again turned inside out, when he saw the untidy bed and the things thrown about in disorder on the chairs and the floor, he knelt down like a child, leaned his breast against the hard edge of the bedstead, buried his head in the bedclothes and wept freely and bitterly as children do. But not for long. Soon he got up, hastily dried his face, looked round him with tired, absent-minded surprise, got out the bottle of vodka Komarovsky had left, drew the cork, poured half a glassful, added water and snow, and with a relish almost equal in strength to the hopelessness of the tears he had shed, drank long, greedy gulps.

14

Something was going on in Yury that made no sense. He was going out of his mind. Never had his way of life been so strange. He neglected the house, he stopped looking after himself, he turned night into day and lost count of the time which had gone by since Lara had left.

He drank vodka and he wrote about Lara, but the more he crossed out and rewrote what he had written, the more did the Lara of his poems and notebooks grow away from her living prototype, from the Lara who was Katya's mother, the Lara who was away on a journey with her daughter.

The reason for this correcting and rewriting was his search for strength and exactness of expression, but it also corresponded to the promptings of an inward reticence which forbade him to expose his personal experiences and the real events in his past with too much freedom, lest he should offend or wound those who had directly taken part in them. As a result, the steaming heat of reality was driven out of his poems and so far from their becoming morbid and devitalised, there appeared in them a broad peace of reconciliation which lifted the particular to the level of the universal and accessible to all. This was not a goal which he was consciously striving for; it came of its own accord as a consolation, like a message sent to him by Lara from her travels, like a distant greeting from her, like her image in a dream or the touch of her hand on his forehead, and he rejoiced at this ennobling of his verse.

At the same time as working on his lament for Lara, he was also adding to the notes he had been scribbling at intervals over the years about nature, daily life and various other things. As had always happened to him when he was writing, a host of thoughts about the life of the individual and of society darted into his mind.

He reflected again that he thought of history, of what is called the course of history, not in the accepted way, but in the form of images taken from the vegetable kingdom. In winter, under the snow, the bare branches of a deciduous wood are thin and poor, like the hairs on an old man's wart. But in only a few days in spring the forest is transformed, it reaches the clouds and you can hide or lose yourself in its leafy maze. During this transformation the forest moves with a speed greater than that of animals, for animals do not grow as fast as plants; yet this movement cannot be observed. The forest does not change its place, we cannot lie in wait for it and catch it in the act of moving. However much we look at it we see it as motionless. And such also is the immobility to our eyes of the eternally growing, ceaselessly changing life of society, of history moving as invisibly in its incessant transformations as the forest in spring.

Tolstoy thought of it in just this way but did not say it in so many words. While denying that history was set in motion by Napoleon or any other ruler or general he did not carry his reasoning to its conclusion. History is not made by anyone. You cannot make history; nor can you see history, any more than you can watch the grass growing. Wars and revolutions, kings and Robespierres, are history's organic agents, its yeast. But revolutions are made by fanatical men of action with one-track minds, men who are narrow-minded to the point of genius. They overturn the old order in a few hours or days; the whole upheaval takes a few weeks or at most years, but for decades thereafter, for centuries, the spirit of narrowness which led to the upheaval is worshipped as holy.

Mourning for Lara, he also mourned that distant summer in Melyuzeyevo when the revolution had been a god come down to earth from heaven, the god of that summer when everyone had gone mad in his own way, and when everyone's life existed in its own right and not as an illustration to a thesis in support of higher policy.

As he scribbled his odds and ends, he made a note reaffirming his belief that art always serves beauty, and beauty is the joy of possessing form, and form is the key to organic life since no living thing can exist without it, so that every work of art, including tragedy, witnesses to the joy of existence. And his own ideas and notes also brought him joy, a joy so tragic and filled with tears that it made his head ache and wore him out.

Samdevyatov came to see him. He too brought him vodka and told him of how Antipova and her daughter had left with Komarovsky. He came by trolley along the railway track, and he scolded Yury for not looking properly after the horse and took it back, refusing to leave it for three or four more days as Yury wished him to, but promising to come back for him within the week, and take him away from Varykino for good.

Sometimes, after losing himself in his work, Yury suddenly remembered Lara as vividly as if she were before him, and broke down from tenderness and the sharpness of his loss. As in his childhood, when after his mother's death he thought he heard her voice among the bird calls in the summer magnificence of Kologrivov's garden, so now his hearing, accustomed to Lara's voice and expecting it as part of his life, played tricks on him and he heard her calling, 'Yura!' from the next room.

That week he had other hallucinations as well. Towards the end of it, he woke up in the night from an absurd nightmare about a dragon who had his lair underneath the house. He opened his eyes. A light flashed from the gully and he heard the crack and echo of a rifle-shot. Astonishingly, a few moments after so unusual an experience, he went back to sleep, and in the morning told himself that it had been a dream.

15

And this is what happened a day or two later.

Yury had at last decided that he must be sensible, that if he wished to kill himself he could find a quicker and less painful method. He promised himself to leave as soon as Samdevyatov came for him.

A little before dusk, while it was still light, he heard footsteps crunching on the snow. Someone was calmly approaching the house with a firm, easy step.

How odd. Who could it be? Samdevyatov had his horse, he would not have come on foot. And Varykino was empty. 'It's for me,' thought Yury; 'a summons or an order to go back to town. Or they've come to arrest me.—No, there would be two of them and they would have transport to take me back. It's Mikulitsin,' he thought joyfully, imagining that he recognised the step. The visitor, still unidentified, fumbled at the door with its broken bolt, as if he had expected the padlock to be there; then he walked in confidently, certain of his way, opening the connecting doors and closing them carefully behind him.

Yury had been sitting at his desk with his back to the door. As he rose and turned to face it he found the stranger already on the threshold, where he had stopped dead.

'Who do you want?' Yury blurted out the first non-committal words that came into his mind, and was not surprised when there was no reply.

The stranger was a powerful, well-built man with a good-looking face. He was dressed in a fur jacket and trousers and warm goatskin boots and had a rifle slung over his shoulder.

Only the moment of his appearance took Yury by surprise, not his arrival in itself. The traces of occupation in the house had prepared him for it. This, evidently, was the owner of the stores he had found and which, as he knew, could not have been left by the Mikulitsins. Something about him struck Yury as familiar, he felt he had seen him before.

Neither did the caller look as astonished at seeing Yury as might have been expected. Perhaps he had been told that the house was lived in and even who was living in it. Perhaps he even recognised Yury.

'Who is he? Who is he?' Yury racked his brains. 'Where have I seen him, for heaven's sake? Surely not . . . A hot morning in May, God knows in what year. The station at Razvilye. The commissar's coach promising nothing good. Cut-and-dried ideas, a one-track mind, harsh principles and unlimited self-righteousness . . . Strelnikov!'

16

They had been talking for hours. They talked as only Russians in Russia can talk, particularly as they talked then, desperate and frenzied as they were in those anxious, frightened days.

Apart from the nervous talkativeness he shared with everyone, Strelnikov had some other reason of his own for talking ceaselessly.

He went on and on, doing everything possible to keep the conversation going; he wanted to avoid being alone. Was it his conscience he was afraid of, or the sad memories which haunted him, or was he tormented by that self-dissatisfaction which makes a man so hateful and intolerable to himself that he is ready to die of shame? Or had he taken some dreadful, irrevocable decision and was he unwilling to remain alone with it and anxious to delay its execution by gossiping with Yury and staying in his company?

Whatever it was, he was evidently keeping to himself some important secret which burdened him, while pouring out his heart all the more effusively on every other subject.

It was the disease, the revolutionary madness of the age: that in his heart everyone was utterly different from his words and the outward appearance he assumed. No one had a clear conscience. Everyone had some reason to feel that he was guilty of everything, that he was an impostor, an undetected criminal. The slightest pretext was enough to launch the imagination on an orgy of self-torture. People slandered and accused themselves, not only out of terror but of their own will, from a morbidly destructive impulse, in a state of metaphysical trance, carried away by that passion for self-condemnation which cannot be checked once it has been given free rein.

As a soldier of rank who had often presided at military courts, Strelnikov must have heard and read any number of confessions and depositions by condemned men. Now he was himself seized by the impulse to unmask himself, to reappraise his whole life, to draw up a balance sheet, while monstrously distorting everything in his feverish excitement.

He spoke incoherently, jumping from confession to confession.

'This all happened near Chita. . . . Were you surprised at all the outlandish things you found in the drawers and cupboards? That all comes from the requisitioning we did when the Red Army occupied Eastern Siberia. Naturally, I didn't bring it here by myself. I've always had trusty, devoted people round me; life has been very good to me in that way. These candles, matches, coffee, tea, writing materials and so on, all come from requisitioned military stores, partly Czech, partly English and Japanese. Odd, don't you think? "Don't you think" was my wife's favourite expression, I suppose you noticed. I couldn't make up my mind whether to tell you when I arrived, but I might as well admit it now—I came to see her and my daughter. The message saying that they were here didn't reach me until too late. That's how I missed them. When I learned through gossip and reports that you were with her and your name was mentioned to me, for some inexplicable reason, out of the thousands of faces I'd seen in these years, I remembered at once a Dr. Zhivago who had once been brought to me for questioning.'

'And were you sorry you hadn't had me shot?'

Strelnikov ignored the question. Perhaps he had not even heard it. Lost in his thoughts, he continued his monologue.

'Naturally, I was jealous—I'm jealous now for that matter. What could you expect? . . . I only came to this district a few months ago, after my other hide-outs further east were uncovered. I was to be court-martialled on a trumped-up charge. It wasn't difficult to guess the outcome. I wasn't guilty. I thought there might be a hope of defending myself and clearing my good name at some time in the future, when things are better. So I decided to disappear while I still could, before they arrested me, and hide for the present, lead a hermit's life, move about. Perhaps I would have succeeded if it hadn't been for a young scoundrel who wheedled himself into my confidence and gave me up.

'It was while I was escaping westwards across Siberia, on foot, in winter, keeping out of people's way and starving. I used to sleep in snowdrifts, or in trains—there were endless rows of them standing buried in the snow all along the main Siberian railway.

'Well, I came across this boy, a tramp; he said he had got away from a partisan shooting squad—they had lined him up with a lot of other condemned men, but he was only wounded, and he crawled out from under a pile of dead bodies and hid in the forest and recovered, and now he was moving from one hide-out to another, just as I was. That was his story, anyway. He was a bad lot, vicious and ignorant; he had been kicked out of school for idleness.'

The more details Strelnikov added to his description, the more certain Yury felt that he knew the boy.

'Was his name Terenty Galuzin?'

'Yes.'

'Then everything he said about the partisans and the shooting was true. He didn't invent a word.'

'The only good thing about him was that he was devoted to his mother. His father had been shot as a hostage and his mother was in prison and the same thing was likely to happen to her. When he heard that, he made up his mind to do all he could to rescue her. He went to the local Cheka, gave himself up and offered to work for them. They agreed to give him a chance on condition he made some important betrayal. He told them where I was hiding. But fortunately I got away in time.

'By an enormous effort and after endless adventures, I crossed Siberia and reached this part of the country. I am so well known here, I thought it was the last place they'd expect to find me; they wouldn't suppose I'd have the nerve to come here. And, in fact, for a long time they were looking for me round Chita, while I was hiding either in this house or in one or two others I knew were safe in this neighbourhood. But now that's finished. They've got on to me. Look here, it will soon be night-time and I don't like it, because I haven't been able to sleep for ages. You know how unpleasant that is. If there are any of my candles still left—good, aren't they? real tallow!—can we go on talking a bit longer? Let's go on talking for as long as you can stand it, right through the night, in luxury, by candlelight.'

'The candles are all there. I've only opened one packet. I've been using the paraffin I found here.'

'Have you any bread?'

'No.'

'Then what have you been living on? But what a silly question! Potatoes, of course.'

'That's right. Any amount of those. The people who used to live here were good housekeepers, they knew how to store them; they're all safe and sound in the cellar, neither rotten nor frozen.'

Strelnikov suddenly switched to the Revolution.

17

'None of this can mean anything to you. You couldn't understand it. You grew up quite differently. There was the world of the suburbs, of the railways, of the slums and tenements. Dirt, hunger, overcrowding, the degradation of the worker as a human being, the degradation of women. And there was the world of the mothers' darlings, of smart students and rich merchants' sons; the world of impunity, of brazen, insolent vice; of rich men laughing or shrugging off the tears of the poor, the robbed, the insulted, the seduced; the reign of parasites whose only distinction was that they never troubled themselves about anything, never gave anything to the world and left nothing behind them.

'But for us life was a campaign. We moved mountains for those we loved, and if we brought them nothing but sorrow, we never meant to harm a hair of their heads and in the end we suffered more than they did.

'But before I go on, there's one thing it's my duty to tell you. You must leave Varykino; don't put it off, if you value your life. They are closing in on me and, whatever happens to me, you'll be involved. You are implicated already, by the very fact of talking to me now. And apart from everything else, there are a lot of wolves round here. I had to shoot my way out of the Shutma the other night.'

'So it was you shooting.'

'Yes. Of course, you heard me. I was on my way to another hide-out, but before I reached it, I saw by various signs that it had been discovered. The people who were there have probably been shot. I won't stay long with you. I'll stay the night and leave in the morning . . . Well, I'll go on, if I may.

'Of course it wasn't only in Moscow or in Russia that there existed these Tverskaya-Yamskaya Streets [1] with young rakes in fancy hats and spats rushing about with their hired girls in their hired carriages. That street, the night life of the street, the night life of the past century, and the racehorses and the rakes, existed in every city in the world.

'There was that. But what gave unity to the nineteenth century, what set it apart as a historical period was the birth of socialist thought. —Revolutions, selfless young men dying on the barricades, journalists racking their brains about how to curb the brute insolence of money, how to save the human dignity of the poor. Marxism arose. It uncovered the root of the evil and it found the remedy, it became the great force of the age.

'And Tverskaya-Yamskaya Street was all that—the dirt and the heroism, the vice and the slums, and the proclamations and the barricades.

'You can't think how lovely she was as a child, a schoolgirl. You have no idea. She had a school friend who lived in a tenement next door to us ; most of the tenants were Brest line railway workers—it was called the Brest line in those days, it's been re-named several times since.—My father—he's a member of the Yuryatin revolutionary court now—he was a station foreman. I used to go to that house and see her there. She was still a child, but already then, the alertness, the watchfulness, the disquiet of those days—it was all there, you could read it all in her face, in her eyes. Everything that made that time what it was—the tears and the insults and the hopes, the whole accumulation of revenge and pride, all of it was already in her expression and her carriage, in that mixture in her of girlish shyness and grace and daring. You could indict the century in her name, out of her mouth. It was no trifling matter, you must agree. It was a sign, a destiny. Something nature had endowed her with, something to which she had a birthright.'

[1] The Piccadilly of nineteenth-century Moscow.

'How well you speak of her. I too saw her in those days, just as you have described her. A schoolgirl and at the same time the heroine of a secret drama. Her shadow on the wall was the shadow of helpless, watchful self-defence. That was how I saw her, and so I still remember her. You put it perfectly.'

'You saw and you remembered? And what did you do about it?'

'That's another story altogether.'

'Yes. Well. So you see, the whole of this nineteenth century—its revolutions in Paris, its generations of Russian emigrants starting with Herzen, its assassinations of tsars, some only plotted, others carried out, the whole of the workers' movement of the world, the whole of Marxism in the parliaments and universities of Europe, the whole of this new system of ideas with its novelty, the swiftness of its conclusions, its irony and its pitiless remedies invented in the name of pity—all of this was absorbed into Lenin, to be expressed and personified by him and to fall upon the old world as retribution for its deeds.

'And side by side with him there arose before the eyes of the world the immeasurably vast figure of Russia, bursting into flames like a light of redemption for all the sorrows and misfortunes of mankind. But why do I tell you all this? To you it must be so much empty noise.

'For the sake of this girl I studied and became a schoolmaster and went off into the unknown, to Yuryatin. For her sake I devoured books and absorbed a great mass of knowledge, to be at hand and useful if she should need my help. To win her back after three years of marriage I went to the war, and when the war was over and I returned from captivity, I took advantage of the fact that I was thought to be dead, and under an assumed name plunged headlong into the revolution, to pay back in full all her wrongs, all that she had suffered, to wash her mind clean of these memories, so that it should not be possible to return to the past, so there should be no more Tverskaya-Yamskayas. And all the time they, she and my daughter, were close by, they were here! What an effort it cost me to resist the longing to rush to them, to see them! But I wanted to finish my life's work first. And what wouldn't I give now for one look at them! When she came in it was as if the window flew open and the room filled with air and light.'

'I know how much you loved her. But forgive me, have you any idea of her love for you?'

'Sorry. What was that you said?'

'I asked you, had you any idea how much she loved you?—more than anyone in the world!'

'What makes you say that?'

'Because she told me so herself.'

'She said this? To you?'

'Yes.'

'Forgive me, I realise it's an impossible thing to ask, but if it isn't hopelessly indiscreet, if you can, will you tell me exactly what it was she said to you?'

'Gladly. She said that you were the example of what a human being should be, a man whose equal she had never met, that you were unique in your sincerity and that if she could go back to the home she had shared with you, she would crawl to it on her knees from the end of the earth.'

'Forgive me, if it isn't intruding on something too intimate, can you remember the circumstances in which she said this?'

'She had been doing this room, and she went outside to shake the carpet.'

'Sorry, which carpet? There are two.'

'That one, the larger one.'

'It would have been too heavy for her—did you help her?'

'Yes.'

'You held it at either end and she leaned far back, and threw up her arms high as on a swing, turning away her face from the blowing dust, and screwed up her eyes and laughed? Isn't that how it was? Don't I know her ways! And then you walked towards each other folding up the heavy carpet first in two and then in four, and she joked and pulled faces, didn't she? Didn't she?'

They stood up and went across to different windows and looked out in different directions. After a time Strelnikov came up to Yury, caught hold of his hands, pressed them to his breast and went on as hurriedly as before:

'Forgive me. I realise that I am touching on things which are dear and holy to you. But I should like to ask you more questions, if you'll let me. Please don't go away. Don't leave me alone. I'll be going soon myself. Just think—six years of separation, six years of inhuman self-restraint. But I kept thinking that freedom was not yet wholly won. When I'd won it, I thought, my hands would be untied and I could belong to them. And now, all my calculations have come to nothing. They'll arrest me to-morrow. You are near and dear to her. Perhaps you'll see her one day . . . But what am I saying! . . . I'm mad. They'll arrest me, and they won't let me say a word in my own defence. They'll come at me with shouts and curses and gag me. Don't I know how it's done!'

18

At long last, Yury had a good night's sleep. For the first time in many nights he went to sleep the moment he lay down. Strelnikov stayed the night; Yury had put him in the next room. The few times Yury woke up and turned over or pulled the blankets up to his chin, he was conscious of the strong refreshment of sleep and he dropped off happily again at once. Towards morning he had several short, kaleidoscopic dreams of his childhood, so detailed and logical that he thought they were real.

He dreamed, for instance, that his mother's water-colour of a place on the Italian riviera fell down from the wall. He opened his eyes. 'No, it can't be that,' he thought. 'It's Antipov, Lara's husband, Strelnikov, scaring the wolves in the Shutma, as Bacchus would say.' But no, what nonsense! It was the picture. There it was, lying in pieces on the floor, he assured himself, back in his dream.

He woke up late, with a headache from having slept too long. At first he couldn't think who or where he was.

Then he remembered: 'Strelnikov's in there. It's late. I must get dressed. He must be up by now. If not, I'll wake him up and make some coffee, and we'll have it together.'

'Pavel Pavlovich!' he called out.

There was no answer. 'He's still asleep. He's a sound sleeper, I must say.' He dressed unhurriedly and went into the room next door. Strelnikov's fur hat lay on the table, but he was nowhere in the house. 'Must have gone for a walk. And without his hat. Getting into training. I ought to be leaving Varykino to-day, but it's too late now. Again I've overslept, it's the same every day.'

He lit the kitchen range, picked up a bucket and went to the well. A few yards from the door, Strelnikov lay across the path with his head in a snowdrift. He had shot himself. The snow made a red lump under his left temple where he had bled. Drops of blood which had spurted away and rolled in the snow made beads like iced rowan-berries.

Conclusion

ALL that is left to tell is the brief story of the last eight or ten years of Zhivago's life, years in which he went more and more to seed, gradually losing his knowledge and skill as a doctor and a writer, emerging from his state of depression and resuming his work only to fall back, after a short flare-up of activity, into long periods of indifference to himself and to everything in the world. During these years the heart disease, which he had himself diagnosed earlier but without any real idea of its gravity, developed to an advanced stage.

He came to Moscow at the beginning of the NEP, the most false and ambiguous of all Soviet periods. He was even thinner, more neglected and unkempt than at the time when he came to Yuryatin after escaping from the partisans. In the course of his journey he had again gradually discarded those of his clothes that had some value, exchanging them for bread and a few worn old rags to cover his nakedness. So he had lived off his second fur coat and suit, and arrived in the Moscow streets dressed in a grey sheepskin hat, puttees and a worn-out army greatcoat stripped of all its buttons like a convict's overall. In this get-up he was indistinguishable from the countless multitudes of Red Army men who flooded the stations and the streets and squares of the city.

He had not come alone. Following him wherever he went was a good-looking young peasant boy who was also dressed in army cast-offs. They both of them turned up in this condition in the few Moscow drawing-rooms which still remained, those in which Yury had spent his childhood, in which he was remembered and welcomed with his companion (after tactful enquiries as to whether they had been to the baths—typhus was still raging), and in which he was soon told of the circumstances of his family's departure from Russia.

Both Yury and the boy were shy and their extreme shyness made them avoid going among people separately, for fear of having to talk. Usually, when these two lanky figures made their appearance at any gathering of Yury's friends, they retired to some corner, where they could spend the evening in silence, without having to take part in the general conversation.

Dressed in his rags and accompanied everywhere by the boy, the tall, gaunt doctor looked like a peasant 'seeker after truth' and his companion like a patient, blindly devoted and obedient disciple.

Who was his companion?

2

Yury had made the last stage of his journey by train, but had covered the earlier and much longer part of the way on foot.

The villages he went through looked no better than those he had seen in Siberia and the Urals, after leaving the partisans. Only then it had been winter, while now, at the end of the summer and the beginning of a warm, dry autumn, the weather made things easier.

Half the villages were empty, the fields abandoned and unharvested as after an enemy invasion—such were the effects of war: the Civil War.

For three days at the end of September his way followed the steep bank of a river. The river flowing towards him was on his right. On his left the wide, unharvested fields stretched from the road to the cloud-banks on the horizon. At long intervals they were interrupted by woods, for the most part oak, maple and elm. The woods ran in deep gullies to the river, dropping precipitously and cutting across the road.

In the abandoned fields the ripe grain spilled and trickled on the ground. Yury gathered it in handfuls and at the worst, if he had no means of boiling it and making gruel, he stuffed it into his mouth and ground it with difficulty between his teeth. With even more difficulty he digested this raw, half-chewed fodder.

Never in his life had he seen rye so ominously rusty brown, the colour of old, dimmed gold. Usually, when it is cut on time, its colour is much lighter.

These flame-coloured fields burning without fire, these fields silently proclaiming their distress, were coldly bordered by the vast, quiet sky, its face already wintry and shadowed by ceaselessly moving, long, flaky snow-clouds with black centres and white flanks.

Everything was in ceaseless, slow, measured movement: the flowing river, the road running to meet it and Yury walking along the road in the same direction as the clouds. Nor were the rye fields motionless. Something stirred in them, something which filled them from end to end with a small incessant rummaging and which nauseated Yury.

Never had there been such a plague of mice. They had bred in unbelievable multitudes such as had never been seen before. They

417

scurried over Yury's face and hands and inside his sleeves and trousers at night when he was caught by darkness and forced to spend the night in the open; they raced across the road by day, gorged and teeming, and turned into squeaking, pulsing slush when they were trodden underfoot.

Shaggy village mongrels, turned savage, followed him at a respectful distance, exchanging glances as if to decide on the best moment to fall on him and tear him in pieces. They fed on carrion, did not disdain mice and eyed Yury from the distance, moving after him confidently as though waiting for something. For some reason they never went into a wood, and whenever he came near one they gradually fell back, turned tail and vanished.

The woods and the fields offered a complete contrast in those days. Deserted by man, the fields looked orphaned as if his absence had put them under a curse, but the forest, well rid of him, flourished proudly in freedom as though released from captivity.

Usually the nuts are not allowed to ripen, as people, and particularly village children, pick them green, breaking off whole branches. But now the autumn-wooded hills and gullies were thick with rough, golden leaves dusted and coarsened by the sun, and festive among them, as if tied with ribbons, were bulging clusters of nuts, three or four together, ripe and ready to fall out of their husks. Yury cracked and crunched them as he went and stuffed his pockets and his bark satchel full of them; for a whole week he fed on hazel nuts.

He felt as if he saw the fields in the fever of a dangerous illness and the woods in the relief of convalescence, as if God dwelt in the woods and Satan were lurking in the fields.

3

At this point of his journey Yury came to a deserted, burnt-out village. All the houses had stood in one row on the side of the road opposite the river. The strip of land between the row and the edge of the steep river-bank had not been built on.

Only one or two burnt and blackened houses were still standing, but they too were empty. Nothing was left of the others but piles of charred rubble with black stove-pipes sticking out of them.

The cliffs facing the river were honeycombed with pits where the villagers had quarried rock for mill-stones—by this they had made a living. Three such unfinished stones were lying on the ground in front of the last house in the row, one of the few that had remained standing. Like the others, this house was uninhabited.

Yury went inside. It was a still evening; but it seemed as if a gust of wind burst into the house as he stepped over the threshold. Tufts of straw and hay slithered across the floors, remnants of paper flapped on the walls and the whole cottage stirred and rustled. Like the whole countryside, it swarmed with mice which scampered off, squeaking, in all directions.

He came out. The sun was setting on the edge of the fields behind the village and its warm gold flooded the opposite bank with its creeks and bushes, their fading reflections reaching out into the middle of the stream. Yury crossed the road and sat down on one of the mill-stones which lay on the grass.

A fair, shaggy head came up over the edge of the bank, then shoulders, then arms. Someone was climbing up the cliff path with a bucket of water. Seeing Yury he stopped, still only visible above the waist.

'Would you like a drink of water? If you won't hurt me, I won't hurt you.'

'Thank you. Yes, I'd like a drink. But come over here, don't be frightened. Why should I hurt you?'

The water-carrier was a boy in his teens, barefoot, ragged and dishevelled.

In spite of his friendly words he fixed Yury with a worried, suspicious stare. For some reason he seemed to get more and more excited. Finally, putting down his bucket, he rushed towards Yury but stopped half way, muttering:

'It isn't . . . it can't be . . . I must be dreaming. Pardon me, Comrade, if I ask you, but it came into my mind that I knew you . . . Yes! Yes! Surely! Aren't you the doctor?'

'And who are you?'

'Don't you know me?'

'No.'

'We were in the same train from Moscow, in the same carriage. They'd conscripted me for labour.'

It was Vassya Brykin. He threw himself on the ground before Yury, kissed his hands and wept.

The burned ruins were those of his native village, Veretenniki. His mother was dead. When the village was destroyed, Vassya hid in a cave in the quarries, but his mother, thinking he had been carried off to town, went mad with grief and drowned herself in the river, that very river Pelga which flowed at the foot of the cliff on which they were sitting and talking. His sisters Alya and Arya were said to be in an orphanage in another district but he knew nothing of them for certain. He went on to Moscow with Yury, and on the way told him of many terrible happenings.

4

'That's last winter's corn going to waste in the fields. We'd just finished sowing it when our troubles began. It was after Auntie Polya went away. Do you remember Auntie Polya?'

'No. I never even knew her. Who is she?'

'You never knew Auntie Polya! She was with us in the train! The one that was stout and fair, and looked you straight in the eye.'

'That's the one that was always plaiting and unplaiting her hair?'

'That's it! The one with the plait, that's the one!'

'Yes, I remember her. Wait a moment, now I come to think of it, I met her later in a town in Siberia. We met in the street.'

'You don't mean it! You met Auntie Polya!'

'Hey, what's the matter with you? Why are you shaking my hands like that? Mind you don't pull them off. And what are you blushing for like a girl?'

'Well, tell me quickly, how is she? Tell me.'

'She was all right when I saw her. She spoke about you and your people. Didn't she say she'd been staying with you, or have I got it wrong?'

'Of course she did, of course she did. She stayed with us. Mother got as fond of her as of her own sister. She's quiet and a good worker, very clever with her needle. We had plenty of everything in the house as long as she was living with us. But they made her life a misery in Veretenniki with all their talk.

'There's a man in the village called Rotten Kharlam. He was making up to Polya. He's a slanderer, and his nose has rotted away. She wouldn't even look at him. He had a grudge against me for that, so he spoke evil about me and Polya. That was how it all started. In the end she left, she couldn't stand it any more. And that was the beginning of all our troubles.

'There was a terrible murder near here. A widow was killed in a house in the woods near Buyskoye. She lived all by herself on a farm on the edge of the forest. She used to walk about in a man's boots with elastic straps. She kept a fierce dog on a long chain—it was so long that the dog could run all round the house. Gorlan she called it. She did all the work about the house and on the farm by herself, without any help. Well, last year the winter came on before anyone expected it. The snow was early, and the old woman hadn't dug up her potatoes. So she comes to Veretenniki and says: "Help me," she says. "I'll either pay you in money or give you a share of the potatoes."

'I said I'd do it, but when I got to the farm Kharlam was there, he'd taken the job on before me and she hadn't bothered to tell me. Well, I wasn't going to fight him about it, so we did the work together. It was wicked weather—rain and snow and mud and slush. We dug and we dug, and we burned the tops to dry the potatoes in the smoke. When we'd finished she settled with us, fair and square, and she let Kharlam go, but she gave me a wink as much as to say, I should stay on or come back later.

'So I went back again and she said: "I don't want to give up my surplus ¹ to the state. You're a good boy," she says, "I know you won't give me away. You see, I'm not hiding anything from you. I would dig a pit myself, but you see what it's like outside. I've left it too late, it's winter, I can't manage by myself. If you dig it for me, you won't be out of pocket."

'So I made the pit in the proper way for a hiding-place, wide at the bottom and narrow at the top, like a jug, and we lit a fire again and warmed and dried it with the smoke—all in a howling blizzard. Then we put the potatoes into the pit and the earth back on top. A very neat job it was. Of course, I didn't say a word to a living soul, not even to my mother or my sisters. God forbid!

'Well, hardly a month went by before the farm was robbed. People coming past from Buyskoye said the door was wide open and the whole place was cleaned out. No sign of the widow and Gorlan had broken his chain and bolted.

'A bit later still, there was a thaw just before the New Year; on St. Basil's eve it rained, so the snow was washed off the high ground; you could see the bare soil. Then Gorlan came back to the farm and found the place where the potatoes were buried; the snow was all gone and he started rooting up the earth. He dug and dug and threw the earth about, and there were the old woman's feet sticking up out of the hole in those boots with elastic straps she used to wear—gruesome it was!

'Everyone in Veretenniki was sorry for the old woman. No one suspected Kharlam. How could you suspect him? How could you

---

¹ Under 'War-Communism' (roughly 1917 to 1921) the peasants were supposed to deliver to the state the 'surplus' of their produce, i.e., any produce not consumed by the producer and not ear-marked for seed. The deliveries were enforced sporadically by armed detachments which often met with considerable resistance. These conditions changed after 1921 when, under the NEP, the peasants had to deliver a fixed part of their produce as a tax in kind but could sell the rest of their surplus.

even think of such a thing? If it had been him, would he have dared to stay in Veretenniki and strut about the village? He would surely have run away, they thought, he would have run as far from Veretenniki as he could.

'The ones who were pleased about the murder at the farm were the village kulaks.

'Here's a chance to stir up trouble in the village, they thought. "There you are," they said, "that's what the townspeople have done to you. They did that to give you a lesson, a warning, so you shouldn't hide your grain and bury your potatoes. And you think it's bandits from the woods that killed her, fools that you are! Just you go on doing what the town people tell you. They've got a lot more up their sleeve, they'll take everything, they'll starve you out. If you wish to know what's good for you, then listen to us, we'll teach you some sense. When they come to take away what you've earned by the sweat of your brow, tell them we haven't so much as a grain of rye, never mind surpluses. And in case of trouble, use your pitchforks. And if anyone goes against the will of the village, he'd better look out!" Well, the old fellows talked and held village meetings, and that was just what Kharlam wanted. Off he went to the town with his tale. "Fine goings on in the village," he says, "and what are you doing about it? A Committee of the Poor [1], that's what we need. Give the word and I'll have them all at each other's throats in next to no time." Then he made off somewhere and never showed up in our parts again.

'What came after happened of itself. Nobody arranged it, nobody's to blame. They sent Red Army men from the town and they set up a court. And they started on me—that was because of what Kharlam had told them. I'd dodged the labour service. I'd run away. And it was me that had killed the old woman and stirred up the village, they said. They locked me up, but luckily I had the sense to pull up one of the floor boards and get away. I hid in a cave in the old quarry. The village was burned over my head—I never saw it, and my own mother drowned herself in a hole in the ice and I never knew. It all happened of itself. They'd put the Red Army men in a house by themselves and given them vodka and they all got dead drunk. In the night the house caught fire through carelessness, and the fire spread to other houses, from one to the next. When it started, our village people jumped out of their houses and ran away. But the people from the town—mind you, nobody set fire to them—naturally

---

[1] Committees of landless peasants set up in order to foment 'class-warfare' in the villages.

they were all burned to death. Nobody told our people to run away or to stay away from their burned-out houses. But they were frightened in case something else should happen. The kulaks spread a rumour that every tenth man would be shot for sure. When I came out of the cave, they'd all gone. I didn't find a soul—they're wandering around somewhere.'

5

Yury and Vassya arrived in Moscow in the spring of 1922 at the beginning of the NEP. The weather was fine and warm. Patches of sunshine glancing off the golden domes of the Church of the Saviour played on the square below, where grass was growing in the cracks between the paving stones.

The ban on private enterprise had been lifted and trade within certain narrow limits was allowed. Deals were made on the scale of the turnover of a rag and bone merchant in a flea market and their pettiness led to profiteering and speculation. No new wealth was created by these transactions and they did nothing to relieve the squalor of the town, but fortunes were made out of the futile selling and reselling of goods already sold a dozen times over.

Several owners of modest private libraries took down their books from their shelves and put them all together. They notified the Town Council of their wish to start a co-operative bookshop. They applied for premises and were given the use of some warehouse which had stood empty since the first days of the revolution when the shop to which it had belonged had closed down, and beneath its spacious vaults they sold out their small and haphazard collections.

Professors' wives who, when times had been hard before, had secretly baked white rolls and sold them in defiance of the regulations, now traded in them openly at some shop or other which had been requisitioned and left unused all these years. They changed over, accepted the revolution and now said 'Sure thing' instead of 'Yes' or 'Very well.'

On arriving in Moscow Yury said :

'You'll have to work at something, Vassya.'

'I'd like to study.'

'That goes without saying.'

'Another dream I have is to draw my mother's picture from memory.'

'That's a good idea too. But for that you'd have to know how to draw. Have you ever tried?'

'When I was apprenticed to my uncle I used to play around with charcoal when he wasn't looking.'

'Well, why not? We'll see what can be done.'

Vassya did not show any great talent as an artist but he had sufficient average ability to be trained as a craftsman. With the help of his friends Yury got him into what had been the Stroganov Institute; there he first took a course in general subjects and then specialised in printing, binding and book design.

Yury and Vassya combined their efforts. Yury wrote booklets of a couple of dozen pages each on various subjects and Vassya set them up and printed them in small editions as part of his practical work at the Institute. They were then distributed through the second-hand bookshops which had recently been opened by their friends.

These booklets contained Yury's philosophy of life, his views on medicine, his definitions of health and sickness, reflections on evolution and the mutation of species, his theory of personality as the biological basis of the organism, and thoughts about religion and history (his views had much in common with those of his uncle and Sima), as well as his poems, short stories and sketches of the Pugachev country he had visited.

They were written in an easy conversational style but were anything but works of popularisation, since they advanced opinions which were controversial, arbitrary and unproved; but they were always lively and original. The booklets found an easy sale and were much appreciated by their readers.

In those days, when there were specialists in everything including the composition of poetry and the art of literary translation, and when treatises were written and institutes were founded for the study of the theory of everything under the sun, there arose all sorts of Palaces of Thought and Academies of Artistic Ideas. Yury acted as medical consultant to fifty per cent of these sham institutions.

For a long time he and Vassya remained friends and shared lodgings, moving from room to tumbledown room, all of them wretchedly unfit to live in.

Immediately on arriving in Moscow, Yury had revisited his old home in Sivtsev Street. He was told that his family had not stayed there on their way through Moscow. Their banishment had completely altered their status. The rooms registered in their name had been given to new tenants and there was not a sign of their belongings. Yury himself was regarded as dangerous to know and was avoided like the plague.

Markel was no longer there. He had gone up in the world and

had been appointed house-manager at Muchnoy Gorod (where the Sventitskys had once lived). The manager's flat had been put at his disposal but he preferred the old porter's lodge, which had floors of beaten earth but which also had its own water pipes and an enormous Russian stove. In the flats all the pipes and radiators burst in the cold weather, but the porter's lodge was always warm and dry and had running water.

There came a time when the friendship between Yury and Vassya cooled. Vassya had developed remarkably. He no longer thought or spoke like the ragged, barefooted, dishevelled boy from Veretenniki. The obviousness, the self-evidence of the truths proclaimed by the revolution attracted him increasingly, and Yury's talk, with its obscurities and its imagery, now struck him as the voice of error, doomed, conscious of its weakness and therefore evasive.

Yury was making calls on various government departments. He was trying to get two things : the political rehabilitation of his family and permission for them to return to Russia, as well as a foreign passport for himself and permission to fetch them from Paris.

Vassya was astonished at how lukewarm and half-hearted his efforts were. Yury seemed always to be in a hurry to believe that his efforts had failed ; he spoke with too much conviction and almost with satisfaction of the futility of undertaking anything further.

Vassya found fault with Yury more and more often and, although Yury did not take offence at being justly criticised, his relationship with Vassya gradually deteriorated. Finally their friendship broke up, and they parted company. Yury left the room which they had shared to Vassya and moved to Muchnoy Gorod, where Markel was all-powerful, and had set aside for him a corner at the back of what had been the Sventitskys' flat. It consisted of a derelict bathroom, a room with a single window adjoining it, and the dilapidated, crumbling kitchen and back entrance. After he had moved in Yury gave up medicine, neglected himself, stopped seeing his friends and lived in great poverty.

6

It was a grey Sunday in winter. Smoke was rising in pillars from the roofs and in thin black jets from the windows which, in spite of the regulations, were still used as outlets for the metal pipes of cooking stoves. The amenities of town life had still not been restored. The tenants of Muchnoy Gorod went about unwashed, they suffered from boils, they shivered and caught colds.

As it was Sunday, Markel Shchapov and his family were all at home.

They were having dinner at a large kitchen table. At this same table in days gone by, at the time of the bread rationing, all the tenants' coupons were collected and cut, snipped, counted, sorted, and wrapped in pieces of paper or tied into bundles according to their category, before being taken to the baker at dawn; and here, too, later in the morning, when the bread had come from the baker's, it was cut, sliced, crumbled, weighed and distributed according to the rations. But all this was now only a memory. Food rationing had been replaced by other forms of control, and the Shchapovs at their midday meal ate their fill and champed and chewed with relish.

Half the room was taken up by the squat Russian stove, which stood in the middle and had bedding on top of it and quilts hanging down over the sides.

Near the entrance a tap (which really functioned) stuck out of the wall over a sink. Benches ran down two sides of the room; under them were kept the family belongings in trunks and bundles. The table was on the left and had a plate-rack fixed above it.

The room was very hot. The stove was going full blast. In front of it stood Markel's wife Agatha; her sleeves were rolled up over her elbows and she was using a long pair of tongs to move the cooking pots inside the oven, crowding them together or spacing them out according to need. Her sweating face was in turn lit by the blaze in the oven and misted over by the heat of the cooking. Pushing the pots to one side, she pulled out from behind them a pie on an iron plate, flipped it over and put it back to brown. Yury came in with two buckets.

'Good appetite.'

'Make yourself at home. Sit down and have dinner with us.'

'Thank you, I've had mine.'

'We know what you call dinner. Why don't you sit down and have something hot? You needn't turn up your nose at it—it's good stuff, baked potatoes, pie and kasha.'

'No thanks, really . . . I am sorry to keep on opening the door and letting in the cold. I want to take up as much water as I can. I've cleaned the bath, now I'm filling that and the tubs. I'll come in another half dozen times and then I won't trouble you again for a long time. Forgive me for bothering you like this, but I can't get water anywhere else.'

'Help yourself. If you asked for syrup, we couldn't give you any, but there's plenty of water. Take as much as you like—we won't even charge you for it.'

They all laughed.

By the time Yury came to fill his third and fourth buckets, the tone had changed.

'My sons-in-law have been asking me who you are. I told them but they don't believe me.—You go on running the water, don't mind me. Only don't slop it on the floor, clumsy! If it freezes over I can't see you coming to hack it up with a crowbar. And shut the door properly, you oaf, there's a draught coming in.—Yes, so I was telling them who you are but they won't believe it. The money that was spent on you! All that learning and where has it got you, I'd like to know?'

When Yury came in for the fifth or sixth time, Markel frowned.

'Just once more and then you give over. There's a limit to everything, old man. If our little Marina didn't keep sticking up for you, I'd lock the door for two pins. You remember our Marina, don't you? There she is, the dark one at the end of the table. She's gone all red, look. "Don't hurt his feelings, Dad," she keeps telling me.— As if anybody wants to hurt your feelings. She's a telegraphist at the Central Post Office—she knows foreign languages. "He's unfortunate," she says. She's so sorry for you, she'd go through fire and water for you! As if I'm to blame that you're a poor fish! You shouldn't have done a bunk to Siberia, leaving your house at a bad time. It's your own fault. Look at us here—we sat it out through the famine and the White blockade, we didn't flinch—so here we are, safe and sound. Blame yourself. If you'd taken proper care of Tonya, she wouldn't be tramping about abroad these days. Well, it's your business. What do I care? Only what I'd like to know, begging your pardon, is what do you want with all this water? Hired yourself out to make a skating-rink or something? You and your water! I can't even get mad at you, you're such a wet hen!'

Again they all laughed, except Marina, who looked round angrily and flared up. Yury was astonished by the sound of her voice, though he could not as yet have said what it was in it that moved him.

'There's a lot of cleaning to be done in the house, Markel. I've got to scrub the floors and also wash some of my own things.

The Shchapovs were amazed.

'It's a shame that you should say such things, let alone do them. You'll be starting a Chinese laundry next.'

'Let me send my daughter up,' said Agatha. 'She'll do your washing and scrubbing and your mending if there is any.—You don't need to be afraid of him, my dear. You can see how well brought up he is, he wouldn't hurt a fly.'

'What an idea, Agatha Mikhailovna! I wouldn't dream of letting Marina do my scrubbing. Why on earth should she dirty her hands for me! I'll manage all right.'

'You can dirty your hands and I can't, is that it?' Marina broke in. 'Stop being so awkward, Yury Andreyevich. I suppose, if I come up to see you, you won't drive me out?'

Marina could have been trained as a singer. She had a pure, well-modulated voice of great range and strength. Her voice was not loud but it gave the impression of being stronger than was needed for ordinary conversation; and it did not seem to be a part of her, but could be imagined as having a life of its own. It seemed to come from behind her back or from the next room. Her voice was her protection, her guardian angel; no one could wish to hurt or distress a woman with such a voice.

So it was from this water-carrying on Sundays that a friendship sprang up between Yury and Marina. She would often come up and help him with his housework. One day she stayed with him and did not again go back to the lodge. Thus she became Yury's third wife, though he was not divorced from the first, and they did not register their marriage. They had children. Markel and Agatha spoke of their daughter, not without pride, as the doctor's wife. Her father grumbled that there had never been a proper wedding either in church or at the registry, but Agatha said: 'Are you off your head? With Tonya still alive, that would be bigamy.'—'It's you that's off your head,' said Markel. 'What's Tonya got to do with it? It's just the same as if she were dead. There's no law to protect her.'

Yury sometimes said jokingly that theirs was a romance in twenty buckets, as you might have a novel in twenty chapters.

Marina forgave Yury his increasing oddities, the dirt and disorder he made in the house, his moods and his fancies; they were those of a man who was letting himself go and knew it. She bore with his grumbling, his tempers and his nerves.

Her devotion went even further. At times they fell into great poverty through his fault, and in order not to leave him alone at such moments she would give up her own job at the Post Office (where, fortunately, her work was so highly thought of that she was always taken back after her enforced absence). In obedience to Yury's whim, she would go out with him, doing odd jobs from house to house. They chopped wood for a good many of the tenants on the different floors. Some of them, particularly racketeers who had made fortunes at the beginning of the NEP, and artists and scholars who stood close to the government, were setting up house on a comfortable scale. One day Yury and Marina, stepping carefully in their felt boots, so as not to dirty the carpet with sawdust, were carrying wood into the study of a tenant who remained insultingly engrossed in something he was reading and did not honour them with so much as a glance. It was his wife who gave the orders and who settled up with them.

'What has the pig got his nose into?' Yury wondered. The scholar was scribbling furiously in the margins of his book. As he passed him with a bundle of logs, Yury glanced over his shoulder. On the desk lay an early edition of one of the booklets which he had written and Vassya had printed.

7

Yury and Marina were now living in Spiridonovka Street and Gordon had a room in Bronny Street near by. Marina and Yury had two daughters, Kapka (Capitolina), who was six years old, and the baby Klazhka (Claudia), who was only six months.

The early summer of 1929 was very hot. Those who lived within a few streets of each other would run across to pay calls, hatless and in their shirt sleeves.

Gordon's room was part of a curious structure which had once been the premises of a fashionable tailor. The shop had been on two floors, connected by a spiral staircase; and both looked out on the street through the same large plate-glass window on which the tailor's name and occupation were shown in gold letters.

Now the premises had been divided into three. By means of extra floor-boards another room had been fitted into the space between the lower and the upper sections. For a living-room it had a curious window, about three feet high, starting at floor level and partly covered by the remnants of the lettering. From outside, anyone in the room could be seen up to the knees through the gaps between the letters. This was Gordon's room. With him at the moment were Zhivago, Dudorov, Marina and the children, who, unlike the grown-ups, were entirely visible through the glass. Marina soon went away with the little girls, leaving the three men together.

They were having one of those unhurried, lazy, summer conversations which men enjoy who were at school together and have countless years of friendship behind them.

People who have sufficient words at their disposal to satisfy them talk naturally and coherently. Only Yury was in this position.

His two friends were always at a loss for an expression. To eke out their vocabulary they paced up and down, puffed at their cigarettes, gesticulated and repeated themselves ('That, plainly, is dishonest, old man; dishonest, yes, yes, that's what it is, dishonest').

They were unaware that this excessive drama, so far from being a sign of their warmth and expansiveness, was, on the contrary, the result of their limitations and inadequacies.

Both Gordon and Dudorov moved in good university circles, they spent their lives among good books, good thinkers, good composers and music which was as good yesterday as to-day (but always good!), and they did not know that the misfortune of having average taste is a great deal worse than that of having no taste at all.

Neither Dudorov nor Gordon realised that even their admonitions to Yury were caused less by a friendly wish to influence his conduct than by their inability either to think with freedom or to guide the conversation freely. Like a runaway cart, it failed to take them where they wished to go. Unable to turn it, they were bound, sooner or later, to hit something, and so they hit out at Yury and showered him with sermons and instructions.

To Yury the springs of their emotion and of their reasoning and the shakiness of their sympathy were as clear as daylight. But he could hardly say to them: 'Dear friends, how desperately commonplace you are—you, your circle, the names and the authorities you quote, their brilliance and the art you so much admire! The only bright and living thing about you is that you are living at the same time as myself and are my friends!'—But how could anyone confess to such a thought?—So, in order to spare their feelings, he listened to them meekly.

Dudorov had recently come back from his first term of deportation; his civil rights had been restored to him and he had been allowed to resume his research and his lectures at the university.

Now he was confiding to his friends his feelings and his state of mind in exile. His comments were not influenced by cowardice or by any external consideration.

He was saying that the arguments of the prosecution, his treatment in prison and after he came out, and particularly his heart-to-heart talks with the interrogator, had 'ventilated his brains', 're-educated him politically', opened his eyes to many things he had not seen before and made him 'grow in stature as a person'.

These reflections appealed to Gordon just because they were so hackneyed. He nodded his head with sympathy and agreed with Dudorov in everything. It was the very triteness of Dudorov's feelings and expressions that moved him most; he took the textbook orthodoxy of his sentiments to be a sign of their common humanity.

Dudorov's pious platitudes were in the spirit of the age. But it was precisely their correctness, their transparent sanctimoniousness, that exasperated Yury. Men who are not free, he thought, always idealise their bondage. So it was in the Middle Ages, and the Jesuits always played on this. Yury could not bear the political mysticism of the Soviet intelligentsia, though it was the very thing they regarded as the highest of their achievements and described in the language of the day as 'the spiritual top-flight of the age'. But this he also kept to himself in order to avoid hurting the feelings of his friends.

What did interest him in Dudorov's story was his account of a cell-mate of his, Boniface Orletsov, a Tikhonovite priest[1]. Orletsov had a six-year-old daughter, Christina, who was devoted to him. His arrest and subsequent fate had been a terrible blow to her. The labels 'minister of religion' and 'deprived of civil rights' seemed to her the stigma of dishonour, a stain of which, perhaps, she had sworn in her childish heart to clear her father's name some day. This distant purpose, conceived so early and nursed with a burning resolution, made of her already then a disciple, fervent beyond her years, of what seemed to her irrefutable in communism.

'I must go,' said Yury. 'Don't be cross with me, Misha. It's stuffy here, with all that heat outside. I haven't got enough air.'

'But the casement is open, look, down there on the floor . . . I'm sorry, we've been smoking too much. We keep forgetting that we shouldn't smoke with you there. It isn't my fault that it gets so stuffy, it's the idiotic way the window is made. You should find me another room.'

'I must be off, Misha. We've done enough talking. Thank you both for worrying about me . . . I'm not pretending, you know. It's an illness I've got, sclerosis of the heart. The walls of the heart muscle wear out and get too thin, and one fine day they'll burst. And I'm not yet forty, and it isn't as if I were a drunkard or burned the candle at both ends!'

'Nonsense! We aren't playing your funeral march yet. You'll last us out.'

'Nowadays there are more and more cases of small cardiac haemorrhages. They are not always fatal. Some people get over them. It's the common illness of our time. I think its causes are chiefly

---

[1] Tikhonovite priest: a priest who remained loyal to the patriarch Tikhon, the head of the Russian Orthodox Church, who was persecuted for resisting the seizure of church valuables by the state. Tikhonovite priests were opposed to the 'Living Church' which, at that time, enjoyed a measure of support from the government.

moral. The great majority of us are required to live a life of constant, systematic duplicity. Your health is bound to be affected if, day after day, you say the opposite of what you feel, if you grovel before what you dislike and rejoice at what brings you nothing but misfortune. Your nervous system isn't a fiction, it's a part of your physical body, and your soul exists in space and is inside you, like the teeth in your head. You can't keep violating it with impunity. I found it painful to listen to you, Nicky, when you told us how you were re-educated and grew up in jail. It was like listening to a circus horse describing how it broke itself in.'

'I must stand up for Dudorov,' said Gordon. 'You've simply got unused to hearing human beings talk, their words don't reach you any more.'

'It may very well be, Misha. But in any case, you must let me go now. I'm having difficulty with my breathing. Honestly, I'm not exaggerating.'

'Wait a moment, you're just trying to get out of it. We won't let you go until you've given us an honest straightforward answer, from the heart. Do you or don't you agree that it's time you changed your ways and reformed? What are you going to do about it? To start with, you simply must get things straight with Tonya and Marina. They are human beings, women who feel and suffer—not disembodied ideas for you to juggle with in your head. And secondly, it's a scandal that a man like you should go to waste. You've got to wake up and shake off your idleness, pull yourself together and look at things without this arrogance which is quite unjustifiable. Yes, yes, without this inexcusable haughtiness in regard to everyone. You must go back to work and take up your practice.'

'All right, I'll give you my answer. I've been thinking something of this sort myself recently, so I can really promise you that there's going to be a change. I think it's all going to come right. And quite soon at that. You'll see. No, quite honestly. Everything is getting better. I have an indescribable, passionate desire to live, and living of course means struggling, going further, higher, striving for perfection and achieving it.

'I am glad that you stand up for Marina, Misha, just as you were always sticking up for Tonya. But you know, I haven't a quarrel with either of them, I am not at war with them, or with anyone else for that matter. You used to reproach me at first because Marina said "you" to me and called me Yury Andreyevich while I said "thou" and "Marina" to her—as though it didn't distress me too! But you know that the underlying cause of this unnatural state of affairs was removed long ago ; everything has been smoothed out and equality is established.

'Now I can tell you another piece of good news. I've been getting letters again from Paris. The children are growing up, they have a lot of French friends of their own age. Sasha is finishing the *école primaire* and Masha is soon going to it. I've never seen her, you know. I have a feeling in spite of everything that although they've become French citizens, they'll soon be back and that everything will be straightened out in some way or other.

'It seems that Tonya and my father-in-law know about Marina and our children. I didn't tell them in my letters, but they must have heard about it in some roundabout way. Naturally, Alexander Alexandrovich feels outraged as a father. He must be very hurt for Tonya. That would explain why our correspondence was interrupted for almost five years. I used to write to them after I got back to Moscow, and then they suddenly stopped answering.

'Now, quite recently, they've started writing again, all of them, even the children. They write very warmly and affectionately. For some reason they've relented. Perhaps Tonya has found someone else ; I hope to God she has. I don't know. I too write from time to time . . . But I really can't stay any longer. I'll go or I'll get an attack of asthma. Good-bye.'

Next morning Marina came running in to Gordon, greatly distressed. There was no one she could leave the children with, so on one arm she carried the baby wrapped in a blanket and with her free hand she was pulling Kapka, who trailed behind and dragged her feet.

'Is Yury here, Misha ?' she asked in a frightened voice.

'Didn't he come home last night ?'

'No.'

'Then he must have spent the night at Nicky's.'

'I've come from there. Nicky is at the university, but the neighbours know Yury : they say he hasn't been there.'

'Where can he be, then ?'

Marina put Klazhka down on the sofa and had hysterics.

8

For two days Gordon and Dudorov did not dare to leave Marina alone and took turns watching her and searching for Yury. They called at all the places he could conceivably have gone to—Muchnoy Gorod, Sivtsev Street, all the Palaces of Thought and Houses of Ideas he had ever been employed in, they looked up every friend of his they had ever heard him mention and whose address they could discover—but all without any result.

They did not report him as missing to the militia. Although he was registered and had no police record, it was better not to draw the attention of the authorities to a man who, by the standards of the day, lived anything but an exemplary life; so they decided not to put them on his track except as a last resort.

On the third day, letters from Yury came by different posts for all three of them—Gordon, Dudorov and Marina. He was full of regret for the trouble and anxiety he had caused them, he begged them not to worry about him and he implored them by everything that was holy to give up their search for him, saying that it would in any case be fruitless.

He told them that in order to rebuild his life as completely and rapidly as possible, he wished to spend some time by himself, concentrating on his affairs, and that as soon as he was settled in a job and reasonably certain of not falling back into his old ways, he would leave his hiding-place and return to Marina and the children.

He told Gordon that he was sending him a money order for Marina and asked him to take on a nurse for the children, so that Marina could go back to work. He explained that he was not sending the money to her directly for fear of someone seeing the receipt and her thus being exposed to the risk of robbery.

The money soon came and the amount was far above any sum that Yury or his friends ever handled. The nanny was hired and Marina went back to work at the Post Office. She was still very upset, but, accustomed as she was to Yury's oddities, she eventually resigned herself to his latest escapade. All three of them went on looking for him, but gradually they came to the conclusion that it was as futile as he had warned them it would be. They could find no trace of him.

9

Yet all the time he was living within a stone's throw, right under their eyes and noses, in the middle of the district they were combing for him.

On the day of his disappearance, he had left Gordon and come out into Bronny Street a little before dusk. He turned straight for home but almost immediately, within less than a hundred yards, he ran into his half-brother Yevgraf, who was coming down the street towards him. He had neither seen him nor heard of him for more than three years. It turned out that Yevgraf had just arrived in Moscow; as usual he had come out of the blue, and he shrugged off all Yury's questions with a smile or a joke. On the other hand, from the few questions he asked Yury, he gathered the gist of Yury's troubles at once, and there and then, between one turning and another as they walked along the narrow, twisting, crowded street, he worked out a practical plan to rescue him. It was his idea that Yury should disappear and stay for some time in hiding.

He took a room for him in Kamerger Street, as it was still called, near the Arts Theatre. He took steps to get him a good post in a hospital with plenty of opportunities for continuing his research work. He supplied him with money and assisted him in every way. Finally he gave him his word that the ambiguity of his family's situation in Paris would be resolved and that either Yury would go to them in Paris or they would come to him. All these things he undertook to see to personally. As usual, his help put new heart into Yury, and as usual the source of his power remained a mystery. Yury did not even try to guess at it.

10

His room faced south. It almost adjoined the theatre and looked out over the rooftops opposite; beyond them, the sun stood high over Okhotny Ryad but the street below was in shadow.

To Yury the room was more than a place to work in, more than a study. At this time of devouring activity, when the pile of notebooks on his desk was too small to hold all his plans and when the shapes of his projected books were all round him, like unfinished pictures standing with their faces to the walls in a painter's studio, his living-room was to him a banqueting room of the spirit, a lumber room of unreason, a store room of discoveries.

Luckily Yevgraf's negotiations with the hospital were dragging on and Yury's new job seemed to be indefinitely postponed. The delay gave him time to write.

He began by trying to sort out those of his earlier poems of which he could remember snatches, or of which Yevgraf somehow got him the texts (these were manuscripts, some in Yury's own hand and some, copies made by others). But this chaotic material made him disperse his energy even more than he was inclined to do by nature. He soon gave it up and turned to new work.

He would make the rough draft of an article, rather like the notes he had kept when he first went to Varykino, or put down the middle, or the end or the beginning of a poem as it came into his mind. There were times when he could hardly keep pace with his thoughts, even in his shorthand made up of initial letters and abbreviations.

He was in a hurry. Whenever his imagination flagged he whipped it up by drawing in the margins of his notebooks. The drawings were always of forest cuttings or of crossroads in town marked by the sign '*Moreau & Vetchinkin. Seed drills. Threshing machines.*'

The articles and poems were all on the same theme, the Town.

11

These notes were found later among his papers:

'When I came back to Moscow in 'twenty-two I found it empty and dilapidated. It had just come through the trials of the first few years after the revolution; it still looks much the same to-day. But even in this condition it is still a large modern city and cities are the only source of inspiration for a truly modern, contemporary art.

'The seemingly incongruous and arbitrary jumble of things and ideas in the work of the symbolists (Blok, Verhaaren, Whitman) is not a stylistic fancy. This new juxtaposition of impressions is taken directly from life.

'Just as they hurry their succession of images through the lines of their poems, so the street in a busy town hurries past us with its crowds and its broughams and carriages at the end of the last century, or its trams, buses and electric trains at the beginning of ours.

'Where, in such a life, is pastoral simplicity in art to come from? When it is attempted, its pseudo-artlessness is a literary fraud, not inspired by the countryside but taken from academic book-shelves. The living language of our time is urban.

'I live over a busy crossing. Moscow, blinded by the sun and the white heat of her asphalt yards, scattering sun gleams from her top-floor windows, breathing and blossoming with the colour of her streets and clouds, is whirling all round me, turning my head and willing me to turn the heads of others by writing in her praise.

'The incessant rumbling by day and night in the street outside our walls is as much connected with our thoughts as the opening bars of an overture with the curtain, as yet dark and secret, but already beginning to crimson in the glow of the footlights. The incessant, uninterrupted rustle and movement of the town outside our doors and windows is a huge, immeasurable overture to life for each of us. It is in these terms that I should like to write about the town.'

There are no such poems in what has been preserved of Zhivago's work. Perhaps 'Hamlet' belonged to such a series.

12

One morning at the end of August Yury took the tram in Gazetny Street to go to the Botkin Hospital (known as the Soldatenko Hospital in those days); it was his first day at his new job.

He had no luck with his tram; it had a defective motor and kept getting into trouble of every sort. Either its way was blocked by a cart in front of it with its wheels caught in the grooves of the rails, or the insulation went wrong on the roof or under the floor, and the current short-circuited with a flash and a crackle.

The driver would step off the front platform, walk round the tram with a spanner, and squat down and tinker with the machinery between the rear platform and the wheels.

The wretched tram blocked the traffic all along the line. The whole street was dammed up with other trams which had already been stopped, and still others kept joining the queue as far back as the square of the Manège and beyond. Passengers moved from the back to the front of the queue, hoping to gain time, and got into the very car which was the cause of all the trouble. It was a hot morning and the car was crowded and airless. Above the crowds running about in the street from one tram to another, a dark lilac thunder cloud was creeping higher and higher up the sky. A storm was gathering.

Yury sat on a single seat on the left, pressed against the window. He could see the left side of Nikita Street, the side of the Conservatoire. With the vague attention of a man thinking of something else, he watched the people walking and driving past on that side, missing no one.

A grey-haired old lady, in a light straw hat with linen daisies and cornflowers and a tight old-fashioned lilac dress, was trudging along the pavement, panting and fanning herself with a flat parcel which she carried in her hand. Tightly corseted, exhausted by the heat and pouring with sweat, she kept dabbing her lips and eyebrows with a small lace handkerchief.

Her course lay parallel with that of the tram. Yury had already lost sight of her several times, as the tram had started up after a stoppage for repairs and passed her, and she had again come into his field of vision, when it broke down once more and she overtook it.

437

Yury thought of the conundrums in school arithmetic, in which you are asked how soon and in what order trains, starting at different times and going at different speeds, arrive at their destination; he tried to remember the general method of solving them, but it escaped him, and he went on from these school memories to others, and to still more complicated speculations.

He thought of several people whose lives run parallel and close together but at different speeds, and wondered in what circumstances some of them would overtake and survive others. Something like a theory of relativity applied to a human race-course occurred to him, but he got completely muddled and gave it up.

There was a flash of lightning and a roll of thunder. The luckless tram was stuck for the twentieth time; it had stopped half-way down the hill from Kudrinsky Street to the Zoo. The lady in lilac appeared in the window-frame, passed beyond it and moved on. The first heavy drops of rain fell on the roadway, the pavement and the lady. A gusty wind whipped past the trees, flapped the leaves, gave a tug at the lady's hat, turned up the hem of her skirt and suddenly died down.

Yury felt sick and faint. Overcoming his weakness, he got up and jerked the window straps up and down trying to open the window. But he could not move it.

People shouted to him that the window was blocked, it was nailed in position, but Yury, fighting off his faintness and seized by a sort of panic, neither understood the cries nor referred them to himself. He was still trying to open the window and again gave three sharp tugs at the strap—up, down and towards himself—when he suddenly felt a new and mortal pain; he understood that something had broken in him, he had done something irreparable and that this was the end. At this moment the tram started, but it had only gone a short way down Presnya Street when it stopped again.

By an inhuman effort of the will, Yury pushed through the solid crowd down the gangway, swaying and stumbling, and came out on the rear platform; people blocked his way and snapped at him. The fresh air seemed to revive him and he thought that perhaps not everything was lost, perhaps he was better.

He began to squeeze his way through the crush on the rear platform, provoking more snarls, curses and kicks. He paid no attention to them, tore himself free of the crowd, climbed down from the stationary tram into the roadway, took a step, another, a third, fell down on the cobbles and did not get up again.

There arose a hubbub of talk, arguments, advice. Several people got off the tram and surrounded him. They soon ascertained that he was no longer breathing: his heart had stopped. The group round the body was joined by others who stepped off the pavements, some relieved and others disappointed that the dead man had not been run over and that his death had nothing to do with the tram. The crowd grew larger. The lady in lilac came up too, stood a little, looked at the body, listened to the talk and went on. She was a foreigner, but she understood that some people were in favour of putting the body on the tram and taking it to the hospital, while others said that the militia should be called at once. She did not wait to see the outcome.

The lady in lilac was a Swiss national, she was Mademoiselle Fleury from Melyuzeyevo, and was by now very, very old. For twelve years she had been writing to the authorities in Moscow for permission to return to her native country, and quite recently her application had been granted. She had come to Moscow for her exit visa and was now on the way to her embassy to collect it, fanning herself as she went with her documents, which were done up in a bundle and tied with a ribbon. So she walked on, overtaking the tram for the tenth time, and quite unaware that she had overtaken Zhivago and survived him.

13

Through the open door of the passage could be seen a corner of the room and the table placed at an angle to the wall. On the table the coffin, like a roughly carved canoe, pointed at the door with its narrow end, the end which supported the feet of the corpse. It was the table at which Yury had done his writing in the past; the room had no other. The manuscripts had been put away in a drawer and the coffin stood on the top. Yury's head was raised on pillows and his body lay tilted on its eminence as on a hillside.

He was surrounded by a great many flowers, whole bushes of white lilac, hard to find at this season, cyclamen and cineraria in pots and baskets. The flowers screened the light from the windows. The light filtered thinly through the banked flowers to the face and hands of the corpse and the wood and the lining of the coffin. Shadows lay on the table in a pattern of leaves and branches as if they had only just stopped swaying.

The custom of cremating the dead had by this time become widespread. In the hope of a pension for the children, and out of consideration for their future at school and for Marina's position at the Post Office, it had been decided to dispense with a requiem and to confine the ceremony to a civil cremation. The correct authorities had been notified and their representatives were awaited.

In the interval the room seemed empty, like a flat vacant between the going of one set of tenants and the coming of another. The stillness was broken only by the inadvertent shuffling of the mourners as they tiptoed in to take their leave of the dead. There were not many of them, but all the same a good many more than might have been expected. The news of the death of this almost unknown man had flown round their circle with lightning speed. Amongst them were many of those who had known him at different times in his life, though he had afterwards lost touch with them and forgotten them. His poetry and scientific work attracted still more friends, people who had never met the man but had been drawn to him and had now come to see him for the first and last time.

In these hours when the silence, unfilled by any ceremony, was made almost tangibly oppressive by a sense of absence, only the flowers took the place of the singing and the psalms.

They did more than blossom and smell sweet. In unison, like a choir, perhaps hastening decomposition, they unstintingly poured out their fragrance and, imparting something of their scented strength to everyone, seemed to be accomplishing a ritual.

The kingdom of plants can easily be thought of as the nearest neighbour of the kingdom of death. Perhaps the mysteries of transformation and the enigmas of life which so torment us are concentrated in the green of the earth, among the trees in graveyards and the flowering shoots springing from their beds. Mary Magdalene, not at once recognising Jesus risen from the grave, took Him for the gardener.

14

When Yury's body was brought to the flat in Kamerger Street (this had been his last registered address), his friends, notified of his death and shaken by it, came running in straight from the landing through the wide-open door, bringing Marina with them. Half out of her mind with shock and grief, she threw herself down on the floor, beating her head against the edge of the long wooden chest in the lobby on which the body had been left, while the unswept living-room was being tidied up and until the coffin (which had already been ordered) was delivered. She was in floods of tears, muttering and crying out, choking over her words and breaking into loud lamentations. She grieved with an abundance of speech, as peasants do, neither distracted nor made shy by strangers. She clung to the body and could scarcely be torn away when the time came for it to be carried into the room, washed and placed in the coffin. All this had been the day before. To-day the frenzy of her grief had abated, giving way to a weary numbness; she sat in silence, though still only half conscious of herself or her surroundings.

Here she had stayed the rest of the preceding day and all through the night, not moving anywhere. Here the baby had been brought for her to feed, and Kapka with her young nanny had come to see her.

She was surrounded by her friends. Gordon and Dudorov grieved as much as she did. Markel, her father, would sit down on the bench by her side and sob loudly and blow his nose into his handkerchief with a startling noise. Her weeping mother and sisters came and went.

But there were two people in the gathering, a man and a woman, who stood out from all the rest. They did not claim any closer tie with the deceased than the others. They did not compete in sorrow with Marina, her daughters or his friends. But although they made no claims, they had evidently their own special rights over Yury, and no one questioned or disputed the unvoiced authority which they had unaccountably assumed. These were the people who had apparently taken it upon themselves to arrange the funeral and they had seen to everything from the first with such quiet competence that it looked as if it gave them satisfaction. Their composure was remarkable and it produced a strange impression, as if they were involved not only in the funeral but also in the death, not in the sense of being directly or indirectly guilty of it, but as people who, once it had occurred, had come to terms with it, given their consent, were reconciled and did not see it as the most important thing connected with Yury. Few of the mourners knew them, a few others guessed who they were, but the majority had no idea.

Yet whenever the man, whose narrow Kirghiz eyes both expressed and aroused curiosity, came into the room with the casually beautiful woman by his side, they all, including even Marina, at once, without protest, as if by agreement, stirred, got up from where they had been sitting on the chairs and stools placed in a row against the wall, and cleared out, crowding uncomfortably into the passage and the lobby and leaving the couple alone, behind half-closed doors, like two consultants who needed, quietly, unhindered, to accomplish something directly concerned with the funeral and vitally important.

So it was on this occasion. They remained alone, sat down on two chairs near the wall and talked business.

'What have you found out, Yevgraf Andreyevich?'

'The cremation is to be tonight. In half an hour they'll come from the doctors' union to fetch the body and take it to their club. The civic ceremony is at four. Not one of his papers was in order; his labour book was out of date, he had an old trade union card—he hadn't changed it for the new one and the subscriptions hadn't been paid up for years. All that had to be put in order; that was why it took so long. Before they take him away—that's quite soon, we ought to get ready—I'll leave you here alone as you asked . . . Sorry. That's the telephone. I won't be a moment.'

Yevgraf came out into the passage crowded with unknown colleagues of Yury's, his school friends, junior members of the hospital staff, printers and booksellers, and where Marina, her arms round both her children, sheltering them in the folds of the coat she had thrown over her shoulders (it was a cold day), sat on the edge of the wooden bench, waiting to go back into the living room, as a visitor who has come to see a prisoner in jail waits to be let in by the guard. The passage and the hall were overcrowded. The front door was open and a lot of people were standing or strolling about smoking on the landing. Others stood talking on the flight of stairs leading to the ground floor, the louder and more free their voices, the lower down and closer to the street they were.

Straining to hear above the sustained murmur and speaking in a decorously muffled voice, his hand over the receiver, Yevgraf answered questions over the telephone about the funeral arrangements and the circumstances of the doctor's death. Then he went back into the living-room and the conversation was resumed.

'Please don't vanish after the cremation, Larissa Fyodorovna. I don't know where you are staying. Don't disappear without letting me know. I have a great favour to ask you. I'd like as soon as possible—to-morrow or the day after—to begin sorting my brother's papers. I'll need your help. You know so much about him, probably more than anyone. You mentioned that you had only come from Irkutsk a couple of days ago and not for long, and that you came up here by a coincidence, for some other reason, not knowing it had been my brother's flat in recent months or what had happened to him. I didn't understand all you said and I am not asking you to explain, but please don't go away without leaving me your address. The best would be if we could spend the few days we need to go through these manuscripts in the same house or at least quite near. Perhaps in two other rooms in this building. It could be arranged. I know the manager.'

'You say you didn't understand what I said.—What is there to understand? I arrived in Moscow, left my things at the station and went for a walk through some Old Moscow streets.—Half of them I couldn't recognise, I've been away so long I've forgotten. Well, I walked and walked, down Kuznetsky Bridge and up Kuznetsky Lane and suddenly I pass something terribly, extraordinarily familiar—Kamerger Street. That was where my husband, Antipov, who was shot, used to live as a student—in this house and in this actual room where you and I are sitting now. I'll go in, I thought, who knows, the old tenants might still be there; I'll look them up. You see I didn't know it had all changed—no one so much as remembers their name—I didn't find that out till later, the day after and to-day, gradually, by asking people. But you were there. I don't know why I'm telling you. I was completely thunderstruck—the door wide open, people all over the place, a coffin in the room, a dead man. Who is it? I come in, I go up and look. I thought I was mad, raving. But you were there, you saw me, didn't you? What on earth am I telling you for?'

'Wait, Larissa Fyodorovna, wait a moment. I've already told you, neither Yury nor I had the slightest idea of the astonishing associations of this room or that Antipov had once lived here. But what surprises me most is an expression you used just now. I'll tell you in a moment.—About Antipov, Strelnikov, at one time at the beginning of the Civil War I used to hear of him very often, almost every day, and I met him personally two or three times, never realising, of course, that his name would come to mean so much to me for family reasons.—But forgive me, I may have misheard you, I thought you said—it could only have been a slip of the tongue—that he'd been shot. You must surely know that he shot himself?'

'Yes, I've heard that version, but I don't believe it. Pavel Pavlovich wasn't a man to commit suicide.'

'But it's quite certain, you know. Antipov shot himself in that house where, Yury said, you were living before you went to Vladivostok. It happened very soon after you left. My brother found his body. He buried him. How is it you weren't told?'

'I was told something different . . . So it's really true, he shot himself? People said so but I didn't believe it. And in that very house? It doesn't seem possible. It's very important to me, that detail. You don't know, I suppose, if he and Zhivago ever met, if they got to know each other?'

'From what Yury told me, they had a long conversation.'

'Is it really true! Well, thank God, thank God, that's better.' Antipova slowly crossed herself. 'What an astounding, what a pre-

ordained coincidence. Will you let me come back to this and ask
you more about it later? Every detail is so dear to me. But at the
moment I can't, I'm too upset. I'll keep quiet a little and collect
my thoughts. Will you forgive me?'

'Of course! Of course!'

'You won't mind, will you?'

'Of course not.'

'Oh yes. I nearly forgot. You asked me not to go away after
the cremation. All right. I promise. I won't disappear. I'll come
back here with you and stay wherever you tell me and for as long as
necessary. We'll go through Yury's manuscripts. I'll help you. It's
true, I might be useful to you. I know his writing so well, every
twist of it, I know it with my heart, with my life's blood. And then,
you know, there's something I want to ask you too, I'll need your
help. Didn't I hear you were a lawyer?—or anyway, you know all
the present-day customs and regulations. And another thing, I need
to know what government department to apply to for information.
So few people can tell one things like that, don't you think? I'll
need your advice about something terrible, something really terrible.
It's about a child. But we'll talk about it later, when we come back
from the crematorium. All my life I have to go on looking for people.
Tell me, suppose, in some quite imaginary case, it were necessary to
trace a child, a child who had been handed over to be brought up
by strangers, is there any sort of general source of information about
all the Children's Homes throughout the country? And is there
any record of all the waifs and strays, has anything like that ever
been done or attempted? No, don't tell me now, please don't. We'll
talk about it later. I'm so frightened. Life is so terrifying, don't
you think? I don't know about later on, when my daughter comes
and joins me, but for the moment I don't see why I shouldn't stay
in this flat. Katya shows exceptional gifts for music and for acting;
she's very clever at imitating people and she sings whole operatic
arias, all by ear. She's a remarkable child, don't you think? I want
her to go to the junior classes either at the drama school or the Conservatoire, whichever of them will take her, and I must put her down
for a boarding-school. That's really why I've come without her at the
moment, to make the arrangements; when I've arranged it all I'll
go back. Things are so complicated, don't you think, you can't
explain everything. But we'll talk about it later. Now I'll wait a
bit, I'll pull myself together, I'll keep quiet and collect my thoughts
and try not to be afraid. Besides, we've kept Yury's friends out of
the room much too long. Twice I thought I heard someone knock-

ing. And there's something going on outside—they've probably come from the undertakers'. I'll stay here quietly for a bit, but you'd better open the door and let them come in. It's time, don't you think? Wait, wait. There ought to be a footstool near the coffin, otherwise people can't reach up to Yury. I tried to on tiptoe, but it's very difficult. And Marina Markelovna and the children, they'll need it. Besides, it's only right, it's prescribed in the ritual: 'And you shall kiss me with a last kiss.' Oh, I can't bear it, I can't, it's all so terrible! Don't you think?'

'I'll let them in. But just one thing before I do that. You have said so many enigmatic things and raised so many questions which are evidently painful to you that I don't know what to tell you. But there's one thing I want you to know. Please count on my help in all your anxieties. I offer it to you willingly, with all my heart. And remember. You must never, never despair, whatever the circumstances. To hope and to act, these are our duties in misfortune. To do nothing and to despair is to neglect our duty. Now I'm going to let the mourners come in. You're right about the footstool, I'll get one.'

But Lara was no longer listening. She never heard him opening the door nor the people pouring in from the corridor, nor the directions he gave to the organisers and the chief mourners; she heard neither the shuffling of the crowd, nor Marina's sobs, neither the coughing of the men nor the tears and exclamations of the women.

The crowd moving round her, the monotonous sounds made her feel sick and giddy. It took her all her strength not to faint. Her heart was bursting and her head ached. Closing her eyes she abstracted herself in memories, considerations, conjectures. She escaped into them, sank into them, as though carried forward, for a time, for a few hours, into some future which she might not live to see, a future which aged her by several decades, a future where she was old.

No one is left. One has died. The other has killed himself. And only the one is left alive who should have been killed, whom she had tried to kill and missed, the stranger who had nothing in common with her, the useless nonentity who had turned her life into a chain of crimes beyond her knowing. And that monster of mediocrity is busy dashing about in the mythical byways of Asia, known only to stamp collectors, and not one of those who are near and necessary is left.

Imagine! It was at Christmas, and she had set out to shoot that vulgar scarecrow, when she had had that talk in the dark in this very room with Pasha, who was still a boy, and Yury, whose body they were taking leave of now, had not yet come into her life.

She strained her memory to reconstruct that Christmas conversation with Pasha, but she could remember nothing except the candle burning on the window-sill and melting a round patch in the icy crust on the glass.

How could she know that Yury, whose dead body was lying on the table, had seen the candle as he was driving past, and noticed it, and that from the moment of his seeing its light ('The candle burned on the table, the candle burned'), all that was pre-ordained for him had seized control of his life?

Her thoughts wandered. She thought: 'All the same, what a pity he isn't having a church funeral. The burial service is so splendid and tremendous! It's more than most people deserve when they die, but darling Yury would have been such a noble occasion! He's worthy of all the "Weeping which turns into Alleluias".'

Now she felt a wave of pride and relief, as always at the thought of Yury, and as in the short intervals of her life which she had spent beside him. A breath of that freedom and unconcern which had been his climate filled her lungs. She got up impatiently from her chair. Something incomprehensible was happening to her. She needed, if only for a few moments, to escape with Yury's help into freedom, into the open, out of the sorrows which imprisoned her, to feel again the joy of liberation. Such a joy, it seemed to her, would be the joy of taking leave of him, of using the right and the occasion to weep her fill over him unhindered. Full of a passionate haste, she looked round her at the crowd, with eyes as hurt, unseeing and full of tears as if an oculist had put caustic eye-drops into them, and all the people began to move, shuffle and walk out of the room, leaving her at last alone, behind half-closed doors; and she went up to the table with the coffin on it, quickly crossing herself, got up on the footstool Yevgraf had brought, made three broad signs of the cross over the body and pressed her lips to the cold forehead and hands. She brushed aside the impression that the chilly forehead was somehow smaller, like a hand clenched into a fist; she managed not to notice it. For a moment she stood still and silent, neither thinking nor crying, bowed over the coffin, the flowers and the body, shielding them with her whole being, with her head, her breast, her heart and her hands as strong as her heart.

15

The whole of her was shaken by the sobs which she restrained. She fought her tears as long as she could, but at times it was beyond her strength and they burst from her, pouring down her cheeks and falling on her dress, her hands and the coffin to which she clung.

She neither spoke nor thought. Many thoughts, generalisations, facts, certainties, swept and chased through her mind at will, as freely as clouds in the sky, or as their night-time conversations in the past. This it was that had brought them happiness and liberation in those days. Knowledge, not from the head, but warm knowledge imparted to each other, instinctive, immediate.

Such knowledge filled her now, a dark, indistinct knowledge of death, a preparedness for death which removed all helplessness in its presence. It was as if she had lived twenty lives, and had lost Yury countless times, and had accumulated such experience of the heart in this domain that everything she felt and did beside this coffin was exactly right and to the point.

'Oh, what a love it was, how free, how new, like nothing else on earth!' They really thought what other people sing in songs.

It was not out of necessity that they loved each other, 'enslaved by passion', as lovers are described. They loved each other because everything around them willed it, the trees and the clouds and the sky over their heads and the earth under their feet. Perhaps their surrounding world, the strangers they met in the street, the landscapes drawn up for them to see on their walks, the rooms in which they lived or met, were even more pleased with their love than they were themselves.

Well, of course, it had been just this that had united them and had made them so akin! Never, never, not even in their moments of richest and wildest happiness, had they lost the sense of what is highest and most ravishing—joy in the whole universe, its form, its beauty, the feeling of their own belonging to it, being part of it.

This compatibility of the whole was the breath of life to them. And consequently they were unattracted to the modern fashion of coddling man, exalting him above the rest of nature and worshipping him. A sociology built on this false premise and served up as politics, struck them as pathetically home-made and amateurish beyond their comprehension.

16

And now she began to take leave of him in the simple, current words of robust, familiar talk, the kind that bursts the framework of reality and makes no sense—no more sense than the choruses and monologues in tragedies, or the language of poetry or music or any other convention which is only justified by the circumstance of heightened emotion. The justification in this case, the circumstance which strained the tone of her light, unpremeditated speech, were her tears, in which her prosaic, unexalted words bathed and swam and drowned.

It seemed as if these tear-drenched words clung together of themselves and connected into a soft, quick, gentle patter, as when silky, moist leaves rustle, tangled by the wind.

'So here we are again, Yurochka. The way God brings us together. How terrible, think of it! Oh, I can't bear it! Oh, Lord! I cry and I cry! Think of it! Again something just our kind, just up our street. Your going, that's the end of me. Again something big, inescapable. The riddle of life, the riddle of death, the beauty of genius, the beauty of loving—that, yes, that we understood. As for such petty trifles as re-shaping the world—these things, no thank you, they are not for us.

'Good-bye, my big one, my dear one, my own, my pride. Good-bye, my quick, deep river, how I loved your day-long plashing, how I loved bathing in your cold, deep waves.

'Remember how we said good-bye that day, in all that snow? What a trick you played on me! Would I ever have gone without you? Oh, I know, I know, you forced yourself to do it, you thought it was for my good. And after that everything went wrong. What I had to put up with out there, Lord, what I went through! But of course you don't know any of that. Oh, what have I done, Yura, what have I done! I am such a criminal, you have no idea. But it wasn't my fault. I was ill in hospital for three months, a whole month I was unconscious. And since then my life isn't worth living, Yura. My heart has no peace, I can't live for pity and misery. But then I'm not telling you the most important thing. I can't say it, I haven't the strength. Every time I come to that part of my life I can't go on, my hair stands on end, it's so terrible. And you know, I'm not even sure I'm quite normal any more. But you see, I haven't taken to drink as so many people do—I'm keeping off that, because a drunken woman, that really is the end of everything, it's impossible, isn't it?'

She went on speaking and weeping and tormenting herself, but suddenly she looked up and was astonished to see that the room had long been crowded and full of bustle. She got down from the footstool and moved away from the coffin, swaying, pressing the flat of her hand to her eyes as if to get rid of the tears she had not finished weeping, and to shake them off on to the floor with her fingers.

Sir men came up to the coffin, lifted it and carried it out.

17

Lara stayed several days in Kamerger Street. The sorting out of Yury's papers was begun with her help but finished without her. She also had her talk with Yevgraf and told him an important fact.

One day Lara went out and did not come back. She must have been arrested in the street, as so often happened in those days, and she died or vanished somewhere, forgotten as a nameless number on a list which later was mislaid, in one of the innumerable mixed or women's concentration camps in the north.

16

Epilogue

GORDON, recently promoted lieutenant, and Major Dudorov were returning to their units, the one from a service assignment in Moscow, the other from three days' leave. This was in the summer of 1943, after the break through on the Kursk bulge and the liberation of Orel.

They met on the way and spent the night at Cherny, a small town which, although mostly in ruins, had not been completely destroyed, like most of the inhabited places in this 'desert zone' left in the wake of the retreating invader.

Among the heaps of broken bricks and stone ground into fine dust they found an undamaged barn and settled down in it for the night. When Dudorov finally dozed off at about three in the morning, a little before dawn, he was soon disturbed again by Gordon's fidgeting. Clumsily diving into the soft hay and rolling about in it as if it were water, he collected a few clothes into a bundle and awkwardly slithered off the top of the mound of hay, down to the doorway.

'Where are you off to? It's early.'

'I'm going down to the river. I want to wash my things.'

'That's mad. We'll be back with the unit by this evening. Tanya, the laundry girl, will give you a change of clothes. What's the hurry?'

'I don't want to wait till then. They're sweaty, filthy. I'll give them a quick rinse and wring them out properly. In this heat they'll be dry in no time. I'll have a bathe and change.'

'It looks so bad. After all, you're an officer.'

'It's early, there's no one about, they're all asleep. Anyway, I'll get behind a bush or something. Nobody will see me. You stop talking and go to sleep, or you'll wake yourself up completely.'

'I shan't sleep any more as it is. I'll come with you.'

So they went down to the river, past the white stone ruins, already white hot in the sun though it was only a little after sunrise. In what had once been streets, people were sleeping on the ground in the sun, sweating, red in the face and snoring. They were mostly local people who had lost their homes, old men, women and children, with a sprinkling of Red Army men who had lost touch with their units and were trying to catch them up. Gordon and Dudorov stepped carefully past them so as not to disturb their sleep.

'Keep your voice low or you'll wake up the town and then it'll be good-bye to my washing.'

So they continued their conversation of the night before in an undertone.

2

'What's this river?'

'I don't know. The Zusha probably.'

'No, that isn't the Zusha.'

'Then I don't know what it is!'

'It's on the Zusha, you know, that it all happened—Christina, I mean.'

'Yes, but that must be lower down the stream. They say the Church has canonised her. Did you ever get to know more details than what came out in the press?'

'Not really. There was an old stone building, they called it the Stables. It had been used as the stables of a sovhoz stud-farm—now the name will go down in history—a very old place with huge thick walls. The Germans made it into an impregnable fortress; it was on a hill and they had the whole district under fire and were holding up our advance. It had to be destroyed. So Christina, by a miracle of courage and ingenuity, got inside the German lines and blew it up, and was taken alive and hanged.'

'Why do they call her Christina Orletsova and not Dudorova?'

'We were only engaged, you know. We decided in the summer of 'forty-one that we'd get married at the end of the war. After that I moved about all over the place like the rest of the army. My unit was transferred innumerable times, and in the course of it I lost touch with her. I never saw her again. I heard of her feat of courage and heroic death like everyone else—from the newspapers and the army orders. They say they're going to put up a monument to her somewhere near here. I hear Zhivago—the general, Yury's brother—is going round the district collecting details about her.'

'I am sorry—I shouldn't have made you talk about it. I've upset you.'

'No, it isn't that. But I don't want to hold you up. You undress and get into the water and do your job. I'll lie on the bank and chew a blade of grass and think. I may even sleep a bit.'

A few moments later they began to talk again.

'Where did you learn to wash clothes like that?'

'Necessity is the mother of invention. We were unlucky. We

were sent to just about the worst of the punitive camps. There were very few survivors. Our arrival to begin with.—We got off the train. —A snow desert. Forest in the distance. Guards with rifles, muzzles pointing at us, wolf-dogs. At about the same time other groups were brought up. We were spread out and formed into a big polygon all over the field, facing outwards so that we shouldn't see each other. Then we were ordered down on our knees, and told to keep looking straight in front on pain of death. Then the roll-call, an endless, humiliating business going on for hours and hours, and all the time we were on our knees. Then we got up and the other groups were marched off in different directions, all except ours. We were told: "Here you are. This is your camp."—An open snow-field with a post in the middle and a notice on it saying: "GULAG 92 Y.N. 90" [1] —that's all there was.'

'It wasn't nearly so bad with us, we were fortunate. Of course I was only doing my second stretch; it followed automatically from the first. And then I was sentenced under a different article [2], so the conditions were quite different. When I came out, I was reinstated, as I was the first time, and allowed to go on lecturing. And I was called up in the ordinary way, not put into a penal battalion like you.'

'Yes, well . . . That was all there was, the post and the notice board, "GULAG 92 Y.N. 90". First we broke saplings with our bare hands in the frost, to get wood to build our huts with. And in the end, believe it or not, we built our own camp. We put up our prison and our stockade and our punishment cells and our watch towers, all with our own hands. And then we began our job as lumber-jacks. We felled trees. We harnessed ourselves, eight to a sledge, and we hauled timber and sank into the snow up to our necks. For a long time we didn't know there was a war. They kept it from us. And then suddenly there came the offer. You could volunteer for front-line service in a punitive battalion, and if you came out alive you were free. After that, attack after attack, mile after mile of electrified barbed wire, mines, mortars, month after month of artillery barrage. They called our company the death squad. It was practically wiped out. How and why I survived, I don't know. And yet—imagine—

[1] GULAG: *Glavnoye Upravleniye Lagerei*, *i.e.*, Chief Directorate of Camps, a department of the NKVD.

[2] Article: Both Dudorov and Gordon were evidently sentenced for political crimes, but the severity of the sentence depended on the 'article', *i.e.*, the paragraph of the Criminal Code under which the victim of the purge was accused. The most severe punishment was meted out to those accused under article 58 which referred to anti-state propaganda, sabotage, terrorism, etc.

all that utter hell was nothing, it was bliss compared to the horrors of the concentration camp, and not because of the material conditions but for some other reason.'

'Yes. You've been through a lot!'

'It wasn't just washing clothes you learned out there, you learned everything there is to learn.'

'It's an extraordinary thing, you know. It isn't only in comparison with your life as a convict, but compared to everything in the thirties, even to my favourable conditions at the university, in the midst of books and money and comfort; even to me there, the war came as a breath of fresh air, an omen of deliverance, a purifying storm.

'I think that collectivisation was both a mistake and a failure, and because that couldn't be admitted, every means of intimidation had to be used to make people forget how to think and judge for themselves, to force them to see what wasn't there, and to maintain the contrary of what their eyes told them. Hence the unexampled harshness of the Yezhov terror, and the promulgation of a constitution which was never intended to be applied, and the holding of elections not based on the principle of a free vote.

'And when the war broke out, its real horrors, its real dangers, its menace of real death, were a blessing compared with the inhuman power of the lie, a relief because it broke the spell of the dead letter.

'It was not only felt by men in your position, in concentration camps, but by everyone without exception, at home and at the front, and they all took a deep breath and flung themselves into the furnace of this deadly, liberating struggle with real joy, with rapture.

'The war has its special character as a link in the chain of revolutionary decades. It marks the end of the direct action of the causes inherent in the nature of the upheaval itself. By now, secondary causes are at work; we are seeing the fruit of its fruit, the result of its results—characters tempered by misfortune, unspoilt, heroic, ready for great, desperate, unheard-of deeds. These fabulous, astounding qualities are the moral flowering of this generation.

'And when I see such things I am filled with happiness, in spite of Christina's martyrdom and our losses and my wounds, in spite of the high cost in blood of the war. To see the light of self-sacrifice which illuminates Orletsova's death and the lives of all of us helps me to bear her loss.

'I was released just when you, poor fellow, were going through all that torture. Soon after that, Christina came to the university as a history student. I taught her. I had noticed her as a remarkable girl long before that, when she was still a child, at the end of my first term in prison.—You remember, Yury was still alive, I told you both.—Well, now she was one of my students.

'It was the time when the fashion for students to criticise their teachers had just come in. Christina became my most ardent detractor. I couldn't think what I'd done to make her so fierce! She was so aggressive and unjust that sometimes the other students protested and stood up for me. She had a great sense of humour and she made fun of me to her heart's content in the "wall newspaper", calling me by some invented name which everyone could see through. And then suddenly, completely by accident, I realised that this deep hostility was a camouflage of her love for me—a strong, enduring love which she had felt for a long time, and which I had always returned without knowing that she loved me.

'We spent a wonderful summer in 'forty-one, just before and after the beginning of the war. Christina was in a group of students, men and women, who were billeted in a Moscow suburb where my unit was also stationed. Our friendship began and ran its course against the background of their military training. Suburban home-guard units were being formed, Christina was learning to be a parachutist, the first German raiders were spotted from the Moscow roof-tops and driven back. It was then we became engaged, as I told you, but we were separated almost at once because my regiment was moved. I never saw her again.

'Later on, when things were going better for us and the Germans were surrendering in their thousands, I was transferred, after I had been twice wounded, from Anti-Aircraft to the Seventh Staff Division, where they needed people who knew languages. That's how I managed to get you taken on, after I'd fished you up from the bottom of the sea.'

'Tanya, the laundry girl, was a friend of Christina's. They got to know each other at the front. She talks a lot about her. Have you noticed the way Tanya smiles, all over her face, like Yury? You forget the snub-nose and the high cheekbones and you think she's quite pretty and attractive. It's the same Russian type as Yury's. You meet it all over the place.'

'I know what you mean. No, I hadn't noticed.'

'What a hideous, barbarous nick-name, Tanya Out-of-turn. It can't possibly be her surname. I wonder how she came by it.'

'Well, she told us, you know.—She was a bezprizornaya [1] of un-

---

[1] Waif. At various periods, particularly in 1922–25 and after the collectivisation campaign of 1932, numbers of homeless children, whose parents had been killed in the Civil War, disappeared in purges, etc., roamed the country and presented a formidable administrative problem.

known parents. Probably *Bezocherednaya*—"out-of-turn" is a corruption of *Bezotchaya* in the sense of "fatherless", which is what she must have been called somewhere in the depth of the country where she grew up and where the language is still pure. Then in town, where the name wasn't understood and where everything gets picked up and garbled, they turned it into something more topical and urban.'

3

Some time after this conversation took place Gordon and Dudorov were in the town of Karachev which had been razed to the ground. They were still chasing their unit and in Karachev they found some of its rear contingents who were catching up with the main force.

It was a hot summer; the weather had been fine and still for over a month. Sweltering under the blue, cloudless sky, the black soil of the Bryanshchina, the blessedly fertile region between Orel and Bryansk, was sun-burnt to a coffee-chocolate brown.

The main street cut straight across the town and joined the highway. On one side of it the houses had been blown up and turned into piles of builder's rubbish by mines; these ruins were surrounded by the uprooted, splintered and charred trees of orchards which had been levelled to the ground. On the other side, the waste plots had probably never been built on; fire and demolition had therefore largely spared them, since there was nothing to demolish.

On the side where there had once been houses, the homeless inhabitants were poking about in the still smouldering ash, picking up odds and ends in different corners of the ruins and putting them all together in one place. Others were hurriedly digging trenches for makeshift underground dwellings and cutting strips of turf with which to roof them.

The waste plots across the road were white with tents and crowded with lorries and horse-drawn wagons belonging to all kinds of auxiliary services—field ambulances cut off from their divisional staffs and sections of every sort of commissariat and depot, lost, mixed up and trying to sort themselves out. And here too, thin, weedy boys from the draft reinforcement companies, in grey forage caps, with heavy, rolled-up greatcoats on their backs, their faces earthy, drawn and bloodless with dysentery, rested their packs and had a sleep and a snack before trudging on further west.

Half the gutted, blown-up town was still burning and there were explosions in the distance where delayed-action mines were still going off. Every now and then, people digging on their plots felt the shock-waves under their feet; they straightened their backs, leaned on their picks and rested, turning and gazing in the direction of the blast.

There, the grey, black, brick-red clouds of smoke, flame and rubble rose into the sky, first in jets and fountains, then more lazily, like heavily rising scum, then fanning and spreading into plumes; finally they scattered and sank back to earth. Then the diggers went on with their digging.

Among the waste plots opposite the ruins, there was a field bordered by a hedge and overshadowed by great, spreading trees. Shaded and enclosed by the trees and the hedge, it seemed as cut off from the rest of the world as a cool, private, dusk-filled, covered courtyard.

Here Tanya, the laundry girl, with several service people from her regiment including Dudorov and Gordon, as well as others who had joined them, had been waiting since morning for the lorry which had been sent to fetch her. The regimental laundry entrusted to her care was packed in several crates which stood piled one on top of the other in the field. Tanya watched it conscientiously, never moving away a step, and the rest of the group also kept it in sight for fear of missing the chance of a lift.

They had been waiting a long time, over five hours. With nothing to do, they listened willingly to the girl, who had seen many things in her life and who chattered incessantly. At the moment she was telling them of how she had met Major-General Zhivago.

'Certainly I did, yesterday it was. They took me in person to see the general, Major-General Zhivago himself. He was passing through here, and he was interested in Christina, asking questions about her. He wanted to see eye-witnesses who had known her. So they pointed me out to him. They said we'd been friends. He told them to bring me along. So they came and fetched me. And he wasn't a bit frightening, nothing special about him, just like everybody else. He's got slit eyes and black hair. Well, I told him what I knew. He heard me out and said thank you. "And who are you?" he said to me. "Where do you come from?" Well, naturally, I wasn't going to tell him. What have I got to boast about? I'm a bezprizornaya, you know how it is, in and out of reformatories, always on the move. But he wouldn't leave me alone. "Let's have it," he says. "Don't be shy. There's nothing to be ashamed of." Well, at first I only said a word or two, being shy, then I told him a bit more, and he kept nodding his head, as much as to say, Go on, so I got bolder. And it's true I have a lot to tell. You wouldn't believe it if I told you, you'd say: "She's making it up." Well, it was the same with him. When I finished he got up and started walking up and down the hut. "Good gracious," he said. "That's an extraordinary thing. I'll tell you what," he says, "I have no time now. But I'll find you again, you can be sure of that, I'll find you and send for you again. I never thought I'd hear things like this. I won't leave you here," he says, "I've just got to clear up a few details. And then, who can tell, I might put myself down as your uncle, you'll be promoted to being general's niece. And I'll send you to college," he said, "have you educated. Anywhere you like." Honest to God, that's what he said. Such a one for laughing and teasing, he is.'

At this moment, a long empty cart with raised sides, of the kind used for carting hay in Poland and West Russia, drove into the field. The two horses in their shaft harness were driven by a soldier from the horse transport corps who in the old days would have been called a forage driver. He pulled up, jumped down from his seat and began to unhitch the cart. Everyone except Tanya and one or two soldiers crowded round him imploring him to take them wherever they were going, telling him, of course, that they would make it worth his while. But the driver refused, saying that he had no right to use the cart or the horses except as he was ordered. He led the horses away and was not seen again.

Tanya and the servicemen, who until then had been sitting on the ground, all climbed into the empty cart which had been left standing in the field. The conversation, interrupted by its arrival and by the argument with the driver, was resumed.

'What did you tell the general?' asked Gordon. 'Tell us if you can.'

And so she told them her terrible story.

4

'Yes, it's true I've got a lot to tell. They say that I'm of gentle birth. Whether strangers told me or I myself kept it in my heart, I don't know, but I've heard it said that my mama, Raïssa Komarova, was the wife of a Russian cabinet minister, Comrade Komarov, who was in hiding in White Mongolia. But it seems that this Komarov was not my real father. Well, of course, I'm not an educated girl, I grew up an orphan without a father and mother. Perhaps what I say will seem funny to you, but I'm only telling what I know; you have to put yourselves in my place.

'It all happened beyond Krushitsy, the other end of Siberia, beyond the Cossack country, near the Chinese border. When we, the Reds that is to say, moved up to the chief town of the Whites, that same Komarov, the minister, he put my mama and all their household on a special train and ordered it to take them away. My mama was frightened, you see, she didn't dare to move a step without him.

'But about me he didn't know, Komarov didn't. He didn't know there was such a person at all. My mama had me when she had been parted from him for a long time, and she was frightened to death in case somebody let it slip out and he heard about it. He hated children, he yelled and stamped his feet when he saw them. They only bring filth and worry into the house, I can't stand it, he used to shout.

'Well now, as I was saying, when the Reds began to come up to the town, my mama sent to Nagornaya Station for Marfa, the signal woman. That was three stations away from the town. I'll tell you how it was. First there was Nizovaya, that was down in the valley, and then there was Nagornaya, that was up on the hill, and then there was Samson's Pass. Now I think I understand why Mama knew this signal woman. I think this signal woman, Marfa, used to come and sell milk and vegetables in the town. Yes, that must have been how it happened.

And I think there's something there I don't know. It seems they tricked Mama, they didn't tell her the truth. The Lord only knows what sort of a tale they told her, I suppose they said it was just for a time, for a day or two, just till the commotion was over and things settled down. But not about me going to strangers for ever. To be brought up by strangers. Mama could not have given up her own child like that.

'Well, you know how it is with a child. "Go and talk to Auntie, she'll give you a sweet, nice Auntie, don't be frightened of Auntie." How afterwards I cried my eyes out, how as a child I wore my heart out with misery—I'd better not start telling you that. I wanted to hang myself, I nearly went out of my mind as a small child. That was all I was at that time. I suppose Aunt Marfa got money for my keep, a lot of money.

'There was a good farm that went with the signal post, a cow and a horse and of course all kinds of fowl, and a big plot for vegetables— out there you could get as much land as you liked—and of course no rent and a government cottage down by the railway. When the train was coming from home, it could hardly get up the hill, it was so steep, but coming from your parts, from Russia, down it came so fast they had to use the brakes. Down below, in the autumn, when the woods thinned out, you could see Nizovaya Station like on a saucer.

'Uncle Vassya, Aunt Marfa's husband, I used to call him Pappy like the peasants. He was a kind and cheerful man, only terribly trusting, specially when he was drunk. Everybody knew all there was to know about him. He'd turn his heart inside out to every stranger he met.

'But the signal woman I never could call Mama. Whether it was that I couldn't forget my own Mama or for some other reason, but she really was terrible. She really was. So I called the signal woman Aunt Marfa.

'Well, time went on, years went by, how many I don't know. I was beginning to run out to the trains to wave the flag, and I could bring the cow in or unhitch the horse. Aunt Marfa taught me to spin, and as for the housework, it goes without saying I did that. Anything like sweeping or tidying or doing a bit of cooking, that was nothing to me, I did all that. Oh yes, and I forgot to tell you, I looked after Petya. Our Petya had withered legs, he was three but he couldn't walk at all, so I carried him about. It's all those years ago, but I still get shivers down my back when I think of how Aunt Marfa used to squint at my strong legs as much as to say, why weren't my legs withered, it would be better if I had withered legs instead of her Petya, as if I'd put the evil eye on him. Can you believe that there are such spiteful and backward people in the world?

'But now listen to what I'll tell you. All that was nothing to what happened later, you'll be astonished.

'It was the time of the NEP, a thousand roubles was worth a copeck. Uncle Vassya sold a cow down at Nizovaya and got two sacks full of money.—Kerenki it was called—no, sorry, they were called lemons [1] by then, that's what they were called. He had a drink and told everyone in Nagornaya how rich he was.

'I remember it was a windy autumn day. The wind was tearing at the roof, it nearly knocked you off your feet and the engines couldn't get uphill because the wind was head on. Suddenly I see an old beggar woman coming down from the top of the hill, the wind was tugging at her skirt and blowing off her kerchief.

'She was walking along and moaning and clutching her belly. She asked us to take her in; we put her on the bench. "Oh," she yells, "I can't stand it, I can't stand it, my belly is on fire, death has come upon me. In Christ's name," she begs, "take me to the hospital, I'll pay you whatever you like." Well, Pappy hitched Udaloy, the horse,

---

[1] Lemons: Slang for 'millions', as million-rouble banknotes were called at the peak of the inflation in 1921-22.

to the cart, put the old woman in the cart and took her fifteen versts away to the hospital.

'After a time we went to bed, Aunt Marfa and I, then we hear Udaloy neighing outside and the cart driving into the yard. It seemed a bit too soon for them to be back. But anyway Aunt Marfa lit a light, put on her jacket and undid the bolt without waiting for Pappy to knock.

'She opened the door, but it wasn't Pappy on the doorstep, it was a terrible, dark stranger, and he says: "Show me," he says, "where the money is you got for the cow. I've killed your old man in the wood," he said, "but seeing you're a woman I'll let you alone if you tell me where the money is. If you don't tell me you know what will happen, you'll only have yourself to blame, and better not keep me waiting, I've no time to hang around."

'O, Lord almighty, dear comrades, the state we were in—put yourselves in our place! We were shaking all over, half dead with fright and we couldn't get out a word—such horrors! First Uncle Vassya had been killed, he'd said so himself, he'd killed him with an axe, and now we were alone with him, alone in the house with a bandit, a bandit in our house, we could see he was a bandit.

'I suppose it was at this moment that Aunt Marfa went out of her mind, she being heart-broken for her husband and not able to show her sorrow.

'First she fell at his feet. "Have mercy on me," she says, "don't kill me, I don't know a thing, I've never heard about any money, I don't know what money you are talking about." But he wasn't going to be put off with that, he wasn't such a fool, the devil. "All right then," she tells him. "The money is in the cellar. I'll open the trap-door for you." But he saw right through that. "No," he says, "you go down, you know the way, you get it. I don't care if you go down to the cellar or up on the roof, all I want is the money. Only mind you don't try anything on," he said, "it doesn't do to try to make a fool of me."

'Then she says to him: "God forbid you should have such doubts. I'd gladly go down and get it for you myself, but my legs are bad, I can't manage the ladder. I'll stand on the top step and hold the light for you. Don't worry, I'll send my daughter down with you," she says. That was me, she meant.

'O comrades, can you imagine what came over me when I heard that? Well, that's the end of me, I thought, and everything went black in front of my eyes and my legs wouldn't hold me up, I thought I'd fall down.

'But that devil, he was all there, he takes one look at both of us and screws up his eyes and gives her a crooked kind of leer, as much as to say: I know your tricks, you can't fool me. He could see that I meant nothing to her, I wasn't her own flesh and blood, so he makes a grab at Petya and picks him up in one hand and pulls up the trap-door with the other. "Let's have a light," he says to her and down he goes—down the ladder under the ground with Petya.

'I think she was already out of her mind and couldn't understand anything, she had gone quite mad. As soon as he had gone down with little Petya, bang, she slammed the trap-door and locked it and began to drag a heavy trunk on top of it, nodding and beckoning me to help her, because it was too heavy for her. She gets it into place and sits down on top of it, as pleased as Punch she was, the crazy woman. No sooner had she sat down than the bandit started yelling and banging on the floor. You couldn't make out what he was saying, the floor-boards were too thick, but you could tell from his voice what he meant: let him out or he'd murder Petya. He roared worse than a wild beast to frighten us. "Now your Petya's for it," he yelled, but she couldn't understand a thing, laughing and winking at me as much as to say: "Let him brawl to his heart's content, I'm sitting on the trunk and I've got the key in my hand." I did everything I could with her, I screamed right into her ears saying she must open up the cellar and save Petya, and I tried to push her off the trunk, but I couldn't, she was too strong for me and she wouldn't listen.

'Well, he was banging, banging on the floor and the time was going by, and she just sat there rolling her eyes, not listening to anything.

'Well, after a time—O Lord, O Lord, what haven't I seen and been through in my life, but such horror as this I'll never come across again. As long as I live I'll hear Petya's thin little voice—little Petya screamed and groaned under the earth, the holy innocent—that devil bit him to death.

'Now what shall I do, what shall I do with this mad old woman and this murderer, I thought. And the time was going by. No sooner had I thought this than I heard Udaloy neighing outside; he'd been standing out there in the yard ready harnessed all this time. Yes, that was how it was. Udaloy was neighing as much as to say: "Let's fly quickly, Tanya, and find some good people and get help." I looked out of the window and I saw that it was getting near to dawn. "All right," I thought, "thank you for putting the thought into my head, Udaloy. So be it. We'll go." But hardly had I thought this when again I heard as if it were a voice calling from the wood: "Wait, don't hurry, Tanya, we'll do it another way." And again I knew I wasn't alone in the wood. An engine hooted down below, like a cock crowing in our own yard. I knew that engine by its whistle, it always stood under steam at Nagornaya—a banker they called it—to help goods-trains up the hill. This was a mixed train going by, it always went by at that time every night. Well, I heard this engine I knew, calling me from below. I listened and my heart leapt. Am I off my head, I wondered, like Auntie Marfa, that every living beast and every dumb engine speaks to me in plain Russian?

'Well, it was no good thinking, the train was getting near, there was no time to think. I grabbed the lantern—there wasn't much light yet, and I raced like mad to the track and stood right in the middle, between the rails, waving the light up and down.

'Well, what more is there to say? I stopped the train; because of the wind it was going slowly, slowly, thank goodness, as you might say at a walking pace. I stopped it, and the driver, who knew me, leaned out of the window of the cabin and called out something; I couldn't hear what it was for the wind. I shouted to him, the signal hut had been raided, murder and robbery, a bandit in the house, help us, comrade uncle, we need help straight away. And while I was saying this, Red Army men came jumping out of the train, one after the other—it was an army train, that's what it was—they jumped out on the track. "What's up?" they asked; they couldn't make out why on earth the train had stopped in the wood, on a steep hill at night and was standing still. When they heard all that had happened, they dragged the bandit out of the cellar; he was squealing in a voice thinner than Petya's: "Have mercy on me, good people," he says, "don't kill me, I won't ever do it again." They took the law into their own hands. They dragged him out on to the sleepers, tied his hands and feet to the rails and drove the train over him.

'I never even went back for my clothes, I was so frightened. I asked them to take me along in the train, and they put me on the train and off I went. After this, I wandered over half our own country and others with the bezprizornys—I don't know where I haven't been. I'm not exaggerating. What happiness, what freedom, I knew after all the sorrows of my childhood! Though it must be said that there was much evil and misfortune too. But all this came later, I'll tell you about it some other time . . . That night I was telling you about, a railway official came off the train and went to the house to take charge of the Government property, and to give orders about Auntie Marfa, to arrange what was to be done with her. Some say she never recovered and died in a mad-house, but others say she got better and came out.'

For a long time after hearing Tanya's story Gordon and Dudorov strolled about under the trees in silence. Then the lorry came; it turned clumsily off the road into the field and the crates were loaded on to it. Gordon said:

'You realise who she is?—Tanya, the laundry girl?'

'Yes, of course.'

'Yevgraf will look after her.' He added after a silence: 'This has happened several times in the course of history. A thing which has been conceived in a lofty, ideal manner becomes coarse and material. Thus Rome came out of Greece and the Russian Revolution came out of the Russian enlightenment. Take that line of Blok's, "We, the children of Russia's terrible years": you can see the difference of period at once. In his time, when he said it, he meant it figuratively, metaphorically. The children were not children, but the sons, the heirs of the intelligentsia, and the terrors were not terrible but apocalyptic; that's quite different. Now the figurative has become literal, children are children and the terrors are terrible. There you have the difference.'

5

On a quiet summer evening in Moscow, five or ten years later, Gordon and Dudorov were again together, sitting by a window high above the immense city spreading away into the dusk. They were turning the pages of a book of Yury's writings which Yevgraf had compiled, a book they had read more than once and almost knew by heart. In the intervals of reading, they exchanged reflections and followed their own thoughts. It grew dark so that they could no longer make out the print and had to put on the light.

Moscow below them and reaching into the distance—Moscow, the author's native town and the half of all that had befallen him—now appeared to them, not as the place where all these things had happened, but as the heroine of a long tale of which that evening, book in hand, they were reaching the end.

Although the enlightenment and liberation which had been expected to come after the war had not come with victory, a presage of freedom was in the air throughout these post-war years, and it was their only historical meaning.

To the two ageing friends sitting by the window it seemed that this freedom of the spirit was there, that on that very evening the future had become almost tangible in the streets below, and that they had themselves entered that future and would, from now on, be part of it.

They felt a peaceful joy for this holy city and for the whole land and for the survivors among those who had played a part in this story and for their children, and the silent music of happiness filled them and enveloped them and spread far and wide. And it seemed that the book in their hands knew what they were feeling and gave them its support and confirmation.

ZHIVAGO'S POEMS

HAMLET

The noise is stilled.   I come out on the stage.
Leaning against the door-post
I try to guess from the distant echo
What is to happen in my lifetime.

The darkness of night is aimed at me
Along the sights of a thousand opera-glasses.
Abba, Father, if it be possible,
Let this cup pass from me.

I love your stubborn purpose,
I consent to play my part.
But now a different drama is being acted;
For this once let me be.

Yet the order of the acts is planned
And the end of the way inescapable.
I am alone; all drowns in the Pharisees' hypocrisy.
To live your life is not as simple as to cross a field [1].

[1] The last line is a Russian proverb.

MARCH

The world swelters in the sun,
The wooded hollow storms into frenzied life,
Work seethes in the hands of the spring,
That strapping dairymaid.

The snow is wasting away
In little branches like weak blue veins,
But the cowshed smokes with life,
The teeth of the pitchforks bristle with health.

These nights, these days and nights:
Rain drumming on the window at noon,
The thin dripping of icicles on the roof,
Chatter of sleepless streams.

Everything is thrown open, stables and cowshed.
Pigeons are pecking oats in the snow.
The culprit and the life-giver
Is the dung with its smell of fresh air.

IN HOLY WEEK

It is still the dark of night
And still so early in the world
That the stars in the sky are without number
And each is bright as day,
And if it could, the earth
Would sleep through Easter
To the chanting of the Psalms.

It is still the dark of night
And still so early in the world
That the square lies like an eternity
Between the corner and the crossroads
And dawn and warmth
Are a thousand years away.

The earth is still quite naked,
Has nothing to wear at night
While it rings the bells
In response to the choir inside.

And from Maundy Thursday
Till Holy Saturday
The water burrows into the river banks
And spins the whirlpools.

The forest is stripped bare,
And at the season of Christ's Passion
Its crowding pine-trees stand
Like worshippers at a service,

While in town, bunched together
Like a meeting,
The naked trees
Gaze through the church gratings,

Awestruck. Their alarm
Is understandable.
Gardens burst through fences,
The earth's foundations quake :
God is being buried.

They see the light at the royal gate [1],
The black pall and the row of candles,
The tear-stained faces :
Suddenly the procession
Advances on them with the shroud
And two birches at the gate
Have to make way.

The procession walks round the churchyard
And back, along the pavement's edge,
Bringing spring and spring talk
From the street into the porch,
And air with an aftertaste of communion
    bread
And the spring smells of charcoal.

And March scatters snow
To the crowd of cripples at the porch,
As if a man had carried out the ark,
Opened it and given away
Everything to the last shred.

The singing lasts till dawn.
Having wept their fill,
The Psalms and Acts
Reach more softly
Into the empty, lamplit street.

But at midnight beasts and men fall silent,
Hearing the spring rumour
That as soon as the weather changes
Death can be vanquished
Through the travail of the Resurrection.

[1] The gate in the screen which, in a Russian church, divides the altar from the
nave.

WHITE NIGHT

I see a distant past
And a house on the Petersburg Quai [1].
Daughter of a small landowner of the steppes,
You had come from Kursk to be a student.

You were beautiful, young men loved you.
Through that white night we two
Sat on your window-sill
Looking down from the skyscraper.

Like gas butterflies the street-lamps,
Touched by the morning, trembled.
I talked to you softly
Like the sleeping distance.

And we, like Petersburg spreading away
Beyond the shoreless Neva,
Were held in timid fidelity
To a mystery.

Out there, far off, in the dense forest,
On that white night of spring,
The nightingales filled the woods
With the thunder of their praisegiving.

The mad trilling rolled on,
The voice of the small insignificant bird
Roused a bustle of delight
In the depth of the spell-bound forest.

Thither crept the night,
Hugging the fences like a barefoot tramp,
Trailing behind it, from the window-sill,
The wraith of that conversation.

Petersburgskaya Storona: a riverside district.

Within the reach of its echo,
In fenced gardens,
The branches of apple and cherry
Put on white blossoms,

And white as ghosts, the trees
Crowded into the road
As though waving good-bye
To the white night which had seen so much.

SPRING FLOODS

The fires of the sunset were dying down.
Through the dense forest,
Along spring-flooded tracks,
A weary horseman rode towards a solitary Urals farm.

The horse champed at the bit;
In the funnels of the streams
The water chased after
And answered the ringing horse-shoes.

But when the rider dropped his reins
And slowed down to a walk
The spring flood rolled
Its thunder past.

Someone laughed, someone cried,
Stone was ground on stone,
Uprooted trees
Crashed into whirlpools.

In the fire of sunset,
In the charcoal distance of branches,
A nightingale raged
Like an echoing tocsin.

Where the weeping willow
Dipped her widow's veil over the hollow,
There, like the Robber-Nightingale [1] of old,
He whistled the notes of the seven oak pipes.

What misfortune, what fever
Did this violence foretell?
At whom was this grapeshot aimed,
Flying in the thickness of the forest?

[1] Cf. p. 260. According to the legend Robber-Nightingale 'whistled on seven oaks'.

It seemed that at any moment the nightingale would come,
Like the spirit of the woods, from the convicts' hide-out,
And meet the mounted or infantry patrols
Of the local partisans.

Earth, sky, forest, field,
Caught the madness, pain, happiness, torment,
Which had their part
In that rare sound.

EXPLANATION

Life has returned with as little reason
As once it was so strangely interrupted.
I am in the same old-fashioned street
As then, on that summer day and at that hour.

The same people, the same worries,
And the fire of sunset has not cooled
Since the evening of death which nailed it
Hurriedly to the wall of the Manège [1].

Women in cheap striped cotton
Still wear out their shoes by night,
And are crucified in attics,
On the iron roofing.

Here is one who steps wearily
Out on the threshold,
Slowly climbs from the basement
Up the steps, crosses the yard.

Again I make ready my excuses
And am again indifferent to everything.
Once again the woman from next door
Walks round the alley, leaving us alone.

*   *

Don't cry, don't pucker your swollen lips,
Don't gather them into creases,
For that would crack the dryness
Formed by the spring fever.

Take your hand off my breast.
We are high-tension cables.
Look out, or unawares
We shall again be thrown together.

---

[1] Manège Square where there was street fighting during the revolution.

Years will pass, you will marry.
You will forget these unsettled ways.
It is a great step to be a woman,
To drive others mad is heroism.

As for me, I have the reverence
And lifelong devotion of a servant
Before the miracle of a woman's hands,
Back, shoulders, neck.

However many rings of pain
The night welds round me,
The opposing pull is stronger,
The passion to break away.

SUMMER IN TOWN

Conversation in a half tone.
With a flurry of haste
The whole sheaf of hair
Is gathered up from the nape of the neck.

From under the heavy comb
A helmeted woman looks out,
Her head thrown back
With all its plaited hair.

Outside, the hot night
Promises a storm,
The passers-by scatter,
Shuffling home.

Brief thunder
Echoes sharply,
And the wind stirs
The curtain at the window.

Sultry
Silence.
Fingers of lightning
Search the sky.

And when the dawn-filled,
Heated morning
Has dried the puddles in the streets
After the night rain

The centuries-old, scented,
Blossoming lime-trees
Frown
For lack of sleep.

THE WIND

This is the end of me, but you live on.
The wind, crying and complaining,
Rocks the house and the forest,
Not each pine-tree separately
But all the trees together
With the whole boundless distance,
Like the hulls of sailing-ships
Riding at anchor in a bay.
It shakes them not out of mischief,
And not in aimless fury,
But to find for you, out of its grief,
The words of a lullaby.

INTOXICATION

Under the ivy-circled willow tree
We seek shelter from stormy weather,
A cape covers our shoulders
And my arms circle you.

I am mistaken. The trees of this thicket
Are circled not with ivy but with hops [1].
So better spread the cape
Flat on the ground.

[1] *Khmel* is both 'hops' and 'intoxication'.

INDIAN SUMMER

The leaf of the black currant is coarse as canvas.
In the house there is laughter and the sound of ringing glass.
They are slicing, pickling, peppering,
Putting cloves into jars.

The teasing forest scatters all this noise
Down the steep slope
Where the sun has scorched the hazel
Like a camp-fire.

Here the path leads down into the hollow
And you feel sorry for the fallen trees
And for autumn, the old rag-and-bone merchant,
Who sweeps everything into the gully :

Sorry that the world is simpler
Than some clever people think,
Sorry for the drooping thicket,
Sorry that each thing has its end :

Sorry that there is no point in staring
When everything before you is burned up,
And autumn's white soot
Drifts through the windows like a cobweb.

A path has broken through the garden fence
And loses itself in the birch-wood.
There is laughter and hubbub in the house
And the same laughter and hubbub far away.

THE WEDDING PARTY

Crossing the edge of the yard
The wedding guests
Have come to the bride's house
To feast till morning.

Behind the landlord's
Baize-lined door
Snatches of chatter
Are stilled from one till seven.

But at dawn,
When you could sleep for ever,
The accordeon sings out again
Leaving the wedding.

Again the player scatters
The splash of clapping palms,
Glitter of beads,
All the party hullabaloo.

Again and again
The chatter of the dance tune
Bursts into the sleepers' beds
Straight from the feasting.

A girl as white as snow
Glides like a peacock
In the row and the whistling,
Swaying her hips,

Nodding her head,
Waving her right hand,
Dancing on the pavement
Like a peacock.

Suddenly the gaiety and noise of the game,
The tapping of the ring-dance,
Dropping through to Tartarus,
Sink as in water.

The noisy yard is waking up.
A businesslike echo
Mixes in the talk
And peals of laughter.

Whirlwind of grey-blue patches,
A flock of pigeons
Taking off from the dovecots
Rushes the heights of the limitless sky,

As if someone on waking
Had thought to send them chasing
The wedding party with wishes
For many years of life.

And life itself is only an instant,
Only the dissolving
Of ourselves in all others
As though in gift to them ;

Only a wedding, bursting
In through the windows from the street,
Only a song, a dream,
A grey-blue pigeon.

AUTUMN

I have allowed my family to scatter,
All my dear ones are dispersed.
A life-long loneliness
Fills nature and my heart,

And here I am with you, in a small house.
Outside, the forest is unpeopled like a desert.
As in the song, the drives and footpaths
Are almost overgrown.

The log walls are sad,
Having only us two to gaze at.
But we never undertook to leap the barriers.
We will perish honestly.

At one o'clock we shall sit down to table,
At three we shall rise,
I with my book, you with your embroidery.
At dawn we shan't remember
What time we stopped kissing.

Leaves, rustle and spill yourselves
Ever more splendidly, ever more recklessly,
Fill yesterday's cup of bitterness
Still more full with the pain of to-day.

Let devotion, desire, delight,
Be scattered in the uproar of September:
And you, go and hide in the crackling autumn,
Either be quiet or be crazy.

You fling your dress from you
As the coppice flings away its leaves.
In a dressing-gown with a silk tassel
You fall into my arms.

You are the good gift of the road to destruction
When life is more sickening than disease
And boldness the root of beauty.
This is what draws us together.

A FAIRY-TALE

Once upon a time
In a fairy-tale kingdom,
Spurring over
The burs of the steppe,

A horseman rode to battle.
Through the dust a dark forest
Rose to meet him
In the distance.

Uneasiness
Scratched at his heart:
'Beware of the water,
Tighten your girth.'

He would not listen.
Galloped
Full tilt
Up the wooded slope;

Followed the channel
Of a dried-up stream,
Passed a meadow
And crossed a hill;

Strayed into a defile,
Came on the spoor
Of a wild beast
Leading to water,

And deaf to the sound
Of his own suspicion,
Rode down to the gully
To water his horse.

*   *

Over the water,
Across the ford,
The mouth of a cave
Lit up like sulphur.

Crimson smoke
Clouded his vision.
A distant cry
Sounded through the forest.

The rider started ;
In answer to the call,
Picked his way gingerly.
Now he sighted—

And gripped his spear—
The head,
Tail,
Scales of the dragon.

Light scattered
From its blazing mouth.
It had trapped a girl
In three coils of its body.

Its neck was swaying
Over her shoulder
Like the tail of a whip.
The custom of that country

Allotted a girl,
Beautiful
Prisoner and prey,
To the monster of the forest.

This was the tribute
The people paid
To the serpent, ransom
For hovels.

Free
To savage her
The serpent twisted
About her arms and throat.

The rider raised eyes
And prayer to high heaven,
Poising his lance
For battle.

*   *

Eyes closed.
Hills. Clouds.
Rivers. Fords.
Years. Centuries.

Knocked down in battle
The rider has lost his helmet.
His faithful horse
Tramples the serpent.

Horse and dead dragon
Are side by side in the sand,
The rider unconscious,
The girl in a daze.

Blue gentleness lights
The vault of noonday.
Who is she? A queen?
A peasant? A princess?

At times excess of joy
Triples their tears,
At times a dead sleep
Holds them in its power.

At times his health
Comes home to him,
At times he lies motionless,
Weak with loss of blood.

But their hearts are beating.
Now he, now she
Struggles to awake,
Falls back to sleep.

Eyes closed.
Hills. Clouds.
Rivers. Fords.
Years. Centuries

AUGUST

Just as it promised
The early morning sun entered between the
    curtains
And a slanting, saffron streak
Reached the sofa.

The sun's hot ochre
Covered the near-by woods, the village houses,
My bed, the wet pillow
And the wall behind the bookcase.

I remember why the pillow is wet:
I dreamed that you were coming,
One after another, through the wood
To see me off.

You walked in a loose crowd.
Then someone remembered
That by the Old Calendar
To-day was the Sixth of August, the Lord's
    Transfiguration.

Usually, on this day, a light without a flame
Comes from Mount Tabor,
And autumn, clear as a sign,
Draws all eyes to itself.

You walked through the small, beggar-naked,
Trembling alder thicket
Into the graveyard's ginger-red coppice
Which glowed like a honey cake.

The sky was the grand neighbour
Of those hushed treetops,
And distance called to distance
In the long-drawn-out crowing of the cocks.

Among the trees, in the middle of the churchyard,
Stood death like a government surveyor,
And looked into my dead face to measure
How large a grave to dig for me.

All could clearly hear
A quiet voice near by.
This was my own past voice, prophetic,
Untouched by dissolution :

'Goodbye, azure and gold
Of the Transfiguration.
Soften with a woman's last caress
The bitterness of the hour of my death.

'Goodbye, timeless years
And woman who challenged
The abyss of humiliations.
I am your battle-field.

'Goodbye to the span of outstretched wings,
Free stubbornness of flight,
Image of the world revealed in speech,
Creativeness, working of miracles.'

WINTER NIGHT

Snow swept over the earth,
Swept it from end to end.
The candle on the table burned,
The candle burned.

Like swarms of summer midges
Drawn to the flame
The snowflakes
Flocked to the window.

The driven snow drew circles and arrows
On the window pane.
The candle on the table burned,
The candle burned.

On the bright ceiling
Fell the shadows
Of crossed hands, crossed feet,
Crossed fate.

Two shoes fell to the floor
With a thud.
From the night-light
Wax tears dropped on frock.

And everything was lost
In the white-haired, white, snowy darkness.
The candle on the table burned,
The candle burned.

A draught from the corner
Puffed at the candle's flame,
And like an angel, the heat of temptation
Raised two wings in the form of a cross.

The snow swept all through February,
And now and again
The candle on the table burned,
The candle burned.

PARTING

From the threshold a man looks in,
He cannot recognise his house.
Her departure was like a flight
And everywhere are signs of havoc.

All the rooms are in chaos;
Tears and an aching head
Prevent him from seeing
The measure of his ruin.

Since morning there has been a roaring in his ears.
Is he awake or dreaming?
Why does the thought of the sea
Keep pushing into his mind?

When the great wide world
Is hidden by the frost on the window,
The hopelessness of sorrow
Is even more like the desert of the sea.

She was as near and dear to him
In every feature
As the shores are close to the sea
In every breaker.

As after a storm
The surf floods over the reeds,
So in his heart
Her image is submerged.

In the years of trial,
When life was inconceivable,
From the bottom of the sea the tide of destiny
Washed her up to him.

The obstacles were countless,
But she was carried by the tide
Narrowly past the hazards
To the shore.

Now she has gone away;
Unwillingly perhaps.
The parting will eat them up,
Misery will gnaw them, bones and all.

He looks around him.
At the moment of leaving
She turned everything upside down,
Flung everything out of the chest of drawers.

Till dusk he roams about
Putting back into the drawers
The scattered scraps of stuff,
The patterns used for cutting out,

And pricking himself on a needle
Still stuck in a piece of sewing,
Suddenly he sees her
And cries quietly.

MEETING

When snow covers the roads
And lies heavily on the roofs,
I'll go out to stretch my legs, and see you
Standing at the door,

Alone, in an autumn coat,
Hatless, without snow-boots,
Chewing a handful of snow
And trying to be calm.

The trees and fences
Vanish into the dark distance.
Alone in the snowfall
You stand at the corner.

Water drips from your kerchief,
Trickles into your sleeves
And sparkles like dew
In your hair.

A lock of bright hair
Lights up your face,
Your kerchief,
Your figure and your shabby coat.

The snow is wet on your lashes
There is pain in your eyes.
You are engraved on my heart
With a chisel dipped in acid[1].

And in my heart the humility of your expression
Will remain for ever,
And now the hard heart of the world
Is not my business.

[1] Literally antimony.

This is why the snowy night
Doubles itself
And I cannot draw the frontier
Between you and me.

But who are we, where do we come from,
When of all those years
Nothing but idle talk is left
And we are nowhere in the world?

CHRISTMAS STAR

It was winter.
The wind blew from the steppe
And it was cold for the child
In the cave on the hillside.

He was warmed by the breath of an ox.
The farm animals
Were stabled in the cave,
And a warm haze drifted over the manger.

Shaking from their sheepskins
The wisps of straw and hay-seeds of their bedding,
Half asleep, the shepherds gazed
From a rock ledge into the midnight distance.

Far away were a snowy field, a graveyard,
Fences, tombstones,
The shaft of a cart in a snowdrift,
And above the graveyard the sky full of stars.

Near, never seen till then, more shy
Than the glimmer in the window
Of a watchman's hut,
The star shone on its way to Bethlehem.

It flamed like a hayrick,
Standing aside from the sky
And from God;
Glowed like a farm on fire,

Rose like a blazing
Stack of straw.
The sight of the new star
Startled the universe.

Its reddening glow
Was a sign ; the three star-gazers
Hurried to the call
Of its unprecedented light.

Camels followed them loaded with gifts,
And donkeys in harness, one smaller than the other,
Minced down the hill.

In a strange vision all time to come
Arose in the distance:
All the thoughts, hopes, worlds of the centuries,
The future of art galleries and of museums,
All the pranks of goblins and deeds of magicians,
All the Christmas trees and all the children's dreams:

The shimmering candles, the paper chains,
The splendour of coloured tinsel . . .
. . . Angrier and more wicked blew the wind from the
            steppe . . .
. . . All the apples and golden bubbles.

Part of the pond was hidden by the alders,
But from where the shepherds stood
A part could be seen between the rooks' nests in the
            treetops.
They watched camels and donkeys skirting the pool.
'Let's go with the others,' they said,
Wrapping themselves in their sheepskins,
'Let's bow to the miracle.'

They grew hot from shuffling in the snow.
On the bright plain bare footsteps,
Shining like glass, led round the hut.
In the starlight the sheep-dogs growled at these tracks,
As though they were burning candle-ends.

The frosty night was like a fairy-tale.
Invisible beings kept stepping down
From the snowdrifts into the crowd.

The dogs followed, looking round apprehensively;
They kept close to the youngest shepherd, expecting
    trouble.

Through the same countryside, along the same road,
Several angels walked among the crowd.
Bodiless beings, they were invisible;
Only their steps left a trace.

A crowd had gathered by the stone at the entrance.
Day was breaking. The trunks of the cedars were plain.
'Who are you?' asked Mary.
'We are a company of shepherds and envoys from
    heaven.
We have come to praise you both.'
'You can't all come in at once. Wait a little by the
    door.'

Shepherds and herdsmen stamped about
In the ashy dusk before the dawn.
By the wooden water trough
Men on foot and horsemen swore at each other,
Camels roared and asses kicked.

Day was breaking. The dawn swept the remaining stars
Like cinders from the sky.
Out of all the great gathering Mary allowed
Only the Wise Men through the opening in the rock.

He slept in the oak manger,
Radiant as moonlight in the hollow of a tree.
Instead of a sheepskin,
The lips of the ass and the nostrils of the ox kept him warm.

The Magi stood in the shadow,
Whispering, scarcely finding words.
All at once, a hand stretched out of the dark,
Moved one of them aside to the left of the manger.
He looked round. Gazing at the Virgin from the doorway
Like a guest, was the Christmas Star.

DAYBREAK

You meant everything in my destiny.
Then came the war, the disaster.
For a long, long time,
No trace, no news of you.

After all these years,
Again your voice has disturbed me.
All night I read your testament.
It was like reviving from a faint.

I want to be among people,
In a crowd, in its morning bustle.
I'm ready to smash everything to splinters
And bring them to their knees.

And I run down the stairs
As though coming out for the first time
Into these snowy streets
With their deserted pavements.

All around are lights, homeliness, people getting up,
Drinking tea, hurrying to the trams.
In the space of several minutes
The town is unrecognisable.

The blizzard weaves a net
Of thickly falling snow across the gate.
They all scurry out to be on time,
Leaving their food half eaten, their tea unfinished.

I feel for each of them
As if I were in their skin,
I melt with the melting snow,
I frown with the morning.

In me are people without names,
Children, stay-at-homes, trees.
I am conquered by them all
And this is my only victory.

THE MIRACLE

He was walking from Bethany to Jerusalem
Weary with the sadness of presentiment.
The prickly shrubs on the hillside were scorched by the sun,
Over the near-by cottage no movement of smoke;
The air was hot, the reeds motionless,
And motionless the quiet of the Dead Sea.

In the bitterness of his sorrow
That matched the bitterness of the sea
He walked with a small following of clouds.
The dusty road led to the town
And to a meeting of the disciples at somebody's inn.

He was sunk so deep in his thoughts,
The dejected field began to smell of wormwood.
Everything was still; he stood in the middle, alone.
The dazed country lay flat as a sheet.
Everything got mixed up: the heat and the desert,
The lizards, springs and streams.

Near by stood a fig tree,
Fruitless, nothing but branches and leaves.
He said to it: 'What joy have I of you?
Of what profit are you, standing there like a post?

'I thirst and hunger and you are barren,
And meeting you is comfortless as granite.
How untalented you are, and how disappointing!
Such you shall remain till the end of time.'

The doomed tree trembled
Like a lightning conductor struck by lightning,
And was consumed to ashes.

If the leaves, branches, roots, trunk,
Had been granted a moment of freedom,
The laws of nature would have intervened.
But a miracle is a miracle, a miracle is God.
When we are all confusion,
That instant it finds us out.

THE EARTH

Spring bursts impertinently
Into Moscow houses.
Moths flutter from behind the wardrobe
And crawl on summer hats,
Fur coats are hidden away in trunks.

In the windows of the wooden storeys[1]
Stand pots of stock and wallflower,
The rooms breathe a spacious open-air scent
And the attics smell of dust.

The street makes friends
With the bleary window,
The white night and the sunset
Are inseparable by the river.

In the passage can be heard
What's going on outdoors
And April's casual gossip
With the dripping waters of the thaw.
April knows a thousand stories
Of human sorrow,
And along the fence the twilight grows chill
Spinning out the tale.

In the open air and in homely comfort
Is the same mixture of fire and uneasiness;
Everywhere the air feels unsettled.
The same pussy-willow twigs,
The same white swelling buds
On the window-sill, at the crossroads,
In street and workshop.

Then why does the horizon weep in mist
And the dung smell bitter?

[1] Many private houses in Moscow had stone ground floors and wooden storey above them.

Surely it is my calling
To see that the distances should not lose heart,
And that beyond the limits of the town
The earth should not feel lonely?

That is why in early spring
My friends and I gather together
And our evenings are farewells
And our parties are testaments,
So that the secret stream of suffering
May warm the cold of life.

EVIL DAYS

When in the last week
He entered Jerusalem
Hosannahs thundered to meet him,
Crowds ran after him with branches.

Each day was harsher and more menacing than the last,
Hearts were not to be moved by love,
Eyebrows frowned in contempt;
Now was the epilogue, the end.

With the whole of their leaden weight
The skies rested on the roof-tops.
The Pharisees seeking proofs
Fawned on him like foxes.

And the dark forces in the temple
Delivered him to the mob for judgement.
Fervently as they had praised him
They cursed him now.

The crowd gathered outside,
Looked in through the gates,
Jostled awaiting the outcome,
Pushed backwards and forwards.

A small whisper crawled about the neighbourhood
And rumours came from many sides.
He now remembered like a dream
The flight to Egypt and his childhood.

He remembered the majestic mountain
In the wilderness, and that pinnacle
From which Satan tempted him
With world power:

And the wedding feast at Cana,
And the company marvelling at the miracle,
And the sea over which, in the mist,
He had walked to the boat, as on dry land:

And the gathering of poor in a hovel,
And the descent into the cellar with a candle,
And the candle snuffing out in fright
When the resurrected man stood up.

MARY MAGDALENE

I

As soon as night falls my tempter is beside me.
He is the debt I pay to my past.
Memories of debauchery
Come and suck at my heart,
Memories of myself, a slave to men's whims,
A fool, out of my mind,
To whom the street was shelter.

A few moments remain,
Then comes the silence of the tomb.
Having reached the end of the world
I break my life before you
Like an alabaster box.

O where would I be now,
My teacher and my Saviour,
If eternity did not await me
At the table, at night,
Like a new client
Caught in the net of my craft?

But tell me, what is the meaning of sin,
Of death, hell, fire and brimstone,
When before the eyes of all
I have grown one with you in my boundless sorrow
As the graft grows one with the tree,

And perhaps, Jesus, holding your feet on my knees
I am learning to embrace
The square shaft of the cross,
Losing consciousness as I strain your body to me
Preparing you for burial.

MARY MAGDALENE

II

Before the Festival comes the spring cleaning;
Away from the crowd,
With myrrh from a little pail
I wash your most pure feet.

I feel for the sandals and cannot find them.
I see nothing through my tears
And the strands of my hair
Cover my eyes like a veil.

I have planted your feet on the hem of my skirt,
    Jesus.
I have watered them with my tears, I have wound
    them round
With a string of beads from my neck,
I have cloaked them in my hair.

I see the future in detail
As though you had stopped it.
At this moment I am able to prophesy
With the foresight of a Sibyl.

To-morrow the veil of the temple will be torn,
We will huddle together in a little group, apart
And the earth will sway under our feet,
Perhaps out of pity for me.

The columns of the guards will re-form
And the horsemen will ride away.
Like a windspout in a storm, the cross above my head
Will strain towards the sky,

And I will fall at its feet,
Silent and dazed, biting my lips.
Your arms will spread out to the ends of the cross
To embrace too many.

For whom in all the world
Is your embrace so wide,
For whom so much torment,
So much power?

In all the world
Are there so many souls?
So many lives?
So many villages, rivers and woods?

Those three days will pass
But they will push me down into such emptiness
That in the frightening interval
I shall grow up to the Resurrection.

GETHSEMANE

The turn of the road was lit
By the unconcerned shimmer of distant stars.
The road circled the Mount of Olives;
Beneath it flowed the Kedron.

The field tailed off
Into the Milky Way.
Grey-haired olive trees tried to walk the air
Into the distance.

Across the way was a vegetable garden.
Leaving his disciples outside the enclosure,
He said to them : 'My soul is sorrowful unto death,
Stay here and watch with me.'

Unresisting he renounced
Like borrowed things
Omnipotence and the power to work miracles;
Now he was mortal like ourselves.

The night was a kingdom of annihilation,
Of non-being,
The whole world seemed uninhabited,
And only this garden was a place for the living.

He gazed into the black abyss,
Empty, without beginning or end.
Sweating blood, he prayed to his Father
That this cup of death should pass him by.

Having tamed his agony with prayer
He went out through the garden gate.
There, overcome by drowsiness,
The disciples lay slumped in the grass.

He woke them: 'God has granted you to live in my time,
And you loll about like this . . .
The hour of the Son of Man has struck,
He will deliver himself into the hands of sinners.'

Hardly had he spoken when from who knows where
A rabble of slaves and thieves appeared
With torches and knives
And in front of them Judas with his traitor's kiss.

Peter resisted the murderers,
Struck off an ear with his sword.
'Steel cannot decide a quarrel,' he heard:
'Put back your sword in its scabbard.

'Could not my Father send a host
Of winged legions to defend me?
Then no hair of my head would be touched,
The enemy would scatter and leave no trace.

'But the book of life has reached the page
Which is the most precious of all holy things.
What has been written must be fulfilled,
Let it be so.   Amen.

'You see, the passage of the centuries is like a parable
And catches fire on its way.
In the name of its terrible majesty
I shall go freely, through torment, down to the grave.

'And on the third day I shall rise again.
Like rafts down a river, like a convoy of barges,
The centuries will float to me out of the darkness.
And I shall judge them.'

FAIRY-TALE[1]

Once, in times forgotten,
In a fairy place,
Through the steppe, a rider
Made his way apace.

While he sped to battle,
Nearing from the dim
Distance, a dark forest
Rose ahead of him.

Something kept repeating,
Seemed his heart to graze :
Tighten up the saddle,
Fear the watering-place !

But he did not listen ;
Heeding but his will,
At full speed he bounded
Up the wooded hill ;

Rode into a valley,
Turning from the mound,
Galloped through a meadow,
Skirted higher ground ;

Reached a gloomy hollow,
Found a trail to trace
Down the woodland pathway
To the watering-place.

Deaf to voice of warning,
And without remorse,
Down the slope the rider
Led his thirsty horse.

*   *

[1] This translation, made by Lydia Slater, conveys the metre of the original.

Where the stream grew shallow,
Winding through the glen,
Eerie flames lit up the
Entrance to a den.

Through thick clouds of crimson
Smoke above the spring
An uncanny calling
Made the forest ring.

And the rider started,
And with peering eye
Urged his horse in answer
To the haunting cry.

Then he saw the dragon,
And he gripped his lance,
And his horse stood breathless,
Fearing to advance.

Thrice around a maiden
Was the serpent wound ;
Fire-breathing nostrils
Cast a glare around.

And the dragon's body
Moved his scaly neck,
At her shoulder snaking
Whiplike forth and back.

By that country's custom
Was a captive fair
To the forest monster
Given once a year.

Thus the neighbouring people
From a peril grave
Tried their own existence
And their homes to save.

Now the dragon hugged his
Victim in alarm,
And the coils grew tighter
Round her throat and arm.

Skyward looked the horseman
With imploring glance,
And for the impending
Fight he couched his lance.

    *   *

Tightly closing eyelids.
Heights ; and cloudy spheres.
Rivers. Waters. Boulders.
Centuries and years.

Helmetless, the wounded
Lies, his life at stake.
With his hooves the charger
Tramples down the snake.

On the sand, together—
Dragon, steed, and lance ;
In a swoon the rider,
Maiden—in a trance.

Blue the sky ; soft breezes
Tender noon caress.
Who is she ? A lady ?
Peasant girl ? Princess ?

Now in joyous wonder
Cannot cease to weep ;
Now again abandoned
To unending sleep.

Now, his strength returning,
Opens up his eyes ;
Now anew the wounded
Limp and listless lies.

But their hearts are beating.
Waves surge up, die down ;
Carry them, and waken,
And in slumber drown.

Tightly closing eyelids.
Heights ; and cloudy spheres.
Rivers. Waters. Boulders.
Centuries and years.